STEALING STARLIGHT

Tomes of Potem'aku

Stealing Starlight

Cover Design: Autumn Rae Hayes / Mitchie Copeland

Interior Design: Autumn Rae Hayes / Mitchie Copeland

Formatting: Mitchie Copeland

Distributed by IngramSparks / Amazon KDP

First Edition: 2025

Trigger Warning

Stealing Starlight is a standalone book.
However, the events and characters in this novel will be used in other books in the series.
This book contains depictions and/or mentions of PTSD episodes, drug abuse, sexual assault, ritualized murder, and kidnapping.
This book is intended for mature readers due to its sexually explicit content.
Your mental health is important to us.
If you choose to embark on this journey, we hope you enjoy the ride.

I can't even express how much this entire journey has meant to me. Not only have I been living my dream of creating works of fiction, but I have been able to write my very first one with my best friend. We have poured our hearts and souls into every single character, into the world building, and into the emotions of every scene, every chapter. It's been a privilege to have this opportunity, an opportunity I have been dreaming of since I was a little girl sitting on the back of a pick up truck listening to my mother read to me.

I suppose you could say *Ella Mental and the Good Sense Guide* by Amber Deckers started it all. (And yes, it is still on my shelves to this day.)

I truly hope that every single one of you falls in love with these characters as much as we have. Thank you for taking the journey.

Capulli'ana awaits,

Autumn Rae Hayes

It's hard to believe that this started with me, my best friend, and a
roleplay Discord server.
"If you don't write a book about this man, I'm going to be so upset,"
is what started it all.
Little did we know that what began as *my* male character and *her* female character would evolve into what has become... a wonderful mix
of minds that took characters that once "belonged" to an individual,
made better by the joint efforts of two like-minded people.
"You'll have to write it with me because she is your character, and I
have absolutely no idea how to write a book," was my response.
Every bit of Autumn that has trickled into who Kiernan is now has
made him a thousand times better than before, and I hope that everything I contributed to who is now Sitara helped bring her to life.
Thank you for reading our debut novel, *Stealing Starlight*.
And welcome to our little world.
Mitchie Copeland

P.s. Thanks for your support, Grandma. I love you so much, but you
can stop reading here.

For Grandma —
Thank you for listening to my stories for hours on end over the phone.
I miss those times more than you could ever know.
To Mr. Timothy Schroer —
I can finally say I am living Brave, Bold, and Courageous. Thank you
for everything, all of the encouragement and gentle guidance.
Donec iterum conveniamus.

For my sister, Kaitlyn —
Thank you for reigniting my passion for reading.
It's an honor to be on your shelf.

Prologue
Kiernan

The evening sun hangs heavy on the horizon, its golden hues painting the sky in vibrant strokes of pinks, oranges, and purples stretching endlessly. The ocean breeze carries the salty scent of the sea, mingling with the distinct aroma of the island—something clean and pure that I can never seem to peg down. The air is thick with the calls of gulls, their raucous cries echoing over the water as they dive and swoop for fish that dart around the hulls of the ships.

It is the perfect evening to dock and unload our goods.

Almost.

It *would* be the perfect night to unload our cargo if it weren't so hot on this fucking island.

The air is heavy, each breath a struggle, and the humidity clings to the skin like an unwanted prostitute from Port Thomas.

Capulli'ana is an affluent island, lush and vibrant and teeming with life.

Its dense jungle and fertile land are a stark contrast to the arid climates we often find ourselves in. The island's fruitfulness is evident in its bounty: bananas and mangos with their sweet aromas wafting on the breeze, and oranges, those golden orbs of juice that are our saving grace, are heavily sought after by merchants and traders across the southern continents.

The tribe's people flock to the port village of Puka'qui, eager to trade. They bring goods that are as valuable as they are exotic: woven baskets, carved wooden trinkets, and the rare, aromatic spices that only this island can produce.

In exchange, they seek our wax candles, our wool, and our spices. It is a trade that benefits both parties, a mutual exchange that has been honed over years of interaction.

This is my livelihood.

This is how I make my living; how I provide for my crew and ensure that our bellies are full and our pockets are lined.

Sort of.

The lines are often blurred, and the truth is far more complicated.

I suppose some might call me a pirate. A lawless plunderer of the seas. A man without conscience or morals. But I prefer a different title, one that reflects the nuance of my profession.

I am a procurer of fine goods.

A facilitator of trade, if you will.

A man who knows how to get what others want.

My men and I operate in the gray areas, the spaces between legality and illegality, where the lines are blurred and the rules are flexible. We take from those who have more than they need, and we sell to those who are willing to pay. It is a delicate balance, one that requires skill, negotiation, and, at times, force.

I'm not going to sit here and say we don't hurt people.

We do.

There are times when the situation calls for it, when the only way to get what we need is to take it by force. I mean, we do what is necessary.

But I don't particularly end a life if I don't have to.

At least there is that.

Now, what my men decide to do during those times...

In reality, the only harm done is a few broken bones, the occasional bloodshed, and the already burning pockets of the rich.

At Puka'qui, we barter and negotiate, exchanging our goods for theirs. The tribe's people do not carry currency; their economy is based on trade and exchange rather than coins and notes. Yet, the goods they offer hold high value in other parts of the world, where the demand for such exotic items is great. It is a system that works well for us, allowing us to gather the things we need to make a profit in the southern ports where merchants are willing to pay handsomely for the spices and wares of Capulli'ana.

This is why we come here twice a year, timing our visits to coincide with the changing of the seasons. We gather what we need, stockpile our goods, and set sail for the markets that will bring us wealth.

My men, seasoned sailors and traders, are often weary and unsettled by the looming jungle that stretches along the southern border of the island. Its dense canopy seems to breathe, to pulse with a life of its own. It's a reminder of the unknown that lies within.

They try to rush me with these dealings to complete the trade quickly. I don't truly understand it, if I'm being completely honest. There is something about this place that unnerves them, a feeling that they cannot shake.

I suppose there is, however, some distant memory of being a young lad, standing on the deck as we first approached this island. The fear and trepidation were palpable, a knot in the stomach.

Those feelings have long since been removed from me, replaced by pragmatism, an acceptance of the world as it is.

I have faced many dangers, overcome many challenges, and the fear has been worn away by experience.

Though I can understand why my men would feel uncomfortable here. The constant reminder of the magic that permeates this land is everywhere. It is in the air, a force that can be felt but not seen. The jungle thrums with it, a steady beat that echoes through the trees like a heartbeat that seems to synchronize with the people who dwell inside.

The people themselves are a testament to this power, moving with a grace and ease that belies the strength they possess.

They start fires with a mere thought, summoning flames from the wood with a flick of the wrist. They move water without a bucket, channeling it from one place to another with a gesture.

For many of us who live beyond these shores, who harbor no unique magical ability, their power is both fascinating and terrifying. It is something that demands respect and fear, a reminder of our own limitations.

I don't really care as long as I can make my wage at the end of the day.

The people of Capulli'ana have never given me a reason to think of them as a threat. If they are friendly with me, I will be friendly with them.

It is a simple philosophy, one that has served me—Benedict, before me—well over the years.

The port market is bustling with activity, a cacophony of sights and sounds that assault the senses. Merchants and traders, from both our world and theirs, set up along the docks. Voices rise and fall, a constant roar, as deals are struck and items are bartered. The sound of the market is almost deafening, a mix of laughter and argument, of haggling and agreement.

It is a symphony of commerce, a dance of supply and demand.

The distant crashing of waves upon the cliffs to the west provides a rhythmic backdrop, a reminder of the vast expanse of ocean that lies beyond this small, bustling village. Tribal children rush in and out of the tiny schoolhouse that was provided to teach them English. Their laughter echoes through the air, a stark contrast to the shouts of the merchants. Their teacher shouts something in their native tongue, his voice rising above the din. The children respond, their voices high-pitched and enthusiastic, as they learn the language of their visitors.

No one would guess the dangers that lie beyond the treeline. That the world beyond that line is as treacherous as the legends say. It is a truth that few from my part of the world have ever seen, if any. The strict rules that govern our visits to this island are clear: no one is allowed to go past the line of trees, to venture into the jungle beyond. The consequences of doing so are dire, and the rumors paint a grim picture.

Some say that the jungle itself will eat you alive. That the plants and animals will conspire against you. That the very land will rise to defend itself. Others claim that the mythical gods, the deities that the people of this land worship, will come and smite us without hesitation. To punish those who dare to trespass.

The stories are varied, but the message is clear: stay near the water, and out of that place.

It is a warning that I have no desire to test. I have no wish to have my bones licked clean by whatever lurks in that jungle.

Once we are fully tied off, I start helping my men carry crate after crate of our goods from the hull to the docks. The sun beats down on us, its rays relentless, baking the skin and draining the energy from our bodies.

Seriously, it shouldn't be this goddamn hot. Not this time of year. Not this close to the water. The breeze from the ocean *should* bring in some relief, but it is warm and heavy, offering little respite from the heat.

It's as though it isn't even the same fucking sun!

I swear that only a mere twenty miles south, the air is crisp and cool. A refreshing fucking seventy-five degrees.

One by one, our goods are hauled off, each man's body glistening with sweat under the boiling sun. My shirt clings to my back, soaked through with a mixture of ocean spray and the sweat dripping from my pores. It's as if my body is defying the very real threat of dehydration, pouring out water as though it's infinite.

As I bend down to lay a smaller crate on top of another, I feel the sudden, unexpected weight of someone running into me. The impact is jarring, but not quite enough to throw me over. My first thought is that it's a child—there's no way a grown man could hit me with such force without knocking me flat on my ass. Which would have pissed me off.

But as I look down, I'm surprised to see a small woman scrambling to steady herself. She's disheveled, her curls wild and unkempt as she pushes them away from her face.

She is *exquisite.*

She's a work of art brought to life.

A masterpiece that seems to have been crafted solely to tempt men and inspire envy in women.

Every feature, every curve, every angle of her face and body seems deliberately designed to enthrall.

It's as if the gods themselves decided to create the perfect specimen of humanity.

And here she stands, breathing and moving and existing in the same space as me.

I can instantly recognize her as one of the tribe's women here on the island. The banded gold and white tattoo along her left arm is a clear indication of her heritage amongst the Ma'tawi tribe.

During my many stops in this port, I've come to recognize the different tribes and the ways to tell them apart. While Puka'qui is home to primarily Mundanes—the name those like myself were given—the jungle is home to three distinct tribes, each with its own unique markings and customs.

The Han'alli tribe, for instance, is known for its black ivy and golden stone tattoos, which seem to shimmer in the light as if infused with a subtle, otherworldly glow.

The Cali'ako tribe, the snobbiest of the three in my opinion, ink their skin with blue waves and green coral, symbols of their deep connection with the sea.

And then there's the Ma'tawi tribe, as evidenced by the golden poppy flowers intertwined with white Glanthus that adorn this woman's arm, who are known for their peaceful nature and their fiery spirits.

I don't know the significance behind these tattoos, but I've learned that they're more than just decorative. All I know is that if you look closely enough, you can tell which tribe someone belongs to.

I snap my attention back to her, unable to help myself. Her hair cascades down her back in a mess of fiery copper curls. Her face is youthful, dotted with freckles that seem to dance across her cheeks. Her eyes are large and russet-colored, like the earth itself has come to life and is staring back at me.

There's something about her that's magnetic, something that draws me in and refuses to let go.

Where I'm from, we would call that a witch.

As she tries to compose herself, I let my gaze wander. I trace the lines of her body from the top of her fiery head down to her delicate nose, over the curve of her full lips. I admire the long expanse of her neck, those slight shoulders, and the swell of her breasts beneath the flimsy cloth that the tribespeople call clothing.

It's as if every curve and dip of her body has been sculpted by the hands of gods long forgotten by my people.

I bet she would fit so perfectly in my mouth.

Perfectly shaped to be devoured whole.

The thought is instantaneous, primal, and undeniable.

It's as if my body has a mind of its own, reacting to her presence in ways I can't control. Every inch of her seems to have been crafted specifically for me.

Clearly, someone, somewhere, knew exactly what I wanted.

What I need.

What I *crave.*

My eyes snap back to hers, and I'm immediately ensnared in their earthy pools. She's apologizing, her voice soft and melodic, with just a hint of an accent.

"Oh! I am so sorry!" she says, her words tumbling out in a rush.

It's surprisingly fluid, almost like she's been speaking English her entire life.

She must have taken English at the schoolhouse in her youth.

I hear the rumbling timbre of Benedict, my first mate, as he clears his throat. He's been hovering impatiently, shifting from foot to foot as he waits for me to finish this task and move on to the next.

"Any day now," he barks, his tone sharp with irritation.

Reaching out almost absently, I hand off the crate I'm holding to him. He grunts his acknowledgment, taking it with practiced ease.

"You're too pretty for the docks, lass. You lost?"

It's a truthful statement.

There isn't a single man here who wouldn't try to do one of three things to this delectable creature standing in front of me.

The best-case scenario is that they want to fuck her, to claim her as their own, and satisfy their basest desires.

The less enjoyable scenario is that they want to load her up and sell her, to treat her as nothing more than a commodity to be traded and discarded.

And the worst-case scenario is they want to do both.

"No," she says briskly, her voice firm despite the delicate sound of it, "I'm just looking."

The subtle lift of her chin in defiance is my undoing. It's a small act of courage, a tiny rebellion against the world around her.

I laugh at her adorable attempt at pride, my shoulders shaking with mirth. It's infectious, this confidence of hers, and for a moment I forget about everything else—the heat, the work, the dangers that lurk in every shadow.

After I regain some sort of composure, I cock a brow and turn to grab the next crate from the new guy... What's his name again?

Andy? Albert? Arnold?

Fuck, I don't know. It starts with an "*A*".

"It's not safe for you to be out here unaccompanied."

Oh no, it isn't safe at all.

If I am imagining every filthy little thing I could do to her—and I am—then I know every other man on this dock is too. And there are far worse men in this world than me.

"I'm not unaccompanied. I have my brother and friend with me," she says matter-of-factly, then looks back to find that neither of those particular people is standing beside her. "Oops..."

She is probably the most intoxicatingly innocent creature I've ever met, and I am damn near drooling over the prospect of breaking that innocence. There's something about her that's primal, something that calls to me to break her in like a prized broodmare.

The way her lips purse in the absence of her companions, the subtle indication of wheels turning behind those warm eyes, it all combines to sear a brand into a long-forgotten part of me that I can't quite place.

"They're around here somewhere." The mundane way she turns back to me and shrugs her shoulders scrapes at my insides. It's a simple gesture, one that speaks of a quiet confidence and determination that I find both infuriating and irresistible.

"People falling behind in a crowd like this *is* considered being un-accompanied." I point out nonchalantly, though my eyes start to roam over the crowd in search of the familiar gold and white tattooing on the left arms of other men and women passing by.

I don't want some random man snatching this girl up when no one is looking. It happens all the time on these exotic islands. They are loaded onto slave vessels and taken to the continents, where they are sold to the highest bidder.

And she is *prime* stock.

I don't want that.

I will not allow some limp-dick Nottley to take my prize away from me.

I will be the one snatching her up.

Because I have already decided she is *mine*.

And I don't allow people to touch what is mine.

"I'm fine." She waves away my feigned concerns and chuckles, the sound going straight to my groin. "I'm just looking at the ships. I'll do better about staying out of the way, though. Sorry again for bumping into you!"

She walks around me, sending chills down my spine as I catch her scent on the breeze—an intoxicating mixture of fresh water, earth, and something uniquely her.

Yes, because *that* is certainly the problem, isn't it?

Her being *'in the way'*.

I spin around, my eyes locking onto her as she moves barefoot along the worn wooden planks of the docks. The sea air carries the faint sound of her soft footsteps, and her big, expressive eyes are wide with a mix of curiosity and awe. She's like a wild animal untethered, her wonder unchecked as she takes in the sights and sounds of the bustling village.

I can feel the men around me unloading my cargo, their rough voices and the clatter of crates filling the air, but I tune it all out. My focus is on her—her careless joy, her obliviousness to the dangers that linger in every man's eye.

As she approaches the corner of the dock, her gaze fixed on something in the distance, I break away from the line of men. They're unloading my shit, my goods, but none of it matters right now.

I follow her, my boots thudding softly against the wood as I keep her in my sight. She's weaving through the crowd of sailors and dockworkers, her movements light and effortless. Like a bird flitting through a storm.

She's so carefree, so fucking oblivious to the fact that she's walking through a place where danger hides in every face, every gesture.

Then she stops. Someone else has caught her attention—a fat, sweaty fuck with a grin that makes my gut twist. He's offering her a tour of his ship, and I can see it in his eyes. The way he's looking at her tells me he's a predator, and she's walking right into his trap. Judging by the way she spoke to me earlier, so casual, so unaffected, I wouldn't be surprised if she takes him up on it. She may very well be *that* stupid.

Well, at least you don't have to be smart to ride cock.

That's what I tell myself, but it doesn't sit well. I don't want her anywhere near that filthy bastard.

I don't want her anywhere near anyone but *me*.

I'm about to do something I don't want to do, something I know I shouldn't do. I'm about to step in and take control. I'm about to scoop her up and carry her back to my ship if she wants a fucking tour that badly.

But then she does something unexpected. She declines his offer, her voice soft but firm as she tells him she needs to find her brother. I can see the disappointment in her eyes and the way she glances at his ship before turning away.

She wants to explore, to see what's out there, but she's making the smart choice.

Good girl.

She's still too nice, too gentle, too fucking trusting.

If it were me, I would have told the slimy dick to go fuck himself, but... tomato tomahto.

As she continues down the pier, I keep my eyes on her. It's easy for me to inch closer with each step, thanks to my size. Benedict's always saying I'm built like a fucking brick wall, and right now, that's working in my favor. I can keep up with anyone, even someone as slippery as her.

And slippery she is.

She darts back and forth, her attention caught by one thing after another. Her red hair is a flash of color in the crowd. If I weren't so focused on her, she'd be gone in an instant. Just a blur of movement.

But I'm not like that.

I'm a bloodhound, and now that I've caught her scent... I won't let go.

Her bright eyes and smiling face are like a knife to my nerves. Not because they're not temping. Not because they're not fucking adorable. They are.

But they are not directed at me. She's giving those smiles, those looks of wonder, to everyone but the one person who's actually worth her attention.

That's going to change. I'm going to make damn sure of it.

After what feels like hours of her darting around like a rabbit in a hunt, I hear a shout.

"Sitara!"

The sound stops her in her tracks, her head snapping to the side as she tries to locate the source of the sound.

So that's her name.

Sitara.

It means 'starlight' in some languages, but I can't picture stars when I look at her.

She's not something you look at and feel calm.

She's a fucking force of nature, a blazing sun that's burning everything else out of my vision.

Then I see him. Her brother, apparently. Larkin. Black hair, tanned skin, familiar. Too fucking familiar. I've seen him before, trading with Thomas at the tavern.

He's been holding out on me, the little shit.

Who knew he had a sister like her? A sister so tempting, so infuriating, so completely out of his league that you'd never guess they were related.

This is my chance.

My chance to step back into her orbit, to make her see me.

Larkin and I, we're buddies, right?

Or at least, that's what I'll let her think.

I take a step forward, my grin already forming, when a hand grabs my shoulder and stops me cold.

"So... are we officially taking bodies now, or are you just thinking with your cock?"

The voice is familiar, and it belongs to the fucking devil himself. Benedict. *Fucking* Benedict.

"Cock," I snap, turning to face him, "Always cock."

"Well, tell your cock we have shit to do," he growls, his expression as annoying as his voice.

I could punch him. I could punch him right now, send him sprawling onto the dock, and tell him to go unload my shit himself. But I don't.

Because that's not how I want her to see me.

Not yet, at least.

I need her to think I'm charming. She needs to think I'm someone worth trusting.

So instead of splitting my knuckles over his face, I clench my jaw and growl, following him back toward my ship.

But my mind is made up.

Maybe not today.

Maybe not the next time I'm in this port.

But one day, that innocent, wild little thing is going to be mine.

She's going to be under me, in my bed, screaming my name until she can't scream anymore.

And when that day comes, no one—not Benedict, not Larkin, not even *she*—will be able to stop me.

1

Sitara

Three years later

The chill of the morning dew wakes me from my sleep. It is a welcome respite from the sweat that has filmed on my skin through the night. Sitting up on my pallet of furs, I look around my tent as I try to blink away my lingering grogginess.

It's still dark outside. The sky is just now changing from the deep void of night to the deep hue of purple that settles just before dawn.

I shift under my blankets, flicking my wrist to light my candles in the corner, washing the inside of my dwelling with a soft emerald hue.

The light plays on the bowls—some carved from wood, some made of porcelain that I have acquired from a small trade in Puka'qui—that lay stacked in the corner. Rugs and furs line the dirt base of the tent, creating a more floor-like look to the space.

I lift my hands above my head, stretching the stiffness from my muscles languidly. A small smile curves the corners of my mouth as I rise to my feet and move to the water basin in the left-hand corner by the entryway. I splash my face, letting the cool freshness wash over my cheeks, neck, and breasts. It always feels so good to wash the grim of the night off my skin in the morning.

After refreshing myself, I step out of the tent into the crisp morning air. The sun is still low in the sky, barely casting long shadows across the earthen paths between the other tents. The village is quiet at this hour, most still asleep. But for those of us who wake early, there is a certain peace to the solitude.

I walk barefoot through the grass, enjoying the way the dewy blades tickle my toes. This is always my favorite part of my day. Well, one of them anyway. When almost everyone else is still asleep, and it's just me.

My mind is always quietest right when I wake up, before my thoughts have fully woken and my duties call for my attention. In the early morning, the expectations have yet to rise from their slumber along with the rest of the village.

Sure, I may be on my way to see Djar before helping Heira with the morning meal, but even those tasks are minuscule compared to the expectations of trying to seem... normal in front of the rest of the Ma'tawi people. Djar doesn't expect that of me, and neither does Heira.

I take in the fresh air of the morning, making my way toward Djar's hut for morning prayer. I work my way between the tents and huts that make up our little village, which is snugly nestled in the southeastern part of the jungle.

Each hide-constructed tent and woven reed hut holds inside a piece of what makes this village alive.

Our homes are orbited around the central firepit in the center, laid out in five rings much like the layout of our sacred temple that sits in the center of the jungle.

My home is part of the fourth ring, where most of the single-occupant tents rest. Among the larger family homes of the second ring sits Djar's hut. It is the only home that doesn't face toward the firepit.

Instead, it faces toward the temple, like the other two shaman huts in the other two villages here on the island.

As I approach the entrance to his hut, I spot movement inside. I approach quietly, peering through the flaps. None to my surprise, Djar is already awake, kneeling there alone. His eyes are closed, head bowed in silent prayer.

I linger just outside for a moment, watching the play of the light from the sacred fire on his braids of silver hair and the serene expression on his wrinkled face, which has a long braid of facial hair hanging cleanly from his chin.

After a moment, I walk in and kneel beside him.

This is part of my daily routine.

Every morning after I wake, I come here to pray with him around the sacred fire. It is said that when our people were blessed by the goddess, Coli'hanu—our village's matron deity—she gave a piece of her flame to the first shaman. Since then, part of the shaman's duties has been to feed the eternal flame with their own and keep it alive.

I suppose you could think of it like a breathing heart; something that ties our people to the ancients before us.

I lower my head reverently, pressing my eyes shut as I prepare to focus my thoughts and connect. It doesn't take long for the familiar restlessness to creep in.

My knee begins to ache from the stillness, and before I know it, my eyelids flutter open to take a glimpse at the man sitting beside me.

Djar appears completely at peace, as though the world around him has melted away. There is an air of certainty about him, a quiet confidence that anchors him to the present moment. Watching him stirs something deep within me, a longing I struggle to articulate. It is as though I yearn for the same sense of calm he embodies, the ability to find contentment in the stillness. The silence. Yet, it is something I have never quite managed to achieve. My mind wanders, my body shifts, and the silence is oppressive rather than comforting.

Stillness has never come naturally to me.

In a way, I envy him.

Sitting still makes my skin crawl, my legs restless, and my hands itching for something to do.

As I try to refocus on the prayer, my leg begins to twitch involuntarily, and my fingertips find themselves drumming a rhythm against my knee.

Instead of the clarity of mind I seek, I am acutely aware of every sound around me: the steady rise and fall of my own breathing, the slow, deliberate breaths of Djar beside me, and the gentle chirping of birds awakening in the trees overhead. My brows furrow in frustration, and I attempt to quiet my thoughts, but even the air seems to hum with distractions.

I take a deep breath, hoping it will steady my mind, but it doesn't. It draws my attention to the crackling of the eternal flame within its hearth.

After what feels like an eternity—though in truth, it is no more than six heartbeats—I concede to my restlessness. My eyes snap open, and I steal a glance at Djar, who remains perfectly unmoving. He hasn't so much as winked an eye.

Though I suppose it would make sense that he is better at this than I am. After all, he's had a lifetime to practice compared to me.

I silently remove myself from his presence, allowing him to enjoy his solitude in peace, without my constant restless energy beside him.

He's never complained, but I know it would drive me up the wall if I were in his place.

So, I retreat and carry my agitation elsewhere.

Making my way through the last ring of the village, I can see that smoke is already rising lazily from the central firepit.

Heira must already be kindling the fire for this morning's meal. I smile as I see my friend crouched down, throwing log after log into the already roaring flames.

Heira and I have known one another since we were children, as have most of us in the village. We grew up together, lived through the journey into womanhood together, and even shared a taste in a warrior or two during our younger days when having a crush was more of a blushing habit than a search for a suitor.

I arrive at her side just as she's rising from the ground, her curvaceous form towering over mine every bit of three inches. Which isn't actually a feat. I'm not that tall of a woman to begin with.

"Starting without me this morning?" I grin, picking up one of the baskets we'll need to gather our supplies for breakfast.

She smiles at me, shaking her head with a chuckle. Her dark hair shifts around her rich-skinned face.

"No, I saw you coming, and you look to be in one of those '*let's get the day going*' kind of moods today."

She knows me well.

Too well if you ask me.

I roll my eyes, passing her the other basket before we begin making our way toward the grove of trees where we grow shade-resistant herbs between them.

"I'm feeling pretty good today, so... Yes, I suppose I am in one of those moods."

"I figured, since it took you about three seconds to give up on your prayers this morning," she teases, giving me a mocking side glance.

I let out a gushing sigh, dramatically slumping my shoulders. "It really is the hardest thing the old man asks me to do."

"Your spirit is such a restless one," she chastises me playfully. "I can't even picture you sitting for hours on end. Though, if you want me to be honest... I'm pretty sure I caught Djar snoring during evening prayers last week."

I look at her.

She looks back at me.

Then we burst into laughter.

"That old man! The gods gave him the gift of falling asleep any-where at any time. Did you see how he was practically falling off that log yesterday?"

"I'm really just not sure how he *didn't* fall over..."

We start gathering the ingredients needed for the morning meal and placing them into the baskets at our hips.

Somehow, we have come to an unspoken understanding of who gathers what items. We have always been especially in sync when it comes to this particular routine.

We both pause, lifting our gazes to one another.

"The rope," we say in unison, then go back to our task with a bout of giggles.

Once when we were children, Djar had been sleeping in a tree, and we couldn't figure out how the hell he hadn't fallen out. His entire body had been half-hanging off the limb. When we had asked him how the hell he'd done it, he merely claimed the power of divine sleep.

It didn't take us long to figure out he had tied himself around the tree trunk.

Cheeky old man.

We work in comfortable silence for a while, the only sound between us being the sound of plucked herb stalks and the occasional rustle of our skirts against the leaves.

Heira clears her throat, straightening up before asking quietly, "How are you doing with... well, everything?"

Her eyes shift downward toward the infamous space below my navel and then back up to my eyes.

I keep that space hidden underneath my clothing for a reason.

This exact reason.

People tend to stare.

Her shoulders droop slightly at the obvious wince I give to the question, unable to hide my reaction to her well-intended question.

"You don't have to answer. I'm just... checking in."

I school my face into a tight smile, a smile I'm used to giving… especially during this time of the year. "I'm fine, really. It was three years ago, Heira. I hardly even feel the phantom pain anymore."

That's a lie.

I feel the memory of it like it was yesterday, the pain and the fear still fresh in my mind. But I refuse to let it win. I refuse to let it own me.

I can't tell if she believes me or if she's just decided not to push the subject. Either way, we finish gathering our supplies in silence.

By the time we've finished cooking, the village has begun to stir awake. The sounds of children laughing and adults calling greetings to each other begin to drift on the breeze, growing louder as they make their way to us. The air caresses my skin, giving play to the fact that the heat will soon consume even the dense shade of the jungle.

A flash of movement catches my eye, and I glance over to see a familiar figure emerging from his own dwelling nestled among the first ring of the village.

Larkin, my older brother, stands there, stretching like a great cat with lean muscle and sinew. His dark hair falls in disarray around his angular face, his eyes crinkling at the corners when he spots me. He starts making his way to where Heira and I stand next to the boiling stew.

"Pali chute, Sitalli'ara," he rumbles, his voice still husky with sleep, "Sleep well?"

I can already see the glaze in his brown eyes, the opium he trades with the Mundanes at Puka'qui lingering in his dilated pupils. It breaks my heart to see him this way, but asking him to quit would be like asking me to stop wandering off on my own.

I can acknowledge the fact that we deal with our past the way we see fit, without liking his self-destructive tendencies, though. I want to scold him, and normally I would, but I don't want to break the tranquility of the morning just yet.

So, instead, I smile back at him, tilting my chin up slightly.

"I did, thank you. And yourself? How was your hunt last night?"

Larkin grins, flashing even white teeth against his tanned skin. "Successful. We brought down a stag and a few rabbits. Plenty for everyone."

I can tell that he's proud of himself and that warms my heart. Though I won't deny the irritation that blooms in my chest when he slurs his words like a newborn calf trying to bleat.

"That's wonderful news."

I am also proud of him, despite my growing disappointment in his morning activities. Larkin is an exceptional hunter when he is lucid; when he can refrain from clouding his mind with the smoke that fogs his senses and slows his brain function. He's one of our best, in fact.

Again... *If* he can keep his mind clear.

Looking around the gathering place, I notice that it is now swarmed with men, women, and children ready to share a meal before our day begins.

Well... their day begins. Heira and I have been awake for about two hours now. Some of us will go out to gather herbs and nuts for the off-season, others will go to the groves of fruit trees that we cultivate to trade with the Mundanes, and then there is me, who will go to Puka'qui and teach the children English. Just as I had been taught.

Djar thinks that it is good for me to get out and enjoy the throng of the port, even if it's just for six hours out of the day. While the school day isn't that long, I spend plenty of time afterwards getting ready for the next day. It gives me something to do. Keeps my hands and mind busy. I can't say that I disagree with him. I am far too curious in nature to be able to sit and shell walnuts all day.

It gives me too much time to think.

To remember things I don't want to remember.

My fingertips tingle at the thought, aching to reach down and scratch at the space that had been not-so-subtly pointed at by Heira earlier this morning.

If I could just rub my skin clean... Just for a moment...

I shake my head, pulling myself from that train of thought before it consumes me. To think about it is to give it power. And it has been given enough.

I dish out a bowl of the beautiful rabbit stew for Djar when he removes himself from his prayers before giving myself a bowl and allowing everyone else to dig in. It is tradition in our village for someone to serve the shaman first, even if they are the last to eat. It's a respect thing, an acknowledgement of the work they do to preserve our spiritual connection to the gods and the world by staying late to commune. It's a way we ensure the shaman is fed.

I volunteer to do this every single day. It's one of the reasons I agreed to morning meal duty in the first place. It's the little things I do to try to repay Djar for taking my brother and me in when we needed someone the most. He had brought us into his home, unflinching and unwavering, and raised us as his own. He had taken the village's uncertainty of whether we would end up like our parents, and helped mold us into people any one of them could trust–despite our vices. It is a debt Larkin and I will never be able to repay in full.

Not that he expects us to.

After my meal, I watch the others move about the village with a smile on my face. This is my home. This is where I am meant to be... I think. I can't help the gnawing feeling of my spirit clawing at my insides, screaming at me to find the true purpose of my existence. It's like a deep wave of energy that coils in my gut, growing more and more taut the longer I sit idle. If I don't do something, *anything*, to release that energy, I feel like I might implode. That purpose is here somewhere... I hope... It's just elusive—that's what I keep telling myself.

But there is no time to dwell on that now. I need to get to the schoolhouse in Puka'qui.

Not to mention, I am excited for the bi-annual ships to sail into port.

I've always loved watching them, ever since I was a little girl. To me, they signified freedom, adventure, and a taste of life outside of Capulli'ana. I've always admired the sailors who were brave enough to journey across the ocean to a land they didn't know in hopes of making a living. Sometimes, I wonder what sort of lands they have seen.

Are they anything like mine?

Or are they so far removed from the life I know that I would get a culture shock if I even *thought* about leaving the island?

Making my way through the animal-created paths toward Puka'qui, I can't help but veer off from time to time to look at a strange plant or follow an interesting animal as it goes about its day.

I should *also* go about my day, but I can't help myself.

I move through the thick, green foliage, catching sight of a massive female miz'geru as it slinks along the underbrush. She's beautiful, all lean muscle and sleek fur that glistens in the dappled light filtering in through the trees. The play of light on the yellow and green patterns along her body is mesmerizing, enchanting even. Her tails, like dual whips, flick lazily behind her as she stalks through the bushes.

A smile draws up my lips, and I lower my body into a crouch to follow. I know this feline well, having followed her journey from a young cub to the fiercely graceful creature she is now. I even decided to give her a name: Mizka, which is a play on her species name, but hey... I was a child when I named her.

Her graceful head turns to look at me, and I stare back. Her large yellow eyes blink slowly, an indication that she's comfortable with my presence. Then, she turns away, flicking her tail in a clear indication for me to follow, and I take the invitation with enthusiasm.

I can't help myself.

I have to follow and see where she decides to lead me, lest that festering energy explodes.

I half expect her to take off running, like usual, but she doesn't. Instead, she moves at a leisurely pace, jumping from low branch to low branch with a skill no human could match.

I follow suit, my movements—while still graceful compared to someone who hasn't lived in this jungle their entire lives—look clumsy and off balance compared to the cat.

Before I get over the last branch she has led me to, I notice she's begun to move faster.

Little thing is toying with me.

I almost snicker at my own thought; the idea of Mizka being a 'little thing' is as preposterous as seeing Djar without facial hair.

It happened once... Never again.

Just as we are about to really amp up the speed, the massive tree root I'm perched on flicks me off. Like a person flicking a bug off their arm. I land on my back on the soft shade grass, the air momentarily knocked out of me.

"Hey!" I bark, sitting up with a slight groan, only to have Mizka plop her massive frame right on top of me. "What was that for?"

I glare up at the tree, my body now pinned to the forest floor by a gigantic lapdog with claws. She rubs her head against mine, and I bring my hand up to scratch behind her ear.

The roots shift, moving the feline from on top of me. I hardly have time to stand and brush myself off before they start to flick at my feet, pushing me toward Puka'qui.

Even the damn jungle acts like a scolding mother when it knows you're supposed to be doing something...

"Alright, Alright!" I chuckle, giving Mizka's head one more soft pat, "I'm going!"

Either way, the message is received.

The roots cease their prodding, and the jungle seems to relax, content that I'm on my way.

2

Kiernan

"You think they will cry like little women like last time?" Benedict snickers at my side, his body practically vibrating with anticipation and barely contained violence, "I love it when they squeal."

He's always been like this—hard to contain and never controlled. The only reason why the motherfucker listens to me is because he *wants* to. Some might think it's because I could crush him with my bare hands, but... That's actually far from the truth. While, yes, I could probably put in a few good punches, the bastard is a fucking monster.

He just likes to put on a show for the crew.

If people are scared of me, they should be terrified of Benedict.

It's always been that way.

I watch as the men scurry about. They're all practically foaming at the mouth. Rabid animals. All of them. And I fucking love it.

My brow slides up in amusement. "I don't think you'll give them any other choice."

A hush falls over the crew as we glide up toward the North Kent Shipping Co.'s flagship, *The Ethereal*. We have been tailing this small fleet of five for about three days. Now that night has fallen, the water is blanketed in a mild covering of fog, and we can move in.

A hush falls over my crew as they all turn to look at the two of us when our ship draws close enough to board. We can hear the captain of the adjacent ship shouting orders at his own crew to prepare for a fight.

Though the conditions are perfect to have been more inconspicuous, Benedict has a thirst for making ourselves known before we actually cross that line. He likes to watch them move around like little ants. Honestly... so do I.

My men are basically bouncing on their toes, ready to be set loose, to wreak havoc and procure those goods that provide the means to... well, live our lives the way we see fit. A.K.A. booze and boobs.

However, they know that they're not to step foot off of this ship until I release Benedict.

When you are faced with a man and his dog, you should always be afraid of the one holding the leash... Until the dog has been released. Then... you should run.

Ben looks over at me, his shoulder-length brown hair pulled back with a bandana, and grins. This isn't his normal grin, no—this is his *'I'm about to rip at some flesh and drink the tears of my enemies'* grin. I can't say I don't miss the look, really. Just another thing Enna has taken away from me.

I look over *The Ethereal* with a darkened gaze, watching as we give them plenty enough time to arm themselves. It's a little request from Ben. The last time we didn't, it was over too quickly, and he got bored.

I fold my arms over my chest, nodding once without looking at him. "Fetch."

"Fucking yes!" he bellows, his feet over the railing faster than the eye can blink. Benedict's entire body coiling like a spring, and he leaps over to the other ship, his arm already finding the first unfortunate soul.

The crew lets out something like a war cry, following their deranged leader like a pack of hungry wolves. I, on the other hand, wander over on my own time. I'm in no hurry to sully my new shirt in the blood, sweat, or tears of these wet-nosed, silver-spooned, wuss-puss men. Don't get me wrong, I have no aversion to violence, but I don't need to bathe in it like Benedict does.

By the time my boots land in unison on the deck of *The Ethereal*, Benedict is cackling like a maniac, and the others are working on tying up opposing crew members. I whistle as I cross the deck to the small flight of stairs that takes me below deck. I heard that this particular ship is carrying a hefty prize.

I'm hoping that this shopping trip will hopefully be the last we need to make before we set sail for the gates of some random ass sun god's realm. Actually... I'm not sure if the Kana'te people have a sun god... They should, with how fucking hot that goddamn island is.

I swing open the door once I've reached the hull, a wicked grin spreading across my face. Look at that. All the fucking wool, spices, and threads we could ever need to trade on that luxurious island. With this, we could make a fortune.

I skip steps two at a time on my way back to the upper deck. New guy, whose name starts with an 'A', gets sent down to start hauling my newly acquired goodies over to the Nureus. I did actually learn his name. It's Arthur. However, I still call him anything *but* that, mostly because it makes his shoulders drop every time I do it.

And that makes me chuckle.

Everyone needs a good chuckle.

Joffrey and Becket also get sent down to help him. I might be an ass, but I'm not cruel. Am I?

"Benedict... You've made the poor man shit himself," I groan, approaching where Benedict has the captain by the throat, hanging him over the railing. Sure, not too scary until you realize Ben's fingers are trying to dig the poor bastard's eyeball out of its socket.

I snap my fingers, scolding him with a grin. "Bring that man back on this deck right now."

I can visibly see the captain's breath rattle his chest as Ben hoists him back up, and I place my arms around his shoulders.

Fuck... He smells awful.

I was only joking about him shitting himself, but I *do* think he might have pissed.

"Now, I need you to do one tiny little thing for me. Say, '*Captain Kiernan Slater, you can have all the fun things I have in the hull,*' for me will you?"

The man frantically nods, his eyes wide as they continue to follow Benedict's every move. "Y-Yes! You can have it all!"

I point to Ben with a grin, and he smirks back. "You heard that right?"

"I did." He chuckles.

"Alright then."

I pat the fucker on the chest and push him back toward Ben, who is all too eager to shove his fingers in the poor fucker's throat and lead him around like a bitch in heat.

Walking into *The Dancing Daisy* is like walking into a second home.

Is it because of the massive amounts of booze that flow from the tap like a river? Yes.

Is it also because of the women flaunting themselves around looking for someone to take up to their rooms and fuck for money? Absolutely.

The answer to that question is yes.

All of the above.

And so much more.

Not that I've seen much of the latter in the last three fucking years...

I sit down in my usual seat at my usual table in the corner of the brothel. Benedict had scared a pair of wet-eared pups out of it on his way in.

Most people know us here, specifically the female workers. The inside is abnormally clean for the den of debauchery that it is. Idaliah's exact words have always been *'Just because we're whores doesn't mean we have to live in filth'*.

The interior is a white wash of plaster and warm woods, the pine flooring well-maintained and polished.

In reality, *we* look like the bums in this situation—all smelly and covered in sweat and seasalt.

"Well, if it isn't the two most batshit crazy motherfuckers I've ever had the displeasure to know!" Idaliah, the madame and owner of this particular establishment of sin, comes rounding the corner out of the back room, wiping the corner of her mouth with a serpentine grin on her round, heart-shaped face. Moments later, the bartender also comes strutting out like he's the happiest motherfucker in the world.

"Giving for free now, are you, Idaliah?" Benedict grins, leaning back into his chair. The two of them go way back, further than even he and I.

I met Idaliah for the first time when I was still a young lad, and I personally hold her responsible for ninety percent of my coming of age.

Idaliah chuckles, licking at the corner of her mouth where she had wiped earlier, and waggles her eyebrows.

"Call it work compensation. Can't have my boys walking around with their glow sticks aching like it's Sunday, now can I?"

"Afraid they'll jump your girls?" I tease as the aforementioned bartender basically floats over to pour us drinks. He's fairly new, new enough that I've only seen him one other time. He's a blocky fellow, though not nearly as large as most of the crew. He probably sits somewhere between Arthur's lean, fit build and Beckett's honed muscle.

I watch him glance sideways at Idaliah, using the opportunity to take in her blessed hourglass figure and the inky silk of her hair.

Poor fucker... He's going to get wrecked.

It's the only thing that comes to mind when I see that look on his face. It's the same look I've seen on Benedict's when he looks at his wife, Enna.

"If any of the males jump my girls, I end their *employment*."

I had been entirely joking, but she isn't having any of it. That's how Idaliah is. She's many things, but loyalty to her girls ranks top. Always.

"Ah! Don't mind little Kiernana over here, Idaliah! He's just a little blue-balled, is all," Benedict snickers, wrapping his arm around my neck in a chokehold.

Idaliah, obviously, eats this up.

"Still on about that girl, are you?" she laughs, the sound far too sultry to belong to a human.

"He sure is," Ben's voice takes on a pouting lilt to it as he sticks out his bottom lip and begins rubbing my hair like I'm a fucking dog, "Oh! I have a thought! Got any redheads? On me tonight."

"I don't need you to—" I try to protest, but Idaliah isn't going to let me take pay from her. Especially since I *used* to be a very... *loyal* customer.

"Of course I have redheads, Benedict! What do you think this is?" She summons a straight-haired, red-headed beauty from across the room.

Before I can decline further, Ben slaps his money down on the table, which is quickly snatched up by Idaliah. They both grin at me.

"Don't be wasting my hard-earned money, now," Ben quips, waving his hand as if to shoo me away.

Fucking Benedict...

The redhead pulls me up from my chair and leads me up the large staircase that sits off to the side of the bar. This will lead us up to the rooms where the women live and work.

I have to hand it to Idaliah; all of her girls are well taken care of, and probably some of the more enthusiastic people when it comes to living life. Usually, that is a calling card for my more base urges.

But right now, the only thing I can seem to do is pick this fucking woman apart.

That pisses me off.

She's fucking beautiful. A goddamn temptress with heels and a bosom perfect for burying your face in.

But her hair is too straight, too managed.

Her skin isn't translucent and almost bruisingly delicate.

Her eyes aren't brown enough, aren't *alive* enough.

She's not... *breakable* and *innocent* enough.

I close the door behind us as we step into the room. It's simple, with a bed, a dresser, and a few accents to show that someone actually lives here. As the woman seductively drops each article of clothing to the floor, I continue my onslaught of unfair comparisons.

The curve of her waist is too deep.

Her legs are long, but they aren't toned enough.

Oh, for fucks sake!

I remember a time when you couldn't have convinced me not to bury myself so deep in this woman's body. When I would have had her on her knees, gagging on my cock before the door latched closed.

But I'm not hard in the slightest at the sight of the bare woman before me. She's not even eliciting so much as a twitch of interest, because apparently, my cock has decided it will only pay attention to one singular woman. A woman I haven't even seen fucking naked yet.

Sitara.

The goddamn witch who decided I was the man to fuck with.

The woman I'm currently staring at with so much indifference it makes my temper flare sashays with slow movements toward where I stand near the door. Even as her hands slide up my chest, I don't have it in me to grow one. All it does is inflame my rage. Rage brought about by my sudden lack of bodily response.

"What's the matter, baby? You're all tense," she purrs, the sound scraping at my nerves.

Her voice isn't right either.

It isn't high-pitched enough.

It isn't breathy enough.

It isn't *hers*.

I can't name the countless nights I've had to rub one out in the privacy of my fucking cabin while my mind imagines that voice saying my name in all manners of shrieking moans and whimpering cries.

This woman's voice isn't *right*.

"Long trip."

I don't even bother trying to sound convincing. The only thing on my mind right now is how much closer to Puka'qui I could be if we hadn't stopped here. I want to get my ass back on the *Nureus*. That exact exigency is making it rather difficult not to toss this woman onto the bed and walk out.

Fuck Ben's coin.

"I can make it better," the woman coos, pressing herself into me until her breasts smash into my chest.

That's another thing: she's too tall.

Sitara's would be right about—

My hands wrap around her arms, and I walk her back until her knees hit the bed. The excited giggle that she gives is enough to make me angry.

Violently so.

As her ass hits the mattress, she reaches up to stroke my clothed dick, which has yet to even show her any manner of kindness, and her smile falters.

Fuck, now not only will I be known as the fuck who can't seem to break the spell he's under, but I'll also be known as the fucker who can't get it up.

"I don't think so, lass. Have you ever been under a spell before?"

Storming down the staircase, I find Benedict right where I left him, liquor in hand. He's apparently still having a fucking blast with Idaliah, who's perched on the chair next to him.

When he notices me, his grin only widens, and it takes everything in me not to punch him in the fucking face.

"Have fun, mate?" he slurs, clearly too drunk to notice just how much fun I did *not* have.

"Shut up." I kick Joffrey out of my chair with a swift kick to the back and sit down with a huff.

Moments later, the woman I was just with walks down fully clothed and makes her way to Idaliah to explain the entirety of the situation. Her eyes are wide as they flick from me back to Idaliah, and she leans in to whisper in the ebony-haired woman's ear.

Catching on to what has happened, Benedict groans, rubbing his face into his palm. "Kiernan... Nooo... Please tell me you didn't start in on the fucking spell lecture again?"

I really hope my glare can pierce straight through the cocky bastard's skull. Really, I do. He's done nothing but refuse to admit that I am under the spell that I clearly am.

When have I *ever* not performed in the bedroom of all places?

I point a finger in his direction, the scowl so deep in my brows I can physically feel the skin bunch up. "You've fucking seen it. It's true."

"K, seriously? None of those people has the power to do that!"

I lean back in my chair far enough that the two front legs come off the floor and fold my arms. "You have no idea what they can do! No one does!" I argue, "There is no other explanation." The huff I let out causes a rogue strand of my hair to be blown out of my face, my irritation growing by the second.

I just want to leave. I could be a solid four days closer to those fiery, wild curls.

Benedict rubs his palm over his face again with a deep, chest-rattling sigh. "Kiernan, you haven't seen the lass in six months. She could be married with her first child on the way for all you know."

Fuck that...

I am immediately on my feet, kicking the chair away from my ankles. I won't be at this port for another damned minute if *that* is what could be waiting for me in Puka'qui.

"Get your ass up and gather the men," I say as I start for the door, "We're leaving. Right now."

"K..."

"Now, Ben!" I shout over my shoulder as I swing the door to the brothel open and step out into the cold night air.

I faintly register the bartender as I bound for the exit.

"Is he alright?" he asks, though I don't stay to hear a response to his question.

3

Sitara

As I emerge from the dense foliage of the jungle, the expanse of Puka'qui unfolds before me. The village is a hive of activity, with vendors scrambling to set up their stalls in preparation for the influx of traders and sailors arriving on the fleet of ships docking at the port. The air is thick with the hum of commerce and the distant calls of seagulls wheeling overhead.

My path always brings me out of the jungle on the far northeastern edge of the village, and I make my way through the dusty, uneven terrain toward the bustling heart of Puka'qui. Along the northern border, I pass by a cluster of Mundane homes, their sturdy structures a stark contrast to the more temporary shelters my people are accustomed to. Built from rough-hewn stone and timber, these homes stand as a testament to the Mundanes' preference for permanence, while the tents and huts of the Kana'te remain hidden deeper within the jungle, blending seamlessly into the natural world we call home.

Between the docks, where ships unload their cargo, and the homes, vendor stands line the space in two orderly columns, a mix of Mundane and Kana'te traders offering their wares. The vibrant colors of fabrics, the gleam of polished metals, and the earthy scent of exotic spices create a sensory overload that is both chaotic and exhilarating.

This is Puka'qui—a place where two worlds intersect, where the mundane and the extraordinary coexist in a fragile harmony. It is a melting pot, a living proof that despite our differences, we can find common ground and build a life together free from hatred.

Of course, no place is without its imperfections. The village is not immune to the darker shadows that plague any community. Drugs, like the ones Larkin indulges in, find their way into the hands of those who seek escape or solace. And then there are the occasional disappearances—Kana'te women vanishing after nights spent in the tavern with Mundane men. Whether these disappearances are by choice or force remains unclear, leaving behind only whispers and unease. Yet, these issues are rare, and for the most part, the village remains a place of relative peace and prosperity.

As I weave through the crowd, it doesn't take long for me to fall into the rhythm of the vendors calling out their daily specials or the sailors haggling over prices. The village is alive with sound—the cacophony of people competing for attention, the sharp barks of captains directing their crews, and the laughter of children playing in the streets as they wait for the school day to begin. It is a symphony of life, chaotic yet beautiful, and it never fails to leave me in awe.

For me, Puka'qui represents the closest glimpse I've ever had into the Mundane world. A small but significant number of Mundanes have made this village their home, and their presence has shaped it into the thriving hub it is today. And yet, despite its importance to both our peoples, Puka'qui remains primarily Mundane territory. The Kana'te prefer the safety and familiarity of our jungle, our little slice of paradise hidden deep within the trees. It is not out of mistrust or animosity that we keep to ourselves, but rather a deep-seated need to protect our way of life.

Still, that does not stop us from enjoying our visits to the village—whether they happen weekly, as is customary for most, or daily, as is my habit.

As I make my way further into the village, my eyes are drawn to the tavern standing at the far western end. Its walls, made of muddy brick, seem to sag under the weight of years, and the red-painted shutters hang crookedly, in desperate need of repair.

It is the only establishment in the village where sailors can find food and rest, and yet, it seems to be in a state of perpetual disrepair. I find myself wondering, not for the first time, how Thomas Sr. can afford to keep the place running, even during this busy time of year. Our humble huts back in the jungle are cleaner and better maintained than this crumbling building. And to think, my schoolhouse sits right next to it, just to the north. It's almost as if the tavern's neglect casts a shadow over the place where I work so hard to give young minds new opportunities.

Pausing for a moment, I watch as the ships are guided into port, their massive forms dwarfing everything else around them. I find myself pondering, as I often do, the incredible amount of time and labor that must go into constructing such vessels from the ground up.

How many hands must have worked tirelessly to shape the wood, to weave the ropes, to bring these floating giants to life?

These are questions I ask myself nearly every time I come to the village, and ones I hope to one day have answered.

Taking one final look at the ships, I continue on my way to the schoolhouse, eager to begin the day's lesson and share the magic of this place with the children.

My school, a simple one-room building, is a place of modest beauty. Its clay walls are covered in the handprints of every child who has ever walked through its doors. Including my own and Larkin's, though they may be long faded by now.

At the far end of the room, opposite the door, hangs a large black slab of stone that the Mundanes call a "chalkboard." We were taught to use it to write letters and numbers with sticks of compacted dust, a tool that has become indispensable in our efforts to bridge the gap between our worlds.

The floor is lined with colorful rugs, their patterns of blues, reds, and purples mirroring the vibrant designs found in my tent back in the jungle.

To the left, a set of bookshelves holds a collection of books from the Mundane world, their pages filled with knowledge and stories that I strive to share with my students.

On the right, a table serves as a snack station, stocked with fruits and nuts donated by the tribes, ensuring that no child goes hungry during the day.

I move to the table and reach underneath it to retrieve the crate where I store the small, personal chalkboards for the children. Today, I've decided to take advantage of the village's energy and the presence of the ships to give the children a lesson they won't soon forget.

We'll venture out into the village, using the bustling streets and the towering ships as our classroom. The children will practice writing and saying the words for the things they see—the ships, the sailors, the goods being traded. It's an opportunity for them to connect the lessons they've learned in the schoolhouse to the real world.

Expecting children to remain indoors all day is a sure way to breed restlessness, and I've learned that some of the best lessons come from stepping outside the familiar walls of the school. The village is alive, and today, it will be our classroom.

As I slap the surprisingly heavy box down on the table, the sound of footsteps echoes through the room, drawing my attention to the open door. I usually leave it open to allow air circulation, and sometimes the invitation for company while I prepare for the day. The creak of the wooden floorboards signals the arrival of familiar faces, ones I've grown to cherish over the years. My friends, Ivelle and Te'lei, walk in with their contributions to the children's snack table, their presence instantly filling the room with a sense of camaraderie.

Ivelle is a Mundane woman who lives here in Puka'qui with her father. Her long, strawlike blonde hair flows down her back, draping down to stop just past her backside, catching the light in a way that makes it seem almost otherworldly. Her hazel eyes always seem to be sparked with excitement and mischief, which tends to get me into my own more often than not. In her slender arms, she carries a basket of pastries, no doubt baked by herself. Since her mother passed, that seems to be her escape for everything. When the air in Puka'qui is wafted with the smell of sweet sugar, we know Ivelle is more than likely in the kitchen.

Te'lei, on the other hand, is a massive oaf of a man with a goofy grin and warm brown eyes that seem to hold a perpetual kindness. His large hands are empty, but the swirling pool of water he's just sloshed into the drinking bucket in the corner is evidence of his contribution. He turns around to face Ivelle and me, a cheeky smirk on his sun-kissed face, his skin bronzed from hours spent under the open sky.

"Now you don't have to go do it yourself," he beams proudly, his voice laced with a satisfaction that only comes from knowing he's been helpful.

Ivelle and I look at one another with playful eye rolls. Leave it to a Cali'ako tribe male to find any excuse to use his gift of magically playing in puddles. It's a quirk that's both endearing and exasperating, a reminder of the unique abilities that set our people apart from the Mundane.

Though I am grateful, I'm unable to refrain from teasing him a little, so I decide to bring up our upcoming celebrations. Xu'solsi is the Kana'te people's summer solstice, one of many celebrations where all three tribes come together to celebrate the longest, hottest day of the year and the turning of the tide. It's a time of unity, of shared joy, and tradition.

"Have you asked Hiera'yolku to celebrate with you yet, or are you still too shy to look her in the eye?" I ask, my words laced with a playful jab.

At the mention of Hiera, Te'lei's cheeks begin to burn profusely. He rubs the back of his neck, shifting from foot to foot, his usual confidence faltering. I can see the gleam in Ivelle's eyes as she wraps her arm around his shoulder, their height difference making the gesture completely absurd-looking.

"You're going to miss your opportunity, Taylee!" She bats her eye-lashes up at him with horribly feigned innocence, "What if Ko'chi asks her?!"

The gasp that rips up her throat is a little too forced. I know that might very well be an earnest concern of hers, given her feelings for Ko'chi. It's a delicate dance of emotions, one that we all navigate with care.

Te'lei scrunches his nose at the pronunciation of his name, patting her on the head. "I think you should stick to English, Ivelle."

He and I burst into laughter, fueled by the indignant expression of embarrassment that floods her face. She tries, we know she does, but she really shouldn't. We have English versions of our names for a reason.

She crosses her arms, scrunching her mouth to the side. "I thought I did it better that time!"

Te'lei wraps an arm around her head and begins to pet her like a wounded puppy. "We know, Ivy, but... that might have been the worst one yet. It's Tay-lay, for the love of the gods. It's not that hard."

"Then why is it spelled weird?!" she squawks.

I shake my head, a small smile curving at the corner of my mouth. The two of them have always had that playful banter, ever since Ivelle joined our group a couple of years ago. She likes to tease him. Honestly, I'm not sure how his gentle heart has withstood it.

Ivelle catches the telling jerk of my head as I see Hiera'yolku walking toward the building, and wraps her arms around him.

"If only I were allowed to go to your festivities!" she straightens up, tilting her chin to look up at the big oaf, "I'd want to go with you!" She lets out a long, overly dramatic sigh and puts the back of her dainty hand to her forehead, "But alas! I am tethered to this side of the trees!"

The way Te'lei rolls his eyes nearly breaks her beautiful theatrics, so I press on with a comment of my own. "I bet taking another woman to Xu'solci would get Hiera'yolku to see you—"

In the middle of my spiel, Tay's head snaps over to the sound of more shuffling feet. He quickly shoves Ivelle away as Hiera and Ko'chi enter.

"Shut up, you two!" he hisses under his breath, "Or I swear to Teo'Kan..."

Ivelle giggles, stumbling into me. I catch her, trying to steady both of us.

"We told you we could fix that, if only you would go with us to the temple," Hiera says as she sets down a basket of baked bread onto the table, having heard Ivelle's playful teasing.

The blonde's face falters slightly, and none of us says anything further for a moment.

It isn't that Ivelle doesn't want to, but her father isn't exactly in good health. Not to mention the fact that when her mother died, it had been within the barrier. Ivelle's mother was a healer here in Puka'qui and had gotten the blessings from the gods to venture beyond the barrier. On that fateful day, she had been attempting to find a rare herb that only grows in certain sections of the jungle, desperate to heal a Kana'te man who lay dying in her healing shack.

After that, Ivelle's father has been less than welcoming to our people, believing that if she hadn't been out in the wilderness, the beast that killed her wouldn't have had a chance. He won't allow any of us into his home, nor would he be happy to know that she still spends time with us.

"It's probably for the best, anyway," Ko'chi interjects, setting down a large bag of roasted nuts that he and Hiera most likely flamed themselves. Regular fire-wielding is the most common gift among the Ma'tawi tribe. "If you did, you'd be stuck with this limp noodle all evening."

Te'lei shoots Ko'chi a glare, to which he simply smirks back. The two of them have been like this since their coming of age. Mana'Oka, or The Hunt, is the male's Rites of Passage. This is yet another custom that all the tribes celebrate together. That is how Te'lei came to be a part of our little group when he met Ko'chi, and a friendly rivalry bloomed between them.

Ko'chi, with his dark, rich skin that seems to absorb the light around him, looks at me with a fleeting glance. His warm brown eyes, framed by thick lashes, hold a depth that makes me uneasy. His braided black hair, adorned with small beads that catch the light, frames his face perfectly.

I turn away quickly, fixing my eyes on Hiera as she begins to pull out the snacks they've brought. The sight of the woven basket is a welcome distraction. I can feel Ko'chi's disappointment like a weight in the air, but it's simply not something I wish to unpack right now. Not today, when the tension between us feels thicker than the humidity in the summer air.

Kaiko, or Kay'Kaio as she's natively known, is the last of our little group to arrive at the schoolhouse. Her timing, as always, is impeccable—not late enough to miss the awkwardness that has just taken place between Ko'chi and me, but late enough to make an entrance.

She rescues me by clearing her throat loudly, a sound that commands attention, and holding up her basket, which is filled to the brim with sweet potatoes and marigolds. There's also a small satchel of vanilla beans, their sweet aroma wafting through the air, which she hands off to Ivelle as soon as she notices our friend's eyes light up at the sight of it.

"How is it I'm always the last one here?" Kaiko asks, her voice mockingly frustrated.

I give her a grateful glance, taking the basket from her to begin assembling the vegetables on the table. My hands move with a practiced ease, arranging them on the table alongside the other offerings. It's a task that brings me a sense of calm, a grounding ritual that I've grown accustomed to over the years.

"Probably because you live the furthest away," Te'lei responds, his voice smooth and unaffected. He's oblivious to the tension that lingers in the air, or perhaps he's choosing to ignore it. His words are met with a soft chuckle from Hiera, who's busy arranging the pastries in a woven pattern.

Kaiko is a young woman from the Han'alli Tribe, evident not just by the pe'aboros of gold and black inked down her arm, but also by the way she carries herself with a quiet confidence and authority. Her icy blonde hair, a stark contrast to the deep browns of her skin, falls in loose waves down her back. Her dark eyes, sharp and observant, miss nothing and see everything, a trait that has often proven to be both a blessing and a curse.

Kaiko and I met during our training in the temple of Potem'aku, a place of ancient power and wisdom, where we were trained by the goddesses Gula'ci and Coli'hanu. Our abilities are considered special, rare gifts that set us apart from the rest. And there had been no one else who could teach us to control them besides the deities themselves.

I was born with the ability of Cold Fire, a gift that has only been received by one other person in our history—Coli'hanu herself. Though all fire is fickle, mine seems to be even more so. Having the ability to give myself frostbite had been a dangerous reality for me as a child, a constant reminder of the power I wielded and the control I struggled to maintain. It still is, but I've learned how to expel it before it has a chance to build up and harm me. It's a delicate balance, one that requires constant vigilance and a deep connection to the element.

Similarly, Kay'Kaio had been born with Planetary Manipulation, a power that is as vast as it is unpredictable. While it isn't as rare as my own Cold Fire, most Han'alli people are only able to manipulate one of the elements that are encompassed in its description.

Not Kaiko.

Just like the Goddess of Earth before her, she developed the ability to manipulate it all: weather, the environment around her, mountains, oceans, metals...

Back then, when she was upset or angry, you'd know. I think a few of the holes in the outer rings of the temple—now nothing more than rubble save for the two inner circles—were put there by her outbursts. The memory of it brings a faint smile to my lips, a reminder of the chaotic beauty of her power.

I can't place much judgment on that, though. I had plenty of my own outbursts back then, too, and it would take Coli'hanu herself to thaw the crackling emerald flames out of the God of the Sea, Teo'Kan's, hair. It's a memory that still makes me laugh, a rare moment of levity in the otherwise intense days of our training.

Standing among my friends, I feel just a sliver of what Ivelle must feel as the only Mundane in our group. Just as she is an outsider of sorts, so am I. I'm the only one of us whose parents left their village to join the Miqui'oh people. They aren't really a 'people', so to speak, but rather a cult, formed by a collective mass of Kana'te people from all over the island. It's a decision that has always left me feeling disconnected, a bridge between two worlds that I don't fully belong to.

Normally, I wouldn't think much of it if it weren't for the fact that I can feel them edging around me more than usual. It's due to the anniversary coming up, a singular memory that rattled the very bones of the tribes as a whole. When I was the only one to come back—

"Right, Sitara?" Te'lei's voice rings out, breaking my almost-slip into a very, very dark train of thought. His tone is sharp, slicing through the silence like a knife. He's obviously offended by something that has been said, though his eyes gleam with mischief. I have been so consumed in my self-pity that I have no idea what he's asking me about.

Thankfully, Ivelle seems to notice my confusion, bracing her hands on the table I've been so focused on filling, and leans back. "Ko'chi said no woman can handle his horrible jokes, and he rebuked him by saying that *you* laugh," she explains, her voice soft but clear.

Kaiko rolls her eyes, shaking her head before going to stand next to Hiera, who has leaned against the handprint-covered wall next to us. Her movements are fluid, a testament to her connection to the earth and its rhythms.

"Sitara is too kind-hearted to wound your ego by *not* laughing, Te'lei," she says.

Still slightly confused by how much of the conversation I've seemed to miss, I quickly chime in. "I think Tay is funny." The words feel a bit hollow, but they seem to be enough.

From the corner of my eye, I notice Ko'chi's face tighten slightly. I push the discomfort away, giving Te'lei a stiff smile. It's a fragile peace, one that I'm not sure will hold, but it's better than the alternative.

In order to get the group out of this increasingly uncomfortable conversation, Hiera steps forward, changing the topic entirely. "Enough about Tay and his unique sense of humor," she says, her voice warm and reassuring. She moves next to me, looping her arm through mine. Her touch is comfortingly familiar, a reminder of the bond we share. "Have you decided what you'll be gifting the Sacred Three this year?"

She really does know me better than anyone. I've become a master at pretending, or at least I think I have, but it never fools her. It never has. Not once.

I relax into her, the tension in my muscles slacking imperceptibly. "Well, I know what I'm giving Coli'hanu... She's sentimental, you know. I've been working on a little '*thing*'," I say, trying to sound confident.

The truth is, I haven't. I completely forgot how close Xu'solsi had gotten, and I haven't done jack. But it won't be hard, at least not when it comes to the Goddess of Cold Fire. For the others, however... I might be royally screwed.

She gives me a look, completely unconvinced. "Mhm..."

"What?" I glance over at her sheepishly, a small grin forming on my lips. "I'll figure it out."

It's a promise I hope I can keep.

Ivelle lets out a soft, wistful sigh, dramatically placing her hand down on my shoulder. "I'm envious," she says, her voice tinged with longing, "You guys can see them whenever you wish to."

Ivelle is one of the few Mundanes who genuinely embraces the materialism of the Living Gods. Whether this stems from her convictions or the relentless persuasion of all of us, who have witnessed their existence, is a matter of speculation. Nonetheless, I find her belief endearing, as it makes moments like these less strained and more harmonious.

"Well, if you would just—" Te'lei begins, only to be abruptly silenced by Kaiko, who clamps her hand over his mouth.

"We are *not* diving into this debate again," she declares firmly, "A debate, I'm certain, you've all had countless times before I arrived here."

Her ability to discern everything, even events that transpire without her presence, is uncanny. Ivelle offers her a grateful smile, acknowledging her perceptive nature.

Glancing out the window, I notice the sun ascending higher into the sky. "The children will be here soon," I mention casually.

"Let me guess, *'outside class today, children'*," Ivelle teases, her playful jab met with chuckles from the group, even coaxing a smile from Ko'chi.

My cheeks warm slightly, and I press my lips together in an attempt to maintain a serious demeanor. "Outside class is beneficial. It's good for them."

"It's also closer to the Mundanes' ships," Ko'chi counters with a mischievous grin, easing the tension between us.

I respond by sticking my tongue out at him, yearning to return to our comfortable banter.

"I think it's kinda charming that she finds them so captivating," Ivelle remarks, her eyes twinkling with amusement.

"Of course *you* do. You're Mundande," Te'lei retorts, his tone laced with mocking sarcasm.

"Hey, there's nothing wrong with showing appreciation," Hiera interjects, defending Ivelle's perspective.

Before the conversation can escalate into another debate, I gently nudge everyone toward the exit. I playfully shove the guys, fully aware that Te'lei and Ko'chi are far too robust for me to budge. They stand their ground, arms crossed, clearly enjoying the playful exchange.

"What if I want to learn how to add two plus two?" Te'lei whines mockingly.

"Sitalli'ara! I want to see the big boats too~" Ko'chi chimes in, feigning childlike innocence.

As the group finally moves forward, their lively chatter filling the air, Ivelle lingers for a moment. This is a usual practice, ensuring she isn't seen departing with the rest of us, so no one gives it much thought.

"I brought you this..." she says softly, extending her closed fist toward me. I hold out my palm, my brows furrowing in curiosity. She places a small pouch of herbs into my hand. "I know things can be challenging. I thought these might help."

Her gesture is accompanied by a sympathetic smile, and she gives me a quick hug before leaving the schoolhouse, taking a different path from the others.

I open the pouch, examining its contents. Devil's Claw catches my eye, likely imported from a drier, southern climate. It's used for alleviating phantom pain, a condition all too familiar to me.

While I appreciate her kindness, the gift also stirs unease. It serves as a reminder that my friends are aware of my struggles, confirming my deepest worries. Their concern is touching, yet it underscores the reality I've been trying to evade.

Pushing these emotions deep down, I tuck the pouch into my pocket. Taking a moment to compose myself, I pick up the crate of chalkboards and position it by the door. A gentle smile forms on my lips as the first students begin to arrive.

"Good morning, girls," I greet them in English. I teach in the same way I was taught: only English is used in the classroom unless you are just beginning to learn or you can't figure out how to describe what it is you are trying to say.

Evara and Meona, two young girls from the Han'alli tribe, enter first, their giggles filling the room as I hand them their chalkboards. They respond in unison, "Good morning, Miss Sitara," their voices bright and cheerful.

Their ages remind me of when I first started school—Evara is seven, Meona nine, while I began at eight. Here, education isn't forced; children attend when they're ready, a concept that seems foreign to many Mundanes.

As more students arrive from the three tribes, I notice an older boy, Hakimos, proudly wearing his newly adorned pe'aboros, a symbol of his coming of age. His excitement is palpable, and I can't help but admire the intricate green and blue patterns of the Cali'ako tribe inked into his skin.

"Look at you, Hakimos! All grown up!" I exclaim, patting his cheek affectionately. "Your parents must be so proud."

Hakimos beams with pride, though he remains silent, for he was born mute. Yet, his determination to learn and communicate through reading and writing is admirable. He takes his chalkboard and joins the younger children, ready to embrace the day's lessons.

Once all twelve students are seated at my feet, I clap my hands excitedly. "Okay, children! Today we're going on a trip to the docks to learn about sailing terms!" I announce, my voice filled with enthusiasm.

The room erupts in excited chatter and laughter. Learning outdoors always brings a spark of joy to their faces. Leading them out of the schoolhouse, we make our way down the dirt path toward the towering boats, the world outside promising an engaging and memorable lesson.

4
Kiernan

Capulli'ana comes into view just as the sun is beginning to break over the horizon, shattering the waves into golden gems dancing on the surface. The familiar heat of this region begins to force perspiration to break out along my brow, but I don't mind.

I barely notice.

I'm too captivated by the sliver of land that grows larger and larger the further we sail North.

This year will be the year. I don't give a shit if she's married. I don't give a fuck if she likes it or not. I refuse to leave this port without her on my ship, in my quarters, in my bed. I will not be letting anyone—not Ben, not the half a dozen children that follow her around the village half the time, no bystander or onlooker—stop me from taking what I want.

Every time we've docked here since that fateful day, I have lusted after her, following her as she milled about the village. I've watched her from every vantage point possible, especially after she took up a job at the schoolhouse. It gives me four or five hours a day to plan out the perfect way to take her.

But each time I have almost gotten my hands on her, someone has interrupted at the most inopportune time. The children under her care pose as a hindrance most of the time, enough so that I often have to remind myself that I'm above throwing a child into the bay.

The ocean spray beats on my face as I lean over the railing, trying to formulate yet another plan to snatch her the fuck up.

This woman has me wound up so damn tight that I feel like a fucking boy who barely knows how to yank off his own rection, let alone take another woman to bed. After the incident at Idaliah's, my blood is boiling over, steam practically rolling out of my pores. Hate fucking... It's going to be a whole hell of a lot of hate fucking at this point. How can a woman twist a man's insides for three fucking years without him even having *touched* her?

It's the fucking spell, of course!

It's so goddamn maddening that I've even contemplated joining Geralt a time or two, but I can't give that fucker the satisfaction of his eternal torture by my hands.

My frustration only grows the closer we get to the island. So much so that I hardly even hear Benedict as he comes to speak to me.

"Ready to cast in, 'Cap?"

When I don't respond, my eyes scanning the port in search of a mess of red hair, he suddenly lands his knuckles right into my shoulder blade.

"Kiernan! For all that is fucking divine, don't start this shit before we've even tied off!" Benedict's brows furrow, the irritation on his face evident as I finally rip my gaze from the shoreline to him.

I look at him, furrowing my brow slightly. "Well?" I pause, looking past Ben to the crew standing there waiting for an order.

"Get us to port, you lazy fucks! Get your asses in gear!"

And thus, the scrambling begins.

Benedict pinches the bridge of his nose with a deep, exasperated sigh. "You know what... I'll pay the woman *myself* if it'll keep you from being such a fucking prick every time we come here."

I ignore him, pacing the bow of my ship, agitation coiling my muscles taut. His words are drowned out into nothing but a ring in my ear as I spot her surrounded by a horde of tiny, dirt-covered children. I can feel that deep-seated need rearing its ugly head like a dog nipping at my heels for scraps.

Though I get to see her twice a year, she never ceases to stop me right in my tracks.

I can hear someone's distant mumbling, but it's muffled, too far away for me to register. All that exists is that mess of fiery locks and the gentle sway of those hips. My hands flex at my sides as they ache to grab and take and take and *fucking* take.

A heavy hand roughly collides with my shoulder, forcing me from my hot-blooded gawking.

Arthur.

Of course it's fucking Arthur. The boy won't wipe his own piss off his dick unless I tell him to.

I swiftly turn, knocking him on his ass with a sharp jerk of my arm. *That's for startling me, you little shit.* Or maybe I'm irritated that he interrupted me. Either way, he deserves it.

"Don't sneak up on me while I'm thinking."

Thinking... Yes, that's what I was doing. Thinking about my rough hands on soft skin and my cock buried in—

"Sorry, Cap!" Arthur scrambles to his feet, his young body hoisting itself up in a flourish. He motions toward the crew, all of whom have confused looks on their faces. Except Benedict. He looks downright pissy. "We are waitin' for orders."

I give the entire crew a look of irritation. After all these years, you'd think they'd have gotten over their fucking fear about this place. Any other port, they would have just done what was expected of them.

Now that I think about it, Ben might have something to do with that, too.

Fucking Benedict...

"Have none of you bastards docked this damn ship before?" I jab my finger in the direction of the cargo, "Unload my fucking ship!"

I roll my shoulders, wringing my hands before pushing my way through the crew to pick up the first crate. I'm not like some captains who are above pulling their own weight. I unload cargo from my vessel just like the rest of them. After all, if I don't busy myself until I can come up with a plan, I'll go insane.

Insane enough to do something stupid.

Insane enough to rip her out of that schoolhouse in front of a dozen or more children.

Insane enough to take her in front of someone and then have an entire village of Kana'te people throwing fucking fireballs at me.

I have managed to make four passes from deck to dock.

Well, I have nearly made it back to the dock the fourth time. I have just planted my right foot on the boardwalk when she knocks into me, causing me to nearly squash a child with the crate I have perched on my shoulder.

Ah, just like the good old days... She hasn't changed a bit. And I should know, I've been stalking the little vixen since day one.

All I can do is look down at her, taking in the subtle details that elude me when I'm at a distance. "Watch your step, lass. I'd hate to turn your tiny army into pancakes."

Smooth, Keirnan... smooth.

Let's threaten to squash a child. That'll make her roar and ready to go.

I think I even hear Ben let out another exasperated sigh somewhere behind me.

She looks up at me, those smoldering earthen orbs punching the air from my lungs. Her slender fingers push back the titian locks away from her face with a practiced movement.

Fuck... It only serves to reignite the flame of desire that's been eating me alive for three years.

It just isn't fair for something like her to exist in this world, teasing and tempting without any promise of relief or peace.

If it wasn't for the fact that I would have an entire island after my ass, not to mention a mass of young witnesses, I would snatch her up right here, right now, and leave this godforsaken island without bartering a single fucking thing.

What a fucked up time for an opportunity to arise.

"I am so sorry! The children just wanted to see the ships." Her breathy voice reaches out and wraps itself around my throat.

Deja'vu anyone?

The children huddle around her, tugging on her poor excuse for a skirt—the edges fringed and pieces torn from years of wear and tear—as they point around at the ships, the cargo, the men.

That's when I am struck with a *genius* idea.

I give her my most convincing smile, trying to hide my devious intention behind an air of innocence. "Well, we can't disappoint the *children*, now can we?"

I can tell by the look in her eyes—the same wide-eyed excitement that has been there since I first saw her—that the children are here because she has duties as their teacher. The children may very well want to see the ships as well, but it is *she* who really wants to be here.

"Why don't you bring them onto the ship, and I'll make sure you get a grand tour?" I offer, my skin practically buzzing.

I watch as the most mouthwatering blush dusts her cheeks. It is clear to me that I have just given an offer she *can't* refuse. She looks down at the children, their wide eyes filled with excitement almost equal to her own. Almost.

"What do you think, children? Want to see a sailor's ship?"

I almost lose it. She really has no idea what I actually am. She has no recognition of the difference between us and the 'respectable' seafarers that port here alongside us.

Perfect.

The children cheer and start babbling in a roar of laughter. They are all so enthusiastic that they've moved on to speaking in their native tongue. Even if it weren't in such an uproar, I wouldn't be able to understand any of it.

She looks up at me, and for a moment, I feel something click into place like so many times before. It's most likely just more of that burning, gnawing mania brought on by the fucking curse she's had me under. A curse that has kept me awake night after night, year after year.

Leading them all up on deck, I make sure to keep close enough to practically taste her on my tongue. We Mundanes have always been under the impression that the Kana'te peoples are not the cleanest. After all, they live in the jungle in huts and bathe in rivers—or so the stories go. But there is nothing that screams filth about the smell of her. It's a sweet intoxication that has been forcibly branded into my memory.

The expression on her face as she looks around the deck sparks all kinds of fantasies, the images running wild and unabashed through my mind. I bet she would just *love* to be ravished on this ship under the stars.

I pull myself from my own *glorious* filth, catching the sight of her reigning in the children. I can't help but admire how well she maintains her composure as the children begin to grow restless, wandering eyes and hands wishing to see and touch everything, with little feet that want to run.

Personally, I would have thrown a couple overboard by now.

Catching Arthur as he passes by, I grab a hold of his shirt and whip him around to face the group I have just led onto the deck.

His brows furrow deeply, clearly unamused by my latest extreme.

"Arthur, give the children a tour, will you? They're just *dying* to learn all there is to know. Be a good lad and humor them."

I almost burst into laughter at the look that crosses the boy's face.

Yeah, I know, my gentle, enthusiastic tone probably has him thinking I've lost my damn mind.

I lean in, just close enough so the woman and her little pack of monsters can't hear the deep rumbling threat on my tongue.

"Do it, or sleep in the sand tonight."

Arthur gives me a look, one that tells me he's completely confused by my sudden willingness to allow several young children onto the ship. I pay him no mind, clapping him on the shoulder with another sickeningly sweet grin. His eyes snap from me to Sitara, back to me, and I can see the recognition seep into his boyish, baby-blue eyes.

He hangs his head, his shoulders slumping slightly as he nods his agreement. Apparently, sleeping in the sand was a great enough threat. Not that he really has a choice in the matter, but I'll allow him to think he does.

As Arthur moves toward the little crowd of tiny monsters, Ben shuffles to my side with a sigh. "This is low, even for you," he murmurs, side-eyeing me with a knowing glance.

"Not for you, though," I remark dryly, "I'm just taking a page out of the Book of Benedict."

Clearly, my first mate doesn't approve of my actions, or my motivations behind them, but I really couldn't possibly care less about what *Benedict* thinks of it.

I watch as Sitara starts shuffling the children across the deck, following closely behind Arthur. The innocent wonder radiating from her is absolutely delicious! I could watch every small emotion flash across her face all day long and never get bored. Actually, I have watched every small emotion flash across her face all day long. Last time we came to port. I had spent an entire week doing nothing but standing outside the schoolhouse for hours upon hours.

That's probably why Benedict is so fucking uptight about it. He had to do all the heavy bartering last time.

I follow the group closely, shooting daggered glares at any of the men who dare to look in her direction. Each one averts their gaze, and Becket is lucky I haven't thrown him overboard after catching him craning his neck to look at her ass.

Luckily for me, she isn't paying attention to what I am doing a few feet behind her. Actually, now that I think about it, I'm not okay with how *little* she cares that I'm even breathing the same air as she is.

I lengthen my strides to close the distance between us, my hand already outstretched before I've even made it to her side. My palm is itching, and touching her is the only thing that will scratch it. The moment my hand meets the exposed skin of her lower back, just above the waistline of her skirt, I have to bite back an appreciative groan. Yes, she's just as soft as I had imagined all these years, and it has done absolutely nothing to 'itch that scratch'.

I want more.

"Enjoying the ship?" I ask, leaning down just shy of her ear.

She turns her face to meet my gaze, and I'm not sure if that makes me feel triumphant or even more irritable that she's just given me the same polite smile she's given *every other man* on this ship.

I can't say why I had expected anything more.

This woman *really* gets on my nerves. She's as infuriating as she is alluring.

"I am, thank you," she nods, "I'm sorry, I didn't catch your name."

"It's Kier-" I'm cut off by the irritatingly loud shriek of a child in front of us. Her attention snaps to a young girl who somehow managed to get her leg caught in one of our nets.

How in the fuck... Seriously?

I might as well be a damn bug on the wind compared to the inconveniently placed child in a snare.

I wait—very impatiently, I might add—trying to keep my patience. When she finishes helping the girl, I try again.

"It's Kiernan. Kiernan Slater."

"Keetan... Nice to meet you."

She's not even fucking looking at me!

I'm not sure which irritates me more: the fact that she is blatantly ignoring me or that I'm trying so hard.

We shuffle through my ship to below deck, my hand moving back to her skin with increasing persistence. Flashing her another charming smile, I demand her attention a little more than the last time.

I clench my jaw tightly when there is *still* no reaction to my touch. The realization that she is surrounded by a horde of children who seem to be taking up space makes thoughts of feeding them to sharks more and more appealing by the second. I didn't bring them aboard to distract my prize over and over again. I brought them to get *her* here.

Arthur clearly isn't doing his job correctly.

The perfect opportunity to really get my hands on her presents itself in the form of a massive oaf by the name of Jeoffrey as he clumsily shuffles through the children with his arms overflowing with cargo.

I curl my fingers around the dip in her hip and pull her closer to me with a sudden jerk.

"Careful, darling," I coo in her ear before grabbing Joffrey by the scruff of his neck, nearly causing him to lose his grip of the crate on his shoulder. "Apologize to the lady."

"That's not—"

"He nearly crushed you."

I never break eye contact with the idiot, making sure he knows my unspoken threats hold. "Apologize. Don't make me tell you again." Of course, he hadn't *actually* almost crushed her, but she wasn't paying attention enough to know that. I am also well aware of the animosity Jeoffrey holds for the Kana'te people.

He comes from a long family line that dates back to the War of the Great Divide almost four hundred years ago. While many of us had long since let the tension from the past fester into no more than annoyance, some families seem to hold onto it as though it is a personal injustice. Most of their prejudice is directly linked to the idea that the gods had given up on those without magical ability and favored those who did.

I could care less, but the glowering stare Joffrey is giving her seems to work in my favor.

His clear disdain for her seems to spark a flicker of annoyance in Sitara herself as she folds her arms over her chest and stares back. From what I have learned in my years of watching and observing her interactions, Sitara is friendly until you are not.

"Shouldn't have filthy little cante getting in the way," Jeoffrey grumbles, though he isn't brave enough to look away from me.

Sitara stiffens in my grasp, the generations-old vulgarism clearly forcing its way down like a bitter pill. Her skin seems to grow icy to the touch, almost painfully so, but I don't let go. Actually, I do the opposite. My grip on her tightens slightly.

"That did *not* sound like an apology to me," I growl through clenched teeth.

The fact that this motherfucker doesn't open his mouth or do as I've just instructed makes my blood boil. Him completely ignoring an order in front of an outsider—not to mention that outsider being *her*—on *my ship* has just set in stone exactly how the rest of his visit in Puka'qui is going to play out.

He's just ruined his entire week all on his own.

Just as I've made up my mind to grind him under my boot, to throw my carefully placed facade of decency over the railing, Benedict strolls up to us. He takes a deep breath as if to start inconveniencing me with something trivial, but I don't allow him to utter a single word.

"Ah, Benedict! Perfect timing."

The look of fear that flickers through Joffrey's eyes tells me all I need to know about his bravado.

Yeah, you just fucked up.

I throw my free arm around Ben's shoulders, and he gives me a subtle eyebrow twitch in response. "I have an issue that I need dealt with. Mind taking care of it for me?"

I watch his murky green eyes take in the scene unfolding, flicking from me to Sitara to Joffrey, who has now begun to shift uncomfortably.

Benedict's lips curve into a friendly smile—well, friendly to anyone who doesn't know him personally—and tilts his head as he assesses the oaf in front of us with a predatory gaze.

"Sure thing, Cap."

Ben jerks his head toward the deck, and Joffrey listens, quickly making his presence in front of me scarce.

The rest of the tour moves along about as smoothly as the first half. It consisted mostly of me trying to gain her attention like a young pup vying for a scrap of food. My patience had grown thin, so thin in fact that I had contemplated simply taking her behind a crate. By the time the tour finishes and she herds the children down the gangplank, I'm practically vibrating with irritation.

I am Kiernan fucking Slater, and here I am debasing myself in the attempt to appear less selfish than I am. Why? To keep her from being afraid of me. Because it's not time for her to fear me yet.

It's not the time for her to run away.

Even if she tried, I won't allow it.

I watch her mess of curls move further and further away as she takes the children back into the schoolhouse, my muscles coiled tightly. My jaw aches from clenching so hard, and I've decided.

I'm done waiting.

There will be no more games.

Not after today.

However, I have a rogue rat to deal with first.

I find Benedict leaning against the railing at the stern of the ship, his elbows propped up against the wood. His face is lowered to the water, that usual gleam of sadistic pride swimming in his eyes.

Making my way to stand beside him, I look down into the water as well, grinning despite myself at the scene playing out on the surface of the water below. Joffrey hangs, his ankles and wrists hog-tied with a length of sturdy rope. His body is pressed against the ship with each wave that crashes.

"I figured you wouldn't want your little plaything to see what qualifies as discipline just yet," Ben explains, his voice laced with amusement as more and more of the men come to watch the show. Joffrey gasps for breath after each wave that tumbles over his face and knocks his head into the side of the ship. "So, I decided to threaten him with meeting dear old Gerald for a spell."

"You know me too well." I playfully roll my eyes at his enthusiasm, watching the man below squirm and sputter. "He doesn't seem to be too grateful for your generosity, my friend."

I give him a quick glance, chuckling at the depravity of it. Ben is an excellent knotsman. The poor bastard doesn't stand a chance in hell of freeing himself. What makes it all the more amusing is the fact that, for Ben, this is *mild* in comparison. Imagine what would have happened if I hadn't silently demanded subtlety.

He turns to face the opposite direction, leaning back against the railing as though he's just sold a young child a litter of kittens rather than practically drowning one of our best crew members.

"He will be, when I have him on swab duty from here to the next port."

I roll my shoulders, groaning with satisfaction as a symphony of crackling rolls down my spine. "Pull him up and we will see if he is ready to see reason."

Benedict wastes no time hoisting the bastard up, and I am still amazed someone of Ben's size holds the capacity for the level of strength. He's not a small fellow, but he certainly isn't nearly as large as myself.

Joffrey rolls onto the deck with a loud thud, coughing up bouts of ocean water from his mouth and nose. His clothes are soaked to the bone, rivulets of water cascading down his pudgy face.

I squat down next to the gasping man as he rolls onto his side, wheezing and spitting like a foul rodent. "I'm sure after that nice, refreshing cooldown that Benedict so generously offered you, you're ready to follow orders when they're given the *first* time?"

It's posed as a question, yet I've brooked no argument on the matter. The lesson is clear. Either he will do as he's told, or the next time I won't be so kind. Nor will I hold any rein on Benedict's leash.

After the gasping has subsided enough for him to speak, he rasps out a response, his voice hoarse from the salt water he's undoubtedly ingested. "Aye, Aye, Cap."

I loom over him for a moment longer, tilting my head to the side as I study his sincerity. Satisfied with what I find, I rise to my feet and brush myself off with a light huff, turning to Ben with a grin.

"Well, Benedict, put my ship to bed. I'm going for a walk."

I move toward the gangplank without so much as another thought. I can hear the skepticism in Benedict's voice as he shouts after me. "A walk?"

"A walk," I repeat, turning to look over my shoulder at him, "I have a little witch to grab."

5

Sitara

Walking through the crowded pathway a while later, I am beaming with residual excitement, the kind that lingers long after the initial thrill has passed. My cheeks are still flushed with exhilaration, and my heart's still pounding with anticipation. The smell of salt and tar lingers in my nostrils, and the creak of wooden rigging echoes faintly in my mind.

I had gotten to see the inner workings of a sailing vessel! The intricate web of ropes, the towering mast, and the rhythmic calls of the sailors as they worked had left me in awe. When I woke up this morning, it was the last thing I had expected to happen today, but I couldn't be more thrilled that it had. Life in Puka'qui is never dull, but moments like this remind me of why I love this village so much.

As I walk, the sounds of the village fill the air: the clatter of pots from nearby food stalls and the chatter of villagers. The sun is beginning to dip, casting long shadows across the pathway.

I feel tiny fingers wrap around my hand, tighter, bringing me out of my dazed stupor. I look down at the young boy, his dimpled smile and green eyes greeting me. Thomas is the only Mundane child who shows up at the schoolhouse out of the four that reside here on the island.

His mother and father own the only tavern in Puka'qui, a bustling hub of activity that comes alive in the evenings when sailors and travelers pour in seeking rest and refreshment.

They often send him out during the day so that they can prepare for the evening rush, but Thomas would rather be anywhere but home. He is a sweet boy, though a little young, in my opinion, to be running around trying to attend school. The boy is only four years old, after all. I know I have no room to judge anyone—I'm not a parent—but the seemingly obvious lack of attention he gets at home bothers me.

He reminds me of a younger version of myself, constantly trying to understand why his parents never seem to have the time for him. To see the confusion in the eyes of someone so young... It simply shouldn't be that way. I remember the days when I felt the same way, when I wished for just a moment of my parents' attention. It's a pain that I wouldn't wish on anyone, and seeing it in Thomas cuts deep.

"Are you ready to go home, Thomas?" I ask him, gently squeezing my hand around his with a soothing, firm grip.

I try to keep my tone light, but I can sense the reluctance in his small frame. He looks up at me with those big green eyes, and I can see the hesitation there. He *doesn't* want to go home. If he could, he would most likely walk around the streets until the sun dropped from the sky. It is sad to see such a young, sweet child tire of going home, to the one place he should feel the most at peace.

I kneel to his level and brush a strand of hair from his face. "It will be okay, Thomas. I'll see you tomorrow, alright?"

Thomas's little mouth pinches at the corners, and he nods. I give him a reassuring smile and a gentle pat on the back.

Looking around the streets of Puka'qui, I scan the buildings once more before we round the bend toward the tavern. The village is starting to come alive with the sounds of the evening. The smell of cooking meat and fresh bread wafts through the air, mingling with the salty sea breeze. I've felt eyes on me all day, as per usual for this time of year.

I can't quite explain it, but it always feels like someone is watching me, hiding away in a corner of the village I can never see. As unnerving as it is, I try to ignore it. After all, I'm sure a lot of people feel that way when ships of strangers begin to filter into the coast. But still, the feeling persists, a nagging at the back of my mind.

Still, it never ceases to send a cold sweat down my spine. The idea that someone could be watching me in the schoolhouse, or as I walk to and from the jungle's treeline, always drops down into my gut like heavy stones. It always makes my palms sweat, and I have to rub them on the front portion of my skirt to keep them dry. I quicken my pace, my eyes darting from one shadow to the next, but I see nothing. Just the usual village life.

As Thomas and I approach the tavern, the candles just starting to flicker with the lowering sun, I notice a familiar figure slipping out of the entrance. His skin is taut, pale despite the tanned melanin. His dark locks hang over his face as he moves toward the jungle, his muscled frame sluggish and slow.

Larkin.

My brother.

My heart sinks as I see him, the familiar signs of opium use evident in his sluggish movements and pale complexion. I feel a surge of anger mixed with worry. What is he doing here?

"That's the big guy I was telling you about," Thomas blurts out, pointing toward my brother. His voice is innocent, but it cuts through me like a knife.

My blood rushes to my feet, leaving me feeling iced out. The heat of my previous elation is now gone as I recall a conversation I'd had with Thomas all of five or six days ago.

He had come to school tired and upset. His clothes had been hastily put on, and his blond curls were disheveled and unkempt. When I had asked him if he was okay, he had looked up at me with weary eyes and proceeded to tell me that his parents were loud all night long with a—and I quote— *'big, scary man who breathes smoke like a dragon'*.

I had dismissed it at the time, thinking it was just a child's imagination running wild, but now I realize that it was true. Larkin had been at the tavern, and he had scared Thomas.

Horror quickly turns to rage, my cheeks tingling with the overflow of emotion. How could he be so reckless? I know Larkin is messed up, but this? This is a new low.

I motion Thomas toward the entrance to the tavern and give him a tight smile, trying to hide my building frustration and disappointment. "Go on inside, sweetheart. I'll see you again tomorrow, okay?"

I watch him toddle off toward the door, his bouncing baby curls swaying side to side as he does. It isn't until he is safely inside for the evening that I rip my gaze from the door and hurry after my brother.

"Larkin. Larkin!" I shout, though he pays me no mind, too far gone from the amounts of opium he has just put into his body.

I run after him, my skirt catching on the underbrush as I go. He disappears through the trees, his form becoming harder and harder to make out under the heavy shading of the Cecropia trees. I quicken my strides, the bubbles of irritation in my chest popping like boiling water.

Who the hell does he think he is?! Does he have any idea how much pain he's causing? How much he's hurting the people around him?

Just as I take a step over the barrier, I feel the slight brush of something against the skin at my lower back. The waistline of my skirt tugs enough that I can feel the subtle pull of the fabric. I whirl around to see if perhaps a low tree branch had gotten snagged on my clothes, my hand reaching back to make sure it hasn't frayed. There is nothing in my path. Nothing but the flickering candles in the windows of buildings in front of me and an abundance of foliage at my back, where Larkin has disappeared.

I can feel those eyes on me again, the same feeling that makes my heart race and my ears buzz. My eyes scan the trees, darting from shadow to shadow. My fingertips tingle, the familiar wave of cold pumping through my veins.

The flicker of emerald flame begins to swim over my skin, lapping at the raised hair on my arms. This time, I am almost positive someone had tried to touch me, but there's no one there. Just the trees swaying in the breeze. I let out a breath and try to calm myself down. It's probably just my imagination, but the feeling lingers, a cold dread that I can't shake.

When I don't see movement or hear even the faintest sound of breathing or footsteps, my shoulders relax imperceptibly. I don't have time for this, nor do I want to get into a fight with a ghost right here on the barrier line.

I shake my head and turn back toward the jungle, my mind still racing with the strange feeling that someone is watching me. But for now, I have to focus on finding my brother and making sure he doesn't hurt anyone else.

I turn back toward the direction Larkin has gone, the crunch of dried leaves and twigs beneath my feet echoing the turmoil in my chest. The warm breeze carries the faint scent of the jungle, but it does little to calm the storm brewing inside me. I begin to jog, my strides purposeful, driven by a growing frustration.

Finally, I catch up to him, my fingers closing around his arm. He spins around, his eyes narrowing as he shakes off my hold.

"What?!" he growls, his voice low and menacing, like a predator cornered. His face twists into a snarl, and for a moment, I'm taken aback by the raw anger in his eyes. I blink rapidly, trying to process the sharp edge in his tone, the way it cuts through the air like a blade.

"Um, excuse me? What the hell is your problem?" My voice rises, each word sharper than the last, my pitch climbing in disbelief. My brows furrow deeply, forming a tight coil between my eyes as I struggle to contain the surge of emotions threatening to spill over.

Why? Why does he always act this way? The question echoes in my mind like a refrain. It's a familiar ache, one I've grown all too accustomed to over the years. His attitude, his distance, his constant defiance—it's a shield he's built around himself, one I've tried to breach time and again, only to be met with more walls, more barriers.

"I don't have a problem, Sitalli'ara," he huffs, his tone dripping with disdain. The use of my native name cuts deeper than I care to admit. It's not the name itself that stings—it's the way he growls it, as if it's a curse, a burden, an inconvenience. It's the way he spits it out, as though I'm nothing more than a nuisance, a fly buzzing around his head.

"Don't just go around grabbing people while they're walking," he adds, his voice laced with irritation, his jaw clenched tight. I feel a surge of anger at his deflection, at the way he twists everything to make me the villain.

"I wouldn't grab you if you were paying attention to me when I yelled for you," I shoot back, my voice sharp, my frustration boiling over. I can feel my heart pounding in my chest, the rhythm fast and frantic, like a drumline in my ears.

Larkin folds his arms over his chest, his posture rigid, defensive. He stares at me, but I wouldn't say he *sees* me. His eyes are glazed, unfocused, like a film has been pulled over them, dulling the sharpness of his gaze.

"What do you want?" he asks finally, his tone flat, detached, as though I'm a stranger, not someone who's known him my whole life.

I won't lie and say it doesn't sting. The pain is sharp, biting, and I can't tell if the reason I want to cry is because my feelings are hurt or if I'm simply *that* pissed off. Probably both. The mix of emotions swirls inside me, a toxic cocktail of anger and hurt, each fueling the other.

"Are you serious, Larzoma'kin?" I demand, throwing my hands to the side in frustration. My voice rises, each word a betrayal of the calm I'm trying to maintain. "That little boy is terrified of you! He came to school saying you were breathing smoke like a dragon! What is wrong with you?"

The words hang in the air, and for a moment, I feel a flicker of regret. But then it hits me—*the realization,* like a punch to the gut, forcing my jaw to drop in disbelief.

"Is... Are they the ones who supply you with that Mundane garbage you put in your body all the time?" I ask, the accusation slipping out before I can stop it.

It's the wrong thing to say. I know it the moment the words leave my lips. His face darkens, what little color is left draining from his cheeks as he leans in slowly, his eyes narrowing, his lips curling into a snarl.

"That is none of your damn business," he hisses, his breath hot against my face, his voice low and dangerous. "Why don't you go do something productive instead of standing here lecturing me like a child?"

"Productive?" I repeat, my voice incredulous, my laughter sharp and bitter. "Really, Larkin? I spend all day at the school, teaching young minds how to read and write and do math. So that they have options in their future. What do you do? Smoke your crap every waking moment and snag a stag from time to time if you can keep your head clear enough not to shoot someone else instead of the damn deer!"

The words spill out, a torrent of anger and frustration, each one a dagger aimed at the walls he's built around himself. I can feel the tightening in my chest, the pressure building, making it hard to breathe. My hands begin to tremble, and I clench my jaw so hard I worry I might chip a tooth.

How dare he treat me as though I'm the problem! The thought blazes through my mind like a wildfire.

I've done nothing but look after his ass for the last fourteen years, covering for him any time he was too messed up to come out of his tent and take care of his responsibilities. I've been understanding, or at least I've tried. Yet, here he is, brushing me off like I'm no more than a bug that's landed on his shoulder.

"Just because you can go about your life acting like our parents didn't try to gut you like a pig for slaughter, doesn't mean I can," he spits, his voice dripping with malice, his tongue slurring every other word. There's a venom in his tone, a poison that seeps into my veins, chilled and deadly. "I don't need you to watch over me or take care of me. Maybe you should start worrying more about yourself."

His words hit me like a sledgehammer, each one a blow to the chest, leaving me breathless and reeling. I freeze, my heart stopping, the world around me narrowing to the sound of his voice, the way the words cut through me like a knife. It's so painful that I fear my sternum might crack open and spill everything inside me.

I can barely register him now, barely see his face through the red haze that clouds my vision. Everything tilts, and I feel like I'm falling, like the ground has been pulled out from under me, leaving me weightless, directionless.

He has gone too far, and judging by the slight softening of his jawline, he knows it too. There's a flicker of something in his eyes, a hesitation, but it's too late.

The damage is done.

I dig my nails into the meaty portion of my palms, the pain grounding me, anchoring me to the moment. Two things can pull me back from the brink: adrenaline and pain. Neither feels like they will work at the current moment.

Before I can give him a chance to retract his statement or, worse, continue his beratement, I turn on my heel and walk away. To where,

I don't know. I don't care. I just need to get away from here. Away from him.

Everything is spiraling, and I can't seem to stop it. Right now, I wish the ground would open wide and swallow me whole.

I feel my body sway and tilt as I walk, my muscles trembling with the force of my accelerated heart rate. I can't get my breathing to come out in anything but shallow, jutting gushes of air. It's as if someone has reached into my chest and wrapped their fingers around my lungs, squeezing tight.

Flashes of memory come rushing to the forefront of my mind, and I have no way to shut them off. Nowhere to run away.

He didn't mean it.

He didn't mean it.

Or did he?

His words, despite his compromised state, were so full of conviction. Like he means it.

Why?

Why did he have to say that?

Why couldn't he have left that as nothing but a distant memory?

Why does he act like it happened to him? It didn't happen to him! He's only using it to justify his self-destruction.

I walk to the beach on the far side of Puka'qui, the sand shifting under my feet as I move. When my toes hit the cool sand, I contemplate simply throwing myself into the waves. Maybe if I swim long enough, I'll find another little island and...

No. No, that's not really what I want. I don't know what I want right now.

With a single sentence, my brother has managed to open every last healing wound he could find. I stop along the shore, having made a beeline for the edge of the water.

I let the frigid liquid snap me from my fast descent, and I suck in a sharp intake of air as it laps at my ankles. It doesn't, however, manage to keep me from finding it harder and harder to keep myself together.

My shoulders are shaking violently now, and I rake my hands through my hair, tugging at the strands as though I'm trying to peel away my skin and become someone else entirely.

And that is when the tears come, the salt-like acid on my skin as it flows freely and drips onto my collarbone. *Damn it...*

I bury my feet into the wet earth and sigh, the sound cracking against the force of my sobs. I hate crying. Crying never does anyone a bit of good, though Djar says the opposite to me often.

I rub my arms, trying to warm my chilled body. It is like all the heat has drained from my blood, and I can feel the cold fire begin to simmer under my skin. If I'm not careful, it'll explode.

As my hands graze over my upper arm, I can't feel the familiar scrape of fabric on my palm. My Tilona'matli isn't where it should be; the absence of the thin strip of cloth suddenly leaves me feeling bare. It has been a constant piece of who I am for fourteen years.

The Tilona'matli is a marking band that the children of those who left the villages to join the cult of Hu'yimona were forced to wear. In the beginning, it was due to their lack of trust in us—the fear that we may grow up to be just like our parents. Even though the village trusts me and Larkin now, it doesn't change the fact that there will always be that small seed of doubt.

Honestly, I'm confused as to how it could have fallen off. In fourteen years, it has *never* fallen off. The intricate knotwork is meant to stay. The damn thing is even washed on my body, as though it has become a part of my skin.

Panic begins to set in, for just a moment.

What if they think I took it off to go join my parents? Which isn't possible since they are dead.

Listening to the sound of the waves sloshing onto the shore, I can't help but feel somewhat liberated by the fact that it is *not* there. Even still... I'm not sure how it could have disappeared.

Finally, I take a deep breath, letting my soul ease slightly as I begin to work my wounds back to a trickling stream rather than a raging river.

6

Kiernan

I had been so close—agonizingly, painfully, close—to finally having her right where I wanted her. My fingers had nearly hooked into the fabric of her skirt. The opportunity had been perfect, the setting ideal. Larkin, that self-absorbed prick, had been so intoxicated, so completely out of his mind, that he wouldn't have even noticed what was happening.

And Sitara? She had been so engrossed in the argument brewing between them, so caught up in the tension, that she hadn't even realized how close I had gotten.

It had all been falling into place so beautifully, so flawlessly.

It had been *perfect*.

And then, as if the universe itself had decided to mock me, she stepped through that barrier at the last possible moment. The barrier Mundanes are never, *ever* supposed to cross.

Just like every other time, my carefully laid plans had been ruined before I could even see them through. My moment, my perfect, shining moment, had been snatched away from me.

Needless to say, it has left me in a foul mood—one that can only be described as utterly shitty.

Though I will admit, my near miss had almost cost me more than just my pride. I had never seen her use her abilities before, and I wasn't entirely sure what they were. To be honest, it has always been one of the few things about her life that I *hadn't* managed to uncover, to dissect, to understand.

Now I know why.

The sight of those emerald flames, flickering across her pale skin like a mesmerizing dance, had left me utterly entranced. It was the most captivating thing I had ever seen her do—and that is saying something.

I have been watching her for three long, grueling years. Three years of waiting, plotting, and pining for the perfect moment to take what I want. And every single time, the universe seems to find some way to step in, to interfere, to ruin everything.

But I am not one to give up easily. No, not me.

Take now, for example.

I should be heading back to the Nureus, crawling into my bed, and trying to forget the entire scene I have just witnessed on the edge of the forest. I *should* be leaving this all behind, letting it go.

But I can't.

And I won't.

The opportunity to place myself directly in her path during a moment of such vulnerability is too good to pass up. That fight between her and Larkin has left her rattled in a way I have never seen before. I have every intention of exploiting that, of using it to my full advantage.

Still, it doesn't stop me from fantasizing about turning around, crossing that treeline, and bashing Larkin's face in. I wouldn't wish the expression I had seen on her face on my worst enemy, let alone my sister, which I do have. The very idea of it opens up a whole new line of questions in my mind.

What had her parents done to her to cause such a reaction at the mere mention of them?

It is a question I will have to save for another time. Right now, there are more pressing matters at hand. Matters that have everything to do with the undeniable burning desire coursing through me.

And it shall have her.

As I walk along the shore, breathing in the fresh ocean air, I finally see her standing motionless a few yards ahead of me. I give her a moment, though not one out of any kindness on my part. No, I simply want her calmed enough to notice my presence before I make my move.

After all, a vulnerable woman is easy prey, but a hysterical one is beyond reason.

It only takes a few more steps for the full picture to come into focus, for my heart to begin pounding wildly in my chest.

This is it. The moment I have sacrificed so much for, the moment I have been waiting for all these years.

She is standing alone in the sand, as though she has been placed there just for me. My reward, finally, for all my efforts.

She buries her feet in the sand, wiping the back of her hand across her face. The warm ocean breeze catches her long, copper-colored hair, sending strands of it dancing around her.

A sinister smirk tugs at my lips as I find myself thanking whatever imaginary gods might be out there. As I approach her, I take the time to soak in every little detail—the twitch of her lips, the curve of her jaw, the tight fists at her sides, the glistening tears on her cheeks.

She is still crying.

And I plan to make her cry even more. But when I do, it won't be for the reasons that have brought her here to this beach. It will be for something far more pleasurable.

I have always known Larkin could be a piece of shit, but this... This is something else entirely. I have done many things, terrible things, but making my sister cry like this? That is a new low, even for him.

"You're a long way from home for such a late hour," I say finally, stopping just a few feet away from her. My voice is low, rough with the excitement coursing through me.

She startles at the sound of my voice, quickly drying her face as she turns to look up at me. She has been so lost in her thoughts, her pain, that she hadn't even noticed me approaching.

That's okay. After tonight, she will never *not* notice me again.

I tower over her, my larger frame dwarfing hers as we stand here in the sand. My eyes roam over her face, drinking in every expression.

"I'm on an adventure," she says bitterly, her voice cracking with emotion she is trying to hide.

"Sounds like you're thrilled about it," I say with a chuckle.

She glances up at me, her hair blowing across her face as she tries to tuck it behind her ear. She wraps her other arm around herself, as though to shield her body from the compromising position she has found herself in—alone on a beach with a Mundane in the dead of night.

"Sawyer, right?" she says, her tone uncertain.

Seriously?

My jaw clenches tightly as I force myself to smile through the irritation rising inside me. The woman is infuriating! Absolutely, mind-bogglingly airheaded.

I make a mental note: I will have to make sure my name sticks in that beautiful, stubborn little head of hers.

"Kiernan," I grit out, forcing myself to take a deep breath. I have to keep my eyes on the prize, and what a delicious prize she is.

"So, where is this adventure taking you, Sitara?" I ask, her name rolling off my tongue, sweet and addictive. I have been dying to say it out loud.

She narrows her eyes, suspicion flickering across her face. "How do you..."

I realize my mistake almost immediately. She hasn't introduced herself to me, and I haven't been around when others have addressed her. I quickly smooth it over, forcing a charming smile onto my face.

"I heard one of the children call you by name during the tour," I lie, my tone light and innocent.

It works.

Her shoulders relax, and I see the spark of recognition in her eyes. Just like that, I have established a rapport.

She shrugs, a heavy sigh trembling through her body as she returns to my initial question. "I don't know. I'm just on an adventure."

I can tell she is debating how much to reveal to me, despite having seen me before. The people of her tribe aren't exactly known for being open with us Mundanes. Not emotionally, anyway.

I press on, tilting my head to the side to make myself look curious rather than probing. "So, you don't have a destination, then? Are you traveling alone?"

I go to great lengths to keep my voice neutral, to mask the excitement bubbling just beneath the surface.

"Yes," she replies simply, her voice flat.

She doesn't even seem to realize the implications of what she is saying. She is too caught up in her pain, her grievances, to think about the dangers of traveling alone or to pick up on the underlying currents in my words.

It is perfect.

Absolutely, gloriously perfect.

I might just become a religious man yet.

I reach out, wrapping a long strand of her hair around my finger. "Well, that isn't very safe *or* smart," I say, my tone playful, "You know, there are pirates out this time of year."

She shrugs again, the motion both endearing and frustrating. "What would a pirate want with me?"

Oh, Pet, you have no idea...

A deep, rumbling chuckle bubbles up my throat, my finger tracing the bridge of her nose in a gentle, teasing gesture. "You're a very pretty lady, lass. I think that should be an easy thing to guess. Why *would* a pirate want you?"

I can't believe my luck.

She stands here, her wide eyes sparkling with the same naive innocence that captivated me the day we first met. It's almost as if the world hasn't touched her, hasn't hardened her, hasn't stripped her of that radiant purity. And it's precisely that innocence that makes her so dangerously alluring and easy to lead astray.

And lead her astray I shall. I can hardly resist the urge to guide her down a path she doesn't even realize she's stepping into.

I shake my head, a slow, amused smile spreading across my face as I let my hand drop back to my side. No need to reveal my intentions too soon. Thus far, she seems to be interpreting my touch as nothing more than a playful gesture, a harmless tease, but it won't remain that way for much longer. I can see the spark of curiosity in her eyes, the way she leans in just slightly when I'm speaking. She doesn't realize it yet, but she's already caught in my web. In the same way, she has had me caught in hers.

To my disbelief, she lets out a soft scoff, her lips curling into a coy smile as she rolls her eyes. It's a smile that speaks volumes, a silent admission that I'm exactly where I want to be.

"Trust me, they'd bring me right back," she says, her voice laced with confidence, though I can hear the faintest undertone of uncertainty beneath it.

"Think so, do you?" I ask playfully.

"I would," she replies, her voice steady, though her eyes flicker for just a moment. It's a small crack in her armor, one she probably doesn't even realize she's revealed to me. The self-loathing.

Her words strike a chord with me, and I quickly realize something: She has no idea how absolutely captivating she is. No idea how her gentle nature is like a beacon, drawing in men who crave power, who want to dominate, who want to destroy. She doesn't see how the way she carries herself, with such effortless grace, could bring lesser men to their knees and weep.

Unless you're me.

I won't be the one kneeling on my knees tonight.

"Ah, but being taken by a pirate would be an adventure, yes?" I say, my voice low, smooth, as I let a smirk play on my lips. It's a provocative statement, one designed to test the waters, to see just how far she's willing to go.

"I suppose it would be," she admits, "Too bad Puka'qui seems to be fresh out of those."

I'm about to lose my composure. My gut twists with a mixture of anticipation and amusement, the two emotions warring for dominance as I struggle to keep my expression neutral.

But I know I'm on the right track.

I can feel it in my bones, that undeniable pull that tells me I'm pushing her in exactly the direction I want her to go.

"Do you have a place to stay tonight?" I ask her, keeping everything light, unthreatening. It's a simple question, one that could go either way, but I already know the answer. I can see it in the way she hesitates, in the faint furrow of her brow.

I watch as she tilts her head back, her gaze drifting upward to the night sky. She lets out a deep, chest-rattling sigh.

"I'll more than likely trek back home before much longer," she says finally, her voice tinged with resignation.

Well, that would certainly spoil my plans.

I can feel the frustration rising, the impatience burning in my chest. I've come too far, waited too long, to let this slip through my fingers again.

"Or..." I begin, drawing out the word just enough to catch her attention, "I happen to know the man who runs the tavern. And he just so happens to owe me a favor. I could get you a room for the night, instead of you having to hike *all* the way back home."

She takes a step to the side, her eyes narrowing as she side-eyes me. A faint blush rises to her cheeks, barely visible under the pale light above.

"Are you trying to get me naked?" she asks bluntly, her voice steady despite the obvious embarrassment.

I shrug, my face a mask of calm, unbothered innocence. "I would lie," I say, my voice smooth, "but I was raised better than that."

It's a lie, of course. I wasn't raised better than that. But she doesn't need to know that. Not yet, at least.

"Besides," I continue, "I've had a long day, and you certainly look like you could use a... destination for your adventure."

I watch as she contemplates my offer, her expression unreadable. I keep my smile perfectly charming, perfectly non-expectant, as I wait for her response.

It's not uncommon for Kana'te women to spend a night in the tavern with a sailor or two during their visits. In their culture, such an act isn't as taboo as it might be in other parts of the world.

Then, it happens.

A coy grin spreads across her lips, and I feel a rush of triumph, hot and overwhelming, as I realize I've won.

It's almost too easy to read her, to know which buttons to press. Sitara has always been the type to chase a thrill—or to run from whatever plagues her—and offering her a respite from the heaviness that surrounds her has worked in my favor tonight.

Without another word, I let her lead the way to Thomas's tavern, my pace steady and deliberate as I stay barely half a step behind her. My hand rests on her back, just between her shoulder blades, my fingers tangling in the messy strands of hair at the nape of her neck. It's a possessive touch, one that sends a spark of electricity through me as I feel her warmth beneath my palm.

As we walk through Puka'qui, I pay no attention to the village around us. My focus is singular, narrowed down to one thing and one thing alone: getting her to the tavern.

Once inside, I waste no time, striding around the bar to the keys that hang along the wall. Anticipation is building in my veins, a burning, restless energy that demands to be satisfied. I don't have time to trifle with Thomas or his pointless small talk.

He and I share a fleeting glance as he stands behind the counter, scrubbing a mug with a dirty rag. For a moment, I think he might try to protest, might try to assert some semblance of control over the situation. But then he thinks better of it. He knows better than to cross me, especially after all the favors he owes me. So, he says nothing, his eyes dropping as I snatch the key from its hook.

I glance down at the tag attached to it. Room three. Perfect.

It's not too far down the hallway, just a short walk.

I turn back to Sitara, guiding her toward the staircase with a nonchalance that belies the urgency burning inside me.

All it will take is one time. One time, and I can be free from the shackles she's had me in for years. One night, and it can all be over. I can walk away, live my life as though I've never laid eyes on her.

As we climb the stairs, the wait feels interminable. The thirty-second walk to the room stretches on for miles, every step a torturous test of my patience. The moment is finally within my grasp, and the delay is almost unbearable.

But I know it will be worth it. I'm about to be rewarded for all my efforts, and no amount of waiting can diminish the satisfaction that's coming my way.

I shove the key into the lock, the mechanism clicking loudly in the quiet hallway. My muscles are tense, coiled beneath my skin, urging me to get her inside those four walls before she has the chance to evaporate like a damn ghost. It's irrational, I know, but after watching her for so long, after chasing her for so long, one can't blame me for feeling like she's an apparition.

I push the door aside, focusing instead on the task at hand. It swings open, and I step aside just enough to let her enter first. And she does, crossing that threshold. As my hungry gaze bores along her form, I feel it—a sense of victory, of conquest, of finally achieving what I want.

The world around us fades into a blur as I close the distance between us in less time than it takes for a single heartbeat. She is in my arms before I can even process the thought, her body pressed tightly against mine. Our lips meet in a fiery collision, a passionate tangle of desire and pent-up frustration. It's as if every moment of longing, every ounce of unspoken tension, pours out of me.

The transition from standing to hovering over her on the bed is abrupt and rough, driven by a primal urgency that leaves no room for gentleness. This isn't a moment for tender glances or soft, sweet touches. There's no time for slow, sensual foreplay or the kind of quiet intimacy that comes with it. This is raw, unbridled need, a carnal hunger that demands satisfaction. I don't have the patience for anything less than immediate, unrelenting gratification.

But then, something unexpected catches me off guard—Sitara's response. Her passion is a force to be reckoned with, rising to meet mine with a ferocity that leaves my very bones scorched. Her body reacts with a heady intensity that matches my own. I feel a mixture of surprise and exhilaration as her hands claw at me, her hips pressing up to meet mine.

My fingers explore every inch of her, tracing the curves and dips of her body like a cartographer mapping uncharted territory. It's a moment of pure, unadulterated need, and yet, I can't help but marvel at how different reality is from the fantasies I've harbored.

For years, I have imagined what it would be like to touch her, to taste her, to have her beneath me. But nothing—*nothing*—could have prepared me for this. The feel of her skin under my hands, the taste of her mouth, the way her body responds to mine—it's all so much more vivid, so much more alive, than anything I could have conjured in my mind.

And yet, for a moment, I'm torn.

Part of me is thrilled, even awed, by the sheer intensity of it all. Another part of me is irritated, almost resentful, that the reality could so utterly surpass the fantasies.

How could I have spent so long imagining her when the real thing is so much more intoxicating?

But I let the thought go.

It doesn't matter now.

She's here, she's mine, and I'm not wasting another second on doubts or distractions.

I tear at the scraps of fabric that separate us, sending them tumbling to the floor without a second thought. Her clothes are gone, discarded with the same urgency that drives me closer to her.

I break the kiss just long enough to trail my lips down her neck, nipping at the tender flesh there. Her moan is like a spark of fire, igniting something deep within me. It's a sound I've heard a thousand times in my head, but the real thing is so much sweeter. I groan in response, my body thrumming with need.

She arches into my touch, practically pleading for more. My hands are everywhere at once, tracing the lines of her hips, cupping her breasts, skimming down her thighs. Every touch ignites a new spark, a new wave of desire that courses through us both like electricity.

I continue my descent, my mouth following the path of my fingers. Her stomach is taut and warm beneath my lips, and when my thumb brushes against the apex of her thighs, she whimpers.

The sound is like fuel to a fire, driving me forward. I chuckle low in my throat, the sound dark and primal, as I circle her sensitive pearl with the pad of my finger. She writhes beneath me, her body responding to every touch with a raw, unfiltered honesty that leaves me breathless.

I groan at the heat I find there, the slickness of her arousal coating my skin and smoothing the way for my touch. It's intoxicating, a heady mix of musk and sweetness that I can't get enough of.

As I nestle between her spread legs, the scent of her fills my nostrils, rich and primal. My cock throbs in response, eager to claim her.

She trembles, her body responding with an almost palpable need. I lean down, dragging the flat of my tongue along her dripping slit. The taste of her essence is like nothing I've ever known, a mix of sweetness and heat that leaves me groaning. She arches and cries out, her voice ringing through the room exactly as I've imagined all these years.

"I'm going to make you sing for me, kitten," I promise, my voice low and rough, a growl that sends shivers down her spine. "And then, I'm going to eat you alive."

I'm pacing back and forth in my cabin hours later, the floorboards creaking beneath my boots as the memories of the night's events still sear the backs of my eyelids. Every second, every touch, every sound is etched vividly into my mind, refusing to let me escape it. The taste of her lingers on my tongue, a haunting reminder of what I can never truly let go of. Her scent clings to my skin, a maddening mixture of earth and floral, driving me to the edge of my sanity. The feel of her body, soft yet unyielding, wrapping around me like a vice, replays over and over in my mind, a torment so exquisite it borders on agony.

My hands curl into fists at my sides, the frustration boiling in my veins as I imagine her now, fast asleep in that rustic tavern room, blissfully unaware of the storm she has unleashed within me.

I should feel elated. I should feel relieved. I should feel like the weight of three long, torturous years has finally been lifted from my shoulders.

But I don't.

Instead, there's this gnawing, insatiable hunger that claws at my gut, a fire that roars to life with every passing second. Having her once—just one fleeting, glorious taste—has only made the craving worse. It has sharpened the edges of my obsession, turning it into something jagged and unrelenting.

This has been one of the best nights of my goddamn life, but it is never going to be enough. One night will never be enough.

I will not leave this fucking island, this cursed little slice of paradise, until she is mine. Here, on my ship, in my possession. Where I can keep her, touch her, taste her, and never let her go.

At least not until I feel satisfied.

I want more.

And more.

And fucking *more.*

With a growl of impatience, I fling open the door to my cabin, the sound echoing sharply through the quiet of the night. The crew is asleep, their peaceful slumber a stark contrast to the turmoil raging inside me. I don't care. I don't care about their rest or their comfort or anything else that isn't *her.* I make a beeline for Benedict's hammock, my movements driven by a singular focus. Without hesitation, I reach out and tip him unceremoniously onto the floor, his stocky frame hitting the wooden planks with a loud, jarring thud. It's louder than I expected, and for a moment, I freeze, half-expecting the entire crew to stir. But aside from a few muttered curses and the shifting of bodies in hammocks, no one bothers to investigate. They know better than to interfere when I'm in a mood like this.

Benedict, however, is not so easily ignored.

He scrambles to his feet, his fists clenched at his sides, his broad frame squaring off with me. There is a menacing intensity in his eyes that would have shattered a lesser man. His face is a map of irritation and unspoken threats, his sharp jawline twitching as he fights to rein in his temper. If I were anyone else—someone weaker, someone less accustomed to his loyalty—he would have already flattened me on my back. But I'm not just anyone. I'm his captain, and that fact alone stays his hand, even if his expression screams a thousand creative ways to end my life.

"*Captain*," he growls, the word spat out like a curse through his clenched teeth. I barely register it, too caught up in my impatience to care about his tone.

"I have an errand I need you to run," I say, the urgency in my voice betraying the restless energy coiling in my muscles like a spring about to snap.

He raises an eyebrow, his sleep-addled gaze narrowing into a sharp, piercing stare. "Before the sun rises?" he growls, his tone laced with disbelief and a healthy dose of irritation.

I nod once, sharply, folding my arms across my chest. "Right now."

Benedict's groggy, murky gaze slices through me, his eyes filled with a thousand unspoken threats and a healthy dose of resentment. If I weren't the captain—if I weren't me—there's little doubt he'd have already acted on at least one of those threats. But I *am* the captain, and he knows it. Reluctantly, he seems to accept that fact, though it's clear he's not happy about it.

"What is it now, Kiernan?" he grumbles, his voice low and rough, like the scraping of gravel against stone. There's something in his tone that catches my attention—a flicker of irritation, a hint of the boy I once was, scrubbing the decks of this very ship. I don't know if it's the irritation I find amusing or the fact that, deep down, some part of him still sees me as that simpering, wide-eyed teenager. Either way, it's a distraction I don't need right now.

"She's in room three of the tavern," I say, my voice smooth and commanding, a smug, self-satisfied smile spreading across my face like a slow-burning fire. "Go get her."

Benedict groans, dragging a hand through his messy, sleep-tousled hair as he scratches at his scalp in blatant annoyance. "And this requires *me*, why? Do it yourself, you massive asshole."

I cross my arms tighter over my chest, glaring down at him with a look that brooks no argument. "I am your captain."

It's a card I've never played with Benedict, not in all the years he's served under me. I know damned well he'll make me regret it later, but right now, I don't care. Right now, nothing matters except getting what I want.

"I am not required to give you a reason to do my bidding," I say, my voice cold and unyielding, a sharp contrast to the burning anticipation coursing through my veins.

For a moment, he just stares at me, his jaw ticking like a clock about to explode, his nostrils flaring with suppressed rage. Then, without a word, he turns and grabs his pants, yanking them on with quick, jerky movements that betray his irritation. He doesn't break eye contact as he dresses, doesn't speak, but the tension between us is palpable.

I watch him with a smirk, knowing full well I'll hear about this later. Knowing full well he'll find a way to make me pay for this. But for now, I don't care. For now, nothing matters except the prize at the end of this little errand.

I follow him out onto the deck, leaning against the railing as I watch him stalk toward the tavern with the predatory grace of a man on a mission. The moon is high overhead, casting a silver glow over the sleepy little island, and the sound of waves crashing against the shore creates a soothing backdrop to the chaos brewing inside me.

My prey, as I've come to think of her, is asleep, unaware and vulnerable, completely at the mercy of the monster I've just set loose to fetch her.

The thought sends a shiver of excitement coursing through me, and I press my lips together to stifle the laugh that threatens to burst free. My shoulders begin to shake, my nerves stretched taut like a bowstring about to snap. The facade of calm I've worn all day cracks and crumbles, falling to the deck in shattered pieces. A dark, satisfied chuckle rises in my throat, growing louder and more menacing until it spills out of me in a wicked, uncontainable laugh.

After three long, agonizing years of waiting, plotting, and starving myself of the one thing I've craved more than air itself, my little kitten is just moments away from being exactly where I want her—curled up in my sheets, where I'll make her purr until I've had my fill.

7

Kiernan

The sun has climbed high into the sky, long before my prize shows any sign of stirring. The wait is maddening, and with each passing moment, my patience wears thinner. I find myself questioning how much chloroform Benedict might have forced into her system to keep her unconscious for so long.

That's a conversation I'll be having with him later.

For now, I allow myself a brief reprieve from my duties, leaning against the rough wooden planks of the cabin next to the door. The sound of fabric rustling and a low, discomforted groan finally breaks the silence, signaling that she's beginning to stir.

The window above my bed creaks open, slamming forcefully against the outer hull of the ship. She's awake now, and from the frantic shuffling and labored breathing, it's clear she's in a state of panic.

Panic is good. It means she's aware of her predicament, and awareness will make this game far more entertaining.

Still harboring resentment over how he undermined my authority during the tour, I snatch an untouched plate of food from Joffrey's hands. His pale face twists in horror, as if I've just committed some unspeakable crime against his mother. I hand the plate to Arthur, who happens to be strolling by without a care in the world. I pull him in by the shoulders, tilting my head toward the door with a knowing smirk.

"Why don't you give our guest some food like a gentleman, Arthur? I'm sure she'd appreciate it."

I know she won't, which is exactly why I'm not delivering it myself. Not yet. My plan consists of being the most welcoming and familiar presence when she finally emerges onto the deck. When she realizes she's trapped aboard this ship with twenty men who have a certain taste for the finer sins of life. I'll be the one she turns to. The one she trusts.

Arthur shoots me a confused look, but does as he's told. He knocks on the door, his voice booming loudly enough to ensure she hears him. "Cap said ye might be hungry, lass!"

The response is immediate and venomous. "I'm *not* hungry!" Her voice trembles with a mix of rage and confusion, the emotion so raw it can be felt even from where I stand a few feet outside the door.

Arthur turns to me, his expression lost and uncertain. I wave my hand dismissively, signaling for him to give her space. Space, of course, is something she'll have very little of once she steps out of that cabin. Every moment from then on will be carefully controlled.

She's not ready yet, and that's fine. I have all the time in the world to play this game.

"Aye then, lass," Arthur mutters, shoving the plate back into Joffrey's pudgy hands with a bit more force than necessary. He's never been a fan of him, due to Joffrey's constant tormenting of Arthur.

My actions no doubt confuse them all. It's been seven years since I last sailed with a woman aboard my ship, since the complications with my sister. The memory still lingers, a sharp reminder of why I've avoided this until now.

But this time is different.

This time, it's calculated.

I can hear her pacing the cabin, her bare feet thudding against the floor with growing urgency. The sound brings the faintest trace of a smirk to my lips. She's trying to make sense of her situation, wondering what she's gotten herself into.

In three... two... one...

The door bursts open, and she rushes out, her eyes fixed on where the gangplank *should* be. It's no longer there, of course. I'm not stupid enough to linger in Puka'qui after she was brought aboard. She's probably praying to her gods that we're still docked, hoping against hope that there's some way to escape.

Her body jolts to a halt as she leans over the railing, staring down at the water as if it's transformed into a pool of acid. Even from where I stand, I can see the wheels turning in her head, the realization dawning on her that she's completely trapped.

She straightens her form, her posture defeated, as the sound of boots approaches from behind her. The crew gathers around her like sharks sensing blood in the water, their faces split with eager grins, their clothes reeking of sweat and salt. All except Arthur, who looks like a placating puppy, his eyes darting between her and me as if pleading for some kind of intervention.

I hate the boy sometimes, I really do.

Joffrey, with his tall, pudgy form, unkempt beard, and fat fingers that look as though they couldn't hold so much as a grape, leans in closer. She backs up, her face twisting in disgust, her nose scrunching up as if his smell alone is enough to repulse her.

"Did ye slumber well in the cap'n's bed?" he asks, his tone a peculiar mix of irritation and amusement, like a man who knows he's getting under someone's skin.

"For the cap be snoozin' in the nest," he adds, his words dripping with a mocking familiarity.

Her fists are balled at her sides, though I can see the faint tremors in her hands even from where I stand. She clenches her jaw tightly, her muscles coiling like a spring ready to snap. She's not a very large or physically powerful woman, but there's a fire in her eyes that makes me certain she'd fight them all if she had to.

"Back up, fatty," she growls, her voice steady despite the slight tremble that betrays her bravado.

I choke on my saliva, the sound catching in my throat as I try to keep myself from doubling over in laughter. A little spitfire! I love it.

Jeoffrey moves closer to her, a feral grunt rolling up his throat like an animal preparing to strike. "Ye don't be lookin' too grateful, me lass," he says, his voice low and menacing. "What'd our poor cap'n say if he were seein' such disrespect from ye, eh?" He's goading her, pushing her to see how far she'll go before she snaps.

"I said. Back. Up." Her voice is firm, steady, but there's a hint of desperation lurking just beneath the surface. She's trying to keep her cool, but it's clear she's on the edge, ready to do whatever it takes to protect herself.

A broad, wolfish grin curves my lips as I watch my men close in on her, forming a semicircle around her like predators circling their prey. I wait a moment, soaking in the almost primitive look in her eyes, the way she seems to be sizing them up, searching for any weakness she can exploit. So... My little kitten has claws after all. The thought is almost too delicious to bear.

I take a step toward their backs, chuckling under my breath as I listen to Joffrey slur through his lecture. He isn't wrong. I had, indeed, slept in the nest last night. That is not something that will be happening again. My bed belongs to me as much as she, herself, now does. The thought sends a shiver down my spine, a mingling of possessiveness and desire that I can't quite untangle.

Arthur steps forward, his palms up in a nonthreatening manner, his voice soft and placating. "Joffrey, come on noo. Leave the wee lassie alone. She's scared enough wi'oot ye pressin' her agin' the railin'." His words are calm, but there's an undercurrent of something else there, something that makes me clench my jaw in frustration.

I really, *really* do hate him sometimes. I still cling to my initial assessment of him—that he wasn't built to be a pirate.

Before the chaos can escalate further, I give an audible chuckle, the sound low and gravelly. "I'll make a pirate of you yet," I laugh as my men part like the Red Sea, leaving me a generous path to walk.

There it is! The look of utter horror as all her unanswered questions click into place like pieces on a chessboard. Her eyes widen, her breath catches, and for a moment, she's frozen in place, her mind racing to keep up with the revelation.

"Kiernan." Ah, so she finally remembers my name the first time. Good, my face, my name, has finally become worthy of her acknowledgment and memory. The thought sends a surge of satisfaction through me, a twisted sense of pride at having made an impression on her.

The horror on her face is quickly replaced by a delicious rage that fills me with a sick satisfaction. It's like watching a storm brew, the kind of rage that makes your blood run hot and your heart pound in your chest.

"You have got to be *kidding* me!" she snarls, that rage coiling its grip up her spine as she visibly shudders. She's trembling with it, her hands clenched into fists at her sides, her eyes blazing with an almost feral fire.

I take another step closer, my grinning face being met with a fist to the jaw. I hardly move, my smug expression never wavering. All she's managed to do is hurt herself, which is evident by the grimace she's trying to hide. I can see the pain flashing across her face, the way her hand instinctively goes to her knuckles as if to soothe the ache.

I chuckle again as she rubs her fingers over her knuckles. I do not doubt that her hand will bruise. Pity. I don't take kindly to my property being damaged. The thought is dark, twisted, but it's there nonetheless.

"Careful there, Pet," I say, my voice low and smooth, like honey dripping from a spoon. "I don't need you breaking those pretty little fingers in the first five minutes I have you. I suspect they will be very useful to me later." The words are a promise, a thinly veiled threat that makes my blood run hot.

I reach out and take her hand in mine, examining her fingers as if they're some kind of fragile treasure. This, of course, earns me a swift slap across my right cheek.

That one kind of stings. How adorable.

The sting is sharp, but it's nothing compared to the rush of excitement that follows.

"You son of a bitch!" she growls, attempting to pull her hand out of my grasp. I don't release her. Instead, I wrap my fingers around her wrist and tug ever so slightly. Her anger fills me with something warm, gooey, and disgustingly arousing.

It's like a drug, something I can't get enough of.

"Met my mother, have you?" I grin, every fiber of my being itching to fuel her rage, to see how far I can push her before she cracks. I don't have much memory of my mother, to be honest, but that's beside the point. The point is to see her squirm, to see her break.

"Take. Me. To. Shore," she commands through her still clenched jaw. I can see every vile, awful, horrible thought she's having about me in the way she glares.

Oh, she is a wicked little thing, isn't she?

It's enough to stir the insatiable beast in my gut, to bring images of another filthy, hate-filled tussle in my sheets to the surface of my eyelids. Watching the emotion flicker in those russet eyes is like the first taste of fresh water on a hot day. It's intoxicating, addictive.

"Oh, you naive little thing," I grin, hoping it conveys every ounce of victorious pride I am feeling. "You've been asleep far too long.

Turning around now isn't an option, Pet." The words are cruel, but they're true. She's in this now, and there's no going back.

I have to stir the pot. I can't help myself. I tug on her arm again until she is flush against me, the memories of her skin against mine playing unabashed through my mind as I wrap my arm around her. The woman would have steam rolling out of her ears if her anger boils any hotter. I can see the glimmer of emerald flame that licks at her skin, but is unable to be used.

Oh, yes, I know the law *well*. If she uses her magic outside of Capulli'ana, she will never be allowed to return home, and I am counting on her being such a devoted daughter of the gods to heed the law.

She tries to pull away from me again in vain. "You kidnapped me, you fucking psychopath!" The words are venomous, spat at me like a curse. I can feel the heat of her breath against my skin, the way her body trembles with rage.

Capturing the delicate curve of her jaw in my ironclad grasp, I force her to tilt her head back and look at me. Her skin is still so soft against my rough fingers. Like a peach. Easy to bruise. Easy to ruin, but, oh, so sweet. The thought is dark, but it's there, lingering in the back of my mind.

"Psychopath?" I give her a look of mock hurt and lean in closer so the hush of my tone will rumble in her ear and vibrate into her chest. Gods, she smells so *good*. So good that it makes it hard not to flick my tongue out and taste her skin again. "At least I am on a path, darling. You can't even figure out your own life, let alone give it a heading. After all, we did say that being taken by a pirate would be an *awfully* big adventure, did we not?" The words are a taunt, a reminder of the conversation we once had, the one that led her here.

She composes herself, her eyes fluttering closed in a deep sigh. I watch the green tint in her skin disappear as she opens them again, meeting my stare for stare. Her face coils into a viperish grin, her eyes narrowing into slits as the distance between us closes.

"Maybe you're right. This is *quite* the adventure." The words are laced with sarcasm, but there's a hint of something else there, something that makes my heart pound in my chest.

A rush of pleasure ripples down my spine as she runs those delicate hands up my chest until her fingers wrap over the firm muscle of my shoulders. Her breath fans over my face, and I let my eyes roll closed, plunging into the sensation of her willing contact. My hands slide down to grip her hips, my thumbs digging into the divots there. It's like she's melting into me, like she's finally giving in.

Just as I think victory is within my grasp, that she can see the logic in giving in to the possibility of another night with me, this damn girl has to go and ruin it by making my grandchildren wince at the sight of her raised leg for generations to come. Her knee collides with my groin, my crew sucking in bated breaths and giving small grunts of their own as a pained snarl rips from my lips.

"How's that for *fucking* adventure?" she spits, her voice venomous as she scurries through the horde of men, barreling for the door of my quarters. I clench my jaw, struggling to catch my breath even as I manage to stay upright. The pain is sharp, a deep burn that radiates through my loins, but it's nothing compared to the fury that's rising in me now.

This just won't do!

I straighten myself from the slightly bent position I've found myself in, not doubled over but certainly in slight discomfort.

"Sitara," I growl, making my way to the door of the cabin. I can feel the fire of irritation burning its way up my spine.

I'm not about to take a blow to the testicles sitting down.

I would kick the door in if it belonged to any other person on this ship. But no, this is my door, and as I have mentioned before, I don't take kindly to my things being damaged. Even by me. So, instead, I will turn the damn key.

She scrambles back a few steps, eyeing me wearily as I fling open the door. The look of horrified surprise splattered across Sitara's face at my abrupt entrance is almost comical. Does she really think I will let her bruise my ego and walk away?

Not likely.

She has realized the gravity of how badly she's just fucked up.

Good. At least she has *some* brains.

Instead of falling to her knees and begging me not to hurt her like a normal woman in her situation, she reins in her shakes and clenches her fists once more. Honestly, she *really* needs to stop doing that. At this rate, her nails will pierce the soft, unblemished skin of her palms, and I fully intend to make use of those delicate hands later. I can already imagine how they'll feel grazing against my skin once more.

She squares her shoulders as I take a deliberate step toward her, her chin lifting in a feral, almost animalistic defiance that stirs something equally primal within me. Her eyes gleam with a mixture of fear and fury, a potent combination that I find undeniably intriguing.

Without so much as a glance behind me, I close the door, the sound of the latch clicking into place echoing through the room like a death knell. It's not exactly how I envisioned our second encounter, but if she insists on playing dirty, then I'll happily play downright filthy.

"You know," I murmur, taking slow, taunting steps toward her, "kneeing a man in the balls might be considered foreplay to some." My voice is low, teasing, and I can see the flush rise to her cheeks as she backs away, her eyes darting wildly around the room for an escape or a weapon. I watch her with a molten, predatory stare, my gaze narrowing in on the frantic rise and fall of her chest. It's almost hypnotic, the way her body betrays her fear even as her spirit refuses to back down. "Not me, personally," I continue, my tone laced with amusement, "but my point still stands."

Her back hits my tall, ornate dresser, and she wastes no time in scanning the area for anything she can use to defend herself. Honestly,

I'm a bit insulted by the assumption that I would truly harm her, especially after the heated encounter in the tavern and all the effort I put into getting us to this moment. But I suppose fear can make people do reckless things. Example one being the heavy bookend she grabs off the shelf to her left, her fingers wrapping around it like a lifeline before launching it straight at my face.

"Get away from me, you vile, loathsome ogre!" she spits, each word intended as a dagger to my pride.

I sidestep with ease, the airborne bookend whizzing past my face, barely a breath away from making contact. It lands with a loud thud against the wall, an audible reminder of her desperation.

"*Ogre*, am I?" I muse smugly, "Strange, I seem to remember a completely different term falling from your lips mere hours ago that would make witness to the contrary."

I glance from the dented wall back to her, taking another step closer. "And it's not kind to throw people's belongings, Pet," I chide, my tone light despite the undercurrent of irritation.

When I'm finally mere arm's length away from her, I reach out and grab her by the waist, pulling her to me until our faces are only centimeters apart. Her soft, delicate features are hardened by fear and loathing, but even amid her panic, she's lovely. *So* lovely.

And so *mine* until further notice.

"Furthermore," I continue, my voice dropping into a low growl as I grab her face with my free hand, squeezing her cheeks enough to make her full, pouty lips pucker for me, "it's extremely rude to bruise the jewels of the man who so generously surrendered his bed for your sleeping pleasure."

Her head cranes back at the angle I hold her face, the smooth, untouched expanse of her skin making my mouth water. I can see her heartbeat fluttering under her skin at the hollow of her throat, and it sends a shiver down my spine.

I lean in, running my nose along her jaw, letting her scent fill my senses and make my head swim. "I think you should apologize."

"What is *wrong* with you? Why the hell would you force me onto your nasty ship?!" she squawks.

She attempts to slap my hand away in a fury, to push me back, but I tighten my grip, pulling back to force her to meet my glare head-on.

There's a fire in her eyes, a spark of defiance that only fuels my desire. Desire to break her. To tame her. To make her mine. There will be no running away this time. No games. I am done waiting. I am done being *denied*.

Her insult to my ship cuts through my pleasurable haze, my brows furrowing as the indignation registers. How dare she speak of my *Nereus* in such a manner! Especially after I've watched her for three years, her eyes lingering on my ship like a lover's caress.

"What do you mean by '*nasty ship*'? I seem to recall you roaming about the deck giving my *beautiful*, well-kept ship your most convincing come-fuck-me eyes!"

Her eyes widen at the accusation, her lips parting in an exasperated scoff. "I was *not* looking at your ship with come-fuck-me eyes! Someone has an over-inflated ego!" she snaps, folding her arms over her chest in a futile attempt to create a barrier between us. She stares right back at me with that same defiance that belies the anxiety visible in every tense muscle of her body.

I roll my eyes at her dramatics, a smirk tugging at the corners of my mouth. "You were," I say simply, watching as the anger builds in her eyes.

She's like taming a dragon, a wild, untouchable force of nature. She's so far removed from the accommodating young woman on the beach who simply wanted to forget her sorrows. And it is the most delicious thing I have ever witnessed. If I thought her gentle innocence was erotic, then this is downright cock jerking.

"You took me from my home!" she lashes out, "Why didn't you just throw me to your wolves while you were at it?"

Is she being serious? After the night in the tavern, it should be pretty *obvious* why I didn't.

Why I *couldn't*.

She is mine now, and I don't like to share my things.

"I didn't *'throw you to the wolves'* because watching my men pile drive you into oblivion—night after night—on my ship, burdening my ears with the sound of your incessant moaning, is not my idea of a good time."

Unless, of course, I'm the one making her scream.

I chuckle as her eyes widen beautifully in horror, her mouth falling open in shock.

For the love of her infuriating gods, there isn't a thing about this woman that is a turn-*off*, is there? Her anger, her defiance, her fear—it's all perfectly designed to draw me in deeper.

She isn't a witch. No, she's a fucking siren, singing into the night to lure sailors to their death.

"You better close that pretty mouth of yours, Kitten," I purr, my thumb slipping past her lips to press down on the flat of her tongue. She shudders against my invading touch, her body betraying her yet again. I rub the pad of my finger deeper, hooking it into her cheek. "You never know what manner of filth might land in it when you leave it open like that."

She snaps her mouth closed, her teeth digging into my flesh. I pull it out with a smirk, bringing my saliva-coated thumb to my mouth. Her lips press into a thin line as I watch her watch me. Her cheeks flare with color, and she quickly changes the subject.

"My name is Sitara," she declares, the quiver beneath her firm tone amusing, "Si-tar-uh. Not *kitten*. Not *darling*. Not *pet*. Sitara."

I admire her spirit—really, I do—even as I dismiss it. I give a bored sigh, bringing my thumb back out of my mouth with a lewd pop.

Though in reality, I am anything but bored. This woman has proven to be everything I knew she would be and more, keeping me on my toes in only a few short moments we've had thus far.

I pull away just far enough to give an exaggerated bow, dramatically rolling my wrist on my way down before bringing my hand back to the warmth of her back.

"Kiernan," I reintroduce myself, "Charmed, I'm sure."

The sarcasm in my tone isn't lost on her, but I don't care. I'm too busy enjoying the way her muscles tense under my touch, the way her breath hitches when I'm near.

However, I can tell she's had enough for now, her body so taut with tension that I fear she might hurt herself just standing here. I can't have that, now, can I? She won't be any fun if she breaks before I can put her back together again. There's no need to send my sweet little plaything into a hysterical fit before I've had my fill.

Finally, I allow her to move away, letting my hands fall back to my side as I step back, giving her the illusion of freedom.

"You should eat, *Sitara*," I advise, emphasising her name for my amusement, "The food gets worse by the day, and the boys don't take pity on those who are late to chow. So, I suggest the next time food is offered to you, you take it."

I watch her deflate, and to my surprise, I don't enjoy this side of the game we've been playing at all. I expected to feel triumph over taming such a wild thing, but as I watch her shoulders slump and her voice quiver as she says, "I don't want your food. I want to go home," I feel anything but gleeful. She looks like a kicked puppy, broken and helpless, and for a moment, I question my own actions.

I shake off the feeling, stomping it down as quickly as it arises. What a little minx she is, making me feel bad and shit, no matter how fleeting the feeling is.

I cross my arms, walling myself off from whatever long-forgotten part of me she's managed to touch. "I see nothing holding you here,"

I say coolly, "which must—in turn—mean you are not trapped. When we reach land, you are free to go if you want, but just know that you won't make it back to Capulli'ana with no money and no favor."

I will take her back… eventually. Once I've had my fill of her, once I've sated the obsession that's been burning inside me for years.

As soon as she frees me from her spell, I'll free her from mine.

8

Sitara

This man is completely out of his mind!

He's parading around like he somehow has the right to barge into women's lives, snatch them out of their beds, and then act like it's all some twisted game. It's appalling, and yet... here he is, doing just that.

He's standing here, staring at me with this unnerving intensity, like I'm some kind of curiosity he's never seen before. It's unsettling, and not in the way that might spark some fleeting attraction or fascination like it did on the beach. No, this is the kind of unsettling that makes your skin crawl, that makes you wonder if you're looking at someone entirely insane. And then, to make matters worse, I feel the sting of tears welling up in the corners of my eyes.

Oh, no. No, no, no!

I will not—I absolutely will *not*—give this son of a bitch the satisfaction of seeing me cry. I won't let him have that power over me, no matter how much he seems to think he already does.

But the truth is... he does.

That realization cuts deeper than anything he could say or do. I can't use my cold fire here—this strange, flickering power that's always been my shield, my weapon, my security. Without it, I feel raw, exposed, vulnerable in a way I've only experienced one other time. The only difference this time is that I don't have eight other women to try to be brave for.

It's just me.

It's a terrifying feeling.

And I hate him for it.

Dismissing his previous statement about food, I look up at him with far more bravery than I feel right now.

"What do you want with me, you shit goose?" It's the only insult I can come up with. The only way I can somehow stick it to his stupid ego. But instead of anger or hurt, he looks... amused. Worse than that, a laugh escapes him, deep, rich, and far too enticing for someone as unhinged as him. It makes me want to scream, to lash out again.

Gods, this man is absolutely, mind-bogglingly infuriating! And to think, just last night, I found him attractive!

I have no taste in men. None whatsoever.

"Did you just... call me a 'shit goose'?" He's grinning now, biting the insides of his cheek to hinder another laugh so he can speak. "What a novice you are, Pet," he says, his voice dripping with mock affection.

He bends down at the waist, meeting my gaze with those unnerving, electric blue eyes. The eyes that had caught my interest in the first place.

"Don't worry," he adds, "I'll give you dirtier things to call me later."

I almost let my jaw fall open in complete mortification, but then I remember the way he had shoved his thumb into my mouth earlier. I wouldn't put it past him to do something even worse—something even more invasive, something designed to prove his dominance in the most disgusting way possible. Like some kind of animal asserting its control over another.

"Absolutely not!" I snap, trying to keep my voice steady, "Stop touching me with your grimy, disgusting hands!"

He counters immediately, seemingly unbothered. "That's not what you were saying last night," he says, and I can feel the heat rising to my face like a tidal wave as he moves to the bathing room.

My blood races through my veins, pounding in my ears, urging me to deny it, but I'm trying to keep my wits about me. To not let him get under my skin.

"What do you want, Kiernan?" I repeat as he makes his way back out. His name feels like a curse on my lips, and I mean for it to be.

He pauses, tapping his chin thoughtfully as if he's considering some grand, life-altering decision.

"You needed adventure," he finally replies, "And I needed *you*. I provided us with both. A girl like you would never have agreed to climb onto my ship and leave your comfortable little box."

As if he expects that to be the end of the discussion, he gestures to a small bowl of fruit that sits on a table in the corner of the room. "You're welcome to that if you're going to be... What was the phrase? Oh, yes. If you're going to be a little shit goose and refuse to go down to the gully for food."

I watch him carefully as he walks over to the wardrobe, pulling out a shirt that isn't sweat-soaked and salt-covered. I respond to his proximity by shuffling slowly toward the corner of the room, trying to put as much distance between us as possible. I don't want him near me. I don't want to look at him. I don't trust him as far as I can throw him, and validly so, if I might add.

"The bath is in there," he says casually, as if the tension isn't riding on the razor's edge of suffocating. His incredibly large hands snatch me by my shoulder, his grip tight and unyielding, as he turns me toward the bathing room. The movement is sudden, jolting, and I stumble slightly under his strength. My heart races in protest, my breath catching in my throat as I'm propelled forward.

Once we're inside, the door clicks shut behind us, and I hear the unmistakable sound of a lock being turned. My body tenses, my muscles coiling like a spring ready to snap. Panic claws at my chest, its icy fingers digging deep into my lungs, making it hard to breathe. My legs twitch with the instinct to bolt, to run, to escape—to do anything but remain trapped in this small, stifling space with him.

At this point, jumping off the ship seems like a viable option, a desperate but preferable alternative to being so close to him, to feeling the suffocating space between us growing smaller and smaller.

My insides turn icy, a cold dread pooling in my stomach like water filling a sinking ship as I feel my power lashing at my gut. But there's nowhere for it to go, no escape, no release. It freezes into a hard, unyielding lump, a heavy, burdensome weight that presses down on me. My body feels rigid, unresponsive, as if rooted to the spot, while my mind races with panic.

"A girl like me? You don't even know me," I finally manage to say, the words tumbling out of my mouth like a desperate plea. My voice is shaky, uneven, but there's defiance still left, a spark of resistance that I cling to.

I'm trying to sound braver than I feel, stronger than I am. But he doesn't seem to notice—or care.

He simply grabs a pitcher off of what looks to be a makeshift wood heating element and continues to pour hot water into the large, round trough that serves as a bathtub, the steaming liquid splashing against the metal with a rhythmic, almost soothing sound that only heightens the tension in the room.

"A girl like you," he confirms, his voice calm, steady, and maddeningly self-assured. He keeps his back to me, his attention focused on the water as he continues with his task. "A hollow, afraid, lonely little thing with no intention of actually fulfilling herself with anything she truly longs for."

His words are like a blade, sharp and cutting, slicing through my defenses and striking at the very core of me. They hurt deeply, and I feel the sting of them like a slap across the face.

He begins to peel off his shirt, the fabric parting to reveal the toned, muscular planes of his torso. I've seen his body before, but it still shocks me, still unsettles me just how large this man is. How powerful he is.

Every scar that dots his sun-kissed skin is familiar, etched into my memory like a map. The small constellation tattoo on his forearm glints in the dim light, a reminder of the man he is—complex, enigmatic, and utterly intimidating even with such a delicate piece of art on his skin.

He pulls his shoulder-length, auburn brown hair free from its tie, the strands falling around his face like a curtain of warm earth. And I realize with dread what is happening. What he is expecting.

I want to flee, to run, to escape. But my legs won't move, my feet rooted to the floor as if anchored there by some unseen force. And yet, despite my fear, despite my panic, I can't help but admire him—his strength, his beauty, the raw, unbridled appeal of his physique. It's infuriating, humiliating, and deeply, *deeply* unsettling. I remember the heat of his body against mine, the way he felt, the way he made me feel. And I hate myself for it.

I'm hit with a blood-chilling realization: I am completely helpless here. There is nothing I can do, no way to fight back, no way to escape. I'm trapped, alone, and vulnerable, with a man who seems to know me better than I know myself.

I take a deep breath, forcing myself to calm down, to push the fear below the surface. But it's hard, so hard, when every part of me is screaming to run. My hands tremble, my mind racing with thoughts of everything that could go wrong.

"You're a fixer," he continues, turning to face me. His eyes lock onto mine, "So until you *fix* whatever it is that needs tending to, you'll stay put right where you are. I hate to break this to you, Darling," he says, his tone softening almost imperceptibly, "but you can't fix him. You can't fix someone that doesn't want to be fixed."

The words hit me like a physical blow, knocking the breath out of me. I flinch, my body jerking backward as if slapped, as the full weight of his words crashes down on me.

He knows.

He knows about my life, about my struggles, about the secrets I've kept hidden for so long. The realization drops a rock into my gut, a heavy, unyielding weight that presses down on me, making it hard to breathe.

"Only he can decide that the euphoric smog he fills himself with day in and day out is fucking him more than it's helping him," he adds, his voice filled with conviction, with certainty. His words are like a knife, twisting in the wound he's already made. "And until he does, you, my dearest darling, are watching grass grow."

His words are like a series of blows, each one hitting harder, hurting more than the last. He might as well have slapped me across the face repeatedly, over and over again, until I'm raw and bleeding and broken. Hurt and fear swirl in my gut, a toxic mix of emotions that fogs my mind and makes it hard to think, to reason. I want to scream, to yell, to thrash and fight him tooth and nail. I want to lash out, to hurt him the way he's hurting me.

But I can't. As much as I hate it, as much as I hate him at this moment, he's right. He's right, and we both know it.

Despite my longings and wants, I've never been able to bring myself to leave Larkin. He's the only family I have left, the only person who hasn't left me, who needs me. The thought of him wasting away, of him falling further and further into the abyss of his own making, while I chase pipe dreams and thrills, would kill me.

It would destroy me.

So I stay, no matter how much it hurts, no matter how much it costs me. Because I have to. Because I can't leave him. Because I can't abandon him.

My chest rises and falls with violent breaths as I try desperately to keep my emotions in check, to keep them all from spilling over again. My hands clench tightly into fists, my nails digging into my palms as I try to ground myself, to focus on the physical pain rather than the emotional turmoil. I bite the inside of my cheek, the tangy copper taste of my blood filling my mouth.

"What do you even know about it?" I murmur, the words barely escaping my lips. My voice is still shaky, uncertain, and I hate it. I hate the way I sound, the way I feel. "You're just making assumptions like you know anything about me or my brother..." I trail off, the words dying on my lips as I meet his gaze.

He rolls his eyes, a subtle hint of frustration flickering across his features before he sighs deeply, the hard mass of his chest rising and falling with the movement.

"You would have told me that you'd think about it, and then left me looking like a fool, wanting in the morning. You would have gone home if it weren't for me. You would have continued to wallow in your misery while you watched him wallow in his." He rakes his fingers through his hair, the movement rough, before he uses his free hand to unclasp his pants. He removes them with a practiced ease, stepping into the bathwater as if it's the most natural thing in the world.

Even though I've seen his body before, even though I've been this close to him before, I can't shake the unsettling feeling that settles in the pit of my stomach. I wrap my arms around my torso, feeling raw and exposed, as if I'm the one standing naked in front of him.

He might as well be stripping me, too, because it's as if he can see right through me, as if he can read me like an open book. And I don't enjoy it in the slightest. I hate the way he looks at me, the way he talks to me, the way he makes me feel, attraction conflicting with loathing.

"I saw the fight between you two," he continues, "I have seen the way you cover for him when he doesn't do what he's expected to do. And I have seen the look on your face when he continues to disappoint you time and time again. I saw you crying on that beach. I know *plenty*."

The eyes I felt, the constant tingling sensation that skittered across my skin in Puka'qui during port season... It had all been him. Watching me. The tug on my skirt during my pursuit of my brother... That had also been him. My only saving grace must have been the barrier. But now, here, there's no barrier, no protection, nothing stopping him.

I move until my back hits the hard surface of the door, my face twisting into something that borders on terror and disbelief.

How long has he been watching me? The question drops like a stone in my gut, rippling the surface of my already unstable composure.

"A good cry never hurts anyone," I manage to say. My voice cracks under the weight of my personal life being aired out, laid bare at my feet, slapped into the space between me and this practical stranger.

It's humiliating, degrading, and painful.

He slips into the water, sighing as his eyes roll back slightly and his muscles relax against the heat. His eyelids flutter shut as he gives in to the comfort of the bath, his body going limp, relaxed. But the storm inside me is raging, thrashing, and beating against my chest like a wild animal trapped in a cage.

"You should relax," he says, peeking at me through one slitted eye. His voice is smooth, lazy, and there's a predatory amusement in it that makes my blood run cold. "If you would, you might just enjoy yourself, Sitara." The 'r' in my name rolls around on his tongue, a sensual, intimate sound that sends a shiver down my spine. "Now. I'll not have you smelling like Thomas's sewer of a tavern in my bed. Get in."

My eyes widen at his demand, my heart stuttering in my chest as his lazy gaze locks onto me with an intensity that raises goosebumps on my skin and the hair on the back of my neck. I shake my head wildly, my frantically beating heart threatening to explode. It's as if—now that he has already seen my body once—I have become a right and not a privilege.

I don't mind being naked; I bathe in the streams and hot springs with others of my tribe all the time. But it's the expectancy in his voice, the implication of the situation he is placing me in, that makes me squirm.

"You're welcome to bathe in the brig if you'd rather not use my private chambers," he says, a grin spreading across his face. "I'm sure the boys wouldn't object."

He's cornering me, and he knows it. He knows there's no real choice, no real option. Fear wraps its way around my spine, tightening like a vice. I want to slap him. But—as recent events have made plainly evident—it would do me no good. It would only make things worse.

I weigh my options, though both of us know which one I will pick. One madman is better than twenty. My third option is to smell like the sewer tavern, which is no more desirable than the other choices I'm faced with. Besides, he'd probably hold me down under frigid water if I refuse. Even still, I can't bring myself to give in so easily. I don't want to be anywhere that close to him again.

"I'll bathe when you're finished," I counter, muttering 'pig' under my breath. It's a small act of defiance, a tiny spark of resistance in a situation where I feel utterly powerless.

His eyes remain locked on mine, which are probably as round as saucers right about now. He gives me a piggish snort before hunkering down further into the steaming liquid.

"I'm offended by that term, Pet," he says, his voice dripping with mock offense. "I take great pride in my personal hygiene. Hence, you will not spend another moment smelling like Thomas's filthy tavern. Besides, the water will be cold by the time I'm finished." He extends his hand over the edge of the trough demandingly. "Now, I won't tell you again. Get in the tub."

When I make no move to comply, my feet frozen in place, he rises from the water in one swift motion. He stalks toward me, his naked body glistening with water, his movements confident and unyielding. He wraps an arm around my waist, his grip tight, unbreakable.

"Have it your way then," he says, his voice low, rough, and infinitely dangerous.

He lifts me off my feet with an ease that belies the tension in his muscles, and my body responds instinctively, kicking and thrashing. But it's like battering against a brick wall. He doesn't flinch, doesn't falter, and before I can process anything, I'm submerged in the warm water, clothes and all. The fabric clings to my skin, heavy and uncomfortable, as the heat of the water seeps through my bones.

The sound of my blood rushing through my ears is a deafening roar, a cacophony that drowns out everything else. I'm livid, my anger burning hotter with every passing second. I'm mortified, the humiliation of this situation pressing down on me like a weight. And beneath it all, lurking just below the surface, is a fear I refuse to acknowledge aloud.

Fear of Kiernan's intentions, of where this is all heading.

Fear that I might not make it home, that I might never feel the familiar heat of Capulli'ana again.

Fear that Larkin might not be waiting when I return.

The tub is enormous, far larger than I expected, and Kiernan fills it with an imposing presence. It isn't until I'm sitting in the water, my knees pulled up to my chest, that I realize just how deep it is. The water laps at my chin, and I can feel it rising with each breath, a reminder of just how vulnerable I am.

I glare at Kiernan, my eyes locked on his, searching for any sign of what's going through his mind as he sinks back down into the tub. Every twitch of his muscles, every flicker of his eyes, is a clue, and I'm desperate to read him, to understand what he's planning.

I remain unmoving, my wide eyes fixed on him with an intensity that borders on desperation. I curse myself for not being able to hide the fear that's clawing at the back of my mind, for not being stronger.

I wrap my arms around my knees, pulling myself into a tight ball, trying to create some semblance of distance between us. My gaze bores into his face, willing him to feel the weight of my hatred. But he's oblivious, or maybe just indifferent, as he nonchalantly starts washing himself, the rag in his hand moving over his skin with a familiarity that makes my gut twist.

"You're so uptight, aren't you, Kitten?" he says, his voice laced with amusement. The nickname grates on my nerves like nails on a chalkboard. I snarl, a raw, animalistic sound that even I don't recognize. It's a reaction that feeds into every stereotype he probably has about Kana'te people, and the realization only fuels my anger.

"I was kidnapped by a psychopath who now has me in his bath. Yes, maybe '*a little uptight*' is an understatement." My voice is venom, each word a dagger aimed at his smug, self-satisfied expression.

He chuckles, the sound low and rich, and I feel a surge of rage at the amusement dancing in his eyes. "I've seen you naked before. Quite intimately, in fact," he says, the memory hanging in the air like a challenge.

His words are a reminder of a moment I'd rather forget, and the smug look on his face only adds to the insult.

"You'll sleep in my nightshirt tonight. When we dock again in a few days, I'll make sure that you have suitable things to wear." The offer is gracious, almost kind, but it's laced with an underlying possessiveness that makes my skin crawl.

I turn away, my eyes finding a speck of dirt on the far wall, anything to avoid looking at him. "Fine," I mutter, the word barely audible over the pounding of my heart.

He sighs, the sound heavy and exaggerated, and I can feel his eyes on me, weighing me, probing for weaknesses. "And still, you're blaming me for this adventure you told me you were on in the first place. You know, a thank you would be wonderful when you're done hissing and scratching like a soggy cat."

I glance at him, a sideways look that's meant to convey defiance, to hide the fear that's threatening to overwhelm me. I want him to see the hatred in my eyes, to believe that it's the only thing driving me. "I didn't want to leave my brother and go with a pervert who likes to read phantom meanings behind the simple phrase *'I am on an adventure'*."

He laughs again, the sound this time tinged with a boyish charm that only makes me angrier. It's as if he's enjoying this, enjoying the power he has over me. Without my cold fire, I'm defenseless, a sitting duck in a pond full of crocodiles.

He reaches for the pitcher of water on the table beside us, the liquid cascading over his broad shoulders as he rinses off the soap. I watch, transfixed, as the water clings to his tanned skin, each bead a reminder of the strength, the power that lies beneath.

How is it that someone who looks like him can be just as equally unhinged? He's a paradox, a man who embodies both beauty and danger, and the combination is intoxicating and terrifying.

"Think of all the wonderful stories you'll have for dear old Larkin when you see him again, Pet!" His enthusiasm is twisted, a cruel mockery of the situation.

My teeth grind together, the pressure building in my jaw as the anxiety swirling in my stomach threatens to boil over.

His words bring back the fear, the uncertainty, and for a moment, I'm teetering on the edge of a meltdown. What if Larkin isn't there when I get home? The thought churns bile in my throat, a cold dread that seeps into my bones. It's a fear I can't afford to show, a vulnerability I can't let him see.

"You're insane," I spit, the words a last-ditch effort to keep him at bay, to maintain some semblance of control.

"Thank you," he beams, his pride almost childlike, as he reaches out to grab me. I hug myself tighter, pulling away from his grasp, desperate to keep some part of myself safe, untouched.

"You are not sleeping in my bed again, covered in filth," he growls, his fingers fisting into the fabric of my top as he tugs me closer. I try to resist, to pull away, but he's too strong, his grip unyielding.

And it is in this moment, I realize just how trapped I am, just how little control I have over what happens next.

9
Kiernan

I feel my right eye twitch with irritation as she glares at me, her expression bristling at the mere suggestion of her coming closer. It's almost as though the idea of proximity to me offends her very being.

Well, I'm not about to let her sit there and wallow in her defiance, neglecting herself out of spite.

No, I have standards.

I like my possessions well taken care of, and I won't tolerate anything less.

It's a matter of pride, really.

Not that she's my prisoner, of course. I did take her without her consent, yes, but that's a technicality. The fact remains that she's here now, and I'm not about to let her sit in her own filth.

I grasp at the fabric of her top, my other hand wrapping around the delicate flesh of her arm, and pull her toward me. She resists at first, but I'm not having it.

Once she's nestled snug between my legs, I reach around and begin to loosen the tie that binds her top at the back. She squirms, trying to fight me off, but I'm stronger, and I manage to manhandle the fabric off her. Then, with the same ruthless efficiency, I remove her skirt as well.

Water sloshes out onto the floor as her small, claw-like hands begin to paw at my grasp, her nails digging into my forearm.

"Let go of me!" she squawks, her voice shrill enough to grate on my nerves. Her nails break skin, and for a moment, the sensation teases at something that might be arousing under different circumstances.

I reach out with my free hand, clamping it over her mouth. The washrag, forgotten in the chaos, sinks beneath the soapy water as my fingers press into her cheeks, muffling the screeching that threatens to split my eardrums.

"You have such a pretty voice when you aren't using it for pure evil," I growl, my patience wearing thin.

I pull her closer, resting my forehead against hers. My eyes lock onto those warm brown orbs. "I'm not going to hurt you, Sitara."

Her squirming lessens, though, doesn't disappear completely, as I loosen my grip on her face, the pressure easing just enough to release the divots my fingers have left in her cheeks.

"Now, be a good girl and grab the damn rag," I demand, "Or my hands will wander to places you don't wish them to be."

She hesitates, her chest heaving with panicked breaths as the water laps at her skin. She's beautiful, even like this.

Her trembling fingers finally reach out, grabbing the rag from the bottom of the tub. As she hands it back, I notice the muscles in her jaw ticking beneath her skin, a sign of the fear and panic she's desperately trying—and failing—to hide.

But I've watched her for too long to miss the signs. I know her every move, every tell, every futile attempt to mask her emotions.

"You listen so well, Pet," I praise her, taking the rag and running it over her nearly flawless skin. It's a relief to see her clean, to scrub away the dirt and grime that's been marring her perfection. I like my things clean, and as long as she's mine, I'll make sure she's exactly as I wish her to be.

I tilt her chin upward, washing away the dirt caked in the crook of her neck. Her skin is flawless beneath it all, smooth and unblemished, save for the endearing splatter of freckles along her body. I caress the soft expanse of her throat, leaning in to feel the supple flesh beneath my tongue.

It's intoxicating, this quiet power I have over her.

And to my explicit delight, her struggles have ceased. For now.

This woman is dangerous—lethally so, even as she sits here trembling like a scared animal. There's something about her that draws me in, something that makes me want to unravel her, to break her down and rebuild her in my image. And yet, I know better than to underestimate her. She's a storm waiting to happen, a powder keg of fury and defiance just looking for a spark.

As I continue to clean her, my hands trail over her newly scrubbed skin, reacquainting myself with the soft curves of her body. It isn't until I reach her stomach that she jerks away, her reaction sharp, as though I've pressed a branding iron to her flesh. At first, I think it's because I'm too close to the apex of her thighs, but then I notice her hands resting on her pelvis, and I realize it's something else entirely.

There's a scar there, one that mars her otherwise perfect complexion. I remember noticing it last night in the tavern, though I hadn't given it much thought at the time.

Now that I think about it, she had been careful to keep it hidden, shifting away from me or guiding my hands to other places. It's clear that this scar is a sensitive subject, one she doesn't want to discuss. So I keep my questions to myself, silently vowing to uncover the story behind it when the time is right. It's a kindness I am willing to afford her.

I'm a bad man, but I am not completely wicked.

For now, I spin her around and begin washing her back, letting the silence between us fill the room.

Once I'm satisfied with her cleanliness, I move on to her hair, my fingers raking through the fiery locks as I lather them with a reverent care.

It's a shame she's been neglecting it.

I can only imagine how stunning it would look when it's clean, well-kept, and properly combed.

I make a mental note to buy her soap of her own when we dock, something that doesn't smell like me. I want her to smell the way she did on the beach, like salt and florals and temptation.

As I work, I notice her beginning to relax against my touch. Not because she trusts me, of course—she doesn't, and I wouldn't expect her to. But her body is tired, her mind worn down by the adrenaline that's been coursing through her veins all day. It's only natural that she'd start to give in to the exhaustion.

Finally, when I'm satisfied, I stand, the water cascading off me in a thunderous downpour. I reach for a towel hanging on a nearby hook and nod toward her. "Stand up," I tell her, my voice firm. "The towel won't do you any good down there, Darling."

For a moment, I consider leaving her where she is, kneeling in the water below me. The view is... perfect from this angle, and I find myself lingering on it longer than necessary.

But I have to be practical.

I reach down and grab her by the arm, pulling her to her feet. The towel wraps around her like a sheet, clinging to her dripping form as she steps out of the water. I watch as she clutches it tightly in her hands, her knuckles white with tension. I can already tell the wrinkles from her grip will linger long after she's let go.

After wrapping myself in my towel, I take a moment to appreciate her perfection before grabbing the shirt I'd brought in earlier. I hold it out to her, my palm open in offering. When she doesn't move, I tighten my fingers around it and grin.

"If you'd rather sleep in nothing but the sheet, be my guest, Kitten," I say mockingly.

She snatches the shirt out of my hand, and I laugh as she pulls it over her head. It's too big for her, the hem stopping just above her knees. It's going to be... interesting, lying next to her tonight, with all that tempting expanse of smooth, pale thigh on display.

As I dry myself, I can't help but watch her. I adjust myself in my cotton pants, cursing my inconvenient sense of decency. I don't get off on unwilling partners, not really, but there's something about her that makes me question my self-control. It's a character flaw, I'm beginning to think.

This is the spell she's cast over me, this little vixen.

Once I'm dry, I open the door, allowing the thick steam that has built up in the bathing room to roll out into the rest of the cabin like fog. The cool air shocks my overheated skin, and I stand there for a moment, letting it ease the burning sensation left behind by the scorching bath.

The sudden chill is almost refreshing, but it does little to calm the aching need that has been building inside me.

I take a deep breath, letting the air fill my lungs, before walking over to the bed and stretching out over the covers as I wait for her to exit the bathroom after me.

My eyes follow her intently as she steps out, the sound of her bare feet padding softly across the wooden floor of the cabin filling the space. The anticipation grows in my gut as she draws closer, her body heat radiating against mine even before she reaches the bed. My mind races with thoughts of having her pressed against me as I sleep.

Yep, the death of me. She'll kill me yet.

But to my surprise, she doesn't even glance at me. Instead, she reaches over to the other side of the bed, grabs a blanket and a pillow, and moves to tuck herself into the plush armchair in the far corner of the room. Her petite body curls into a ball, her head lying down on the pillow as if she's settling in for the night.

Oh, *absolutely* not. I swear this woman is doing everything in her power to irritate the ever-loving shit out of me.

I look at her, then at the empty place next to me in the bed where she is supposed to be. After all that I have put myself through to get to this point, I will not be settling for anything less than her lying beside me, her head on the pillow next to mine.

"Just because I call you Kitten," I say, my voice firm, "does not mean that you are going to be sleeping on the furniture like an animal. Get in this bed." I smack the space next to me with enough force that the sound can be heard across the room, making it clear that it's not a request. "Now."

But she doesn't move. Instead, she curls up further into the chair, her beautiful eyes sparking back to life as she looks at me. I can see the flames of resistance burning within her, and, while I love that fire, I'd much rather not have to deal with it at this particular moment.

"No!" she hisses at me, covering her face with the blanket that she has draped over her body like a shield. "I'm not getting into bed with you!"

"You forgot the word: again." I let out a malicious chuckle as I hurl myself off the mattress, gripping the arms of the chair so tightly that my knuckles blanch. "It wasn't a request, Pet," I say, my voice low and menacing. I jab my pointer finger in the direction of the mattress. "Bed!"

She glares back at me with an intensity that damn near has me seething. She's playing with fire, and I'm not sure how much more restraint I have left in me tonight.

"I am not your 'Pet,'" she spits back, "I am not your property. I am not getting in that bed!"

She wraps the blanket tighter around her shoulders and, to my complete disbelief, turns her entire body away from me like a child, leaving me staring at the planes of her back and shoulders. Her hair drapes over the pillow in a maddening display of curls, and I can feel my patience wearing thinner by the second.

I clench my jaw, the muscles working under my skin as I try to keep my temper in check. I lean forward, my nose buried into her soft hair, my breath whispering against the shell of her ear.

"I'm not a patient man, Sitara," I say, my voice low and dangerous. I straighten myself, cracking my neck to ease the tension that is building there, before walking over to my armoire and pulling out a lovely little neck scarf.

This... Yes, this will do nicely.

I tuck the fabric into my waistband and walk back over to her. I spin her toward me with a firm grip, and I'm met with a pure, hate-filled sneer.

"Sometimes we don't always get what we fucking want, now do we, Kiernan?" she says, her accented voice dripping with disdain and malice. The way she says my name, mixed with the sweet, sultry sound of her voice, forces me to release an angry, hungry growl.

Perhaps there are gods out there after all, and they are testing every last nerve I have in my goddamn body.

In one swift motion, I have her out of the chair and over my shoulder. My hand grips the supple expanse of her thigh as I adjust my hold on her, my other hand landing on her asscheek with a resounding smack.

"You have a dirty little mouth," I say, my voice gruff with annoyance.

I walk across the cabin, crawling onto the bed. I toss her down onto the mattress, her dainty form bouncing lightly before settling flat on her back. Straddling her hips, I grin down at her as I take in the wide-eyed expression on her face. I take one of her narrow wrists in my large hand and the neck scarf in the other.

I'm an expert with knots, and I find myself rather proud of the one I use to bind her to the rail that anchors my bed to the wall.

I'm done playing games. I just want to go to sleep, knowing my prize is nice and warm under the covers beside me.

I lean down, letting my lips graze the shell of her ear. "You'll do best to learn quickly that I'm the last person you should attempt to defy. It won't ever work well in your favor."

She lets out a frustrated whine, which fills my chest with a sick, triumphant pleasure. She tugs at the scarf, cursing all manner of profanities at me. I'm pretty sure I even heard the term 'shit goose' thrown in there again.

I chuckle against her skin, the sound so sinfully deep and smooth that it surprises even me.

The things this woman is doing to me... I might be losing every vestige of sanity I have left.

I take one final inhale of her scent before I dismount her and cover her in the blankets with a gentleness that belies the harsh encounter from mere seconds ago.

"Do be a dear and don't snore too loudly," I say, grinning as I sink into the blankets next to her.

I let her beautiful, irritated grunts and growls of frustration lull me to sleep, my lips curved into a perpetual smirk.

10

Sitara

Did he really just tie me to the bed and fall asleep?!

The sheer audacity of the situation is staggering, and yet, here I am, bound and helpless, while he rests peacefully. This entire day has been nothing but one problem after another. Even still, the fact that this particular situation could have gone so much worse sends a tidal wave of discomfort crashing through me.

I tug at the scarf, trying to dig my nails into the tight knot that sits against my wrist. For the love of the gods, this man has tied it so tight that it will take me forever to loosen it, if I can even manage it at all.

Letting out a rattling sigh of defeat, I roll my body over and lift myself onto my knees, the movement awkward and strained due to my restraints. Quietly, I push myself up and shift myself to the window above the bed, carefully opening it to lean out into the cool night air. The waves below crash against the ship, their rhythmic motion doing little to soothe me. I try to take deep breaths, hoping to calm the emotions threatening to consume me like a parasite.

Now that I have no choice but to sit still and contemplate my life, I realize that I have found myself at a crossroads. On one hand, I could continue to fight tooth and nail, making this man's life as miserable as

I can during my time here. Or, on the other hand, I could accept what is for the time being and muscle my way through it, biding my time until I can escape.

Although the first option is tempting—oh, how tempting it is—I am exhausted. Everything I have thrown at him, Kiernan has taken with ease and reciprocated with something of his own. I can't physically harm him, not in any meaningful way, and especially not now, without my abilities. He seems to have an equally impenetrable mind, as if nothing I do or say can faze him.

I had been in a state of despair, feeling lost and vulnerable, and he had waltzed in, giving me sweet promises of a delayed journey back home.

That had been my first mistake, falling for his flirtations so readily.

I had been fooled by his provoking charm, ignoring my intuition even as it screamed at me to turn around and go home.

He had played me like a fiddle, expertly using my thirst for new experiences and my hesitation to return to his advantage.

And by the gods, it had worked.

It also hadn't helped that, unfortunately, when it comes to appearances, Kiernan is exactly my type. Tall, broad-shouldered, with piercing eyes and a sharp jawline that seems to be chiseled from the very stones of the earth. His auburn brown hair is perfectly tousled, and his smile is the kind that can disarm even the most guarded of women.

But of course, there is the crazy.

The manipulative games, the lies, the way he seems to take pleasure in my misery.

If I had known what I know now, I wouldn't have stood on that godsforsaken beach and entertained the idea of his offer. The knowledge that I had fallen for such blatant deceit is horrifyingly embarrassing.

I take a moment to look around the cabin, trying to come to terms with everything I have learned today. The idea that someone—seemingly a stranger—seems to understand me better than I even know myself is deeply uncomfortable. It's as if he has seen into the very core of my being, uncovering part of me that I have tried to keep hidden. I don't know if I want to think too deeply into how much of my life, of me, he's seen.

Obviously, he would have only followed me around Puka'qui, but there were times when I would slip away to take a private moment, just to breathe, just to be alone. I'm sure he's even seen those private parts of my life, too, the moments I thought were safe from prying eyes. It sends shivers down my spine, a rock of disgust forming in my gut.

The room is dim, the only light afforded by the moon's reflection off the waves that filter through the windows. The soft, silvery glow casts long shadows across the walls, making the space feel both intimate and oppressive.

Everything in this room screams organized chaos. Papers and ledgers are scattered over the surface of a desk that sits just a few feet from the foot of the bed, half-melted candles having dripped beads of wax onto some of them. On the far wall sits the wardrobe and dresser, as well as the bookshelf, which I had snatched the bookend earlier in the day. Everything is well-kept and dusted, despite the clutter. Minor repairs can be seen scattered throughout the wooden furniture, a testament to Kiernan's meticulous nature. He wasn't joking when he said he doesn't like his things damaged.

Not that I appreciate being placed among said possessions.

It isn't until I have been sitting here for some time, my mind racing with thoughts of escape, that something catches my eye. Draped over a nail that is being used to hold up a world map, swaying gently with the rocking of the ship, is something familiar. My tilona'matli, with its clay-stained fibers and charcoaled band, hangs there like a trophy.

That son of a bitch...

I bury my face in my free hand, groaning in disgust at my own lack of self-control and foresight. The idea that he had been watching me all day sends my blood running cold, a shiver wrapping itself around my spine. I had practically laid myself on a silver platter for him. I gave him the impression that I am nothing but a wide-eyed, naive child. And, truthfully, I haven't exactly given him any other impression thus far.

How could I have been so stupid?

Djar had warned me time and again that my recklessness, my habit of diving headfirst into situations without thinking, would get me into trouble one day. And now... the day has come. I swear that old man can see the future. He'd been right all along, and the realization stings like salt in an open wound.

I turn my gaze toward the man sleeping next to me, his dark lashes brushing against his sharp, high cheekbones as he dreams. In this state, it's almost easy to forget that he's absolutely mental. His face is smooth, relaxed, the smug, self-satisfied grin he usually wears now nothing more than a faint twitch at the corner of his mouth. His chest rises and falls in steady, rhythmic breaths, his broad shoulders moving slightly with each inhale and exhale.

He looks... peaceful.

Calm.

Almost normal.

Like I've said before, if he could keep his crazy in check, he might even be an appealing prospect. But of course, that's a big *if.*

His dark bronze hair is beginning to dry now, aided by the cool ocean breeze streaming through the open window. The dim reflections of the waves outside dance across his tanned skin, giving him a faint, glistening aura. I find myself leaning in, drawn to the sight of him before snapping back to my senses.

What the hell are you thinking, Sitara?!

Even with the full, horrifying knowledge that he's completely sadistic, I still let my curiosity get the better of me.

Maybe I'm dumber than I originally thought.

But as I sit here, I do come to one small, begrudging conclusion: as bad as this situation is, it could have been worse. *Much* worse. I could have ended up in the hands of someone far more dangerous, far more cruel. Maybe the gods are looking after me in some way, shape, or form.

The thought doesn't comfort me as much as usual, though, but I'll take what I can get.

I tug once more on the scarf wrapped around my wrist, my fingers working at the knot with a desperation that borders on panic. Somehow—don't ask me how, because I have no idea—the knot finally slips free. I have to stifle a triumphant whimper, the sound clawing at my throat.

Freedom!

I take a moment to compose myself, letting out all my jittery nerves in a slow, shaky sigh. If I don't take my time, if I let my anxiety get the better of me, I risk waking him up, and that's not something I want to do.

I inch toward the edge of the mattress, sliding my hips inch by agonizing inch. I don't even dare shift positions, as small a movement as that might be. Every so often, I stop, holding my breath as I watch his chest rise and fall consistently.

Must be nice to sleep like a baby after acting like a complete...

I bite back the rest of the thought before it can fully form.

It's not worth the risk of distracting myself.

He doesn't stir. Not even a little. So, emboldened by his stillness, I continue my slow, painstaking journey across the sheets until my feet finally hit the footboard.

I let out a quiet breath, my hands grasping the wooden frame for balance as I carefully drape my legs over the side. My knees wobble slightly as I lower myself to the floor, my weight sending a faint creak through the wooden planks beneath me. My heart leaps in my throat at the sound, my eyes snapping immediately back to the bed.

He still doesn't move.

I exhale and take a moment to do a little jig, my arms waving in a ridiculous, silent celebration. I even go so far as to flip him off. Ivelle said it was called *"flipping the bird"*.

Yes, it's childish, but it feels *so* good.

Take that, you psychotic piece of seaweed!

With that small act of defiance out of my system, I turn my attention to the door. My gaze lingers for a moment on my tilona'matli. I contemplate taking it, but the idea of taking so much time to do so is enough to deter me. It's just a piece of cloth, after all.

It's not like it's ever brought me much luck.

If it means that much to *them*, they can stitch a new one onto my arm when I get home.

I tiptoe toward the door, each creak of the floodboards making my heart stutter and my eyes dark back to him. My breath comes in short, shallow gasps, my hands trembling as I reach out for the cold metal handle. I have to stifle another triumphant cry as my fingers wrap around it, the feeling oh so satisfying. I crack the door open, peeking my head out just enough to see if the deck is empty.

When I'm sure it is, I slip out into the night, closing the door behind me as slowly and quietly as I possibly can. My heart is pounding in my chest, my blood racing with a mixture of fear and adrenaline as I scan the ship, trying to dredge up any memory I have of its layout. The tour I had been given feels like a lifeline now. What started as a massive advantage for him has now turned the tables, screwing him over all the same.

I rush toward the davit on the side of the ship—it doesn't matter which one—and begin examining it frantically.

Of course, there are more knots.

Why wouldn't there be?

My breathing comes out in sharp, frustrated gushes as I struggle to free the stubborn rope, the rough fibers digging into my palms. I curse under my breath, the words barely audible over the sound of my labored breathing. My efforts yield nothing but a growing rope burn, and I grit my teeth in annoyance. Desperate, I brace my foot against the railing for leverage, but it doesn't help.

It's almost a pointless as trying to convince Te'lei that his jokes aren't that funny.

I'm not sure how much time passes before I hear a deep, amused voice behind me.

"I was wondering how long it would take you to give him the slip," it says quietly.

I whip around, my hair flying into my mouth. I spit out the strands, my heart racing as I take in the sight of the man standing there. His arms are crossed, and he's grinning cheekily, a piece of orange in one hand. His mossy green eyes sparkle with amusement, and his brown hair, slightly longer than Kiernan's, is held back by a blue bandana.

Benedict, I think.

I'm not entirely sure—I only remember hearing the name once during the tour.

My stomach drops as he approaches, his movements casual and confident.

"I-I was..." I start, but my voice trails off.

Benedict shrugs and moves closer, not directly toward me but the rope, where he leans against the davit. "Yeah, he can be a bit much sometimes, huh?" he teases, taking another bite of his orange.

"He's a nightmare," I blurt out before clamping my mouth shut, afraid of saying something that might get me into even more trouble.

Benedict chuckles, nodding dramatically. "He can be, yes." Then, to my surprise, he reaches out and tugs on a piece of rope I hadn't tried yet. "See this? All you have to do is pull the right one, and the boat will drop right into the water."

Sure enough, it does.

The small, rickety wooden boat splashes into the waves below.

I rush to the railing, peering down at the water in relief.

But the real question is—why did he help me?

I turn to eye him warily, suspicion written all over my face. "Why are you helping me?"

He wipes his hands on his pants, then slaps them together as if dusting them off. "Oh, I'm not helping you. Just showing you how it's done."

Before I know it, I'm lifted off my feet and flung over his shoulder. His arm wraps tightly around my waist, holding me in place. I scream, my fists pounding against his back as I kick and claw at him.

"Let go of me! What is wrong with you people?! You can't just toss people around like this!"

He chuckles, his grip tightening. "Wanna bet?"

Then, he detours to kick open the door that leads below deck, his voice booming. "Arthur! Wake up, boy! Get up here and get the fucking boat out of the water before Kiernan throws you overboard with it!"

I hear only a groggy grunt in response.

Once Benedict is done, he carries me back toward the captain's quarters. I'm still kicking, screaming, and throwing a full-blown tantrum as he swings the door open. Kiernan jolts upright, rubbing his eyes in confusion.

"Kidnapping is only the first step, bud," Benedict says smugly, "You're far too comfortable for someone who hasn't finished the job."

He flops me back onto the bed, right where I started.

Kiernan watches, his voice low and gravelly. "You little minx..."

"If you're going to keep a pet, you should leash it better," Benedict remarks.

Are these people serious right now?!

"Then you fucking do it," Kiernan retorts.

"Not my pet. Mine's at home."

My eyes widen in disgust as Benedict moves to tie me up again anyway. What does he mean he has a pet at home?! Is there some poor woman tied to his kitchen table?!

I struggle against the ropes, but Benedict's knots are even tighter than Kiernan's. I can see my fingertips turning purple in the dim light.

"You're too soft," Benedict scolds Kiernan, grinning as he steps back.

At least he hadn't smelled as bad as the drunk man from earlier.

"I didn't want to bruise the skin," Kiernan replies casually, draping his arm over my waist to keep me still. "Thanks, buddy."

Benedict rolls his eyes and leaves.

Now it's just Kiernan and me again, and I slam my head back against the pillow in defeat.

Kiernan's growling chuckle sends shivers through my body as his lips brush against my ear. "Now that we've established you won't be escaping me, be a good girl and go to sleep."

Dammit... I failed.

I knew it was a long shot, but being caught, manhandled, and thrown back into my original position is pathetic.

I groan and let the sound of the ocean lull me into a calmer state. As I close my eyes, Kiernan stirs under the sheets. I hold my breath, thinking I might have woken him, but he's still asleep. His brows furrow, his lips pressing into a thin line.

I watch as his body tenses, his veins bulging slightly. Sweat breaks out on his face and chest as he jerks again.

Is he... having a nightmare?

Before I can stop myself, I reach out and place my cold palm against his forehead. My fingers rake through his hair, trying to soothe him. It's not due to any real fondness for him, but I don't want him jerking and rolling over to crush me when I can't protect myself from being squashed.

He lifts his hand, holding mine to his face and burying his nose into my palm. It's such a gentle gesture from someone so crude and cruel.

When he finally lets go, I pull my hand back and close the window. I realize now that the best course of action is to obey and do as I'm told for now. Today was hard enough, and I don't need to make my time here any harder than it needs to be.

I keep a wary eye on him, hoping he doesn't have another episode and crush me in my sleep. It takes me a while to get comfortable, but eventually, I drift off, the ship's rocking motion acting like a lullaby.

I slowly come to, roused by the faint sound of shuffling footsteps echoing through the cramped cabin. My vision is hazy, blurred by the remnants of sleep, as I struggle to open my eyes. I rub my hands over my face, trying to scrape away the lingering fog of slumber, the so-called *"sandman's dust"* that clings stubbornly to my eyelids. The air is thick with the scent of worn wood and salt from the sea, familiar and unpleasant.

As my gaze finally clears, I see Kiernan moving about the room with an unusual energy in his steps. His boots scuff against the floor, the sound grating against my nerves. Despite the rhythmic thud of his footsteps, there's an unmistakable pep to his stride, a liveliness that seems out of place given the tension that's been simmering between us since my arrival on this ship.

I sit up slowly, wincing as a sharp ache shoots through my back and shoulders. I must have slept in the same awkward position all night, and now my body is paying the price. The faint creek of the bed frame beneath me seems to echo my discomfort.

Kiernan turns toward me, and I catch a glimpse of something black clutched between his teeth—a tie, I realize, as he begins to pull his hair back. His mouth is set in that infuriating, self-satisfied grin, the one that makes my blood boil. It's the same smug expression he's worn since the moment I stepped foot on this vessel, the one that tells me, without a word, exactly where I stand in his eyes. My stomach twists into knots as I meet his gaze, any fleeting hope that things might have changed overnight evaporating in an instant.

There's no mistaking it—*yup, he's still the same asshole.*

He saunters over to the bed, his movements deliberate and confident, like he owns the place—yes, I'm aware he *does* actually own it.

Extending a hand toward me, he seems to expect me to let him help me up. My body tenses instinctively, bracing for the rough handling I've grown accustomed to. I know better than to trust him, to let my guard down for even a moment. My eyes snap shut, preparing for the inevitable—another yank or a calloused grip that leaves me squirming. But instead of the expected manhandling, there's a pause, a moment of silence that stretches on long enough to make me uneasy.

Curiosity gets the better of me, and I reopen my eyes to find him standing there, still smirking, his expression more arrogant than ever. It's the kind of look that makes me want to slap it right off his face, to wipe that unrelenting grin away for good. But before I can react, he reaches out and tugs on a tiny, insignificant piece of the scarf.

It's such a small movement, but the effect is instantaneous. The knot slips undone with an ease that leaves me speechless, the fabric falling away as if it had never been tied in the first place.

"No locks today, Kitten," he says, his voice low and laced with a deep satisfaction that makes my skin crawl. He's taunting me, the full weight of what just happened hitting me like a ton of bricks, my mind reeling in stunned disbelief.

Are you kidding me?!

I could have gotten out of the godsforsaken scarf the *entire* time?

All I would have had to do is pull on the right spot?

I realize with shameful clarity that it had been the exact type of knot Benedict had shown me how to until last night, the same one that had been on the rope. He had taught me how to undo it, and all I did was lie down like a defeated animal!

I flop back onto the bed, my frustration boiling over. I bring my hands to my face, covering my eyes as a groan escapes me, rough and raw, trying to process the sheer audacity of it all.

11

Sitara

I've been on this stupid boat for three days now, and today is the first day I've come out of the cabin without being forced. The last few mornings, Kiernan has resorted to throwing me over his shoulder and hauling me out onto the sunny deck. Even still, I haven't spoken to him if I can help it.

Take now, for example. He's standing at the helm, doing whatever he does, while I sit perched on the railing to his right, my arms crossed. He's tried to get me to participate, to interact with him, but I've refused to do so.

Until today, apparently...

Just as I'm about to look away from him, he catches my gaze and beckons me to him. I glare, clenching my jaw tightly as I shake my head. I look back out over the water, letting out a deep huff. I know I'm acting like a child, but I can't help myself.

I can hear one of his men fail to stifle a snicker when I blatantly ignore his request. I won't lie, it gives me great satisfaction knowing I've made him look like a fool, even just a little.

I hear him let out a heavy sigh as he quickly lashes the helm—a term I learned from a crewmate named Henry, and his twin brother Viktor—which will supposedly hold the course of the ship for a moment.

Well... That's not good.

He turns, taking a few long strides toward me, getting into my personal space. His movements are swift and smooth, and before I have time to resist or put up a fight, he has his hips wedged between my thighs, his hand in my hair to force me to look at him.

My heart kicks into overdrive, hammering against my ribs. His blue eyes bore into mine, and I feel like I can't breathe.

"I've shown you far more patience over the last few days than I should have," he growls, the sound vibrating through his chest and into mine, "You seem to be under the impression that my requests are optional. I'll have you know, they are not. If you won't come of your own free will, I will move you with mine." His free hand comes up to brush his thumb over my lips. "If I beckon, you come. If I say eat, you open wide. If I tell you to sit, you plant that juicy ass of yours on my lap and get comfortable."

He's so close to me that I can feel the heat radiating off his skin, searing into mine. His breath ghosts over my face, and I have to remind myself why I have been so difficult to begin with.

He's insane.

He's narcissistic.

He's a complete and utter wackjob.

It shouldn't be this hard to keep my own traitorous body from reacting. But it is, and it does. It's reason number two why I've kept my distance. I don't want him lowering my inhibitions. I can't afford it.

"I don't want anything to do with you," I bark, pressing my hands against his chest to push him away.

He uses my action to grab me firmly by the wrist, pulling me back to the helm. Once he has me facing the large, mahogany wheel, he places my hands on the spokes, wrapping his own over my fingers.

"You best get a firm grip, or my Nureus will grow a mind of her own, and carve her own path." Then, he steps away from me! Every line of my face is pinched tightly, my shoulders rigid.

"Are you *kidding* me?! Kiernan, I don't know how to steer this damn thing!" I squawk, my knuckles white as I grip the spokes tightly.

He lets out a sultry chuckle as he moves to stand beside me once more, taking one of my hands to a better spoke with a far gentler hand this time. He uses his foot to knock my feet into a better stance, then lets go of me completely.

"Much better."

Dang it... I can't stop the warming of my cheeks and the dusting of blush I know is to follow. So, I give him a shitty look in response, my brow raised and my nose scrunched up as I purse my lips.

"Port is left. Starboard is right," he begins to explain, but I am only half listening. The other half is still trying to recover from the beginning of this encounter by the railing. "The bow is the front of the ship, and the aft is the rear."

He walks back to his charts and maps that sit on a table just next to where I stand like a doe-eyed statue, bending over the table without looking at me again.

"So, if I told you 'to starboard two notts', you would adjust your hands two pegs to the left, causing the ship to turn right," he continues.

It takes me a moment to realize that it is actually a command, then do just that.

"Couldn't you have someone more... qualified to do this?" I say, cursing the nervousness that shakes my voice. I'm not comfortable with this. I don't *want* to do this.

"Oh, come now, Pet! Adventure is about learning new things!" he barks with an amused chuckle. He finally lifts his gaze from the table, leaning against it and folding his arms over his chest to watch me.

I don't want him watching me. That's all he's done since bringing me on this ship. I don't like it... It makes my skin crawl. Well... Yeah, it makes my skin crawl. Anything else would be unacceptable.

"So," he adds, "to answer your question, yes. I *could* find someone 'more qualified' to guide my precious ship. However, I promised you adventure." He looks down, as if to calculate something. "Two notts port."

I move my hands exactly the way I'm supposed to, hearing his pleased grunt at my side. I set my jaw into a firm line, keeping my eyes planted forward. I can only focus on one thing at a time right now, and looking at him would be a mistake. One of many as of recently.

I'm given a short reprieve from the tension before Benedict comes up the stairs from the lower deck, taking them two at a time. His eyes are sparking with some form of excitement, their pupils narrowed into pinpricks. A wide grin spreads across his face as he reaches the top. I can practically feel the vibrating restlessness in the man's muscles as he begins to speak.

"Bodies, Cap, six notts, starboard."

Bodies?! What the hell does he mean by bodies?!

Are there people floating in the ocean somewhere? There hasn't been anything but a completely open ocean all day, and I suddenly feel the need to vomit.

Kiernan grins, turning to me. "You heard the man, six notts starboard."

I do, counting them out in my head due to my distraction from dead bodies.

Thank the gods for learning simple math...

Kiernan stands to his full height then, turning to Benedict, who is still damn near bobbing on his toes. "Have Arthur prep the powder, and tell the men it's time to play."

The laugh that rumbles out of Benedict sends a shiver all the way down my body, cooling my bones as if I were just doused in ice-cold water. Te'lei did that to me once, having had his cousin chill it before. It sucks. This might suck even more.

Benedict hurries back down the stairs, shouting something I can't even make out over the sound of the rest of the crew jeering and cheering.

I look over at Kiernan questioningly, my brows knitting tightly. "What are bodies?"

He picks his spyglass up off the navigation table, extending it. I try to focus on him rather than the chaos that has now ensued below. Men scramble to grab their weapons, Benedict gives orders with more excitement than I think I have seen in the last few days, and the mess of red hair that I've come to recognize as the man named Arthur, rushes around gathering powder guns, which I had never even seen before coming aboard this ship.

Kiernan steps forward until my back is flush with his abdomen and pelvis. It's just another excuse to touch me, and I feel the skin of my back burning. With him behind me and the helm in front of me, I have nowhere to run.

He grips the helm, handing me the instrument in his hand ,and points.

"That ship..." he begins, pausing to wait for me to peer through the glass. I do, catching sight of a poorly kept ship with a red flag sailing out ahead of us.

"That ship is a slave tradeship. When captains are taking a load of slaves, they call it 'moving bodies'," he continues, stooping low enough to bury his face in my hair and inhale deeply, "Understand, Pet?"

Tingles skitter along my skin, and I chalk it up to the new information I've just been given. I'm not willing to admit that it is anything more.

Slaves...

The idea sends a deep, gut-retching feeling into my stomach, making it flip and flop around like a wet fish. All I can think about is the Kana'te women who sometimes go missing in Puka'qui.

Are there women, who once could have been growing up right alongside me on that ship? I can't help but ask the question, turning my head to look up at him with wide eyes.

"Are there Kana'te people on these ships?"

"Almost certainly," he informs, snatching the spyglass away from me. He peers into himself after I take over the wheel once more. "The *Makara*, which is the name of that specific ship, seems to deal mostly in Anthichee people, and other pondscum... However, Kana'te people are a rare commodity, so I wouldn't be surprised if there are one or two of them on it."

My blood runs cold, a gentle yet useless reminder of the power simmering under the surface. If there are Kana'te people on that ship, they are just as stuck as I am, unless they break the decree and use their abilities. If they were to do that, they might as well stay on that ship anyway. That's how I would feel if I were them.

"They are just sitting ducks away from the island..." My voice cracks, my gaze lingering on the silhouette of the ship ahead of us.

"They are indeed," he nods, then breaks away from this uncomfortable topic. He calls down to Benedict, who is still helping grab weapons and ammo. "Oi! Did you happen to see the title of that ship?"

The furrow in Benedict's brow tells us that he hadn't, his body growing still for a moment in anticipation. There's a pause, whether that for dramatic effect or for Kiernan's own personal pleasure, I can't be sure. I startle as his voice suddenly booms over my head again. "Makara!"

The shift in Benedict's body is almost instantaneous, not to mention startling. The excitement in his eyes morphs into something dark, menacing. It's as if he had started as a crazed psycho ready to crack skulls and has now turned into a monster ready to devour them completely whole. The entire crew gives him a wide berth as he storms to the front of the ship, peering out over the water.

"Get me to that ship, K, before I decide to swim there."

I turn back to Kiernan again, my brows furrowing deeply. "Is there something special about that ship?"

He takes over the helm, caging me between his hard body and the steering column once more.

"That ship is where Benedict plucked his own *pet*," he chuckles.

The ship creaks under the stress of the turn, and I find myself bracing my hand on his arm. We watch as Benedict climbs onto the railing, every sinew of muscle tightly pulled at the ready.

"Blood will flood the deck tonight, boys," Benedict growls, the sound so incredibly hate-filled that fear begins to leak from my pores.

I look up at Kiernan as if I might find some vestige of sorrow or remorse, but the grin on his face gives me pause. I have questions. So many, many questions... I search his features for the answers, and it becomes clear to me I won't find them.

As the *Nureus* glides up parallel to the *Makara*, both crews scrambling at the ready, Kiernan immediately shouts over the noise. "Benedict! Go fetch!"

Everything turns to chaos as the smaller man drives his foot into the first opposing crewmember's face before ever even touching the *Makara*'s deck. The rest of Kiernan's crew follows, save for the redhead who stays behind to reload pistols, and the sound of battle clashes through the air. The scene begins to blur into a messy tangle of bodies.

The sound of steel against steel and the deafening pop of gunpowder igniting rises over the roaring shouts and curses.

Kiernan's arms are around me in an instant, carrying me down the staircase like a child. He sits me down in the alcove that holds the door to the captain's quarters, that evil-looking smirk still planted on his face.

"Now, stay here, Pet. Be a good girl and watch," he commands, his lips grazing my temple, "If you don't wish to, you could always go wait for me in bed."

Then he's gone, joining the fray without giving me a chance to protest his disgusting insinuation.

Little does he know—or maybe he does—this '*pet*' doesn't like to be told what to do.

There is no way that I'm going to risk my own people being locked up on that ship, let alone countless others, and not try to help them.

I make my way to the railing, searching for a way over to the other ship. The gap is too wide for me to jump like the rest of them did, so I snatch a rope that hangs from the mast. The redhead is too distracted, handing out reloaded pistols, and the rest of the crew is in the middle of a bloodbath. None of them will notice if I simply swing over and make my way to the brig.

So, with a lot of 'lady balls', as Kay'Kaio likes to call it, I swing over the railing and land with a hard thud on the other ship.

And a bloodbath it is...

Bodies litter the floorboards, blood flowing like a fountain, staining the wood red. I can't even keep my bare feet from sludging through the warm, wet goop as I try to break through to the other side. Bile rises up into my throat, and I drop to my hands and knees to slip through the legs of someone cutting their way through the bones of another. My hands slip in the red lake, and I smack my face on a boot that shuffles by. It stings, but it wasn't hard enough to leave lasting pain.

My ears ring from the sheer volume of the screams and shouts, and I scramble to my feet once I've broken through the horde of men. I turn around to look in horror.

I've never seen anything like this before, though I have seen my fair share of the grotesque. But this is something different. What I had been involved in all those years ago had been silent panic, calm malice. This... This is pure, unfiltered chaos.

And in the center of it all is Benedict.

He holds a pistol in one hand, a sword in the other, alternating between cutting into the intestines of men who find it wise to test him, and shooting through the temporal lobes of nearby, unsuspecting bystanders. Well... bystanders isn't the right word. They are all involved in this nightmarish little war that's taking place, but my meaning is clear enough.

His face is twisted up into something akin to a snarl, though it might very well be a sneer considering the deep, throaty, unhinged laugh that rips from his throat. He isn't a man, not right now. I don't think he's even a monster. He is just a cold, bloodlusting devil, covered in the blood of the people around him.

Well... he'll give me nightmares for the rest of my life...

Just as I'm about to turn and try to descend the staircase, I feel the rough, calloused hands of someone grabbing my shoulder. He spins me around, and I'm met with the cruel, hungry gray gaze of a middle-aged man whose teeth have seen better days.

I start to panic, his arms wrapping around my waist to lift me off my feet. I begin to kick and scream, though my voice is lost in the crashing sounds already happening around us.

No one can hear me.

No one is coming to help.

I open my mouth to scream louder, ready to resort to screaming out for Kiernan, but his nasty, blood-soaked hand clamps down over my mouth. I can taste the copper of some stranger's blood on my tongue, and it's enough to make me gag. My stomach churns, and I realize I can't breathe.

The stupid asshole has his hand over my nose, too!

My eyes begin to sting at the corners, but I refuse to let some stinky, bile inducing man half the size of Benedict get the better of me without a fight.

I thrash my head side to side until I've managed to pry my mouth free, biting down as hard as I can on the man's fingers. They taste like urine, which is disgusting to even acknowledge, but I muscle through, letting my jaw pop with the force of my bite. Flesh splits under my lips, and bone begins to crunch.

The man's snarled howl rings in my ears, causing me to go temporarily deaf in the right ear. But I don't let go, I don't falter.

"Stupid, crazy little bitch!" he growls, attempting to beat me off him with his other fist. The blow to the head sends me reeling, but it isn't enough to sedate me. He continues to do this, over and over again, until I think my skull will split in two. My vision begins to darken around the edges, but I don't let go.

Just as I'm about to brace for another blow to the head, he goes still, his hand growing limp in my mouth. Confused, I release my teeth, taking chunks of skin with me. I spittle onto the deck, trying to get the taste out of my mouth, and stumble slightly on my feet.

And then I'm snatched up again, this time with less thought, but a gentler touch.

"For such a smart woman, you are the dumbest thing I've ever seen in my life," Benedict's voice calls out, though it's muffled slightly in my right ear. He throws me over his shoulder, something I truly hope doesn't become a habit for these people, and walks me to the railing of the ship.

I look behind us at the man who had just been manhandling me, and start to dry heave. Benedict, somehow, had severed his head from his body.

Before I can even come to terms with it, my body is airborne, flying over the rail of the *Makara* and into the waiting arms of someone else.

Arthur.

"Arthur! If anything else happens to that woman, it's your ass, not mine!" Benedict shouts and then disappears back into the crowd.

"What do you think you're doin', lass?" Arthur shouts as he places me on my feet, shoving me behind him to hand off another gun, "Are you askin' to be sliced into wee bits?"

I let out a huff, trying to steady myself after the sudden transition from weightlessness to being upright on my feet.

"I just wanted to help!" I protest, narrowing my eyes.

"Well, I dunno!" he barks back at me, though his is definitely bigger than his bite, unlike the other men on this crazy crew, "I've just been put in charge o' you, and I cannot risk you dyin'. I cannot lose this job! So stay put."

After that, he turns away from me and back to what he was doing.

I have no idea what he means by '*I can't lose this job*', but something in his voice sounds almost... desperate. That desperation alone makes me stay put for the remainder of the battle.

After the fighting has settled down and all of the people from below the deck of the *Makara* have been loaded onto the *Nureus*, I scan the sea of faces for any that look familiar to me. Sure enough, there is one woman, with dark, soot-covered skin and pale eyes, bearing the mark of the Kana'te people. Up her left arm are the intricate designs of the Cali'ako tribe, the blues and greens starkly bright against her dark almond skin.

I take a step forward, moving to comfort her regardless of not knowing her personally, but a massive brick wall of muscle blocks my view.

"What in the hell do you think you were doing?!" Kiernan shouts, causing my eyes to snap up to his face.

He's angry.

No... He's *pissed*.

"I was just trying to—"

"I told you to stay put!" His snarl causes silence to fall over everyone else aboard the ship, and I think I see Henry and Viktor shuffling the rescued 'bodies' below deck.

My entire body goes still, my heart hammering in my chest. I've never seen Kiernan like this before.

Irritated? Yes.

Frustrated? Absolutely.

But completely outraged? Never.

"You can't just tell me what to do and expect me to just listen to you!" I retort, my anger originating from startled fear rather than true rage.

I can see the vein popping out of his temple, pulsing with each racing heartbeat. His jaw clenches, ticking audibly. His eyes harden like cold diamonds against his sun-kissed skin, which is splattered and stained red.

"You *will* listen or learn the hard way," he grits out between clenched teeth, and scoops me up harshly into his arms.

I cry out, startled by the suddenness as he carries me to the edge of the ship. My eyes scan the deck, realizing that no one has stayed to watch.

Not a single one of them.

My heart stutters in my chest as he sits me down on the rail, pushing my upper body off balance until I'm only held up by the fist he has wrapped in the fabric of my top.

"If you're not going to listen to me, then you're as good as dead already," he rumbles, his voice suddenly laced with a cold finality, "I may as well chum the waters with you now!"

My entire body trembles, and my fingers scramble for purchase on his shirt. Not his wrist or his hand. I don't want him to drop me into the unforgiving water below. My eyes grow wide, panic lacing through my body.

This isn't the same panic as before. This is hotter. It's like all the power I've had built up over the course of my time on this ship has vanished, leaving only me and him, with nothing to protect me if he were to choose to let go.

"K-Kiernan!" I stammer, my hands finally twisting into his shirt.

He holds me here, as if contemplating it, and I begin to count the heavy rises and falls of his chest to keep myself somewhat grounded. But how grounded can one really be when they are hanging in the grasp of a man who has their life in his hands?

"I told you to stay," he repeats, his voice now low and steady.

"I-I know..." I swallow thickly, unable to keep the perspiration from making my vision swim, "I'm sorry."

"When I tell you to stay, you fucking stay."

He shakes me slightly, as if that alone will get his point sinking into my thick skull. I snap my eyes shut, my chin quivers as a whimper escapes from between my lips.

There is a moment of silence, then I feel his warm breath on my face as he draws me up from over the edge. His forehead rests against mine, and I open my eyes again to meet his crystal stare.

"I almost lost you today, because you can't take a simple fucking order," he breaths, his jaw twitching under the skin.

"I'm sorry..." I repeat.

"From now on, you will listen to every word I say, every single command I give you. If I tell you to swing from the mast like a fucking ape, you will do it."

I nod, the message loud and clear. I hadn't expected him to react like this. Sure, I thought he would be angry that I disobeyed him, but I didn't think he would be so... What is that emotion flitting across his face? Fear? Concern?

Doubtful. This is Kiernan Slater we are talking about. He's just angry that he almost lost his little plaything. Nothing more, nothing less.

He takes a step back, pulling me to stand on the deck, though I'm still pinned between the railing and his hips. His eyes rove over my body, like taking inventory of his goods, and he leans in to bury his face in my hair.

"You're filthy, Darling. Let's go clean up."

12

Kiernan

I step into the room the next morning, greeted by the sight of Sitara's defeated form sprawled across the bed. The morning light filters through the windows, casting a soft glow over her as she flops onto her back, letting out a groan of frustration. It's undeniably endearing, watching her writhe in discomfort, her body splayed out in a messy, disheveled state on my bed. There's something about her helpless demeanor that stirs a twisted sense of satisfaction within me.

She doesn't fight back the way she used to, and I can't help but wonder if it's because of the fear I instilled in her with that little display on the railing. Part of me feels guilty for pushing her that far, but then I remind myself of the events that transpired—her blatant disregard for my orders, for her safety, the blood, the chaos, the sheer recklessness of it all. If she hadn't put herself in such a precarious position, I wouldn't have had to resort to such extreme measures.

But she did, and now here we are.

As I stand here, I can't help but admire the way the fabric of my shirt rides up her thighs as she moves. It's a simple, innocent thing, yet it ignites a fire in my belly, a head that's laced with something unfamiliar. Something I can't quite put my finger on. I'm not sure how to process these strange, foreign emotions that this woman keeps stirring up in me.

She's dangerous—more dangerous than I ever could have anticipated—and I'm starting to realize just how much of a challenge she's going to be.

My mind drifts back to the moment I learned she'd been aboard the *Makara* during that battle. The way my chest tightened at the thought of her being in harm's way. The way my blood ran cold when I heard about Ben having to cut a man's head off to protect her, to keep her from being hurt worse than the nasty bruise she was given.

I didn't like it then, and I still don't like it now.

The idea of her being in danger... It's something that sits unsettled in my gut, something I can't seem to shake.

"Good morning, Pet. Sleep well?" I say finally, tearing myself away from the blatant ogling that seems to have become a habit whenever she's around. My voice is light, almost playful, but beneath it lies a layer of tension, a reminder of the unease she's been causing me.

I walk over to the desk where I'd set out our breakfast earlier this morning. It's simple fare—salted pork, cheese, and a few slices of orange I added to her plate. It's not much, but it's enough to keep her from going hungry.

As for the oranges, well, she's not in any danger of scurvy, but I figure it's better to start these habits early. After all, I take care of my possessions, and I intend to take care of her the same way.

Whether she likes it or not.

Picking up her plate, I make my way back to the bed, settling myself down among the disarrayed sheets. I reach out, wrap my fingers around her wrist, and pull her up, turning her hand over so I can place the plate in her grasp.

"Eat," I command, my voice firm. I'm confident that after yesterday's events, she won't dare refuse.

For a moment, I think she won't. She looks up at me, her face etched with exhaustion, the remnants of sleep still clinging to her expression. Then her gaze drops to the food in front of her, and I think she'll comply.

But then she takes only a few small, nibbling bites before pushing the plate away. My jaw tightens, my mouth turning downward as I frown.

"Eat more," I demand, crossing my arms over my chest and nodding sharply toward the food. "If you don't want to eat that, I'll feed you my cock instead."

Her reaction is immediate. Her face twists in revulsion as if the very suggestion revolts her. It's almost as if she believes I've brought her aboard this ship simply to use her body for something wet, warm, and tight to fuck. And while that is, of course, part of the plan, it's not the only reason. However, looking at her now, I can't help but wonder if that's *exactly* what she thinks. If that's all she believes she's worth to me.

"No part of your filth will be anywhere near my mouth, let alone inside of it," she says.

But then I see it—a flicker of softness in her eyes, a glimmer of something that doesn't quite match the fiery defiance she's been clinging to since the moment she woke up here. It's a rare sight, one I haven't seen since she first boarded with the children for that ill-fated tour.

It's a small crack in her armor, a small sign that maybe she's starting to realize she's exactly where she should be. While the sight is almost pleasant, it doesn't change the fact that she's still as stubborn as ever.

I take a deep breath, trying to summon what little patience I have left. This woman, I swear, seems to exist solely to test my limits, to push me to the edge of my restraint. And right now, she's doing a damn good job of it.

"So bold of you to assume the word '*never*' is in my vocabulary, Pet," I murmur, only to be interrupted with a sharp, annoyed sigh. My jaw clenches as I force myself to relax, to keep my patience from shattering completely.

"Suit yourself, you stubborn little thing," I finally say, letting the words come out through gritted teeth.

I'm being far more lenient than I want to be, but this infuriating woman has brought out all kinds of new feelings and reactions. Even amid my rage, while I had her hanging over the edge of the ship, a single quiver of her bottom lip had run my hot blood cold. She might as well have dumped a bucket of snow over my head.

I turn toward the door, reaching for the handle. She's frustrating me already this morning.

Just as I am about to swing open the door and leave her to her sulking, I hear her voice filter through the air behind me.

"I would like what is mine returned to me." Her voice is firm, yet far calmer than I have yet to hear. It's a new side to her; a side I have the sudden need to poke and prod at.

A catholic smirk spreads across my face as I turn to look at her, possessiveness surging through my veins as I am met with a cold, solid stone gaze.

"I beg your pardon?" I say as I shift to lean against the still closed door, "What belongs to *you*?" The honey smooth chuckle that escapes my person rumbles through me, displaying the amusement that skitters along my skin at her choice of phrasing. "I'll have you know, Pet, that everything within the walls of this ship belongs to *me*."

I kick off the door, sauntering toward her at my full height, just for dramatics. "*My* ship. *My* crew. *My* room filled with *my* things." Each item I list off earns me a step closer to her until I'm towering over her petite form that is still perched delicately on my bed. "And *my* Kitten."

She furrows her brow, her eyes hardening as they narrow. Honestly, I wouldn't mind that expression staring up at me while I fuck her face. It would certainly be a change of pace from the fawning, ecstasy-filled ones on the faces of lesser women.

After all, everyone loves a good hate fuck now and again.

I watch as her slender arm raises, her movements stiff and robotic. She points toward the wall above my desk, her pouty lips pressing into a deep line. "That is *not* yours. I want it back."

My gaze follows the line she has created with her arm until it lands on the little strip of cloth I had so easily slipped off her upper arm as she was floating about the deck with the children.

Ah, so she has noticed it after all.

What an observant little thing when she isn't thrashing around like a fish caught on a hook.

I had originally taken it without any knowledge that I would have *her* in my cabin later that very same week. I had wanted a piece of her. Just a tiny memento to get me through another painstaking six months without the pleasure of her proximity.

An idea springs to life, and I turn to give her a wolfish grin. "You're welcome to it," I say with a challenge, "As soon as you get it down. Until then, it remains mine."

I know damn well how high that nail holding her precious cloth is. After all, my large, six-foot-five-inch ass had to stand on a chair to get it up there. I also know damn well that she won't be able to reach it without valiant effort.

The change in her body language is intoxicating. I finally get to see that spark of life reignite in her eyes.

"I'll see you on the deck."

With that, I leave her to her devices, walking out of the room with a sense of triumph.

As I go about my morning, I wait with sick amusement to see her walk out of the cabin to join the fray upon the ship after having failed. As time ticks away, my anticipation builds.

Is she really going to sit in there and sulk all day over a stupid scrap of cloth?

Annoyed at being denied my victory, I make my way back to the cabin door. My eyes immediately focus on the bed where I expect her to be upon my entry. To my surprise, she isn't there. My gaze follows the sounds of shifting and exertion, finding her well-toned body high above my head.

I don't fucking believe it...

She took the challenge literally, and now I have to eat my words. I don't like shoving my foot in my mouth. No one but Benedict has ever shove it there before. Yet, here she is, standing atop a stack of books on the desk.

The tower of literature sways with the rocking of the ship, but her footing is sturdy, unwavering. I watch her slender fingers wrap around the cloth, pulling it off its perch on the nail with a whine of triumph.

I watch in fascination, having completely forgotten the agility most of the tribal people have. When she plops down into the sitting position on the mountain of books and leans her elbows onto her knees. She grins at me, a look that is both intoxicatingly delicious and frustration-inducing, and swings the cloth that is now dangling between her delicate little fingers. "Next time, make it a real challenge."

I find that my mouth is now hanging open despite myself. This little woman amuses me greatly, and her confidence as she sways with the movement of the ship, never once seeming to falter in her balance, creates a fire that begins to burn in my belly.

Oh, she and I are going to have so much fun, I can feel it.

"I'm impressed," I laugh, shaking my head in disbelief at her audacity. That little bit of cloth must be something significant if she went through all the trouble to get it back.

Good. I like a woman who knows what she wants and isn't afraid to take it.

"New challenge. Put my damn books back." I gleefully watch as her adorable button nose scrunches up in distaste, her eyes moving toward the bookshelves. All of those books had been neatly organized before she had so savagely unshelved them.

"Hurry up, you're wasting daylight." I back myself out of the room, something resembling pride swelling in my chest, "I have more for you to do when you're done." I laugh as I lean against the railing of the upper deck, waiting for her to finally finish with her task.

It takes her all of fifteen to twenty minutes to walk out of the cabin, having traded in my large sleepshirt for her original clothing. Her hair is braided back into a long rope of amber. I was right, the sun catches each lock like an extension of itself when it is freshly washed and combed.

I catch a glimmer of mischief in her eyes and the subtle tug of the left side of her mouth. There is no way she put those books back on the shelf correctly. For a moment, I let my imagination wander into the bedroom, trying to imagine the clusterfuck of a bookshelf she has left me.

For now, however, we have things to do, and I have a little plaything to put to work.

She climbs up the steps to the upper deck, her movements graceful and determined, where I remain leaning against the railing, admiring the soft angles of her profile from where I stand. The way the light of day dances across her features is still captivating to me, even as I notice the way she adjusts her clothing. However, I would hardly call the outfit proper clothing, not by the standards of my world, at least. It leaves too little to the imagination, and I find myself bristling at the thought of other men ogling what is undeniably mine.

Note to self: while I am getting her some soap of her own, I should make sure to procure less revealing clothing for her to wear while she is walking about the ports.

"So," she addresses me, her tone laced with a vexatious pride that borders on defiance. "What else are you wanting me to do, your highness? I hope it's more of a challenge than your poor attempts as challenges thus far."

As much as I reveled in her rage and panic when I tried her to the bed, I think I might enjoy this vindictively kittenish side of her better. There's something about her sharp wit and the way she spars with me verbally that sends an entirely new sensation of thrill coursing through me. It's dangerous, this game we're playing, one where the stakes are as high as the tension between us.

I'll admit it; I'm enjoying this little game between us. A game where we see who can outdo the other. If I'm keeping track correctly, she's at two while I sit at a perfect lead of six. And I have every intention of keeping that lead.

"Wow, you finished that faster than I expected you to." I turn toward her with a guileful grin, my voice dripping with amusement. "Good job."

I'll let her bask in her false victory for a while. After all, what's the fun in a game if you can't play with your opponent a little first? I watch as she straightens her shoulders, her expression radiating a willingly offered sense of triumph. Damn... she really is adorable. Too bad I'll have to disappoint her later by ripping that victory away from her. Like taking a bowl of milk from a kitten.

I cock a brow at her, resuming our conversation about her responsibilities aboard the ship. "Can you sew?" I ask, my fingers rubbing over my jaw in contemplation, my tone casual despite the underlying seriousness of the question.

She nods, her eyes filled with the same skepticism she gave me on the beach. I do love that look. "Yes. Is that all you have for me? That's hardly considered manual labor."

My face spreads into a maliciously amused grin as she leans onto the railing, her arms folding over her chest. "Can you cook?"

She rolls those pretty eyes and nods, pursing her lips. "Yes, I can cook too."

Perfect.

I know exactly how to spark that fiery temper in my beautiful, perfect little minx.

"It's clear that you have too much time on your hands. I guess I'll have to keep your hands busy," I say, my voice low and teasing as I motion for her to follow me. I crank my first two fingers, leading the way down toward the kitchen.

As we descend into the bowels of the ship, I continue to listen to her prattle on about how she doesn't think cooking qualifies as manual labor either. I remain silent, basking in the anticipation of the reaction I know will come soon enough. It isn't the cooking that will test her paper-thin patience, and I am counting on a good show.

Once we've finally arrived at the door that leads to my entertainment for the evening, I swing it wide and shout into the room for Todd, the man who has been serving as a poor excuse for a cook since our last cook, Gerald, had a sudden... accident involving a shark.

How he ended up in the water is still a complete mystery.

I wait impatiently for Todd to work his way through the mess, the clanging of pots and pans echoing through the room as he steps over them. I roll my eyes, reaching in once he's gotten close enough for me to grab him. His dull blue eyes widen as I drag him out, his medium-built frame tensing under my grip.

He's not a big man, smaller than Benedict but larger than the lanky twat Arthur. His sun-scorched skin pales as I practically lift him over the last of the piles of shit littering the floor.

I take a moment to give Sitara a mocking glare. She is currently holding her hand over her mouth in complete horror and disgust, her wide-eyed expression forcing a victorious chuckle to rumble up my chest. I think this makes my score a seven.

"You have been feeding me food... from here?!" Her voice pinches in repugnance, her throat bobbing as though she might vomit right on the floor. I do hope she keeps it off my boots if she does.

"You said you wanted something to challenge you," my voice is laced with uncontrollable levity, my amusement at her disgust evident.

"I am not touching that!" she scoffs, her wild mane thrashing side to side as she shakes her head.

"Well then, I'll have to keep those pretty little fingers busy in other ways," I say, my tone dripping with suggestion.

I back her up against the door frame, pressing my body into hers. Her eyes widen, and she attempts her signature move of pushing me away. I take the opportunity to grab her hand, trailing it down my body with a smirk.

Leaning in, I bury my face in her hair once more. I can't help it. She just smells so perfectly tempting, so perfectly mine, with the lingering scent of my shirt still clinging to her skin.

I let out a low groan as I press her hand into the growing bulge in the front of my pants, and start grinding into her palm.

"We can always go back to the original arrangement we made on that beach if you really, really don't want to clean the kitchen," I murmur, nipping at her earlobe.

Sitara stiffens, letting out a mousy little squeak.

Arthur, fucking Arthur, happens to be walking down the stairs at just the right moment, ruining my fun.

"You. Come here. You're helping me with this stupid disaster," she barks, attempting to push me off her again.

I let her this time, albeit reluctantly.

"And you," she points to Todd, "Don't you dare come back into this kitchen."

Arthur's eyes widen in surprised dismay, and he looks to me for confirmation. I shrug, folding my arms.

"You heard the lady, Arthur. You get to play maid for the day. May she have mercy on your soul."

Arthur's head falls, his chin touching his chest as he makes the walk of shame toward the minefield that is the kitchen.

I laugh darkly, watching the two as they begin to sift through the room. I adjust myself, grunting in frustration that she's managed to evade me yet again.

I suppose it's my fault.

I gave her a choice.

13

Sitara

I can't believe what I am seeing! I put food in my mouth from this kitchen! The repulsion of even looking at this mess sends a shudder through my body, as if my very soul is recoiling at the sight. To make matters worse, I can hear Kiernan's dark chuckle echoing through the air as he walks back up onto the deck. The sound grates against my nerves, and I clench my teeth in frustration.

Fucking prick...

I give a side glance toward the tall, lanky redhead standing beside me. The look of dread etched on his face mirrors the same emotions swirling in my chest. This job is going to take us all day, maybe even longer, and the thought of it is exhausting.

The room is a complete disaster, a nightmare come to life. The old cast-iron stove is caked with dust and Gods only know what else; its surface is so grimy that it looks like it hasn't been cleaned in years. The ladles hung along the beam above it are streaked with dried-on grime, their once-shiny surfaces now dulled by neglect. Fish remains are scattered across the wooden countertop, their rotting flesh creating a foul-smelling stench that clings to the air. The lack of ventilation in the cramped space only exacerbates the odor, and I can feel the nauseating stench burning inside my nostrils.

"And here I thought he liked his things clean," I grumble under my breath, taking a hesitant step into the kitchen. My bare feet press against the filthy floor, and I can feel the sticky residue coating my skin. The sensation is vile, and I swallow down a lurching wave of nausea that rises in my throat, fighting to keep my breakfast from making an unwelcome reappearance.

This is the first time in my entire life I wish I had a pair of Mundane shoes.

I glare down at the floor as if it's personally offended me. Arthur's eyes track my movements, his blue gaze dull compared to that of his captain.

"Aye, he does. He's just not been in the kitchen ever," he says quietly.

I glance back at him over my shoulder, eyeing him down with not-so-subtle annoyance. "It's still part of his ship. He should care about every bit of it if he's going to go around lecturing people about it," I say bitterly.

I look around the room, searching for a decent place to start, but every surface seems equally vile. The air is thick with the stench of rotting food and stale sweat. Deciding on a heading, I move to the barrels stacked and secured to the left-hand wall, but the moment I lift the lid off the first one, I'm hit with a rush of putrid air. The contents are spoiled, their once-edible state long since passed. I gag, moving quickly to close it back up. Even Arthur scrunches his nose, his expression paling as he realizes too late that he might as well have been watching out of the garbage this entire time.

No, correction, even that would have been more sanitary.

Moving to the broom closet nestled in the far corner of the room, I yank open the creaky door to pull out the mop and bucket. The mop head is dry and brittle, its fibers frayed and worn, and the bucket looks like it hasn't been used in years. I roll my eyes, trudging back toward the door with them in hand.

I jerk my chin toward the barrels, grimacing in contempt. "Get that filthy crap out of here, Arthur. Throw it overboard if nothing else. No one is putting that in their mouths."

He moves to comply, and I practically stomp out of the kitchen and up the narrow staircase that leads onto the deck, seething with a dubiousness that has me reeling.

The crew above deck is laughing, and I can feel their eyes on me as I pass by. Their amusement only fuels my irritation, and I clench my fists at my sides as I walk. As I move past a set of three burly men, one of them leans his head around the shoulder of another to look at me, a sly grin spreading across his face.

"Having fun, little lady?" he asks sarcastically. Obviously, he is being facetious, his toothy grin nothing more than an annoyance I don't have time to deal with.

I take hold of the hook and rope used to hoist buckets of water up the side of the ship, gripping it tightly in my hands. Without thinking, I swing the wooden container purposefully wide, knocking it against the side of his head with a loud thud.

He grunts, his hand flying out to the side of his face as his murky eyes narrow at me. I unhook the handle off the rope, glancing over at him as I shrug one shoulder.

"Oops," I say dryly, my voice laced with mock innocence. I raise my brows in a challenge, daring the brute to say one more gods-damned word to me.

The other two men standing beside him begin to laugh, their identical smiles splitting their faces. The one on the left, who has a strangely dual-pupilled left eye, slaps the larger man on the shoulder as his brother practically doubles over, his laughter echoing across the deck.

"How's your face, Becket?" he asks, wheezing between bouts of laughter.

The first man composes himself just enough to add in his own jab. "It's an improvement! The ladies at the next port are going to *love* that shiner!" he says, chuckling.

The one, namely Becket, throws the lanky man hanging on him to the floor. Despite the thud, he seems unfazed by the violence just inflicted on him.

"Viktor! I know what to call him!" the one with the double-pupilled eye says to the other excitedly.

The two men stare at each other for no more than a heartbeat before chanting in unison. "Becket the Bucket Boy!"

Becket doesn't seem to like this, pulling the rag he's had stuffed into his waistband and walking away with a grumble. "Stupid bastards," he mutters under his breath, but I don't care.

With that, I fill my bucket with fresh water from the barrels on deck, a small smirk playing on my lips, and walk back to the kitchen. Arthur and I scrub and remove the filth from our presence, slowly falling into casual conversation as we work. I'm standing on the counter, taking a rag to the walls as we bicker and banter back and forth.

Arthur, perhaps, is the most normal among those on this dang ship. He's not as rough or as crude as the others, and he doesn't seem to take pleasure in riling me up. It's a small comfort, but it's something.

"You know," he finally says as he begins hanging the freshly washed utensils back where they go, "you're not so bad for a tribal lass." His tone is light, almost teasing, and I shoot him a playful grin over my shoulder, rolling my eyes as I go back to focusing on my task.

"Thank you, I guess?"

I can hear his laughter rumbling around in his chest as we go back to cleaning in comfortable silence. Maybe that is what I appreciate most about Arthur. He doesn't seem to want to rile me up or make me uncomfortable. It is something I am grateful for, something I don't often find among the rough-and-tumble crew of this ship.

"So," he finally breaks the silence, his voice rising above the sounds of our scrubbing cloths raking against the wood surfaces, "What made you want to be a teacher?" His question catches me off guard, and I pause for a moment, soaking the rag in sudsy water again before responding.

That's right... Arthur had been the one to give the children and me our tour of the ship. Man, he really does get thrown into a lot of piddly bullcrap, doesn't he? But despite all of it, he seems to handle it with a quiet resilience, a steadfastness that I admire.

"Well, it was mostly my guardian's idea," I say honestly, reaching down to soak the rag in sudsy water again. "But I do enjoy the children. I like to be around them. They are naturally curious."

I go back to scrubbing the wall, paying close attention to a particularly stubborn spot that refuses to wipe off. It's crusty, and I'm not even sure if it could have qualified as food in the first place.

What happened here? Did they have a full-on food fight while they were cooking?! The thought is almost too ridiculous to fathom, but given the state of the kitchen, I wouldn't be surprised.

"You do seem like the type o' woman that'd like that stuff," Arthur says, nodding slowly as a wide, crooked grin spreads across his face. "But you seem a bit daft too. You don't use your head much in the real world."

He does have a point. If I were more self-aware, more skilled at foreseeing consequences, I probably wouldn't be here right now, scrubbing down a grimy, foul-smelling kitchen on a creaking ship in the middle of the endless ocean.

The rag in my hand feels rough against my raw palms, and the bucket of now murky, soapy water beside me reeks of salt and grime. I toss the rag back into it with a splash, then hoist myself up onto the worn countertop, sighing heavily as I flick my water-pruney fingers dry. The cool ocean air filtering through the small porthole does little to ease the heat of the cramped kitchen.

"Fair enough," I chuckle.

I've been enjoying this casual back-and-forth with Arthur. He's easy to talk to, his demeanor relaxed and unhurried. Earlier, he'd mentioned being young and new to the crew, explaining that jobs like this—scrubbing kitchens, hauling barrels, and doing other menial tasks—were just his way of "paying his dues." There's something admirable about his acceptance of his place on the ship, his quiet determination to prove himself. It's a stark contrast to the bitterness I've felt since being dragged onto this vessel. He seems at peace with the hand life has dealt him, and that's something I can't help but envy.

I push a stray lock of hair out of my face, tucking it behind my ear as I glance around the small, cluttered kitchen. Pots and pans hang from the ceiling, swaying slightly with the gentle rocking of the ship. The air smells of salt, sweat, and the faint tang of last night's dinner, which we haven't managed to get out.

"Can I ask you a question?" I say, turning my gaze back to Arthur.

He nods, his carrot-red hair catching the dim light streaming through the porthole. "Shoot."

"Why *this* ship?" I ask, my curiosity getting the better of me. "Why do you put up with all the crap Kiernan throws at you? He's awful, possessive, arrogant, cruel, and morally gray. Honestly, I can't name one good thing I've learned about him so far."

Arthur pauses, his hands stilling as he wipes them absently on his trousers. His expression shifts, thoughtful, as he searches for the right words. "The captain's not that bad, Sitara," he says finally, his voice soft but sincere. "He's a good lad once you get to know him and earn his trust."

The idea of Kiernan being anything other than the self-serving, manipulative man I've observed is hard to wrap my head around, but I can see the genuine admiration in Arthur's eyes as he continues.

"He looks after his crew," he says, his tone steady. "Once he trusts you, he's got a soft spot for his people. But to get there, I need to prove myself. The other lads say it'll all be worth it in the end."

His words spark a new round of questions in my mind. "Don't you have anywhere else to go?" I ask, tilting my head slightly. "A home to go back to, I mean?"

Arthur shakes his head, his expression somber as he shrugs and picks up his rag again. "My reasons for bein' here far outweigh any need for home I once had," he says quietly, his voice carrying a weight that suggests there's more to his story than he's letting on.

It's clear that Kiernan has a way of drawing people in, even those who might otherwise have a life to return to. And yet, despite the captain's abrasive nature, Arthur's respect for him is undeniable. I find myself wondering what it is about Kiernan that inspires such loyalty, but the answer remains elusive.

We fall back into a comfortable silence, the only sound the faint creak of the ship and the occasional splash of water against the hull. My mind wanders, trying to reconcile the stark contrast between Arthur's view of Kiernan and my own. At first, I think it might be because I'm a woman and perhaps see things differently, but then I remember how I've seen Kiernan treat Arthur harshly, without any sign of the softness Arthur claims he possesses.

The hours pass slowly but steadily as we work. Finally, we step back, side by side, to admire our handiwork. The kitchen gleams now, the surfaces clean and the floors spotless. We both grin, a sense of camaraderie settling between us. Arthur slings a friendly arm around my shoulders, his touch warm and reassuring.

"Good job, Starlight," he says, his voice tinged with amusement.

The nickname is new, something he'd started using after I'd told him the meaning of my name during one of our earlier conversations. He'd been curious, knowing that in my tribe, names often carried deeper meanings. Since then, "*Starlight*" had stuck, and I'd grown to like it. It felt endearing, a far cry from the belittling terms like "*kitten*" or "*pet*" that others on the ship had tossed my way.

I return the gesture, wrapping my arm around his slim waist in a show of solidarity. "You too, Pip," I say, using the nickname I'd decided on for him. It suited him—youthful and charming, with just a hint of mischief. He'd earned the affection behind it, being the only person on this ship who'd shown me any real kindness.

As we break apart, I glance down at myself and groan. My clothes are filthy, stained with who-knew-what, and my skin feels grimy. I turn to Arthur, tugging at the clinging fabric of my shirt. "Where do you all usually wash your clothes?" I ask, feeling more disheveled than I had in weeks.

He jerks his head toward a large tub in the corner, a scrub board propped up inside. "We usually give them to Todd to wash," he says.

The thought of Todd handling my clothes is less than appealing. If he washed laundry the way he cleaned the rest of the ship, I'd rather not risk it. "Thanks," I say, forcing a smile as I move toward the tub.

Arthur makes a low, grunting noise as I start to strip off my skirt and top, tossing them into the tub. He quickly averts his eyes, his cheeks flushing slightly. I roll mine, amused despite myself.

Mundanes really do care far too much about nudity, don't they?

Once I've freed myself from the confines—and, frankly, the filth—of my clothes, I walk back toward the door with a newfound sense of freedom. My plan for the evening is simple: take a bath, then return to wash my clothes. I'm sure Kiernan won't mind if I borrow yet another shirt from his collection. He seems to have more than enough, and I've already taken a liking to his cotton ones.

I waltz up the staircase, ignoring the wide, bulging eyes of the men around me. By the love of all that is holy, what is with all this propriety? Back home, nudity was never this big of a deal. People had more important things to worry about than the sight of a bare body.

I find Kiernan on deck, his strong hands working to untangle some of the ropes. His piercing, crystalline eyes flick to me as I approach, and they widen in a mixture of surprise and disbelief. I bound toward him, shoving the list of supplies Arthur and I had made while cleaning into his hand.

"Here," I bark, watching with slight amusement as his mouth drops open.

It seems like the cat's got his tongue.

I take my pointer finger and press it to his chin, closing his slack jaw with a mischievous, almost malignant grin.

"Careful," I tease. "You never know what kind of filth might land in there if you leave it open like that."

With a pride burning in my belly—and a sense of triumph I couldn't ignore—I lift my chin high, spin on my heels, and make my way toward the cabin. My skin is still coated in the grime of the day, and I'm eager to scrub it all away.

As I disappear into the cabin, I hear the scream of the man standing next to Kiernan, followed by the sound of a wet splash.

"Anyone else?" Kiernan growls, his voice loud and commanding.

I notice all of them quickly avert their gazes, their faces turning red as they focus painfully hard on their tasks.

Just as I close the door behind me, I hear Benedict's vindictive voice echo from outside. "Really, K? He was our best ropesman," he says, his tone laced with amusement.

There's a pause, and then a resigned sigh. "Well... Gerald seems to have some company now."

After spending ample time scrubbing the day's grime off my skin, I walk back out of the bathing room wrapped in one of the large towels. I'm in such a good mood. Not only have I spent the entire day with someone who seems to understand the world around them, but I've finally managed to one-up Kiernan at his own game. The expression on his face when I walked onto that deck fills me with a triumphant, almost smug fire.

I make my way to the wardrobe, swinging the door open to find everything perfectly folded and in place. It's starting to occur to me that this man might have a serious control problem. I yank a simple cotton shirt from the second shelf and slip it over my shoulders, feeling the soft fabric settle against my clean skin.

Now that I'm scrubbed clean, I can feel the exhaustion creeping in. Maybe I should take a moment to enjoy my little victory and crawl into bed. Or perhaps I should revel in the fact that I'm done for the day and leave washing my clothes until the morning.

Just as I'm about to crawl under the magically smoothed covers—the bed had been a mess when I left the cabin this morning—Kiernan walks through the door. The look of irritation on his face is immediate, and it only makes my smug grin spread wider.

His brows are drawn in, his face so tense that I think he might break his own jaw.

He looks at me, and the low, growling sound that escapes his throat makes my smirk falter.

"I thought I told you to put my books away," he says.

It isn't a question. There's far too much finality in his tone for it to be anything but a statement.

What is his *problem*?

"I did," I reply, gesturing to the bookshelf. All the books I'd used to grab my marking band—which is now securely back on my arm—are placed back on the shelves.

"Did you put them back the way you found them?" he asks, his long strides carrying him toward the wall where the bookcase sits.

"I don't know how I found them," I answer, staring him down in disbelief.

Why does it matter? The books are back on the shelf!

"You found them in alphabetical order," he snaps. "Where I can find what I'm looking for when I need it."

Before I can process what's happening, he hooks his hand behind one of the rows of books and swipes them onto the floor with a loud crash. I startle at the sound, my eyes widening in confusion. Why is he so angry? I did everything that was asked of me today. With minimal resistance, no less. All I'd done was play the game he's been playing since I arrived here.

Clearly, some people can dish it out but can't take it.

His jaw still clenched, he swipes the second row of books off the shelf and straightens himself once more. "Do it right," he growls.

I stare at him as he stalks toward the bathroom, the door clicking shut with a deafening echo throughout the room. I don't understand his behavior at all.

With a groan of dismay, I slide myself off the bed and walk over to the pile of books scattered across the floor. This is going to take forever.

My mind wanders back to the conversation I'd had with Arthur earlier. There's no way in hell Kiernan is anything but a selfish, over-bearing, mean man.

Give him a chance, my ass.

14

Kiernan

Watching Sitara walk out as bare as the day she was born makes me just about lose my godsdamn mind. My blood boils at the sight, and I can feel my pulse pounding in my temples like a blacksmith hammering away at molten steel. When I had left her this morning in the kitchen, she had been in a foul mood, her arms crossed and her lips pursed into a tight, angry line. She had been fully clothed then, grumbling and bitching under her breath. Her irritation had been palpable, like a thick fog hanging in the air, and I'd found it oddly comforting. It was familiar, like the predictable tides of the sea.

But somehow, throughout the day, Arthur had managed to make her talk to him like it was a normal afternoon. Like they were old friends or something. I couldn't believe what I was hearing.

Oh, yes. I had heard everything I needed to hear. More than I wanted to, in fact.

I had originally walked down to the kitchen to see how things were going, to scratch the itch of hearing her sweet little grumbles and irritated growls. There's something about her anger that draws me in. What I was met with instead was a casual, lighthearted conversation about their lives. Arthur had been leaning against the counter, easy and carefree, while Sitara had been sitting perched on said counter. The boy even had her laughing.

Laughing!

Not that I object to the sound, not really. But the fact that someone else had warranted such a reaction from her turns something nasty in my stomach.

"I've noticed you fiddlin' with that thing six times today. What is it?" Arthur had asked, like he was inquiring about the weather. It took me a moment to realize he was talking about the scrap of cloth that had been the object of our earlier game.

My game.

Mine.

Sitara had grown quiet, as if contemplating how much to say. Her fingers fidgeted with the fabric, her eyes narrowing slightly as she considered her response. Then she sighed, the sound soft yet weighted. "It's my Tilona'matli band."

"You'll have to give me more than that, Starlight," Arthur replied, his tone light and teasing. "I have no idea what that is."

Starlight? The little prick gave her a nickname. My jaw clenched so hard it ached. At that point, I had almost blown my cover, almost ripped the little twig right out of the room.

How dare he.

How dare he try to claim a piece of her like that.

"It's the band our tribes marked some of us with after our parents left to join the Miqui'oh cult," she had explained, though her voice was tense and reedy, like the strings of a harp stretched too tight. There had been a vulnerability in her tone that made my gut twist even harder.

"Who are they?" Arthur asked, his curiosity genuine.

My thoughts exactly.

I had heard the name whispered around some of the ports in my youth, but had never come into contact with them. It had been no more than hushed whispers, the kind of stories you told to scare children into behaving.

"We call them the Maggot Cult," she had explained. "They are followers of Hu'yimona."

Now that is a name I never thought I'd hear again.

Hu'yimona, the Shadow Beast of Wrath—for us Mundanes—is nothing but a bedtime story our parents used to tell us to keep us in line. A boogeyman, a monster under the bed. But hearing the tremble in her voice, I'd wager he is something far more tangible for the Kana'te people.

Something real.

Something terrifying.

I'm not sure what game Arthur, or rather '*Pip*,' seems to be playing, but I will have his fucking fingers if he thinks about stealing away what is mine. I bet that wet-nosed pup doesn't know the first thing about pleasuring a woman. He's just a boy, a naive little boy playing at being a man.

He doesn't deserve her.

He can't possibly understand her.

Which brings us to the other disastrous point of the day. How had she gone from being pissed off this morning to walking across the deck buttass fucking naked with a huge grin on her face? I swear to her farcical gods, if I find out Arthur has lied to me and did, in fact, lay his hands on her... Well, let's just say he will be joining Gerald with the sharks. And this time, there won't be a rope to save him.

These reasons are why I can't seem to prevent myself from showing my ass as I roughly toss all the books from my bookshelf back onto the floor. The sound of leather-bound spines hitting the wood is satisfying, but it does nothing to calm the storm raging inside me.

Sitara looks at me from her place on the bed with such a befuddled expression that it makes her look almost as though she has no idea the can of worms she has just opened. Her brows are furrowed, her lips parted slightly in confusion, and for a moment, I wonder if she is that oblivious.

I storm into the bathroom, securing the lock behind me. The click of the latch is final, a sound that echoes in the small, enclosed space. I make my way to grip the sides of the trough that serves as a hand and face washing station, my fingers digging into the worn wood. The surface is cool under my touch, but it does little to calm the fire burning inside me.

Who does she think she is, walking across my deck like that?

Naked.

Uninhibited.

Like she owns the place.

Like she owns me.

What was she trying to do?

Does she enjoy having every man on this ship gawking at her naked body?

Does she have any idea what that does to me?

What it makes me want to do?

And what the fuck could Arthur have said to make her smile like that? It was probably something so fucking dumb and childish that it reminded her of her students. A pity laugh. I'm going to chalk it up to a pity laugh to save my sanity. Otherwise, I might actually lose it.

I begin boiling water for my bath, pacing the room as I wait for the bubbling sound to start. The kettle whistles, shrill and loud, and I pour the steaming water into the tub with a violent flourish. I strip off my shirt, my muscles tense with the raging possibilities.

She despises me. Her words were so hateful and filled with malice that there is no doubt she hates me. Her words roll around in my head like a mantra: *I can't name one good thing I've learned about him thus far.*

How could she not like me? I have given her the thing she asked for! I have given her an adventure. I have given her the thrill she so obviously craved. I have given her the best bed on the ship. I have let her use my bathing room, with the warmest water afforded to anyone on this vessel.

Maybe it's not enough.

Maybe she needs more.

Maybe she *expects* more.

But what more could I possibly give her? I have rescued her! I freed her from a life of *"what ifs."* I have saved her from the ball and chain that is her opium-crazed, shithole of a brother. I have given her everything she could possibly want.

And then... threw her into an inhabitable kitchen.

Then... let my anger get the better of me, throwing two whole shelves of books off onto the floor at her feet after she had finally had a moment of enjoyment here.

Good job, Kiernan. You probably just scared the fuck out of her.

How can I say that I like my things well taken care of if I try to break them the first time they test me?

Thinking back on the altercation outside this door, I remember the look that had been on her face when I stormed in here. It was a look of confusion, the first look of genuine fear of *me* and not of the situation as a whole. I had taken her so off guard that she hadn't even been able to muster up any of that defiance I so desperately crave from her. Her eyes had widened, her lips had parted, and for a moment, she had just stared at me, frozen in disbelief.

I lean back over the troupe again, raking my hands through my hair in frustration. I can't begin to imagine the thoughts that must be running through her mind at this moment. I have just confirmed to her that there is, indeed, nothing good to be seen in me. The weight of that realization settles heavily in my chest, and I can't help but wonder how I let things escalate so quickly. I've always prided myself on my control, my ability to remain calm and collected, no matter the situation.

But then she came along, and everything changed.

I can't believe I allowed myself to act out that way in the first place. I've never behaved in such a way before. No other woman has ever elicited such a response. All I know is when she laughed and joked with Arthur in the kitchens, when she walked toward me in all her bare glory without a care in the world that anyone else was looking at her besides me, I couldn't bottle it up fast enough. It has to be whatever spell she has on me; whatever magic she has used to keep me chained to her like a willing dog who's loyal to a fault.

There's no other explanation for the way I feel, the way I react when she's around. She's different, and I can't deny it any longer.

Yeah, that's it.

After all, I haven't been able to look at another woman the same way since I met her. Even when I tried, the only face I could picture was hers. The only touch I was able to imagine was hers. It's as if she's imprinted herself on me, leaving an indelible mark that I can't erase, no matter how hard I try.

And I have tried.

Gods, I've tried. But every time I think I've moved on, she's there, haunting me, reminding me of what I can never have.

She's the only woman who has not swooned and fawned when met with my charm. I thought that once I had her, this would go away. Once I indulged in the sight of her writhing beneath me, these feelings would go away. Once I had tasted triumph, I could go about my life as though I had never been graced with her magnificent perfection.

But that's not what happened.

Instead, everything only got worse. The more I tried to push her away, the more I wanted her. The more I tried to convince myself that she meant nothing, the more I realized she meant everything.

And yet, none of that has done anything to break this curse she has endowed upon me.

The sight of her practically cowering on the floor, the lack of defiance that I have grown accustomed to, breaks something deep and long forgotten within me. It's at this moment that I realize the gravity of my actions. She had taken two steps toward being comfortable here, and I just pushed her back three. I think about all the times she's stood up to me, all the times she's challenged me, and I realize how much I've taken that for granted. I've always known she was different, but I've never stopped to think about how much that meant to me. Now, seeing her like this, I can't help but feel a sense of regret.

I take slow, steady steps toward her, kneeling to look into her face. She stiffens more, if it is even possible, and shifts away from me again. She never pauses in her attempt to clean up the books, her hands continuing to shake as she picks up another from the floor. I watch her, my heart pounding in my chest, as I try to find the words to say.

I want to apologize, to tell her how sorry I am for what I did, but the words feel stuck in my throat. I've never been one for apologies, but something about this moment feels different.

I slowly take the book from her grasp, gently moving it from her white-knuckled grip. She finally looks at me, and for the first time in so many, many years, I feel regret.

It's a deep, aching regret that I've never experienced before. I see the fear in her eyes, the uncertainty, and I realize that I've broken something between us. Something that I don't know how to fix.

"I'm sorry," I say genuinely. Pausing, I place the book back onto the shelf before gazing back down at her recoiled form. "You did well today. Go get some rest, darling."

The words feel inadequate, but they're all I can manage. I watch as she slowly gets to her feet, her eyes never leaving mine. For a moment, I think she's going to say something, but then she turns and walks to the bed in silence.

Throughout the next week, Sitara has barely spoken to me as she goes about her new duties aboard my ship. She moves with a quiet efficiency, her hands deftly preparing meals in the cramped galley, the smell of exotic spices mingling with the salty air. She washes the clothes, her slender frame bending over the tubs as she scrubs the fabric with a strength that belies her delicate appearance. She settles into a casual rhythm of day-to-day life among the crew, her presence becoming almost routine. But despite her integration into the crew's dynamics, there's an undeniable distance between us—a chasm that feels both familiar and frustrating.

She has been spending more time with Arthur than I am particularly pleased with, but what else am I going to do? Scare her again until she does nothing but sit in my fucking bed all day?

The memory of her wide, fearful eyes haunts me, a constant reminder of the line I've crossed. I want her trust, her respect, but I'm not sure how to earn it without breaking down the walls she's built around herself.

This particular morning is port day, the crew is in an excited uproar at the prospect of feeling solid land beneath their feet. The air is alive with their chatter and laughter, the clatter of boots on the deck as they prepare for shore leave. I find myself trying to find that same excitement in Sitara, hoping to draw her out of the shell she's retreated into. Unfortunately, she has been uncharacteristically solemn in my presence as of late. I can't tell if that is due to residual fear or deep contemplation. Her expression is a mask, unreadable and unnerving.

I beckon her to me, glancing over to where she stands against the railing, her silhouette sharp against the bright blue horizon. The sea breeze tugs at her hair, and for a moment, I'm struck by how small she looks, how fragile, yet how fiercely she holds herself together.

We will be docking in the next hour or so and staying for the night. When she doesn't even acknowledge my summons, I give Arthur—who is standing near her—a look. He taps her shoulder, sending her attention toward me. I watch her face go from a softened contentment to a mass of hardened lines. Her shoulders stiffen, and she narrows her eyes so slightly I almost don't catch the shift in their setting.

Almost.

She makes her way toward me painfully slow, a hint of reluctance in her stride as she does. "What?" she lets out a sigh, her tone laced with a quiet defiance that makes my jaw tighten.

"We will be dropping anchor at our first port shortly," I give her a hint of a grin, trying to keep my voice light despite the tension between us. "The crew will be taking to town and gathering supplies." I pull out the list of kitchen supplies she had given me the day of her naked voyage across my deck from my pocket. "I'll make sure that you find all of the items on your list, as well as find you some clean, proper clothing and soap."

She stares up at me with an almost immovable hardness. It's unsettling; going from the fiery brimstone of her defiance to this cold, icy facade. "I think I'm going to stay on the ship." Her voice comes out in an almost monotone form that has my jaw clenching. "I'm not feeling well."

My brow furrows, my shoulders dropping slightly with disappointment. "You're not going to leave the ship?" A twinge of something like anger starts to fill my chest, pressing painfully on my sternum. The whole point of bringing her was so she could see something other than that bloody island! Right? "This is the first port since leaving Puka'qui. Don't you want to see it?"

The delicate line of her left brow twitches slightly, something I've begun to notice when she's irritated, and she sighs. "I'm on my cycle and I don't feel well. I'm sure there will be other ports for me to look at some other time."

I know that is a blatant lie. I've not noticed a single speck of red on my sheets since she's been sleeping in them. Yes, I've been checking.

I feel the muscles in my face work under my skin as I try to keep my temper in check. "Suit yourself."

I don't mean it.

I want to tell her that she has no other choice but to explore the town with me. I want to spend time with her. I want to see her face light up as she discovers new things... I want to see that spark in her eyes that she had every time our ship docked at Capulli'ana. But after the incident with the books, I've done my best to keep my temper under control. To not give her any more reason to believe me to be unredeemable.

After we dock and unload our cargo, making our money's worth off the goods we had managed to barter in Puka'qui, I set out into the town. Before separating from the men, I threw the kitchen supply list at Arthur.

"Here, *Pip*, you helped make the list; you can spend your time filling the order."

The boy gives me his usual look of obedient dismay and nods stiffly. "Aye Aye, Cap.'"

And thus the fun begins.

I move to the nearest boutique and skim through the premade gowns lined up along the wall. The woman running the shop comes up to me with a fawning smile and begins to ask me exactly what I'm looking for, clearly trying to gauge whether I am looking for something for a wife. She bats her eyes as I look down at her and smile, running my fingers along the hanging line of silks, linens, and lace.

"I am looking for a specific size," I admit, giving her my most charming smile. There's no doubt I will be getting a pretty discount from this encounter as the woman's face immediately flushes scarlet.

"O-Of course! What size are you looking for, sir?"

I hold my hands out in front of me, picturing Sitara standing before me as I change the distance of my hands periodically. "Approximately 33.5 inches in the bust, 30 inches to the waist, and... 38 inches in the hips. Yes, I believe that's about right."

I love it when my charm works in my favor. I walk out of that boutique with half my money still burning in my pocket. It only cost me a little white-lied promise of coming back to visit soon.

I hold the wrapped garments under my right arm, pleased with the selections I have picked out. I have kept the designs of the gowns simple, mostly a cotton undergown with equally light bodices and overskirts. I didn't bother getting her any undergarments. She'd probably slap me again for even trying to place her in such restrictions.

It's the colors of the gowns I am most proud of, however. I have selected light blush colors to make her russet eyes pop, emeralds that I know will contrast beautifully with her hair, and violets to bring out the porcelain of her skin. I think she will like them, so long as she gives the Mundane wear a chance.

After procuring some soap that smells exactly the way I remember her, I make my way back toward the ship, my gifts in tow. I stop along the way, my line of sight catching on a golden hairpin perched in a display at one of the vendor stands. At the end of the two prongs sits an oval brooch-shaped image of a honey bee, bordered with emerald jewels.

She would like this. I know she will. That is one thing I have never seen in the tribe's lands, so I doubt she has ever seen one either. Once my final purchase has been made, I finish my trek toward my docked ship.

I find myself swelling with a boyish, almost overwhelming pride as I glance down at the haul I've managed to procure. My arms are loaded with gifts, treasures I've carefully selected for my prize. The weight of them in my hands is satisfying, a tangible reminder of the effort I've put into this.

But as I make my way up to the deck, a flicker of unease catches my attention. My cabin door is cracked slightly open, just a sliver of space where it should be firmly shut. My mind pauses, a seed of concern planted in my chest. The entire crew is ashore, likely indulging in drink and women, their voices and laughter probably carrying on the wind. But here, on my ship, it's quiet.

Too quiet.

And my door shouldn't be open.

I push it the rest of the way with my shoulder, my eyes immediately scanning the room for any sign of her. "Kitten?" I call out, the nickname slipping easily from my lips.

There's no response.

I set my treasures down on the bed, the clatter of objects against the fabric filling the silence. I move to the bathroom, the door creaking as I push it open.

She's not there either.

My heart begins to pound in my ears, the sound drowning out everything else. My mind races, spiraling through every possibility, every worst-case scenario. She said she wouldn't leave the ship. So where is she?

I force myself to think clearly. Maybe she's in the kitchen, helping Arthur with the supplies. That makes sense.

The thought calms me slightly, enough to slow my heart rate as I make my way down to the lowest level of the ship. But when I get there, she's not in the kitchen either.

Confusion and frustration gnaw at me. Am I missing something? Did she hide herself away somewhere, and I just overlooked her? The possibility makes me grit my teeth. I'm sure she's enjoying this, wherever she is. I'm sure she's laughing at me, at my foolishness.

I turn on my heel and make my way back to my quarters, my strides long and quick, driven by growing impatience. Once inside, I begin searching the room, looking for anything out of place. Anything missing.

At first glance, everything seems as it should be. But then, after a long, anxious moment, my eyes land on my desk. Something's wrong. My key is gone. I know I left it on the hook that hangs off the side of my desk. I can picture it there, gleaming in the dim light. Now, it's just... gone.

A surge of anger rises in me, hot and uncontrollable. Did she steal it? Did she take it and leave? The thought burns in my chest. Would she do that? Would she try to escape in the dead of night, without a word?

I march toward the hold in the belly of the ship, my determination hardening with every step. When I reach the door and find it locked, my blood begins to boil.

"Sitara!" I slam my fist against the wood, the sound echoing through the empty hallway. "Unlock this door!" I demand, twisting the knob again, but it doesn't budge.

My patience snaps.

This is *my* ship, and no one—no one—locks me out of any part of it.

I take a step back, giving myself room to build momentum. Then, with a roar, I lift my leg and kick the door with every ounce of strength I have. The wood splinters under the force, the sound of it cracking like a gunshot in the silence.

The door swings open, slamming against the wall with a loud, resounding smack. And there she is.

Sitara stiffens at the sudden intrusion, her body whipping around to face me. Her eyes are wide, her pulse pounding visibly at the base of her throat. I can see the fear in her, the shock. But something else too—something that makes my nostrils flare. Rage, yes, but also... something else.

Not wounded pride, exactly.

Not irritation.

Not even disappointment.

It's deeper than that, a feeling I can't quite put my finger on. It unsettles me, makes me question myself.

I'm at war with myself.

Normally, I wouldn't let go of what I want so easily. I've worked far too hard to get her here, to keep her here. But... I remember the promise I made to her. I remember the words I spoke when we first took port. I told her she wasn't my prisoner, that when we reached the first port, she was free to leave if that's what she wanted.

And I meant it.

I am a man of my word, if nothing else.

But now, seeing her here, seeing the look in her eyes... It's a struggle to hold to that resolve.

I storm over to her, my movements rough, and grab the coin from her hand. "If you want to leave so badly, then go," I spit out the words, the bitterness tasting sharp on my tongue. "But you'll not be taking anything from me in the process."

Nothing but my sanity.

She stares up at me, her expression a mixture of shock and uncertainty. She's shocked that I've given in so easily, despite everything. And she's uncertain of what I might do next, of what I'm capable of.

Her fingers curl into fists, her knuckles blanching as if she thinks this is another one of my games.

It's not.

But God, how I wish it were. I wish I could take it all back, wish I could keep her here, wish I could make her stay.

But I don't.

Instead, I watch as she rushes past me, her bare feet echoing off the wooden floors as she runs out the door. I stand there, frozen, listening as her footsteps fade into the distance. Down the hall, up the stairs, across the deck...

And then there's silence.

15

Sitara

I don't stop running until I am halfway down the length of the docks. The wooden planks creak under my feet as I finally slow to a halt, my chest heaving with exertion. I pause to catch my breath, resting my hands on my knees and tilting my head back to let the cool ocean air fill my lungs.

The salty breeze stings my face, but it's a welcome relief after the chaos I just escaped. I am still shaken, still reeling from the sudden shift in Kiernan's behavior. I can't believe he actually let me go. The memory of his twisted expression as he took the coin from my hand lingers in my mind, confusing and bothering me more with every passing moment.

I straighten up, brushing my hands against my thighs as I finally catch my breath. Letting out a sigh, I rake my hands through my hair, the tangled strands catching my fingers.

I take in my surroundings, the bustling docks alive with activity. Sailors shout orders, gulls cry overhead, and the smell of saltwater and tar fills the air. Each person who passes by gives me one of two looks: either curiosity or disdain. Some glance at me with a mixture of both, their expressions a blend of suspicion and intrigue.

I'm hoping the reactions I'm eliciting won't hurt my chances of getting a ride back home.

I need to find a ship willing to take me, and fast.

Well, I suppose I can finally say I have found a redeeming quality in Kiernan. He didn't go back on his word like I thought he would. Though his face as he took the coin from my hand will certainly confuse and bother me for some time. Why had his face been so twisted up with betrayal? Surely, he would have known I wasn't placating on that ship.

Surely, he had to have known that kidnapping someone would have its repercussions.

Had he really expected me to just accept my fate and comply without resistance?

When he had kicked down the door, I thought he was furious. My blood had run cold, and I was certain I had finally pushed my luck too far. After all, I had lied to him this morning and said I didn't feel well. I then proceeded to snatch his precious key and had every intention of stealing from him. I had planned on grabbing what I could—anything I could—that would give me favor to use as a bartering chip to get back home. It wasn't my finest moment, but desperation has a way of driving people to do things they wouldn't normally consider.

My biggest regret in the entire situation was how I had wittingly brought Arthur into the mess. I needed to figure out where Kiernan kept the key to get through the door to where they kept their loot and supplies.

I had slid the question into our casual conversations as though I were nothing more than an ignorant passenger trying to learn everything I could. I do feel bad, like I had manipulated him, but... a girl has to do what she has to do, right?

Still, the weight of that guilt presses down on me now, especially as I think about how his friendship had been genuine, while mine had been tinged with deceit.

I certainly wasn't going to ask Kiernan, because it would have turned into a million questions as to why I wanted to know. He would have been suspicious, and I wouldn't have been able to talk my way out of it.

So, I used Arthur instead. It wasn't right, but I told myself it was necessary.

Now, standing on the boardwalk while I try to figure out my next move, I feel something shy of shame swell in my gut. It's not a full-blown regret, but it's there, gnawing at me.

No, I have nothing to be ashamed of.

Kiernan kidnapped me.

He forced me into a bath with him.

He tied me to his bed.

He forced me to scrub his disgusting kitchen.

And he showed me exactly who he was when he threw those books off the shelf, like I was nothing more than a serving wench.

I have nothing to be ashamed of. I did what I had to do to get back home.

It is nothing personal.

Well... Maybe it was a little personal.

I mean, I might be willing to admit that I did want to peeve him off a little one last time before I left.

He had done nothing but do the same to me time and time again during my time with him.

Fair is fair.

I wasn't going to let him get the last word, not when he had already taken so much from me.

The last straw was his wording on *"proper"* clothes.

My clothes are proper, thank you very much. They are perfectly acceptable in my world, and for him to expect me to change and debase my culture to fit into his... Nope, no way. Not when he is the one who dragged me into this mess in the first place.

His arrogance knows no bounds.

Standing like a lost puppy, I'm not sure what I should do next. I guess I could go asking for the captains of each ship until I find one willing to take me. I hear a familiar voice from behind me, the sound of Arthur's cheerful words reaching my ears. My heart sinks a little at the sound of his voice, knowing I'm about to have to tell him the truth.

"Starlight!" I turn to find his big, goofy grin staring down at me. His eyes are bright with excitement, and for a moment, I forget about everything that's happened. "You're out o' bed! That's great! Where's the captain?" His eyes scan the area around us, his face falling slightly when he doesn't see Kiernan.

"I'm leaving, Pip. I'm going home," I say, feeling more guilty than ever that I had manipulated his friendship the way that I had. Now, after seeing his smiling face, I feel like the lowest scum imaginable.

How could I have used him like that?

How could I have lied to him?

"Leaving? What are you doin' that for?" Arthur's tone changes, his excitement replaced by confusion and concern.

"I'm going to find a ride on another ship. One that will take me straight back," I explain, trying to keep my voice steady.

I can't look him in the eye, not now.

I'm afraid of what I might see there.

I watch as Arthur's face falls completely, his enthusiasm replaced by a solemn frown. "You need to be careful doin' that, Sitara. We aren't the worst ones out there," he warns, his voice soft but serious.

"No one could be worse than Kiernan Slater," I grumble, folding my arms loosely over my chest.

I stand by my original statement.

Not to mention, I forgot to add that he almost threw me off the side of the ship into the dang ocean to fend for myself.

What rational human being behaves like that?

Arthur shakes his head, mimicking my actions with his arms over his chest. "You're wrong, Starlight. In a good few ways, you're wrong." He tilts his head to the side slightly, looking down at me with a questioning, yet knowing, gaze. "Do you really think there aren't worse men out there? Has the cap forced himself on you?"

"Not in *that* way, but—" I start, but Arthur cuts me off.

"Has he let anyone else have their way with you?" he continues, his voice firm but gentle.

"No," I state flatly, shuffling from one foot to the other.

I don't like where this is going.

I don't like being reminded of just how lucky I've been.

"That's a far better ride than most women get aboard a pirate ship," Arthur says, his tone softening.

He's trying to make me see reason, to understand that things could have been much worse.

I press my lips together, chewing on the inside of my cheek. "Are you trying to tell me that just because he didn't force penetration, he should get brownie points for touching me and manhandling me around when I don't want him to?" I ask, my voice laced with frustration and anger.

Arthur shakes his head again. "No, Sitara. That's not what I'm sayin'. I'm just tryin' to get you to see it could be a bloody sight worse. And I'm worried about you," he admits, his voice filled with sincerity.

"Help me find one that won't be worse, then," I say, meeting his gaze finally. I need his help, and I know it.

I just hope he's willing to give it to me after everything I've done.

He rubs the back of his neck, sighing as he catches sight of one of the other crew members from the Nureus. "Aye, I reckon I could lend a hand. Just make sure you find yourself a decent ship."

He hands over the supplies, promising to put them away himself after he helps me.

He really is a sweet young man.

I'm sure a woman will be very lucky one day to call herself his. Given that he remains this way and doesn't let Kiernan ruin him.

As we walk, I can't help but feel a pang of guilt for manipulating him, for using his kindness for my gain. But I push the feeling aside, telling myself it was necessary.

After all, survival often requires making difficult choices, and I'm just trying to make it back home in one piece.

We walk side by side as I begin asking for passage. Most of the ships we stop by aren't even going toward Capulli'ana, which I suppose makes sense. Most ships only sail that far north twice a year, if at all.

The port is bustling with activity, sailors shouting as they load and unload cargo, the smell of salt and tar filling the air. I've been at this for hours, and my feet ache as I trudge along the dock, Pip beside me. The sun is beginning to set, casting a golden hue over the water, and I'm starting to lose hope.

Walking up the ramp of yet another ship, I find it easy to spot the captain on the deck. He's a man who commands attention, his voice booming as he shouts all manner of foul profanity at his men. They scramble to obey, their faces pale as they scurry about their tasks.

He's an older man, his dark coils of black hair wound into tight locks that billow around his shoulders like a storm cloud. His beady eyes sit deep in his skull, giving him a cunning, almost feral look. His hooked nose sits atop a large handlebar mustache, perfectly waxed and curled at the ends. His gaunt cheeks emphasize his sharp cheekbones, and the weight of his unkempt beard makes his face look even more haggard. The ashy complexion of his skin seems like a stark contrast to the black and golden accents of his sailing uniform, which looks well-worn and faded. He's a far cry from the type of sailing captain I've come to be accustomed to—polished, refined, and courteous. But he doesn't seem all that bad at first glance. There's something about him that feels rough but not entirely untrustworthy.

"Excuse me!" I shout over the uproar of his men, my voice carrying across the deck. His eyes snap to me, and to my surprise, a pleasant smile spreads across his face, revealing crooked, yellowed teeth.

"What can I do for you, lass?" he asks, his voice deep and raspy, like the scraping of rough wood against stone.

I relax a little. Okay, he doesn't seem all that bad at all.

"You wouldn't happen to be going toward Capulli'ana, would you?" I ask, giving him a sheepish look and trying to appear as apologetic as possible. "I don't have any money, though," I admit, my shoulders hunching in defeat.

He chuckles, a rough, gravelly sound, and rubs the handle of his mustache thoughtfully. "Aye, we do happen to be heading that way," he says finally, his eyes flicking to Pip, who is still standing quietly beside me. "We'd be mighty willing to help ye get back home, Miss. One tiny lass doesn't take up much space, but I'd reckon there ain't enough for two."

"Oh, no," I say quickly, shaking my head. "He's not coming. It'll just be me." My shoulders drop as I sigh in relief, thanking him before turning back to Arthur.

Pip gives me a soft smile, but it doesn't reach his blue eyes at all. It's not even enough to poke his dimples into his cheeks, and for a moment, I feel a pang of guilt for leaving him behind.

"Are you sure you want to do this?" he asks, wrapping his arms around my shoulders in a goodbye hug. His voice is soft, laced with concern, and I can feel the tension in his body as he holds me close.

"I'll be fine, Pip," I say, trying to reassure him. "When you guys port in Puka'qui again, come see me at the school. Only you, though," I add, making him smile a little. I hug him back, wrapping my arms around his lean waist and holding on for a moment longer than necessary.

"Aye, I'll come to see you when I can," he says, his voice tinged with sadness. "Take care o' yourself, Starlight."

After we've said our goodbyes, Arthur descends the gangplank, leaving me alone aboard the ship. I watch him go, feeling a strange sense of emptiness as he disappears into the crowd on the dock. The crew begins to bustle around me, preparing to set sail, and I'm ushered aside as they work.

As the ship sails away from the port, I let the ocean breeze caress my skin, the salty air filling my lungs. I stand at the bow of the ship, looking out at the horizon as the mainland grows smaller and smaller in the distance. The sun dips lower in the sky, casting a golden path across the waves, and I contemplate the events of the last week. I hate to admit it, but Kiernan was right.

This *has* been quite the adventure.

But it's almost over now, and soon I'll be back home, where I can live out my life as I was supposed to. The thought brings me a sense of comfort, and I close my eyes, letting the cool breeze wash over me.

As the sun begins to dip below the sea, painting the sky in an array of colors—blues and purples bleeding into oranges and reds—I enjoy the view for some time. The beauty of it distracts me from the growing unease in my stomach. But then a jolting realization hits me. The sun sets in the west... and from our placement on the waves... we are going south.

A cold sweat rolls down the back of my neck as I hurry toward the upper deck, where the captain is talking to a few of his men. My heart pounds in my chest, and my breath comes in shallow gasps as I approach him.

"Captain Nottley," I say, trying to keep my voice steady. "I thought you were sailing north. I said I needed to go north, not south."

The smile that curls around his teeth sets a blaze of dread burning in my gut. It's not the friendly, crooked smile he gave me earlier. This one is predatory, sinister, and it makes my blood run cold.

Oh... Oh gods, I've fucked up...

"An' I said we be heading that way," he says, his voice low and menacing. "I didn't say we be heading that way immediately, now did I?"

The looks on the faces of his men fill me with a fear I've never felt before. Their eyes gleam with a knowing glint, and their smirks make my stomach twist with nausea.

There's an instant, overwhelming need to flee, a primal, desperate panic to get away. I don't think—I just act. I rush for the railing, my hands gripping it tightly as I look out at the water. We hadn't left the port that long ago. The mainland is still visible in the distance, a faint line on the horizon. I'm young, strong enough—stamina enough—to swim back to shore from here. Without hesitation, I throw my legs over the railing, preparing to jump overboard.

"Take a deep breath, Sitara," I tell myself, my mind racing. "Jump. Jump!"

Just as I go to fling my body off the ship, a pair of muscular arms wrap around my waist, whipping me back over with a harsh jerk that snaps my head forward with the momentum. I begin to claw, to scratch, to inflict all manner of pain I can to make him release me. My nails dig into the arms that hold me, but they don't budge.

"Let go of me! LET GO!"

I scream at the top of my lungs, praying that someone will hear me from the port despite the fair distance of the ocean between us. Maybe Arthur will get a spark of intuition, as I should have, and come looking for me. Maybe he'll say something to Kiernan...

But Pip's words ring in my mind as a second man grabs hold of my legs to help the first keep his grip. "We aren't the worst ones out there," he had said to me. I hadn't realized how true his words were. I had been so consumed with my ideal of who Kiernan was, who I perceived him to be from a shallow level of examination.

As the men drag me into the belly of the ship, I search my surroundings for anything to grab hold of, my hands gripping the bars of a cage. And that's when I see it. That's when I completely understand the situation I've gotten myself into.

This is a true nightmare.

Nothing like the perceived one I thought I'd been in.

The hold of the ship is dimly lit, the air thick with the stench of filth and sweat. Cages are filled with women and men, their tunic-covered bodies stained and soiled as they watch the scene unfold with empty, hopeless eyes. This was a slave ship... and I had walked right onto it like a willing offering.

"Kiernan..." I think, my mind racing with desperation. "Maybe he'll come for me. Maybe he'll change his mind and come to retrieve me. By the gods, Kiernan, please..."

I don't even realize the implications of the plea that screams inside my skull as they throw me into one of the iron rod prisons, slamming the door shut with a loud clang. The sound echoes in my ears, final and unyielding, as the darkness closes in around me.

I'm beginning to believe I might just be the dumbest person alive. All I have managed to do is trade one freak show for a worse one.

I've spent the last few hours sitting in the corner of my cage, debating—debating whether I should take the chance and use my Cold Fire. The weight of that decision presses down on me like the heavy iron bars that confine me.

Didn't I just say a few days ago that people on the other ship might as well stay on it if they used their abilities and couldn't go home?

Didn't I say that's how I would feel?

Yes, yes, I did.

I know the sun has set long before now, only because it had already begun to set when I was thrown in here. Everything is dark, damp, and not nearly as well taken care of as the gleaming exterior of this ship. The wooden planks beneath me splinter into my skin in certain places, which I try to avoid once I've found them. The smell of rodents and human filth permeates the air, swirling around with no proper ventilation to escape. The only sounds that can be heard are those of the boots shuffling above us and the shifting bodies packed tightly all around me.

It's too familiar. Far too familiar.

It's taking everything in me just to remain present, grounded, and sane. My mind threatens to spiral at every turn, and I'm grasping for anything—anything at all to keep myself tethered to reality.

I move my hand along the floorboards, using one of the rough, splintered areas to create a grounding discomfort. Pain, at least, is something tangible. I can't afford to lose it now. I can't afford to spiral.

"Be careful, Ichka'ima..." A raspy voice calls out to me, and a long, slender finger pokes through the bars of the cage. It points to my hand, which is still seeking purchase on the rough floor.

My head snaps toward the sound, my eyes narrowing as I try to make out the face behind the voice. It's too dark, but I can tell by the tallish shadow and the tone of his voice that it's a man. My eyes immediately jump to the pe'aboros markings on his left arm, squinting to try to see them through the darkness and the grime that coats his skin.

"I Ian'alli," he offers, and I can hear the effort in his voice as he tries to swallow, to find enough saliva to wet his parched throat. When he fails, a nasty, dry cough grinds its way up his esophagus like sandpaper.

"You're Kana'te..." I mutter, mostly to myself, and scramble to his side of the cage. I poke my head between the bars, my fingers grasping them so tightly that my knuckles grow bone-white. "Do you know where they are taking us?"

"Catcher's Bay," he tells me quietly, once he's managed to catch his breath. His voice is low and gravelly, but there's a faint hint of something else beneath it—something like resignation. "It's the midway point for every slave ship."

The two of us glance over at the guard who is sitting on his stool next to the door. He's half-asleep, his back slouched against the wall, completely unaware of the conversation happening just a few feet away. And then we begin to speak in our native language, Lo'pillkat, our voices hushed but urgent.

"And what happens from there? How long have you been away from the island?" I ask, my panic mounting rapidly.

"Slaves are sold in the 'underground,'" he explains quietly. His breath catches in his throat, and for a moment, I'm not sure if he'll be able to continue. "Once you're purchased, you depart for your new dwelling." His words remain soft, but there's a bitterness to them. "Sometimes, that's in Catcher's Bay, and sometimes you set sail again."

So what he's telling me is... I could be trapped in this cage for days, weeks, months... I don't know if I'll be able to survive that. The thought alone is suffocating, and I have to fight to keep my breath steady.

His voice cuts through my spiraling thoughts once more after he takes a moment to collect himself. I can see the sadness in his eyes, even in the dim light. "This is my fourth voyage. Nine years away from the island..." His voice cracks, and he pauses, swallowing hard before he continues. "I wish I were allowed to see it again..."

My eyes widen in a mix of sympathetic anguish and fear as he begins to explain that once we're sold, Kana'te people are required to use our abilities to serve our masters. That is our value as slaves, whether that's for manual labor or entertainment. If we refuse, the consequences are dire.

When we are sold, returning to the island is no longer an option.

My blood runs cold, and I have to take gulping breaths of the foul-tasting air to keep from completely crumbling apart. The truth slams into me like a tidal wave as I think longer and harder about the laws set in place for our people.

Yes, it probably gives the Mundanes a feeling of ease, of reassurance. But for us... For us, it might as well be a death sentence.

"I wonder sometimes if the Sacred Three would make an exception," he says, his voice tinged with desperation. "Pardon my transgressions due to the circumstances." He leans his forehead against the bars between us and sighs, the sound heavy and defeated. "Being rescued is a fool's dream, but... Hope is all we have to keep us alive, yes?"

I nod, swallowing the saliva that I have a feeling will be as precious to me as water soon. I can feel my lip quiver, and I clamp down my jaw to keep it from betraying me.

"They have to," I murmur with conviction. "They have to. It's not right to take away someone's home over a circumstance they couldn't control..."

Silence falls over us for what feels like an eternity, though I know it's probably only seconds. When I speak again, I turn my head to look at him more closely. In the dim light, I can make out the sharp line of his jaw and the high cheekbones that sit atop his gaunt, hollowed-out cheeks.

"I don't think being rescued is a fool's dream," I whisper. My hand comes to rest on his shoulder, a small gesture of solidarity in this bleak, hopeless place.

His eyes swim with emotion as he looks at me, as though he's trying to muster up the same certainty that I seem to have.

"How can you be so confident?" he asks, his voice trembling. His hand comes up to rest on top of mine, his fingers thin but warm.

A small smirk tugs at the corner of my lips, and a renewed fire ignites in my belly. If I've learned anything in the last week or so, it's that I'm right.

"Because I happen to know a first mate who enjoys killing slave traders," I say quietly. "And a captain who doesn't like to be told no."

16

Kiernan

I let her go.

Why in the hell did I let her go?! What the fuck is wrong with me?!

I pace the deck furiously, my boots thundering against the weathered floorboards like a storm rolling in. The wooden planks creak beneath my feet, echoing the turmoil in my mind. My hand claws through my hair, tugging at the strands as if trying to pull the frustration from my scalp. The other hand clenches into a fist at my side, ready to strike the first person brave—or foolish enough to approach me. The crew keeps their distance, their murmurs hushed as they watch their captain unravel.

"K, what the fuck has crawled up your ass?" Benedict calls out, his voice laced with amusement as he walks up the gangplank. He's always been one to test the waters, to see how far he can push before I snap.

Today, he's playing with fire.

"Keep talking, Ben," I growl under my breath. "See where it gets you."

Okay, the second person foolish enough to approach me.

Dear gods... if you're real... Let it be Arthur.

But it's Benedict, of course. He's always been a thorn in my side, with his clever remarks and that infuriating smirk.

I flash him a look that could freeze blood in its tracks, my glare sharp enough to cut steel. Benedict, to his credit, doesn't back down. He knows better than to push me when I'm like this, but he doesn't retreat either. Instead, he leans against the railing, crossing his arms over his chest as if daring me to take a swing at him.

He's one of the most intelligent men I've ever met—brilliant, even—but right now, I don't care. I don't care about his cleverness or his loyalty or his damn sense of humor.

All I care about is the knot twisting in my gut, the bile rising in my throat, and the voice screaming in my head that I made a mistake. A colossal, idiotic, unforgivable mistake.

I'm still trying to wrap my head around it. How did I let her go? How did I stand there, staring into those eyes, and let her walk away? I've never been one to hesitate. I take what I want, by charm or by force. It's always been that simple. But this time... this time, I hesitated.

Is it because I'm tired of the fight? No, I love the fight. I thrive on it. The fire, the chaos, the adrenaline—it's what keeps me alive. So why did I let her go without so much as a struggle?

Was it the look in her eyes? That flicker of fear when I burst through the door, the way she flinched as if she believed I'd hurt her? That thought makes my stomach twist into knots. Or maybe it's the cold dread that gripped me when I found her locked in that room, alone and scared. Relief—relief!—that she was safe, that no one had touched her.

Me.

Captain Kiernan *fucking* Slater almost vomited due to relief.

The memory makes me nauseous. My hand tightens into a fist, and for a moment, I'm tempted to punch something—anything to vent this boiling rage.

I'm not sure if I'm angry with her for making me feel this way, or if I'm just angry that I let her go so easily.

Probably both.

Benedict raises an eyebrow, his expression a mixture of confusion and concern. "What the hell has gotten into you?" he asks, his voice softer now, tinged with genuine worry.

"At this point, I'm questioning that myself," I admit, the words bitter on my tongue. "I remember thinking you'd lost your damn mind when Enna left the ship. If it felt anything like this, then I was right. You had lost your mind..." The admission burns, leaving a foul taste in my mouth. "Now I understand why you acted that way."

Benedict's brows furrow deeply, and he shakes his head. "Do you?"

"Yes!" I shout, slamming my fist against the railing. The sound echoes across the deck, and the crew flinches. "It is infuriating!" I cross my arms over my chest, leaning back against the railing as if trying to hold myself together. "How could she have been so... *ungrateful* for everything that you had done?! You rescued her! Apparently, women don't know when to say thank you."

Benedict's eyes widen, and he blinks several times, as if trying to process my outburst. "Clearly, you were not as much a fly on the wall in that whole situation as you think you were," he says finally, his voice dry. He pauses, his expression darkening as realization dawns on him. "Wait, backpedal... Sitara's gone? You could have just led with that instead of bringing my wife into it."

"Keep up, Benedict," I snap, rolling my eyes. "Obviously, Sitara is gone! Why else would I be comparing Enna leaving to my current situation?!" I resume my pacing, my boots thudding angrily against the deck. "I found her in the hull. She had locked herself in there and was gathering coins to escape with!"

Benedict mocks me by placing a hand over his chest, his expression one of exaggerated horror. "Noo... The audacity of the woman! You stole her away from her home, and she had the balls to steal coin from you?! How dare she!"

I shoot him a look that could kill, my anger boiling over. "You think this is funny, don't you? You think it's hilarious that she tried to leave me, to steal from me, to defy me after everything I've done for her!"

"And what, exactly, have you done for her?" Benedict asks, his tone biting. "Kidnapped her? Imprisoned her? Oh wait, no, you're a pirate, so it's all just part of your charm, right?"

Before I can respond, a loud voice interrupts us. "Ahoy, Cap'n! I be bringin' ye a—"

I don't let Joffrey finish. My fist connects with his jaw, sending him sprawling to the deck. The whiskey he was carrying spills everywhere, soaking his clothes as he grunts in pain. I feel a momentary rush of satisfaction, but it fades quickly.

"I feel better now," I say, turning back to Benedict with a forced smile.

"Do you?" Benedict asks, raising an eyebrow. His expression is judgmental, but he knows better than to push me further.

"I do," I lie, flexing my hand to ease the sting of the punch. "I pictured your face, and it brought me peace."

The crew begins to gather, their faces a mixture of curiosity and fear. The twins, ever the loyal ones, help Joffrey to his feet while Becket hops over him, earning a loud groan from the fallen man.

"I bet you did," Benedict mutters under his breath, turning his head as Arthur comes aboard.

Arthur. The little bastard has shown up four people too late.

"Where the hell have you been?" I demand, my anger redirecting toward him.

"I was just helpin' Starlight find a jaunt home," Arthur replies, his tone smug and nonchalant.

"Of course you were *'helpin her find a jaunt home'*," I mimic his accent poorly.

Helpful little prick...

"Which '*jaunt*' did you put her on?" I ask, my voice low and dangerous. "Which ship would possibly give her passage to Capulli'ana with no coin? You'd best find the name in your memory before I give you a taste of what I gave Joffrey."

Arthur pales, his eyes darting to Joffrey, who is still nursing his sore jaw. "It was... It was a ship called the *Cordelia*... The captain seemed good enough."

I freeze. Benedict does the same beside me.

"Oh, boy," Ben grunts, shaking his head. "You just fucked up my redheaded little friend."

"You put her on Nottley's ship?!" I growl, my anger exploding. "You stupid, ignorant, insufferable little shit! Do you have any idea what you've done?!"

I grab Arthur by the collar, shaking him violently. His eyes widen in fear as I back him up toward the gangplank. "You'd better thank Sitara when you see her," I hiss. "Her fondness for you is the only thing keeping me from chumming the waters with your scrawny ass."

I release him with a shove, and he stumbles down the plank, nearly falling over. I turn to Benedict, who is seething with anger. He doesn't like Nottley any more than I do. Hell, he might hate the man more than I do, considering the man had him held up on that ship once upon a time.

"Get their heading," I order, my teeth grinding together. "I don't care if you have to beat it out of the wharfie to get it." I point to the gangplank, my anger boiling over.

"Fetch."

17

Sitara

I press my nose against the narrow crack that has split the wood, the rough grain scraping lightly against my skin as I try to draw in what little bit of clean air I can. The smell of damp earth and mildew fills my nostrils, contrasting heavily with the salty, stifling air that clings to the rest of the hold. Water trickles through the crack in minute amounts, and the faint sound of the waves outside lapping at the rigging echoes in the silence.

I cup my hands carefully, trying to gather the precious droplets to wash my face. The coolness of it is a fleeting relief against my parched skin. I turn to offer some to Saolo'ki, the man sitting in the cage next to mine, but he waves it off with a tired smile. It doesn't matter much anyway; the water is salted, rendering it undrinkable.

We've been given meager rations of leftover scraps to eat, barely enough to keep someone alive, and even less water. My throat burns, a dry pain that refuses to subside. The stench in the hold is overwhelming, a nauseating mix of sweat, mold, and the faint tang of sea salt. It's hard to breathe without gagging, and so I find myself puffing air through my mouth instead of my nose. Even that offers little relief, as the taste of the air clings to my tongue like a rotten egg.

Saolo'ki shifts in his cage, his movements slow and deliberate as he stirs from the lightest of cat naps. We'd talked long into the night, sharing stories and quietly acquainting ourselves with one another. There's something about him that reminds me of my father—my real father, not the man he became in the end. He reminds me of the father who used to carry me on his shoulders through the jungle, who told me stories of the ancient rivers and the spirits that lived within them. He reminds me of the man who would toss Larkin into the Lake of Mirrors on sweltering summer days, laughing as the water rippled and shimmered under the sun. He reminds me of a simpler time, a time before the world seemed to unravel and everything got messy.

Saolo'ki is even around the same age my father would have been, had he still been alive. There's a quiet strength in him, a resilience that I find comforting in this bleak place.

After wiping my hand along the mossy, damp wood of the wall, I reach out and press my palm against his forehead. The heat radiating from his skin is almost unbearable, and I can feel the sweat slicking his temples. I try to care for him as best as I can, offering what little comfort I'm able to muster. He needs it far more than I do.

"You have a kind heart, Sitalli'ara," he whispers in our native tongue, "How did someone get their hands on you, dear one?"

He moves to sit against the bars of my cage, and I wipe my hand down the wood again, collecting as much moisture as I can before pressing it against the back of his neck. It's a small comfort, but it's all I have to offer him.

"I... made a mistake," I admit, the words tasting bitter on my tongue. A hard rock of guilt settles in my stomach, weighing me down. "I was taken by the captain I mentioned earlier. He doesn't trade slaves or anything, he just... took me. When I left, I tried to board this ship to get back home. I didn't know it was a slave trading vessel."

Saolo'ki shakes his head, a mixture of disappointment and understanding in the shadowed outlines of his face. "So, you left your captain's ship and walked onto this one..." he trails off, and I can feel that shame burn colder in my gut. "What's done is done now. Tell me about your captain."

He settles in, his silhouette turning to face me. I scrunch up my nose in distaste, and a low chuckle rumbles in his parched throat. I'm assuming his eyes have acclimated to the dark better than mine have, and I feel silly for the way my cheeks burn with embarrassment. I purse my lips stubbornly.

"He's not *my* captain," I clarify quickly, defensively. "He's horrible, actually. He's bossy, rude, arrogant, thinks he can just force people to do what he wants them to do, and he even made me clean his disgusting kitchen. It took me all day, even with my friend's help!" I pause to catch my breath, my chest heaving slightly. "He's temperamental, overly possessive, and he acts like it's his gods-given right to have women fawn all over him."

Sao is silent for a moment, though I can see his lips twitch in amusement with the barest of light that is now coming through the cracks of the ship. The entire time I'm ranting, he's been quietly chuckling to himself, his eyes crinkling at the corners.

"The boy seems to really ruffle your feathers, Sitalli'ara," he teases, "You're more puffed up than a pissed-off Coa'hesa." Another wave of heat rushes to my cheeks. "He is a captain. A *pirate* captain at that. The life of a pirate takes a certain... charm? He's probably used to getting what he asks for."

"He doesn't *ask* at all," I huff, folding my arms over my chest and leaning my shoulder into the cool iron bars. "Not since..." I tail off, and more color rises to my face.

I think my skin will melt off at this point.

"Mhmm," he cocks a brow at me, his tone playful. "My point still stands, dear one. He must be doing something right, or you wouldn't have so much faith in him coming to claim you once more."

"What are you—" I'm cut off by the sound of the shouts echoing overhead. We both look up at the ceiling, our brows drawn in concern. The sudden noise startles many of the other prisoners, their gasps and whimpers filling the hold.

Large thuds, almost like the sound of boots hitting the deck, rattle our confinement. The guard who has been sitting on a stool in the corner lurches to his feet, grabbing his weapons from the wall behind him. The door to the hold swings open, and an equally unpleasant man bursts through with a bark.

"Get your ass up here, Jacob! We're being boarded!! All hands on deck!"

Confused, I watch as the two of them barrel through the threshold just as the sound of clinking weapons and battle cries begins to resound through the ship. Scuffling and scrambling can be heard through the wood above us, thuds and loud bangs forcing many of the other prisoners to gasp and tremble. I, however, just want to know what's going on.

"This would be the perfect opportunity you need to get out without using your abilities," Saolo'ki murmurs, his voice low but urgent.

"The keys! Where are the keys?" I ask, my voice a rushed, frantic garble.

He points to the far wall by the stool, and I scramble to the back end of the cage, my eyes scanning the dim light. I see the faint sheen of metal hanging against the far wall.

Okay... Okay... All I need is something to grab them with.

I can find something to grab them with.

Is anyone else closer to them than us?

My eyes search the room just as the door slams open on its hinges.

I whip my body around, catching sight of a prodigious shadow standing in the doorway. His broad shoulders heave with ragged breaths, the air thick with the smell of sweat and blood. The man's boots beat against the floorboards, the sound frantic and hurried as his feet stumble over themselves in a panic.

It doesn't take me long to recognize those incredibly blue eyes, even in the dim light of the hold. They're searching the faces of those around me, and when they lock onto mine, something shifts in the air.

"Kiernan... He came," I whisper, mostly to myself. I'd put my faith in his stubbornness, and he'd delivered.

"So, that is your captain, is it?" Saolo'ki murmurs beside me. I nod, unable to protest it or deny it like I had moments before.

I feel all the tension leave my body, replaced by a strange, buzzing numbness. I choke down a sob of relief as his eyes meet mine, the weight of his gaze steady and unyielding.

He seems larger somehow, more imposing than I remembered. Maybe it's the dim light playing tricks on my eyes, but he looks every bit the pirate captain he is.

His broad frame fills the doorway, his disheveled appearance a testament to the chaos that must have ensued above deck. His shirt is torn, his boots scuffed, and his face smeared with grime and blood that doesn't belong to him.

But even so, there's an air of confidence about him that's impossible to ignore.

I watch as he quickly fixes himself, raking his hands through his tangled hair and straightening the hem of his shirt as he approaches. He wipes the blood from his face, his movements rough but precise. As he moves closer, his lips quirk up into a smirk, though his eyes betray the intensity of his emotions.

"Oh, there you are, Darling," his deep, husky voice reverberates through the space between us, a familiar sound that both soothes and irritates me.

I am still holding my breath, my eyes wide as I take in the sight of him. A sight I never thought I would be grateful to see.

"Seems like you have gotten yourself into quite the pickle," he says, his voice carrying out into the space between us like a blanket. He wraps his large fist around the door latch of my cage, his muscles flexing as he gives it a hard yank. The sound of the door breaking free is loud, a sharp clang that echoes through the hold. "Allow me to get the door for you."

I can't stop the sobbing laugh that rips up my throat as my feet surge forward. I wrap my arms around his middle, burying my face into his chest. His arms wrap around me in response, holding me tightly as if he's afraid to let me go. For the first time in what feels like an eternity, I feel safe.

18

Kiernan

After I've gotten Sitara settled on a barrel back aboard the *Nureus*, I watch as Benedict and the twins help the others who had shared captivity with her onto the deck. The weathered planks creak underfoot as people move about, their murmurs filling the air. I can see her eyes scanning the chaos, as if she's looking for someone. Her gaze flicks across the crowd, her brow furrowing slightly.

"Kiernan…" she starts, not even protesting the hand I still have around her waist, my fingers resting lightly on her side. "I have a favor to ask you."

I turn my attention from the others to give it to her fully. "You have a '*favor*'?" My voice is tired, laced with the wariness of a long day and the weight of everything that's happened. It's way past my normal bedtime, and while I usually would be irritable about it, I don't care. She's safe now, and that's all that matters.

She doesn't know that she could ask for the moon right now, and I'd pull it down for her. I'd do anything to keep that look of relief in her eyes. To keep that same comfort in my presence in her posture that had been there when she ran to me on the *Cordelia*.

The tension in my muscles has been slowly melting away the longer I have my fingers on her skin, the longer she doesn't push away my touch. It's a small thing, but it's enough to soothe some of the frayed edges of my nerves.

"I've rescued you from a life of servitude for the second time," I continue, my tone light and teasing. "What more could you possibly desire?" I watch the play of emotions on her face, the flash of shame in her eyes. She looks down, her lashes lowering as if she's embarrassed to be asking for anything at all.

"I know..." She takes a deep sigh, closing her eyes briefly before lifting them to meet my gaze. Her voice is soft, hesitant, and I can tell she's struggling to ask. She tilts her head slightly, as if searching for the right words. "It's not really for me. Arthur told me you have a place for people... and, well..."

I raise an eyebrow, intrigued despite myself. "A place for people?" I repeat, my tone curious.

She nods, her hands fidgeting slightly in front of her. "There is a Kana'te man who had been in the cell beside me," she says slowly, her words careful. "His name is Saolo'ki, and he can't go back home."

As she speaks, I begin to gather a decent picture of what she's about to ask me. It's not hard to tell that whoever this Saolo'ki is, he's somehow managed to crawl under her skin. She's always seemed to have a soft spot for strays, and I suppose this man is no exception.

"You want me to take a stranger... to Rhazden," I say, my voice flat. It's not a question, because I already know the answer. If she were quite literally *anyone* else, I would laugh in her face, tell her there's no chance in hell.

But she's not anyone else.

She's Sitara, and if this is her '*moon*'... I can give it to her.

That doesn't mean, however, that I'm not going to make her think I'm mulling it over.

I scratch my jaw, looking up at the fluffy white clouds drifting lazily in the sky as though it's a difficult ask. After all, if it were anyone else, it would be. But for her, I'd do just about anything.

"Please, Kiernan..." she murmurs, looking up at me with those big brown eyes, like a puppy seeking praise. Her voice is soft, tinged with a quiet desperation. "He's been a slave for nine years. He has used his abilities, and he can't go home. He would, if he could."

A warm sense of triumph spreads through my chest. This would mark the first time she's begged me for something. It's not exactly the begging I'd pictured all those times I'd imagined her surrendered and at my mercy, but it's close enough. I'll take what I can get.

My thumb caresses the exposed skin of her waist, a gentle, reassuring touch. I give her a subtle nod, my expression softening. "Okay, Sitara. Okay."

Her face lights up with a measure of gratitude that I've never seen before. It's like an inner light shining from somewhere deep inside her, radiating outward until her entire expression glows with it. "Thank you!" she breathes, her words barely above a whisper. "I'm going to go tell him!"

She steps away from me, pulling out of my grasp, and I let her go. I watch as she disappears into the crowd, her small form weaving through the people on deck. The warmth of her gratitude lingers, a strange, unfamiliar feeling in my chest.

It has been a solid three days since I retrieved Sitara from Captain Nottley's ship, and she seems much more content here now. Her laughter, once a rare and guarded sound, now rings out frequently, rich and authentic, a melody I find myself drawn to again and again. She still plays the game with me, but now it's out of genuine playfulness, not the irritation that once edged our interactions. Her demeanor has shifted back to that of the wild and carefree young woman I first met, a transformation that brings both comfort and an unfamiliar emotion.

I've also noticed the increasing time she spends with Arthur. While this development isn't exactly thrilling to me, I've chosen to step back, wary of pushing her away as I did before. That mistake led her to a slave trading ship, a consequence I don't wish to repeat. So, I've decided to let it be, at least for now, and revisit it when the time is right.

However, this particular morning, Sitara is acting strangely. Her usual vivacity is replaced with silence, barely a word spoken even to Arthur. Her shoulders, normally held high, have been slightly hunched, and her face wears a disgruntled look that lingers even during our customary banter. I've kept my distance, not wanting to intrude on whatever storm brews in her mind. From time to time, I catch her gazing out at the water, her expression distant and contemplative.

The questions swirl in my mind. Has she changed her mind? Does she want to return home after all?

The thought stirs an unfamiliar ache in my chest, one I struggle to comprehend. All I know is that I don't want her to go.

Yes, I want her to stay with me. This realization is both profound and debilitating, a truth I find myself grappling with.

I've tried to rationalize it, telling myself I just don't want her to end up on another slave ship. But then, why do I care so deeply about that either?

These are the questions that have haunted me all day, making it hard to focus on my duties. Sitara, lost in her own thoughts, remains unaware of my turmoil.

As night falls, I lie awake, restless, pondering what's happening to me. I need to clear my head, to understand why I'm so unsettled by this sudden change in her demeanor.

A week ago, I would have relished in irritating her, but now, that face she's worn all day only makes me yearn to be tender, to soothe the storm raging inside her.

I slip out of bed, moving slowly to avoid waking her, who rests fitfully. Seeking solace, I climb to my usual sanctuary, the nest, where I find peace and can detach from life's chaos.

What if she decides to leave me?

What if she chooses to return to teaching at Puka'qui, to her brother, and the life that once bound her?

Why does it matter if she does?

That was always the plan, wasn't it? I would have my fill of her and send her back, broken or whole, without a second thought.

But now, the thought of losing her is unbearable.

I grip the edge of the nest, leaning heavily on the rails, lost in my thoughts. Time passes, and I'm unaware of how long I've been there before I notice a shadow moving across the deck—a small, feminine figure emerging from the darkness.

The path of her hands catches my attention as they move to rest over her pelvis, her body bent forward just enough that I can see it from here. The dim light of the moon casts long shadows across her form, illuminating the gentle curve of her spine. I don't like seeing her like this. In fact, it's my least favorite of her many sides. There's something about her vulnerability that tugs at me, unwilling to let me stand idly by.

I notice the subtle shake in her shoulders well before I realize that she's crying. Her sobs are silent, yet they speak volumes.

Compelled by something unknown to me, I call to her before I can stop myself. "The view is much better from up here, Darling."

Her head snaps up, her body turning sharply as she searches for the source of my voice. When her gaze finally finds me, her eyes are red-rimmed and puffy, the trails of dampness on her cheeks glistening in the faint light. She wipes at her face frantically, as though she can erase the evidence of her tears before I notice.

But I've already seen it.

I would be lying if I said I don't notice the tantalizing display of skin that peeks out of the collar of my nightshirt, even at a time like this. I, of course, hadn't bought her any sleepwear of her own during my shopping spree in the port. Seeing her in my clothes—soft, oversized, and utterly impractical—is far too satisfying to give up.

Still, the moment of vanity is fleeting, overshadowed by the instinct to comfort her. It's not something I'm used to, this urge to soothe, to fix whatever it is that's broken. I've seen her cry before, more times than I care to admit, and each instance leaves me feeling frustrated, furious even.

She shouldn't be crying.

Not ever.

Now, though, as I look at her, something feels different. Her defiance isn't laced with fear or anger, not this time. It's something else entirely, something I can't quite name.

She shakes her head, her fiery mane shifting as though it's alive, the strands curling around her face like flames.

"I'm good down here," she says, "But... thank you."

"Come here, Sitara," I say, my tone firm but oddly gentle, as though I can't bring myself to be as demanding as usual, "Don't make me climb *all the way* down there just to toss you over my shoulders like a sack of flour and haul you back up here."

The threat is idle, perhaps, but I can see the flicker of doubt in her eyes. She knows better than to test me, to push me when I'm in this mood. Still, she hesitates, her hand pressed against her abdomen, her feet rooted firmly to the deck.

"Alright then," I mutter, swinging my leg over the shallow wall of my perch. "Don't say I didn't warn you."

She steps back, her hands lifting in a futile attempt to stop me. "No, really, Kiernan. I'm fine. You don't have to—"

But I'm already moving, my descent swift and sure. Before she can finish, I've closed the distance between us, one arm scooping under her to lift her easily, the other free to steady myself as I climb back up. She wraps her arms around my neck, her body pressed tightly against mine, and for a moment, I forget everything else. The stars, the sea, the weight of the world—it all fades into the background, leaving only her.

When we reach the crow's nest, she looks around, her eyes narrowing at the cramped space. "There isn't much room up here," she says hesitantly. "Maybe I should just go back down."

I roll my eyes, though the satisfaction of having her close is almost overwhelming. I wrap my arm around her waist, holding her firmly in place against me.

"I can be stubborn too, Darling," I say, "Just come here. You'll love it. I promise."

For a moment, she stiffens, her body tensing against mine, and I have to loosen my grip to keep her from pulling away. The proximity sends a spark of memory through me, sharp and vivid—the day I'd rescued her from Nottley, the way she'd clung to me, her body trembling with fear and relief. I want more moments like that, moments where she's close, where she's mine.

The space is small, as she'd said, but I don't care. If anything, it's an excuse to hold her, to keep her pressed against me. Her warmth seeps into me, soothing the tension in my muscles and calming the restless energy that has been plaguing me for days.

However, I notice something odd—a strange, almost imperceptible burning sensation in her lower abdomen, just below where my arm rests. It's fleeting, and I brush it off as a trick of my imagination, or perhaps some overflow of her own power.

Shifting my weight, I reach up and grasp the handle of the lantern hanging from the mast. I bring it to my lips, blowing out the small flame with a smile. The darkness seems to deepen around us, the stars shining brighter now that the light is gone.

I hook my finger under her chin, tilting her face upward toward the sky. "There," I murmur, my tone almost reverent. "See?"

Her eyes widen, her lips parting in awe as she takes in the view. It's breathtaking, the stars spread out above us like diamonds scattered across black velvet. Her face lights up, a look of pure wonder crossing her features. For a moment, I forget to breathe.

She's beautiful, heartbreakingly so, and I can't look away.

I don't want to.

"Wow," she breathes, her gaze still fixed on the sky. "You get to see this whenever you want?" She pauses, a small laugh escaping her lips. "The jungle obstructs most of the view at home. Unless we make the pilgrimage to Potem'aku."

I frown, unfamiliar with the term, and she notices.

"It means '*Temple of the Sacred*'," she explains, "It's the home of our gods."

I nod, though I don't fully understand, and she laughs again, the sound soft and melodic. Just for now, the world feels still, the only sound being that of the gentle lapping of waves against the ship's hull and the quiet rhythm of our breathing.

She continues to tell me about her home and the customs she is accustomed to, her words painting vivid images of a life so different from the one we share now. Somehow, I scarcely hear much of it. My mind drifts, and my attention is captured by something far more captivating.

The almost blue moonlight cascades through her hair most perfectly, as if it were a gentle rain of light, casting a soft violet hue across the embers of her locks. It reminds me vividly of the green light that once danced across her skin the day she awoke after I had taken her. The memory of that moment flashes through my mind, as vivid as the starlight that now reflects in her eyes.

Her eyes light up with a deep devotion as she speaks about her people and her gods, and I find myself utterly taken by the way the stars dance within them. It is as if the very night sky itself has come alive in her gaze, and I am powerless to look away. But beneath this enchantment, a deep, burning need begins to gnaw at my center—a feeling I have never experienced before. It is a hunger unlike any other, and it grows more unbearable with each passing second.

My heart leaps into my throat, the realization choking me with its weight. Owning this woman, possessing her, is no longer what I desire. The truth hits me like a storm, and with it comes a fear that I have not felt in years. It is a fear of the unknown, of the uncharted territory that lies before me. For the first time in my life, I am forced to confront the depth of my own emotions, and it terrifies me.

I crave for her to want to stay here with me. Not because she is bound to me, not because she has no choice, but because she desires to be here. I wish for her to stay because she wants me, needs me, as desperately as I need her. I realize that I do not want to break the hold she has on me. I don't want to break free from the bond that has formed between us. The very idea of it is unthinkable to me now.

Becoming hyper-aware of her presence, more so than I have ever been before, I pull her closer to my chest. I dip my head, burying my face in her hair, and breathe her in deeply. Her scent fills me, grounding me in this moment, and I let her presence wash over me until there is nothing else but her.

But then, I notice something strange. A faint, wispy black flame flickers through the fabric of her shirt, its tendrils curling outward like dark, ethereal fingers. My curiosity piqued, I reach out to touch it, my fingertips inching closer to the strange phenomenon. She stops me abruptly, her hand wrapping tightly around mine, her entire body tensing with a mixture of fear and urgency.

"Don't touch it," she says, a command rather than a plea. I pause, my fingers intertwining with hers as I give her a look of confusion. I'm curious about this reaction, and about the strange flame that seems to emanate from her very being. This is not the first time I have seen her react this way, and I can't help but wonder what it means.

"What is it?" I finally ask. I want to understand, to know what this flame is, and why it seems to hold such power over her.

Her jaw clenches, and I see her shoulders shudder slightly before she begins to explain. "When I was eight years old, my parents left the village to join this... radical group." She takes a deep breath, the motion rippling through her body as if the very act of speaking these words is a burden she carries with her. "After they left, my brother and I were raised by the village shaman, Djar."

I remember her mentioning this before, in vague terms, when she spoke to Arthur in the kitchen. But now, as she continues, the full weight of her words becomes clear. "This particular group follows a god by the name of Hu'yimona," she says, her tone laced with disdain. "He claims himself to be one of the sacred gods, though I hardly see him as such. They seemed harmless at first, inactive, until young women between the ages of eighteen to twenty began to go missing from the villages. I was eighteen at the time when that began."

I listen intently, my anger growing with each word she speaks.

"Djar had the entire village on lockdown," she continues. "No woman was allowed to leave without an escort for what felt like forever. But me being me... I went off on my own one night because I wished to see the aquatic firebugs in the Atesk uoi Skafes—Lake of Mirrors. My brother refused to go with me so late at night, and I didn't see the harm in it..."

Her voice cracks, and I can see the pain welling up in her eyes as she struggles to continue. "That's when I ran into my parents. I was so excited to see them that I didn't even think about the possibility that they would do anything to me. I mean... I was their daughter after all. They kept us locked away for I don't know how long, and eventually, I was bound and standing in a line with eight other young women as we were led toward the sacrificial altar of Hu'yimona."

I watch as her throat bobs, as she swallows hard to keep herself from breaking down. The image she paints is one of unimaginable horror, and it fills me with a fury I have only felt once before—in the days following my sister's death. A fury so intense, so consuming, that it threatens to overwhelm me entirely.

"They began to perform a ritual," she continues, her voice shaking slightly as she forces the words out. "Feeding our... feminine essence, as they called it... to him. I was the last in line, and I had almost met the same end. I was lucky enough to have the grace of the gods on my side, though. They appeared just as they were... in the process of it. But the ritual was left incomplete, so it rears its ugly head every year, and there isn't anything anyone can do about it, not even my Maku'ome, Coli'hanu. I simply have to endure it."

As grateful as I am that she is finally opening up to me, I can feel my muscles growing rigid with anger and frustration. I can taste the bitter, metallic tang of my blood as I clench my jaw, my teeth sinking into my cheek in an effort to keep my emotions in check. The flame continues to flicker along her scar, fueling my rage further. The image she has painted—the thought of her walking toward her own death, being forced to watch as the other women were murdered right before her eyes, knowing that her parents had willingly handed her over—it's all too much for me to bear.

I will still take her home if that is what she chooses, but I will not rest until I find the miscreants who caused her such pain. I will hunt them down, and I will end them, no matter the consequences. This is a vow I make to myself, one that I will not break. And with that promise solidified in my mind, I tighten my hold on her, pulling her closer to me as if to shield her from the horrors of her past.

I will lay siege to those who have harmed her. I will desecrate their bodies in the most vile, violating ways for bringing such pain to the woman I love.

My love.

My love.

Love.

The word echoes in my mind, a truth I can no longer deny.

I will gladly give up everything—time, reason, sanity—if it means keeping her here, safe in my arms.

19
Arthur

My dearest Millie,

I wish I had enough time to tell you everything that has happened in full detail, but unfortunately the Cap' is a right slave driver. So much has happened since my last missive. Some of it is so crazy to even try to explain that you might not even believe me.

Do you remember the Kana'te woman I mentioned after my first voyage to Capulli'ana—the one that has been driving the Cap' into lunacy? Well, Kiernan took her right off the beach and she's been sailing with us since. That's right, he kidnapped a woman like cargo.

Between the explosive drama that ensued during her first days here, being forced to clean Todd's mess up in the kitchen, and running off to get snatched by slave traders, I had almost begun to believe she was as good as dead on this ship. Luckily, she's a mighty tough little lass.

I think you would like her. She's spirited, opinionated, and could very well melt a heart of ice. She certainly has with Kiernan. I've never seen the man like this, so docile and complacent. It might even be enough to crack a wee laugh about.

I know time seems to stand still as we wait, but I'm almost done. Soon, very soon, I will come to get you, and we can have the life we always wanted. Just hang in there for me just a little longer.

I love you.

Always,

Arthur

I wipe my quill on my trousers, corking the ink well closed with a heavy sigh. Looking around at the mess of hammocks swaying lightly with the movement of the ship, I can barely tell that it's already early morning. If it weren't for the oil lamp I have hung over my head, the faint glow just barely enough to allow me to see, I wouldn't have been able to even write this letter.

I never write to her during waking hours, not wishing for them to know. They all seem like decent lads, but I would rather keep Millicent separate from this life until absolutely necessary. There will be a time when she will have to board this ship, and I'll be a nervous wreck the entire time. But that time will only come once I've secured my place in Rhazden.

Men start to turn and stir in their hammocks as the collective internal clock begins to rouse them from their sleep, and I quickly shove the quill and ink back into my pack, which hangs on the rafter behind my head. I pull at the spool of coarse thread I have buried in the front pocket, quickly folding and tying the letter closed. I won't be able to send it out until our next port, so I shove it into the side pocket with the five others I've managed to have time to write to her since our last one.

Just as I'm about to grab for the tie in my pocket to pull my grown hair back away from my face, I feel a sharp jab to my back as Joffrey, who bunks in the hammock below me, throws his fist up.

"Oi, ye tiny turd, rise and shine! I'm starvin' like a hungry sea dog!" he barks, and a wave of irritation floods my system. It'll pass as it always does, but something about that guy in particular rubs me the wrong way every time he opens his fat mouth.

I jump down from my designated sleeping place, and rub my eyes as I make my way toward the kitchen. Sitara and I have been 'blessed' with the responsibility of making sure no one on this ship dies of food poisoning, which had been a high possibility during Todd's time. I can already smell the food as I descend the stairs to the lowest level of the ship.

Walking into the kitchen, I tie my hair back—a task that had been rudely interrupted by Joffrey. Maybe I should see if Starlight knows how to clip hair...

I smile at the image painted in front of me, Sitara bustling around in an attempt to finish what smells like stew on the stove. Her hair is pinned back using a golden hairpin the Cap' must have bought her, coiled strands falling to frame her smiling face as she notices me.

"Pali Chute, Pip," she greets me, her native tongue completely lost on me.

"I'm going to assume that means *'Good mornin'* and not *"Fuck off, Pip',"* I chuckle, grinning as I get to work helping her slice the morning orange rations.

I will have to admit that my latest job is far more bearable than the last few years have been. Sitara has become a good friend during her time here, which is more than I had before. She's an intelligent conversationalist, reminding me greatly of my Millie. I wasn't lying when I said I think the two of them will get along. Though Millicent isn't nearly as loud and hyper as Sitara seems to be on a good day, there is something about the two that I find comparable personality wise. I just haven't put my finger on it yet.

Her playful grin as she stirs the pot is enough of an answer to my comment. I'm right, that must mean 'good morning' in Lo'pillkat.

Once breakfast is prepped, and we can hear the men beginning to congregate in the mess deck, I give her a salute like a soldier heading off to battle. I may as well be when it comes to these brutes. Getting between any one of them and Sitara's cooking is like willingly walking into an open fire. Though, I can't honestly blame them. They've not had a decent meal about this ship for literal years.

I've only been damn near trampled once. It had been quickly stopped by Starlight and a wooden ladle. Poor Viktor had a goose egg for three days afterward, which Henry continued to poke at until it was irritated and sore. I honestly don't understand those two. Sometimes they seem like they have that unconditional brotherly bond, then the next they seem like they cherish getting on each other's nerves.

"What's taking so long in there, Starlight?" one of the twins holler through the wall.

I can't say I'm not pleased that my little nickname has stuck. I'd say it's probably my first lasting contribution, as small as it may seem.

"The longer you bother us, the longer I'll make you wait!" she barks back, eliciting a laugh from my throat.

After breakfast has been served, and Sitara and I have scrubbed down the kitchen—Sitara having said, and I quote *'I'll be dead before it ever gets that bad again'*, we go our separate ways. When I say separate ways, I mean I watch Becket teach her how to work and mend the sails while I sit on the deck and perform maintenance on the artillery.

She's begun to grow more comfortable with us I think, once the crew started realizing exactly how magnetic she really is. Sitara gives a good name to the Kana'te people, a name that previously had been obscured by our own history on them.

Well, everyone else besides Joffrey has grown to like her, but no one can expect much else from the giant arsehole.

I glance up from my work from time to time, just to keep an eye on Becket, to make sure he's being polite. I've grown rather protective of her during her time here, and I'm beginning to realize that our friendship might be more like an adopted siblinghood. If I *were* to have a sister, I think Sitara would be exactly what I envision.

I grin as she utilizes the proper knotwork that Benedict had shown her a few days ago after she had asked him to teach her for '*just in case*'. But we all know it's because she wants to be able to get out if she finds herself tied to a bed again.

Kiernan is good about that: created unneeded trauma. But he's also a good lad at heart.

"Well, damn," Becket grunts as they finally get the main sail down from the mast, "Looks like the hole is bigger than it seemed from way up there. Grab that box with the needle and thread in it, will ya, Star?"

I watch her hurry to do as he asks. When she returns with the box in hand, I watch her take in every word Becket says to her. She seems to learn everything so fast. I won't be surprised in the slightest if she picks up the skill within the first lesson or two.

"Alright, so first you want to measure and cut the patching cloth," Becket explains, laying the sail down as flatly as he can, "Alright, there we go." He cuts the fabric to size with a knife and quickly holds it up to check it. "Then, you're going to fold the hemming about half an inch. Yup, just like that."

I watch Sitara fold the edges, Becket going behind her to sew everything together. Honestly, I'm surprised their proximity hasn't led Kiernan down from the upper deck to rip Becket away yet. The captain *has* seemed to be a little less violent lately.

Perhaps Starlight is thawing out that frigid heart of his too. Not that he wasn't already completely consumed by the woman, but it has changed into something different. Still possessive, yes, but gentler.

Still, that doesn't keep Kiernan from watching her like a hawk from afar, his face etched in a carefully stoic line of observation. Either Sitara is *really* good at ignoring him at this point, or she hasn't noticed him staring into the back of her head. Probably the former.

It isn't until Becket finishes with showing Sitara the repairs, and starts hoisting the sail that Kiernan moves. He's stayed on his side of the ship longer than I had expected him to honestly. The man hardly ever stays further than arm's reach from her anymore. Perhaps it's because she's trying to learn the ins and outs of the ship, or maybe it's because she's trying so hard to keep herself busy. Kiernan had ordered us to find her things to do if she began to sulk around again.

I know Cap is getting frustrated. We all thought that allowing that old man aboard the ship, promising her his safe transfer to Rhazden without having to take the three year trial, would have changed her constant distance from him. Somehow, it only seems to give him less and less physical contact with him.

Kiernan Slater does not like this, you see. He doesn't like that she's spending more time with every other man on this ship but him. Well, aside from Joffrey, who she's continued to give a wide berth.

"You're picking up fast, Pet," Kiernan grins, causing Sitara to startle at his sudden proximity.

Eww... Pet? The nickname still doesn't sit well with me, but he's not the first man on this ship to call a woman that. I still don't like it, but Sitara seems to have gotten used to it.

She takes a step to the side, creating just a sliver of distance between them, but Cap's hand is already at the base of her spine. Sometimes, I just want to look at him, and tell him to knock it off, but he'd just throw me off the side of the ship.

"I'm a fast learner," Sitara responds casually, pushing her hair out of her face. If one thing can be said about her appearance, it would be her hair. Anytime any of us has described her by anything but name, it's been something to do with that massive mane of curls.

Kiernan chuckles, leaning up against the mast to pull her to him. Sitara stiffens, whatever it is he whispered to her makes her face the same color as said hair.

That is something I've noticed... She doesn't fight him anymore. She hasn't specifically told me if her feelings for him have changed at all, but she doesn't fight and squirm away like she used to. Now, she certainly doesn't hang all over him, but she's begun to stand still during moments like this, as though she's simply decided to ride through it rather than reject it all together.

Her head snaps up to look at him, her lips pressing into a thin line. "No."

Kiernan just laughs harder, and I think I might be able to discern what that conversation is about given my knowledge of the man.

I turn my eyes to the sky, having started to notice that daylight seems to be fading far earlier than it should. "Cap, there's a storm brewin' up," I call over.

He shoots me a look, one I've gotten more times than I can count over the last few years. It's a look that says '*of course it's you*'. I'm starting to think that I'm his least favorite person on this ship. Or maybe all together. I can't be sure.

The breeze kicks up not long after, and everyone's face turns toward the sky collectively. Clouds have rolled in faster than you'd think were possible, the waves beginning to rock the *Nureus* harsher than usual.

Kiernan pulls Sitara to the helm, quickly turning to change the course slightly. We won't be able to get around it completely, but if we can stick to the outer edge of the storm, we'll be fine.

I quickly gather up the pistols and cleaning utensils I had been using as Benedict begins to bark out orders. We all rush around, reducing sail area and switching to the storm jibs, which are smaller, reinforced sails that will help Kiernan maintain control over the ship without causing rig strain.

The rest of us begin to batten down the hatches and ballast management, making sure everything is secured and evenly distributed throughout the ship to keep from risk of capsizing.

It isn't long before the waters are rough, less than forgiving, and begins to throw us around on the desk. I think I remember seeing Cap shuffle Sitara into the cabin earlier, which is probably the best place for her to be.

Joffrey is taking his sweet time tying down a crate, his meaty hands working slow to tie the rope. When the ship suddenly pitches left, the big oaf loses his footing, and falls to the deck with an inaudible crash. The poorly tied down crate tumbles with him, the corner colliding with his arm.

The twins rush over to pull it off him, and it doesn't take long to find the bloody gash across his bicep. By the time we get past the stormy winds, his arm is stained red.

I'm almost certain he's going to need stitches.

I hurry to his side with a wet rag, but he pushes me away with a grunt. I don't particularly like him, but bleeding out on this ship isn't going to help anyone. Even though Joffrey is growing old and slow, he's invaluable to the crew with his knowledge of the sea.

"Leave me be, lad. I be needin' no aid from ye!" he barks, and I falter for half a second.

Stubborn arse old man...

Even bleeding and in pain, he is a damn arsehole.

I don't get the opportunity to protest or try again before Sitara comes up behind me, and takes the rag from my hand. She saunters over to him, crouching down beside him.

And of course, the stubborn jack shoots her a glare that could curdle milk.

"An' I be needin' no aid from *ye*!" He goes to jerk out of Sitara's grasp, but she whacks him in his bad arm with the rag, eliciting a hiss from between his clenched teeth.

"Stop it," she retorts, though her voice is far more forgiving than I would have thought after the way he's treated her and spoken about her people.

To my surprise, Joffrey doesn't protest again.

Sitara proceeds to clean his wound, her movements gentle despite the look of concentration on her face. "Pip, go get me the needle and thread please," she murmurs, and I rush to do as she asks.

By the time I have come back with the items, Joffrey's jaw has relaxed slightly, though he's still tense. Whether that is from the pain or Sitara's proximity is yet to be seen.

I have also had the mind to grab a small bottle of alcohol on my way back, so she can sterilize her supplies. We don't need the old man living through the bleeding just to die of infection.

Everyone one of us watches as she pours the amber liquid over his open wound, and then over her needle. She hands him the remaining contents of the bottle.

"I'm sorry to tell you that this is going to sting, and you may want to get in a good swallow or two before I begin," she says, threading the needle while Joffrey does just that with a grumble.

When she begins to move in with the needle, we all continue to stare intently, leaning forward in case he loses his mind. Joffrey hisses, spitting a bit of whiskey out as she begins to dig the needle into his flesh.

"What be ye tryin' to do?! Dig into me bones?" he growls, but Sitara doesn't flinch.

"No, I'm barely going below the skin. Now, stop being a big baby, and let me finish."

Sitara does indeed finish, but not without a lot of noise from Joffrey.

After she has finished, Kiernan takes her back to their cabin for a bath, the tone in his voice suggesting that it isn't a request. From my understanding, Sitara takes every bath with Kiernan, and he is extremely anal about keeping her clean.

The rest of us scatter, some up to the upper deck, and some to their hammocks for the night. I join the former of the two. I'm surprised that the sky has cleared by the time night hits, and it is alive with stars. The twins have followed me up, mumbling back and forth amongst themselves about how Sitara is a better man than either of them. They go on to say that—after the way he has treated her—if it had been them, they would have left him to bleed out. I can't say that I disagree completely, though I also can't say I would have let him bleed out.

After all, he treats me just as shitty, but I went to his aid as well all the same.

The three of us move to sit against the railing, and begin to watch the skies. My Millie would love this... I'll make a point to bring her out to the deck when we make our move to Rhazden.

"Shooting stars!" exclaims one of the twins, though I'm not sure which one. I'm ashamed to say I still really struggle to tell the two apart. Which brings us to yet another endearing trait of Sitara's. In a matter of days, she knew them by name and by face. How she did it, I have no clue, but she has not once gotten them mixed up.

"Mon dieu, Starlight would *adore* this," the other responds.

"Why don't one o' you two go see if she wants to watch?" I suggest.

The first grins at me, a knowing look in his eyes. "Why don't you go get her, and see what happens, oui?"

I chuckle, rolling my eyes as I lean my head back against the wood. "Aye, I know Cap's gonna tan my hide. But you two might have a wee more o' fighting chance."

"Good point!" the second laughs, moving to rush to the cabin door before the show is over.

Moments later, Sitara is sitting between myself and one of the twins, looking up into the sky in awe. Kiernan is leaned against the rail by the helm, clearly displeased with their nightly routine being disrupted.

"Wow..." Sitara murmurs, her face lighting up with a brilliance that seems to make anyone around her melt. She really is a good, sweet lass with a strange sort of pull to her.

To know her is to adore her.

And now I have figured out why she reminds me of Millicent. Millie is the same way. There isn't a person in their *right* mind—again, I repeat, right mind—who can't love her while in proximity to her. I know I certainly fell for her charms, and still keep falling even miles upon miles apart.

Sitara continues, her voice laced with a sense of nostalgia, "I've only seen the sky fall like this one other time."

"You have seen this before in the jungle, have you?" one of the twins teases, and she laughs with a shake of her head.

"No, not under the trees, but I spent plenty of time at Potem'aku as a child," she explains. I remember her telling me about the great temple that is nestled in the center of the island, where the Kana'te gods—or the ones that stayed—reside. "One night, after a particularly rough training session, my friend Kay'Kaio and I were shuffled up onto the roof by the Sacred Three. They said it was a surprise."

"Sooo, have you actually *seen* the living gods we hear so much about then?" the other twin asks.

Sitara laughs, shuffling to lay flat on her back. "Yes. Many times actually. I was taught how to control my power from the Goddess of Cold Fire herself."

Silence falls over us for a moment, as though we all are trying to wrap our heads around her conviction. Then, I break the ice to keep the flow. "And what happened durin' your time on the roof?"

"She told me about another god she used to know, one that doesn't live in the temple anymore," she says, propping her head up on her hands, "His name is Ma'dai, Demon of the Stars. She had told me that he was a mysterious god, and had always been so, but that the stars began to fall more often after his rebirth. Something in the way she looked up with such a deep sigh, the melancholy in her voice, tells me there was much more to that story than she let on."

Something about her tale resonates, and I look back up at the sky. I think I can understand how that goddess had felt on that roof, just from what little Sitara has disclosed of the encounter.

It's probably similar to how I feel right now, wondering if Millie is also standing under the blanket of night, watching the stars dance across the black void.

20
Sitara

I wake up one morning, later than I had intended. The dull ache behind my eyes lingers from another night of restless sleep, and I blink slowly, willing the grogginess to dissipate. The air in the cabin is warm, thick with the scent of salt and wood—familiar and comforting to me now. The midmorning sun filters through the clouded glass of the windows on the far end of the room, golden shafts of light cutting across the wooden floorboards, illuminating specks of dust that dance lazily in the air.

Shifting beneath the covers, I stretch my limbs, relishing the comfort before my fingers instinctively brush over the mark on my skin. My scar. The familiar, jagged line that has burned for days finally feels cool to the touch. A deep, trembling relief washes over me, causing me to let out a slow, tranquil sigh, as if expelling all the tension I've been carrying.

This year had been worse than most. The stygian flame clung to me with stubborn persistence, malevolent heat searing through my dreams, twisting them into nightmares that left me gasping awake in the dark.

Now, at last, the torment has subsided.

Sitting up, I rake a hand through my tangled curls, wincing at the knots. The sounds of the crew outside the door reach me—boisterous laughter, the heavy tread of books, the occasional creak of the ship's timbers as it sways gently on the waves.

The *Nureus* is alive with movement today, as she always is.

The door to the adjoining bathing room clicks open, and Kiernan steps out, steam rolling off his bare skin as he ruffles his damp hair with a towel. The sight of him, bronzed and glistening, sends an embarrassing flutter through my chest. One I stubbornly ignore.

He wears nothing but a towel slung low around his waist, revealing the hard planes of his torso, the faint scars that map his body like a map of his history. I've found myself stealing glances at him more often than I should, tracing the lines of old wounds with my gaze.

Stop staring, Sitara.

He smiles—slow, knowing—as if he can hear my thoughts.

"Good morning, Darling," he purrs, the words dripping with amusement. The steam curls around him like a lover's embrace before dissipating into the room. A part of me is surprised he didn't drag me into the bath with him, as he usually does. He must have let me sleep, recognizing the exhaustion that weighed on me.

It's a small mercy, and one I'm silently grateful for.

I'm still half-trapped in the remnants of sleep, my voice rough with disuse. "Mhm," I grunt, rubbing the heel of my hand against one eye before brushing the wild tangle of curls away from my face.

He pauses in the act of retrieving his clothes from the wardrobe, tilting his head as if I've said something particularly puzzling. Then, with that effortless confidence of his, he stalks toward me. My throat goes dry as he stops just before the bed, his finger hooking under my chin to tilt my face up to meet his gaze. His eyes are luminous, that unnatural, captivating hue of blue that always unsettles me just a little. He hasn't changed, not really. He's the same infuriating, arrogant bastard he's always been.

And yet—

"I said, '*Good morning, Darling.* '"

A lump forms in my throat. Heat creeps up my neck, staining my cheeks.

Good gods, Sitara, get a grip on yours! It's ridiculous. The man rescues you one time, shows you the stars, and suddenly you're a flustered schoolgirl! *Pathetic.*

"Good morning," I manage, my voice barely above a whisper.

His finger slides from my chin, trailing down the column of my throat, skimming the sensitive pulse point there. I swear he can feel my heartbeat stutter.

"Good girl."

And with that bombshell, he releases me and saunters back to the wardrobe as if he hasn't just reduced me to a breathless, stammering puddle of goo. A shiver rolls down my spine as he dresses, pulling on his shirt, fastening his belt. He moves with an easy grace, as though the moment meant nothing at all.

By the time I've gathered my scattered senses, he's already fully dressed, boots laced, hand on the doorknob. Then—just as I think I'm safe—he pauses. That slow, smug grin curves his mouth, and he turns his head just enough to glance back at me.

And he winks.

Winks! Like the smug, self-satisfied psychopath he is.

Then he's gone.

I sit here, heart hammering like a wild thing against my ribs, cursing myself for reacting like some blushing maiden. I blame the sway of the ship for my unsteady breathing.

He's insufferable.

Since the first night after he rescued me from the *Cordelia*, I've found myself settling into life here in ways that I never expected. I won't forgive him for kidnapping me—dragging me out of that inn bed like some prized trinket—but I could have been taken by worse me.

I *have* been taken by worse men.

Things are... easier now. Pip and I have become fast friends—after I groveled for forgiveness for using him to sneak into the hold. Well, he forgave me pretty quickly, and I doubt he was even mad at me at all, given the way he still banters back and forth with me, but it's the thought that counts. He's taken over breakfast duty for the crew, a task that was both of ours until Kiernan decided my mornings are better spent elsewhere.

Like in the bath. With him.

Honestly, it has become routine, and I've stopped protesting it.

We've fallen into a rhythm, the crew and I. Arthur and I cook together in the evenings. Sometimes, when the skies are clear and the sea is calm, I stand at the helm with Kiernan, learning the feel of the ship beneath my hands and the heat of him at my back.

"You might even enjoy yourself if you stopped scowling all the time," he'd told me once.

Turns out, he was right.

With a reluctant sigh, I drag myself from the bed and cross to the wardrobe. Kiernan has cleared a space for my things, meager as they are. The clothes are still unfamiliar—Mundane garments, rough-spun and simple—nothing like the beaded embroideries I'm used to. But blending in is survival, and I'd rather not draw more attention than necessary.

I do, however, draw the line at shoes.

The earth—even the shifting, restless sea beneath the *Nureus's* hull—speaks to me in ways most wouldn't understand. The vibration of the waves, the deep thrum of life beneath the surface. Shoes mute that connection, leaving me adrift.

After dressing myself in one of the emerald cottons from my bor-rowed wardrobe, I step out of the captain's quarters and onto the main deck. The air is crisp with the scent of brine and damp rope, mingling with the faintest hint of spice from the cargo below.

For a moment, I pause and close my eyes, tilting my face upward. The sun presses against my skin, seeping into my bones with a quiet contentment. It's the kind of warmth that promises adventure, that hums with the energy of a ship about to dock, of a crew buzzing with purpose.

When I open my eyes again, the world sharpens into focus. Movement draws my attention to the starboard side, where Arthur helps toss the warping lines over the edge. Sensing my gaze, he looks up, and his face splits into a grin so infectious I can't help but mirror it.

"Pali chute, Starlight!" he calls, the syllables of my native greeting rolling effortlessly now off his tongue.

The fact that he's learned it, that he uses it—so freely, so easily—sends a warmth through my chest. He respects my culture. More than that, he embraces it.

I return the greeting with a smile, lingering another heartbeat before shifting my focus.

My gaze seeks Kiernan, scanning the deck until I find him where he always is—commanding from the helm, his voice ringing with authority as he barks orders to the scrambling crew.

His usual sharp-edged intensity is softened, replaced by an eager energy that hums beneath his words. He's not just commanding; he's animated. The sight piques my curiosity.

What has put him in such a mood?

I move toward the staircase leading to the upper deck, my fingers trailing along the polished railing as I ascend. Each step gives me a better vantage to watch him—the way his hands gesture sharply when he speaks, the way his eyes gleam.

And then, he sees me.

His head snaps up, and for once, there's no guarded amusement, no sly calculation—just a grin so genuine that it knocks the breath from my lungs.

"She lives!" he declares, throwing his arms out in a theatrical gesture, laughter rich and resonant in his chest.

I roll my eyes, but the effect is ruined by the smile tugging at my lips. Without hesitation, I take my place at his side. His hands settle on my waist, firm and warm, turning me toward the docks where the ship is being secured.

"Port Hammond awaits." His breath brushes my ear, low and satisfied.

I watch as he moves to the navigation table, gathering his maps with efficient precision. The parchment whispers as he rolls them, tucking them into their designated sleeves.

"I'll be quite busy today," he muses, glancing at me sidelong. "Therefore, you are more than welcome to explore to your heart's content, Pet."

I scrunch my nose at the offer, unable to suppress the memory of my last unsupervised '*exploration*' in a port village—a misadventure that had ended with me narrowly avoiding servitude.

He laughs, shaking his head. "Don't worry. This is the safest place for you to do so, outside of Rhazden, that is."

The name alone is a lure, a mystery whispered among the crew like a secret too sacred to speak aloud. It's the one place Kiernan guards fiercely, the one destination no one is permitted to see until they've sailed with him for three years.

Well, apart from Saolo'ki, whom I swallowed my pride and begged for.

"Will I get to go?" The question slips out before I can stop it.

He nods slowly, deliberately, as if savoring the weight of his answer. "It's our next stop. You'll be the first person I've taken there on the voyage. Besides your cage buddy, whom you were so insistent that I take."

I huff a laugh, but my mind whirls. First. There's significance in that. A privilege, because I didn't have to beg for myself.

His voice cuts through my thoughts as he shouts for Arthur, issuing brisk instructions about gathering belongings for an extended stay in Port Hammond. The way Pip merely nods—as if he'd known he wouldn't be continuing with us—only deepens the enigma.

"I guess we should feel special, then?" I quirk a brow at Kiernan, unable to resist teasing him.

His chuckle is like dark velvet as he responds. "No, *you* should feel special. Your friend is just lucky you are."

With the ship secured, Kiernan strides toward the gangplank just as Benedict lowers it to the dock.

"You should stop by the bakery on Third Avenue," he calls back over his shoulder, his tone easy, familiar. "There's a lovely little lady there by the name of Annie. She'll feed you. Just tell her to charge '*Nan*'."

The nickname—Nan—catches me off guard. Before I can ask, the sound of boys shouting from the shore steals his attention.

"Captain Nan! Captain Nan!" Their voices ring with excitement, their small hands waving furiously.

And Kiernan—my captain, the man whose very presence commands reverence—grins like a boy himself, lifting a hand in greeting.

People know him here. Not just as a feared name, but as someone welcomed. Someone loved.

How interesting.

He leaves without another word, disappearing into the bustle of Port Hammond with a stride so light it's nearly a skip.

And I?

I should go to the bakery. I should explore. I should do as he said.

But the truth is, I won't.

Because I am far too curious not to follow.

I want to see what has put that rare, unguarded joy in his step. I want to watch him move through the town like a man unshackled, to witness the way the streets seem to brighten around him.

And most of all—I want to understand why.

I linger at the top of the gangplank for only a brief moment. The *Nureus* creaks softly behind me, its massive hull swaying ever so slightly with the tide. I finally walk down the plank, letting myself adjust to the solid weight of the dock beneath my feet after so many days at sea.

Saolo'ki appears beside me with that unhurried swagger of his, falling into step as if we've walked like this a thousand times before. And in a way, we have—though never quite like this.

He moves more easily now, his lean frame no longer trembling from exhaustion, his muscles no longer taut with the memory of chains. Proper food and rest have done wonders for him: the ashen pallor of his earth-toned skin has deepened into a warm, sunbaked clay. His tightly coiled dreads, once matted with grime, now shine black as raven feathers, pulled back from his face in a loose tie that exposes the sharp angles of his cheekbones.

But the most striking change is in his eyes. They were dull before, clouded with resignation, but now—now there's a spark there. A glimmer of mischief, of life. It reminds me of the way he used to look before the slavers took him, back when we were just wild things racing through the highgrass of the southern plains, careless and free.

He's still too thin, his frame still carrying the hollows carved by years of starvation. The borrowed trousers hang loose on his hips, the fabric cinched tight with a belt lest they slide right off. He'll fill out in time, I remind myself. Already, his ribs don't press so sharply against his skin. Already, he stands taller.

He's foregone a shirt entirely, and shoes as well—much to Henry's amusement. The Mundanes aboard the *Nureus* had offered him both, but he'd wrinkled his nose at the scratchy weave of the linen and refused outright.

"Nothing can be scratchier than dried hide and burlap," Henry had laughed. "Yet here you are, fussing like a spoiled princeling."

Fair point.

Still, I don't blame him. There's something freeing about bare feet on sun-warmed wood, about the breeze against bare skin.

As we step onto the dock proper, I brace for the usual disdainful stares—the ones Mundanes so often level at my bare arms, my uncovered legs. But today? Nothing. Or at least, nothing obvious. A few sidelong glances, yes, but nothing like the outright glares I've endured in other villages. Kiernan must have bribed or threatened someone into civility. Or perhaps it's simply that I'm not quite as scandalous as usual—no corset, true, but at least I'm wearing trousers that don't leave my thighs exposed.

Saolo'ki, however, draws a few more arched brows than I do. I frown. Is it really so strange for a man to walk shirtless here? Back home, it was commonplace, especially in the heat of the dry season. But here, amid the starched collars and stiff woolen vests of the Mundane villagers, his bare chest seems to unsettle them.

He doesn't seem to notice—or if he does, he doesn't care. His focus is elsewhere, his dark eyes darting from shadow to shadow as if expecting an ambush. It's an old habit, one beaten into him over years of captivity. Even now, with his chains gone, his muscles tense at every sudden movement—a merchant slamming a crate down, a child shrieking in play.

I loop my arm through his, squeezing gently. You're safe, the gesture says. No one will take you again.

For a long moment, we walk in silence, our bare feet scuffing against the weather-smoothed stone of the pathway. The sensation is strange after weeks of unsteady decking—too solid, too unmoving.

Then, softly, he speaks.

"Where are we going, Sega Asilama?"

The endearment—*dear one*—catches me off guard, even now. It's not the casual se'lama of childhood friends, but the deeper, rarer variant. A term reserved for those held closest to the heart, for those who are kin in all but blood.

Before I can explain that my original plan—scouting for information—has been temporarily derailed by the tantalizing scent of freshly baked bread, my stomach growls with such ferocity that Saolo'ki's eyebrows shoot up.

A slow, knowing grin spreads across his face.

"You spend all that time in the kitchen, and you mean to tell me that you neglected to feed yourself?" He shakes his head, clicking his tongue in mock disapproval. "Sitalli'ara!"—Hopeless.

"In my defence," I counter, laughing as my stomach gives another indignant rumble, "I woke up late!"

Kiernan hadn't jolted me awake at dawn like usual, and by the time I'd stumbled from my berth, the crew had already devoured half the morning's rations. No matter. The village ahead promises something far better than the ship's biscuits.

The bakery's aroma is impossible to resist—rich yeast, honeyed pastries, the earthy sweetness of rye. It pulls us forward like a lodestone. Even Sao, who usually feigns indifference to Mundane food, looks nearly giddy, his steps quickening.

The shop itself is achingly quaint, like something from one of the illustrated storybooks in the schoolhouse. A railed porch, painted a cheery red, wraps around the front, and a creaking rocking chair sits in one corner. An old man occupies it, his gnarled hands folded over his stomach, his face a map of wrinkles beneath a thatch of white hair.

As we approach, his milky eyes flick up to us.

"Good mornin'," he rasps, smiling like we're expected.

"Good morning," we chorus back.

Walking into the bakery, the scent of freshly baked bread wafts through the air, a warm and yeasty embrace that instantly makes my stomach rumble. The space is small and cozy, with a simple, inviting charm. A sturdy wooden countertop bisects the room, its surface worn smooth by years of use. Behind it, the bakery was a hive of quiet industry. To the right, shelves stacked high with proofing baskets hold mounds of dough in various stages of readiness.

In the center, a large, flour-dusted wooden table serves as the kneading station, its surface covered in baking flour. A tiny, laddered staircase clings to the wall, hinting at a second floor above, undoubtedly used for storage or perhaps the baker's home. Dominating the back wall is a massive stone oven. Flames dance and flicker within, visible through the opening.

I hear Sao's stomach let out a low rumble that betrays his hunger. Turning toward him, I offer a playful grin. "Did you forget to eat this morning, too?"

I already knew the answer.

Sao is like a bottomless pit, a walking black hole for food, devouring everything he can get his hands on. Now, that could be one of two things: either the residual hunger from the last nine years of forced starvation, or he has always possessed an insatiable appetite.

As the bell jingles merrily above the door frame upon our entry, an elderly woman, who has been shuffling about her work, halts her movements. She looks up, offering us a warm, flour-dusted smile.

She is a kindly looking woman, her wrinkled face radiating warmth and genuine hospitality. Her hair, still thick despite her age, has grayed considerably, yet remnants of its former auburn hue cling stubbornly to wisps and tufts around her head. Her eyes, dulled with the privilege of her many years, hold a reservoir of wisdom.

"What can I do for you, children?" Her sun-kissed features remain warm as she moves toward the counter. "I don't think I'm familiar with that pretty face of yours, sweetheart, so you'll forgive me if I've somehow forgotten."

She turns to Saolo'ki, her eyes brightening. "Nor do I know this handsome man either. My, you look like you could use a nice warm loaf or two. What are your names, lovies?"

I immediately feel a kindred familiarity with her, a sense of comfort and connection that settles over me like a warm blanket. She reminds me of Djar back home. I am almost certain Sao feels the same, as I feel him relax slightly beside me, his shoulders easing.

Saolo'ki speaks up first. "Oh, we're not from around here, so you needn't worry about forgetting me," he explains gently, waving a placating hand in her direction.

I give a soft, reassuring smile, tucking a stray strand of hair behind my ear as I follow up with, "Um, 'Nan' said I could charge his account and get us something from here."

Her eyes light up at the mention of Kiernan's nickname.

"Oh! My sweet Nan is home?!" Her hands fly up to her cheeks, leaving faint flour prints on her skin. She is giddy with delight, nearly skipping in place behind the countertop.

Are we even talking about the same Kiernan?

"Anything you want, my dears. It's on the house. You just make sure to send that boy of mine in for some food before you all take off again." She radiates joy as she speaks, her elderly features lit up brightly, reminiscent of the Lake of Mirrors shimmering under the moonlight. "Tell me your names, sweet girl. I want to know just who managed to lasso our little Nan. He's never brought anyone to see me besides those brutes he calls friends."

I laugh softly at the expression on her face as she mentions the crew, her wrinkles pinching up into a comical scowl. She seems so sweet and gentle, yet I don't doubt for a moment that she would scold those pirates like unruly children, even throwing them over her knee if she felt it necessary.

"Well, this is Saolo'ki," I say, gesturing to Sao, then to myself, "My name is Sitara, ma'am. We are simply... taking a joy ride with Kiernan until he rounds back to our ports."

It probably wouldn't bode well for him if I reveal to her that her *sweet Nan* had kidnapped me and is sailing around with me like cargo.

"Sao and Starlight..." she murmurs, almost whimsically, then offers me a sweet roll glistening with glaze and Saolo'ki a strange powdered bun with another of her warm smiles. Or perhaps it is the same one. I can't be sure, as she hasn't stopped smiling since we walked through the door.

"It's so good to meet a friend of our boy," she continues, "Nan doesn't just bring passengers for... joy rides." She reaches across the counter to pat my hand gently. "My name is Annie. I hope you enjoy your time with us, my dear. You as well, young man. It's been quite some time since I've seen Capulli'ana beauty grace our shores."

Saolo'ki and I share a surprised glance, taken aback by her knowledge of our origins based solely on our names. It would explain how she knew what mine meant, at least. There had been others from our homeland here before. Now, I am more curious than ever. Maybe I can come back before we leave and sit with her for a while, hear her stories.

But for now, I have a tall pirate to stalk.

21
Sitara

Saolo'ki seems content to prolong his stay within the bakery's comfort. With a respectful gesture, I raise my hand, palm open and facing forward, elbow bent in a graceful curve—a traditional greeting and farewell of our people. It feels like ages since I've last used this simple custom with someone who truly understands its significance. Sao returns the gesture with a knowing smile, then gently places his hand over his heart, a silent acknowledgment of our shared heritage.

I step back out of the bakery, giving the old man—most likely Annie's husband or brother—an incline of my head, and then move into the bustling streets of the town.

The village is a hive of activity, homes and businesses crammed together, lining the cobblestone streets in a vibrant tapestry of browns, deep greens, and cream colors. Some shopkeepers had flung open their doors, beckoning customers to browse their wares. I move through the throng of people, weaving between shoppers and traders, and I begin to realize that this bustling town, despite its larger size and louder energy, isn't so different from my quiet village of Puka'qui.

Reaching the crest of a hill, the town having been built to flow with the natural curves of the land, I pause and smile. Below, the ocean stretches out like a scattering of precious jewels, lapping gently at the village's edge. Ship masts poke up above the rooftops in the distance, and the sky is filled with the white and grey streaks of gulls swooping and diving. As I wander down a particularly noisy street, a familiar sound cuts through the general din.

It's Kiernan's hearty laugh.

Curiosity piqued, I move closer to the gathering crowd, the volume of the laughter increasing with each step. Peering around the broad chest and muscular arm of a particularly large man, I finally see the source of the commotion.

To my utter astonishment, Kiernan, with a young girl who can't be more than four years old perched precariously on his shoulders, is kicking around a crude ball with two older men and a gaggle of teenagers. The little girl squeals with pure, unadulterated glee as Kiernan darts about, playfully dodging and weaving with the other participants.

He is teaching them Malizapopo... a tribal game I had grown up playing. A game so deeply ingrained in my childhood and culture.

The scene unfolding before me is completely unexpected. Kiernan, sharing a piece of my heritage, is bridging a gap I hadn't thought possible. It's as if they are embracing a part of me, a connection forged without even knowing who I am.

I watch him celebrate a winning goal, his face alight with genuine joy. A warm feeling begins to blossom in my chest, spreading upwards until my face flushes with unexpected emotion. This is a side of Kiernan I have never witnessed, a depth of character I hadn't imagined existed. I would have never guessed he is so comfortable with children, and that he possesses such a natural charisma.

Joining the other bystanders, I clap along, a bubble of delighted laughter rising in my throat. It isn't long before Kiernan's eyes meet mine, and a wide grin spreads across his face. He quickly makes his way toward me, still carefully balancing the little girl on his shoulders, eager to draw me into the playful fray.

I shake my head, waving my hand dismissively. "Oh! No, no... I think I'll just watch." I can feel the heat rising in my cheeks as more and more of the crowd turns to glance at me, drawn by Kiernan's boisterous approach.

Kiernan peers up at the little girl. "I think we've scared her with our impressive goal." His tone is playful, almost taunting, stirring the dormant competitive spirit within me. "I know Ahvi, here, looks very intimidating, but I promise she'll take it easy on you." He tickles the girl's side, eliciting a series of delighted squirming and giggles.

I can't help but chuckle, placing my hands on my hips with a theatrical flourish. "I don't know... She seems a bit cheeky to me," I tease, raising an eyebrow with a playful grin as I look at the adorable girl now known as Ahvi. "You promise to take it easy on me?"

Ahvi nods emphatically, patting Kiernan's cheek with a small hand.

It is now that I notice it—Ahvi is missing her left leg from the knee down. The realization washes over me, making the scene even more touching. That Kiernan would take the extra care and consideration to ensure that she can participate, that he would make her feel included and valued.

The game continues for a while longer, and eventually, I succumb to the contagious energy and join in. The joyous atmosphere of the players and the surrounding crowd is infectious, leaving me flushed and content with how my day has unexpectedly unfolded.

Ahvi giggles, a smooth, yet high-pitched battle cry, amidst the older boys and men jeering with laughter. When I manage to steal the ball from Kiernan, sliding under his bulk with my inherited quickness, Ahvi tugs on Kiernan's hair in excitement, forcing a surprised grunt from his lips.

"Come on, Nan! She's getting away!"

"No, she's not!" He laughs, the sound much closer than I anticipated. Suddenly, his free arm wraps around my waist, hoisting me off the ground.

I squawk in surprise, instinctively gripping his arm as he spins the three of us around in a dizzying circle. With a well-placed kick, he sends the ball sailing back in the opposite direction.

"Hey! That's cheating, you big cheater!" I reprimand playfully, eliciting a dramatic gasp from Ahvi.

"Ah! Nan! You big cheater!"

He releases me with a lingering chuckle as the game comes to an end, gently lifting Ahvi off his shoulders and tucking her securely into the crook of his arm. "I need to take Ahvi home now. I'll meet you back on the ship."

I nod, having no intention of returning to the ship just yet. I wait, watching him turn the corner, Ahvi resting her head contentedly on his chest.

Something deep within me stirs awake, catching me completely off guard. Affection. It is a surprising, unfamiliar warmth. Affection for the man who has, in his own way, begun to show me what life can be outside the strictures of my home. Thinking back on my time with him, despite the rocky start, I have to admit... I have enjoyed myself.

I have enjoyed myself with *him*.

Driven by an irresistible impulse, I follow behind him at a discreet distance, wanting to observe more of this unexpected behavior that has suddenly brought these conflicting feelings to light.

Wait... Wait, wait, wait! No, no, Sitara... this man kidnapped you, for gods' sake! These feelings surely can't be real, right? *Right!* There's no way. *No way....* This has to be some sort of Stockholm Syndrome or something. I have to nip these feelings in the bud before they take root.

I quickly turn around on my bare heels and walk back the opposite direction from where I had been headed. A palpable need for clarity drives my sudden retreat.

I need to clear my head of the confusing fog that seems to settle whenever he's near. I need to give myself some separation, a buffer zone of space and silence, to think without the immediate influence of his presence. I need time, precious, uninterrupted time, to figure out this baffling internal conflict.

Why does my heart still beat rapidly, a frantic drum against my ribs, when he's near, even though the fear that once gripped me has largely subsided?

And why does my face burn, a betraying flush creeping up my neck, without the presence of anger to ignite it?

Making my way back toward the gentle curve of the shoreline, my gaze sweeps across the landscape until it snags on a promising sight: a rugged cliffside jutting out over the water.

Perfect.

That's exactly what I need.

Standing above the ocean, suspended between earth and sky, letting its salty winds whip through my hair and calm me with their relentless power—it's a ritual, a comforting habit. It's something I do often at home. It's also something I had been doing on that beach back home, the night my life took a sharp, unexpected turn—the night I officially met Kiernan.

For the worse?

Or the best?

If you had asked me three weeks ago, wallowing in self-pity and resentment, I would have told you nothing good could possibly come of that night.

But now, standing here with the memory of his touch still lingering on my skin, I'm not so sure.

However, standing this high above the ground, feeling the raw power of nature surge around me, it gives me that adrenaline rush that always seems to help me recollect my thoughts, to untangle the knotted threads of my emotions.

A nervous smile creeps onto my lips as I cautiously approach the cliff's edge, hanging my toes precariously over the precipice. I look down into the water below, a vast expanse of blue that appears fairly calm from up here.

Or at least, it looks calm.

I know better than to be deceived by appearances. It's not like I'm going to jump, anyway.

This isn't some dramatic gesture of despair.

Standing this close to the edge, feeling the dizzying pull of gravity and the exhilarating rush of danger, is all the thrill I need to get my heart pumping and my mind silenced.

Just as I feel my muscles prepare to turn around and walk back to the *Nureus*, I feel a powerful embrace snatch me by the waist, yanking me backward with alarming force.

My back hits the ground with a deafening thud, the wind instantly knocked out of my lungs, leaving me gasping for air. My eyes widen in shock and confusion at the sight of Kiernan, heaving for breath as he looms over me. His eyes frantically scan my person, his gaze darting from my head to my toes and back again, a raw cocktail of concern and fear twisting his usually composed features into a mask of barely suppressed panic.

His gaze darkens, the fleeting vulnerability replaced by a surge of anger, hardening his face in an attempt to mask the lingering panic that I can still see flickering in his eyes. "Do you have a fucking death wish?!"

The unexpected sharpness in his voice takes me completely off guard, so far removed from the gentleness and teasing affection he had shown me earlier. His hands are planted flush with the ground on either side of my body, effectively pinning me in place, his fingers digging into the soil beneath us as if trying to anchor himself to the earth.

"For fucks sake, Sitara!"

I quickly look back at the cliff, then back to him, my eyes as large as round disks. I take in sharp, exerted breaths, my chest brushing against his as we breathe in tandem, our bodies close and connected even in this moment of chaos.

"I-I wasn't jumping. I was just..." I can't speak properly. The words are caught in my throat, tangled and jumbled by the residual shock. I can't make them come out fast enough to explain myself.

However, I don't think he can hear me past the roaring in his ears, the overwhelming fear and panic that has taken hold. His voice continues to rise in intensity, fueled by a potent mix of relief and fury.

"You were about to jump off a cliff on a strange island you've never fucking been to?! Are you out of your mind?" He rakes his hands through his dark hair, his muscles coiling tightly beneath his skin as I watch him begin to pace in a sharp, tight space in front of me, his movements jerky and agitated.

"You want to jump from rock to rock in a stream? Fine, knock yourself out. You want to jump out of a treetop where you can see clearly what is beneath you, where you know the landing? Be my *fucking* guest. You want to cliff dive into unfamiliar waters? You find me first! You tell me what you're planning! Is that understood?"

He walks over to pick up a large limb that is lying on the ground nearby, a piece of driftwood, no doubt carelessly brought this way by a storm. Walking back, he roughly grabs my arm, hoisting me to my feet with a force that borders on violent. I can't stop the whimper that escapes my throat, an involuntary sound of protest scraped raw by the sudden, jerking movement.

He tugs me over to the cliff's edge, where he grips my chin in his hand, his fingers digging into my skin but not enough to cause pain.

He angles my face toward the water, holding me there with an ironclad grip as he tosses the piece of wood over the edge. It disappears under the water with a loud, echoing plop, then resurfaces a moment later in eight different pieces, splintered and broken.

"This is the Razorath coastline, Sitara. You were just about to inadvertently sign your damn death certificate." He jerks my face toward him as he shoves a finger from his free hand into his chest, his eyes blazing with a mixture of anger. "Then *I* would have had to go tell your drugged-up brother that you fucking jumped! That his little sister had thrown her life away on some foreign beach for no reason!"

My blood runs cold as I watch the broken wood drift and slam against the jagged cliff wall, the force of the impact sending sprays of water into the air. I could have been seconds away from accidentally offing myself. I could have slipped on the loose dirt, or the earth could have given way under my weight.

I tremble as the full realization of the danger crashes over me, a wave of nausea washing through my body, and I instinctively take a step back away from the edge, my fingers fisting into the fabric of my skirts, as if trying to anchor myself to solid ground. I manage a deep, steadying breath, trying to regain some semblance of composure before Kiernan speaks again, his voice still rough with contained fury.

"What do you need?" I can tell he's still seething, the muscles in his jaw tight and clenched, though I can sense the effort he's making to try to soften his tone, to rein in the wildness of his emotions. "Do you need a damn cliff to stand on? I will take you to one that won't end your fucking life. Do you need to be chased down by some rabid beast to get whatever fix you're out here looking for? I have you covered there, too. Just let me know. Just do *not* go running off to do something that reckless by yourself again. Understood?"

"I'm sorry..." My voice quivers, a fragile whisper lost in the wind, my hands still shaking as I move closer to him, instinctively reaching up to cup his face in my hands. The reach up feels like more of a stretch than usual. I suppose it could be due to not having done it since Cordelia. Still, he feels... bigger now. The same way he had on the Cordelia. "Kiernan, I wasn't going to jump. I was just... standing there. I realize now I was standing too close, it was stupid, I get it, but I wasn't jumping."

I can feel the muscles of his jaw work beneath the rough skin of his face, a testament to the inner turmoil he's still battling. He says nothing, only giving me those blazing blue eyes, their intensity softened by a glimmer of something I can't quite decipher. I continue softly, my thumb subconsciously caressing the sharp curve of his cheekbone, drawing soothing circles against his skin. "I'm sorry I made you so angry. It wasn't my intention."

He lets out a sigh, a heavy release of pent-up tension, leaning slightly into my touch, as if seeking solace and reassurance in my presence. His eyes close for a brief moment, the dark lashes fanning against his cheeks, then open again, revealing calmer seas within their depths. They aren't steady, not yet, but not the brewing hurricane they had been just moments before.

"I'm not mad," he murmurs, his voice rough with emotion, the words barely audible above the crashing waves. "You scared me, Darling. There's a difference."

It's in this moment, looking into the depths of his eyes and feeling the raw vulnerability beneath his rough exterior, that I realize I can't deny what I already knew in my bones. I can't deny the way my heart flutters when he looks at me, the strange comfort I take in his presence, the fierce protectiveness that flares in him.

Kiernan has somehow, inexplicably, ingrained himself under my skin and seeped into my bones without me ever being the wiser.

22

Sitara

I wake up the next morning, burrowed into the warm body at my side. Kiernan usually wakes up before me, then comes back in for our bath when I finally open my eyes. However, he's stayed this morning, his arms wrapped around me and our legs an intertwined mess.

I blink the grogginess of my eyes, looking up to find him already awake, grinning down at me. I rub my face with the back of my hand, mostly to hide the reddening of my cheeks I know has started to creep up to my ears. He still looks at me like he always has, though I've noticed the tenderness beginning to mix with the possessive flare that is always there. I'm not sure if it makes it better or worse. My body certainly seems to react on its own more often than not now.

"Were you... watching me sleep?" I ask, trying to take the attention off my already flustered state this morning.

He nods as he uses his free arm to stretch. "I was, but only after I noticed the dribble of drool that was about to dip onto my chest."

Mortification flashes across my face before I can hide it, and he laughs. It's genuine, filled with amusement and mirth.

"I don't drool..." I protest, quickly sitting up to create distance between us. "Even if I did, you should have moved me away then."

He gives me a crooked grin. "You're not as bright as I gave you credit for if you think for one second that a little drool is going to determine whether or not I touch you."

I'm pretty sure my ears are red at this point. Thank gods for my hair.

I rise off the bed before him, climbing over his legs to let my feet hit the cold wood floor. I shove his shirt down my thighs for good measure and move to the bathing room without a word to begin our daily routine. I don't know what to say. I'm far too flustered to make even the snarkiest of comments.

I can feel him watching me walk away, his eyes boring into me from behind as I make my way into the bathing room. I can *feel* him, where his eyes land, and it sends a series of tingles up from the base of my spine. Once I'm out of his view, I take a moment to breathe, deciding to start warming up the water. Normally, that is his job, but I've decided to take care of it this morning. It'll keep me busy, giving me less time to just stand there and watch him.

He follows after me, appearing in the doorway moments later. He pauses, watching me, before he begins to undress. His eyes never leave me as I start filling the tub.

I'm not sure we have ever gone this long without him piping off with some perverted comment or me backlashing with a rude remark. The silence stretches on, well into us having sunk into the warm water. My skin blazes as he pulls me into my usual spot between his knees, pressing my back against his chest.

He begins running a warm rag along my skin, muttering to himself about how the scent of the soap he had chosen is perfect. I pull my hair over one shoulder, clearing the way for him to continue as he always does.

Once my body is clean, he moves on to my hair. He's made it abundantly clear in the past that this is his favorite part of every bath we take. It's also the bit he takes the most time on. Arthur had once teased

Kiernan—much to his disdain after being made to swab the deck for comparing our hair colors—that he should get special treatment for also having red hair. Kiernan simply refused to see the resemblance.

I don't fight to hide how much I enjoy this part anymore. The feeling of his fingers massaging the soap into my scalp makes my head fall back slightly, my eyes close as I savor it.

We sit in comfortable silence, the first of such we've ever had, until both of us are scrubbed clean. We both dress in that same unspoken comfort that has somehow developed over the last few weeks, then he leads us out of the cabin and onto the main deck.

As Kiernan moves to the helm, I catch sight of Arthur walking up on the deck with his bag in tow. He gives me a goofy grin, his dimpled cheeks broadening as he does.

"Aye, Starlight! Come here and gimme a hug before you leave!" He stretches his arms out to the sides, and I give him a bright smile, moving into his embrace. I'm not looking forward to not having Arthur on the ship. I've enjoyed the friendship that has blossomed between us, feeling closer to him than anyone aboard this ship.

Even Kiernan.

"Take care of yourself, Pip. Don't get into too much trouble, yeah?" I chuckle, wrapping my arms around his waist in a friendly hug.

Arthur rests his chin on my head, one hand wrapping around the back of my head, the other wrapped around my shoulders. "Don't have too much fun without me."

As soon as our goodbyes are said, I move up to the upper deck where Kiernan is standing. I perch myself on the edge of the navigation table, watching as he sets us out to sea once more. The silence between us finally breaks with the sound of Benedict's raspy chuckle.

Ben's mossy green eyes flick between the two of us, his arms casually wrapping around Kiernan's waist in a mocking hug. He grins, laying his head on his shoulder. I can't stop the giggles that pour out unstifled at the display.

"Awfully quiet up here…" he pokes fun, batting his eyelashes up at Kiernan, "Aw, K, are you sad that one of your little gingers is gone? I remember a time when I used to be enough for you."

Kiernan shoves him off playfully, rolling his eyes.

"I think I've made it abundantly clear how I feel about that ginger in particular," Kiernan teases back, sighing with a shake of his head, "You *were* enough for me, Benedict, but, alas, I have moved on to better curves and a prettier face."

He motions back to me, and I can feel my cheeks start to heat up again. Benedict grips his shirt, groaning as if he had just been stabbed in the chest. "You wound me, Kiernan…"

"I remember the pain of rejection well. Remind me to say hello to Enna when we dock by the way." He grins, wiggling his eyebrows at the other man.

My face scrunches imperceptibly, trying to decide if they are serious or if it is just playful banter. Sometimes, the two of them *do* make you wonder.

Ben proceeds to slump over to me, dropping to one knee as he lays his head down in my lap. "See what you've done, Starlight? Do you see it! My little bluejay…" I can faintly hear Kiernan in the background say *'don't call me that'*, but Benedict's whining is too loud to be sure. "…is leaving the nest! Too soon! Too soon!"

I'm in a full fit of laughter by this point, clutching my sides. I can't even give him a proper remark due to gasping for a breath. Benedict lifts his head, grinning up at me with a wink before throwing me over his shoulder.

"Hey!" I cry out, still laughing to the point my ribs hurt.

Ben rushes down to the main deck, shouting over his free shoulder at his captain. "Fair is fair, Kiernana!"

Kiernana? That makes me laugh harder, even as he flips me over into his arms and pretends like he's going to toss me overboard.

I hear Kiernan's laugh roar out behind us as he pummels Ben, careful not to knock me onto the floor with him. After coming to my rescue, Kiernan tucks me under his arm like a loose puppy and totes me back to the helm, where he sits me back down on the navigation table.

We sail straight through the day and into the night, Kiernan and I taking turns steering the helm. By the next morning, he has removed me from the steering column as everyone grows silent. I have never seen the crew so perfectly still. I want to ask questions, but I'm too afraid to break the seemingly mandatory quiet.

As the tiny sliver of land that had been off in the distance a few hours ago breaks into view, all I can see is a mountainous line of jagged rock and sharp cliff sides. I don't see any docks or a bustling village anywhere in sight. I glance over to Kiernan in question, though he is far too engrossed in what he is doing to notice.

When we round the ship toward the eastern cliffside, I begin to put two and two together. As the sails begin to be drawn, slowing the momentum of the massive boat to a snail's pace, a large cavern opening comes into view. Just large enough to fit a single ship.

I watch on with blatant wonder as Kiernan steers the ship perfectly between the rocks, the ship breaking through a curtain of coiling ivy at the other end of the short passageway. We are met with a slowly rising chatter of men coming out to greet the ship upon its arrival.

"Oh...wow!" I move to the railing, looking around the cave and its surplus of supplies.

The moment the ship is warped to the docks and the gangplank is drawn down, we all begin to move, working to unload the cargo. I can't help much in this department, but I can take a few of the smaller things off the ship with some hard work and gusto. I move to grab a few of them that are sitting off by themselves, but Kiernan stops me before I can even make my way over there.

"Leave those few," he instructs me, nodding toward the two small crates that I am going for. I turn on my heels and immediately go to see if there is anything else I could move.

Once the rest of the cargo is unloaded, Kiernan shuffles over to gather up the two parcels that have been segregated. He turns to Benedict, who is still waiting to be dismissed. "I have to take these where they go. Make sure Sitara is comfortable."

I step forward excitedly, curious as to where those particular packages go. "I could help carry one if you wanted."

"No," he says abruptly yet smoothly, "I'll be doing this one on my own." He walks off, turning to Ben as he does. "Get our new friend settled into one of the vacant houses on your way, will you?"

I turn toward Benedict with a questioning look, which receives a dismissive wave. "Don't worry about it." He throws his arm over my shoulder with a gentle squeeze. "How about a grand tour?!"

Oh, I'm going to worry about it. I want to know everything about him, to feel closer to him. I told him my biggest secret, about what had happened to me. I only want the same in return.

Saolo'ki approaches us from the side, his face a mask of external calm. I can tell he's nervous, unsure of what the future holds for him. I can't blame him. The unknown would—no, *has* terrified me in the past. I reach out and wrap my hand around his, giving it a gentle, reassuring squeeze.

He returns my gesture with a small smile before looking to Benedict. "I don't have anything to put in a home."

My chest clenches a little. I only had a taste of what life must have been like for him the last nine years, and that was enough for me. Slaves are seen as possessions; therefore, they don't have belongings to account for.

Benedict shakes his head, the understanding in his eyes softening his features far more than I think I've ever seen from the hound. "Most of the people Kiernan brings home don't. The house will be modestly furnished already. As for other items or wants, we work on a barter system, much like those in Puka'qui. I'll have Enna help you get your hands on everything that you may need outside of what is already provided by Kiernan."

I can feel Sao relax at my side, his lung finally inhaling as though a massive weight has just been lifted from his shoulders. Butterflies form in my belly as I think of the implications of Benedict's words.

Arthur was right again. Kiernan is a far better man than I gave him credit for.

With that finally established, Ben looks between the two of us and grins. "Let's go, you two."

As we walk along, I notice Saolo'ki making note of where each landmark is that Benedict points out: the village square where people congregate and town meetings are held, the barter market on the eastern side of the village, certain crew members' homes in case we would ever need to find someone familiar while here.

Sao's designated home isn't far of a jaunt from the market, only a level above. The village is built in levels, climbing up the inner cliff face by carved paths into the rock. It's a testament of engineering and utilization of the land around it.

Saolo'ki's new dwelling is modest, with barren walls, but the inside is warm and humble, with everything he would need to get started. A bed sits in the far left corner, with a quilt that looks to have been sewn together by hand. A wood stove provides warmth and a place for cooking in the little alcove to the right, reserved as a kitchen space. A wooden table sits in the center for company and meal times.

He will be okay here, and that is all that matters.

"I'll make sure Enna comes by before the end of the day." Benedict steps aside, letting Sao in to explore his new surroundings.

I can visibly see the shudder in his shoulders, as though everything—his pain, his fear—has finally melted away. It's like watching a bloom quiver and rise after a drought.

The turns, pulling me into a tight hug. I wrap my arms around him, savoring the gentle embrace of my friend, my kinsman. He places a kiss on my hairline, murmuring in a soft whisper. "Yechooma ot, sega asilama."

My eyes well up with tears—not of loss or goodbyes, for I know I'll see him again, but of relief to finally see him at peace. I pull back just enough to place my hands on either side of his face, pressing our foreheads together. "Mete lien vaheka uoi Maki laza ot chute aigvo."

As Benedict and I walk out to allow Saolo'ki some time to adjust, he glances over at me. There is only the sound of our feet scuffing the dirt for some time before he finally asks, "What did you say to him? It was rather long, wasn't it?"

I smile, peering up at him. "It means '*May the winds of Maki bring you good favor*'. It's how way wish each other well," I explain. I've never actually seen the God of Winds, but he's out there somewhere. Coli'hanu had said many of the gods decided to leave the temple after the War of the Great Divide, and scattered on the wind to different temples and locations around the world.

I'm surprised when we don't immediately walk back down the path toward the market, instead veering to the right. My brows knit together in confusion as I look up at him. "We're not going back into the main part of town?"

"I need to make a detour first," he says, quickening his stride until I'm practically jogging to keep up.

"Benedict Leighton!" A woman's voice rings out from behind us, causing me to whip my entire body around.

Ben's entire demeanor changes from the rough brute to something soft and gooey, something I've never seen before. The man is practically melting already, even before he whips around with his arms ready to receive the woman who is now nearly on top of him. The genuine smile that lights up his face is a new discovery, his arms wrapping around her slender frame.

"Miss me, did you?" he purrs. Yes, purrs. I've only heard growls and grating laughs that border on feral up until now, but the man is literally purring like a contented tiger.

"I missed *parts* of you," she teases, pressing her lips to his as she wraps her arms around him tighter, "He keeps you from me for far too long at a time."

I stand there awkwardly, taking a few steps back to give them some semblance of privacy. This woman must be Benedict's wife, the one I have heard about a few times during my time with them.

She's beautiful, absolutely beautiful. Actually, it's almost painful to look at her. Her hair is like spun silk, the honey brunette strands pulled back into a long braid. Each angle of her frame is delicate and defined, covered by olive toned skin that is as flawless as granite. Every part of her is symmetrical and proportionate in an almost inhuman way. Even her eyes, which unlike Kiernan's that are a profoundly vivid blue, seem different somehow, as if different hues of the color have been layered upon layers.

She must have noticed the subtle shift of my footing, her eyes snapping over to me as she pulls back from him. Benedict, on the other hand, has his face buried in her neck, leaving a trial of kisses as he goes. Her eyes trail toward my left arm, her eyes widening slightly.

"Benedict Theodore Leighton, please do *not* tell me he actually took that poor girl from Puka'qui!"

Hehe Theodore...

My cheeks flare with color at the prospect that she has heard about me before. I suppose I just didn't realize that I have actually been a topic of conversation.

"Fine," Ben mutters shamelessly against her skin, "I won't tell you that."

Trying to break the uncomfortable bubble that has now formed around me, I give her a shy smile. "Hello. I'm Sitara."

She smiles back at me with an unexpected reply. "I know who you are." She rolls her eyes dramatically, turning back to Benedict. "I can't believe you let him *do* that!"

She pushes her husband away, smacking him in the chest with the back of her hand. I have to stifle a laugh at the wounded puppy expression on his face.

"Hey, what did you expect me to do about it?" Benedict grumbles, trying to snatch her up again.

"Told him you weren't going to go shove drugs in my nose," I deadpan, the opportunity that flickers far too good to pass up.

Her mouth falls open in complete horror. "Benedict!"

That's when I receive a pained look of betrayal from the man himself. "Thanks for that, Sitara."

"*You* drugged her?!" Her eyes narrow for a fraction of a second before turning back to me with a grin. "I wish I could say he's a better man than that, but, obviously, I didn't fall in love with him for his virtue."

I let out a snicker, shaking my head. "It's fine."

"I, however, am going to combust if I don't get this dishonorable creature naked in our bed." She bites her bottom lip, grinning as she backs herself into his chest. "You'll forgive him, won't you?"

"I'll finish showing myself around," I laugh, watching Ben throw his wife over his shoulder without another word. I turn on my heels, letting their giggles and banter fade away as I continue down the path.

This gives me the perfect opportunity to do what I wanted to this whole time, which is find out more about Kiernan.

I roam aimlessly for a while, trying to catch sight of him towering over the others on the street. The usually infuriatingly clingy captain seems to be elusive today. And I want to know why. After weeks of being up my booty almost every second of every day, minus when I've gotten myself into trouble, he's never been this difficult to find.

When I finally spot him walking along a path that leads up to a seemingly secluded level of the village, I make chase, being careful to keep a considerable amount of distance between us. Watching him walk isn't something I've paid much attention to in the past, but now, watching his shoulders sway with each confident stride, makes my heart race.

I slip behind a fairly obscuring bush as he pushes through the trees toward a small, well-kept cottage with a reed roof. His home, perhaps? Why would it be so far removed from the rest of the village? Wouldn't the founder want to be closer to everything that is happening below?

I strain my neck to see, easily remaining concealed in the foliage.

The front door flies open, a wide grin falling across Kiernan's face as a young girl, who can't be any more than five or six years old, comes barreling toward him.

I don't think anything of it at first. There can be plenty of reasons why a child might be excited to see him. There were plenty of children who did the very same thing in Port Hammond.

Though the uncanny similarities in their appearance are what strike me as notable. She has the same auburn strands that frame her round, sun-kissed face. The same set in her jaw. The same eye shape, though they are a vivid green rather than blue. Even the cupid's bow on their lips is the same depth.

Kiernan quickly drops the crates just in time to wrap his arms around the girl upon impact. He swings her around excitedly, the giggling and greetings rising into the air. It isn't until a woman walks out behind the girl that I begin to grow uneasy.

Calm down, it could be anyone... right?

Her hair is a deeper brunette, very similar to the child's in length, as it flows down her shoulders in loose waves. Her blue-hazel eyes are wide, more of a rounded shape. They look similar, if you take in skin tone and hair color, but apart from that...

It's hard not to immediately rush to the conclusion of *exactly* what it looks like.

"Kiernan..." The woman's chipper tone carries through with a breathy voice. She looks tired, eyes slightly glazed.

"Rielle." It is the loving tone of relief in his voice that begins to crack my resolve for not jumping to conclusions. It is when he places his hands on either side of her cheeks, cupping them with such reverence as he kisses her forehead, that sends a sensation of painful tightness through my chest. My heart rages wildly under my breast as I watch the scene unfold. "What have you made for me? It smells so good! I'm liable to start drooling!"

Both the woman and the child giggle, tucking themselves into his waiting arms as he guides them back inside. I can't describe what I am feeling. On one hand, surely he wouldn't have brought some random ass woman onto his ship if he had a wife and a child, right?

Or is this why he had been using Benedict to hide me in town? Is that why he refused to let me come here with him?

Oh gods... oh no no no...

Am I falling in love with a married man?

Have I been reading every little thing as a play when really it hadn't been?

Have I just been used as a toy to entertain him until he could go home to his family?

Tears sting at the corners of my eyes as I hurry back the way I came, rushing toward the docking cavern and back to the ship. I can't be here right now.

I shouldn't have followed.

I should have kept my ass on the ship...

After all, ignorance is bliss...

And now I have ruined mine.

23
Kiernan

Sitara has barely spoken to me—no, barely looked at me—since the first day of our time at Rhazden. The only thing she has uttered to me is questions on when we would be leaving and when we would be going back to get Arthur.

Arthur... Always in the fucking way.

I can't say that I'm not disappointed. I had hoped she would like my little slice of paradise. That it would be just as entrancing to her as it is to me. Then again, I suppose she has lived her entire life in a paradise of sorts. Even at night, I can't get her to so much as look at me. She lies down long before I do, her back toward me, and remains that way until dawn. She washes herself up in our morning bath and immediately gets back out.

I don't get it.

I thought we had been doing well.

I *thought* I had been making headway.

When we dock back at Port Hammond, the three men whom we had left there are waiting for us along the boardwalk. Sitara is damn near down the gangplank before it is even positioned fully. I watch as she throws her arms around Arthur's gangly form, irritation boiling in my gut at the sight of him wrapping his arms around *my* girl in such a casual embrace.

I clench my jaw as I watch the moment between them unfold. Every fiber of my being wants to go down there and rip them apart. I hope he feels my eyes boring into the side of his skull like a searing hot branding iron. Only the sound of Benedict calling out my name nearby breaks my focus.

Well, sort of.

Jealousy grips my gut like tar.

She has her hands on his cheeks. His hands are rubbing her shoulders... I think I might be sick. I don't behave as though that is how I'm feeling, of course. Though it doesn't make it any less true. Sitara loops her arm into Arthur's as they make their way back aboard the ship.

Over the next few days, Sitara manages to avoid me at nearly every turn. She has spent nearly every waking moment talking with *him*. Even when I try to resuscitate our normal playful banter, she will give me short answers, give me any excuse she can to get back to the kitchen, or go sit at chow with Arthur.

Even when I try to find him other things to do so that I can keep his ass too busy to be in the damn kitchen with her, she will follow him around and help him with whatever bloody task I have plopped into his lap.

"It's only fair that I help him with his work when he's been such a help with mine," she will say when I raise the question as to why.

When I offer to help her in his stead, she simply tells me that Arthur already knows how she likes things and it would take more time, more effort, to show me than it would to just help him finish his tasks so that he can help her.

After the third full fucking day of being ignored, I seem to have found myself back in the damn nest trying to wrack my brain as to where exactly I went wrong. I thought I had done so well. I thought giving her time and space to come around was the best option; it was the right thing to do.

Yet, somehow I'm crouched in the damn crow's nest while Arthur is in the gully shoving his face full of her phenomenal cooking, with her scooched up close to him while she laughs and jokes with the crew, who have all come to love her to fucking pieces.

I'm lost in my thoughts when I notice the two of them walking out onto the upper deck toward the bow of the ship. I can't hear a damn word they're saying due to the wind, which is tossing my hair wildly this way and that. But what I can see is more than enough to sour my stomach, threatening to bring my supper back up my throat.

Sitara sits on the railing, with Arthur turned to face her as he leans against it at her side. She looks distressed about something, her beautiful face twisted up into a foul expression. Of course, she would go to him when something is bothering her.

She always has.

The only small glimpse into her heart I've managed to pull out of her was the night up here when she was having trouble with her scar. Other than that, I haven't managed to get her to say a word to me when it comes to what truly lies beyond skin deep.

Arthur mutters something, the grin on his face taunting me. The way he can be so casual with her, even when she's upset, without making things worse irritates the fucking shit out of me.

I can see Sitara's eyes widen slightly, the gears of contemplation swirling in their chocolate depths just before she abruptly leans in and presses her lips to his.

Every facet of my being is screaming. I'll throw him over that railing faster than the taste of her—the taste that he's just stolen—can leave his lips.

I'm sure he'll just love being reunited with his old cook buddy, Gerald, as I send him to the fucking sharks.

She's mine.

Mine!

Not his.

I'll take my damn dinner knife and peel the pink flesh of his lips right off his fucking face. Let's see him try to kiss her then.

I'm reeling as I watch Arthur pull away, his hands brushing over her shoulders gently. He says something to her, but I can't make out the words. Sitara leans her forehead into his chest, and my vision goes red. When he wraps his arms around her, stroking her back in soothing circles, I can no longer stand up here and watch them.

I swiftly climb over the ledge of the nest and slide down to land with a purposefully loud thud.

I'm going to kill him...

I'm likely to chip my damn teeth with how hard my jaw is working. My strides are long and deliberate as I close in on the two, my hands finding Sitara's waist to lift her from her perch on the railing. Once she's safely planted on the deck, I turn to Arthur. I fist my hand into the fabric of his shirt and push his scrawny ass over the railing. The look on his face is comical, fucking priceless.

I don't need words.

He knows what he did.

I take a knuckle-blanching hold on his long hair. His eyes are wide as I press him so hard against the railing that he very well may bruise.

If he lives, that is.

I can faintly hear Sitara scolding me. Wait, no... She is screaming in my direction, but I can't hear what she's saying. The ringing in my ears is too loud.

I have to remind myself that killing this wet noodle of a man is not in my best interest. So, if I can't kill him, I'll just threaten him within an inch of his fucking life. "One unholy glance in her general direction, just one, and I will fucking kill you." My breathing is so gods damned heavy right now that I sound like I've run laps around the deck just before coming to this abrupt stop. "What a shame it will be for you to have worked this long, this hard, and never get to see Rhazden. I suggest you think about that the next time you decide to touch what isn't yours to touch."

I roughly toss him to the side, jabbing my finger in his direction. "Keep your hands to yourself and your cock in your motherfucking pants, or I will remove it from your body with a rusty spoon and send it to Gerald as a peace offering."

I turn back toward Sitara only to see her back growing smaller as she rushes into the cabin. The door slams behind her with a deafening bang, eliciting the attention of several men walking up to the deck from dinner. My nostrils flare as I make my way to her, every nerve ending shot to hell.

I can feel those walls building back brick by brick, the facade snapping over my face with ruthless efficiency. I feel my heart slowing, feel my body falling back into itself just in time to throw the cabin door open.

When she isn't there, I move to the bathroom. The door is locked. Yet again. However, there will be no banging on the door this time. There will be no demands.

I swiftly turn on my heel, snatching the proper key to the door and walk back over, sliding it into the keyhole. It clicks open with a finality that makes my gut flutter, and I push it open.

Sitara is standing on the far end of the room, her back leaning against it as she tries to catch her breath. Her arms fold around her like a shield, but we both know how little that does anything in these situations, especially against me.

"Look at you, you naughty Kitten," I rumble, my shoulder resting against the doorframe as I hold up the key in response to her wide-eyed stare. "I haven't even taken you to the *Dancing Daisy* yet, but you seem to be a natural."

She looks up at me in confusion, and I know she doesn't understand what I'm talking about. But it's how I feel right now—like a fool being played like a fiddle.

"Kiernan..." She quivers out, her eyes bulging from their sockets. "It's not what it—"

"I know what I saw," I growl, cutting her off before that stream of lies can even finish exiting her lungs, "Or are you going to try to convince me that my eyes lie?" She takes a breath, attempting a response, but I shake my head. "It was *exactly* what it looked like."

Sitara cards her hands through her hair, rubbing her face on the down stroke. "No– It... Yes, okay, it was a kiss, but it's still not what it looked like."

"A kiss is exactly what I saw." I straighten to my full height, towering over her until she looks tiny in comparison. "I hope he enjoyed those precious seconds because I'll make his workload hell."

"Kiernan, you're not listening! I kissed *him*!" Her voice cracks as she takes a step toward me. "Yes, I love him, *platonically*. The kiss... I was confused!"

"Confused?!" I roar in irritation, stalking toward her. "What do you mean you were confused?! What could have possibly happened to confuse you to the point that you'd press *my* lips to another man's mouth?"

She groans out, the sound grating up her throat as more of a growl. She holds her fingertips to her skull, squeezing her head tightly until I can see her face turn red. "I... I thought that you... I thought that we were..." She struggles with her words, flustering herself even more as she tries to regain use of her tongue. "I followed you that day in Rhazden. I saw your little family, and I was trying to be logical and work through it before I went into a fit of ragged jealousy and made assumptions that I didn't know were true. So, I've been talking to Arthur. He told me that Becket had once said that the best way to get over someone was to get under someone else. I know it wasn't fair to Arthur, but I... I simply needed to move on. Like I said, I was confused..."

The anger instantly melts away, and I feel a warm laugh threaten to break through. I understand now. I get it.

I walk closer to her, reaching out to gently cup her cheeks in my hands. She pulls away to keep that distance between us, but I refuse her. Taking her chin in the crook of my hand, I force her gaze to meet my own.

"My sister... Sitara, Rielle is my sister." I see a parade of emotions slide across her soft features: comprehension, relief, then embarrassment. Her cheeks turn a beautiful shade of scarlet as she blinks.

"Your sister..." she says slowly, letting my words sink in, "So the child is..."

"My niece, yes." I can't stop the amusement that drips off my tongue. Sitara buries her face in her hands,

"See, this is why I was trying to work through things before I said anything... I was so sure I was just a toy for your amusement..."

My hand finds the back of her neck, pulling her toward me gently, yet firmly. I can't keep it in any longer.

"You have had me intoxicated from the moment you appeared before me on those docks in Puka'qui... I'll be damned if that bean pole out there gets the satisfaction of having you sit on his face, of you coming undone on his fingers, or learning what you taste like. I'll slit his throat faster than the smell of you can leave his nostrils." I swallow the knot of raw emotion that catches in my throat. "I'll be damned if he gets to touch what I decided long ago is mine."

She visibly shudders under my gaze, her lips parting every so slightly as her chin quivers. Tears begin to spill over her cheeks. The sight would normally anger me, but right now, all I feel is a deep tenderness, a tenderness that's been building for a while now.

And suddenly, all my walls are gone.

"You're leaking, Darling." I run the pads of my thumbs over the curve of her cheekbones, catching the salty perspiration with a reverent touch. Her eyes search mine, the faintest of sighs parting her tear-dampened lips.

"Then fix it."

24

Kiernan

That one breathy reply falling from her lips breaks every vestige of control that I have been scrambling to hold onto since she woke up on this ship.

The distance between our lips is gone in a matter of seconds, and I devour her mouth with a ferocity that surprises even me.

This is not a slow, sweet kiss like I've come to expect it to be.

No, this is raw, hungry; all tongue and teeth and the mingling of breath. It's a deep-seated need that fuels the fires of desire within my gut.

She tastes even better than the first time.

Perhaps because this time she is truly mine.

Even though I have already had experience with what her body molding against mine feels like, it's different.

It's not like the first time.

There's no resentment, no preconceived notions of spells or deception or manipulation.

I break the kiss first, boring my gaze into hers as she looks up at me with half-lidded eyes and glistening, swollen lips.

Gods, this woman...

"Stop me now if you expect me to leave you in Puka'qui…" I rasp out, my hold on her tightening.

I can't tell where the line of my possessiveness stops and my plea begins anymore.

And that is fucking terrifying.

I don't want her to make me stop. I want to gobble her up and leave nothing behind, fuse myself under her skin until she can't live without me.

Just like I can't live without her.

But I know, now that my tongue has parted those beautiful, luscious lips, that one inch further and letting her go will not be an option that doesn't kill me.

She lets out a shuttering breath, the air from her lungs wafting over my face and I breath it in like it's the only thing I need to survive. Sitara's bottom lip draws between her teeth, her eyes darkening, pupils browning wide with desire.

It's an image I will remember for the rest of my fucking life.

"I don't want to stay in Puka'qui," she says, her voice barely above a whisper.

She's mine.

Of her won volition, she is choosing to be mine.

It's all the permission I need.

All the validation I require.

My hands are around her before I can blink, fingers digging into her asscheeks as I lift her into my arms. Her legs immediately band around my waist, and I find her responding with eager compliance.

My mouth finds hers agains, nipping at the supple flesh of her lower lip before soothing it with my tongue, eliciting a pretty little gasp. My teeth scrape along her jawline, a hungry growl escaping the depths of my chest. Every nerve is alive, searing my flesh everywhere her skin makes contact with mine.

"I am not one of your gods," I rumble, pressing my lips to the hollow of her throat. "So I'll be damned if I don't worship you in every unholy way."

She cranes her neck, letting out a needy sigh that goes straight to my aching cock, and willingly offers more access to every expanse of skin I can reach.

The scrape of her nails across my scalp forces a shudder to ripple down my body, pooling at the base of my spine. Her equal hunger is intoxicating; the sudden grinding of her hips as they seek friction is almost too much to bear.

My hands slide around to the laces on the back of her dress. While I have never had any trouble unlacing pretty things before, I'll admit that I'm struggling to focus on what my fingers are *trying* to do.

"Off," I demand, growling against her lips.

I have us over to my bed in three long strides, tossing her gently onto the mattress before I join her, sitting back on my haunches.

I grip the collar of her dress in my hands, destroying it with a burst of effort and a twist of my wrists. The sound of the fabric ripping between my fingers melts with the delicious sound of another gasp. It's enough to send me reeling.

"Much better."

Sitara sits up, her fingertips exploring the hills and valleys of my torso. The sensation alone is enough to force my muscles to flex and ripple under her touch as she runs trails of fire along my skin. My head falls back with a grating groan as the feeling of her tongue leaves wet paths along my throat.

Fuck...

If her tongue along my neck can make me quiver like this, I can only imagine what it will do when she runs it along my cock.

Running my hand along her shoulder and down her toned arm, I take hold of her wrist. I can't stop myself from guiding those tantalizingly soft fingers to the hem of my shirt, sliding them underneath. The agonizing suspense of the journey from my chest to my tented pants is met with no hesitation at all.

To my depraved delight, she immediately starts fumbling with my waistband. The moment she's able, she dips her hand in and wraps her fingers around me.

Her palms are like silk against my heated flesh, sending an electrified current of pleasure up my spine. Each torturously slow stroke solicits a groan from my throat. The feather-light nips along my hipbones as she prostrates her face down toward the one place I want to feel her most, where I can revel in her touch the most, is enough to send stars streaking across my eyelids. The warm breath that ghosts over my sensitive skin as she frees my throbbing length forces my hands into those fiery locks of hair.

It takes all of three euphoric seconds to realize that letting her stay in this position can't happen yet.

She'll be my undoing before I even get the chance to taste her. I refuse to be the three-stroke Timmy I warned her about all of twenty minutes ago. I pull myself from her lips with a groan, the wet pop of her mouth as I slide free enough to make my already boiling blood evaporate through my skin. The wide-eyed look that meets my own glazed gaze makes my mouth water.

The way her pink tongue darts out along her lips is enough to make a grown man sob with need.

"Not yet," I tell her, "I want my sheets soaked in your sins before you have the chance to undo me."

I run my hands along the silky smooth expanse of her body, marveling at the feel of her under my calloused palms. I take in every curve and plateau that makes up the beauty that is Sitara. Filling one of my hands with her pert breast, I roll her pebbling peak under my thumb. Her responsiveness as I trail my other hand down her side, enjoying the raised prickling of her skin, sends the heat in my groin to a fever pitch.

The way her body curves and bows off the bed as she keens under my touch, giving me greater view and access to her already exposed flesh... damn...it's everything. Everything in this moment.

The silk-like feel of her leg sliding up my side is enough to make me work for a bated breath, a shudder rolling through me in unison with her trembling form.

Wrapping my arm underneath her, I slide us both further onto the bed. I lean back against my pillows as I kiss her so deeply, I swear she can taste my thoughts. *My gods...* The pounding of her heart just beneath her skin is an attestation to the pleasure that is building. My hands slide up her back, pulling her to meet my mouth once more in a filthy kiss.

I'd never get enough of this; of tasting the honeyed recesses of her mouth, of feeling her tongue so eagerly dance with mine with the same passion and hunger that I never knew I needed. I could easily become addicted to her touch, in the way her fingers glide over my heated skin, like her brother is addicted to his opium.

No, I *am* addicted to it.

I've *been* addicted to it from the first moment her bare skin touched mine in that tavern.

Only my vice is sweet and salty, warm and fucking consuming in all the right ways.

Swallowing her groans, I throw her leg over my body to place her in exactly the position I wish for her to be. I guide her hands to the headboard in a silent instruction to grip the smooth cherry wood with those beautiful hands.

I kiss down the ivory expanse of her neck, nipping at her collarbone before continuing downward. I stop momentarily to lavish attention to her chest, rolling the still hardened peaks with my tongue, grazing them with my teeth.

Her hands card through my hair, to which I respond with a groan before removing them and planting them back onto the headboard. A dark chuckle intumescens up my throat as she growls out in protest. I have just taken her ability to touch me back, and the writhing that has already begun to commence dispatches a sense of pride through me.

"But I want to play too," she whines, the sound like saccharine fruit.

"You can play when I've finished having my fun," I growl, gripping the plush globes of her ass as I lift her upward until she is straddling my face. The whimper that escapes her as I nibble the supple flesh of her inner thigh brings a satisfied grin to my lips.

I blow a cool, teasing breath over her sensitive skin, watching with pure male satisfaction as she quivers above me. I draw her body to my mouth, laving the flat of my tongue from perineum to clit. The taste of her arousal fills my senses, forcing a contented moan to rattle up my throat, vibrating through her body. Her taste is as sweet as molasses, like sin and salvation wrapped up into the most delectable little package.

A gratified swell forms in my chest as I watch her head fall back with a sharp intake of air. My fingers dig into the smooth flesh of her hips, silently instructing them to move against my willing tongue. The sudden compliance sends a rush of quenching pleasure straight to my groin.

Her moans cause a stronger form of desire to take over. It isn't a simple need like hunger. No, it's a taut, elastic compulsion; a burning need to ravage her until she is nothing but an incoherent mess above me.

"That's it, Kitten, purr for me." I revel in the sight of her knuckles blanching against the grip she has on my headboard, her broken moans rising into the air around us, "The louder you are, the harder we play."

I alternate my tongue between broad strokes and tight circles as her moans grow louder.

"Such a good girl," I praise, reaching up to pinch her nipple between the pads of my index finger and thumb.

My free hand lends a resounding smack to her rear, echoing in my ears. Immediately, my hand grips the reddening flesh hard enough to dimple beneath my fingers.

Sitara laments and thrashes above me as her spine bows forward, allowing herself to drown in the throes of pleasure I am providing. I want to overwhelm her senses until I am the only thing present in her mind.

"More. I want more." The sound of her desperation fills my ears, muffled only by the quivering thighs that I'm wearing like a perfect pair of earmuffs.

My tongue plays roughly against the bundle of nerves as I oblige, sliding a single finger into her quivering depths. "Then more you shall have."

The cry that rips from her throat is enough to set my insides ablaze.

Such a wanton little thing, isn't she? So pliant and easy to respond. It amalgamates pride with my already searing arousal like cream to coffee.

A low rumble breaks through my lips as she moves her hips against my tongue, the erotic display drawing my eyes up her body as she keens and begs for friction.

"Another?" I ask, just before strengthening the intensity of the finger I already have occupying the depths of her warmth.

This gives her no time to answer before I have her mewling above me in supplication.

"Yes," she clamors out harshly with raging breaths.

The sound is sweet, dripping like seductive honey even as her tone rages with demand.

I lap at her like a man starved, sliding another finger deep within her. I curl my fingers; the sensation of her quivering against my face causes a deep ache to take over.

"Fuck... Look at you," I praise gruffly, her pleasure beautifully evident in the way she shudders and drips down my wrist.

I slide my head out from between her thighs, my fingers never wavering from their duties. I can feel myself pulsating with need, the strain of blood flow down south too much to ignore with ease. I lift to my knees behind her, removing my fingers. She presses back with a growl of protest, eliciting a wicked smirk from my lips. I angle myself just enough so that my length will give that bud the friction it has been begging me for, my shaft gliding between her thighs with such ease that it makes me moan.

My grip instinctively tightens on her hips as she rocks herself against me. This little vixen is already going to push me to the edge of insanity.

Her feverish panting echoes in my ears as I hold her frustratingly still against the bare skin of my pelvis. My left hand slides up her spine until it tangles into those purifying locks of fire, gently tugging until her neck cranes back to expose that beautiful expanse of skin to my hungry lips.

Trailing open-mouthed kisses along her pulse, feeling it flutter under my mouth, I whisper between each press of contact, "What do you want, Kitten?"

My hips roll forward with a maddening slowness that forces my jaw to lock tight with effort. Each whine that escapes that infuriatingly tempting mouth chips away at my resolve for control, forcing my muscles taut with restraint. When her back bows, her hips lifting to present herself in the most mouthwateringly wanton display, a strangled chuckle—dark and filled with barely contained desire—rips up my throat as I glide myself through her slick heat in taunting.

"You have to use your big girl words." My breath ghosts over her ear, my teeth grazing along the lobe to elicit a full-body shudder that fills me with satisfaction.

"I want..." her breath hitches in her throat as her nails practically chip away at the headboard she is still grappling for purchase on, "I want you. I want to feel you inside me." She rolls herself against me for emphasis, her eyes locking with mine over her shoulder. Those smoldering russet orbs damn near level me with their intensity.

"I'm going to need that pretty word from your lips." I can feel the temperature of my body reach a fever pitch, no longer satisfied with the mere play and tease. "Say please."

Before she even has the time to let the word quiver up her throat, I press myself into her inch by agonizingly delicious inch.

I stop halfway, giving her body a chance to acclimate to the intrusion. The sheer heat of her body is enough to strangle a groan from my lips as I continue forward seconds later, driving myself to sheath until I bottom out in her warmth, my pelvis flush against her ass.

She lets out a cry, the sound a mixture of pain and pleasure. It doesn't take long for her to give me the sign I am looking for; that subtle roll of her body that urges me to move.

However, I have no intention of moving until I wring out the one thing I'm craving, her complete submission. Despite my aching love for her, it is an addiction I can't smother out; the need to hear her beg for me. Just as I have been dreaming about all these years. I pull her head back into an almost back-breaking angle, reveling in the sounds of her blissful enjoyment of my manhandling.

"Do you still want it?" I question with a deep, smooth as whiskey taunt, "There's more waiting for you. All you have to do... is say... please."

As I wait for the word I know will be spilling from her lips in a matter of seconds, my free hand obliges incentive as it explores every curve and hollow of her body. My hands move over her smooth skin in a worshiping fashion that belies the growing sadism within me. I find myself lost in the sensations of her until a strangled whine breaks through the sound of our combined breathing.

She rolls her hips, forcing me to feel every inch of her clamping down around me as though her mouth isn't the only thing begging.

"Please," she croaks out, her voice like music to my ears. So sweet, so pleading, so perfect. "Please, please, please."

She's practically mewling like a kitten begging for cream, and it far exceeds the expectations I have built up in my mind these last few weeks.

With a triumphant growl, I wrap my hand around her throat, squeezing just enough to cut blood flow and make her see stars.

Pulling out slowly, I snap my hips forward, our combined cries of bliss filling the room.

"You feel so good wrapped around my cock," I praise, my restraint gone as I rut into her. My chest swarms with pride at the stream of growled curses and the sight of her eyes rolling.

I begin to set a scorching pace, my free hand moving back to settle on her tailbone. "Tell me, Sitara... Who does *this* belong to?"

I emphasized the word with a particularly deep thrust of my hips, the sound of her sweat-slicked skin against my own, a symphony of debauchery that I will never tire of.

"You, Kiernan..." she cries breathlessly between whines of rapture, "Only you!"

"That's right," I growl into her ear, unable to keep the wicked grin from my face as I plow into her again, my pace growing relentless with a newfound abandon.

She growls, dipping her chin to capture my thumb in her mouth. Her tongue swirls around the digit, tasting the remaining evidence of her own arousal on my skin. Saliva drips down her chin and I can no longer take it.

I have to see it; I have to watch her face as she comes undone in my arms. Without so much as a warning, I flip her around and settle back into pace between her thighs as I slam her back into the wall above the bed.

"Oh!" She arches into me, her hands digging into my shoulders as her petite frame meets me thrust for thrust, wild and untamed. I savor the feeling of her claws as she finds purchase in my skin, the intensity making stars swim behind my eyelids.

My mouth meets hers in a clash of desperation, swallowing down her whimpers like the finest wine.

My left arm wraps under her tailbone to keep her steadily where I want her. My free hand slides down the dip between her breasts, the smooth skin of her torso, until finally my fingers find their mark between us.

Oh fuck... She's absolutely soaked; so wet, so warm, so perfect. The sensation of her muscles quivering and tensing with pleasure under my expert touch, the feel of the vibrations as she growls against my lips, her body pulling me in as though I am the only one who has been built to fill her like this. It's all so perfect. So right.

It's in this moment that I realize she is everything I want, everything I crave, everything I *love*.

I groan as the sensations and realization flood through me.

Never has any woman brought me to my knees like this one has.

Never again will any other woman bring me any satisfaction.

No other woman will ever feel as good against me.

There will be no other woman after her.

Not after this.

"No one else will ever compare, Sitara," I rasp, "No other woman will ever touch what is yours. I am wholly, irrevocably yours."

25

Sitara

The world is quiet as I lie here savoring Kiernan's warmth, his words resonating in my mind like a soothing melody. Him telling me he is mine, giving me that claim, fills me with a foreign sense of pride and belonging. My fingers trace idle patterns along his broad chest, my cheek pillowed on his shoulder. Our breathing is shallow, though sleep has yet to come to us. Every so often, we can hear a hoot or holler from outside the cabin door from a crew member.

They heard us. And to be honest, I don't care.

We've stopped in one more port since that night, and it is to this date the best experience I have had. Kiernan stayed by my side, showing me landmarks and shops he thought I would enjoy. I even managed to convince him to let me see the haggling process. He only had to snatch me up one time when a man said something offensive to Pip, but at least I didn't get into too much trouble... Unless too much trouble consists of being tossed back in bed.

I enjoy being this close to him; close enough to see the subtle freckles dusting his shoulders, the crisp lines of his muscles moving downward over his torso, the way the light catches the subtle hints of auburn in his hair, or the fact that his left eyebrow is naturally arched slightly higher than his right. He's a marvel, a sculpted work of art in motion. It isn't until he looks down at me with those icy-blue eyes that I realize I have been staring at him like an idiot.

His lips twitch as though he's attempting to stifle a chuckle, his eyes filled with mirth as he closes them once more. His head burrows back into the pillow with a smug grin. "If you've left something on my face, I expect you to fix me."

He peeks back down at me with half-lidded eyes. "Otherwise, you staring into my soul may lead you on journeys that you are wildly unprepared for, Darling." I roll my eyes, quirking him a half-sideways grin. The snicker that escapes his lips makes him seem younger in this moment, his free arm tucked behind his head as that slightly higher arch in his bow cocks upward.

I lean into his palm as he moves a strand of my chaotic locks from my cheek. "I was simply admiring—ogling, if you will—or is that a privilege only afforded to men?" I grin, lifting my brow in playful response.

"Oh, by all means," he gestures to himself, "if you wish to '*ogle*', as you so delicately put it, I'm on display for your perving pleasure." My mouth falls open with an exasperated scoff, smacking the back of my hand lightly against his chest. He laughs at me, grabbing hold of my hand to bring my wrist to his lips for a nip. The simple act causes my blood to sing through my veins, heat rising to my cheeks.

"If you think what I've been doing is '*ogling*' you since you've been here, I hate to redirect you to a more crude phrasing, but '*perving*' is more accurate." He flashes me a roguish grin. I watch him, my eyes following his movements with a tentative curiosity.

"You don't have women on board often, do you?" I chuckle, rolling over to my side to prop myself up on an elbow.

He clutches his nonexistent pearls in a gesture of playful offense. "Whatever gave you such an idea?!"

I laugh, hearty and genuine. I like him this way, casual and relaxed, as though I am getting a glimpse of the playful creature beneath all of the brooding sexual tension that has been crackling between us for the last few weeks.

"No," he finally answers with a shake of his head, "You would be surprised how many women turn down my gallant offer to join a ship filled with smelly, sex-starved brutes who would likely take turns tapping in rounds of coital wrestling on the lass if I didn't have control. It might also surprise you to know that I do not have the patience for more than one emotional being aboard my ship at one time. Arthur is a handful."

I throw my head back in amused laughter, shaking my curls around my face as I roll my eyes at his jab toward my poor Pip. "He's a good man, Kiernan. You are too hard on him."

I watch as his lips twitch slightly. "Of course he is. I would not have him working on my ship if he were not." He pauses, stroking my hair as he grows more solemn. "However, if he thinks even for a second that you are-"

I cut him off with a chaste kiss to his lips, shaking my head. "He doesn't have feelings for me, Kiernan. Not beyond that of a friend, that is."

I push myself up into a sitting position, leaning back on my hands as I run my foot along his leg beneath the sheets. "He has someone at home waiting for him." I smile fondly, remembering the way Pip's eyes had lit up at the mention of his love, Millicent, and his desire to earn his way into Rhazden with her in tow.

His brows raise as he gives me a sidelong glance that is laced with a flare of jealousy. The look rears an unwanted sense of guilt swirling in my gut. I had made a mess of things between him and Arthur, and I feel horrible about it.

"That kiss might suggest otherwise," he grumbles, shaking his head as if that could remove the unwanted image he no doubt still harbors in his mind.

I let out a sigh, giving him an apologetic look as I move to straddle his thighs, resting my arms over his shoulders. "I'm sorry. I allowed my confusion to cloud my judgment. I took Becket's words too literally and didn't catch the joking tone in which Arthur said it."

I pepper his face with feather-light kisses; along his forehead, down the curve of his cheekbone, his nose, to the corner of his lips. "I kissed him, and he pulled away. That's when he explained everything to me."

He laces his fingers around the small of my back, holding me flush against his bare chest. His voice reverberates through my body as his breath ghosts over my face, our noses brushing against one another in a tender gesture. "Then be a dear and explain it to *me* before I feel compelled to introduce him to dear old Gerald."

The intimate moment is momentarily clouded by confusion, having heard the name a few times, my brows knitting together as I blink. "Gerald?"

"It's not important," he grins, urging me to explain the conversation I had with Arthur. We would come back to that Gerald thing later.

"Her name is Millicent. Arthur said they have known one another since they were children, and even now, he writes to her every day. It's rather sweet, really," I muse, a soft smile tugging at the corner of my mouth, "According to him, poor Milli has not had an easy life... Pip wishes to bring her to Rhazden once he has earned your favor."

He chews on the inside of his cheek, those mesmerizing blue eyes drifting to the ceiling as he takes and digests what I have told him. I can see the wheels turning behind his pupils, the subtle tension in his shoulders. "New crewmates serve three years before I allow them to move to Rhazden. It has been that way for everyone who has ever lived there, apart from your Sao. By the way, it really is an abuse of power for you to beg me like that."

I slide myself to sit between his knees, my legs still thrown over his thighs as I lean back and look at him, my own wheels turning. "Why is that exactly?" I cock my head to the side, resting it on my shoulder.

"Rhazden is mine. It is a haven I have found and created to keep Rielle safe." His tone shifts, tense and possessive with a hint of something deeper. Rage, maybe? "I'll take you to meet her eventually. I'm just hoping for lucidity when I do."

My brows furrow slightly, noticing the subtle changes in his posture, in the way his muscles twitch under his sun-kissed skin. There is a story there, and I'm not sure if I should even push the subject.

"I suppose I understand why you do it like that," I keep my voice gentle, whimsical in a way, and glance up at the ceiling as well. "Pip is almost done with his three years, isn't he?"

He nods stiffly before shifting his glance back to me. I can see the ticking in his jaw. "When we left him at Port Hammond, that was the last time he would be left behind. His three years are finished, and he'll be coming to Rhazden the next time we dock there."

My heart swells with joyful affection. Pip did it. He can go get his Millicent and bring her somewhere safe. The idea fills me with a gleeful camaraderie and pride. "Good, I'd very much like to meet her. If she's half as enjoyable as her counterpart, I could see us being friends."

"The heavens may implode at such a thing." He chuckles, the smirk on his face a clear indication of the pride he has in himself. His hand slides under me, pulling me back up into his lap. "Speaking of privileges of passage, have Mundanes ever been in the jungles surrounding your villages before?"

I savor his warmth as his hands draw soothing lines up and down my back. I close my eyes, enjoying the scrape of his calluses on my skin. "Yes, but it's a bit of a process. I think it's happened maybe once in my lifetime."

"I've always wondered what you all keep hidden beyond those damn trees," he flashes me a roguish grin, "What's so interesting that it keeps you tethered to it?"

I stare at him for a moment, trying to decide how much I should say. By the time I am done warring with myself, I let out a sigh of mock annoyance and flash him a grin of my own.

"Potem'aku." I watch the blank stare that slides on his face, forcing a laugh to bubble up my throat. "The Temple of the Sacred. It's where our gods live."

"Potem'aku..." he repeated the word back to me sloppily, I press my lips into a thin line to keep from laughing. "Calee'Hanu...Teao'Kane...Goola'See."

I can't stop the incessant giggling that bursts from my lips, spitting accidentally on his face. I quickly wipe his cheeks with my hand, his own cheeks brightening. "Those *are* their names, right?"

I nod, impressed that he knew them at all. "Coli'Hanu, Teo'Kan, and Gula'Ci." I repeat back to him, exaggerating my sounds as I point to my lips.

"Yeah, that." He gives me a look of confusion. "I'm pretty sure that is exactly what I said." He motions for me to continue, seeming surprisingly interested in my world. "What's so special about Casey, Tyler, and Greta that keeps you all so devout?"

I furrow my brows at him, pinching his nose between my thumb and forefinger. "Coli'Hanu, Teo'Kan, and Gula'Ci are the sources of our power. We all share the bloodline of at least one of them."

"Does everyone from your island have god-given special powers?" he teases, tugging on a strand of my hair until I let go of his nose, "Or do Janice, Harold, and Martha pick and choose their favorites?"

"I have never heard of anyone not having magic in their blood. *Coli'Hanu*, *Teo'Kan*, and *Gula'Ci*," I emphasize again, scrunching my nose at him, "Do not have '*favorites*'... However, some of us have rarer powers than others."

"And what are those rare powers that Margaret, Ted, and-"

I pinch his cheeks between my fingers, squishing his lips into a pucker. "Say them with me, Coli'Hanu, Teo'Kan, Gula'Ci." He says each one with me, his face filled with amusement.

"You know, if I had known taking you off that beach would result in my face being manhandled by your spindly little fingers, I might have thought twice about it," he teases.

"So why'd you do it then?" I question him with a grin, a silent challenge to continue our banter. "Surely, I find it a bit hard to believe that anyone would kidnap a random woman off a beach just because she had an inkling for adventure."

"Ah, but it wasn't just an '*inkling*'," he purrs against the shell of my ear, forcing a slow shudder down my spine, "Was it, Kitten?"

His lips trail across the soft line of my jaw. The feeling has me swallowing a stifled groan, my heart fluttering in my chest like a giddy schoolgirl. "No, my pet..." his voice lowers an octave, his rumble vibrating through my chest. "You were *marinating* in it."

In one swift motion, I find myself pinned beneath him with his breath ghosting over my face. His lips hover just slightly out of reach.

"And it was *delicious*."

26

Sitara

I lie in the sheets, attempting to catch my breath, just as the sun is beginning to filter in through the windows. It isn't until now that I realize just how much time Kiernan and I have spent in this bed over the last ten days. The thought has me cracking a small chuckle as I roll over to look at him, propping my head up on an elbow.

"You know, your crew probably thinks I've tied you to this bed by now."

He grins down at me, cocking a brow. "I doubt you have the skill to tie me to the bed. You couldn't even undo the one tying you to my bed the first night you slept in it."

I shoot him a mock look of offense, rolling my eyes as I puff my cheeks playfully. "Who said it had to be a physical rope?" I grin back at him, a smug gleam in my eyes as I tuck myself into the covers again. "Besides, I was taught by someone better than you. After all, if it wasn't for Ben, I would be sailing away in a dinghy right now."

He opens his mouth to make some witty comment, but is cut short by a pounding on the bedroom door. The sound of Pip's disgruntled voice, muffled by the heavy wood, reaches us seconds later. "Please tell me you two are decent?"

I slide down into the covers, Kiernan shifting his body to block out the majority of my nude form. I peek over his shoulder as Arthur opens the door, sticking his copper-locked head through the opening. "'Bout to dock at Catcher's Bay, 'Cap."

At the mere sight of Arthur peeking his head into the room, Kiernan takes a firm grip on his pillow and hurls it toward his face. Pip ducks out of the way, causing it to hit Benedict, who is standing a solid three feet behind him.

"You lot act like ducklings who need their mother to follow!" Kiernan yells in their general direction before burying his face into my hair, "Go dock my fucking ship before I cast you all out or start your three years from scratch!"

I giggle into his shoulder at the comedy of the scene unfolding in front of me. After almost six solid months aboard this ship, I've come to enjoy and even appreciate the banter between them all. It certainly keeps a girl entertained.

Arthur rolls his eyes playfully, scratching an itch on his jaw as he bellows. "Aye Aye, 'Cap! Though I gotta ask... When was the last time the sheets were washed?! Smells spicy in here."

Kiernan slowly lifts his face from my hair and gives him a nasty grin. "You know what, you're *absolutely* right, Pippy ol' boy. Be a good chap and get on that for me, will you?" It isn't a request, and everyone within earshot knows it. I can hear snickering from behind Arthur as he gives Kiernan a look of dismay.

"I think I'll stick to only washin' sheets with my own fluids on them."

"That was a decision you could have made before your ass decided to become my little bitch boy, Artie." My shoulders shake with silent laughter as Kiernan speaks, trying my hardest not to start cackling.

Pip gives me a disgusted look, pointing to Kiernan like a small child throwing a fit after being told no. "You gonna let him treat me this way, Starlight? I thought you *loved* me!"

I peek over Kiernan's shoulder again, a smug grin on my face as I shrug. "He's da 'Cap."

Kiernan buries his face back into my hair once more, flipping Pip off from over his shoulder. To my response, Pip hangs his head, muttering low to himself. "Damn it..."

Pip turns to leave with a grumble. Just as he is about to click the door closed, Kiernan throws the blanket back without any inkling of shame, enthusiastically thumping both feet onto the floor. The brisk half-skip toward the door, butt-ass naked, has me rolling in the sheet in a cackle. Kiernan throws the door back open. "Hang on there, sport!"

Pip watches in wide-eyed horror as Kiernan's naked form moves toward the armchair in the corner.

I can't breathe, laughing until my face is red, as he exaggerates his walk with a dramatic hip sway, his elbows swinging high out to the side. Kiernan rips the throw blanket off the back of the chair and spreads the fabric wide as he hurries back to me with a wide grin. "Come here, you spicy little cabbage."

I can barely move from laughing so hard, my ribs aching so badly, I feel like they might split in half. I manage to pull myself up just as he reaches me, and I wrap my arms and legs around him. He secures the blanket around my body and begins stripping the sheets from the bed. Tossing each item at Arthur's face, Pip attempts to dodge them but fails miserably. The poor guy is hit with every article of fabric besides Kiernan's left sock. "You can't dodge worth a shit, Artie Boy. Remind me to send you below deck if we ever get hijacked." Kiernan laughs, using his foot to slam the door in Arthur's face.

When we are alone in the room once more, Kiernan turns his face and sniffs the air. His nose scrunches up into a playful grimace. "Damn, we do smell ripe."

I gap my mouth into an 'O', feigning offense. "How dare you insinuate that I smell anything but lovely, enchanting, a blessing to your senses!"

"You can be a blessing to my senses after our bath. Until then, you are a rotten cabbage."

"I suppose you believe you smell better?" I lean in, sniffing him under the earlobe. "Nope, decaying cucumber."

"Is this your subtle '*female*' way of telling me you're hungry? I assure you, my cucumber is anything but '*decaying*'."

Pip comes back hours later with the sheets that now have holes in them from his scrubbing. He holds the fabric up, looking through one of the tatters with a grimace. "They won't *come out*!"

Kiernan chuckles darkly as he finishes getting dressed for the day, as I sit on the armchair, lazily swinging my legs off the armrest as I wait. "Oh, I knew they wouldn't," Kiernan's voice is filled with a sick pride that almost makes my cheeks burn, "You'll be taking your '*best friend*' to town to get some new ones."

"Then why did you make me wash them?!" Pip groans in dismay, throwing his head back like a salty child.

"Don't interrupt me again. Next time you'll hang with Gerald."

Arthur's look of terror gives me pause.

Who the fuck is Gerald?!

As we sail into port at Catcher's Bay, I realize very quickly the significance of this place. The residual presence of my people can be seen under the towering wooden homes and shops that hang off the sides of the cliffs. Crumbled ruins, etched with carvings that tell the stories of the Kana'te people, lie buried beneath poor excuses for architecture. Something deep within me mourns the loss of a place I have never set foot in. However, I do remember the stories. Stories that stretch back thousands of years to a time long before the great war of 1245, when our people were not so isolated from the outside world.

I feel Kiernan's furrowed brow from where I am standing, taking in all the history, long removed and tainted by those who do not appreciate it. I'm sure he can see the disgust that has crossed my face, though 'crossed' isn't the right word. Nothing is fleeting about how I am feeling right now.

He walks up behind me, caging me in as his hands settle on the railing on either side of my body. The warmth of his chest seeping into my back does little to warm the ice that has formed in my blood. "I'll take you to see them all as soon as I can free myself from boring 'pirate' business." He rests his chin on my tense shoulder.

My eyes scan the area around me, trying to allow his, what is now, calming presence to ground me to the here and now. It isn't as though the Mundanes had taken this place from us. We left it after the war. Still, it makes my teeth grind to see how little respect they have as a whole for the Kana'te culture and beliefs.

"I would like that," I say softly, giving him my most convincing smile.

He kisses the top of my head with a heavy sigh. "You'll have to spend the day with your Pip today."

I can tell he isn't looking forward to the 'business' he has to tend to, but I also know he will do whatever must be done to acquire the medication for his sister, which he had explained to me earlier in the day.

He's already explained to me why I can't go with him, and I under-stand it completely. So, Arthur and I will be going to the other side of the village to look at whatever our little hearts desire, so long as we stay away from Hemon's Alley.

He had explained that Hemon's Alley is the worst part of the village. Catcher's Bay isn't exactly considered moral to begin with, but that particular area is said to harbor the lowest of the low. I shudder to even think about the fact that Saolo'ki and I would have most likely been taken there if Kiernan hadn't gotten to us in time.

"Think you'll survive?" he teases.

I can tell the shift in the atmosphere of those aboard this ship as we finally dock. It's clear that even among fellow thieves, Catcher's Bay is not a place this crew wants to be.

"I think I can manage," I nod, tapping my fingers on the railing in front of me. "Just be careful."

Kiernan kisses the back of my head, breathing deeply against my hair before sauntering off toward the gangplank and disappearing into the sea of people.

"Alright, Starlight, ready for one hell o' a good time?"

I turn around to find Arthur's cheeky, dimpled smile staring at me, excitement for a day of fun instead of work laced on his face. His grin quickly falters at my, apparently, obvious distaste.

"Well, now, that face doesn't say, *Aye, Pip, let's go romp across Catcher's Bay and have a grand ol' time*, now does it?" He puts his hands on his hips in playful disapproval before leaning in to whisper, "Did Mister Cap' put his foot in his arse again?"

I shake my head with a woeful smile, sighing heavily as I look back toward the village. "No, his foot is no longer up his rear. It's just sad to see my people's structures so... so..." I can't even finish the sentence. What would I say? So disrespected? So crumbled and ruined? All of which are completely true at this moment.

I can tell that he notices the hesitation in my words, quickly wrapping an arm around my shoulder to pull me in tight against his side. He ruffles my hair, which I worked so damn hard to pull back as neatly as I could this morning.

Dang it, Arthur!

"Well, you can tell me all about what's crawled up your arse then." He chuckles as he tugs the tie out of my hair, *'freeing the fire'* as the crew likes to call it. I yank my tie out of his hand, shooting him a mockingly stern look.

"I worked hard on that!" I whine, attempting to put my fiery locks back in place in vain. Pip laughs, leading me toward the gangplank with his arm still slung lazily around my shoulders.

"Nae, you get too worked up over your hair, Starlight. It is meant to be free!" He jests as we plant our feet onto solid land.

"It's not that I get worked up over it." I raise my chin in defiance. "It just gets in the way, so I put it up so I can see."

"Mhm..." he shoots me a knowing look, his eyebrow quirking up in amusement, "And the sudden wish for it to look pristine has nothin' to do with wantin' to look good for a certain captain." My cheeks burn brightly as I squat at him. Though I have to admit, I appreciate the temporary distraction from my earlier unease. He chuckles under his breath as he moves us toward the dilapidated, poor excuse for a town.

The entire town is unbelievably neglected. Most of the wooden slab buildings are missing boards, and the roofs are caving in above their heads. They obviously don't have respect for their own way of living, let alone mine.

Then, he takes a less jesting tone, side-eyeing me with friendly concern. "Tell me what's on your mind, Sitara."

I take in a heaving sigh, looking around Catcher's Bay. "It's just... Look at this. They have no respect for what they've built, let alone what they've covered." I point to one of the buildings further up the cliffs, the beams that hold it in place on the edge of the rock bolted into a mural now no longer discernible.

Arthur's face twists up into a sympathetic smile, his gaze following my line of sight toward the mural, then back to me. "No offense, Sitara, but... What can you expect from people who have been cast aside by their own gods? I mean, you can't blame them for it, can you?"

I look at him, confusion lacing my brow as I process his words. "Cast aside? No one cast the Mundanes aside." I keep my words gentle, though the realization of just how uninformed most of his people are about their own history, the *true* history, eats at my core. "We left because we were told to leave."

I watch as his brows stretch up to nearly touch his hairline. "Told to leave? That's not what we're taught." I know he isn't arguing with me. No, he is simply stating a fact about his rearing. "We were always told that the Cante people were bein' greedy with the magic o' the gods and because the Cante people were favored by the gods, they were able to convince them to go with them, leavin' the Mundane to drown in their own insignificance."

I sit there blinking up at him for a long moment, my eye twitching subtly, trying to wrap my head around his words. I raise a brow, unable to keep the look of bafflement from my face. "You think that is how the gods work, do you?" A small smile creeps up on the corners of my mouth at the sheer innocence of his understanding. "First of all, '*Cante*' is the word your ancestors used to call us '*Holy dogs*'." I give him an understanding smile as a look of shame washes over his face. "It's okay, but next time, try the term '*Kana'te*'. And secondly, that is not what happened at all."

Pip slides his hand into his pocket, his lanky body slumping slightly as he takes in the implications of my words. "Educate me then, lass," he cocks his head slightly, tilting it toward me with a sidelong glance, "If I've been taught wrong, then speak your truth."

I take a deep breath, trying to decipher the best way to keep this history lesson short and sweet. "Firstly, the gods didn't abandon anyone, nor did they favor any one people," I start, raising a brow to keep the snarky banter going with our facial expressions. I let that sink into his delightfully thick skull before continuing with far less tongue-in-cheek. "It's said that at one point, we all lived together fairly peacefully. Some were born with innate gifts, others were not. It didn't matter; everyone helped everyone. I was told it was a world built on neighborly respect. But, over time, the Mundanes became wary of the

Kana'te people, increasingly seeing us as a threat. The war was waged based on nothing more than prejudices and perceived dangers."

I take a moment to run my fingers along part of a stone wall that is now nothing more than a heap of crumbling rock. "When the Mundanes demanded that we leave, the gods decided to isolate all traces of magic on Capulli'ana. It's why I'm not allowed to use my abilities outside of the island. We left to make your people more comfortable."

"So..." His voice is soft but contemplative, "Basically, we were all taught that the Mundanes were victims, that we were abandoned and left for dead basically, when in reality, Mundanes pushed the..." His brow knits together deeply as he tries, in earnest, to use the appropriate terminology. "Kana'te? Did I say that right?"

I laugh, shaking my head with an amusement that belies the seriousness of the conversation. "Kah-nAW-tAy. Not CAn-A-Tee. But good job for trying." I pat his shoulder, rubbing his back in a friendly gesture.

"But we aren't victims," he continues after flashing me a look of gratitude for my linguistic lesson, "We just pushed you all out?"

"That's what it says in our history books anyway," I sigh, nodding solemnly.

We sit in a semi-comfortable silence for some time, neither of us knowing which way to steer the conversation. "Sooo..." I finally break the silence with a small smile, "Have you written to Millicent much recently?"

His face lights up at the sound of her name. The clear display of joy just by the mention of the girl warms my heart. I can tell he must love her very much.

"I have," he rakes his fingers through his messy, wind-tossed hair. "She obviously can't write back, since she never knows exactly where we will be or when we will be there. But I did tell the tale o' you and your nasty stained sheets." He laughs at the redness that creeps up my neck and into my cheeks.

"You did what?! That's a horrible first impression, Pip! Believe it or not, I *want* to be friends with her. Now I'm just going to be '*nasty sheet girl*'!"

He gives me an ornery grin. "It's better than '*naked deck girl*' or '*kitchen slave driver*' or even '*wall-rattling moaner*', isn't it? Though I'm sure she will think o' you as those things too after the horrible light I've painted you in, Starlight."

I smack the back of my hand into his gut, sticking out my chin with a dramatic flourish. "Is introducing someone by their name a foreign concept to you? You could have just said '*Wow, my new best friend, Sitara!*' But noooo... You had to give details!"

"Aye! I needed her to have the full experience!" He throws his arms wide and laughs before returning his hands to his pockets, a contented sigh filtering through his lips. I roll my eyes, shaking my head as a rush of nostalgic warmth spreads through me.

"You know, you remind me so much of how my brother was when we were children; before life decided to kick us both in the butt." My lips press into a thin line as I recall the last conversation Larkin and I had before I was so '*rudely*' taken from the beaches of Capulli'ana.

There is a long, sullen silence, mostly due to my putting myself into a mood. I'm beginning to realize quickly that I am good at doing that. I take a moment to try to compose myself and remove Larkin's last words to me from my mind. Even though I know he wasn't in his right mind when he said it, I still don't deserve to be talked to like that.

After a few more minutes like this, I look over at Pip, clasping my hands behind my back as I sway with dramatic innocence. "Soooo... .speaking of siblings... What exactly is wrong with Kiernan's sister?"

Pip's body tenses, and I watch him stretch as if he is uncomfortable or trying to come up with a way to answer me without getting himself into too much trouble.

Or both. Probably both.

"Rielle?" he asks as if there were any other answer. I give him a look, narrowing my eyes into slits both in play and threat. "Right, right... O' course you mean Rielle. Um, have you asked Cap' about her?"

That would, indeed, seem like the logical way to go about it. However, I haven't particularly tried to bring her up due to the look that passes through Kiernan's face anytime her name is whispered in the wind. It's subtle, but it's there. And it bothers me.

"Nnnno... I haven't. I'm just curious. From the way you're acting, I'm going to assume whatever it is isn't great."

"The most I can say is that she...well, she ain't well." He tilts his head side to side as if he is weighing his words carefully with each one that comes out of his mouth. "She's the reason the crew comes here in the first place, so that Cap' can get somethin' that helps her. It's only available here in Catcher's Bay."

Pip scrunches his mouth to the side and gives a one-shouldered shrug. "Cap' only tells the minor details o' the story to those who are about to be allowed into Rhazden. He only tells the story once, and you're expected to keep it in the back o' your mind. Rielle is to be treated with the utmost respect. You could say she's kind o' the royalty o' Rhazden. She is the one thing that can get you kicked out o' Cap's place with no trial or chance to plead your case."

I take his words in one syllable at a time, a shudder rolling down my spine. I can't be certain, but I feel a sudden kinship with Rielle. As though she and I might have more in common than anyone would guess. It's just a hunch, though, a small intuition that I don't want to linger on too long.

We make it a few more feet along the shops and vendors before I look up at him, the aching suspicion gnawing at my insides. "What do you mean when you say she isn't well?"

Pip's eyes dart around as if looking for anything else to talk about. His gaze lands on a group of people just inside one of the alleyways between shops. "Well, ain't that an odd lookin' group o' people!" he motions to them to distract me.

At first, I open my mouth to protest until I follow his line of sight. My blood runs cold as I halt, my muscles coiling tightly. Every fiber, every tendon, every cell in my body begins to scream danger. Screams at me to run and hide. To leave Arthur in the middle of the street and seek refuge on the ship.

My eyes trail first to the intricate Pe'aboros of swirling black smoke and sickeningly beautiful white scales that have been laid to cover their original tribe tattoos. My heart rate begins to race, whooshing in my ears to deafen me.

Oh god... shit... fuck fuck fuck...

One of them turns toward the direction that Pip and I stand, my heart clenching in my chest and dropping to my feet. There, smack dab in the middle of his forehead, is the brand. The unfinished diamond-shaped sigil with intersecting lines through it screams like a beacon against his pale skin, all plague-inducing greens and infection yellows in color. The mark of death itself... or rather, himself.

"Sitara?" Arthur's voice finally breaks me from my momentary trance, my head snapping up to look at him with—what I am sure are—eyes the size of saucers.

My toes have gone numb, every sensation in my body narrowing into a pinprick at the base of my skull. I need to get out of here. We need to get out of here.

Mustering up the will to speak, I grab his arm and tug him back the way we had come, "We have to go. We have to go *now!*" My voice comes out in shaky, strained bates of breath as I take off toward the ship at full speed. Pip shouts for me to slow down, confusion lacing his voice. But I do not stop. I refuse to stop until I have made it back to the ship.

Back to Kiernan.

Everything else around me falls away until it is just me and the remaining distance to the ship. I don't care how many people I have to topple over and shove out of my way. All I care about is getting the fuck out of here. I can faintly hear Arthur in the background apologizing to people as he tries to catch up to me. But I am faster. More agile. And at this moment, I don't care if I leave him miles behind me.

I bolt up the gangplank, coming to an abrupt halt as the remaining crew on board begins to crowd around me, concern etched in their features. I rest my hands on my knees, my entire body quivering as I attempt to catch my breath.

"Sitara," Kiernan jumps up from where he is leaning against the mainsail mast. I can faintly feel his gaze trying to break through the buzzing of my skin as he assesses my trembling form.

"Where the hell is Arthur?" He barks, wrapping me up in his arms. He holds me firmly to his chest, stroking my hair in a soothing motion. It would be soothing if I weren't on the verge of a complete panic attack.

My ears begin to ring, my feet growing more unstable until all that is holding me upright is him. I can't control my breathing. Gods know I am trying to, but I can't. It's coming out in sharp, fast gushes that seem to have a life of their own. "Whose hands am I severing? Whose tongue do you wish on a platter?" Keirnan fumes, growing increasingly angry with each passing moment, and my panic grows.

As Arthur runs up on deck, wheezing like he'd just run the entire expanse of the bay, Kiernan turns to him, my body still trembling against his.

"What happened?" he demands, the hand in my hair fisting firmly yet gently in my curls.

"I...I don't know Cap. We were walkin' down the street and happened upon some strange-lookin' folk. After that she ju-"

I cut Arthur's words short as I tugged at Kiernan's shirt, my words trying to break through my raging lungs. "We have to go! We have to go!"

He looks down at me with confusion seeping from every pore of his face. He tries to soothe me with his voice, something that might have worked in any other situation. "Go? Darling, you're safe. I've got-"

I cut him off, shaking my head frantically until I think I might fall over from the dizzying action. "No, no, no! I am not safe, no one is safe. We have to go!" My voice grows into a shrill squeak as I try to tug him to the helm. "Kiernan, they're here. In Catcher's Bay."

By this point, I can barely believe I'm still creating coherent thoughts. "Who is here, Sitara?"

The very thought of admitting what I saw in the alleyway out loud makes bile rise in my throat. I shove the feeling down as I wrap my arms instinctively over my lower abdomen. "The Maggots... Hu'yimona's cult is here...."

27
Kiernan

My insides are on fire. She had told me a few things about what had happened to her all those years ago, but never in great detail. To hear the story in full, to know every single detail of the hell she had gone through from such a young age...

I am doing my best to keep the inferno that is my white-hot rage bottled up until I've left the safe space I have created for her. I stay next to her, holding her, stroking her hair, and listening to everything she needs to tell me. Once she is finished, still trembling like a damn leaf, I hold her until her breathing slows, becoming even and shallow, before extracting myself from her side.

Slowly, quietly, I make my way to the door. I'm not surprised to see the crew that adores her so much, all crowded around the pathway to my door. Concern is etched in every line of their faces—even Joffrey, whose first real interaction with Sitara had led to him being tied upside down from the ship, is looking at me as though he had been praying this entire time that she was going to be alright.

As soon as the door latches shut behind me, I allow the fiery rage to show, the blaze of my glance landing on Benedict. "We are casting immediately. Once we are adrift, I want you to make sure every single man is on the upper deck in five minutes. No one is to leave until I release them." I storm to the upper deck just as Benedict begins to bark out orders for cast off to the few members lazing about.

Everyone kicks into high gear as Benedict comes to join me at the helm. "It isn't good, is it?" He glances at me, recognizing the pure *fury* raging behind my eyes.

I gnaw on the inside of my cheek, biting down until I can taste the coppery tang coating my tongue. I can feel my nostrils flare out like a bull, raging toward that red banner with a coursing determination.

"Heads will roll," I growl.

I can feel Benedict staring at me, trying to assess whether this is the time to be my best friend or my first mate. He chooses wisely, letting me stew while he finishes organizing the crew as I had told him to.

I stare down each of them, bracing myself for the information I'm about to deliver. "We have to go back to Capulli'ana. There will be no stops in between."

We need to get her somewhere safe. To warn her people of the dangers they thought long gone.

I run my hand through my hair, letting out a sigh that sounds more like a growl. "Alright, boys, listen closely. I don't want to have to repeat this more than once. If any of you so much as make a mention to my girl about what you are about to learn; if there is so much as a quiver of her chin because you couldn't keep your damn mouths shut, I will hang you from the mast and let the blood drain from your skulls."

Their eyes all widen as I speak, and there is a unanimous single nod given. They all know I'm serious. Hence why Gerald is probably still being digested.

"Not'a word, cap'n," Joffrey's slurred words ring out over the crowd in a solemn tone.

I have to brace myself to continue, steeling my mind to keep the bile that is churning in my stomach at bay. "There are some dangerous people in Catcher's Bay, people who—until just now—Sitara and the rest of the Kana'te people thought to be dead. We have to get back to Capulli'ana so that Sitara can warn them that these people, this *"Maggot Cult"* as she called it, are still very much alive."

An uproar of murmurs begins to emanate from the group, each one voicing their grievances as though there is a fucking choice in the matter.

"A cult? What kind of a cult?" Benedict asks, his face falling into a look of unease.

Henry, a deck swabber in his fifth year with me, grinds out, "What would old-god cultists want in Catcher's Bay?"

I raise my hands to silence them, "Alright, enough. All Sitara told me was this: When she was a young child, members of this Maggot Cult–followers of Hu'yimona… Don't fucking ask me to pronounce that again. Anyway, they began picking up followers all over the island, including her parents. They began stealing livestock and waging battles along the expanse of the jungle. According to her, they wanted to expand outside of Capulli'ana. They succeeded." I motion back toward Catcher's Bay, which is slowly becoming a small sliver of land on the horizon.

The murmuring grows louder once more, the crew becoming more and more restless as they feed off one another. "I wager those cursed deities be the ones that sent 'em!" Joffrey spouts off with a clearly groomed distaste.

"The gods are just a myth, you stupid fuck," Todd snaps out with a shove of his fat fingers on Joffrey's shoulder. The unrest begins to grow, fueling my rage to a fever pitch.

Just before I am about to lose my ever-loving shit, Arthur steps forward with a pale-faced look of dread. "Wait, what does a cult have to do with Sitara, Cap'?"

My fingertips lose all feeling as the implication of Arthur's question sinks in. This is the part I *really* don't want to discuss. The issues that affect my Darling directly. My lips press into a thin line as I lean against my navigation table, rubbing my hand across my face. The murmuring tries to rise once more, eliciting a growl from my throat.

"All of you, shut the fuck up!" Benedict shouts, his voice grating against his clear distress. The crew falls silent, looking to me as they wait for me to place my thoughts together.

"When Sitara was eighteen years old, the Maggots began taking young women of *"proper breeding age"* from all the villages in the area. Nine young women were taken and sacrificed to this *'Cultist god'*. Only one walked out alive. That woman was Sitara."

The crew sucks in a breath in unison, every single one falling completely still, utterly silent. Some men avert their gaze to the deck, others stare at me with a horror that mirrors the sickening twist in my guts.

I don't tell them everything she told me. They don't need to know. They don't need to know what they did to her before lining her up at that altar. They don't need to know that she didn't walk out of there without her lady bits almost spilling out of her body. They don't need to know that she still—even after being rescued from death's grasp—almost didn't make it.

Arthur looks around, his skin a sickly green pallor. "You...You don't think they will try to take her again... Do you, Cap'?"

I clench my jaw, nearly seeing stars due to the intensity of the act. I know that I will not rest easy, not until this is dealt with. "They come anywhere near this ship and they will be met with a gruesome end," I speak between gritted teeth, feeling the crunch of my molars in my mouth.

This is a topic I'd rather skim over and, because of who I am, that's exactly what I'm going to do. "We have just enough supplies to get us to Capulli'ana. I will be rationing the food myself. I don't want to hear any extra bitching about the portions. The faster we get there, the faster this shit can be dealt with and my girl can rest easy." I give a rough wave of dismissal, "Get to work. Now."

Every man begins to scramble out of my sight to make themselves scarce and get to work. I walk toward the railing, leaning against it to look over the deep expanse of the ocean as though I am expecting one of the Maggots to poke their head out of the fucking water. After all, some of them are from the Cali'ako tribe, and some of those people have the power of Aquamancy... Someone could very well be following us below the waves, and we would never be the wiser.

Benedict walks up beside me, silently mimicking my lean on the rail as he looks over the water as well. "Alright, Kiernan. Where is your head right now? I know that look."

I let out a long, tense sigh and grace Benedict with a sidelong glance. He knows me too well. It makes me want to throw him overboard and see if he can find someone lurking in the murky depths below. Of course, that's just my inner turmoil talking at the moment. "What look? The look of *oh fuck, some crazy, human-sacrificing hoard could be after my woman*? Is that the look you're referring to?"

I turn my body, sitting down to lean back against the railing, trying to use the movement to calm my rising panic. "Or is there some other look you're seeing? Perhaps one of '*Shit, I have to take her home and hope that she still wants to get back on this ship when everything is over*'?" I swallow deeply, leaning my head back against the cold wood.

Benedict says nothing at first, but then slowly drops down beside me. "Do you really think she wouldn't come back with you?" His eyes bore into my skull, the question hanging heavily between us like a stone thrown into a river.

I suck in a sharp breath. "Can you tell me that there isn't even the slightest chance that she would stay there in the safety of her island?" I rake my fingers through my hair and let out that breath. I hadn't realized I had been holding it in anticipation of his answer. As if he could read her mind, or she had told him anything that would ease my spiraling thoughts.

He looks up at the sky, now beginning to paint with the colors of dusk, and sighs heavily. "Look, K. I watched you stalk her for three years. I might not have felt the same way as you did, but I watched her in that port every single year. I've never seen her face look so... alive." his voice brooks confidence, as though he truly believes what he is saying to me. "And besides," he pauses, a small smile trying to tug at the edge of his lips, "Sitara isn't the type to hide away under a blanket the rest of her life."

I give him a forced smile, one that probably looks more like a constipated two-year-old, then I look back at the water. "She's not."

He is right about that much. After everything she's been through, after everything that has happened, she is a fighter. I don't know any woman who would stand on the deck of a foreign ship, surrounded by over a dozen men twice her size, and still be willing to clock a man in the balls in front of them all

My mind begins to wander into thoughts of what exactly I would do if she decides to stay in the safety and familiarity of her village.

Would I drag her back to the ship kicking and screaming?

Or would I let her go?

Neither of those ideas makes me particularly happy.

My train of thought is interrupted by the muffled voice of Benedict, who is once again trying to speak to me. "You know, I never thought I would see the day when the great Captain Kiernan Slater would find himself nothing more than a love-drunk pup who doesn't have the confidence to think his love would stay with him. She does have her little hook in you, doesn't she?"

"I told you she had *bewitched* me," I cock a brow at him, "You didn't believe me." I know now that Sitara hadn't actually put me under any spell. But my point still stands.

She might not have used magic to do it, but I am still completely and utterly at her mercy with a single look. The memory of seeing her running up onto this ship, breathless and terrified out of her damn mind, floods back to me. I had never seen her like that before. Even when she was scared to death of *me*, I had never seen her so broken, like a rabbit caught in a snare. I never want to see that look on her face again.

Benedict brings his powerful hand down on my shoulder, patting me as he hoists his muscular body up onto his feet. "Yeah... Guess I owe you that glass of mead, huh? Now that you won't be wasting my money on naked women you won't even touch." He shakes his head with a soft chuckle, shoving his hands into his pockets as he makes for the stairs.

I shoot him a glare. "I didn't waste your money. *You* did."

He pauses, turning toward me with a determined set in his jaw. "Just so you know, not a single man on this ship would let anyone take her without a bloody fucking fight. She might be your woman, but she's *our* girl."

28

Kiernan

The journey to Puka'qui has felt so much longer than it usually feels. Even sailing straight through, the miles have felt like tar under the ship. Finally, however, I see the familiar sliver of land come into view, the distinctive mountain of Capulli'ana stretching into the sky like a forgotten fortress.

Good, my muscles might unclench now... maybe.

I look down from the helm, my eyes landing on the fiery flames of my darling's hair. She's smiling, talking with Arthur, who has put in almost as much effort as I have to get her talking again.

Almost as much effort.

It had taken me two days after our quick departure from Catcher's Bay to even get her to come out of the cabin at all. Fuck, I had even attempted to send Arthur in there to get her to come out from under the covers.

Now that right there is the actions of a desperate man.

It took me every bit of a week to get her to talk, about a week more to get her to smile and joke with the crew again. We all put in the effort to try to help her reclaim her fire. The fire we all love so much.

Benedict's words ring in my ear again for the hundredth time. *"She might be your woman, but she's our girl"*. I suppose I shouldn't take all the credit for her improved mood, though I certainly will take most of it. After all, I didn't see anyone else whispering in her ear in the dead of night, crying to ease her fears in any way that they could. And if I had, they would have been dead by now anyway.

As the sliver of land begins to take shape, I give Benedict a nod, which signals him to start prepping the men to dock. I descend from my place at the helm and amble my way over to her. Arthur takes that as his cue to leave us be.

Good man. He's learning.

I wrap my arms around Sitara from behind. "I wish I made you smile like that," I tease, nuzzling my nose into her hair as I trail my lips down to the nape of her neck. I can feel the shiver that creeps along her skin, which excites me. "I suppose I'll have to try harder," I purr into her ear, watching with glee as the hair on the back of her neck rises with goosebumps.

In my youth, I thought the most prideful thing was satisfying a woman between her legs but while that is still a grand feat to be sure, I've enough experience now to know that these little reactions are what makes the ticking time bomb all the more explosive. Even more so with my cute little kitten.

She turns her face, the remnants of exhaustion still apparent on her features, to look at me over her shoulder with a small, slow, sultry little grin. She knows that look gets me every time. My little kitten has her claws back.

Finally.

"Maybe you should, instead of sulking at the helm all morning." She chirps playfully, leaning back until her shoulders are flush against my chest.

I rest my chin on the top of her head, humming contentedly. "Miss me, did you?" I let my voice rumble deep in my chest so that she can feel the vibrations. "I can fix that," I tease, just as I look to Benedict, reminding me that I *do* still have to guide the ship to its proper place.

I let out a sigh just before an idea strikes me. "Let's test out those skills, shall we?" I take her hand in mine, pulling her along behind me toward the helm. She groans, acting like her feet suddenly become filled with heavy sand. "You know I hate it when you make me do new things." I chuckle, pulling her more insistently.

The unsettling feeling creeps back into the pit of my stomach. Dread? I'm dreading docking in Capulli'ana. The anxiety of her not wanting to leave with me eats away at my stomach. I do my best to shove that feeling down while I direct her in docking the ship, but it won't go away, gnawing on me like a rabid dog, and I am the scraps.

Once we have dropped anchor and the men begin lowering the gangplank, tying us down, I spin her toward me. "You're coming back with me..." My brows furrow deeply as my eyes search her face, looking for reassurance. Part of me feels like a fool, trying to beg without begging. "Leaving with me... right?"

Her bright eyes rove over my face. At this moment, I have never felt more exposed. I can feel the air in my lungs leaving in bated breaths as she finally smiles up at me. "Of course I am."

I run my thumb over her chin and lower lip, grazing the skin ever so lightly as I do. Pure, unadulterated joy surges in my chest at her words. That is all I need to hear to shove those gnawing thoughts away for good.

Or so I thought.

The hair on the back of my neck and arms stands on end as I hear the voice of her brother, damn near screaming her name from the docks. I spin around to look at him just as she perks up and rushes down the staircase. I stare him down, something about his demeanor as he bobs and weaves through the crowded dock to reach the gang-plank of my ship not sitting well with me.

He's not keeping her here. He's too late, and I'll make sure he knows it, too.

He walks up onto my precious ship, meeting her at the bottom of the stairs that lead up to where I am standing. They wrap one another up in an embrace, and that is when Sitara notices what I have already noticed. "You... You look so healthy! When did that happen?"

Larkin rubs the back of his neck, a self-deprecating chuckle falling from his lips. "Not long after you disappeared. I couldn't stand the idea that I was the one who ran you off like that."

I watch her pull away, looking up at him with a furrowed brow. "Ran me off? You didn't run me off." I listen as Sitara starts telling her brother about the joyous little adventure she has had with me, Larkin's face darkening in disbelief with each second that ticks by.

I walk slowly down the stairs to meet them, and as my foot reaches the last step, I am met with a bone-crunching fist to the face.

I let out a grunt as I stumble back, the stairs causing me to take a forced seat upon impact. Honestly, I hadn't expected her brother to be that ballsy. However, this isn't my first rodeo with a broken nose, and it probably won't be my last either.

"Larkin! What the hell?!" Sitara jerks him back, her voice a shrill shock.

I place my fingers on each side of my poor nose and, with a firm, quick, calculated push, I reset my bone. The sickening crunch of the nasal bone popping into place makes Sitara cringe visibly. My eyes water slightly as I spit my precious blood onto the deck of my ship before standing. "Strike a nerve, did I?"

I give a bloody grin as I step into my place beside his sister. She immediately goes to fussing over my face, wiping some of the blood from my lips.

"What the fuck is wrong with you?" she turns toward Larkin, her brows knitting together. The look on Larkin's face as he looks from me to her, and then back to me, makes me want to point my finger and boast like a damn child.

Ha! Motherfucker.

But I am a grown man, after all, and have far more dignity than that.

"Are you *kidding* me, Sitara? Djar and I have been worried sick about you, and you are *enjoying* yourself? This fuck took you off the beach like a sand-dollar and you're upset that I punched him?"

Watch this shit, asshole.

I nuzzle into her hand as she tries to wipe more of the copious amounts of blood from my face, my eyes never leaving Larkin's as I do. "Aye, I did, didn't I? Such a pretty little sand-dollar, in fact."

Larkin goes to lunge at me again, but Sitara stops him with her own body. He halts, his eyes practically bulging from his eye sockets at this point. "Are you—Sitara! You can't be serious right now. He's... He's a fucking psy-"

"Psychopath. Yes, yes, she's already brought that to my attention many times." I grin, pulling Sitara back to my side.

I can feel her eyes boring into me as she silently scolds me for adding fuel to the flames. She should be used to it by now, after all. I give in and look down at her, shrugging one shoulder as if to imply that I hadn't done anything wrong.

She looks back at her brother, sighing heavily as she holds her hand up in an attempt to placate the situation. "It's not what you think, Larkin."

Oh, it *absolutely* is. I know that he knows that she doesn't know what he thinks it is. I also know that he knows that I know we men are on the same page.

"No, it absolutely is," I say with a smug grin.

It's like lightning flashing across Larkin's face as he pales, a growl rumbling low and threateningly in his chest. You know, this is exactly why many Mundanes think Kana'te people are savages. "You didn't... Gods, Sitara! You can't possibly think this man loves you!"

Well, shit, that was a low blow! With wide eyes and flared nostrils, I jab a finger in his direction. "Fuck you!"

This fucker has no idea what I do or do not feel, and his comment is so far off the mark that I am offended.

The sizzle of electricity dancing along his body makes me sneer and roll my eyes. Larkin growls, shoving his finger back at me. "Why don't you take two long strides away from my sister, and we'll see how fucking tough you are then."

"Is that a threat?" I narrow my eyes, clenching my jaw tightly.

"It sure as fuck wasn't a compliment, you fuckin-"

Just as things are starting to get heated, and I think I might have to fight this motherfucker, a rush of chilling cold sensation spreads across our bodies, the temperature just cold enough to elicit a yelp from Larkin and force me to step back a couple of feet.

My eyes snap to Sitara, who is panting heavily, emerald flames dancing across her skin and hair like delicate flower petals dancing on the wind. I watch in awe as her hair ebbs and flows like it is one with the flicker of beryl that caresses through it.

It's a beautiful thing to see her in her element.

Part of me feels guilty for being so dead set on taking her away from the one place she is allowed to access this side of herself, but I quickly push that feeling aside as she shakes out her limbs with a sigh.

"Gods, that feels good," she muses before turning to stare both of us down with those beautiful eyes, both threat and promise swirling within them, "Now, if you two will shut up for two seconds, we might be able to resolve something here."

The two of us stare at one another in tense silence, neither of us willing to break eye contact or say anything more to one another for fear of another freezing ice dump in Sitara's cold fire.

"Well," she looks between the two of us, "I am hungry. Let's go to the tavern, eat, and have a decent conversation like adults instead of gabbing like children."

Once we have chosen a table in the tavern's dining hall, I make sure to slide into the seat next to Sitara, leaving Larkin a seat across from us for when he comes to rejoin our merry trio. He had hesitantly stepped away to take, what he claimed to be, a much-needed piss while we walked inside.

I turn to my woman, propping my cheek on my hand as my elbow sits on the table. "Every rude thing that boy says to me," I cup her chin in the palm of my hand, "You'll be taking care of later." I lean in to brush my lips against the shell of her ear, my voice filled with mirth and playful threat. "Every. Single. One."

The arch of her brow rising is fucking adorable, her lips attempting to tug upwards into a grin, which she denies. "Is that a challenge?"

I straighten myself as Larkin makes his way to our table, disgruntled by the fact that our only available seat is not next to his sister. "I would consider it more of a threat," I whisper as he takes his seat with a huff.

He's refusing to make any sort of eye contact with me now. We each give the slightly annoyed waitress our food requests before Larkin looks at Sitara with a grumble. "I still don't know why you couldn't keep your dog at home for this conversation."

I grin, tapping my forefinger on her thigh once. "That's one, Pet," I whisper melodiously, watching the pretty dusting of color rise to her cheeks.

Let's count, Kitten. I know you love games.

"Knock it off, Larkin. Can we please just have a half-decent dinner?" She frowns at him, lifting her chin defiantly.

"I'll do my best," Larkin bites out hoarsely. *Clearly*, the fuck can't help himself. Right now, that seems to be working in my favor. My hand slides more firmly over Sitara's thigh, and I can feel her press her leg more firmly together at my touch.

"I'm serious, Larkin. You don't get to sit here and lecture me about my life decisions."

Yeah, Larkin.

I scoot a bit closer to her, starting to roll the hem of her skirt between my fingers. I make sure to let the backs of my fingers skim the soft skin of her inner thigh as I do.

Let's see how well you play this game, Pet.

Sitara leans forward, propping her arms on the table as though she is preparing for a heart-to-heart conversation with her brother. We both know, however, she is simply trying to hide what is going on underneath the table right now.

"Okay, I know alright? I'm the last person who should be lecturing you about anything but..." he pauses, running his hand through his hair in exasperation, "Are you at least going to have enough leash to write and visit?" He glares daggers in my direction.

That makes two.

I tap two fingers on the inside of her thigh, feeling the shudder that rolls through her body.

"I do not have a leash," she scoffs, rolling her eyes.

Not yet, you don't... Although... Fucking shit, Kiernan! Pay attention!

My hearing cuts back in as Larkin says, "I don't understand it. But if this is really what you want... and that *thing* isn't forcing anything on you... I just want to know that you're safe."

Oh, don't you worry, bud. She's safe.

I wedge my fingers between her thighs, inching them closer to my intended target. I momentarily tighten my grip on her leg, signaling her to relax and let me pass.

We play by my rules, Kitten.

Sitara slowly unclenches her muscles like a good girl and opens her mouth to go on a tangent. I can tell she's trying to ignore the sensations that are washing over her. It isn't working, though. I won't let her ignore the heat I can already feel radiating from between her legs. "I am safe. All of the men are very respectful, and I'm very well taken care of," she insists, her voice growing tighter by the end of her sentence.

Yeah, you are.

"I do my very best to ensure that she is *well* taken care of," I smirk at Larkin, who snarls in my general direction.

"No one is fucking talking to you," he snaps.

I run three fingers up to the apex of her thighs. There is a satisfaction blooming in my chest at the fact that he is unknowingly making my plans for the evening more and more enticing with every few words that he lets come spilling out of his stupid face.

I stifle a growl that threatens to rumble up my throat at the dewy heat that meets my fingertips. Sitara shifts slightly, attempting to ward off the lump in her throat, given the way she is swallowing. She is doing a fairly good job at pretending her arousal is discomfort by frowning at him.

"Larkin... Stop it. I am enjoying myself. I'm having fun."

Her brother rolls his eyes, scoffing with mock acceptance. "Oh, yeah, Sitara. I'm sure sailing around the world with a goddamn lunatic is such a fucking joy."

That is four, motherfucker.

I slide my fingers to their intended destination, slipping them into the wet folds that are telling me just how much fun she's having. I'm baffled that her brother is so incredibly ignorant of what is happening just under his damn, unbroken nose. I can feel her stiffen against my touch, and I clear my throat in a nonverbal chide for her actions.

"It is, actually," she bites out in response to Larkin's brazen comment, chewing on the inside of her cheek to keep from reacting.

Larkin rolls his eyes, digging into the food that has been brought out to us. I look down at my food, realizing that my hunger has shifted to something completely different.

"I assure you, she has found great joy in her time with me." I stick out the tip of my tongue from between my teeth, waggling my brows at him.

The slight gasp that Sitara gives as I curl my fingers inside of her wouldn't necessarily be noticeable to someone who wasn't listening for it.

But gods, I am fucking listening for it.

I keep eye contact with Larkin, finding too much pleasure in defiling his sister right in front of him while he's none the wiser.

Perhaps I am a fucking psychopath.

He growls at me, not in the slightest ignorant of my meaning. "I'd chop off your fucking hands if I could for what you have done."

You mean, what I am doing?

I widen my eyes in a show of lunacy. If that's what he thinks of them, then I might as well give it to him. "Oh, do tell, what exactly do you think my hands have done to deserve such *malice* from the likes of you?"

I can feel her squirming under my touch, but she's doing such a good job playing my game. Larkin leans closer, eliciting a hitch in Sitara's throat. She doesn't want him to come any closer than he already is.

I, personally, think it's hilarious that he still hasn't caught on.

"You and I both know that no man just takes a woman away from her home for platonic cuddles," he hisses, the storm brewing behind his eyes making this all the more thrilling.

I refuse to break eye contact with Larkin as I continue to pleasure his sister. "Larkin, if that is all I wanted, I would have left her here after defiling her in this very tavern before we left," I muse, curling my fingers to hit that precious spot inside of Sitara as I do.

She is in the middle of a drink of water and has now choked on it. She coughs and sputters slightly, composing herself quickly as I revel in the fact that she managed to hide yet another moan.

Good girl, Kitten.

The subtle increase in the pace of her breathing and the mess she is creating on my fingers is simply to *die* for. I'm quite pleased with her. I plan to let her know just how much momentarily.

His entire face pales, twisting up into a disgusted expression, his eyes darting to Sitara. "Um, *excuse* you?"

He is growing more and more tired of my antics, his head snapping back to me. "You're *really* hard to tolerate, you know that?" His teeth never part, and I'm sure he's giving himself a headache with how hard he is clenching them together.

I can do nothing but smirk, propping my chin up on the table. "Believe it or not, I have, indeed, heard that a time or two. Most of them have come from your sister, in fact."

I slowly turn to look at Sitara as she grabs my wrists tightly. Her nails will leave pretty little crescent-shaped indentations in my flesh. "I'm finished. I'm ready to go back to the ship."

I can't help but grin at her, amused by the fraying control I can see in those warm eyes of hers, how her pupils are blown wide just for me. "You're finished? But you've hardly touched your food, Pet," I purr. I can see Larkin tense up at my little term of endearment, clearly using it as fuel to his fire.

"This conversation has ruined my appetite. I'm ready to go home."

I look back at her brother, giving a one-shoulder shrug as I practically ooze with a mixture of grotesque satisfaction and pure, unadulterated joy. Judging by the look on his face, he had caught it too. She wants to go home, and that home is no longer with him but with me.

On *my* ship.

In *my* bed.

I slowly remove my fingers from her slick folds and bring them to my lips. The look of mortification that crawls onto Sitara's face when I look Larkin dead in the eyes as I clean them with my tongue is wildly satisfactory. "Well, as wonderful as this evening has been, my lady is ready to go *home*. And *I* am ready for dessert."

29

Sitara

"What is wrong with you?" I bellow, my face most likely the color of my hair right about now as we ascend the gangplank.

First of all, what gave him the idea that it was a good course of action? And secondly... Why in the fuck did I enjoy it? The sheer voyeurism of the whole situation has somehow managed to melt my insides and leave me with a pooling lake of magma low in my belly.

"I think the real question is what is wrong with *you*." He grins at me as he scoops me up into his arms and makes a beeline for the cabin. Every cell in my body is screaming, even as my mind tries to chide him for what happened at the inn. Kiernan swings open the door, nudging it back with his foot as he practically skips to the bed with a giddy gaunt.

"Welcome *home*, darling."

He crawls up my body, pressing me down into the mattress for a hungry kiss, my lips parting almost instinctively to let his tongue slide along mine. The appentency that I meet him with is nearly all-consuming. He begins tearing at my clothes, my own hands working heatedly to divest him of his shirt.

I need to feel his skin against mine. I need to know that what my brother said to me isn't true.

You can't possibly think this man loves you.

I keep telling myself that Larkin doesn't understand. That he doesn't know Kiernan the way I do. He hasn't witnessed the man who played Malizapopo with a group of children on the street. He doesn't know the man who would risk Catcher's Bay to get the medicine his sister so desperately needs. Then again, all those people were not some random lady he picked up off the beach.

I don't know why I think sex is going to solidify my denial, but I don't care at this moment, to be honest.

I don't know how, but Kiernan pulls away from me with a questioning gaze as though he had sensed the shift in me. It had been only a subtle blip, a slight moment of questioning, but it was enough for him to notice.

"Where did you go?" he asks, his voice that deep, sultry growl that makes my toes tingle and my heart race.

Physically, I have been right here the whole time, but mentally, I had flickered away for just the slightest moment.

Damn you, Kiernan, and you're incredible observational skills!

"I'm right here," I answer him, hoping that he will drop it and let us enjoy our time together.

I don't want to get into this. I'm sure my reservations are simply because I let Larkin get into my head. He's good at doing that, after all. It'll fade. I'll forget about it so quickly, it'll be as though it was never a thought. Right?

"You hesitated," his brow furrows deeply as he pulls us into a sitting position, perching me on his lap, "So, tell me, Darling. Where did you go?" He gently moves my hair from my face, caressing the length of my neck with the back of his fingers. The heat of his skin is searing, but not in the sexually charged way of mere seconds ago.

It is warm and grounding.

It is safe.

I let out a deep sigh, carding my hands through my hair. My fingers snag on the coiled tangles, but I barely notice the tug on my scalp. "It's not that big of a deal. It's just... What Larkin said to me earlier popped into my mind at such a horrible moment."

"He said a lot of things, Sitara. Which one are we talking about?" His voice remains soothing, though I can faintly detect the slightest irritation. Not at me, but at my brother.

If Larkin were ever to become a living god, he'd be one of assholery.

"About how you couldn't possibly *love* me," I croak out, my voice going tight. I'm not sure why it even bothered me. It isn't like I have told him I love him either. Up until this point, things have been fairly new. We've simply been enjoying one another and learning about where this dynamic will lead us.

He gives an irritated chuckle, his head falling forward for a brief moment before cocking his brow and looking back up at me. His blue eyes swirl with an almost amused haze, their color somehow seeming even brighter at this moment. "Is that all?"

His hands move to cup my cheeks, forcing me to hold his stare. He opens his mouth to say something, but is interrupted by Benedict's voice coming from the slightly ajar door.

Apparently, we were very close to giving the whole crew a show.

"His stupid ass has been obsessed with you for three agonizingly long years. There's no question whether he's in love with you or not, Starlight," Benedict grins, his dimples indenting deeply into his cheeks. He folds his arms over his broad chest, leaning against the doorframe as his eyes pass from me to Kiernan and back again.

"Benedict," Kiernan's tone is threatening, but he doesn't move. His hands remain firmly on my face, eyes boring into mine with the same intensity.

I would have looked at the man standing in the doorway if my face wasn't sandwiched between two massive man-mittens. My eyes widen in disbelief as I let the implication of Benedict's words sink in. "Three years?"

When did I run into Kiernan before the beach? I don't remember seeing him up until that point. You would think I would remember those eyes anywhere.

"Aye, three incredibly annoying and *expensive* years," he gives Kiernan a look of playful irritation as he swaggers to the desk and perches himself on the surface. "I was dead set on having you one way or another. But I hadn't originally planned on taking you off the island."

I remove myself from Kiernan's grasp, crawling to the end of the bed to give Benedict my full attention. "Really?"

Benedict nods, sticking out his bottom lip in a mock pout. "Big ol' Cap over there would be a giddy little lass, talking big and bad about how *this* would be the year that his balls would drop out of his vagina and he would speak to you. Then, he would spend the journey back home depressed and pissed off at himself for being a pussy yet again."

"Benedict!" Kiernan flops back onto the bed with a groan, his hands rising to rub his face. "Get out."

"No, no, Benedict. Do stay." I prop my arms onto the footboard of the bed, laying my chin down on them with a smile. "I'm invested in this now. But... I do have to ask. Where on earth did we meet three years ago?"

"That's the year you started coming to the docks," Benedict laughed, "All it took was your clumsy feet and you damn near knocking him on his ass."

I whip around to look at Kiernan, my eyes wide. My cheeks flush with color, the heat radiating off my skin almost palpable. How had I not remembered him?!

I distinctly remember it now. I had been so excited to see the ships that I had left Larkin and Hiera behind and barreled onto the docks without paying attention to where I was going. When I had almost toppled him over, I was so distracted by my whirlwind brain that I had barely given him so much as a glance as we spoke. All I had cared about was getting a better look at the ships.

In my defense, it hadn't been that long after I had recovered from my deadly encounter with the Maggots, and I was doing everything I possibly could to distract myself from my mind.

You're too pretty for the docks, lass... he had said to me, *It's not safe for you to be out here unaccompanied.*

If I had so much as taken one extra brain cell to contemplate his words, or even so much as look at him, things might not be how they are today.

"Why didn't you talk to me?" I ask. I want to understand why he hadn't said anything to me before ripping me out of the inn room that night.

"You're welcome to exit my room at any point, Benedict." Kiernan sits back up and looks over at me, "I didn't want to scare you. I didn't, and still don't, have the best reputation. The second year, I didn't talk to you because I realized that something I was doing was harming you. I figured you would probably hate me for it, so I put a swift end to it. Then this year, I saw the result of said stupidity first hand and, I suppose, in my own fucked up way... I was trying to fix what I had helped cause. Even if it wasn't directly."

My brows furrow deeply, confusion laced in my face as I press my lips into a thin line. "What did you do, Kiernan?"

He looks down at his hands, his expression filled with shame and self-deprecation. I can see him warring with himself on whether or not to continue, but I will find out eventually.

Surely, he knows that.

"I was the one who originally started supplying Thomas Kai with the opium he sells to your brother." His body visibly tenses as if bracing himself for the wrath he thinks is coming, his eyes darting to Benedict, who shifts slightly against the uncomfortable atmosphere.

I remain silent, unmoving, for what feels like forever. That first year we had all gone to Puka'qui had been the year Larkin's opium addiction started. Knowing that the filth Larkin was putting into his body had been supplied by Kiernan, at least that first year, brands itself into my brain.

However, I can't bring myself to be angry with him. It isn't like he had traded with Larkin directly, and I'm sure Thomas Kai would have gotten his supply from someone else if not Kiernan. Larkin would have still been where he was before I had left Capulli'ana.

I take a deep breath, closing my eyes to ground myself in the moment before staring back at him with a stern look. "I'm angry with you for being stupid enough to even touch something so grotesque. But... Larkin's choices are his own. It's not like you blew it into his lungs yourself."

He looks up at me, slightly surprised that I hadn't given him more of a tongue-lashing.

We stare at one another for a long, charged moment before Benedict decides to speak up. "Kiernan only sold in the first year. The second year was when he realized that Kai was selling to your brother. Hence, he didn't talk to you. He did, however, have a nice little conversation with Thomas. Well, more like a nearly life-ending altercation-"

Kiernan quickly interrupts him. "The only reason it was *nearly* life-ending was that I realized he had a young child. So I left him with a broken nose, two black eyes, and a threat."

My thoughts wander briefly to little Thomas, to his smiling little face and his eyes that hold far too many experiences for a child so young.

"Your brother made it out with less bruising, but no less of a threat. *'Clean up your act, or I'll take her somewhere you can't hurt her'.* I believe those are the words you said," Benedict adds casually.

So that's how Larkin had gotten those bruises on his neck and face. I had honestly just assumed that he and Thomas Kai Sr. had gotten into one of their many brawls.

"Watching you cry on the beach was the last straw." Kiernan looks at me with a fire that damn near makes me shudder, "I couldn't watch it again, so I sent Benedict to get you."

I process every word that comes out of their mouths with rapt attention, pieces of my life that I had decided weren't important enough to care about falling into place. They were minuscule details, but details nonetheless.

"You can leave now, Benedict," I say softly, my tone leaving no room for argument. After he leaves the cabin, the charged silence between Kiernan and me is so thick, I feel like I'm wading in maple syrup. I slowly crawl to where he is sitting on the bed and place myself into his lap once more. Draping my arms over his shoulders, I gaze up at him with all the affection and adoration I feel.

My hands find the soft strands of his hair, my nails grazing over his scalp tenderly. "You are not a *good* man, Kiernan Slater," I muse the insult like a praise, my lips finding the corner of his, "But you are mine, Mea'laz Nem'loa."

His hands skim over my sides, leaving goosebumps in their wake. "What does that mean?" he asks, his rumble low and raspy.

I smile softly, extracting one of my hands from his hair to cup his cheek, running my thumb along his high cheekbone. "It means, *'one to whom I love most'*."

The endearment feels right. Like it was meant to fall from my lips and flutter in the space between us. It's at this moment that I realize how true the words are. I do love him. Every drop of blood in my body sings his name.

I feel him melt into my touch, relief evident in his body language as he closes his eyes to savor the connection between us. When he opens them, my breath hitches in my throat at the intensity of feeling being mirrored back at me.

"I thought I had been waiting three years—one thousand and ninety-five days—for this moment." He pulls me forward, locking me into a feverish kiss which I return with equal fervor. I can feel the manifestation of everything he is feeling absorbing into my soul like liquid fire. When he pulls his lips away, pressing his forehead to mine, I hold him close. Our heaving breaths mingle together.

"Turns out, I have waited a lifetime for you, my dearest Darling."

30
Sitara

As the sun rises into the sky the next morning, I place myself back into the clothes of my people, a small smile spreading across my face at the feel of the familiar fabrics brushing against my skin. I look over at Kiernan, who is watching with rapt attention. His arms are folded over his chest as he leans against the armchair, a deep, worrisome scowl bunching the skin between his brows. He isn't happy that he can't come with me.

"Tell me again why this 'Doja' can't just come to Puka'qui, where I can make sure you're safe?" he lets out a huff of annoyance, watching me dress in—what he likes to describe as—the *'scraps my people con-sider clothing'*.

I shoot him a heated look, my lips pressing into a thin line. "His name is *Djar*, and you will do well to remember it, mea'loa. He's practically my father."

I understand why he is unhappy with the situation, but there is nothing that can be done about it. If he were allowed to go into the jungle, I would have no problem taking him with me, showing him my world. Unfortunately, that is just not something I can do right now.

"And he is the shaman of our village, the elder. He can't just leave to come to Puka'qui. He's a busy man." I counter his proposal for the hundredth time, grabbing my beads off the dresser to latch them around my ankles and neck.

"Djar," he corrects himself with a clenched jaw. I know that look well, the one where he's contemplating tying me to the bed again. "I don't like it. That small rock in the pit of my stomach—you know the one you get when you're about to get into some really deep shit—is acting up."

I do my best not to insult him by rolling my eyes, padding over to where he is standing, and throwing my arms over his shoulders. My fingers caress the back of his neck in soothing circles as I give him a soft, chaste kiss despite his rigid stance.

"You are forgetting one large detail. *Here* I am allowed to use my power. I won't be so easily taken off guard without a fight." When he doesn't respond immediately, my smile falters. "I need you to trust me, okay?"

I can tell he is trying his best to unclench his jaw, nodding with a slight slump of defeat. "You're right," the words still roll up his throat in a tone of disapproval. He clears his voice, sighing heavily as he tries again. "You're right..."

I smile up at him, gratitude swirling in my chest as I rise to my toes, pressing my lips to his once more. When we part, I grab my satchel from the chair—as I had promised to bring back a few things for the kitchen—and aim for the door. "I'll be back before nightfall," I reassure him gently.

Kiernan takes a deep breath, letting it out slowly through his nose. "If you're not, I'll be breaking a *lot* of rules."

I know he's serious. I wouldn't put it past Kiernan to barrel right through that treeline to find me. It's an endearing quality, one that I've grown to love rather than hate. To be so needed—so wanted—that he would risk the consequences to get to me; it's a feeling I will never be able to describe in full. All I know is it warms every facet of my being until I am nothing but puddy in his massive man-paws. Still, as annoying as that is sometimes, I find it oddly comforting.

"I'll walk you as far as I am allowed," he says, barely getting to finish his sentence before my name is heard being bellowed from outside. Larkin. Kiernan's distaste is evident on his face, his body growing rigid once more.

I whip around, poking him in the center of the chest. "Oh, no. Don't you even start," I furrow my brows at him. "I am in a good mood. Don't ruin it."

He cocks his brow at me, a slight sneer tugging at the corner of his lips. "Are you going to give him the same warning, or should I expect the same dumbassery as yesterday?" he taunts as we exit the cabin and walk toward the gangplank where Larkin is waiting on the dock.

"I think after dinner last night, no one's *'dumbassery'* quite lives up to your own, Mea'las Nem'loa," I tease, winding my arms through his to hold him close.

As Larkin comes into view, Kiernan pulls his arm from my grasp and wraps it around my waist, pulling me in tightly to his side. I know what he's doing. It's a possessive gesture. A petty one used to rub against Larkin's nerves. I pinch his ribs, glaring up at him. Kiernan clearly doesn't care; too proud of the expression he's elicited from my brother.

I sigh heavily and loudly, purposefully being dramatic to show them my irritation with their childish games. And here I thought I was the youngest of the three of us. Clearly, only in physical years.

"Ready to go, Sitara?" Larkin asks, his eyes darting to Kiernan for a brief moment. His eyes shoot daggers as he leans in with a slight smirk. "Sorry, Mundanes aren't allowed."

I flick my fingers in my brother's face, sending sparks of flames shooting into his nostrils. Larkin jerks back, trying to dispel them from his nasal cavities. "Shut up, Larkin. He's just walking me to the treeline."

We walk through the streets of Puka'qui toward the treeline, a mixture of different levels of silence clashing in the atmosphere. Kiernan is smug as hell. Larkin is seething. And I am just annoyed at this point.

Once we have reached a few feet away from the line that Kiernan is not allowed to cross, I turn to tell him my goodbyes. I'm met with a crash of his lips, hot and heavy against my own. His hands cup my cheeks, holding me in place. I'm slightly ashamed to say that even with Larkin standing right there, I can't help but melt even as I mentally formulate the verbal lashing I'm going to give later for using me in his petty little dick war with my brother.

Kiernan's tongue slips into my mouth in a not-so-subtle show of affection. I don't need to open my eyes to know that Larkin is broiling with displeasure. By the sound of the thunder crashing above our heads in barely contained rage, if looks could kill, Kiernan would be six feet under right about now. I can feel Larkin's eyes shift to me, his gaze burning a hole in my face with disapproval that I didn't immediately push Kiernan off of me.

Kiernan deepens the kiss further, his hand wrapping into the curls at the nape of my neck to angle my head. Honestly, if he pressed any further into the passion of our joined mouths, he'd be fucking me right in front of Larkin... again.

The heat radiating off Kiernan's body forces a shudder to ripple through me, which is the last straw for my poor brother. Larkin's hand wraps around my arm, jerking me away from Kiernan's embrace. "Alright, that's enough."

I can hear the dissatisfied grunt roll out of Kiernan's throat as Larkin drags me over the line that he isn't permitted to pass. I know for a fact that if he hadn't fled to the safety of the other side, Larkin would have gotten a slug to the face for that. My brother looks over his shoulder, giving Kiernan a self-congratulatory look.

I roll my eyes, biting my tongue before I make things worse. I don't want to get into another lecture about my long-lost virtue or the question of Kiernan's feelings for me again. I jerk my arm out of his grasp, glaring at him from my peripheral vision. I throw a leaflet of green flames at his bare foot. He stumbles to the side, kicking his toes out to dispel the subtle burn. I can hear Kiernan's rumbling chuckle behind us before rounding the corner of the path and out of view.

The walk toward the village is taking an agonizingly long time, even more so with Larkin muttering under his breath every two seconds. It makes me want to roll my eyes and flick another flame in his face, but I restrain myself, unwilling to let this reunion with my homeland be squandered because he can't keep his loud mouth shut.

I swear, all that opium melted his brain.

"Are you fucking serious?" Larkin mutters.

Yup, I sure am.

"He practically licked your tonsils right in front of me!"

Yeah, he did. The man has no shame.

As we move deeper into the jungle, my silence seems to only agitate him more. His voice becomes more shrill by the second as we pass the few telltale signs that we are getting close to the village.

"What did he do, brainwash you? You're better than that piece of pond scum."

Really? Because your bipolar ass hasn't treated me much differently in the last few years.

"I mean, come on, Sitara! The guy kidnapped you!"

He's right. He did. And he got a nice knee in the testicles for it, too.

We break through the trees in the clearing where our people's tents and huts sit, and I take in the familiar smell of herbs and spices and smoke from the communal campfire.

"It doesn't even matter," Larkin runs his hands through his ebony locks, sighing heavily. "He's a Mundane and can't stay here anyway. And I'll be damned if you think you're leaving with him again."

Last time I checked, that isn't your fucking choice, Larkin.

I almost open my mouth to say something about that one, my head snapping toward his as my lips part to take in a large intake of air. Before I can say a word, however, the familiar smoky rasp of Djar's voice chimes in from behind us.

"That is enough, Larkin." The old man's voice is soft-spoken, but his tone is as firm as nails. The look of utter shock on Larkin's face is enough to earn him a stern look from under Djar's bushy gray brows. "You do not get to decide what is or isn't in Sitara's best interest, my boy. You do not control her path any more than she controls yours."

Djar slips between the two of us, patting my hand gently as he moves to his hut just a few feet in front of us. He holds the flap open for me to enter, halting Larkin in his attempt to lead the charge. "I think it's best if this discussion is solely between Sitara and me, until your head is clear of bias."

I can't help but flash a bitter smirk in my brother's direction, narrowing my eyes at him as I walk through the entrance of Djar's hut, the smell of ancient smoke immediately filling my senses. From the sound of the grumbling outside growing distant, Larkin has refused to defy our shaman, as he should.

My elder lays soft eyes upon me, a swirl of mischief in his gaze. "You have gotten his britches in a bunch, haven't you, my girl?" He lets out a quiet chuckle, stroking at his long beard with spindly, aged fingers.

He moves to sit on the rugged floor in front of me, our knees touching in an intimate gesture of respect and care. His wise eyes meet mine, a silent invitation to say my piece. I take a deep breath, smiling as I bask in his presence for a moment. I simply want to soak in the feeling of his calm for some time before reality crashes back down on my shoulders.

"I'm surprised you aren't telling me all the reasons why my choices have been wrong," I admit. Djar has never been judgmental, but he isn't above letting you know that you have done something completely stupid.

"Does it feel wrong to you?" He eyes me knowingly. The question takes me off guard, but I instinctively shake my head.

"No."

"You may be impulsive, Sitara, but your intuition is rarely wrong." He pats my knee lovingly before taking in a deep inhale from the pipe he has used his thumb to light.

"I'm waiting, dear girl. I am an old man, I might wither away before you have finally told me why you are here with such urgency behind your ears," he grins at me, playfulness mixing perfectly with his insistence, "So, say your piece before I lie down for my nap."

Shaky laughter bubbles up my throat, and I sigh, suddenly feeling that same lump in my gut that has not wanted to leave since we departed from Catcher's Bay. "There are two things, actually..." I trail off, eyeing him closely as he takes another drag of his pipe, his hand extending in question. "Djar... I saw... The Maggot cult was seen outside of Capulli'ana, in the old site of Maku'yol. I saw them with my own eyes."

My heart pounds wildly in my ears as I wait for his reaction to the information I have just divulged.

Djar's brow furrows slightly. "They are in Maku'yol?" he repeats softly as he scratches his chin through his snowy facial hair, "You are sure of this?"

I lift my chin, giving him a stiff nod in response. "Yes... I was given a clear view from where I was standing. The brand. The etching over their Pe'aboros... It was them."

He lets out a long, smoky breath, the cloud pluming between us like fog. "I see..." he mulls the information over, chewing on the end of his pipe—his one bad habit. "We will need to start making preparations then."

"What do you need me to do, Djar?" I stare at him, determination laced in the fine lines of my face.

He shakes his head, his eyes closing for a fraction of a second before he looks at me once more. "I need time to think about it. I'm not exactly sure of the magnitude of the predicament yet."

His eyes gloss over momentarily as he thinks deeply on the matter, his eyes burning into the eternal flame sitting to the side of us in the center of his hut. I swear I can see him communing with the flame sometimes when he goes into deep contemplation like that.

"What was the second topic you needed to discuss with me, my dearest?" He focuses on me once more, giving me a look of concern. "By the sacred three, I do hope you didn't save the worst for last."

I shake my head, the unease in his tone causing my gut to churn with discomfort. "No, no... It is more of a question," I assure him, suddenly becoming very nervous under his scrutiny, "I was wondering if it were possible to gain your favor to take Kiernan to the temple for the blessing to stay... here... with *me*... from time to time." I rush through the first part of the sentence, though I find the words difficult to say by the end of my spiel.

"...from time to time?" he repeats. It is obvious that he is suppressing laughter, the corner of his mouth twitching under his mustache before he clears his throat to keep it from bubbling over. "I know he will be staying with you. I highly doubt he would be staying here with Larkin."

His little quip about my emphasis on the fact that Kiernan would be here with me is almost embarrassing. He squints at me, leaning into my personal space. I can smell the smoke from the pipe on his breath, a scent I had grown up with. It should be revolting, but it's not. It is soothing.

Well... It would be soothing if I weren't feeling as though my soul is being analyzed.

"You know that if I give my blessing, he will still have to be approved by the Sacred Three. And pass the rites if he chooses to remain beyond the veil."

"Yes, I know," I squeak out, leaning back as he presses further into me with a cheeky smirk. "But he needs a shaman's blessing to even make the journey to the temple?" I remind him, the statement coming out as a question, my voice far more shrill than normal.

He grins at me, his entire body radiating with mischief. He lifts his hand to my face, pinching my nose between his curled index finger and middle finger. He lifts a brow, holding me like that long enough that I am forced to breathe out of my mouth, rascality laced in his face.

"But does he?"

31
Kiernan

"Look what I found," Benedict comes out from below deck, holding up two pints of rum. I cock a brow, shaking my head with a smirk. "You do realize that it's before noon, right?" I throw my head back in laughter as Benedict starts rambling on about *several* other instances where we were either still inebriated or drinking with the arrival of the morning sun.

"Besides, K! This is as close to a day off as we ever get. You can't go into the jungle with ya lady, and I certainly will not be going to the inn with the other riff raff. Indulge me, will ya. I have something to celebrate!" He flops down on the deck, tossing me one of the glass jugs.

I give him a playfully offended look as some of the rum sloshes out of the mug when I catch it. "What exactly are we celebrating?" I ask as I take a seat next to him, drawing out a mouthful of alcohol. I let it coat my throat, feeling the burn in my belly.

Benedict smiles brightly, barely able to contain the excitement that glimmers in his eyes as he props himself up on his elbows to take a large swig of his own bottle. "You are looking at a newly branded father, mate!"

"Oh shit! Which of those poor bar wenches wrapped her legs around and wouldn't let go?" I gasp, clutching my imaginary pearls, "Oh my fuck, it was Ginny, wasn't it? I knew she was a hoe!"

"Well, I had to get my money's worth somehow, you celibate fuck!" He laughs, taking another smug swig of his drink.

"I *tried* to tell you not to spend your money! I told you her gods-fueled magic was too strong for your pimping ways!"

"Ah, but it wasn't magic, was it? It's your pure wittle hearty-heart," he sticks out his bottom lip in a mock pout, batting his eyelashes tauntingly.

"Oh my god, I have one of those?!" I look around, bewildered, "Damn, someone should have warned me." I patted him roughly on the back. "Congratulations, my friend. I pity your poor wife, but congratulations!"

He gives me an overly cheeky grin, the dimples in his cheeks defining his face. "Hey now, last time I checked, Enna has me in a pretty strong chokehold... Literally and figuratively." He wags his eyebrows suggestively.

I raise my brows and shrug my right shoulder, feigning indifference. "I never said leaving was what I pity her for," I ruffle his hair, "If your head were any larger, you'd be top-heavy and I wouldn't be able to keep you upright." I grin, which elicits one from him.

"Don't worry about me being top-heavy, friend. I have a kickstand."

"Oh, I know, even at half-mast it gives so much wind resistance it slows your ass down and you're nearly useless first thing in the morning." I take another swig, watching as Benedict throws his head back in a roar of laughter.

"Well, *my* woman doesn't get to scream at the top of her lungs in the middle of the sea while the rest of the crew is forced to listen. Besides, no one would hear her anyway. She'd be too busy choking on it."

We burst into hysterical laughter, the kind that makes your ribcage burn after a while. As we both settle for a drink and catch our breath,

I let my mind wander. What would it be like to have children of my own? With Sitara especially... It isn't a thought I have ever entertained before.

I lean back, resting my weight on my elbows as I stretch out my long legs. "Can you imagine if *I* had kids?" I muse, looking up at the bright, fluffy clouds above us.

Benedict spits out his mouthful of rum as he tries and fails to stifle a laugh, startling me in the process. "Now, that one... I would feel sorry for *you*, friend! They would murder you in your sleep!"

My mouth falls open in obvious offense. "In my sleep? My children would have the balls to do it with my eyes open, thank you!"

He leans forward, eyes swimming with goofy amusement. He's drinking far too fast. "Do you think they would spit fireballs from their mouths?"

"Frankly, I'd be disappointed if they didn't," I say in an almost authoritative tone before snickering and shaking my head, "I don't think I've ever heard you mention wanting kids." My voice falls into a murmur as I swirl the amber liquid in the bottom of my bottle, staring into the neck with a contemplative expression.

"I didn't know I wanted them until she told me it was happening," he responds in equal quiet, but the smile that creeps onto his face conveys his glee perfectly. "Besides, you know well that there isn't a single thing I wouldn't give her. What she wants is what I want."

The thought pulls me back to the history we share. I was there when Benedict met Enna. Back then, he was as wild as he was ruthless, and—somehow, someway—the witch of a woman managed to ensnare the beast.

I had never understood that statement. '*What she wants is what I want.*' At least, not until Sitara. I had always thought that made him a damn fool—the way his eyes would soften even by the mention of Enna; how his entire being would go gentle by a single touch from her hand. I used to think that no woman should ever have that kind of power over you, and if she did, that said something about you as a man.

Boy, was I fucking wrong.

I realize now that it has nothing to do with the woman having *'power'* over her man and everything to do with the man wanting to provide for his woman, wanting to be the one who brought her peace. Somehow, it is different.

I now understand why he looked at me like I was a dumbass every time I would voice that ignorant opinion in the past.

"I told you," he smirks softly, side eyeing me like he can read my mind, "That one day, you would have to eat those words. I will admit, however, that I'm going to miss beating the shit out of you when you open your arrogant little mouth." He chuckles lightheartedly, taking another drink before clicking his tongue.

"Oh, give it time, Benny Ol' Boy, you'll find some other ridiculous reason to hand my ass to me on a silver platter," I grin, taking the last mouthful of rum out of the container. "Damn, you drilled a pinhole in the bottom of this bitch, didn't you?"

I survey the bottom of the empty bottle in my hand. "There is no good reason this thing should be empty already."

Benedict grins, shaking his head as he also finishes off his own. "Perhaps, it's because you are a camel where rum is involved, you great oaf."

He falls silent as he leans his head back to savor the now early afternoon sun. We sit in comfortable silence for some time, letting our minds wander to our women and whatever else happens to find its way into our intoxicated train of thought. When he finally speaks again, his voice is filled with nostalgia. "I'd say I'm running out of reasons to kick your ass. You're turning into quite the fine young man."

I let out a sarcastic sigh, leaning over to lay my head on his shoulder with a grin. "Aw, thanks, *Dad*."

Benedict proceeds to lay his head down on mine, slapping my cheek as he chuckles. "Anytime, Buddy. Daddy is always here for the praise, you little mutt."

I give a drunken chuckle, pushing his head off of mine as we both wobble back into our respective positions. "You've been good for that since about day three," I inform him, reminiscing on those days that feel so long ago they could have nearly been another lifetime.

Back then, Benedict had been the captain of this ship. He had held a notorious reputation for taking what he wanted, when he wanted it, and didn't give a damn about who he hurt in the process. Despite that fact, he was just as good a man as he is now, though he is far more docile these days. That is, until one of my men pisses him off.

I suppose I have Enna to thank for that.

Before her, Benedict had taken me on his ship as a seventeen-year-old lad and taught me all I needed to know about being a pirate. Even back then, he had a code, though it was hard for many people to understand it.

We both continue to talk and bask in the rays of the sun as it drags along the sky. When the light begins to fade, washing the world into a blanket of darkness save for the torch lights, Benedict claps me on the shoulder. He uses me as an anchor to rise to his feet, a grin spreading across his face. "Well, I'd say my hammock is calling me."

Just as he moves to shuffle his drunk ass below deck, I catch a glimpse of red hair from around his large form. Benedict pauses to ruffle Sitara's copper locks, placing a paternal kiss on the top of her head. "Welcome back, Starlight. I got him all warm and fuzzy for ya," he chuckles, staggering off to enjoy the rest of his inebriated night.

I also stand as soon as I realize my girl is finally back home. The wobble that happens as I bring myself upright is enough to elicit a small smile from her perfect lips. "Welcome home, Pet," I grin, opening my arms wide for her as a loud hiccup escapes my lips.

Sitara chuckles, though there is no hesitation as she eliminates the distance between us and wraps her arms around my midsection. I would blame the feeling on the alcohol if I didn't know better. The feeling of knowing she is no longer hesitant about me - about us - brings me more joy than I will ever care to admit aloud. I don't even think there are enough words in my vocabulary to describe it anyway.

"Did you enjoy your day off, 'Cap?" she tilts her head back to look at me, laying her chin on my chest. Even through the intoxication, I can tell she's amused by my antics.

I give her a wolfish grin, wrapping one arm around her shoulders. "Well, I spent most of this *'day off'* getting insulted by Benedict."

My arm swings in a drunken motion toward a no longer present six-foot-four-inch behemoth. There is a momentary look of confusion at his absence before I yell after him. "I'm going to be your spawn's *favorite*! I hope you know that!"

I hiccup again.

Damn, these things are violent!

I'm taken off guard by Benedict's booming chuckle coming up through the deck floorboards. "You're barely *Starlight's* favorite!"

I snap my head back toward my fiery-haired vixen with a wide-eyed look of shock. "What?!"

Sitara's head hangs as she begins to burst into laughter, her shoulders shaking with the force of them. I take my time admiring her as her head falls back, still laughing at us. "Of course! Becket is my favorite. He's the only one who takes my buckets to the head without complaint."

Just as she says this, Arthur walks up the gangplank from wherever he had been in town. "Um, excuse you! I believe I was the one cleanin' nasty sheets!" He balls his fists up into his shirt at his chest, pretending as though he had been stabbed in the heart. "I even dealt with you kissin' m-"

"Arthur," I flash him a drunken snarl, sloppily pointing toward the railing of the ship. "*Gerald*!"

The boy holds up his hands, a small smile playing on his lips despite the color draining from his face. His eyes shift to Sitara, giving her a grin before continuing below deck. "That's my cue. Night, Starlight. See you in the morn."

I look back down at Sitara, her brows furrowed in confusion. Her expressions are just the most adorable thing. "Who the heck is Gera-"

"Shh," I cut her off, placing my finger to her lips. I lean down, grinning against her cheek with a playful snarl. "Take me to bed, Pet."

32
Sitara

The sky is blue... So iridescent blue.

When was the last time the sky was this bright? White fluffy clouds roll in over the treetops as I walk along the animal-made paths through the jungle.

My eyes scan the landscape around me.

Everything is green - green grass, green leaves, green bushes breaking up the thick brown trunks of the trees.

When was the last time I slowed down long enough to appreciate the world around me?

As I admire the deep hues and gentle breezes pushing past the breaks in the thick jungle, I can hear the melodious sound of a familiar voice calling out to me from some distant space further ahead.

"Sitara, come, child. Stop lagging," my mother calls out to me.

My head snaps around to find her standing there - the obsidian silk of her hair glistening in the sunlight filtering in through the trees. Her skin is healthy, her pale cheeks flushed with color and slightly tanned by the sun. A warm smile spreads across her lips, the playful mirth swimming in her eyes. "I swear, you are the most distracted child I have ever met."

My chest clenches at the sight of her, her playful chiding forcing tears to sting at the corner of my eyes. I ache to reach out and touch her. To feel her arms wrap around me and hold me close.

I want her to make me feel safe.

I want her to make me feel loved.

When was the last time she looked at me like that?

My legs seem to have a mind of their own as I rush to her, my blood pumping through my veins.

She's home!

She's home and she's beautiful.

She's right here in front of me.

When I reach her, I realize quickly that I have to crane my neck back to look into her warm brown eyes. Confusion knits my brows together, and I reach out to grab her hand, only to find that it engulfs my own.

Her thumb rubs soothing circles over my knuckles, bringing me the peace I once felt in her presence. It is a feeling that all children should experience in the embrace of their mother.

"Come here, Sitara," she coos, lifting me and wrapping me into her arms with a warmth that soothes the churning in my stomach. I wrap my young arms around her neck, burrowing myself into her.

"I miss you, momma..." I sigh, those pesky tears now streaming down my face.

"Shh," she strokes my hair, running her fingers through the thick curls, "Oh, my sweet child, when will you learn?"

I am confused by her question.

My eyes open as I attempt to tilt my head to look at her, but I am met with resistance. She wraps her arms around my head more firmly and begins to squeeze. My panic sinks in as I flail against her, trying to push her away from me.

"Momma? Momma!" I protest in vain. It's as if she can't hear me, like she's in a trance as she mutters under her breath something I can't make out.

Just as I think I can't take any more, as I believe the pain and the betrayal will swallow me whole, the world falls away into nothing.

At first, I think I am dead, but then I find myself in Djar's hut. I take in my surroundings. The familiar smell of herbs hanging out to dry and hide being oiled permeates the small space. Everything is just as I remember. The fire crackles in the center of the space, the distinctive pop of the eternal flame that the shaman of our village has always guarded breaks the silence.

I turn my face toward the warm body standing next to me - a younger version of Larkin, his long onyx locks pulled back into intricate knot-work. The last time he wore his hair long was right after we were given our Tilona'matli bands.

I was eight at the time, and Larkin was twelve.

I watch as his youthful face pinches, clearly in distress. That's when I notice it... The freshly created Tilona'matli band wrapped around his left arm, the black ooze of the tar still dripping down his flesh.

That's when I feel it - the burning sensation of my own as it tries to adhere to my skin. I look down at myself, remembering how afraid I am supposed to be.

Will it come off?

Or will it become permanently stuck to my flesh?

My fear is quickly washed away when I realize that Kiernan had once taken it off with a simple slip of his wrist.

Looking over at Larkin, he turns his head and stares down at me. The expression I am greeted with haunts me... will haunt me for the rest of my life.

"This is all your fault, Sitara," he lashes out through clenched teeth, "If you hadn't told them where Momma and Papa had gone, none of this would have ever happened. Why can't you just keep your loud mouth shut?"

His words sting like acid. I would rather he slap me than hiss his venom in my face.

"Now they can never come home!" he whips around, leaning in to shout mere inches from my face, "Why do you always have to ruin everything?"

I flinch as if he had struck me.

That's right.

I remember now.

When Djar had asked me where my parents had gone, I told him they had left with a strange-looking man with a brand on his forehead and dark tattoos etched over his Pe'aboros.

I was supposed to have been asleep, but the sky had held me captive outside our tent until the late hours of the night. I wasn't supposed to be awake, let alone see that my parents had left the village.

I feel that harsh lump of coal form in the pit of my stomach - the guilt almost overwhelming in its intensity.

Just as Larkin opens his mouth to shout at me again, I am pulled away from him by some unseen force. However, that's not before he says what I know he had said to me then, his childlike face twisted in agony.

"We were happy before you were born!"

When my vision is restored, I am standing on the edge of the Lake of Mirrors. It is a place that once sent my blood soaring with elation and promises of better days. Now, it only gives me a sick feeling in the pit of my gut. What once used to make my heart sing now only fills it with pain.

But why am I here?

What could have possibly compelled me to come back here?

The moonlight filters through the trees that crane overhead like ancient ancestors, watching over the once tranquil waters. I can feel them judging me, watching my every decision and move.

Oh, that's right... The aquatic firebugs.

The only creatures alive that are as much a contradiction to themselves as my cold fire is.

I have come to see them.

Leaning forward, I settle myself on my knees to look into the vast pool. Like the mimicking of starlight, soft twinkling dots scatter the depths of the clear waters. It's like a vast night sky, contained within a deep chasm in the earth.

"Sitara, my daughter," a deep, grating voice rings out from behind me. My spine stiffens as I turn my face. I know that voice. It's one that used to give me all the comfort a little girl could ask for.

I turn just in time to see the tall, imposing figure of my father standing in the moonlit clearing, his arms outstretched for me.

His fiery locks, from which I inherited my own, shift around in the soft midnight breeze. His skin is paler than I remember - Larkin having gotten his caramel skin from him, more gaunt around his cheekbones and eyes.

The putrid festering of the brand on his forehead can be seen even in the dimly lit clearing. I know I shouldn't go to him, I should curse him and walk away.

He's a traitor to his village.

A betrayer of the Sacred Three.

But I can't help myself.

I miss him so much that I can practically feel my chest crack open and ooze with it.

I scramble up, my bare feet and hands searching for purchase in the dew-dampened grass as I race toward him.

The moment our bodies meet, he melts away as though he were never there.

Everything shifts, and suddenly I am in a dark, cold place. The stone walls encase me in dread.

I know this place.

My bloodstream runs cold as I snap my eyes shut, unwilling to face it for a second time.

I am deceptively calm as I sit on the filth-covered floor, huddled into a group with seven other young women.

All the women around me cower as the eighth - a woman no older than me with blonde locks - is shoved back into the cell. Her hazel eyes are haunted, distant in a way that tells me all too much of what is to await the rest of us.

The guard saunters in behind her. Grabbing up Imogen as she buries her heels into the dirt with meek protests.

The air is stale, the stench of mildew and rot broken up only by the scent of our clammy skin. My blood whooshes in my ears, heart hammering so violently against my ribs that I think it might have cracked one. It hurts to breathe, though I force myself to take the acrid air into my lungs.

The taste is bitter and rancid on my tongue.

Whimpers filter through the air from the women around me, a few of them I recognize. Deara and Imogen are two women from my village.

From the looks of it, there are three women from each of the three villages here.

There is no light in here.

I'm not even sure where 'here' is.

All I know is that I'm trying to keep it together.

I'm not sure how long we have been here, the days bleeding together like spilled paint. In a world of complete darkness, save for the torches burning further into the swell of the stone fortress, it is easy to lose track of time. The mysterious creatures breathing low and gruff are created by the drafts that run through the stone like ice-cold tendrils threatening to swallow me whole.

"Sitara..." Deara looks over to me, her teeth chattering wildly in her jaw. Her cinnamon locks are matted, smaller locks stuck to the sweat sheen on her face.

I am almost certain that I look just as disheveled and filthy.

"Sitara, what do we do?" Her voice cracks under the weight of thirst and fear. Her body is trembling like a leaf.

Is there something wrong with me?

Why am I not behaving like the others?

Is it because I know that it is futile to snivel and cry? That it will only waste what little energy I have left...

It's because I want to remain strong for the others. In some backwards way, I feel responsible for them.

A mother hen.

"I don't know," I say softly, looking around the warded cell, the runes etched into the walls keeping our powers hindered. It is a smart move on the cult's part.

They wouldn't be able to contain us quite as easily without the advantage. From my village alone, there is one woman with the power of fire manipulation, electrokinesis, and then, of course, my Cold Fire.

As I understand it, there is a mixture of Behemoth Physiology, Earth manipulation, Ice magic, and healing magic among the other tribe women.

The world tilts on its axis as my vision narrows in on the point of Imogen's burgundy-red head being drug around the corner.

My heart rate picks up into a wild crescendo as everything goes black once more.

This time, I can't see anything—my memory being kind enough to save me from reliving it fully.

Now that I think about it... I had my eyes closed from the moment they threw me into the chamber.

The stench of mildew and the smell of sex mingle in the air around me.

But that isn't the scent that brands itself into my nostrils.

The scent of his skin is sweat, filth, and musky oud. The smell is unpleasant. And it makes this experience all the more unhinging.

The bed on which I am lying atop is damp from sweat and tears, the lingering evidence of my sisters seeping into my skin like poison.

"You should feel honored. To be chosen for such a cause."

His voice is raspy, baritone in a way that would be cruelly attractive if not for the hollowness of it.

"I'm giving meaning to your worthless life."

I can feel the sting of his teeth in my lip, tasting the copper on my tongue.

I am in pain.

But I will never let it show.

Even as he attempts to force my eyes open, to revel in the fear he finds in them, I keep them clamped shut.

And I decide, right now, right here, that I will never let them see my fear again.

It is as if I have fallen asleep, and suddenly I am met with the back of Deara's cinnamon head. The weight of the heavy chains wrapped around my neck and wrists is almost too much. Chainlinks are connecting each of us.

Terror coils up my spine as I realize exactly what is happening. The chamber is wide, lit with a deceptively warm glow of torches circles around the vast auditorium-like space.

Dozens of men and women are circling a massive stone slab in the center, the rock etched with symbols I do not recognize. Their bodies are clad in thick ceremonial hide, which has been dyed with blackest tar and crimson red.

I bite down on my tongue, refusing to let the overwhelming horror of what I am witnessing take hold.

Don't let them see you cry.

Don't let them see you break.

Don't let them see how terrified you are.

I tell myself these things as I watch the chain be removed from around Deara's throat, her body thrashing as she screams and pleads for her life.

That is another thing I will not do.

I will not beg.

Despite my best efforts, my body begins to shake and spasm uncontrollably as I watch her get tied to the altar.

He *stands at the head of the slab, licking his lips as trails of red ooze out from between his lips.*

The sudden need to vomit overtakes my senses, growing lightheaded as I realize exactly what he has just ingested.

Deara's screams are short-lived as one of his faithful plunges the knife into her body and begins to carve.

Before I can so much as process the scene, my body is shoved forward until I am slammed back onto the cold stone.

Bile rises in my throat as I feel the scorching life force of my friends beneath my nude form, the pungent metallic smell filling my nose.

"Ah, there you are, my Flower. I have indeed saved the best for last."

Kiernan

"Sitara!" I call out to her, attempting to shake her awake. What started as whimpers and stiffening of her body about twenty-five minutes ago has now turned into full thrashes. She screams at the top of her lungs, so loud that several of our crew members have flung open my door.

I am too worried about waking her up to appreciate the fact that any one of these men would have been willing to murder me in my bed if these screams were a result of my hand.

I fling the covers off of her, her back arching almost painfully as she lets out another guy curdling scream. She is in one of my shirts, just like she is nearly every night, but I don't care if the crew sees more than I would like at this moment. It's an afterthought that I barely give value to.

"Arthur, the door." I scoop her up into my arms, her body still fighting against my hold. Without me having to give him any further instruction, Arthur throws open the bathing chamber door and stands aside as I take my love to the tub.

I sit her convulsing frame into the empty basin, nodding to Benedict, who has just run in with a large pail of ice-cold water.

She immediately wakes when he drenches her, though not awake enough to understand what has just happened. She claws at me, attempting to get away.

"No, nononono NOO!!" she screeches, her nails finding purchase against my cheek.

I barely notice the sting as I grab her wrists in an attempt to stabilize her. "It's me! Sitara, baby, it's me!" I raise my voice, not to scare her but to hopefully gain her attention, "It's Kiernan! You're safe, baby, I have you..."

Her wide, unfocused eyes finally clear, her pupils dilating out as recognition washes over her face. The broken sob that rolls up her throat is enough to threaten my own. I have to swallow it down to keep from breaking at the sight of her like this.

I try to wipe away the tears that have spilled over her face like a dam breaking against the force of a river. Her chest heaves as she tries to catch her breath, the attempt being stifled by the choked sobs of panic still lingering in her throat. I take her into my arms, sitting down on the bathroom floor, uncaring about how soaked my clothes are getting.

I say nothing as I look back over my shoulder at the men standing behind us, crowding into the doorway. They understand without words and shuffle back out of the room in silence.

I start rocking, pressing her against my chest once I am sure my heart has slowed enough to be soothing. She clings to me like a lifeline, her fists curled so tightly around my shoulders I think she might be strong enough in her terror to bruise me. Her nails have undoubtedly left crescent-shaped divots in my skin. My hand rubs slow circles on her back as the other cradles the back of her head.

"Talk to me," my voice comes out as more of a plea than I had intended, my throat tight with the emotions that threaten my composure.

When she doesn't answer me, I just go back to my ministrations, trying to calm her. The silence stretches out for what feels like forever - the only balm to my frayed nerves being the slowing of her breathing. I don't speak again until her breaths were even and steady.

"Does this happen often?" I ask, concerned for her safety during these moments (and if I'm honest, my own as well).

"Not often... Not anymore, anyway," she whispers, pressing her cheek into my chest. I can feel my heartbeat under her ear, her own finally beating in rhythm with it.

Once I think she is calm enough to move, I lift myself with her in tow and walk back out to the bed. Lying her down on the bed, I slide in beside her and draw her to my body. All I can do is hold her, the muttered words from amid her dream still ringing in my head:

Don't let them see you cry; Don't let them see you break; I will not beg.

33

Sitara

I open my eyes, my eyelids swollen slightly from the tears and terror of the night before. My head blooms with a throbbing pain as I sit up and look out the window. Everything is so bright. Too bright. It forces that pounding in my skull to creep into my already burning pupils.

I shift slightly, feeling Kiernan's warmth still pressed up against my hip. I turn to look at him, his arms instinctively wrapping around me. My heart clenches with gratitude as I think back on the night before. All of them, every last one of the men on this ship, had come running. It feels good... Knowing I have so many people who care enough about me to barrel through a door to come to my aid. It isn't something I have ever experienced before.

Of course, I know that Djar cares for me, but his alliance will always hold to the greater good of the eternal flame. In his own fucked up way, I know Larkin loves me too, but he would most likely still be the cause of my sorrows, not the resolution. And my parents...

My gut twists with the aching gnaw of their betrayal, and I place my hand over the scar through the thin fabric of Kiernan's shirt.

Kiernan's eyes are closed, but I know he isn't sleeping. Every move I have made since the events of last night has woken him up. I turn, his tightening grip and soothing fingers would drag me out of my own sleep just in time to feel his lips brush the top of my head. It was a long, sleepless night—more so for him than me—so I assume he has put Benedict in charge of the crew until he and I emerge from the cabin when we are good and ready.

I lift my hand slowly toward his slightly tense face, running a finger along his brow to unwrinkle them from one another. "Kiernan?" I address softly, my voice still hoarse from the screaming I had done the night before. I feel ashamed and embarrassed.

When I came back from the Ma'tawi village, I was in a good mood. I had managed to receive Djar's token of favor to take Kiernan to the temple. When I arrived, I was warmly welcomed back by two drunk-happy idiots I call family now. After that, Kiernan and I went to the cabin, and I enjoyed listening to his drunken antics. I'm not sure where my mind had gone after we went to sleep. But it is a sudden turn that makes me feel raw and exposed, just as it had when those nightmares would come to me frequently.

"I'm sorry for worrying you so much." I continue, pushing a loose strand of his hair away from his cheekbone.

"Shh," he tilts my chin to press his lips to mine in a chaste kiss, "After the night you have had, you don't owe me any apology, Darling." He shakes his head as if to ward off the memory. My hair is soft under his loving strokes, though his fingers still tangle in it; the thrashing I had done last night seems to have knotted it significantly.

I press my forehead to his, closing my eyes to savor his warmth and gentleness. I can still feel that ever-present rock in my stomach, perhaps lower into my uterus if I am being honest with myself, that seems to have gotten harder to ignore these past few weeks.

"Djar said he needed time to think about what our people's actions should be before moving forward," I explain, running my hand through his chestnut locks. In truth, I am simply trying to steer the topic away from myself. "He'll most likely be gathering the other two shamans... Until then, I managed to get what I needed to take you to Potem'aku."

He gives me a jocose grin, one filled with mirth, "I get to cross the border?" I can see the petty amusement all over his face. His first thought isn't that he gets to go on an adventure of his own, but that Larkin will be pissed if he even steps so much as a toe across that line.

It's written across his forehead like a banner, flying high and proud. I lift an eyebrow at him, my tone brooking an energy of playful irritation.

"Not that your first thought isn't '*Wow, Sitara, what an honor*!'" I fold my arms, huffing loudly as I turn my cheek away from him. I try to keep my grin at bay, which isn't as difficult as I would like it to be due to the events of last night.

His mouth falls open in a forgery offense. "Who says that wasn't my first thought?" He barely finishes his sentence before I shoot him a look, and he starts chuckling.

"You know me too well, Pet," he teases me, burying his face into my hair.

"Don't go making a scene with Larkin in the village. I'll freeze you both into dummy-pops and let the hounds have you to cool their bellies," I fold my arms over my chest, jabbing him in the ribs lightly.

"I would *never* do such a thing," the mischievous grin that takes over his face is halted by my hand as I grip his cheeks between my slender fingers, "Okay, so I would..."

"Yes, you would," I say sternly, squeezing his cheeks more firmly in my hand as I push them in and out, making his lips pucker and unpucker in rhythm, "Do not embarrass me. Show some common sense. The gods know Larkin can't."

"You have a lot of misplaced faith in me," he chuckles, though the look of stern defiance I give him makes him hold both of his hands up in surrender, "Fine, Fine. I'll behave to the best of my ability."

The gods know that his ability to behave is minimal at best.

I sigh, releasing his face from my hand as I lean back against the wall next to the bed, my thoughts traveling elsewhere. I look out the window, finding it more and more difficult to keep my racing thoughts at bay. Usually, when I get into moods like this, I do something impulsive and stupid, trying to halt them before I begin to spiral. However, I know that Kiernan isn't going to allow me to do such reckless reprieves.

I can feel Kiernan's frown boring into the side of my head, his brows undoubtedly knitted together in a deep line. They are. I can see it as he hooks his forefinger under my chin to bring my gaze back to where he is sitting next to me.

"Come back to me," his voice is gentle, as though he knows that what my mind is focused on is important, all while still attempting to reel me back into our little bubble, "What can I do to keep you here, present here with me?"

If I didn't know Kiernan so well, I would have almost taken his words as a plea. I take a deep breath through my nose, tucking the snarled locks of my hair behind my ear. I don't know how to keep my thoughts at bay, not when I've spent most of my life trying to deal with them in ways that haven't always been the best. My mind flickers back to those early months after I was rescued and healed enough to walk around.

It had felt like everyone could see the damage, their stares slicing through me like hot branding irons. To have to watch Imogen and Deara's family mourn for them while I was alive and breathing had been the hardest thing I had ever had to watch. Imogen's father couldn't even look at me after that, his face always pinched up away from me.

They all knew that my mother and father had been the ones to take us, and Deara's mother had made it clear that it wasn't fair for the daughter of traitors to have survived while her daughter was slaughtered in cold blood.

She wasn't wrong. I had thought the same things during my long recovery time as I lay in Evelle's mother's healing hut, staring up at the ceiling. Why did I get to live, and all of them had to die? Why didn't the Sacred Three get to us sooner?

That rock in my core hardens once more, and I place my hand over my pelvis, an equally indismissible lump forming in my throat.

Kiernan's eyes follow the path my hand trails along the scar that runs from hip bone to hip bone. His hand follows mine, gently removing it to replace it with his and moving the bits of clothing that cover it. I tense in his arms, feeling ashamed of the lives lost that I feel it represents. In this moment, it is something horrid that I don't wish for him to look at. All it does is remind me of the look on my sisters' faces as identical cuts were made, ones that they never recovered from.

He traces it gently with his middle and ring fingers, goosebumps rising on my skin. Part of me enjoys his soothing hands on my body, even as a small part of me wants to push him away and cover myself. "Is this what's keeping you so far away?" he whispers, questioning me as though he doesn't already know the answer. His lips skim the shell of my ear, forcing a shudder of warmth to roll down my spine. "You think this scar makes you less?"

Doesn't it?

If I hadn't allowed my parents to enter the village, if I had immediately run to Djar when my father found me by the Lake of Mirrors, instead of running toward him, they wouldn't have had time to grab the other girls.

He kisses the corner of my jaw, bringing me back to the present with him once more. I open my mouth and take a deep breath as if I'm about to tell him exactly why my opinion is fact, but he cuts my words short by grazing his lips along the long expanse of my neck to plant another kiss on my collarbone. My heart flutters wildly in my chest, and I have to swallow down the soft whimper that wants to escape me.

Gods, the things this man does to me when I'm trying to be moody.

"I see nothing but perfection," his voice rumbles in his chest, vibrating into my body, which evokes another shudder. He begins trailing kisses down my sternum, my chest clenching with the force of his gentle attention. I can't help but place my hand against the soft trusses of his hair, my fingers tangling in the strands.

"This," he continues, trailing his fingers along my scar with grander purpose, "Is no different than this." His lips meet the splatter of freckles along my shoulder. I have to bite my tongue to keep the broken whine that wants to roll out at bay. "Or this," his fingers wrap around my wrist, bringing my hand to his mouth where he plants another open-mouthed kiss to the tiny scar I had gotten on my palm when I was a child during a game of chase through the jungle, "It is just another beautiful stop on the roadmap of your skin; just another glimpse into who you are, and who you are is resplendent."

Treacherous tears sting at the corners of my eyes, the liquid like acid to my already overused tear ducts. I swallow hard, trying to find my voice again, which proves more difficult than I wish it were. I am of two minds at this moment. There is a part of me that swells and oozes with gratitude and longing for the man in front of me. And another part that is still telling me I don't deserve to be here.

"I didn't-" my voice catches in my throat as I try to articulate what it is I am thinking, what I'm feeling, "No one wanted anything to do with me after everything that happened. Right now, I am finding it hard to believe that I am desirable to anyone."

There. I confessed it. I know it is just a fleeting thought. Kiernan has done nothing but make me feel desirable since the first time we finally confessed how we felt. However, right now I feel nothing but dirty and wild and completely adrift on the sea of my own self-loathing.

Kiernan's eyes close, as if he is attempting to gain control over his temper. His nostrils flare, though his hands remain gentle on my skin.

At first, I think my words have upset him, though that doesn't make them any less true right now.

"You are desirable to *me*," his voice rolls out like a low, grumbled growl, "*You* are perfection to *me*." His hands run along my sides, and I instinctively arch into his touch, my lips parting in a gentle sigh. He leans in, inhaling my scent deeply, greedily. It's enough to send a roll of fire through my veins that pools between my thighs. "You are mine. No one needs to pay you any attention because I will take their eyes for seeing anything other than goddess-like magnificence."

In a matter of minutes, he has brought me back to our little world, holding me hostage here with him. I don't mind. I welcome it, my brain short-circuiting with the magnitude of emotions and sensations that have led me to this appetitive prison. My fingers begin to wander away from his hair, sliding along his skin where he grounds me. Every move, every muttered praise, every tentative touch draws my attention away from my worries and doubts.

My other hand, which is still embraced in his ironclad grasp, shifts to cup his cheek as I rise to my knees, sitting back on my heels. I lean in until our noses brush together, my heart hammering in my chest like a caged bird ready to take wing if only I would open the door.

"Remind me," I whisper, my voice a husky groan due to the damage I had caused it in the middle of my hysterics last night.

One of his hands wraps around my waist, roughly pulling my pliant body to fit against his hardened planes. The other continues its ascent to the back of my neck, where he angles my face perfectly, crashing his mouth into mine. My lips part immediately, letting him swallow down any sound I may or may not be making.

I didn't have to ask him twice.

When we break apart for air, his eyes bore into mine, the scintillating blue of his irises swimming along my features reverently. I stare back at him, wrapping my arms around his shoulders to pull him down with me onto the mattress. As I do, my thighs spread to let him settle between them, my mouth latching onto the sensitive skin of his neck, my tongue grazing just below his ear. My fingertips scramble to find any inch of warm skin I can touch, desperate for him to remind me of exactly why I am still here, why I am still breathing.

If my only purpose is this—being here with him—that is enough for me to live a long and happy life.

He groans as I nip at him, his hands making quick work of removing my clothes. I lift my hips for him, helping him pull my skirt off my hips. I kick it carelessly to the side, uncaring of where it falls. My own hands work on the cotton night briefs around his waist, attempting to remove the barrier that sits between us and everything we both crave. His eyes scan every inch of my flushed form, my gaze roving over him with equal hunger.

"I hope you look at me like that always," I say breathlessly, feeling the heat of his attention like a sinful caress along my body.

"Darling," he rumbles, his hands following the path his eyes make until his fingers find purchase at the apex of my thighs, "you have no idea the constant starvation I feel for you—the need to have you in any manner you will allow. It is something that will never be sated. Not now. Not in a hundred years when you are old and gray, wrinkled and hunched."

I gasp, the breath stolen from my lungs as his fingers work over my clit with that maddening precision. The same intake of air catches in my throat when he lowers his face to the scar just above where his fingers play, placing a filthy—yet tender—kiss to the marred skin. "I will never see anything other than pure, untainted flawlessness in you."

34
Kiernan

As we approach the treeline that is supposed to keep me out of Sitara's world, I feel my muscles tense unconsciously in apprehension. Some part of me wonders if there will be some big feeling that comes in a wave as I pass through to her side of the barrier. I hesitate, looking over at her with a less than phlegmatic expression. "Are we completely confident that I'm not going to get smote...smotted...smitten...uh... burned alive, if I cross over?"

She laughs at me, her hand flying over her adorable little grin as she attempts to stifle it.

Fucking Benedict...

I suppose I should pay him the twenty silver pieces we wagered all those years ago. Even the simple act of seeing her smile eases my inhibitions just a bit.

"Do you have the token Djar gave you?" she asks, hooking her forefinger in the lip of my pocket and tugging playfully.

I nod, shoving my hand into my pants to retrieve it. You know, just in case. The palm-sized gem listens in the filtered sunlight that breaks through the branches overhanging the veil, the yellow topaz coloration seemingly pulsing in my hand. It's like it is alive, an extension of the collective heart of Sitara's tribe.

"As long as you keep that with you, the jungle won't know the difference between you and me," she explains with a sweet, reassuring smile.

The jungle won't know the difference?

Are the fucking plants alive now, too?

I place the stone back in my pocket with dutiful care and reach for her hand, lacing our fingers together. If there is *any* chance that I will die on the other side of this line, I'll be damned if I am not holding her hand when I go. "Here goes nothing..."

I take a deep breath, planting one foot in front of the other as I cross over that seemingly invisible—yet oh-so-evident—line between the Mundane and the unknown. I continue to hold that breath as my body arrives fully on the other side. There was no big wave of feeling, other than the sweet relief of not being *dead*. My shoulders relax substantially. "Well, that was...anticlimactic."

The offended expression that tightens the corners of her eyes and mouth tells me I probably should have—could have—chosen a better turn of phrase. She gives me an annoyed grin, and I can practically see the vein bulge out of her forehead.

"You're so dramatic," she snides, taking me along the animal-created pathway. I'm not sure why I expected there to be a road. I suppose I am very acclimated to my side of the universe.

I shrug one shoulder, a grin spreading across my face. "I expected some big feeling. Like coming up out of the water or something." I squint suspiciously, bobbing up and down on my feet like a dumbass. I'm doing it on purpose. I'm trying to keep her here with me and not off somewhere else that feels so far away when she gets that reticent look in her eyes. "But there is nothing but normal, solid ground on this side... Just like on my side," I remark, motioning for her to continue the charge through the dense jungle.

The further into the foliage we go, the more the world comes alive. I'm assaulted with sights and sounds I have never witnessed before. As we walk along, I watch the confident stride of my woman as I follow. I am the one out of my element now. She vaults fallen trees, never stumbling once, along the narrow path, which is barely registered by me. If I weren't following her, hypnotized by the sway of her hips, I'd have already gotten lost in this gods-forsaken place.

The jungle is oppressively humid, and I feel like I can't breathe deeply enough to catch my breath. It makes me wonder if my pet has gills to breathe in all this perspired air so effortlessly. Now I know how she felt in her first few hours aboard my ship. I had watched her stumble about at the slightest jerk of waves underneath us and had thought it amusing at the time.

Payback is most certainly an evil mistress.

We walk under massive canopies of human-sized leaves that hang heavily on the branches of the ancient trees, the vibrant ferns and oddly colored flowers below seeming to grow despite the overcast shadows created by the dominant plants. The ground itself, a mixture of soft, shifting dirt and large slabs of stone, seems to pulsate under my feet. Each mile we make toward our destination seems to bring about a deeper feeling of connection. Even Sitara, who is no less human than I, seems to melt into our surroundings as though she is meant to be there, as if she were born from the very ground we tread.

"So, tell me again where we're going right now. To see...uh..." I do genuinely try to pronounce the damn names, but her language is not my first.

Or my second.

Hell, it isn't even my third!

She looks pleased that I didn't *purposefully* fuck up their names. The way her eyes light up with sterling approval before turning back around to follow the indiscernible path causes a smile to spread across my lips.

Gods damn, I feel like a young whelp brimming at the seams just for that.

"Tell me about them."

"We are going to Potem'aku," she says, the excitement laced in her voice almost palpable, "It is the home of Teo'kan, Gula'ci, and Cal-li'hanu."

The relaxed set in her shoulders is a stark contrast to the tension I know is still coiled in mine, though not nearly as bad as before. The gentle sway of her hair as she moves so effortlessly, so gracefully, is like a bright beacon against the backdrop of green.

"Make sure you are on your best behavior, Kiernan," she says to me, a slight sternness in her tone that has my lips tugging for a smirk, "They are not known for their patience."

"Neither were you when this all started," I tease, bumping her with my elbow right before nearly tripping over a root that I swear wasn't there before.

The damn plants are out for my blood. Maybe I'll get to see her precious temple, or maybe I will die via an angry tree root. The answer of which one is still in the air at the moment.

She laughs at me, a melodious sound despite it being at my expense. Her face lights up everything when her laughter is unreserved and unabashed like that.

"It tried to bite me!" I drone, pointing a finger back at the root, "See! I think it moved!"

She blinks rapidly at my stupidity, raising a brow with a tone that is undecidedly teasing or serious. "It is a root, Kiernan. They don't have teeth." I open my mouth as if to indulge her in her lack of knowledge in her own home when she wraps her hand into the fabric of my shirt and tugs me to the other side of her body. "But that does. You should pay more attention."

I look around the verdure for whatever it is she is talking about, my brows bunching up in confused wariness. "I don't see-"

Oh, I see it now.

Her nonchalant tone when she had warned me of the danger just doesn't seem to match the urgency of death I just about found myself in. There, amid the greenery, is an equally green feline cat. Its body is every bit the size of two fully grown men, the speckled green and brown of its fur allowing it to blend into the landscape so efficiently that it would have bitten my head off before I would have even been able to register that said head was detached.

How in the hell had she seen that thing?!

It stares at us, its yellow eyes absorbing our forms. Probably determining which one of us is tastier. It's going to be me. Sitara is beautiful, but probably not nearly as filling.

Apart from its abnormal coloration, it seems like a perfectly normal jungle cat. Until I notice the dual tails swishing lazily off the branch. "What is that thing?"

"It's a miz'geru," she answers casually, as if the damn thing isn't practically licking his jaws at us.

"Oh, just a miz'geru, huh?" I pronounce the word like a damn three-year-old, panting heavily as I try to slow down my frantic heart. Place me on a ship with thirty men with swords? No problem. Place me in a jungle with a three-hundred-pound cat with teeth as big as my thumb? I become a little bitch. "Well, if I had known *that*, I would have pet the pretty thing."

I roll my shoulders, trying to ease the tension that continues to rapidly rebuild in them. The thing is fucking massive and, frankly, its sudden appearance had scared the shit out of me. I look at her just in time to see her roll her eyes at me, a smartass look painted all over her face as she strolls right up to the damn thing and reaches out her hand.

Her fingers glide along its furred side once, then she leaves it be, walking back to where I am standing with—no doubt—the dumbest look I have ever had on my face.

I take a step forward, holding out my hand to let it sniff me. When the massive beast makes no move to gobble me up like a feast, I stroke my fingers up its head to scratch behind its ears.

"Come on, big guy," Sitara chuckles, flitting along the trail like a satisfied child.

Smartass woman.

I close my ajar mouth, following behind her closely. I reach out, poking her side with a look of petrified horror. "That thing could have bitten your hand off if it had wanted to! Then where would *I* be? How could you be so selfish?!"

The laughter that follows is unlike anything I have heard from her before. She's at home here. She knows this land like the back of her hand and is at perfect ease.

"I guess you would have been wandering around trying not to get eaten," she crows far too enthusiastically, "Don't worry. *Most* of the creatures here are docile unless provoked."

"I take it your brother missed that memo," I give her a furtive glance, pressing my lips into a thin line as I try my damndest to stifle my amusement.

I'm fucking hilarious.

She shoots me a look of disapproval, and I quickly avert my eyes, scanning the trees for any other creatures I should be aware of.

The branches are filled with brightly colored birds and strange-looking primates, but it is the creatures at the base of another nearby tree trunk that catch my attention. Two of them seem to be playing a game of chase, hopping, and chittering happily among themselves. Their coloration is strange, however. I can recognize them as some sort of fox-like canines, but their fur is a mixture of deep reds and rich creams. Their tails, far longer than any I have ever seen before, are ringed in alternation of those colors. Like stripes.

"What are those?" I ask, pointing toward them like a child being presented with something interesting for the first time.

"Those are Mat'chich," she responds, a serious tone laced in her voice. "Those are less friendly. *Don't* touch them."

"You mean to tell me, a big scary cat will let you touch it, but cute little floofs will try to eat you?"

What kind of ass backwards world have I willingly entered?

"Actually, now that I think about it, it makes perfect sense. Scary things, nice. Cute things, could murder you in your sleep," I throw an arm over her shoulder, "I should have known!"

At first, I think I might have made her angry with my posturing, but then she smiles, a mischievous glint in her eye that suddenly has me very unsettled. After a while longer, she bends down and snatches up something from the ground.

"Look, you can hold this little guy." She grabs my wrist, plopping a seemingly ordinary mouse into my hand.

"Well, look at that," I muse, holding the tiny ball of fur in my palm.

Just as I am about to relax a little, Sitara ducks under an invisible branch, and I am left looking around in confusion. A few precious seconds later, I see a streak of white feathers barreling toward me. I duck just in time to avoid its head, accidentally tossing the mouse in the process. The beast snatches it right out of the air in passing, smacking me across the forehead with its tail.

"What the hell?!" I turn to look at what had just assaulted me.

Oh, great. They have flying, feathered snakes... I *hate* snakes. I have always hated them since I was a child. Having wings makes it worse.

Sitara bursts into a fit of hysterics, unable to keep her body upright anymore. She tumbles over, clutching her sides as she doubles.

"Hey! What was that for?! I could have died!"

"I thought," she takes in a deep gasp, "It was better than '*murdering you in your sleep*'."

My eyes grow wide at the murderous thing she has just forced upon me. "That poor little mouse! You just sacrificed it to the feather boa!

Your temple sitters are *never* going to let me hang around here if you continue to make me do your dirty work, sacrificing tiny fuzzy mice."

I jab a finger in her direction, which only makes her laughter roar to life with renewed vigor. After she has finally composed herself, she wipes away her mirthful tears and stands.

"I watched it stalk that mouse for every bit of five minutes. It was getting eaten anyway."

"You don't know that! Maybe he would have scampered home to his wife and eight little mouselings. You just made that poor mouse wife a widowed, single mother!" I cross my arms, turning up my nose at her. "I hope you are proud of yourself!"

Sitara snickers, holding her hand over her mouth. "Those mice reproduce asexually."

Is nothing in this damn jungle normal?!

35

Kiernan

Sitara and I stand just shy of the clearing where the temple, Potem'aku, sits. I stare at it, surprised by what lies before me. I was expecting an impenetrable fortress guarded by an army of those nasty Feather Boas. One where those who decide they wish to enter must have a password, a special handshake, and a secret language to get in the front door.

Instead, I am met with a fucking garden party.

The domed ceiling grapples high into the sky, held up by the massive carved pillars of the outer ring. Every inch of the oddly colored stone used to compose this place is covered in vines and iridescent flowers. A staircase carries visitors in through said outer ring into the inner circle of the temple.

"Are you ready?" Sitara asks, squeezing my hand reassuringly before tugging me toward the entrance.

I return the gesture, clearing the dryness from my throat. "I am *not* going to fit in here," I mumble—mostly to myself.

Once we have broken through the outer ring, I can see everything more clearly. We stand on a meticulously crafted annulus flooring, the stone glittering in shades of gold and jade. Below us is a pool of crystal clear water that wraps around a five-tiered dais in the center, which is layered like massive steps and bears the same carved pillars as the space we have just entered, though. Within that pool, I notice strange-looking salamanders, their skin bioluminescent blues and pinks. They swim under the water lilies, floating along the surface and crawl up the central dias. In the center of said dais is what looks to be the same flickering violet flames I have seen dance and pulse along Sitara's body.

Then, my gaze centers on three figures lounging lazily on the tier-like ledges, their bodies poised and relaxed in equal measure.

My eyes are drawn to the male first. From the long history lesson I was given on the way here—due to Sitara demanding I have some knowledge before walking in to face them—this man is Teo'Kan, God of the Sea. His massive body sits perched on the edge of the bottom step of the dais, one foot hanging over to submerge in the pool at the base. The salamanders skitter along his leg as though they belong to him, which they probably do. His other leg is drawn up toward his chest, his arms resting on it as though he is bored.

His face is angular and cold, the black flow of his mane only broken by the pointed tips of his ears poking through the strands. His skin is a mixture of hues, laid out like a pattern on his well-built body. From his hairline to his cheekbones is a strange shade of teal, which halts to reveal pale, smooth alabaster skin until it continues once more from his jawline. If I squint hard enough, I think I see scales lining certain angles of his body.

He is giving me a distrustful look, his yellow eyes vibrant against the backdrop of his face. I'm honestly surprised he isn't cross-eyed with the angle at which he is glowering down his nose at me. I would love to say that I could take him in a fight, but—if I'm being completely transparent—I know there is no way in hell. He leans his body weight against the one erect knee, giving a long sigh of inconvenience as we approach the water's edge.

My attention is then shifted to one of the two women sitting on either side of him. The one to his left looks as if she has been carved from the purest of ebony, her flowing tendrils of hair equally as dark. Vein-like patterns line her skin as though she were once shattered and then placed back together again with molten gold. Her eyes are equally metallic, no irises or pupils to be found. She is standing at the top, one shoulder leaning against a pillar, picking at her nails absentmindedly before her eyes lift toward us.

This one must be Gula'ci, Goddess of Earth.

One side of her mouth ticks upward into a snarky sneer just before she shifts her eyes toward the man and whispers something far too quiet for my ears to register.

I don't have a chance to get a good look at the second woman before I find myself face down on the floor. With a groan, I turn my face toward Sitara, who has prostrated herself into a deep kneel. She, however, is not tasting the dirt that films over the stone beneath our feet.

"It is usually customary to bow in the presence of gods, is it not?" Gula'ci's voice registers through the tranquil space, though there is amusement in her tone where I expected there to be distaste.

I take a moment to adjust myself, sitting up on my heels as I pull my face out of the dirt. I place my hands on my thighs, my knees still firmly planted on the stone slabs beneath me.

"My apologies." My tone is less than enthusiastic, but I manage to maintain a note of respect. The ebony woman looks over me longer and harder than the others do, then gives them a look as if to communicate something without words.

While this is happening, I take a moment to look over the goddess to the male's right. She is exactly as I expected, only due to Sitara's doting description of her. Coli'hanu, Goddess of Cold Fire and my Sitara's progenitor.

She is the smallest of the three, though it does nothing to hide the coiled power I feel radiating off of her. She can, however, still hold her own with the other two. Her skin is the color of fresh snowfall, no active warmth to be found besides the subtle flush in her lips. A mixture of orange and green flames coils and dances along her skin as if alive, just as I have seen the emerald dance across my woman's. Her hair is of an equal snowy hue, which also translates to her eyebrows and eyelashes. However, it is her eyes that unsettle me the most. Her irises are like glowing orange coals, rimmed with a burning violet color that matches that of Sitara's gift.

She lies along one of the tiers halfway up the dias, lounging carelessly on her side with her head propped up on an elbow. She doesn't stay like this long, however, as a wide smile spreads across her face and she rises. Coli'hanu spreads her slender arms wide, her voice unexpectedly low and authoritative. "Sitara, Ko'u'con. Come, let me have a look at you."

I watch as Sitara rises, a soft smile gracing her face as she makes her way toward the woman. There is the narrowest of walkways over the water that leads to the base of the central structure, and she all but runs across it to stand before the oddly icy goddess. I, however, do not risk standing until told to do so. I'd rather not taste the soil a second time.

The interaction between my darling and the living goddess is a stark contrast to what I was expecting. Coli'hanu wraps her arms around Sitara's slight shoulders, kissing the top of her head with an almost motherly affection.

"My, how you have grown. You really shouldn't make me wait so long between visits," the goddess chides.

"I apologize, Maku'ome," Sitara's voice is almost reverent as she refers to the goddess as her *Mother Creator*.

See, I can retain new things when I want to.

Gula'ci straightens her stance, which draws my attention back to her momentarily. She gives me a nod, a huff rolling up her throat in the process.

"Thanks," I mutter, rising now that I have been permitted to. I look to Sitara, waiting for some cue as to what I am supposed to be doing, saying... *not* doing or saying.

She turns around to look at me, her face flushed with excitement. With a warm smile, she holds out her hand, beckoning me to her side.

I make a conscious effort to relax my jaw, which I hadn't realized was clenched until now. My feet move, carrying me across the spare land-bridge that sits between us. It takes every ounce of self-control I have to keep my hands to myself in the presence of her esteemed gods. I also have to remind myself to hold my tongue and not let it run rampant, no matter how tempting it is under the scrutiny of Teo'Kan's glare.

Dying seems like a bad option right about now.

Sitara laces her fingers with mine as I finally stand next to her in front of the three ethereal beings, her touch grounding in the power dynamic. I'm not used to not being the strongest in the room. Though, in reality, I probably haven't been for a while now. Sitara simply couldn't use that power away from the island.

"Maku'ome, Kala'ome, Ana'ome," Sitara begins by addressing them each by their respective titles, "This is Kiernan Slater. I've come to ask for your favor so that he might be allowed to stay within the borders of our jungle."

Teo'Kan is the first to speak, his dark brows knitting inward. "Does he have a shaman's favor?"

Of course, he knows I have a shaman's favor. I wouldn't have been able to cross the damn line without it. Damn, for a supposed *'merciful god'*, this guy is a prick.

I pull the pulsating gem from my pants pocket, flashing it in his general direction before slipping it back into its temporary home. The tangy copper taste that suddenly tinges my mouth is my cue to stop gnawing on the inside of my cheek. I've been biting into it to keep from saying something that would not only put me six feet under the stone floor of this temple, but worse, get me banned from the island. Banishment would only open the possibility of taking my ability to see Sitara away if they were to decide to keep her here.

Coli'hanu tilts her head to the side, sliding a sideways glance toward Gula'ci, who is still standing by her pillar as still as stone. "I see. And you wish to keep a man who enjoys taking our women off the sand like trophies, do you?" She turns back toward Sitara with a coy smirk on her face.

A long sigh escapes me, my eyes closing as I try to keep my composure. *Fucking hell. Of course, they would know about that.*

"Woman," I correct her, "Just one. I had every intention of allowing her to come back."

I really should try harder not to growl at *goddesses*.

Sitara tenses next to me, her fingers tightening around mine in a clear warning.

"Ah, but you didn't just take *any* woman. You took the one I have personally taken under my wing," the Goddess of Cold Fire berates, though there is no real heat behind her words. I'm beginning to understand why said fire is *'cold'*.

Before an apology can come, Gula'ci chuckles, the sound far too melodious for someone who looks so hardened by time. "Oh, he is a delight, isn't he?"

"Well, no one can accuse me of having poor taste, now can they?" I mentally scold myself for being so impertinent. Didn't I just tell myself two seconds ago that dying wasn't a good plan?

Damn it. My mother didn't have the chance to teach me the etiquette that I so desperately need right now, did she?

Sitara's face snaps toward me, mortification clear in her wide eyes. Honestly, I'm just as perplexed by my behavior. Who would have thought that I had the bollock size to be an asshole to a literal god?

"Think it is funny to claim our women like mere chattel, do you?" Teo'Kan's voice rumbles through the space, a low growl in his throat.

"Please," Sitara tries to placate the situation, "It isn't what it— Well, it was, but the situation is far from how it began."

I don't look at the male who is still sitting off to the left of us, but I can feel his eyes boring into the side of my head. Everything in me wants to snap my jaws back at him, though I know it isn't wise. I need this to be over before I end up getting myself into some deep shit.

"How quaint. Captor-Hostage bonding at its finest," Teo'Kan snides, scoffing as I watch him roll his eyes and avert his gaze toward the water once more from my peripheral vision.

I bite into my tongue, using every bit of strength I have left not to growl at him.

"I wasn't aware you were so taken with my children, brother," Coli'hanu surprises me by snapping at him with a less than grateful tone. He shrugs, resting his cheek in his palm.

Is that motherfucker feigning boredom right now?

I turn to Sitara, leaning in to whisper in her ear. "Can we just get through the topic of why we are here?"

Don't ask me what has possessed me to whisper, seeing as they are living gods and probably have impeccable hearing.

"Isn't that what we are doing, *Captain* Kiernan Slater?" Guca'ci chuckles, her obsidian lips curling up to reveal pearl white teeth.

See?

What did I tell you?

Impeccable hearing.

"At the end of the day, we need to treat this as we always have," Coli'hanu sighs, turning back toward Sitara. Her hand snakes out to coil a strand of Sitara's hair around her finger, looking up at my girl with a gentle expression that eases away the tension in her tone mere moments ago.

These deities are bipolar as hell.

"Does he mean that much to you, Sitara?" the goddess asks, her voice commanding but gentle. I hold my breath, my eyes drinking in the silence between them with bated breath.

"Yes," Sitara responds simply. It is a short response, but the magnitude of its meaning is clear.

I am hit with an enormity of feelings. Part of me wants to laugh while part of me wants to cry. Not the kind of tears that come from any sort of pain, but the kind I have seen in others when they are experiencing too much of a good thing. It isn't something I have ever witnessed in myself before.

My entire body feels lighter, even as the weight of what she has boldly admitted aloud to her gods fills me with a deep pride. It nearly has me sinking to my knees before her. A part of me has always known this to be true, but to hear it out loud with such conviction... Sitara, though having gotten better about voicing her thoughts and feelings as of late, has always seemed to hold her emotions at arm's length. To hear it fall from her lips so proudly, so simply, is something I didn't know I needed to balm my insecurities until now.

I smile at her, conveying every ounce of warmth I feel in my chest. I know she can feel it, though she keeps her eyes firmly placed on the goddess before her. I have to war with the nearly uncontrollable urge to kiss her—long and hard, hot and heavy—while simultaneously flipping the arrogant bastard off the stairs into the water as I do.

However, I will be a good boy, settling for a smug grin in his general direction.

Gula'ci moves toward the group, just as her brother stands up with a disgruntled sigh. The three of them move to the top of the dais until they are lined up on the highest tier. The Goddess of Earth holds out her hand, palm up, as if inviting me to step toward them. "We need something from your person, Kiernan Slater. Something of great importance."

Great.

Are they about to ask for my heart on a silver platter?

As if catching onto my thought process, Teo'Kan rolls his eyes. "No, you fool. We only require an item. Perhaps those Ma'tawi beads you have so carefully hidden under your sleeve."

My eyes grow wide in their sockets, the left one twitching ever so slightly as my brows damn near disappear into my hairline.

Busted.

"Kiernan!" my love hisses at me.

"Hmm?" I dare to feign my innocence even though I know it does me no good. I know if I speak with any actual articulation, they will betray me regardless.

"How long have you had those?!"

Her eyes grow nearly three times in size as I quietly inform her that I had slipped them off her ankle, having kept them lovingly tucked away since the last time I found myself between her thighs.

She lets out a chagrin groan, burying her face in her hands. By the color of her ears, she is a tempting shade of scarlet right now. I'm not sure why she is so embarrassed. Surely they know I've had her in my presence long enough for something to have happened between us.

I slowly roll my sleeve, unclasping the strand of beads from around my wrist. With slow, measured steps, I ascend the stairs, holding out the beads in my palm.

Gula'ci takes the beads in her outstretched hand, her skin as un-yielding as stone against mine as I drop them into her palm. Her fingers, tips with equally dark nails, wrap around the piece of jewelry.

The sound of shells and glass being ground down into dust filters through the air until there is nothing but a pile of sand between her fingers. She holds her fisted hand above the other, which is cupped underneath it like a bowl, and begins to allow the dirt to fall like the sand in an hourglass. It slowly builds upon itself, being remade anew. The beads have had their entire making altered to fit that of a male; the beads are now of stone and wood.

What was once an anklet of brown and blue beads is now mute in color, the size more proportionate to my wrist. She then passes it on to Coli'hanu, who tosses it into the green flames behind them, as one would do to fire clay. The item crackles and pops, a slight glow furnishing the beads until she finally sticks her hand into the fire and pulls it out. It now has a slight sheen of orange and violet.

Teo'Kan then takes it from her, his lips moving as if he is muttering under his breath, even though my human ears cannot make out his words. He descends until he is right beside me, tossing it into the water below us. I turn to witness the beaded strand emerging with added renderings of blue and greens. Meanwhile, Sitara has been watching with awe and admiration, soaking in a ritual I assume she's never seen in her lifetime.

The man turns to me, holding his hand out begrudgingly. "Here, mortal. Keep this close to you, and the jungle will accept you as one of its own. Lose it and... well, perhaps one of those *'Feather Boas'*, as you so crudely call them, will decide it would much rather eat you than the mouse."

The other two, who are still standing at the top, grin as if there is a hidden joke that neither Sitara nor I is aware of.

I take the new bracelet from him as he dangles it between his forefinger and thumb, wrapping it back around my wrist with delicate care. *I was wearing it because it was hers... not for fashion.* I chastise myself quickly after the thought for being ungrateful.

"Thank you," I say with forced gratitude. I reach out, pulling Sitara to my side, where I tuck her nicely under my arm. I feel her warmth as she wraps an arm around my waist, pulling me down into a deep bow alongside her.

"Thank you so much. Your understanding is as graceful as your mercy."

It isn't until now that I truly understand the depths of her devotion to the gods of flesh and bone that stand before us. I was always under the impression it had to do with her upbringing. I can see now that she would have worshipped them regardless.

"Do come see us again soon, young ones," Coli'hanu smiles as her brother motions for us to take our leave.

The three of them move with a grace unattainable to mere humans as they resume their original positions along the tiered steps of the dais. That is our cue to leave them to their shared solitude.

"Oh yes. Perhaps next time, our meeting will be a little more... entertaining," Gula'ci concurs, a knowing glint in her eyes as she grins.

Sitara has noticed it as well, looking up at me with a slightly knitted brow. Her eyelashes flutter in contemplation as the two of us try to decipher what the implication of the goddess's tone could have meant. We linger on it briefly before striding off through the outer ring of the temple and into the less oppressive air of the outside world.

36
Sitara

As we had left the temple earlier today, I began feeling nauseous. Something hadn't settled well with that rock inside of me as we stepped out of the outer ring of the temple. My entire body had stiffened, my eyes compelled to look off to the right of the entrance and toward the staircase that opened up out of the earth. It was, what I assume to be, the entrance to the bowels under the temple: Mala'tet, the Cavern of Light.

Rumor has it, it is a beautiful place of glowing stone and colorful crystals. However, no one has been allowed to go in there in four years. No one knows why that is, but we have followed that rule to a letter, as the consequences were brutal compared to any other form of defiance. Perhaps that is what had given me that sickening feeling in my gut.

The entire walk back toward the Ma'tawi village, Kiernan hadn't stopped asking me if I was alright. I kept lying, telling him I was fine. I'm not sure why I had lied; why I hadn't immediately told him that I suddenly found it hard to breathe, that my insides were twisting in on themselves. It just didn't seem important. Especially when the feeling was quickly fading with each mile we placed between us and Potem'aku.

It was a little after noon when I had walked him into the village, my brothers and sisters of the tribe stalling in their paths to watch me lead the massive Mundane man into our home. Some looked at him with awe—amazed that he had been given the gods' favor. Others looked upon him with critical, untrusting gazes. I had squeezed his hand firmly, trying to reassure him that their opinions might not be completely narrowed on him. There were still some tribe members—though they were few nowadays—who still held Larkin and me with disdain for the sins of our parents.

He had squeezed my hand in reassurance, trying to convey that he was okay. The murmuring all around us was probably difficult for him to make out anyway, considering they were all talking so low that we could barely hear them. Not that Kiernan would have understood them regardless. He had already admitted to me that his Lo'pillkat was rusty at best. Even if he had been able to hear them, he wouldn't have understood anything that was being said. I found it rather comical that Kiernan is every bit of a foot taller than most of the people in my village.

Not all, but most.

I pulled him to a stop in front of Djar's hut flap before he had the chance to walk right into it due to his absent-minded observation.

"Djar," I had called out, peeking my head into the doorway to find the crazy old man sitting with his pipe in the same position I had left him yesterday. Had he even moved? I knew the answer without having to ask it aloud. No, he hadn't. He hadn't taken that nap he had threatened, either.

"So, it is done, is it?" Djar grinned, crooking his aged fingers for us to enter, "Where is the man with my relic? I don't like it when my things are borrowed longer than necessary." I bit back a smile, knowing he's simply trying to keep Kiernan on his toes.

It's a game Djar plays with all of us often.

Once Kiernan had ducked to clear the entrance, he began fumbling in his pocket. "Oh uh..." I could see the slight panic in the corner of his eyes before an equally quick flash of relief washed over him, "Here."

Djar held out his hand, where Kiernan plopped the large stone into it. He then quickly slides his hand back into mine, the other making its way back into the now-empty space inside his pocket.

"It is," I said proudly, sitting down on the rug across from Djar, "He was given their favor."

"Even despite proving himself a thief, how interesting." The old man smirked, running his hand through his long beard. I can see Kiernan's head snap up from my peripheral vision, forgetting all about picking at his nails. The look that crossed his face was priceless. Eventually, he will learn that Djar just knows things, and it is best not to lie to him.

"A thief?" Kiernan gave a mock scoff of offense, "I *earned* that bracelet, thank you very mu-"

I quickly cut him off with a swift backhand to the chest, my eyes closing and brows bunching in distaste. He rubbed the 'injured' area, the tone in his voice evident of the bewildered look on his face. "What?! I did!"

Djar had hummed softly, a low, throaty chuckle filling the space inside the hut. "Oh, yes. I'm sure you did. It takes some real talent to take something off someone when they are... distracted."

"Djar!" I snapped, my eyes growing wide with embarrassment. My cheeks are probably still trying to melt off my face.

Thus, here I am, standing next to Kiernan just before dusk as more and more members of the village file in around the communal fire. My fingers are two knuckles deep in colorful oils extracted from some of the bioluminescent plants that grow here in the jungle.

Kiernan is shirtless, as are the others who will be participating in the Mana'Oka—the rites of passage—alongside him tonight. It is a tradition that has been passed down from generation to generation; a ritual that marks the beginning of a young boy's arrival into adulthood.

I know Djar wouldn't have required him to do so if not for the fact that he's a cheeky old man and the Mana'Oka takes place on a New Moon, which happens to be tonight. I remain silent as I paint the oils along his arms and chest, a small smirk rising to my face as I ponder the comedic relief of the situation. All the other men performing the Mana'Oka are either twelve-year-old boys or their fathers.

"Remind me again exactly why I have to do this?" He mumbles, side eyeing me. He knows that I am enjoying every moment of his struggle, but it is more than that. Kiernan's participation in the Mana'Oka is a symbolic thing, a way for him to prove that he is willing to accept my culture and traditions, just as I have for him aboard his ship. Yes, I am finding some sick satisfaction out of this, but I am also filled with a pride that brings a giddy feeling to my stomach. "And who did the old man say he was going to go find?"

I smile, my fingers tracing the oil down the middle of his sternum where it will flare out like fire along his abdomen. "Ko'chi. He is the most renowned warrior in the village," I say simply, feeling the way his muscles move under my hand as I run my fingers from his navel to the small of his back, smearing orange oils along his skin to match the purples along his chest. I pause, looking up at him with warmth and affection. "The Mana'Oka is the mark of the beginning, where a young boy—or in this case a mundane—is considered a man of the village. One of us. It should be seen as an honor to bear the experience of such a thing."

I can see the honor and bruised pride warring on his face as I go back to painting his skin. I know he doesn't like the idea of having an escort. He believes himself capable, and I do not doubt that if it weren't for his lack of knowledge of the jungle, he would be able to do this on his own. However, he has already proven that his observational skills are not as keen when not drifting along the ocean currents. That became evident when he almost ran into the miz'geru earlier today.

"What is it we are supposed to be looking for again?" he asks me.

"A Coa'hesa," I chuckle, feeling a small twinge of guilt for traumatizing him with one earlier. If I had known... "A feather boa," I clarify.

I step back to look at him, admiring my work before dipping one of my fingers into the purple and one into the orange. I begin to slide my fingertips along my face from one temple, along my cheek, across my nose, and stop at the other temple. I then place intricate knotwork around my brows and neck, not needing to look to know exactly what they look like. It is tradition for the woman vouching for the boy, usually his mother—though in this case it is me—to wear the colors along her body as a show of support. That she is with him in spirit. Once the sun has fully set, these intricate lines and knots will begin to glow, creating a tapestry of art on our skin.

He gives me a wide-eyed look of despair, clearly not happy with the information. "I have to catch one of those things?!" he groans, his head hanging low between his shoulders, "Of course I have to get my hand on a damn feather boa..."

I snicker, crouching down to wipe the excess oil from my fingers onto the grass. "Remember the mouse? That trick might prove more helpful than I originally intended it to be."

"You people are demented," he chides, letting out a deep sigh.

"If that's how you want to look at it," I chuckle, shaking my head at his theatrics.

He reaches out to pull me to him when we are interrupted by Djar calling out to me using my tribal name. The look of confusion on Kiernan's face cracks me up. I forgot to tell him my real name isn't Sitara. That is just the name I use for the Mundanes, which is something many of us do.

Kiernan studies the large man walking beside Djar. Ko'chi is probably just as tall as Kiernan, just as broad, too. His sun-kissed skin and dark hair make the hazel of his eyes stand out against the earthy hues. The dark dusting of facial hair around his full lips shifts as he smiles and holds out an arm for a brotherly hug once they have reached a close enough distance.

"Sitalli'ara! It's good to see you home!" Ko'chi grins, wrapping an arm around my shoulders.

I can sense Kiernan stiffening as Ko'chi greets me, hearing the deep breath he draws into his lungs. He halfheartedly forces an uncomfortable smile, one that looks as painful as it does fake. I can read the ticking time bomb behind his eyes, and after returning a greeting and a smile, I slide back to his side, tucking myself under his waiting arm. I can feel Kiernan's shoulders relax as I wrap my arm around his waist.

Ko'chi turns to Kiernan without missing a beat, giving him a smile and a nod in a way of greeting. "I am Ko'chi. I'll be going out into the jungle with you tonight," he says with a friendly tone.

"Kiernan," Mea'loa responds after a deep, calming inhale.

Djar looks Kiernan over with a playfully critical eye, rubbing his fingers through his grey beard in contemplation. "Yes, I'd say you look every bit Ma'tawi with those markings on your body. Sitalli'ara did a fine job."

Kiernan quickly looks to Djar, giving him a much more genuine grin. "She's good with her—" My eyes flare, a sharp flash of violet passing through them as I glare up at him. He damn near chokes on his own words and redirects like a good boy, "Uh— I mean, yes, she did a good job."

I'm pleased that he has changed direction with his comment, though honestly, I know it's only because he doesn't want to get singed by my fire.

"Well, the festivities are about to begin. Kiernan, why don't you follow Ko'chi to line up with the others?" Djar motions, lacing his arm into mine to lead me toward the fire. "You, Ko'u'con, can come with me."

I follow Djar, accompanying him to the front where the families and shamans stand. Kiernan and Ko'chi move to line up next to the others, a small stifled snicker passing through my tightly pressed lips at the sight of him towering over all the young boys in line.

Djar moves to his spot among the other two shamans, pulling out the intricately made lantern that is used to carry a piece of the eternal flame for rituals, healing, and blessing, like tonight. He goes along to each of our participants, giving his blessing and placing a small piece of the glowing orange flame into their palm.

When he reaches Kiernan, a mischievous gleam flashes through his eyes. He reaches up, ruffling Kiernan's hair with a chuckle. "Good luck, buddy."

"Djar..." I give him a warning hiss, and he laughs, his ancient shoulders shaking as he attempts to compose himself. Kiernan flashes me a bewildered look, and I have to cover my mouth with my hand to keep from spitting all over the place.

The old man finally manages some form of professionalism, making direct eye contact with my man, where they stare at one another for a long moment. I can see Kiernan squirming slightly under the old man's scrutiny. I'm not going to lie, I feel a little bad for him, a twinge of guilt for finding so much pleasure in this.

Finally, Djar reaches into the lantern and pulls out a small golf ball-sized piece of the flame, placing it into Kiernan's hand where it pulsates and writhes but doesn't burn his skin. "Mete Coli'hanu yechooma ot, Ko'u'con... again," Djar says, placing his hand on Kiernan's forehead almost lovingly.

I smile, my heart clenching with the pride that quickly washes over me. May Coli'hanu bless you, my child. It is the greatest blessing one from our tribe can receive from our shaman, and it fills me with a sense of warmth.

When the sun finally sets and the oils on our skins begin to glow, the group sets out in their own directions, determination laced in every line of their bodies. I watch Kiernan go, leading the charge with Ko'chi hot on his heels. I giggle, the sound bubbling up my throat before I can stop it, and shake my head.

Of course, Kiernan would continue to be as fearless as ever, walking headfirst into a place he knows nothing about while damn near leaving his escort behind in the process.

37

Kiernan

Ko'chic—whatever his name is—keeps talking as we rummage through the undergrowth of the jungle. But listening to him is like trying to understand someone who is speaking underwater.

It's not registering with me at all.

My mind is elsewhere, thinking back to how Sitara had looked as the sun set and the fiery hues of orange and emerald had lit up across her cheekbones. The way the light had illuminated the delicate lines of her face, making her eyes look larger and brighter than they already are...

It was an achingly beautiful sight. After beholding such a thing, I didn't want to leave. All I wanted to do was spread her out right there on the fucking ground in front of everyone.

But now, here I am, trying to see what is more than a foot in front of me. How did they expect *children* to walk through this shit at night? I guess that is why their fathers accompany them. All the while, this jackass drones on at my backside. He's too pretty for my liking. Far too nice as well. Not to mention, far too familiar with my Si—

"...Sitalli'ara seems to be very happy you are doing this. It's good to see a genuine smile on her face for once," Ko'chi says, snapping me out of my thoughts with ease.

"Why does everyone keep calling her that?" I blurt out, my brows furrowing inward with confusion. Ko'chi blinks slowly; the expression that passes over his face makes me want to punch him for looking at me like I'm stupid.

"It's her name," he says, his words drawn out like he's talking to a child, "Sitara is just her name in your language."

At first, his words don't even register.

All I hear is him calling me a dumbass.

I furrow my brow after a momentary need to throttle him passes.

"Say it again," I demand softly.

I want to be able to pronounce it correctly when I get the chance to use it.

Part of me wonders why she never told me about this *other name*. Then it suddenly dawns on me.

It's probably because I'm a fucking idiot who did nothing but make fun of the pronunciation of damn near every word she has tried to teach me, without making much effort to try.

Dumbass, I chide myself, *no wonder she didn't tell me!*

Ko'chi side eyes me as we continue to make our way through the foliage, not sticking to a path like Sitara and I had on our way to the temple. A small grin forms on his face as he begins to deliberately break up each syllable of her name. "Si-tah-lee-R-uh."

"Again?" I listen to him say it one more time before attempting to say it back to him as perfectly as I can.

To my surprise, Ko'chi doesn't poke fun at me or laugh at my expense. This is probably a good thing, considering my muscles are ready and prepped to break his stupidly perfect nose if he does.

Shit... maybe I am a psychopath... no... well...

"Good, but don't forget to emphasize the 'R' at the end of it," he corrects the slight pronunciation mistake, and I try it again.

"Sitalli'ara."

He grins, nodding enthusiastically as he claps me on the shoulder, his massive hand probably the same size as my own.

"Perfect!"

My inner monologue screams out in my usual bravado, wanting nothing more than to look at him and say, '*I know I am, but thanks anyway*'.

Somehow, the words "Thank you "come out instead.

Damn, she's rubbing off on me.

Ko'chi laughs, waving off my thanks with a nonchalant dismissal. "It's not a problem. It's nice to finally see her... happy," he muses, and that is when it becomes very clear—based on the words and the softness that sets into his eyes—that Sitara, *my* Sitara, means something to him.

Great, just when I thought I had gotten past the urge to introduce him to Gerald...

I barely get through that thought when I stumble over a root that, again, I swear wasn't there a second ago.

This fucking jungle is alive.

I swear by their apparently real gods, it is!

"Glad I can do something right," I say, looking around the area to see if I can detect any movement in the trees.

I mean that honestly.

To have someone tell me she seems happy with me... It's a good feeling.

After a sidelong glance in his direction, I decide this is the perfect opportunity to learn more about my Sitara. "Was she not happy when she was here before?"

Ko'chi's smile falters slightly and he lifts one shoulder in a shrug. "No, not really. Don't get me wrong, she was always smiling, but it was hollow, like it was forced. It never really reached her eyes, you know? But she and her brother have been through a lot. Sitalli'ara even more so."

I swallow hard, the fire in my belly aching to lash out. I know I shouldn't, though. After all, this guy is the only thing probably keeping me from getting eaten by a stripy-tailed fox.

He obviously knows her.

Too well if you ask me.

"Are you this observant with everyone?" The look I give him probably isn't following the tone of innocent questioning I'm trying to aim for. "Or is that strictly reserved for Sitara?"

I turn my eyes forward to watch out for more of those rude tree roots, and I swear by the gods, I saw one move.

I clench my jaw as he mulls over his response, probably trying to gauge how much he should reveal to me.

"No... It's just a Sitara thing," he admits softly, crouching down to look at something in the ferns and vines near one of the larger tree bases, "She's a remarkable woman. Any man would be lucky to have her at his side, so long as he can handle her wild nature."

"Some might find that wild nature charming." I clear my throat, raking my fingers through my hair. "So the observation is there, but the admiration for her *'wild'* spirit isn't?"

I look over my shoulder at him as I place enough distance between us that I can't reach down and smash his head into the tree. I really should learn to check myself before lashing out.

"No, it's one of the things I like most about her," Ko'chi clarifies, shaking his hand as he stands back up to his full height, "She's already rejected me. I offered her a courtship not long before you took her."

He lets out a self-deprecating chuckle, running his fingers through his own hair. "Besides, even if she hadn't, I wouldn't dream of trying to come between her and something that makes her so happy."

Okay, maybe I *won't* introduce him to Gerald.

I give him an empathetic nod, running my fingers along my temple as I contemplate my own thoughts. I remember telling myself that if I ever saw Sitara happy with someone, I would move past my incessant obsession and leave her be. That I would leave her to be happy with whoever she had chosen. I also remember how shitty that thought had felt when I had it.

Great, now I feel bad for the guy. Proof I'm not a psychopath... right?

"I said the same thing once," I admit, feeling some sort of camaraderie with the guy.

"She's not an easy one to let go, is she?" He muses, bending down in another thicket of brush. I momentarily wonder what the fuck he's looking for, then brush it aside as his question hangs between us.

"No, she's not."

I move on to a different topic, one that I had been wondering about but didn't really have anyone to ask before now. Larkin sure as hell wasn't going to be helpful. And Djar would just blow smoke in my direction and laugh, telling me I would figure it out eventually.

"Would you tell me about your customs when it comes to things like courtship?" Part of me questions whether or not I should be asking him this after what he has just revealed to me. I know it would feel like someone rubbing salt in my open wound if it were me. I give him a sheepish smile, rubbing the back of my neck. "I don't have anyone else I can ask."

He looks up from the foliage, standing up once more to move toward another thick patch. A small smile graces his face as he hunches over once more. "I would assume it is much like it is for you Mundanes, in the beginning, anyway. We spend time together, though our court-ing is probably shorter, as we already know each other. Our island is very small," he pauses, his eyes lighting up as he stands erect yet again, "As for the actual *'getting married'* part, there is a special tattoo that is woven into our pe'aboros, at the base of our left wrist. It is tradition for each partner to etch it into the skin of the other."

I scratch at the base of my throat, filing away the information I have just received. Okay, but... what about the *asking* part? For some damn reason, I can't get the words to come out of my mouth, my throat suddenly very dry. Still, he answers the question that is sitting on the tip of my tongue, one that hasn't even been asked yet.

"You ask her however you heart desires," he chuckles.

Am I really that easy to read?!

He is far more eager to help than I would be if I were in his position, and in another timeline, I probably am. I don't believe I could get so lucky in all of my lives. I appreciate his help, and I give him a grateful nod.

Ko'chi then holds out his palm with a smirk, a tiny, stringlike tail poking out from between his fingers.

Another damn mouse.

"Why don't we make sure you can take her home some good news, shall we?"

As the sun crests over the horizon, Ko'chi and I walk out into the clearing that harbors the village. I am grinning, proud of myself for what I have accomplished. Ko'chi grins as well, patting my shoulder before walking off to allow me my victory gait toward my woman, who is sitting with a dark skinned lady by the fire. Her laughter rings out into the air, and I pinpoint it easily, knowing her laugh anywhere.

Her head lifts, scanning the treeline for me as the lot of us stumble our way out of the jungle. When her gaze lands on me, a wide smile spreads across her face, and she removes herself from the ground to meet me halfway. I hold up the damn snake, smiling broadly as I wave it in front of her.

"I caught this. *Midair*!" I say, puffing my chest out with pride.

She laughs at my childish wonder, running her fingers along the snake's feathers reverently. "I knew you could. I'm proud of you."

I slide my free hand into hers, roughly pulling her to me with a chuckle, and plant a kiss on the center of her forehead. She leans into me, sighing softly.

"Ko'chi is a good man," I say, leaning in with a conspiratorial whisper, "Don't tell anyone I said that. Can't have them thinking I'm capable of making friends."

She giggles at my teasing, rolling her eyes as she takes the Coa'hesa from my hand. "Oh, of course. We can't have that, now can we?"

Her sarcasm is refreshing, as I have missed her greatly. It's been quite some time since I have had to be away from her for so long. "Come on, it's time to get started," she continues, pulling me toward the fire.

My eyes widen fractionally, my shoulders slumping in disappointment. "Get started? I just–but I did it... didn't I?"

She spins around to look up at me, and I'm not sure if I enjoy the gleam of mischief in her eyes.

Clearly, she spent too much time with the old man last night.

She wiggles the Coa'hesa out in front of her, a broad smirk rising along the lines of her mouth. "You still have work to do, Mea'loa."

I let out a soft groan, dragging my feet along the ground. "I thought I just had to catch it? What's his face didn't mention having to *do* anything beyond that!"

She ignores my whining, the sinful little grin still planted firmly on her face as she makes her way to where the mothers are waiting for their triumphant sons.

"Am I getting a designated mother too, or is *Ko'chi* coming back?" I tease, waggling my brows at her. She rolls her eyes, slapping the snake back into my hand as she points toward a collection of stools and grinding stones that sit off to the side.

"You still have to prepare it for your pe'aboros. Unless... You've decided not to get one."

There is a challenge in her eyes.

She's daring me to refuse like she doesn't know her wish is my fucking command.

My head falls further forward with a huff as I stalk over to the stools. "You never answered my *designated mother* question," I wave the creature in her face once more, "Who will teach me the ways of feather boa mutilation?!"

Sitara sits down on a stool at my side, jabbing me in the ribs with her sharp nails.

"It doesn't have to be a mother, you idiot," she laughs, "It is the job of the family matriarch to help prepare and bestow the pe'aboros, be that a mother, grandmother, aunt, sister, or... whatever I am."

"Yeah, we're going to have a conversation about *whatever you are* when this is through," I tell her as she settles more comfortably on the stool, angling herself to instruct me on what the hell I'm supposed to be doing.

She gives me a look of wary confusion. "What are you-"

I don't let her finish, putting my finger to my lips and hushing her.

"Shh... I'm trying to listen to the old man." Djar moves to our little group of Kana'te people, smiling broadly at the four of us who had participated in the Mana'Oka.

"Mighty hunters, the lot of you, but you are not finished yet. For the next few hours, you will undergo the transition from boys to men. When your pe'aboros are finished, come to me. I'd very much like to see them." The old geezer turns his attention to me, amusement laced in his face.

If I hadn't already begun to learn how this man works, I would be offended by his insinuation that I'm a mere *boy*.

Sitara gets to work, bringing out bowls of water, oils, and jars that I hadn't even noticed were sitting next to the grinding stone.

Damn, I really don't have good observational skills when I'm being pelted in the face with new things left and right, do I?

When she pulls out the knives, my brows lift into my hairline and my eyes widen. "The meat will go to feeding our bodies, the scales are for the white ink, the venom is for the gold ink, and its feathers are sharp enough to use as the needle."

I listen to her explain, looking from her to the creature I hold in my hand. I guess that makes a lot of sense. Killing it just to kill it would have made far less sense. Sitara patiently shows me how to go about gently butchering the five-foot-long danger noodle.

When the scales and feathers have been put in their respective bowls, she goes on explaining how to extract the venom. The word *'venom'* scares me at first, but she explains that the venom is not harmful to humans, especially once it is diluted with water.

I take the snake by the base of its head and pry its mouth open, fixing its fangs over the film of a jar. I push from the back to the front to squeeze the venom glands on both sides. I watch in amazement as a thick, golden liquid begins to flow from it, dripping down into the bottom of the glass. The creatures here are not much different from the ones I am used to, but still so different. What the fuck is the point of the venom being gold? Sitara quickly hands me the water, which I pour in until she tells me to stop.

The next process is to crush the scales into a fine powder in order to add the oils. The process is grueling and time-consuming, and I'm not sure if I have the damn patience for it more than once. But then, I remember the marriage mark, and I decide I'd better get used to it.

"These are beautiful. Good job," she smiles at me, grabbing the bowls to swirl the contents around.

I watch as she begins prepping the feathers and inks that I worked so hard on, steeling myself for the poking and prodding I am about to endure. She cleanses the tips of each feather reverently, keeping her movements slow and gentle.

I watch as she delicately needles the ink into my skin, the intricate designs of golden Poppies and white Galanthus flowing down the whole expanse of my arm, coiling around one another in an intriguing balance. She is focused and precise, perfecting every line as it materializes on my skin. She uses every trickle of sunlight that she has before the tiny sliver of the moon rises into the sky.

She has worked for hours, finally rolling her shoulders as she straightens, the last prick of the feather sinking into the skin mere centimeters from my cuticle. I roll my arm from side to side, confused as to how flowers somehow do not seem as feminine as I had expected them to.

"All done," she sighs, placing the feather down into the empty bowl where there was once white ink. She rolls her neck, clearly stiff from the hunched-over position she has been in all day.

The old man is now happily droning on about the second night of the celebration, his excitement palpable. I'm not hearing any of it. I have plans, none of which involve smoking myself stupid out of his pretty little pipe.

Well... At least not until after.

I lace my fingers with Sitara's, gently backing us out of the crowd. I press my finger to my lips as she turns toward me to protest, despite the mirth that is swimming in the depths of those russet eyes. I had found a place while I was out hunting that feathery creature, and I knew it would be the perfect spot the moment I saw it. Well, so long as no one gets there before I get my chance.

Hence, why I am luring her away in the middle of Djar's speech.

"Where are we going?" she whines, though the bubbling giggles tell me she is far from disappointed to be missing Djar's ramblings. She wraps herself around me tightly, her delicately arched brow rising in confusion.

"Do you have to know absolutely everything?" I tease in a harsh whisper, "I want to show you something."

She nods, the sparkle that lights up her face as she tightens her grip on me, making my chest swell with something similar to pure worship. Something in the way she looks at me, like she's the happiest she's ever been to have both of her worlds together in one place, sends a flutter into my stomach. Or perhaps it's just nerves.

I'm not sure yet.

I make a dramatic coltish effort to pull her in and out of the shadow-covered hidey holes as if the possibility of getting found could mean trouble. It doesn't. No one would care that two adults have gone off by themselves—save for Larkin, who has done nothing, a 180-degree shift to ignoring my ass completely, her peals of laughter as I do so are worth everything. My eyes grow wide as I snatch her up and cover her mouth with my large hand.

"You're not very good at thi-" I am halted in my playful chastisement when we tumble through the brush, landing on our sides in the grass.

"Who's not very good at what now?" she says between fits of laughter, hair tousled around her face like a fiery halo against the dark greens of the grass beneath us as she rolls over to her back to catch her breath. I position myself above her, my hands splaying on the ground on either side of her head. My muscles flex as I dip my face, pressing a kiss to her lips. Her hands cup my cheeks, the pleasant dance of her lips against mine...

It's a feeling I will never get used to. Never get enough of. Never grow bored with it.

Gods, am I stalling for time? The somersaults my stomach does are answer enough. When our lips part, she smiles at me gingerly, her fingers carding through my hair.

"So, what was this conversation you wanted to have?" I can tell she's been thinking about it since I mentioned it this morning, as evidenced by the growing look of impatience in her eyes.

There's that 'wild nature' I love so much.

I chuckle, moving to stand as I bring her up with me. "I'm getting there. Be patient, my darling." I lead her further into this clearing that I have not-so-accidentally landed us in.

The warm glow of firebugs illuminates the clearing with their vast numbers as they dance along the tall grasses in the bijou meadowed area. Mist filters in subtle puffs from the trickle of the little waterfall that flows over a slight ledge, where it barely moves the water that sits at its base. I feel her hand tighten around mine as I pull her to the water's edge, looking down at the surface where even brighter, white-lit bugs swim under the surface, creating a vast night sky in the voided depths.

Sitara stares into the water, her eyes wide and unreadable. I'd like to think it is awe, but she's probably already been here before. Then again, I guess it could still be awe. Sitara has always maintained a constant level of attention toward things that bring her great emotions, be that anger, fear, joy, or awe.

Except for me.

I managed to get her to change her opinion of me. It is still, to date, one of my greatest accomplishments.

She says nothing, staring down into the water as her eyes follow the movement of the little lights. This is one of those moments where all of my people-reading abilities fail me. I'm not sure what she's thinking.

I turn her toward me, pressing my forehead to hers. My heart hammers in my chest even though I know I've never been so sure about something in my entire life. "I spent so long chasing things that I thought made me happy. The sea. Women. Money. The longer I chased, the further I wandered from myself until I was so lost that I had no hope of finding my way back again."

I can feel her breathing quicken, and can see the way her eyes search mine. I'm not sure what she's looking for, but whatever it is... I will give it to her.

She needs only to say the word.

I wrap my arms around her waist and pull her flush against me. Her heart is beating as rapidly as my own. I can see the soft flush starting to creep up her neck and into her ears.

"Then, my ship docked on your shore," I continue, my voice dropping into a low, emotional murmur as I hold her to me. I had gone through so many different ways to word this while I was on my little rites mission in the jungle last night, yet somehow none of this is what I had rehearsed for hours. "The moment you stumbled into me that first time, all wide-eyed wonder and self-assured defiance, my heart's compass sprang back to life. In that moment, I knew I had found my True North."

I swallow deeply, loosening my tongue to say the next phrase.

"Chilo ko' wahi'ci, ko'lolaz Sitalli'ara."

The way her eyes light up when I ask her to be my wife, spoken perfectly in her own native tongue while using her true name, makes the hours upon hours I had spent letting Ko'chi teach me every word and every syllable—the frustration of endless correction to my pronunciation—all while trying to catch a damn Coa'hesa worth it.

She says nothing for what feels like hours, though it was probably only mere seconds.

"Yes," she says, the word mumbled so softly I barely register it, "i net'i chilo 'ma hostu hi' lep'uic teu."

38
Sitara

I am yours even after the stars burn out.

That is what I had said to Kiernan after his proposal. And I meant every word of it. The effort he had made to ask me in my native tongue fills me with a sense of pride like I have never known. In that moment, I felt as though he sees me for all my aspects; the good, the bad, the in-between. Afterwards, I had learned that Ko'chi had spent hours teaching him until he had perfected the phrase.

Now we are lying in our bed aboard the *Nureus*, snuggled up under the sheet in a tangle of limbs. I am idly tracing his fresh pe'aboros, keeping my touch feather-light on the freshly marred skin. A soft smile is plastered on my face, one that has been there almost consistently since the start of the rites.

Still, I can't help but let my mind wander to other things from time to time, specifically the sudden shift in my brother's behavior. He hadn't spoken to either of us the entire time we were in the village. At one point, I'm not sure he was even there during the Mana'Oka. When he was, his eyes were distant as though he were thinking long and hard about something-the corners of his eyes pinched tightly in the way they do when he is worried about something.

Kiernan kisses the top of my head, his fingers trailing down the line of my spine. "Those eyes look so far away right now." His voice is muffled by my hair as he continues to keep his nose buried there. "What has you so preoccupied that it has you so far removed from me?"

I turn my face to smirk at him, shifting to straddle his waist. I lay my hands flat against the pillow on either side of his head and lean down to kiss the corner of his mouth.

"I was just thinking about all the ways I can give you gray hair for the next few decades of our lives," I tease warmly.

He squints at me, that roguish grin trying to force its way onto his lips. "I think I'd look pretty damn wise with gray hair, so you'd be doing me a favor." He turns his nose up at me, then peeks through one slitted eye. "Wanna discuss those ways? I might have some ideas of my own."

"I could walk naked across the deck again," I chuckle, my eyes swimming with mirthful promise. If I did it once, I'd have no problem doing it again, and he knows it.

Catching me off guard, he has me beneath him in an instant. I yelp, kittenish laughter spilling from my lips as he presses his pointer finger to my nose. "You will do no such thing, or I will start feeding the local sharks eyeball chum." He cocks an eyebrow at me, a heated challenge in his brilliant blue eyes. "They will be *grateful* for it too!"

I roll my own eyes, my breathing harsh due to the laughter of mere moments ago. "Always so menacing. How do you gain any loyalty?"

He shrugs his shoulders impassively. "Well, the whole shark bait thing is a pretty good incentive, I guess." I laugh, shaking my head at him as I lift to prop myself on my elbows, bringing our faces to near touching.

"You're awful," I tease. I then look out the window by the bed, sighing heavily as I move on to the more serious topic at hand. "I think I need to go talk to my brother. He wasn't acting right."

My lips press into a tight, worrisome line as I draw the blankets up over my bare chest to sit up. I move my hair from my face, my fingers catching in the curls due to their debauched state.

He lifts the blanket, peeking beneath it at his naked body. "I should probably put pants on first," he grins, looking back up at me, "Actually, on second thought-"

"You're not going," I interrupt, my face a mask of stern resolve, "The last thing I need is you antagonizing him while I'm trying to make amends."

"You want me to stay behind?" He flops onto his side with a groan, like a toddler who is about to throw a tantrum. I simply stare at him for a long moment, half-ass expecting him to start kicking his feet. "Wait-" He suddenly shoots upright, drawing the blankets up to his chin with a look of mortification. "Do you expect me to entertain myself?!"

"Oh, absolutely not," I purr, crawling out of the bed to grab my discarded clothes from the floor, "I'll have Benedict come in for a playdate."

He whines like a simpering idiot, but moves to grab his clothes from the pile he left them in. Once we are dressed, my hair managed to the best of my ability, we walk hand in hand out onto the main deck where Benedict is already standing with two jugs of Spiced Rum in his hands. He grins at us, holding the liquor out in front of his person. "Can Kiernan come out and play?"

I laugh, lifting to my toes to plant a kiss on Kiernan's jaw before moving toward the gangplank. "Have fun, you two. Do me a favor, Ben, keep him on the ship. The last thing I need is him getting drunk and thinking he can catch another flying snake."

I am pleased to say that I have managed to find Larkin fairly easily, as he is still nestled in his fur pallet in his tent. I walk into the tent flap, sitting down on the rugged flooring. His home looks very similar to my old one, though there is no longer any evidence of his vice littering the corners.

I stare at him for a long moment, debating whether I should wake him yet or not. Larkin's hair is mussed as though he has been tossing and turning fitfully, the dark locks standing every which way. His mouth is slightly ajar, and an occasional snore rumbling from his nose. The gentle sweep of his lashes over his cheekbones cast shadows over his skin.

Gently, I lean forward to press my palm into his shoulder, shaking him lightly. "Larkin... Larzoma'kin, wake up," I whisper, trying to keep from startling him too badly.

Larkin lets out a snort, his body jerking awake as he cracks his eyes open ever so slowly, slightly to look at me. "Sitalli'ara? What are you doing here? Don't you have a *betrothed* to sate?" he asks, his voice raspy from sleep.

I bite the inside of my cheek, not sure what I was planning to say to him, but now that the moment is here, I should probably figure it out. I scratch the hairline at my temple, giving him a look of concern. "I'm worried about you. You haven't said two words to me since the first time I came back to the village." My brother sits up stiffly, rubbing his eyes with the heel of his palm.

"Oh, yeah... I've had a lot on my mind, and I've been trying to figure out how to talk to you about it."

"What is it?" I brace myself for what I expect will be another Kiernan-bashing session or another insult to my intelligence, but it never comes.

Larkin simply sighs, rubbing the back of his neck as he grapples for the words he wants to say. "It's going to sound so fucking crazy, but... Do you have that liquid fire that Coli'hanu gave you when you were chosen to be her apprentice?"

The question throws me off, my brows furrowing in confusion. Of course, I still have it. It is a precious gift from the goddess. I don't always keep it with me, though, after getting a glimpse of the Maggot Cult in Catcher's Bay, I did rush to my tent during my first time back in the village to grab it, keeping it on my person since.

The gift that I had received from the Goddess of Cold Fire is a vial forged by Gula'ci and filled with Coli'hanu's magic tempered down and infused with Teo'Kan's water to create an elixir. I was told that whenever I needed a little more oomph behind my magic, all it would take is a couple of drops. I have never used it, though I wouldn't hesitate if my life were in danger.

"Yes," I tilt my head to the side, giving him a circumspect glance, "Why do you ask?"

He opens his mouth, then closes it, doing this a few times in hopes of finding the right words, until finally he stands. "I think it's best if I just show you."

I'm not sure where he plans on taking me, but if it is troublesome enough to smother the argumentative nature of my brother, then it's worth taking a look at. I nod, rising to my feet as well.

Motioning for him to lead the way, Larkin moves out of the tent to take me into the jungle toward a patch of land that sits directly between Potem'aku and the Lake of Mirrors.

Larkin barely talks to me as we make our way through the landscape with ease, only offering up small comments about needing to trust him and not to freak out once we get there. We can move much faster than

I was able to with my clumsy oaf of a man, my and Larkin's bodies having been groomed to move along the unstable ground since we were born. It takes us no time at all to eat up the distance between the village and our destination.

When he stops at the mouth of a cave entrance, I stare into the abyss. My entire body leans in as though I am trying to listen for something or catch a glimpse of whatever has him so beside himself.

"This is... nice?" I try to be encouraging, though I know it falls flat.

"It's what is inside the cave, Ma'nok," he insults, a dry humor interwoven in the stiffness of his tone. He rakes his hand through his hair, looking at me. I understand him perfectly, as the sun hasn't risen enough to create any light within the tunnel. I hold out my palm, letting the tingling sensation of my power spark to life in my hand. A tiny flame no bigger than a chicken's egg dances between my fingers, sending a cool glow along the inner walls of the nature-made structure.

Larkin surges forward, though I hesitate longer. There is that pesky intuition again. Something doesn't feel right, but I'm afraid that if I back out, it'll only make Larkin feel as though I'm only concerned with my comfort. Due to that, I take a step into the mouth of the tunnel and begin to follow him down the winding natural corridor.

The passage is oddly drafty, the breeze coming from somewhere deeper into the hillside. This means if we walked far enough, following the current of air, we could find our way out again.

Well, at least there's that.

My green flame casts moving shadows along the dark stone as we continue, that knot in my gut growing with each passing second. "Mind telling me what this is all about?" I question. I'm not sure if I had managed to keep the accusatory tone in my voice at bay as my insides gnaw with the instinct to turn tail and run.

"It's really hard to explain. I promise it'll make sense once we are there," he says gently, trying his best to reassure me. We grow silent for a few more painstakingly long moments before Larkin finally breaks the ice with a terrible attempt at small talk.

"So, when are you and the big guy getting married..."

Wow...news travels fast. The only person I had told was Heira'yolku. I suspect Djar had done his strange communion and found out on his own. And he probably told Larkin.

"I don't know. We haven't gotten that far yet," I say simply, the tension in my shoulders growing with each passing step.

"And he makes you that happy?"

"Yes."

My short but definitive answer ends the conversation. Larkin and I have spent so long being the only thing each other has for biological family that it has taken me until now to realize he and I don't talk all that much. We have always been far too busy chasing our poor excuses for comfort to cope with the trials we have faced to sit down and have a heartfelt conversation.

Regardless, I love him, and I know he loves me.

I open my mouth to say something, anything, to break the tension that is progressively building between us, but my attempt is cut short as he halts just before a bend in the path. He turns to look at me, an odd expression on his face that I can't quite place. Sadness? Excitement? Anxiety? Maybe a mixture of all three. I am about to ask him why he stopped when I hear it.

Or rather... I hear *them*.

"Larzoma'kin, you came back!" The excited, raspy tone of our mother's voice echoes against the stone walls.

My eyes widened with a mixture of disbelief and uncertainty, my head shaking subtly upon reflex. No, there is no way that's them. Our parents are dead... Or so we thought. Larkin takes a step back toward me, holding his hand out as if he is about to explain.

He can see it on my face.

I know he can.

Every vile, horrible thing that they had done to us washes over my memory like a monsoon, forcing my knees to weaken and threaten to buckle. I take a step back, preparing to hightail my ass right out of this fucking tunnel and back into the fresh air of the world outside. It is then that I hear a second voice. The low, deep rumble of my father cutting through the silence.

"Sitalli'ara? Larkin, is that your sister?" The excitement in his tone is a far cry from the cool, unfeeling voice I had heard from him the last time I saw him. He must have heard me take a step.

"Yes, she's here," Larkin answers far too quickly for my taste.

"Sitara, come here. Let me look at you after all this time," my mother demands gently, almost lovingly. She, too, doesn't have the same viperish venom laced in her voice anymore, which confuses me.

I freeze, unsure of what I should do. On the one hand, these are my parents, and I love them. On the other hand, they had been willing to sacrifice me to a god of death, forcing me to go through unimaginable pain, all for their ends.

"Sitara," Larkin snaps my attention back to him, "It's okay. Let them explain."

Let them explain? How can he ask that of me? How could he expect me to give them even so much as another millisecond for my life when they have already taken so much from me?

It is the plea of pure desperation written all over my brother's face that forces my hand, and I take a step out from around the corner. My parents stand on the other side of what looks to be a shimmering wall of lavender fog. They look just like they did when I was young, before Hu'yimona's corruption.

My mother stands in all her beauty, the long strands of her ebony hair the same as Larkin's. However, my pale skin was inherited from her. The face staring back at me is so eerily similar to mine. I had almost forgotten how much I look like my mother. My father stands next to her, his messy mop of fiery locks and sun-kissed skin a stark contrast to the slight woman standing next to him. They both still have Hu'yimona's brand on their forehead, though it has healed into nothing more than a scar now.

They stand there, my father's arm wrapped around my mother's waist, giving me the tender smiles I remember as a young child. I hadn't realized how much I needed it until now. The sheer magnitude of emotion that washes over me like a balm forces a quiver to my chin.

"Look at you, my beautiful girl," my father praises in a low, genuine tone.

"You've grown up to be such a strong woman," my mother concurs, pressing her palm against the wall of mist.

I say nothing, still trying to wrap my head around their existence. I have so many questions, but I can't seem to find my voice to ask any of them. Almost as if sensing my turmoil, my mother begins to explain.

"We are so sorry, Sitalli'ara. What we did, what that monster made us do... It was unforgivable."

What did he make them do?

That becomes just another question on the list of unspoken interrogation.

"Everything we did was a product of his control over us," Mapa continues as my mother begins wiping tears away from her cheek, "You have no idea how hard we tried to resist... But we are only human, Sitara. And Hu'yimona has magic that is as powerful as it is corruptive."

I suppose I could see that... I used to wonder why their eyes looked so glazed over, even in their crazed stupors. And I am not one to question the gods' power.

"Why are you here?" I finally manage to say, motioning toward their evident imprisonment.

"Hu'yimona locked them away in there after they had managed to break free of his hold," Larkin chimes in, his voice cracking under the weight of his own emotions.

My mind reels with the implications as I try to remember. That's right... I don't remember seeing them at the sacrificial ritual... That makes the probability of their story far more likely, I suppose.

"Why didn't you break them out?" I ask.

"I tried," he says, his head hanging low as if in defeat, "but it wouldn't budge for me. So... I thought maybe with the liquid fire you would be able to do it."

I'm not sure how I feel about using the goddess's gift to release cult members, former or otherwise, but they are my parents, and they do seem to be clear-headed and...normal.

I push my hair from my face, tugging at the strands in distress. I close my eyes, trying to take a few settling breaths before I finally nod. I can't bring myself to disappoint my brother. Plus, I'm leaving with Kiernan as soon as the cult is dealt with, so it isn't like I will have to be around them myself. This way, Larkin might have someone to keep him in line and keep him happy.

"Alright... I'll do it," I murmur my agreement, pulling the vial of liquid fire out of the herb bag that I keep it in when I'm wearing it on my person. I pull out the swirling elixir, holding it up to the light of my flame. I analyze it, the shimmering metallic emerald catching the light.

With trembling fingers, I slowly uncork it, pouring just a few drops of it onto my tongue. A cool, fresh feeling courses through my veins, the rush of burning ice licking at my insides forcing a gasp from my throat. The flickering flame in my palm sputters, then grows large,r and I look at my parents who are smiling brightly at their impending freedom.

"Step back," I tell them, and they hurry to scramble behind the wall where the tunnel opens up into the larger chamber. I walk over to the barrier, expanding the flames onto my arms and into my other hand. I press my palms flat against the oddly solid wall of fog and begin to push through. My fire snaps and sizzles against it, a rumbling roar filling the resonant space.

"It's working!" Larkin says rhapsodically, "Sitara, it's working!"

With a buzzing sound that vibrates my eardrums–the crackling of the magical barrier finally dispelling is almost painful in its intensity—Larkin and I step beyond the line that had been created. My eyes scan the large, amphitheater—like cavern from just inside the tunnel of the cave, in search of our parents. There is nothing here; no sign of life whatsoever. And our parents are nowhere to be found.

It isn't until we have walked fully out of the mouth of the corridor that my heart sinks into my stomach.

The stalagmites and stalactites jutting out of the floor and ceiling are made of pure crystal, glowing in a soft, ethereal swirl of blue, green, and violet hues. I look around with a mixture of awe and horror as I quickly realize where we are. The Cavern of Light. The one place on this island we are never supposed to be.

"Uh...Sitara..." Larkin calls out to me, his hand moving to grab my arm and pull me behind him just enough that my right shoulder is shielded behind his left.

Peeking out from around him, I follow his gaze toward the center of the massive dome. There, in the center, sits a small tree.

Legends say this was the child plant of the first tree to rise from the dirt of this world. It is said that it was planted by the Sacred Three here upon the death of its parent.

To my horror, the leaves are brown, shriveled up as they coil in on themselves. They look as though they would turn to dust at the slightest touch; crumble away and shift through the draft until they settle into nothing. The branches are twisted and marred, no longer inhabiting the personification of life that the tree was supposed to represent.

My entire body grows cold, my fingers and toes going numb as I behold the form sitting beneath it–his posture lazed as though in deep contemplation. The inky-black strands of his hair coil and writhe around his pale face, caressing his skin as if imitating a lover's touch. The man's long, toned body shifts slightly, as though he's just noticed our presence—the black mural of tattoos along his bare torso shifting and moving as if alive.

Panic begins to set in as Hu'yimona rises from his dirt bed under the dead tree, my heart rising into my throat like bile. I take an instinctive step back, shrinking away as those burning obsidian eyes narrow in on me.

No...No, No No, this can't be happening!

This is not happening!

My inner monologue is screaming, blood-curdling screeches assaulting my ears from within my mind. This is my worst nightmare come to life; something I had feared for months after my near-death experience. That he was alive and that he would find me.

Faster than Larkin and I can follow, Hu'yimona is pressed firmly behind me—the sickeningly warm scent of his skin filling my nostrils. I really am going to vomit now. I can feel the contents of my stomach trying to exit as I go rigid, my wide-eyed stare of horror mirroring Larkin's as he snaps around to look at me and the god who has pressed himself against my back.

I can feel his breath, hot and nauseating, against the nape of my neck. He leans in, the silky smoothness of his lips brushing against the sensitive skin below my ear. He's toying with me, like a cat with a mouse between its claws.

I'm frozen. I can't move without fear of crumbling to the ground in a heaping mess of flesh and bone. Larkin is equally as still, not making a sound save for the strangled sob that rolls up his throat.

When Hu'yimona finally speaks, he wraps his arms around my trembling form to pull me flesh against the hard planes of his chest. The baritone of his voice is laced with amusement as he chuckles, the sound forcing terror to lace through my spine.

"There's my Flower," he murmurs against my skin, his tongue darting out to taste my flesh, which has broken out into a cold sweat, "Such a good girl."

39

Kiernan

Sitara has been gone too long.

I know that she is with Larkin and the others from the village, but something isn't settling well with me.

Something isn't right.

I pace the main deck of my ship; Benedict, Arthur, and Viktor watch me as I do. I can feel their heads follow me with each step, my path so close to the gangplank that it vibrates as I pass it time and time again.

I am growing more and more agitated with each passing second she's gone. Whether it is lack of control or intuition—call it what you will—it still doesn't feel like everything is hunky dory.

"Come on, K. She's with her brother. I'm sure she has just lost track of time," Benedict finally breaks the heavy silence, leaning back against the door of my cabin.

"Did she give a specific time that she would be back?" Arthur chimes in, a wary curiosity lacing his voice.

"She said before the sun is down," Benedict quickly answers, shooting me a look, "The sun has yet to set. Which is why I'm sure she's fi-"

My head suddenly snaps up, my eyes scanning the treeline as I feel the crackling of electricity beginning to swirl in the air. Larkin's lightning. What concerns me more than the power itself is how it *feels*. It isn't angry like it had been when he and I had our little altercation the day we docked.

No, this is panicked. I can feel his terror as though it were a physical thing in the air, and it drains the blood straight to my toes.

Without so much as a glance or a word to any of the men standing on deck, I take off running toward the treeline. My feet eat up the ground beneath me, kicking up sand until that sand turns to dirt. Twigs and vines along the rainforest floor snap and crack against the force of my muscles, propelling me forward.

Where is she?

I can feel the panic start swirling inside of me like a hurricane, a storm that is barely contained by sheer willpower.

I will kill that motherfucker if he has so much as hurt her feelings.

I have absolutely no idea where the two of them are, but I just run toward the magnetic pull of Larkin's overwhelming panic.

"Sitara!" I call out, my eyes scouring the land around me. I strain my ears to hear any trace of sound beyond the thunder of my own racing heart, "SITARA!"

The sudden sound of tizzied breathing not from my own chest and the thud of something heavy hitting the ground causes me to change course. I force my way through the bushes, breaking through a thick wall of them without caring about the scraps and cuts I'm receiving along the way.

On the other side, Larkin lies face-first in the dirt, groaning as he hoists himself up off the forest floor. The fact that he is in such a panic that he—someone who has roamed these trees since infancy—actually tripped tells me that whatever has happened isn't good. My mind races with the worst possible scenarios that it could come up with: She's hurt. She's disappeared. She's dying. She's dead.

I don't hesitate to grab Larkin up by the scruff of his hair, gripping the short strands in my iron grasp. He yelps, but for whatever reason doesn't struggle. That is evidence number three that my intuition is correct. "Where is she?!"

He seems smaller somehow as he lifts his wide-eyed gaze to mine. His pupils are dilated to pinpoints, the whites around his iris visible underneath his drawn-back eyelids.

I give him a rough shake, trying to jerk him from whatever fucked up, anxiety-induced trance he's fallen into. "Where is Sitara?!"

"I-I...She..." he sputters, though most of the words come out as nothing but choked sobs and broken whimpers.

Before he can attempt to finish, I release his hair and crouch down next to where he is sprawled out. An unholy calm washes over me, my focus shifting from panic to a fierce need to protect what is mine, what I have worked so hard—both physically and mentally—to acquire. "If you don't get some kind of hold on yourself and find your tongue quickly, her love for you won't be enough to save your sorry ass."

Larkin finally rises to his knees, then to his feet with unsteady legs. I've never seen a grown man quiver with fear the way he is right now. He takes a few breaths through his nose, trying to regain some semblance of equanimity. "Sitara and I went to this cave... Our parents were there... I didn't know it was a trick. Even she thought it was real..."

He's not making any sense. My brows furrow deeply, my patience wearing thinner than it already is. "Where. Is. She?"

"I-I don't... I don't know..." he runs his hands through his inky locks in frustration, his face pinched into a look of devastation. "I don't know where he took her."

My nostrils flare, my muscles bulging, "*Who* took her?"

How could he be so stupid?! Even if it had been their parents, what made him think it would be a good idea to take her to them? After everything they had done to her.

I don't have the patience to wait for him to answer me, let alone listen to him stutter and stumble through every thought that tries to fall out of his mouth. His mindless babbling doesn't match up to the urgency of the situation.

I can't say that I'm not proud of my next move, which is to sock him right in the nose. Cartilage crunches under my knuckles as blood gushes down the front of his face. Yet still, he doesn't put up a fight. He doesn't strike back with fists or sparks of any kind. This tells me things are worse than I thought. Larkin would only ever let me strike him if he knew he'd fucked up.

"Stop fucking blubbering like a damned fool and tell me where the fuck she is!"

"I told you, I don't know! Hu'yimona took her!" he shouts, finally making a coherent sentence.

Before I have time to rationalize my actions, I have Larkin off the ground by his throat. I slam him against the nearest tree, the bark cracking under the force of his body propelling back. The air is forced out of his lungs, leaving him gulping for breath.

"You let Hu'yimona fucking take her?! What kind of brother are you?!" My blood boils in my veins, the rage behind my eyes evident by the look on his face. The buzzing in my ears grows louder as I pull him away from the tree, slamming him back into it a second time. "No, fuck that! What kind of *man* are you?!"

I drop him, his body crumbling to the ground as he coughs and sputters. His labored breathing does little to sate my burning need to eradicate him from the very face of this planet.

I start pacing once more, raking my fingers through my hair, tugging on the strands until I have to clench my jaw to work through the discomfort.

What the fuck am I going to do?

How the fuck am I supposed to get her back?

"I tried," Larkin croaks, wheezing as he tries to catch his breath, "I threw everything that I had at him. I could only do so much with him using Sitara as a shield."

"FUCK!" I shout in his general direction, and he flinches as though he expects another punch to the face. My pacing resumes, this time more erratic and choppy. "We need help. We can go to the temple and ask the gods! They helped once before, right?!"

Larkin nods, already leading the way in the direction of Potem'aku.

You can't really call what I am doing *'following'* as I am matching him step for step, like I know where I am going. I don't, but I'll ask anyone for help. At this point, knowing what I know, I'll get on my knees and grovel if that's what it takes to save her.

I already know this isn't like when I'm at sea. I'm not the biggest, scariest thing out here. Not by a long shot. The knowledge that I'm not going to be able to do this alone—or the fact that even if I had my crew, it wouldn't be enough—is a fear I've never had to deal with until now. The helplessness I find myself in has never been my reality.

Larkin's body language has shifted now that he's had the time to get his head straight. His shoulders are still quivering slightly, but his jaw is set. By his reaction to the situation alone, I can only assume that Hu'yimona is about as nasty and dangerous as I had expected him to be. And to use Sitara as a human shield to keep Larkin from being able to use the full extent of his power... Fuck, if it were any other situation, any other person besides my love, it's something I probably would have done too.

We break through the clearing of Potem'aku in record time, our purpose narrowed down to a single-minded focus: Get inside and tell the Sacred Three what has happened... If they don't already know. That thought churns in my stomach, threatening to make all of that spiced rum I drank with Benedict earlier come back up. I'm hoping that when we get there, they will be nowhere to be found, already on their way to deal with the problem.

Unfortunately, as we barrel through the outer ring of pillars, we find them exactly as Sitara and I had left them days ago.

I rush toward the three of them as though I'm their equal, which is quickly thwarted by the familiar taste of temple soil.

She put my face in the damn dirt again.

The curses that fly from my mouth as I spit the mud out of my teeth and stand back up on my feet are muffled to my own ears. "What are you three just standing around for?!"

I wipe my face, smearing the familiar crimson on the back of my hand.

Well, shit, my nose is bleeding now, too.

"You can't expect me to believe you don't know what the hell is going on!"

I could slap Larkin for the dumbass face he is making right now, as though propriety is more important than his sister.

I don't care about who they are or who I am. All I care about is finding Sitara and finding her before Hu'yimona can...

Gula'ci raises a black brow at my lack of manners, taking a step down to a lower tier. "We know what has happened."

Her eyes snap over to Larkin, who lowers his gaze to the floor in shame.

My eyes quickly flash to Larkin, my rage bubbling just below the surface. It takes a prideful amount of willpower not to go over to him and connect my fist to his face one more time. I turn my gaze back to the goddess who has spoken to me, my voice rising up to echo through the temple.

"Then why aren't you *doing* anything?!"

"Our involvement was not foretold," Coli'hanu answers, her tone slightly softer, more understanding than the other woman's, "Otherwise, we would."

"*Foretold*?" I'm completely aware that the look I'm giving them is downright disrespectful. "Then please tell me, what was '*foretold*'?" I scoff, shaking my head in complete disbelief.

Fuck these gods and their fucking foresight!

"You will find out soon enough," the Goddess of Earth says, taking another step down the tiers of the dais.

"No. Nope. I don't accept that," I growl, my head spinning with the unbelievable amount of indifference that is taking place, especially from the Goddess of Cold Fire.

"You will have to. Otherwise, you might as well consider your woman no longer yours," Teo'Kan says sternly, his head angling to the side as he stares down at me where I stand, "And we all know the great *Kiernan Slater* doesn't take well to his things being taken... or damaged."

40

Sitara

The last time I found myself in the Maggots' stronghold, I couldn't tell how long I had been here. Things are certainly different now. I know exactly how long I have been here, thanks to the latest cruelty I have been subjected to. On the surface, my accommodations are a far cry from the dingy prison cell I was in the last time. My room is clean with flickering candles hanging from a chandelier bolted to the stone ceiling. The bed, which is definitely of Mundane making, is soft with plush covers and furs. The Gaboon Ebony wood is sanded and polished to shine, fashioned to match the wardrobe in the corner. Rugs line the cold stone of the floor, making it warmer and more inviting. The pillows, draped in the same dark cottons, are filled with the finest feathers in Capulli'ana.

I have been locked in this room for four days.

How do I know? Oh, it's all thanks to the fact that my specific room has a wide, gaping hole in the northern cliffside big enough for a person to walk through. I can see straight out to the ocean and the blue sky, but I cannot reach it. The room is far too high up for me to jump into the water safely, and the cliffside is far too jagged and steep for me to climb down. It's just another one of Hu'yimona's clever ways to torture me. Giving me the view of the ocean, but keeping me just out of reach of what I desire most.

I sit on the floor, leaning up against the mouth of my '*window*' overlooking the sea. I have been sitting here for hours now, contemplating my life. I should have known better than to think that my parents were alive. And even if they were, they would never have looked at me with such warmth; such remorse. The sun is setting, and I know he will be here soon.

Hu'yimona has come to my room with a meal every day since he brought me here. Every evening, he stays in my room and watches me eat while trying to force me into some sort of conversation.

I let out an irritated sigh as a gentle knock sounds from my door. Every meal time, he sends the same girl—I think her name is Eirian—to fetch me in an attempt to get me to leave my room. Every mealtime, I refuse. Today will be no different.

"I'm not going," I snap harshly, leaning my head against the rough edges of the stone.

Hu'yimona steps into the room, the smell of roasted beef, warm bread, and some sort of leafy greens wafting through the air. My stomach growls despite my protests as he comes to sit beside me on the cold floor. I keep my gaze locked on the horizon, refusing to look at him; refusing to so much as breathe in his general direction.

"I knew you wouldn't," he says gently, his tone belying the psychotic monster I know he is, "So I decided to save us both some time. Eat, Flower, I'm sure you're hungry after refusing breakfast and lunch."

He slides the carved plate across the floor as if trying to feed a frightened stray dog, an almost charming smile tugging at the corner of his lips.

Again, *almost* charming.

That is the most dangerous thing about him. He can hide his ruthless, sadistic nature behind the facade of a handsome gentleman.

My jaw works tightly under my skin as I pull my knees up to my chest. I wrap my arms firmly around them, attempting to shield myself in vain.

How the fuck do I expect to shield myself from a *god*?

"I'm not-" My lie is abruptly interrupted as my stomach growls yet again. It is loud enough that I'm almost positive Kiernan should be able to hear it. Maybe that's how he'll find me. I know he's going to come.

He has to.

Hu'yimona clicks his tongue in disapproval, closing his eyes briefly as he shakes his head. "I'm afraid that just won't do, Sitalli'ara." My name drops from his lips like a prayer, his voice far less '*dead*' than I remember it to be. "I'm not about to allow you to starve yourself for a mere act of defiance. Now. Open wide."

He tears a small section of the bread, leaning in to take my chin between his fingers almost tenderly. Pressing the bite to my lips, he mimics the action of opening his mouth for a bite.

I snatch the bread from his hand, my brows furrowed deeply. I jerk my chin from his grasp, shoving the bread into my mouth where I chew it violently.

Like hell I'm letting him feed me!

"I am not eating out of your hand."

A wolfish grin spreads across his full lips as he leans back into his original position, his back pressing against the other side of the opening. "Ah, but I did manage to get you to eat it, now didn't I?"

Fucking prick.

Stupid, manipulative jackass.

I slow my chewing, gathering up every morsel that is inside my mouth. With a dramatic flair, I spit the gooey, chewed-up pieces into his face, all without breaking eye contact with him. "Let's see you make me eat it now."

I don't wait for him to respond, nor do I care what he has to say. Instead, I stand and walk over to the bed to place more distance between us. I plop onto the edge of the far end, placing the majority of the bed between us. My back is to him, but I can hear his body shift with a sigh.

Before I can even blink, I am flat on my back, his large frame looming over me like a hellish shadow. My heart practically stops beating momentarily due to the fear and deja vu that begin to circulate through my mind at an astonishing pace.

With one knee, he easily overpowers my defiance as he kicks my legs apart to nestle himself between them. He pins my hands to the bed next to my head, his calloused fingers wrapped around my wrists. I expect to see rage when my wide-eyed stare meets his, but all I see is subtle annoyance and—what seems to be—slight amusement.

"I'd prefer you to put sustenance into your body, but if this is more to your liking, I would be happy to oblige," he rumbles, his deep rasp vibrating on my skin as he leans in to place a kiss on the hollow of my throat. "You know, you never struck me as the kind of woman to allow a man to claim ownership of her as if she were nothing more than a possession for his pleasure. Though it seems you have changed quite a bit as of late."

I know what he's getting at, and I don't appreciate what he is insinuating. He's talking about my relationship with Kiernan. That much is clear. My lips draw into a deep line as I set my jaw. "He *loves* me."

"Oh, my delicate little flower," he muses, brushing a strand of hair from my forehead before releasing me and rising from the bed. "We all eat lies when our hearts are hungry."

He walks back over to where the plate is still sitting on the floor and gracefully scoops it up in one fluid motion. He ambles back over to where I have sat up and crouches down in front of me. He takes my hand, gingerly placing the plate in my grasp. "And I am well aware that you have been starved for quite some time."

His words slam into me harder than any physical blow ever could. I let out the breath I've been holding since he lowered himself in front of me, my entire body sagging in defeat. The truth behind his words is a nasty revelation I don't want to acknowledge. I've always kept everyone at arm's length, afraid to get too close.

Even Djar.

Even Larkin.

Even the friends I've had since childhood.

I've only ever given over select parts of myself for fear of being hurt. But without vulnerability, there can't be a true connection. So I have, as he says, starved my own self.

Hu'yimona reaches up, sliding his fingers along my jaw until he reaches my chin, where he proceeds to lift my fallen gaze back to his smoldering pools of ebony. "Come now, don't look so dejected. I won't ever let you feel that way again, if you'll only cooperate just a little."

He runs his thumb over the deep furrow that has formed in my brow, his touch painfully forbearing. How does he know so much? How does he know all the right buttons to push to make me feel so small, yet somehow so seen?

"You... You're the reason I've been made to feel this way in the first place." My words spill out shakier than intended. I ball up my hands into fists, clearing my throat as I manage to find my backbone once more. "You're the villain in this story. Not the love interest."

"Are you sure about that?"

His posture softens, the muscles that have been slightly coiled releasing all at once. The look on his face is one of predatory serenity, beautiful and deadly in the same turn. "It has been four days, Sitara. You're no further from your precious captain than you were when you left him the first time and managed to get yourself tangled up with that slave trader. He was to you in hours and yet... Where is he now?"

He leans in closer, his breath ghosting over my face as his hand slides to the nape of my neck. His fingers tangle through the strands of curls there as he holds my head steady, but doesn't make a move to bridge the gap between us—to my overwhelming relief. Instead, he mutters his next words in a barely audible whisper. "The villain will always be the villain if the man considered the hero is telling the story."

I hate that there is a part of me that thinks he is actually making sense. I mean, nothing he has said so far has been wrong or untrue.

I shake my head, dispelling those thoughts before they can force my hesitation further. Memories of my first encounter with him stay firmly placed in my consciousness, an anchor to keep me grounded in the truth. "You've done nothing but prove the hero's story to be true." Hu'yimona stands up and poises his arms out low to his sides.

"You are absolutely correct, Sitara. I have not." He extends his hand to me as if I'm going to willingly take it. Like I'm *ever* going to walk hand in hand with him like I would Kiernan. "Let me show you now."

I slap his hand away from me, folding my arms over my chest. I stand, looking up at him with a narrowed, challenging gaze. "You can *try*."

He lowers his hand back to his side, tilting his head as though he is amused by my blatant lack of respect for him. He motions me to follow, gliding toward the door where he opens it and waits for me to exit before him.

I don't necessarily want to leave my room, but that pesky curiosity has gotten the better of me. I huff, stomping out of the doorway like an agitated child.

I expect him to take me down an elaborate labyrinth of corridors and passageways to get to wherever it is he is taking me. I am already partially convinced that he is going to take me on a wild goose chase. I am surprised when he simply crosses the hallway and opens a door to a long, dark tunnel. The thought of following him anywhere outside of my own quarters is suddenly firing so many warning shots. I almost can't breathe with the intensity of it. I shake my head, taking a single step back toward the illusion of safety that my room holds.

"I don't believe you." My eyes snap toward him. "I don't believe you are taking me down some unlit passage just to prove that you're not the villain. Actually, every fiber of my being is screaming that this is exactly where a villain would lure an unsuspecting woman."

Hu'yimona chuckles, the sound deep and resonant. He folds his arms over his chest in a leisurely protest, lifting one brow. "It is true that I have done unspeakable things in the pursuit of what I want—of what I believe to be right. But never once have I been a liar, Flower," he motions for me to take a step through the door, which I am reluctant as hell to do. "Come, you need some time above ground. Allow me to take you to see the stars."

We've been walking for what feels like forever, the only light in the narrow passageway being my own flame as it dances along my palm. He might not need it to see, but I do. I sure as hell am not trusting him to keep me from smashing my nose against one of the sharp angles of this winding ass tunnel.

Originally, he had offered to carry me through, claiming it would be faster if we did it his way. I am not letting him put his nasty ass hands on me. I don't want him touching me any more than he already has been. He's so far up my ass I can hardly breathe without immediately feeling his own exhale on the back of my neck.

"How much further?" My voice is accusatory and humorless: "We've been walking for hours."

"We would have been there by now if you weren't so infuriatingly stubborn," he purrs, his own voice edged with laughter, "But instead, you have opted for being an obstinate shrew."

We walk in silence for a few more yards before he exhales loudly through his nose, scooping me up into his arms to take off running.

"Put me down!" I swat and kick to no avail. In fact, my resistance only causes him to tighten his hold on me, cradling me more firmly against his chest. The cooling sensation of his skin seeps into mine, forcing a shiver.

"Come now, you were just complaining about the walk. I, for one, do not care to spend this entire night moving at a snail's pace," he adjusts his hold on me, shifting my weight so that our chests are pressed firmly together. He forces my legs to wrap around his waist as he holds my head to keep it from smacking against the sharp turns in the rock, "Now stop flailing like a shore-stuck fish and let me get us there."

I can't say that I am too pleased with this position, but I guess it is better than breaking a bone on the unforgiving rock surrounding us. I watch as the tunnel whips past us at a speed I am not entirely able to keep up with. I finally close my eyes to keep myself from getting motion sickness. What would have taken us another two or three hours has now taken us only thirty minutes or so, forty-five at most.

Hu'yimona halts, the world coming to an abrupt stop. My head spins as he places me back on my feet, holding me by the elbows to keep me steady.

Having already had far too much of his physical contact in the last hour for my liking, I shrug him off of me. "I'm fine."

He does as I ask, motioning for me to step out of the underpass from hell. When I do, everything becomes more familiar. Not far from the mouth of this structure is the very beach where I had my first full-length encounter with my Kiernan. My heart leaps into my throat as I choke on my own excitement and relief.

I'm so close.

From where I'm standing, he could probably hear me if I were to scream out for him. In fact, I take a deep breath to do just that. My lungs expand as I take a few jogging strides out onto the sand, but I immediately gulp it down with the image I see before me. Disappearing into the horizon is the *Nureus*, the cut of his jib billowing in colors of green, blue, and gold.

"Kiernan..." I nearly choke on his name as my heart tightens painfully in my chest.

Where is he going?

Why is he leaving me here?

I swallow hard as I realize that he is heading toward the direction of Rhazden. He is going home... and he is going home without me.

Hu'yimona shifts his weight behind me, and I can feel the chill of his skin as he places his right hand possessively on my shoulder. His left hand cups my chin, forcing me to hold my gaze over the water and Kiernan, who is sailing his way out of sight.

"Look, Flower. Like I said, I am anything but a liar," he sounds almost sympathetic, though the triumph in his tone tells another story. "From where I am standing, he doesn't care about you at all. You were only fun for him while you were *easy*."

My heart shatters, silent tears rolling down my cheek as I attempt to force them down. I can't cry now. Not in front of him. But the tears won't stop coming. He moves his fingers from my chin to wipe them away with the pad of his thumb.

"*I* do care, more than you even realize. Haven't I proven my devotion? After all, I have waited four very long years for you to come back to me."

I remain motionless, my eyes pinned to the spot where the *Nureus* has now become nothing but a pinpoint in the distance.

I can't breathe.

I can't move.

Everything Hu'yimona said has come to pass, and now I am left looking like a fool.

"Give me some time to prove to you that I am not the monster in your story, Sitalli'ara. I can give you what you are too afraid to ask for."

His promises seep into my bones like ice. It takes me some time to even register what he has said to me.

I don't acknowledge him save for the words that barely make it out of my tightened throat. "And what do you think that is exactly?"

He buries his face in the crook of my neck, drawing in a breath that causes the hairs to stand along my skin. "A chance to be seen. A chance to indulge in that darkness you keep so safely guarded and hidden away." He pauses, pushing my hair from my shoulder as his plants small, sickening kisses to my shoulder. "I am the only one who sees that in you and does not cower away. In fact, I welcome it."

When I say nothing, he wraps his arm around me as I stand here looking out over the empty horizon.

Kiernan is gone, and now I have to draw my attention back to my little corner of the world. It's difficult, gut-wrenchingly painful, but I have no choice. I can't stand on this beach forever, praying that he'll come back to me.

I don't fight as Hu'yimona lifts me back into his arms, blocking out all sensation as I begin to spiral into the darker reaches of my own mind.

Maybe... just maybe, if I can keep Hu'yimona happy, keep him distracted, no one else will have to suffer. After all, I have nothing more to lose in my own personal life besides those I care about, and if tying myself to him holds the chance of protecting them, then I have to try.

I'm sure I am well qualified in the art of dancing with Death.

I had done it enough to know the tempo of this waltz.

41

Kiernan

This trip back to Rhazden doesn't feel as good as the other times. Hell, being on this ship doesn't even have the same luster to it. I hadn't realized how much life Sitara had brought to my world, to my crew, until I am standing on the upper deck looking down at everyone as they move about.

This journey has damn near been silent thus far. Neither Benedict nor I have even had to shout to get the men going. I guess this is proof that they all know exactly what they should be doing. Too bad it took Sitara being taken to prove that.

Larkin and I had spent the last four days begging for help within the villages on Capulli'ana. We received one of two reactions. Either they didn't believe us or they were so paralyzed that they refused us, telling us that a single person—let alone a child of cultist members—is not worth barreling into a war blindly for.

I beg to fucking differ.

Larkin hangs over the railing of the Nureus, probably upchucking his dinner yet again. He certainly doesn't have the same sea legs his sister does. We are heading back to Rhazden to try to find some people with a goddamn backbone to help us. People I know will have the guts to do what needs to be done.

Benedict, ever the vigilant guardian, has been staring between me and the man still hanging over the railing for what feels like hours now. He won't leave the upper deck, standing next to the helm with his arms crossed over his broad chest.

"You gonna say something to him?" he asks me, lifting a brow in accusation.

"No. Why should I?" I grumble, barely looking at him as the muscle in my jaw works furiously. It is his fault Sitara was taken in the first place. I don't need or want to say shit to him.

"If you don't fix whatever fuckery is going on with you two, it's only going to get in the way of what is most important right now," he furrows his brow at me, "Which isn't your pride or his bravado. It's Sitara. So go over there and play fucking nice." He points over at Larkin, who is still none the wiser, and grunts like a displeased father.

I clench my jaw harder, blanching my knuckles on the steering column of the helm before turning around to face the Kana'te man who is still groaning, his skin a green pallor. I fix my shirt, making my way toward him with a look of displeasure.

I know that Ben is right... But fuck him.

Fuck him and his good sense.

Larkin finally acknowledges my approach, side eyeing me as I come up beside him and fold my arms over my chest. I lean up against the rails, lowering my head with a furrowed brow.

Honestly, I'd rather gnaw off my left thumb or swallow my own tongue than be the bigger person. It really just isn't in my nature. But for Sitara, I'll do it.

So, I draw in a long breath while I try to figure out what to say. After a long pause and a considerable amount of effort, I finally let words come out of my mouth. "Your sister was far less dramatic than you."

That probably isn't the right thing to say. Actually, it isn't even completely true. She had been dramatic. It just held a different flare to it. She had kneed me in the balls. He is feeding the sharks his insides. "You'd think that you would have an iron stomach with all that hunting you do."

Is this what small talk is supposed to feel like? It makes my mouth dry and my tongue taste like sand, the restless buzzing behind my ears and the ache behind my brow flaring to life.

"Motion sickness isn't the same as being squeamish over entrails," Larkin grumbles, dry heaving before he lowers himself into a sitting position.

I follow his lead, sitting down on the deck across from him. I keep myself just out of punching range, though not that his jello arms could necessarily hurt anything right now. "You've still thrown up four more times than she did, which was none by the way."

"Yeah, well... She might be younger than me, but Sitara has always been tougher than me," he admits, rubbing the place between his brows as he shoves his head between his knees.

I allow my head to fall back against the crate I am using as a backrest, sighing heavily. Well, at least we agree on one thing. I start wringing my hands, annoyance and anxiety warring together in a maddening cocktail.

"I need you to tell me what we are going up against. What I need to warn the people of Rhazden about." I watch as his brows furrow deeply and he lifts his head to assess my question. "They will come just because I ask them to, but I need to know what they're signing up for."

Larkin sighs, pushing his black hair away from his forehead. "There is a lot that happened... The Maggot Cult and, even worse, Hu'yimona are not going to be easy to leash or eliminate. Hu'yimona, himself, is... really fucking powerful. More so than you can even imagine. He's a god, after all."

I nod in understanding, raking my fingers through my hair. "What does he want with Sitara?" The words come out low and barely audible. My eyes rove over the *Nureus*, every inch of it sparking a specific memory of her.

I look at the helm and see nothing but her trying to sail my ship, her brow furrowed in concentration. I look at the kitchen and only think of her grumbling about, scrubbing it clean, and slapping Beckett over the head with her bucket. I can't even sleep in my bed, having opted to sleep anywhere else.

Before I can stop the words from rolling off my tongue, I blurt out the question that has been eating away at me for days. "What are my chances of getting her back?" I'm not sure I want to know the answer, if he can even give me one.

"When we were in the Cavern of Light, he had said something that pointed toward him believing she's fated to be his wife. There were eight women with her that day, when the cult had taken them. It takes a long time to... cut into a person and carve out their insides. I think he has some twisted fantasy; thinks it was fate that kept her alive and not just some really good timing on the Sacred Three's part." His face falls, eyes landing on some distant point in the wooden planks of the deck. "I don't know the chances. It's Sitara we are talking about, so I'm sure she'll hold her own until we can figure something out. She always has."

I stand up, suddenly becoming extremely restless. I look out over the water back in the direction of Capulli'ana, taking in a deep breath of the salty air to ground myself. A part of me is wondering if there is a chance I'm leading my people into a trap, with Sitara as the bait. "You don't think he'll just kill her, right? Or that he hasn't already..."

Apparently, I've lost control of my tongue. It keeps asking questions that I know don't have definitive answers.

"Again... I don't know. But, honestly, the way he looked at her... I don't think that was on his agenda..." Larkin's face scrunches up in disgust, shaking his head as if to dispel the image of whatever happened in that cave. "No... I think he has bigger plans for her than just death."

My blood chills at the implications of what that could mean. I can't help but wonder what kind of people Sitara is being subjected to; what kind of man this god is.

"The Maggot Cult doesn't operate without direct order from Hu'yimona. So if he wants her alive, they won't do anything to her. Everything they do is based on the god's will. Every move they make is because he has ordered them to. I swear it's like they are blind adherents or something." Larkin answers my question, which I had thought was a silent monologue.

"As for Hu'yimona..." his eyes turn downward once more as he finishes answering my question, "He is ruthless, cunning, manipulative, and that is all without him even using his powers. Sitara told me that he was uncanny in his ability to get what he wants before force is even necessary." He pauses, clearly being able to read the question in my eyes. "She met him the last time she was taken. All the girls did..."

I grip the rail, my knuckles losing all color. I seriously think one of two things is going to happen. Either my joints are going to shatter or the wood of my precious ship is going to splinter.

I give Larkin a sidelong glare, unable to keep the accusatory tone from my voice. "How do you know so much about them?"

He closes his eyes, unable to meet my heated gaze, though I know he can feel my barely contained rage from here. "Some of it was just from watching them. Most of it is because they used me a lot when I was a child. I didn't understand what I was doing and..." he trails off, pinching the bridge of his nose, "Our parents aren't exactly good people."

My head drops as I groan. Damn... Their parents really are pieces of shit, huh? I almost feel bad for Larkin now, too.

Sitara really has put a beat to my unfeeling heart, hasn't she?

"What the hell would he want with Sitara?" I release my grip on the ship, flexing my hands in an attempt to make them relax, "Hasn't she been a problem for him? Don't get me wrong, I've been in the position of obsession, but she's a mortal woman and he's a fucking god. He's going to outlive her anyway."

"Well..." he drawls, tilting his head to the side, "The living gods were once human too. If he really intends to do what I think he wants to do, he'll put her through the process of becoming a living god herself."

I stare at him for a good, long while, like what he's just said is nothing but caveman grunts and "ooo aahs". I blink slowly, damn near drooling on myself as I try to wrap my head around it. Become a living god herself? "Okay... I'm going to need you to explain this to me like I am a fucking child. I'm not following this whole *turn her into a living god* thing."

He huffs, rubbing his face as though it should be the most understandable statement he's said so far. "I don't know everything, just the legends of the nine living gods."

"Wait... There are *nine* of those arrogant ba- You know what... It's not important. Just continue." I have realized quickly that I had stopped in expectation of getting a slap to the chest, which never comes.

Damn it. Sitara has wormed her way into my skin until she's taken root and grown me a damn consciousness.

"You remember the temple you went to to gain their favor?" I nod at his question, and he immediately continues, "Gai'vidiga is beneath the Cavern of Light. It is said that the nine living gods, which include the Sacred Three, traveled down there and went through what is called the Pe'tokem or the Trials of Enlightenment. It's dangerous, according to rumor. It's said that a person is faced with unimaginable trials and is judged. If they are worthy, they come out the other side celestial. If they are not, they die."

"So, what I'm hearing is, her options are to pray to the gods that aren't completely fucking insane that we come save her from Big Daddy Death *or* she goes through another traumatic experience and possibly has to live for eternity with the shitgoose that *caused* the trauma in the first place?!"

Larkin scrunches his nose, lifting a brow. "Damn... You really have spent far too much time with my sister, haven't you?"

Yup, I sure have, and I was planning to spend the rest of my life with her, too.

"Anyway... essentially, yes. Those are her options. But it is Sitara we are talking about here," he continues, "She's... special. She can handle it. At least until we get her out of this mess."

I let all the new information swirl around in my mind, a new sense of urgency boiling white hot in my gut, which I didn't think was possible, to add to my urgency and panic. I stare at him, and he stares back at me. His last comment brought needed realizations to my attention.

"You do really care about your sister, huh?"

"Yes," he says simply, "You really do love my sister, don't you?"

"I do."

We both nod to each other, the tension between us dissipating as I make my way back to the helm and look over at Benedict, who gives me a look of approval.

42
Sitara

It's been a week since I freed Hu'yimona from his prison, three days since I saw Kiernan sail off into the distance, and three days since I decided my new purpose is to do whatever I can to keep the God of Death as complacent and pliant as possible. It hasn't been easy, trying to pretend that I chose this path solely because of his appeal, but I'm managing to pull it off with considerable effort. These last few days have been torture—letting him sit in my room and chit-chat like he's not the guy who is attempting to ruin mine and everyone else's life.

In a way, he's already ruined mine.

Tonight is different, though. He has called me to his chambers instead. I already knew this would be a possibility, but it doesn't make my stomach churn any less. If I refuse now, though, it might undo all the carefully placed sedation I've laid out so far.

Since following him back through the tunnel from the beach, he's spent almost every waking moment with me. As far as I can tell, he's kept the Maggots at bay, too interested in whatever it is he wants from me to send them out to do any major harm.

I find myself in front of the large double doors of his bedchambers, the heavy iron etched and smithed with coils of smoke and shadow in an intricate pattern of artwork. The vibrations of my knuckles smacking against the metal reverberate through my bones, traveling into the stone at my feet. The seconds it takes for the door to swing open seem to tick by forever, the pounding in my ears almost deafening. I'm terrified of what he is going to ask of me, and I'm not too thrilled to be going back to this room.

Hu'yimona's face appears in the opening between the doors, his face spreading into a mockery of a gentle smile. "There you are," he purrs, stepping aside to allow me to slip in, but not far enough to keep me from having to brush against him to enter fully.

His room is exactly as I remember—the dark Gaboon Ebony rafters jutting out of the dark gray stone above our heads, the intricate candelabras hanging from the ceiling to cast a falsely intimate glow. The flooring isn't stone in here like in the other rooms; rather, it is the same dark wood as the rafters. Rugs line the floor in a dance of dark purples, blacks, and reds. I look toward the bed, trying my best to suppress a shudder. The dark fabric is cleanly drawn up over the mattress, pillows fluffed and gleaming in silk. I'm sure if you look closely enough, it is still stained with the salty tears of sisters...

I shake my head, looking back toward him as he motions for us to sit on the pillows piled for leisurely lounging in the corner. "Come, Sitara. Let's talk for a while."

I manage to pull the corners of my lips up slightly, my cheeks already burning with the effort. I pad across the oddly warm flooring, placing myself on a single pillow. My back is rigid, and I have to remind myself to breathe normally as he moves to sit down next to me. He's close enough to touch me, but not suffocatingly so. As though he actually respects my personal space, which I know he doesn't.

I look up at him. Even sitting, he towers above me. He's even larger than Kiernan... Shit, I've opened that box again, and now I have to use all my strength to shut the vortex before it can consume me into a pit of despair.

"What are we discussing tonight?" I ask, keeping my voice light despite the subtle tightness to it. Honestly, I probably sound constipated.

The first night of my return to I'cuma, he had asked me about my childhood, before my parents had gone to him seeking things that were not freely given in other places. Last night, he had asked me about my time as a teacher and what I had liked about it. All of which would have seemed like considerate questions if it had been anyone else asking them.

Hu'yimona takes a strand of my curls between his fingers, twisting it as he brings it to his face and takes in a deep breath. "I'm curious about something. What is it about Kiernan Slater that managed to pull you away from your home so easily?"

I quickly look from the curl he is currently twirling between his fingers to his face as I try to gauge his intent. All I can see in his expression is seemingly genuine curiosity. Why would he ask me that?

"It wasn't easily," I look away from him, staring at some far point on the wall, pretending to find patterns in the stone, "He kidnapped me."

It isn't a lie. Kiernan had kidnapped me out of that inn. It also hadn't been easy—the path of falling in love with him had been rocky.

"I see," Hu'yimona hums thoughtfully, dropping my hair from his grasp to run a feather-light fingertip along my cheek to move my hair away from my face. I can feel his eyes boring into the side of my head as his line of questioning continues. "Yet, you had planned to leave with him again? I apologize, I'm simply trying to understand you. Wouldn't that be considered brainwashing?"

"Isn't that what you're trying to do?" I ask, my voice tight.

"Yes, I suppose my actions can be considered as such. Though unlike him, I'm not pretending it is anything more than what it is. I am not wrapping it in a pretty bow and calling it *love*."

My chin quivers slightly, his words slicing through my still raw chest. I clench my jaw to make it stop, blinking to recant the tears of rage that have threatened to well up. I know what he is saying is the view most sane people would probably have if they look at Kiernan and my relationship from the outside. The start had been rocky, almost brutal even. But once we actually found what we were looking for in each other, it was so effortless, as natural as blinking or breathing.

I decide that arguing that point isn't going to be in the best interest of my cause, so I grit my teeth. "I suppose it looks that way."

He trails his finger down to hook it under my chin, bringing my face to the side to look at him, a mock smile of apology spread across his face. "I've upset you."

No fucking shit, you jackass.

He slides gracefully a few inches closer, burying his face more firmly in my hair for a brief moment before pulling back to look at me. "I wonder though... Do you think he feels the same way as he sails back home with his tail tucked between his legs? I don't want to be too harsh, but... Let's be honest, flower. He was only really open to returning your affections when you were complacent. Tame. When you behaved based on his preferences-the baths, the bed, the clothing."

He takes a deep breath, zeroing in on me with a smoldering fire. "You see, flower, some people are more like moths than butterflies, unveiling their painted wings in the moonlight where only someone who isn't afraid to enter the darkness is worthy to adore them," he murmurs, wrapping one massive hand around my waist to pull me in closer, "You are more a moth than anyone has ever given you credit for and I think it is beautiful in all your forms."

My brows furrow slightly, needing a moment to process his words. Somehow, he has managed to make me feel seen again... and that is dangerous. What the hell is happening? I shake my head as if to clear those thoughts. "Comparing a moth and a butterfly is like comparing a Robin to a Macaw. They are similar, yet different in so many ways."

"Indeed, they are, yet so many try to force the moth to be a butterfly when it is perfect just the way it is," he counters.

I clear my throat, racking my brain quickly for my own argument. "I'm not sure whether I should be offended that you just told me I'm only beautiful in the dark or if I should pat myself on the back for my *uniqueness*." I roll my eyes in slight annoyance.

I know well what he meant and how he meant it. The fact that I identify with what he just said makes me more uncomfortable than anything.

"That is what I like most about you, Sitara. You are much like me in the way of mental warfare. You may keep certain thoughts hidden, but every single one out of your mouth is true and pure. You don't let lies taint your tongue."

I take a deep inhale, looking up at him with a determined set in my jaw. "I think it's my turn to ask questions."

The corner of his mouth ticks upward. He's infuriatingly disarming. I'm sure, as a human, he probably was too, only less psychotic. "Go right ahead."

"What is the fuel that feeds the fires of who you are, Hu'yimona?" If he wants to play games, then I can play games too. I've learned how to play them well. He tilts his head to the side, his hand sliding down to rub small circles along the supple skin of my outer thigh.

"Hmm... That is a very important question, isn't it?"

We sit in silence for a moment while he takes time to gather his thoughts on the matter, his caresses continuing in a gentle rhythm. "I suppose it has something to do with the things I have seen in my long life. As a child, I didn't have many friends, only the four that lived with me in the temple of Potem'aku. We were locked away, you see. Hidden from the world to keep the Mundanes... *comfortable*."

His nose scrunches up in an almost endearing look of disdain. Hell, he might even look somewhat soft in this moment. He shakes his head and continues. "Rather than allowing the Mundanes to feel threatened by our very existence, they'd rather coddle them. And what was it all for, dear flower? Nothing, because as soon as the war of 1245 began, we were thrown out into the forefront as the very weapons the Mundanes feared us to be in the first place. I am tired of yielding to men who find fault in the existence of other men simply due to their lack of personal power."

So that's why he doesn't care for the Mundanes...

I can tell by the way that he is looking at me, he's itching for me to ask more. I'm not sure why that is exactly, but maybe if I ask the right questions, I can figure it out.

"Is that what made you this way?" I blurt out, "Mundanes? You give them too much pow-"

"No," he cuts me off, though his voice continues to remain gentle, despite the sudden tension in his shoulders, "and yes. They are only a small piece in what made me 'this way', as you so eloquently put it."

He continues to touch me, though none of his ministrations are threatening. Unwanted, maybe, but not threatening. He takes my left hand in his, tracing the pe'aboros on my skin.

"Darkness is often feared when misunderstood. With that knowledge, one can assume that prejudice is bound to happen from many sources. Even those one may hold closest to them," her murmurs, his eyes turned down to watch the path his finger takes along my skin, "There was..."

He trails off, straightening as he pulls away from me. "Ask your next question, flower. If you have none, I think you should go on to sleep."

I can see pain and betrayal laced in the tension of his lips, the temperature suddenly seeming to drop a considerable amount.

I can see the signs, and I know what they look like. This man has been hurt in the past. Someone, somewhere, has taken something from him that no one may ever be able to give back to him, and it has caused him to lash out with an earthquake that has rattled the very history of the Kana'te people.

It doesn't give him an excuse, but it does explain a lot of things—why it is so hard to hate him when you spend too much time with him.

Hu'yimona may be a villain, regardless, but he is a villain of nurture rather than nature.

I remain silent for some time, trying to formulate the right words. I want to ask him something that has been eating away at me from the moment I first came here all those years ago. Now that I'm back, I feel more desperate for answers, for closure.

"Can I ask you a question?" I finally speak up, though I refuse to look at him.

"Anything you want, flower," he murmurs, shifting closer to me.

"Was it really necessary?" My voice comes out softer than intended, cracking up my throat as it threatens to close up on me.

"Was what necessary?"

I struggle to find my words, struggle to even bring the topic to light. I can feel the moisture begin to drip down the back of my throat, and I think I might get sick.

"Was it necessary to force yourself on all of us before the sacrifice?"

There is nothing but silence for what feels like forever. It stretches on so long that I finally turn to look at him, only to find that his brows are drawn up, a look of confusion twisting his ethereal features.

"Excuse me? Sitara, what are you talking about?"

At first, I don't believe them, then I remember what he had said to me previously. '*I am anything but a liar.*'

"I... All of us were taken to a room and..."

"A room where you were to be held. Nothing more," he explains, confusion slowly turning to anger.

"No." I shake my head. "We were taken there one at a time, then thrown back into the holding cell." I search his face, face hardening into sharp lines. "We listened to each other scream all night long."

Realization floods his face, understanding what I am implying without me having to word it aloud. Every muscle in his body coils, and his nostrils flare with the force of his released breath.

I find myself pulled into his chest seconds later, the scent of sandalwood and sophisticated oud filling my senses. "That is not who I am, Sitara. I have done many unspeakable things, but taking the autonomy from a woman has *never* been one of them."

Wait... This isn't the smell I remember. His natural smell is clean, and I suddenly realize that I don't think he sweats. *That* man had smelled like sweat.

He's telling the truth.

43
Sitara

I wake up to the sound of a knock on the door. It is nothing but a gentle tap, but it feels like a pounding due to the constant throb that has decided to live inside my skull. I groan, rolling over under the covers to look out the opening in the rock wall on the far end of my room. That's weird... The sun is already setting.

Have I really slept all day?

I lift myself into the sitting position, my back stiff from the way I had been sleeping. The stress is getting to me, I think. Between the constant ache in my backside, my pounding head, and the metallic taste in my mouth from—what I assume is biting down on my tongue too often—I'm a complete wreck.

Before I even have a chance to respond to the interruption to my much-needed rest, Hu'yimona comes into the room with a tray of food. I can smell the cooked venison and the citrus. Oranges... It makes me think of *him*.

Which I don't want to do right now, considering every time I do, I almost lose my hard-won composure.

It's been another four days since the night we talked in his bed-chambers. While I understand him to a better degree, I still do not exactly like spending all of my time with him. Maybe that's why I'm sleeping so much-as a way to avoid him.

I do my best not to groan as I sit up, the tightness in my body becoming increasingly apparent as my muscles pop and stretch with the movement. "I didn't realize it was so late..."

It's not an apology but rather a stated fact.

I take the food from him, setting it down on my lap. I begin to tear into the meat, following it with a much-needed drink of water. My throat is dry from sleeping with my mouth open, which I know I do because Larkin used to tell me I snore all the time.

It hasn't been quite as hard to eat since the night Hu'yimona and I talked. I think being able to hear some of his story helped me put into perspective *how* I should go about stopping him. However, the way he watches me, like he has indeed been waiting four years for me to come back to him, makes me want to squirm. Who, or what, he is seems to amplify the intensity of those swirling depths.

"At least you have a good cook," I say, trying to break the tension that is increasingly growing between us. It makes me uncomfortable when he just stares at me like that while I'm stuffing my face full of food.

A wide, genuine smile spreads across his face, revealing the dimples that don't normally show in his cheeks. His eyes light up and, for some reason, it makes him look younger-almost *normal*. "I'm glad you enjoy my cooking, Sitara."

I stop mid-bite. *He cooked this?* I stare for a long moment before I bring the meat the rest of the way to my mouth. If he were going to poison me-intentionally or otherwise would have done it already. "I'm just glad it's not slop."

He leans forward, tucking a strand of hair away from my face with an almost gentle smile. "Now, do you truly believe I would let you eat food barely suitable for a sow?"

"I wasn't sure if *gods* knew how to cook," I side-eye him, bringing another bit of the venison to my lips. I haven't touched the oranges yet. I can't bring myself to. "Even if you had known how, I wasn't sure if four years beneath the earth would have stolen your skill."

I'm surprised at myself for the playful tone in my voice. I don't want him thinking he's hooking his claws in me; that he's getting his way. He chuckles, dipping his head between his shoulders before looking up at me.

Puppy dog eyes? This demented freakshow can do puppy dog eyes? That's just... That's just fucked up.

"I *was* human once," he reminds me with a jestful smirk, one eyebrow sliding upward in a fluid motion that could make a lesser informed woman-one that doesn't know how fucking insane he is, melt.

"That was a very, *very* long time ago," I point out, taking another bite as I lean back into the pillows.

Hu'yimona chuckles, shrugging one shoulder as though I haven't just called him ancient. "Perhaps. However, I seem to have the memory of an elephant... amongst other things."

I finish the rest of my food in silence, thinking to myself as I methodically go over the questions that are still filling up every corner of my mind. I study him with clearer eyes, watching him lounge back on the bed at my feet. There is just so much I don't understand about this enigmatic man. Despite myself, my curiosity seems to be winning out. After all, they say the best way to stay one step ahead of your enemy is to understand why they are what they are.

A crease forms between my brows as I try to formulate my words into some sort of coherent articulation. "Can I ask you something, and you be open with me?" I am well aware that I don't need to ask him to be honest. The man has yet to lie even once since he brought me here. If I'm being honest, he was truthful with his true colors in the short period of time I interacted with him before, too. I want to know more.

I want to understand why he is the way he is. Someone who could so easily be so lovable and adored had to have had something happen to make him this eerie monster he is now.

"Of course you can, flower," he nods, the gesture so mundane that it makes him seem almost human in this moment.

"What are you planning to do with the Mundanes?" I know that Mundanes are only a small part of his plans, even if they aren't the sole targets of his murderous intentions. I make sure to bury the worry and stress I'm feeling behind a cool facade of curiosity.

Kiernan is a Mundane....

So is Pip, Benedict, and Annie. So is the little girl we played with on the streets of Port Hammond. Every single person in Rhazden is. Millicent is. And so is Enna and their unborn child, which I was given the pleasure to be informed about before even Kiernan. I have people now outside of Capulli'ana that I want to protect, and I will do it with all my mortal capacity.

Hu'yimona looks at me with a tender smile. "There is that determination again..." he muses, more to himself than to me, judging by the distant look of contemplation on his face, "If you must know, I don't plan to kill them... *all* of them. No, I simply wish to take back what is rightfully the Kana'te people's place. Why do they get to move about the world with such free ambition, ruining sacred lands that once held so much meaning, while we have confined ourselves to a tiny island all for the sake of their comfort?"

He pauses briefly, running a finger along his chin. "Of course, there will be resistance. And I will have no qualms about ending it by any means necessary. However, so long as they are compliant, I'll have no reason to harm them. As long as they accept their *place*." He says the last word with a rumbling growl. Something has happened to create such animosity. Something big enough to make him believe the Mundanes are beneath us simply for their lack of power.

"It's been peaceful this way for a long time now," I counter, "Will you tell me what happened to make you so dead set on this being the best course of action?"

The look in his eyes is a mixture of surprising emotions. Yes, there is the expected hunger that comes with the idea of power, but there is also something more hidden behind that—hurt, pain, maybe even betrayal. I unconsciously move closer, silently urging him to open up to me. If I can just understand, maybe I can stop his rage before he takes it out on innocent people.

"Peaceful?" he scoffs, rolling those metallic orbs with grudging playfulness, "Please, Sitara, it has hardly been peaceful. The moment a Kana'te person steps off this island, they face persecution from every angle just for existing outside the barrier my fellow gods have created."

"That's not true..." I say, shaking my mane of red curls around my face, "I have been accepted many times..."

"*You* are not just any person, are you?" he rejects my statement, tilting his head to the side as his eyes rove over me before returning to meet my gaze, "You, Sitara, have a light that is not easily ignored, and yet still, you found judgment in places where there was no cause for it."

He's not wrong. There had been plenty of passersby who had sneered at me just for walking down the streets of Port Hammond. Hell, even some of the crew had to warm up to me before I was finally able to break through their defenses. However, I don't believe it was enough to sentence anyone to servitude or death. I've had plenty of similar looks given to me by my own people. "Then will you tell me what happened?"

He shakes his head, rising to his feet. He holds out a palm to me, crooking his fingers in a silent command for me to take his hand. "How about I show you instead."

I place my hand in his to allow him to pull me to my feet. "What do you mean you'll *show* me?"

"You'll see," he mutters, lacing his fingers with mine as he pulls me out of my bedchambers and into the dimly lit corridor. Every instinct in my body tells me to jerk out of his hand; to not give him this unsettling intimacy. However, I know if I do, my cover will be blown and he'll know I'm not here because I *want* to be, which is what I'm trying to convince him of.

Leading me down the hall, Hu'yimona pulls me down tunnel after winding tunnel, the walls growing more narrow as we go. I'm trying to keep my bearings so that I can keep track of where we would be above ground, but I can't keep up. I would be completely lost if not for his hand leading me through the darkness as the torch fire disappears into nothing.

I create another flame in my palm to look around. There is nothing significant about the passageway we are walking down right now. At least, not that I can see. After a considerable amount of walking, he stops. My brows furrow deeply as I look up at him, trying to ignore the way my violent flame highlights the line of his smooth face. He's ...taken us to a dead end?

No, it's not a dead end, I realize as I watch his large frame turn to the side and attempt to slip through a small opening in the rock. His body won't fit through a space that small. I am convinced he'll get stuck until his body turns to shadowy smoke before he solidifies on the other side.

"Come, Flower," he says, squeezing my hand reassuringly.

I slide my fingers of my free hand, the flame dying in my palm, along the surprisingly smooth wall of the opening. Judging by the size, I should be able to just make it through. I take a deep breath and turn my own body sideways, shuffling through the hole until I can see his features clearly once more.

Once I'm inside the small alcove chamber, I can see a small pool glistening as though it is illuminated with its own white light. Stepping closer, it becomes apparent where we are, and my heart clenches tightly.

I am so close to the Ma'tawi village... yet so far away.

I watch the tiny aquatic bugs flit around in the dark depths of the water. Somehow, we are underneath the Lake of Mirrors. I look at him for answers, my eyes swimming with questions that I know he can see.

"The Lake of Mirrors is actually a tunnel connected to the labyrinth here underground," he explains as he gives me what is supposed to be a reassuring squeeze.

But all I can think about is... Kiernan.

"The water here has magical properties for those who have specific forms of magic. I happen to have one of two of those forms," he continues, pulling me to the water's edge.

I stand there, my neck craning back to look up in awe at the shimmering lake above me. It's unlike anything I've ever seen. My mind wanders to what sort of earthly magic would possibly keep the water from draining down into this cavern and flooding everything. His magic? Something else?

"You said there are two forms of magic. Who holds the other one?" Since it's obvious he is going to show me what his is, I'm more curious about the other.

"I'm afraid that question will only lead us to one of two places, my flower," he murmurs, holding his palm against the water's surface, "Either I will become a liar, or your curiosity will cause more harm than good."

I almost feel a small inkling of sadness for the way his voice tightens and his jaw clenches.

I give a slow nod of unspoken understanding. At least he was honest... per usual. "Then show me yours."

A feeling of anticipation comes rushing into my chest as I look back up to where his palm is pressed against the water as though it is a solid substance. "I'm assuming whatever it is will answer my question?"

His brows furrow in concentration as the dark depths of his eyes begin to swirl like mist. His pupils, which are usually hidden by the darkness of his irises, begin to glow a soft, cloudy gray. I bite the inside of my cheek, looking between his face and his hand as inky smoke begins to filter into the water where it moves like a vortex just below the surface.

"Death and shadow have the properties to reveal the past, just as it can make one's life flash before their eyes and contemplate their own existence," he murmurs a soft explanation, "Just as life can reveal the future and all its fickle possibilities. Here, I can show you what has come to pass, and help you understand." The heartbreaking longing in his voice as he explains how this works to me is enough to make even my hatred lessen.

The shadows writhe and twist, spreading out from his palm to coil through the water that we are standing next to. Images begin to swirl and take form within the waterfall, forcing me to lean closer in curiosity.

The first scene he reveals to me takes me by surprise. There he is, a young boy of twelve, the fresh pe'aboros on his arm. My eyes widen fractionally as I take in the white and gold trailing down his skin. Those images are long since gone from his flesh, so I had no idea that he had once come from the Ma'tawi tribe.

My home.

My people.

My family.

I look over at him, my shoulders drooping slightly. "You... were one of-"

He grips my chin with unnerving gentleness, turning my gaze back to the memory flashing above my head. He lowers himself to coo sweetly in my ear, his cool breath forcing me to shiver. "You're missing it."

My eyes follow the images, amazed by how completely normal he seemed. He stands next to an older woman, her silver locks trailing down her back, their hands locked in an intimate gesture. He looks nothing like himself, yet I can easily tell that it is him. He has the same dark eyes, though there is a warmth to them, an innocence that simply isn't there anymore. His skin is a sun-kissed peach that works well with the warmth of his dark, inky locks. He's adorable. He has the face any mother would love. Any tribe would love...

Seriously, what happened to this guy?

"But... *Calandra*," his boyish voice rings out through the cavern, echoing off the walls, *"Why did we have to leave? Coli'hanu and I would never hurt anyone."*

The old woman looks down at him, her dark face warm and inviting, even loving. *"I know you wouldn't, Hu'yimona. You are a kind soul, but that does not disregard the threat that you could pose to the Mundanes. You make them uncomfortable."*

"So... We had to leave our home because they want us to? I don't understand..."

"You will in time, my child. You will in time." The old woman pats his head tenderly, his child-like eyes wide with confusion and hurt.

"We didn't want to leave our mom and dad," he says in the memory, and my heart almost shatters *for* him.

My chin quivers, and I feel a hot tear spill from each of my eyes as I watch that guileless child being ripped away from his parents.

He didn't ask for that.

None of them did.

It's a realization that feels like a punch to the gut.

Then, in a shift of scenery, I see the same young boy comforting an oddly familiar young girl. She sits on a tier of the inner ring of the temple, her hands buried in her face as she cries. Her brown hair spills over her shoulders as she leans in against him. His arm is around her, whispering gentle, soothing comforts to her as he sits there holding her.

Coli'hanu... I would recognize my goddess anywhere.

"Shh... It's okay..." he murmurs to her, his voice cracking with his own wellspring of emotions.

"I just want a visit," her voice shakes and quivers with the motion of her shoulders, *"I know we can't go home, Hu'yimona. I want to go home to Mapa and Maku."*

The next realization hits me like a ton of bricks. Of course, why hadn't I seen the similarities in them sooner...

"She's... your sister," I breathe out, my eyes wide with shock even as I feel another twist of the knife in my gut.

"Yes," he answers simply, his voice strained as he relives these moments. To me, I'm just watching a moment in time. To him, he is reliving some of the hardest moments of his childhood. I can only imagine how that must feel. Actually, I *can* imagine it. It's exactly how I felt when I was faced with him once more. When I thought my parents were behind that barrier.

The image shifts again, and I am met with the living gods I know today. All... five?... of them are standing in the Cavern of Light. I recognize Coli'hanu and Hu'yimona instantly, as well as Teo'Kan and Gula'ci. However, the fifth one standing there is blurred. I can't make out anything besides trusses of dark hair whipping around a feminine figure.

The old woman known as Calandra is standing under the Tree of Life with a broad smile. *"Look at you all... Magnificent. Truly Magnificent."*

The pride I see shining brilliantly on each of their faces warms my heart, though Hu'yimona's face has an underlying sense of weariness to it. *"Are you sure this was wise, Calandra? Wouldn't this just threaten more of the Mundane's precious comfort?"*

"Who is the fifth-" I start to ask. However, I stop as the scene abruptly changes.

There he is, in all his glory, clashing in a field of hundreds if not thousands of Mundanes and Kana'te alike. His skin is drenched in blood, which is something I would most certainly expect from someone like him. It's the still gentle gleam in his eyes that confuses me. He's not yet been ruined to the light, despite the scenes that have been revealed to me thus far.

The sounds of war become deafening in the echo chamber, but I don't look away or cover my ears. To my surprise, the Mundanes seem to be pushing our line of defenses back, their numbers greatly overpowering ours. Hu'yimona appears out of nowhere, grabbing a Mundane by the throat to throw him off a young man who looks like he shouldn't even be on that battlefield. Shadows begin to rise from the ground, taking on a life of their own as Hu'yimona single-handedly evens the odds.

"You were so different..." I can't help but feel my opinions of him beginning to shift slightly. He has made bad choices, and he should still pay karma for all the horrible deeds he's done, but he isn't the cold-blooded monster I originally believed him to be.

"I think we would have been friends," I say as I turn to face him, "Had I been alive then."

There is a flicker of something akin to surprise flash through his eyes, though it is there and gone so quickly that I can't quite make out what it is. His face falls back into that cool facade of calm as he looks back up at the waterfall. I can feel the corners of my mouth pull upward. "Though I'm sure you had enough to keep you entertained."

"I didn't, actually," he responds smoothly as though it doesn't bother him as much as I'm sure it actually does, "But yes, I do think you and I would have gotten along, had things been different. But alas, Life is a cruel mistress who often enjoys teasing her victims with the right things at the wrong times."

The absolute disdain dripping from his words makes me reevaluate my thoughts. I have a feeling, by the way he said that, it goes far beyond a simple metaphor.

44
Sitara

The journey back to my bedchambers has been mostly silent. I don't pull away from his hand when he interlaces our fingers, and the sickening feeling I had in my stomach at his touch has ebbed slightly. I can't say I'm still particularly fond of it, but the crawling sensation on my skin is no longer there. To be honest, I feel more of a kinship to Hu'yimona now that I understand him a little better.

The sound of our bare feet hitting the stone floors mixed with my own mildly labored breathing is the only indication of life within the walls of the tunnels. It must be nice to never get tired; to never have your lungs feel like they've begun to breathe in fire.

Despite my best efforts, my mind still drifts toward Kiernan, to his face when he and I had stood next to that pool of glittering lights and he had asked me to marry him. I can feel that hole in my chest reopening due to being at the Lake of Mirrors. The sight of him sailing off into the distance replays over and over in my head.

Finally, after what feels like hours of silence, I turn to face Hu'yimona. I still have so many questions, but the one that keeps running through my mind the most—when I'm not torturing myself with images of Kiernan—finally slips out of my mouth.

"Why did you leave Potem'aku? Don't you miss your sister? The other gods?"

I notice a small smile tug at the right corner of his mouth, his eyes sliding down to look at me. "I do miss my sister from time to time, but she made her choices and I made mine. As for the others, well, Teo'Kan and I don't really get along. He can be a bit of an ass." I almost spittle on him as I press my lips together to stifle a chuckle.

It's true. Teo'Kan tends to get on the others' nerves and often prides himself on reminding us mere mortals of our insignificance. "Still, don't you ever-"

"One day you will learn something, Flower. Something vital for every person at some point to learn," he pauses, mostly for dramatic effect, I think. He can be a bit theatrical sometimes. "I have found that light shines brightest in those who embrace their darkest parts. That's why I refused to pretend to be something I was not any longer."

"I wish that didn't make perfect sense to me," I sigh, hanging my head between my shoulders.

As much as I hate it, he isn't wrong... *I'm so fucking tired of this guy being right!*

Can't he just be wrong?

Just once?

Wait... What he did to all those girls. That was wrong.

So, so wrong.

I'm going to hold onto that tiny scrap of wrong just to keep myself grounded.

As we walk through the halls, back to the sanctity of my chambers, a familiar scent wafts to me from a group of Miqui'oh passing by. I instinctively freeze, my shoulders bunching up to my ears. My heart begins to race wildly as I plant my feet.

Hu'yimona notices, of course, turning to look down at me from a few feet ahead.

"Everyone, stop." His voice rings out through the space. The sound of their shuffled footsteps ceases, a collective inhale sucking the air right out of the room.

I still can't move, unable to turn and look at any of them as his shadows coil around my body, reaching out to throw and pin each of them to the wall.

The tail end of his shadow caresses my cheek, snapping out of my panic. My eyes meet his, still wide-eyed.

"They can't hurt you, flower. Tell me who it is."

He wraps his arms around me, walking me along the line of people as they all quiver and sputter against the wall, unable to move from under their god's hold.

As we pass by the scent again—a man with, what I can discern from the corner of my eye, long black hair and pale skin—forcing me to tense in Hu'yimon's arms.

I don't need to say anything. He's managed to read my body language. Hu'yimona's shadows release from all save for this man, instead pulling him forward until his face is within the god's reach.

I don't look up, even as Hu pulls him down to look at me. I can faintly see the man's eyes bulging, his cheeks divoted so painfully deep that he's bitten into the inner flesh, forcing blood to trickle down his chin.

"Do you see this?" Hu'yimona asks, though it isn't really a question. "I don't tolerate a man who elicits this kind of reaction from a woman. That is behavior fit for dogs and Mundanes."

Before a response can be given, before Hu'yimona's shadows wrap around him once more. "Allow me to give you a taste."

The shadows tighten around the man, eliciting a startled, pained grunt before they begin to slither and writhe into each orifice of the man's body. I'm compelled to look more clearly, but Hu'yimona forces my head into his chest, denying my attempt. A few more gurgled struggles echo through the hall, then a resounding thud, before silence falls once more.

Without missing a beat, I'm turned away from whatever carnage is behind us and gently led back to my room.

We finally stop in front of my bedroom door, and I sigh in relief. I'm exhausted—probably from all the emotional turmoil I've been subjected to in the last few minutes.

I click open the door and we both walk inside. He releases me, and I expect to be told goodnight and for him to take his leave. Instead, he runs a hand up my arm and over my collarbone until he is cupping my chin in his grasp.

"That understanding—about embracing the darkest parts—is exactly why I believe *we* were made to love each other," he purrs, the pad of his thumb brushing against my lower lip.

Every time this man opens his mouth, he shows me a little more of why he believes what he believes. I let out a shaky breath I hadn't realized I had been holding. I don't particularly agree with his plans for the Mundanes, but I am starting to understand why he believes what he does.

"What are you doing?" The words come out as barely more than a garbled mess of syllables, still reeling from the ordeal that took place moments before.

I harbor no fear that he is going to hurt me. He has proven over the last week and a half that he doesn't want that. It's the way he is looking at me, the way he is touching me... I've seen that look before behind a different set of eyes, and it makes my heart ache.

I thought I had prepared myself for anything and everything Hu'yimona could throw at me, but I was so, *so* wrong.

Let's add it to my mile-long list of wrongs.

My heart kicks into high gear, and I hope he interprets it as anticipation. I want him to think he's burrowed under my skin where another has already taken root. Although I don't wish for it the way I had with *him,* I don't find it as gut-retching an idea as I had before.

"I think it is time you stopped pretending to be some meek, pathetic little girl when I can see every vicious thought swirling like shadow behind those mahogany eyes," he says, taking a step closer until our bodies are almost flush against one another. It takes every ounce of self-control I have not to take a step away-ruining everything I have worked so hard to achieve already. "Be my wife, Sitara."

I work hard to keep my composure, breathing in through my nose and out through a subtle part in my mouth. I work to relax my body, my tongue darting out to wet my suddenly dry lips.

Okay, pull yourself together, Sitara. If this is what you have to do to keep him from blowing a hole in the map...

"How is that supposed to work?" I ask, making sure to keep my tone concerned rather than unwilling, "You're immortal and I am not. Wouldn't the death of a wife just be more unnecessary pain?"

A broad smile spreads across his face as he uses his free hand to finish closing the distance, his fingers splayed out across the small of my back. "Yes, it would. Which is exactly why I plan to put forth a solution to that problem the moment we are man and wife. I will make you a living god, Sitara, just as I was made."

My eyes grow wide, the implications of such a thing overwhelming. "You want to make *me* a living god."

It's not a question, but rather a statement of finality to one of the many I have had since I first arrived here. I start to rack my brain for how I can use this to my advantage. If I'm going to be stuck here with him for however long I live—maybe even forever if he has his way—I need to use this to keep those I love safe.

I take a moment to envision it. I picture myself as a goddess, standing next to him as I use whatever willpower and strength is granted to me to keep him at bay. Sure, it would most likely keep us both isolated as the world moved on without us, but it is a price I think I might be willing to pay for those I care about.

Hu'yimona apparently sees my hesitation as an interpretation of fear because he caresses my cheek with the back of his fingers and begins whispering soothing words in my ear. "Your life will change, my flower, when you realize that this monster is here to protect you."

"If I marry you..." I close my eyes for a moment, bracing myself for what I'm about to do, "*When* I marry you, you must promise me that you won't hurt anyone else."

I can hear his breath catch in his throat, his hand tightening against my back. "I will not harm a single hair on the top of a human's head."

I believe him.

Because Hu'yimona isn't a liar.

I nod, taking in a deep breath as I open my eyes to meet his dark gaze. "Alright... I will marry you."

The weight of the decision I have just made crashes down on me. I feel two-faced and dirty, agreeing to marry him when I was *supposed* to marry someone else. Even if said someone else doesn't want me anymore...

A wide, bright smile spreads across his face, one that lights up his features into something beautiful. "Mea'las Nem'loa," he purrs, and I feel my heart twist tightly in my chest.

Then his lips are pressed to mine.

The slide of his skin against mine is unfortunately more comforting than I would like it to be, but this is what I have signed myself up for, so I might as well let myself get used to it.

The first step to normalcy is pretending everything is fine, right?

I keep my arms at my sides, though his tongue demands entrance by sliding along the seam of my lips, so I have no choice but to move them with his. Insulting him now will get me nowhere.

And that is the worst part, the fact that it isn't unpleasant. Just like everything else about him. After a millennium or two, who knows, maybe I'll learn to enjoy this a little more.

As he deepens the kiss, one hand sliding up to angle my head just right, his other hand splays across the scar on my lower abdomen. I tense, the shock damn near causing me to break the kiss and step away. It isn't until his fingertips begin to sink into my skin, the appendages now nothing more than smoke swirling and lapping at my flesh, that true panic sets into my chest.

He breaks the kiss then, however, pulling his hand back out of my body with a palm-sized black flame between his fingers. The same black flame that always rears its ugly head when the anniversary of my first encounter with Hu'yimona comes around.

He smiles, pulling out my vial of liquid fire from his waistband. Where the hell did he get that?

I instinctively reach for the pocket of my skirt. How the hell hadn't I even thought to look for the damn thing earlier?!

I watch as he uncorks it, letting the black flame slowly meld with the liquid inside the bottle. It's a strange visual, one I wouldn't have thought possible if I weren't watching it with my own eyes.

Hu'yimona swirls it around, placing the cork back into the neck. "There, we'll add that to the gift from my sister."

45
Kiernan

The towering cliff walls of Rhazden come into view as the sun begins to set. We sailed straight through, not even bothering to drop off the men who still had time to spare before being granted admission. I don't care about customs and propriety at this point. I just want to get docked and get the help we need to get Sitara back. Larkin, who finally stopped painting the side of my ship with his insides after almost a full week at sea, furrows his brow in confusion.

His head tilts to the side as he beholds the towering rock walls around my precious home. "Huh... this is... nice?"

I'd chuckle if it wasn't for the fact that his sister had given me a similar reaction. It kills me to even look at him with that expression on his face. It makes him look a lot like her.

"Thank you," I respond dryly as I replace Benedict at the helm, "The second we dock, I want every crew member out gathering all the able-bodied bodies in Rhazden." I practically bark at my first mate, but I know he understands. I draw in a sharp breath to focus.

It won't do Sitara any good if I kill us all while trying to get through the passageway.

"You might want to hold on," Ben suggests, and I can see him nod toward the railing next to Larkin from my peripheral vision, "There are several sharp turns and not a lot of time to brace between them."

This is indeed a fact. This route through the pass is one that, thus far, only I have ever sailed successfully. The jagged rock and narrow path is only part of the fun. Once you add shallows that barely leave inches under the ship, well... things tend to get interesting.

"And you're sure that people are going to be willing to come with us?" Larkin's question is directed at me. I turn my face, partially placing his concerned, almost boyish, expression into my line of sight.

"*Anyone* I ask to go, will go," I answer with tremendous faith, "Not because they are forced to, but because I asked."

There is a slight furrow pinching his dark brows, and I know what he is thinking. It's something we have discussed during our journey here. He's worried that they won't be willing to lend aid because of *where* we are asking them to go. Larkin seems far more acclimated to the Mundane world than Sitara had been when I first snatched her up out of that inn.

"Now, shut up so I don't kill us," I grunt as I make, what should be, an impossible serpentine turn around a bend in rock.

A collective inhale draws in from everyone aboard the ship as I spin the pegs back in the opposite direction. This wouldn't be a difficult move in something small, but the size of the ship makes it difficult. However, I manage to miss the rock with the bow of the ship by mere inches.

As I pull us straight once more, my beautiful Rhazden comes into view. Benedict makes himself scarce, shuffling off to shout docking orders and inform the crew of the expectations once their feet touch shore. Everyone scrambles to do as they're told, Arthur especially hauling ass around the deck to get it done. I look at Larkin, who is taking in the town with awe.

"Welcome to Rhazden," I rumble, turning away from him quickly.

My stomach churns as I think about how Sitara would have loved to be here for her brother's very first view of this little hidden treasure that she would now be sharing with me. She would have liked to be here for his first time off the island, too. There are a lot of things she is missing right now because we weren't there to protect her.

Larkin moves toward the gangplank the moment it's drawn, though I am faster. My long legs eat up the distance at a greater pace than his when we aren't hopping over trees and stumbling over moving roots.

He calls after me, but I don't stop, and I don't slow down. I don't have time to try to show him how to navigate my world. He'll have to figure it out and be back on the ship before I sail.

"Come on, Larkin! I'm not a patient man."

Fortunately, he catches up to me before I turn off the docks, heading toward the center of my little island, where I know Ben and the others will be sending people. Villagers smile at my approach, but their expressions fall quickly into ones of concern. Even the children, who usually run up to me and get underfoot when I first bring their loved ones home, stop in their tracks at the sight of the determined expression on my face.

Once I reach the center, I am assaulted by a small body flinging its arms around my waist. Neoma, my niece, smiles up at me with bright green eyes. Her long chestnut colored hair falls away from her face as she cranes her head to look up at me.

"Uncle Nan, you're home-" she stops, scrunching her nose playfully, "Your face is sour."

I crouch down to eye level, gently taking her hands in mine, "Neoma, I need you to go home, okay?"

She releases me and takes a step back, nodding softly as her expression grows solemn. It pains me to know that at only six years old, she can take an order so well. However, she knows that when I say she needs to do something, I only say it because it's necessary.

I watch her scurry toward the path that leads her home. The footsteps I hear approaching, I know belong to Larkin as they come to a halt behind me. "These people don't know you. Just as your people deserved my respect, my people deserve the same from you," I mutter, watching as people start to surround the central platform that serves many uses, including village announcements and entertainment. Larkin nods, his eyes roving over the crowd as it becomes more compact.

"Believe it or not, I'm not usually one to be a jackass without cause." I open my mouth to argue that point before he cuts me off with a wry smile. "In my eyes, you had given me cause."

Fair point. I did take his sister without him ever knowing the wiser.

Unfortunately, I'm not the only one, nor am I the worst. The rapidly increasing group leaves enough space around us to keep me from feeling encroached upon, all of the spaces around the platform being filled with warm bodies and concerned faces.

"What's going on, Kiernan?" A middle-aged man who works as a blacksmith asks, his dark beard and kind eyes staring at me. A few more mumble their agreement to his question, and I take a deep breath.

I let the same breath out slowly, looking to the first man who had spoken to me-Robert McKlain. "I'm sure many of you saw the girl I brought back with me the last time we docked."

I pause to give them a moment to murmur amongst themselves to confirm that they had seen her.

"Aye, the lass with the wildfire for hair," Robert nods, "I saw her waltzin' about." I give him a nod in return, my face growing more solemn.

"She is mine, and she's in trouble." I look around at the horde of people that surround us as they all collectively give looks of shock. I'm well aware that I was the last person they expected to settle down. "My love has been taken from me. I need your help to get her back."

Once again, the murmurs rise into the air, some still hung up on the *she is mine* bit, others putting two and two together that she is Kana'te by the presence of the Ma'tawi man standing next to me. I look at Larkin, placing a hand on his shoulder, "I need you all to know what we are going up against, if you plan to join me. This man is her brother. If you'll listen, he'll tell you all you need to know about Hu'yimona and his Maggot Cult."

The murmurs rise higher into the air, more panicked. That's when an old, frail voice rises above the noise, hushing the crowd with a single sentence. "Hush, all of you, and listen to the man. If what Kiernan says is true, if Hu'yimona—the Shadow Beast of Wrath—is truly returned, you'll want to know everything regardless of your willingness to save the girl."

Marjorie, an ancient woman who had been given admission along with her grandson, steps forward with a knowing look, nodding toward Larkin to begin. She eyes him with a knowing glance, as if she's seen his people many times before. She probably has. Her snowy hair falls over one shoulder in a long, tight braid, her wrinkled face softening slightly.

I motion him forward, moving to stand before the large group of bystanders who have grown increasingly more attentive and willing to listen.

"My name is Larzoma'kin of the Ma'tawi Kana'te people. I know in the past our people have not necessarily gotten along, but..." He takes a deep breath as though he's attempting to steel himself for the lecture he is about to give. "Stopping Hu'yimona and his cult wouldn't only be beneficial to *my* people. Hu'yimona is ruthless and without remorse. As the elder said, he used to be known as the Shadow Demon of Wrath during the great war. However, there is a reason my people have come to know him as the God of Death."

Robert takes a step forward, his arms folded over his chest as he studies Larkin with a cool analysis. "What type of power does this god possess?"

"I haven't been in close quarters enough to know everything he is capable of," Larkin responds tightly. "However, I do know that he can create shadows that will kill anything they come into contact with, and recently I discovered that he can use his shadows as clones. It's how he tricked my sister and me. By making clones of our mother and father."

The crowd grows uneasy, wary of the implications of such power. To make matters worse, those are only the powers Larkin himself knows about. My stomach lurches as another man by the name of Lucas steps forward, his thick brows furrowed deeply over unsettled blue eyes. "How are a group of Mundanes going to be able to fight something like that?"

Larkin's lips curve into a stiff smile, his arms folding over his chest. The confidence in his voice mirrors that determination in his shoulders. "My sister. She possesses the gift of Cold Fire. Which is the only thing that can hold him. We can't kill him. All we have to do is weaken their defenses enough to buy her some time to seal him away. But the cult members themselves raise another challenge."

"What sort of challenge?" an ebony-skinned man by the name of Yorin questions, joining in the tense conversation taking place.

"Most of their powers are no different than those of the rest of us. However, Hu'yimona has granted them an amplification of that power, so to speak," Larkin responds smoothly.

I do my best to remain focused on Larkin, just as I expect everyone else to be doing. It's hard. It's hard to keep my mind from wandering, from picturing all the different scenarios that we might face. The fact that all these people are so willing and ready to put their lives on the line for me and mine is overwhelming in its intensity. The fact that, even now, as they are being told all of the odds that are stacked against us, proves how honorable every one of them is. Even as it becomes obvious that we have only scratched the surface of what Hu'yimona is capable of, none of them wavers.

Not one of them has yet to walk away or flat-out refuse me.

If I asked, I can say with near certainty that even the women and children would go. I would never ask that, of course. I don't even want every able-bodied man to go. I need some of them to stay behind and keep my sister and niece safe, as well as all of the other innocent people I harbor here. No, I will select the ones I need and leave the other here to protect what I cannot.

As the questions begin to cease, leaving a low hum of murmurs in its wake, I step forward once more. "Anyone willing to fight with me, step forward."

I'm astonished by the sheer number of those who have taken that step. Standing among them are Yorin, Lucas, and Robert. I place my hand on Robert's shoulder with a nod, jerking my head back toward the crowd. "You have a family. I'd rather you stay here and protect the town."

He hesitates but eventually nods, backing up into the fray and pulling his young son into his side. I do this to a few of the others, strategically choosing which of the volunteers will stay and who will go.

Once I've made my selections, the crowd parts, and those who will be departing with us move to gather their bags for the journey ahead. That's when I spot Benedict, leaning against a post with his arm draped over a familiar figure. Enna stands beside him as she rubs the small swell in her lower abdomen that has begun to form there.

Guilt chokes me as I watch her eyes level me with the same look they always have. Enna respects me, cares about me, but she thinks I'm fucking stupid.

She pushes her cinnamon locks, which are coiled into a tight braid, off her shoulder and smiles. I walk up to them where they stand at the edge of the dispersing crowd, running my hand through my hair.

"Ben," I say solemnly, standing before him and his wife. They are my oldest friends, my first true family apart from my sister. "I'm not going to demand that you go. I can't ask you to walk away from your wife and unborn child. Not when I know that the probability of death is astronomical."

I pointedly glance at where Enna's hand rests on her belly, giving her a warm smile. Benedict and Enna glance at one another, and she nods to him with a raised brow.

They've already talked about it.

Of course they have.

Ben slaps his hand down on my shoulder and shakes his head. "We both agree that I'm going to live or die as I always have, which has never been a coward."

46

Sitara

I wake to the gentle knock on my door, one that has become a normal routine for me. I sit up under the covers, expecting to see the slight form of Eirian, my usual deliverer of meals.

She walks through the door, her head of shoulder-length, honey-brown curls bouncing around her face. Her wheat-toned skin is smooth, stretching firmly over firm muscle. Nothing seems out of the ordinary, apart from her hands gripping the tray far too tightly and her steel blue gaze wide with uncertainty.

I've grown fond of Eirian, having formed a friendship in the last few weeks, so her demeanor concerns me. Her eyes are widened, pupils pulled into pinpoints as if she's just seen a ghost. The pallor of her dark skin has paled.

I furrow my brows questioningly, opening my mouth to speak. Before I can manage, however, the spindly, pale form of Morana, the shaman of the Miqui'oh tribe, walks into the room after her.

This woman doesn't elicit the same calming presence that all the other shamans normally do.

Oh no, she radiates chaos, malice, and something far darker.

Her gray eyes always seem to be blown wide with lunacy, much too large where they bed inside her skull. Her skin is ashy, pulled taut over sharp angles that could almost be considered beautiful if they were softened somewhat. Her icy blonde hair is constantly in disarray, framing her face in tousled, chaotic tufts.

"Pali Chute, ko'tasifa," she purrs, though her tone is more mocking than endearing. The hairs on the back of my neck rise as I murmur the greeting back to her.

Eirian starts to arrange my meal on my bedside table as Morana begins bombarding me with item after item on my to-do list for the day. Since agreeing to Hu'yimona's proposal, I've taken on more responsibilities: teaching the Miqui'oh children English, helping the cooks' preservation of meats with my Cold Fire, and overseeing the preparations for our wedding.

"Also," Morana says, the sound coming out more as a hiss, "You're fitting is today. Do try not to indulge yourself with breakfast, will you?"

I bite down on my tongue, mostly to keep the unsettled churn of my stomach at bay, and watch her flit back out of the room. Eirian and I remain silent for some time. I watch my friend move to close the ajar door, peeking out to check that the shaman has truly left.

With a heavy sigh, her shoulders relax, and she turns back to me with a worried expression. "You mustn't trust her, Ko'tasifa. She does not have your best interest at heart." She pauses, slowly sinking onto the edge of my bed. "Honestly, I'm not sure she has *anyone's* best interest at heart."

"What do you mean?" I press for more information. "She's your shaman, Hu'yimona's right hand... Surely she at least has his interest at heart."

Eirian hesitates, the corner of her full lips scrunching into a foul pinch. "I'm not so sure of that either."

More and more cultists have been called to return to I'cuma and the overwhelming number of them is astonishing. I hadn't realized how many people believe he is the path to a better world. Then again, if I didn't know some of the horrible things he's capable of before letting him get his claws in me, I would probably be easily swayed to.

That thought pushes bile up my throat, the nausea burning my gullet with every swallow. I can't afford to think like that. *Why* would I even go down that thought process? The endless amount of responsibilities I have been given in the last week is obviously fucking with my head.

Since that night, I have been required to do more than just hide away in my room. He wants his people to see me now. He wants me to know them. Like it's some twisted little family made up of almost one hundred strong.

The way they look at me is different from the last time I was here, locked away in the dungeons with eight others just waiting to die. They had been cruel then, their eyes simmering with barely contained bloodlust and unimaginable thoughts of all the ways they could hurt us without ruining any of Hu'yimona's plans.

Now, their expressions are almost... *soft*. It makes me uneasy. They've been smiling at me and asking me how I'm doing, and I can't bring myself to answer with anything but "fine". It's hard for me not to forget that all of them used to be one of us. Every single one of them used to be a friend, a partner, a mother, a daughter, a father, a son to someone within the three tribes. Now... They are nothing but hollow shells of their former selves, chasing behind the shadows of greed and corruption.

I stare at myself in the mirroring glass, yet another thing Hu'yimona has adopted from the Mundanes. The red sheer fabric that is draped over my body is a surprising color. I had half expected him to put me in black for this wedding dress, seeing as it is his favorite go-to color. However, it isn't surprising that the hue of this particular shade of red matches the very crimson blood flowing through my own veins.

The woman who is painstakingly hand-stitching this dress for me looks somewhat frustrated. The delicate curve of her brows pushes down ever so slightly as she leans forward, as though to get a better look at the seam she's just created.

She's a larger woman, roughly five feet and seven inches tall–if I use myself as a standard. Her wiry coils of sandy-blonde hair keep falling into her face, and she pushes them back with a look that says she very well might be contemplating shaving her head.

Hu'yimona is standing across the room from me, leaning against the wall as he watches her work. The slight smile on his face is undeniably wholesome, even if it does make me want to punch him all the same. He's wearing his usual cotton breaches, the ones that are dyed as black as his soul and pinch into a firm coil at his ankles. And just like every other day, he's bare-chested, letting his tattoos swirl and dance along his skin like always. I'm not sure if it makes it better or *worse* to know how such a beautiful man turned into such a malefactor.

After the third small huff of irritation from the woman at my feet, I look down at her with a lift of my eyebrow. It's difficult not to glare at them when they have Hu'yimona's mark branded on their forehead. "Is something wrong?"

She shakes her head, the same strand of bristly curl that's been falling into her face all afternoon making its grand appearance over her eyeball again. "No." She tugs on the fabric, pulling it uncomfortably tight in the areas she had premade before coming here. "Nothing a little *extra* work won't fix."

"Extra work?" Hu'yimona grumbles from his place at the wall, his smile fading ever so slightly, "I'm fairly certain I gave you the correct measurements. Are you saying that you can't do your job?"

She takes in a long breath, and I can see her jaw working under her skin. She slowly lets the air back out of her lungs, closing her eyes for a mere moment before taking the needle back to my dress. She continues to fight with the premade fabric, hissing under her breath before addressing him. "You chose me because you've personally worn my work. You honor me by wearing it now."

So she's the one responsible for the tapestry-stitched fabrics he's always wearing that make me ashamed of myself for even contemplating the idea he could be attractive.

I might end her second only to Morana when I become a living god.

"And yet, you do me a *dishonor* by complaining that my perfect bride is giving you trouble." The irritation in his voice is enough to make *me* shudder a bit, and I've gotten used to him.

Well... As used to him as a mere human can.

She tries in vain to pull the fabric together one last time, and I can feel the slight tremor in her fingertips before they settle. So... Even those with spines of steel within the cult fear him at least a little bit.

"You have my sincerest apology if I gave the inkling that this was, in any way, the fault of your bride," she murmurs, sitting back where I can see the wheels turning behind her cold green eyes.

She twists to the small wooden stool that sits off to the side of where we are standing and pulls out the parchment with my scribbled measurements on it and a measuring tape, all of which have been yet another Mundane innovation he's allowed the cult to use.

For someone who hates them so much, he sure likes using their stuff.

She begins wrapping the tape around each point on my body; first my breasts, then the small of my waist, then my hips.

"The measurements seem perfect–" She pauses, wrapping it around my hips to re-measure once, twice, three times. She pulls the fabric away from my skin entirely to place her palm right over the space where my scar sits.

I swallow down a gasp as her cold palm presses against my flesh. The sick feeling in my stomach rises to a boiling mess of bile threatening to come up my throat. To have one of *them* touch the very scar they created... It's my worst nightmare.

"Ha!" she stands up with a triumphant smile, resting her fists on her hips, "Your measurements were spot on, Alatak Hu'yimona. However, babies have a way of causing things like measurements to change significantly."

Immediately, my head snaps up and our eyes lock together. Even he has had his feathers ruffled with that comment, and it's taking a considerable amount of effort for him to shove it back down.

Babies...

My baby...

Kiernan's...

Hu'yimona has gone as stiff as a column of marble, his face dropping into a cool facade of composed shock.

Oh shit...

"Out." That single word, spoken in such an authoritative tone as if she will die on the spot if she doesn't high tail her ass out of this room, makes my stomach drop into my feet.

Oh fuck...

I watch as he follows the woman to the door, the sound of the doorknob clicking behind her louder than usual. He turns around in that slow, predatory way I have seen him do countless times when someone has pissed him off, the power behind it almost enough to make me lower my own gaze to the floor. I do not.

My heart sputters in my chest, my mind racing a thousand miles an hour. There is no way I can cover this one up. No way I can deny who the sire is to save myself or the child I now harbor in my womb.

He stalks toward me, his eyes boring into the same spot on my skin that the seamstress had just been pressing her hand into. It feels like daggers, like a warning before a potential end to everything.

When he finally stands mere inches away from me, I can see the muscle in his jaw ticking furiously. When he crouches down in front of me, tilting his head to the side as if he can actually *see* through me, I almost lose it.

My muscles grow taut, as though I'd be able to do anything at all to stop him if he decided to do what I fear he's willing to– Nay, what I *know* he's willing to do if he really wants to. His head tilts back, his eyes meeting mine once more through a curtain of inky-black eyelashes.

"I knew this could be a possibility," he murmurs, his voice calm despite the raging storm I can see behind his eyes. Gods, if he grinds his teeth any harder, he'll begin spitting them out in pieces. "It's only a minor hindrance."

I force my body to relax, a gush of air coming out of my lungs in a tight release. I jerk my chin in a choppy nod. Deep down, I know that isn't how he actually feels. I can see it in his eyes; the anger, the... hurt.

"Does it change anything?" I ask him, knowing that the most it may accomplish is postponing his plan for my ascension to a living god.

He shakes his head, his hands coming out to wrap around my waist as he rises to his full height once more. Okay, not what I expected.

"No, it doesn't. You will still become my wife. The rest will just have to wait," he mutters, pulling one hand away to rake it through his hair. "However, I can't say that I'm not dismissive of the idea of hunting him down and slitting his throat."

Now, that is exactly what I expected.

My eyes widen, and I open my mouth to protest.

Please don't be a liar, please don't be a liar.

"But I made a promise, and I will hold to it... so long as he remains on *his* side of the world."

"Thank you," I say quietly, trying to do my best not to allow all that pent-up emotion from the last few weeks to flood over. I look passed him to the mirror, needing a retreat from the conversation before I manage to lose all of my composure. "Do you think the seamstress will be able to alter the dress?"

He doesn't take the bait. I can see it on his face as the lines of his mouth harden for a split second before his features soften.

"Calm yourself, Sitara. I am not going to hurt the baby." He's learned that if he says things out loud, I've become prone to believing him. "While the world certainly does not need more Kiernan fucking Slater in it..." He trails off, looking up at the ceiling to compose himself once more before meeting my gaze again. His palms come up to cup my face, his thumbs running over the curve of my cheekbones. "I could never destroy something that comes from you."

47
Sitara

Time seems to go by so fast here, yet not at all. At this point, I've lost track of the sun's rotation and can only guess how long I have been here in I'cuma. The constant reminder of Kiernan that is now growing inside of me leaves me full and empty all at the same time.

To make matters worse, Hu'yimona has been acting strangely... celebratory about the baby. I'm not sure how I feel about that, if I'm being candid with myself. To continue with the unnerving discomfort, he won't leave my side. He's even gone as far as to sleep in my room at night. It's a bit annoying since he doesn't really need to sleep at all; he simply does it for the novelty of it.

Take now, for example. He's following me at no more than three paces behind as I walk down the dimly lit corridor that leads to the communal chamber where the cultists gather for food and drink. The only thing that keeps me from wanting to high tail my ass back to my room is the fact that Eirian will be waiting for me in our usual spot. I've managed to convince Hu'yimona that I should be able to sit at a different table in the same room without him hovering over me like an overprotective hen.

Walking into the mess hall, my eyes immediately seek out dark skin and honey locks of hair, finding them exactly where they have been every morning since I started coming out here to eat. My shoulders slump in relief as Hu'yimona presses his hand at the small of my back to motion me towards my friend before he walks off to take his place at the massive table at the head of the room, where Morana's wiry mane of knotted locks sits perched in her seat next to his. I already know that she's pissed off at me for taking her place at his right hand, especially since he won't let her sit there even if I don't.

It's easy to tell with the way she glares daggers at me every time I walk into a room.

I sit down next to Eirian once I've weaved my way through the scattered crowd of tables, silvery-blue eyes smiling up at me as I do.

"You look less tired this morning. Did you sleep well?" Eirian hands me a roll off her plate, something she has insisted on doing since the day I got here. "Is that appetite back up and running yet?"

I take the proffered bread and bring it to my lips, nodding slowly as my eyes flick back up toward where I'm being melted in Morana's mind. I don't want to admit the fact that having Hu'yimona in my bed at least keeps me warm and not alone. It's not something I'll ever be willing to admit.

"Yeah, guess that's what happens when you grow another human inside of you. You want to eat *or* you can't eat," I mutter, tearing my eyes away from Morana and her crazed gaze.

Eirian looks down at her plate, the ringlet curls that frame her face bouncing as they shift forward. "I volunteered to help Tamzi with the shaman's room this morning..."

She scoops a bite of hot stew into her mouth, making an "O" with her mouth to cool it. My brow twitches slightly as I try to refrain from making any facial expression that might make Morana suspicious. "And?"

"I found some things..." she trails off, offering me a bit of her stew even though Hu'yimona had already ordered someone to bring me some, the steaming bowl already placed in front of me. I accept it, chewing a particularly large chunk of potato as I lean over the table.

"What is it?" I whisper, then make sure to force a smile and glance back at Hu'yimona. No one will question two girls seemingly ogling over a living god.

She gives me a grin and a giggle, playing into my game. Even someone born and raised in the cult, with a firm belief in what Hu'yimona represents, like her, knows that if we are caught, there is a good chance Morana's wrath won't spare us.

"I'm not sure. It's not a name I am familiar with."

Nor am I.

Eirian leans back into her chair, covering her mouth as though she's trying to stifle a laugh. "But Alatak Hu'yimona signed them. *All* of them."

"*All* of them?" I repeat like a parrot.

Clearly, he *did* in fact know a woman by that name. "You're sure?" I know she is, or she wouldn't have said anything to me, but I can't stop the need to confirm.

I have never heard of a woman in history by that name associated with him. Even in our villages, Hu'yimona is still taught among the children as a lesson in greed and mortality, which I have begun to realize is not the truth about him.

She scrunches her nose as if my words have a pungent smell to them. Honestly, it makes me want to blow into my palm to check with the way her button nose crinkles in distaste. "I would know my alatak's signature anywhere. There is no mistaking it for another."

"Right... Of course," I mutter, my back growing ramrod straight as I feel a hand land on my shoulder.

"Sitara." My mother's voice fills the space between us in a sickeningly sweet coo.

Well shit. I have tried my best to avoid them since I got here. I don't want to talk to them, but it seems like my avoidance can only muster so much distance.

I turn to face them, taking in the deeply etched brands in their foreheads and the glazed, glassy looks in their eyes.

"Maku. Mapa," I barely manage to croak, my fingertips buzzing with energy. At this point, I have lost all feeling toward them, knowing that they haven't changed a bit. The last time I believed they had, I ended up here.

Erian relaxes into her seat, continuing with her meal as though my parents' presence is nothing short of natural. I envy that. The fact that she has grown up around them more than I have would almost make me hate her if she weren't so likable.

"We heard you had finally started making friends here," my father purrs, reaching a hand out to pat the top of my head. I pull away before he can and try to settle myself.

"Yeah. I have."

It isn't long before I can see Morana leaning over to whisper to Hu'yimona from my peripheral vision. I always have one eye on her at all times. She points in my direction, and a flash of concern floods his face. He is immediately on his feet, making his way to where Eirian and I sit with Morana hot on his heels.

I've never been so relieved to see the guy in my life.

"I think it's time for you to rest a while, wouldn't you agree?" He holds out his hand for me, and I take it before I can stop myself, chastising myself for how eager I seem.

He gently lifts me from my seat, and I notice Morana's face, my parents mimicking it to the letter. Each one's brow lowers in disdain, their lips pressed into a thin line as they watch the scene unfold. They fold their arms over their chests, and I swear they all clicked their tongues at the same time.

Well, that's weird...

Could they be more loyal to the shaman than they are to him? Honestly, it would make sense. *He* isn't nearly as devious as everyone believes him to be, and *they* are as disgusting as Morana is. It's an unsettling thought, but it has a very high probability.

In reality, all I want to do is curl up into my bed and pretend nothing is amiss. Unfortunately, the thoughts won't shut off, and I spend the entirety of our little '*nap*' staring up at the ceiling while Hu'yimona lies next to me like a content panther.

I sit up in the bed a while later, having been unable to take that nap I had been allotted. Hu'yimona's eyes immediately snap open, and he sits up as well, his hand finding the small of my back as it always does. The man acts like I'm already eight months pregnant.

I have to refrain from rolling my eyes as I move to the mirror to make myself presentable for the class that I am about to teach. To be honest, I'm surprised he wanted me to teach the children English, given his complete disdain for the Mundanes. Though I suppose it isn't the only Mundane thing he has adopted into this little village of his.

"I've been thinking," Hu'yimona begins to speak, following me at an annoyingly close pace despite the fact that I am still in the same room, "I think it would be best if you didn't stress yourself out over teaching the children."

"Is that you talking, or Morana?" I glance at him through the mirror. I haven't exactly been silent with my dislike for her and, frankly, neither has she for me.

"Both," he murmurs, his eyes hardening ever so slightly before they soften again in questioning curiosity, "Tell me, Flower, why is it that you seem to hold my shaman with such disdain?"

I look up at the ceiling and draw in a breath before turning my attention back to him. "She seems to hold a lot of sway."

I pull my hair over one shoulder to work out the knots with my fingers, knowing a brush will do nothing but make it worse. I do my best to word what I'm trying to say without blatantly screaming '*she is manipulating your every move*', which is exactly what I want to say to him. Every time I see her next to him, she is either whispering in his ear or giving me a look of complete disgust. Honestly, I'm simply waiting for the day she finally gets her way and I am dead.

He comes up behind me, placing his hands on both of my shoulders to bend down and rest his chin there, gazing at me through our reflections. "As all shamans do. However, even if you don't realize it, you hold *more* sway."

I highly doubt that.

Not with how deep her claws seem to be in his back without him even knowing it.

I turn around, a tight smile forming on my lips. I take my palm to his chest, double-tapping him twice with as much playfulness as I can muster. "Good. Then, you'll let me go teach."

He stares at me as I make my way toward the door and, just as expected, he follows. I'm pleased to say, however, he doesn't stop me.

The halls are all the same. The same rock, the same winding paths, the same sconces bolted into the sides of the tunnels. Seriously, how do any of them *enjoy* being in this dark, damp fortress underground? I'm practically going stir crazy.

We pass Morana in the hallway on our route to the classroom, the look that is hurled in my direction giving me some strangely deep-seated satisfaction. I give her a smug smile as Hu'yimona takes my hand

and hooks it into the crook of his arm, making a point to move in closer to his side as he leads me into the doorway.

I win.

I hope the slight quirk of my brow relays everything I mean it to. Based on the metaphorical steam rolling off her body, I would say I have, indeed, made my point.

Hu'yimona raises a brow and looks down at me, amusement swimming around in those dark pools. He noticed it too. Good, maybe she'll mess up in front of him and suddenly... She won't be my problem anymore.

I revel in the fact that Morana has been seething through my entire lecture, glancing back and forth between Hu'yimona and me periodically. The satisfied smile on his face as he watches me with the children only seems to fuel her rage. I even make a great effort to smile back at him warmly every chance I get, pretending to be acutely aware of his attention.

Oh, she *really* doesn't like that.

When the children have all been cleared out, I make my way toward them and purposefully tuck myself under his offered arm. I know it's a shitty thing to do; that I'm no better than she is when it comes to manipulating his emotions. But at least *I'm* not using that manipulation to make things worse. *I* am trying to save lives and, perhaps, save myself from—what looks like it will be—a lifetime of misery.

Just as we are about to exit, another glassy-eyed cultist member flings open the door and begins to explain his haste.

"Ko'alatak," the man pants heavily as though he had been sprinting the entire way here, "We have a situation in the southernmost part of the village. Kiska and Min'okia have turned what was a simple disagreement into a full-on brawl."

"That sounds like something that you may need to handle personally, Alatak Hu'yimona," Morana states, her voice clearly a mock of genuine concern.

He pauses, looking down at me before taking his gaze back to the shaman. "I'll handle it as soon as I get my bride safely back to-"

"I can go with you," I interrupt, plastering a smile on my face. I swear he actually considers it before that bitch shakes her head.

"I don't believe his alatak'fa would ever so much as consider putting you in a situation that could be harmful to your child. Environments like the one he will be taking care of are stressful and potentially violent. This could lead to harm to you or your precious heir."

I don't miss the flash of malicious triumph in her eyes as Hu'yimona turns to give me a soft smile, his hand coming up to cup my cheek tenderly.

"She's right, my flower."

Damn it.

Well, that's put a damper on my plans. I had intended to use the opportunity to get a better look at those members, to see if they also had glass eyes in their skulls. Looks like that isn't going to happen now.

I would almost try to argue, but Hu'yimona hasn't seemed to budge much since finding out about the baby. Honestly, how quickly he's jumped into taking *his* place is unsettling.

"You should go on ahead," Morana's shrill voice cuts the air like a knife. I wonder if I can use it to stab her. "I'll ensure that Sitara gets back to her room safely."

Bad.

Worse than bad.

It's a nightmare.

The last thing I want is to be left alone with her. *Sure, let's just hand me over to her like an unsuspecting sacrifice. I bet she eats babies.*

I look at Hu'yimona with slightly widened eyes, trying to convey my extreme discomfort with this solution. He strokes my hair and pulls me in, pressing his lips to my forehead.

"You'll be in good hands, flower," he murmurs confidently.

Like hell I will be! Can we go back to the part where I think she eats babies as appetizers?

He gently turns me to face Morana, who is smiling at me... *fake bitch.*

Does she really think that the strained tug of her lips actually looks disarming? All it's managed to do is make the hairs at the back of my neck stand up.

"The best," she purrs in my direction, motioning for me to walk out of the classroom ahead of her.

"By all means, lead the way," I offer. There is no way in hell I'm having that woman at my back.

She chuckles under her breath and steps out of the room ahead of me. I attempt to leave a bit of space between us as we walk down the corridor, but she keeps slowing her stride to '*let me catch up*'.

We walk all the way to my room in tense silence, the discomfort palpable on my end. My eyes never leave the jagged planes of her back, acutely aware of her every move. I'm not above giving her frostbite with my palms and making her nose fall off.

Once we have finally reached my door, I open it a little too eagerly and spin around to give her a tense smile as I slowly creak it closed. "Well, thanks again. All safe now. Have a *great* rest of your day."

Just as I am about to finally latch the door and find that reprieve I'm so desperately aching for, her hand snaps out with surprising strength and stops me, her palm making a low thud on the wood.

"You know, it amazes me. Out of all the women he could have had, he chose the bottom of the barrel. A simple sheep that was meant for slaughter. It's astounding."

My muscles tense, a natural reflex to her referring to me as nothing more than an animal. My jaw clenches, and I swear I'm going to chip a tooth.

"It really is," I agree, pushing harder against my side of the door.

How is this spindly witch so strong?! It can't be natural.

"He has a plethora of women right here under his nose that would be much more suited to his cause than the likes of you," she grits out, "Like your friend Eirian, for example."

Or you? That's what I'm actually gathering from this little encounter.

"Yeah, well, his taste is apparently a little more refined than that," I quip, chastising myself for my words and their underhanded backlash to my friend.

Morana moves the door with such ease that you would think I wasn't pushing against it at all. The rage in this woman's eyes is intimidating, but I'll be damned if I let her see that. "You're getting under my skin. Stepping on my toes," she growls, and I feel that spark of defiance roll through my stomach, the same one I get every time I'm feeling threatened like a caged animal.

"Well, I'm sure your toes will heal. I suggest, however, learning to cope with a few sore appendages. After all, I'm about to be his *wife.*"

First of all, why I thought antagonizing this psycho was a good idea, I'll never know. Secondly, why that word seemed to roll off my tongue without me flinching... We'll come back around to that at a later date.

My heart races as Morana backs me up against the wall, her palms resting against the cold, hard surface on either side of my head. "I've had about all I'm willing to take from you. I'd keep your nose to your own business; *wedding* planning and *baby* names. The latter seems to be where you should be focusing. After all, you can't exactly name it

'Kiernan Junior', now can you? Plus, women lose babies every day, and gods make new ones just as fast."

My stomach sinks to my toes. Did she just *threaten* my baby? My cheeks burn with a fury I've never known, my palms itching to reach out and smack the *fuck* out of her. She's pushing every single button that I have, and she knows it.

I grit my teeth, forcing a sneer to my upper lip. "Who says I can't have both?"

Of course, I'm just digging myself a hole. I *know* I'm digging said hole. And of course, for some reason, I can't help but stir that pot.

You know... classic Sitara style.

She brings her face mere inches from mine, my senses assaulted by an oddly pleasant smell of mint. Strange... she *looks* like she'd smell like cattle shit.

"Stay out of my way, or you won't have Kiernan's baby to worry about anymore." Her hand comes up to wrap around my throat, her nail lightly grazing along my jugular. "Nor will you have to worry about *replacing* it."

48

Kiernan

Finally.

As the shore of Puka'qui comes into view, my fucking stomach lodges in my throat. I thought once we returned, some of the tension would leave my body, but I was so, so wrong. Nothing will sate my aching muscles. Nothing except having her in my arms again.

The sun beats down on the upper deck of the ship, and each man who had decided to come with me stands in silence. We have ignored the heat. Ignored the need to sleep, to stop for more supplies. We've made due with what we have, which is next to none now. Not a single one of them has complained, and I appreciate that fact.

I probably would have thrown them overboard if they had. My patience—what little I had to begin with—is completely nonexistent now.

My head swims with the never-ending possibilities that have plagued me night and day since that day eight weeks ago. Two entire months... Is there even any Sitara left waiting for me?

As our ship comes into port, guided in by Benedict due to my inability to focus, I shake that thought away. I can't think like that. I have to believe that she is strong enough to endure. She *is* strong enough to endure. She isn't a damsel to be saved, though I'll be fucking dead if I don't go do something to help her.

To my surprise, the first sight I'm met with is that of the old man, Djar, standing on the dock with a look I've not seen on his face before. Pure, unadulterated determination.

He doesn't give me time to speak before he comes toe to toe with Benedict, slapping something into his palm with a force I didn't expect from such a frail-looking mummy like him. Benedict looks almost like he's about to say something, the look of confusion on his face almost comical.

When Djar pulls away, I realize what he had placed in Benedict's hand. The Ma'tawi tribe's relic stone.

Djar's eyes slide over to me, our gazes locking onto one another with equal intensity. "Bring my daughter back home," is all the old man says.

I nod, his words only fueling my conviction. "Can I take them all to the temple with a single relic?"

I motion back toward my men, who have all huddled into a group at my back. I can feel their tension, the wariness that permeates the air around us. But I can also feel their determination, especially from the men who had been sailing all this time with Sitara aboard the ship. She's become precious. To all of us.

Djar points to the treeline where two figures stand just barely into view. It's the other two shamans from the other two villages, their own relics clasped in their palms, awaiting the exchange.

"Be off with you, Kiernan. You're running out of time." Djar all but shouts at me, no patience left in his aged eyes.

I don't give myself time to question how the old bastard knew we would be sailing in today. I don't even give myself time to question how he managed to gain the help of the other villages. I have no doubt each one of them is concerned about letting this many Mundanes into their borders. I just allow myself to be grateful for the damn assistance.

I'm out of breath by the time we near the temple steps. So are my men, who have been jumping and startling at every little thing. I can't blame them. I wasn't exactly the picture of composure my first time in the jungle, either.

Even Ben had cursed a couple of times, swearing up and down that the tree roots were trying to kill him. See, I'm not the only fucking one who believes this damn forest is alive in ways most are not. It's like it has a consciousness all its own.

I can see the deities standing away from their usual places, watching the hoard I've brought as we barrel in their direction. The three stand on the outer part of the inner circle of the temple, each one with unreadable expressions on their faces, save for Teo'Kan, who has his usual sneer of disdain.

There is no hesitation as I fall to my knees at the bottom of the stairs before them, my men shifting in unison at the display. I don't kneel, and they know it. But for Sitara, I'd eat the dirt on my way down.

"I've brought my men here to help me find Sitara," I begin, my voice tight as I try to remain as polite as I can despite my haste to get going, "I would like your blessing for each of them so that they can travel through the jungle peacefully."

My eyes lift to meet the first one I can find, which is Coli'hanu's. Her expression has fallen into one of... gratitude? "Though I should probably warn you that I'm not asking for your permission. Not really. I'm simply honoring my woman by going about this the right way first. I know how much your blessing means to *her*. That is the only reason I even stopped here before reigning down the shit-storm that I'm about to release."

With a flick of her wrist, Gula'ci sends the others behind me to their knees in the same manner she had me on my first visit here. I can still practically taste the dirt and stone in my mouth.

"Holy shit..." Benedict grunts, his voice muffled by the ground that is no doubt between his teeth.

"I see you're not the only Mundane who lacks etiquette," the Goddess of Earth grumbles, too playfully for my taste. This is a serious fucking matter.

"Do they have your blessing or not? I'm running out of patience and precious time," I grit out through clenched teeth before turning my eyes back to Coli'hanu, "Or better yet, come with us and deal with this problem child like you've done in the past."

Something like irritation flares behind the goddess's eyes, piquing my interest for another day. She steps forward until she is mere feet away, the closest I have ever been to one of them. The power that radiates from her, even in a relaxed state, is immeasurable.

"We cannot. It will not do justice to what needs to be done. All is as it should be to renew the balance the world so desperately yearns for," she states simply, holding out her hands and crooking her fingers. "Items."

Her last words come out in a biting manner, as though I have struck a chord somewhere along the line. Benedict is the first to place something in her hand, careful not to let their skin touch. Then Arthur follows suit.

One by one, the men place small possessions into her hands to create the necessary items that will allow them to walk through the jungle unscathed.

Once each one has been placed in her delicate little hands, Coli'hanu takes them over to Gula'ci to begin the process. When she turns back to me, her expression is almost sad, regretful.

"My brother was not always like this, you know," she says, her eyes meeting mine. So that's what had gotten to her... Hu'yimona is her brother, and I had just called him a *'problem child'* like he's a pest needing termination.

Not that I'm wrong though.

We watch in rapt attention as they go through creating each of the items anew, just as they had for me all those weeks ago. Benedict leans in close to my shoulder, a wry grin tugging at the corner of his mouth.

"Thank gods I didn't hand them my wedding ring," he chuckles, bringing his hand down on my opposite shoulder, "Enna would have had my ass if I'd come home with something different."

"Had your ass?" I look at him with as much playful exasperation as I have been able to muster lately, "You'd be dead, mate."

"Aye, but it certainly would be one hell of a death, dying at the hands of a little minx like her."

"There's still time," I taunt, turning my face back toward the progression of blessings taking place on the dias tiers.

Meanwhile, Larkin is standing off to the side like a vigilant guard, keeping his eyes cast up toward the gods. It's clear he doesn't have as close a relationship with them as his sister, seeing as they didn't even address him when we all walked in. If it had been Sitara, Coli'hanu would have practically thrown herself at her...

Still, the respect is there, though I'd wager it is of a more common form than that of my emerald-wielding partner.

My anticipation grows with each step, each item. Gula'ci with her reconstruction. Coli'hanu with her kindling. Teo'Kan with his rendering. I'm struggling to sit still, my fingers twisting the beads of my own bracelet. I want this done. I want to leave.

I want Sitara back.

As they finally finish the last of the items–some formed into necklaces, some into rings, others into bracelets–I take a step forward to retrieve them. My body is practically vibrating with need, with the longing to get the fuck out of here and go do what needs to be done.

Coli'hanu holds up her hand, pinning me with a stare that could melt precious metal. "You must stay for a night."

"Excuse me?" My nostrils flare, my body growing taut with tension at the mere mention of delaying any further.

"You heard her," Gula'ci's voice slices through the air like a dagger.

"Are you serious?!" I take a step forward, preparing to attempt to rip the fucking jewelry from the Goddess of Cold Fire's hands. Benedict's fingers wrap around my arm, and I send a shattering glare over my shoulder. He simply shakes his head.

"You will be of no use to anyone in your current state," Teo'Kan folds his arms over his chest and leers down at us with that infuriatingly sneering lip, "Or do you wish to not only kill your entire crew but also leave Sitalli'ara alone with the very beast you're trying to rip her from?"

Well shit... I can't exactly argue with that.

My men are exhausted and, frankly, so am I. It doesn't mean that I'm happy about it though.

The sun set hours ago, and I swear if I hear one more snore that isn't my own, I'll lose my goddamn mind. The temple is quiet at this hour, though the loudest silence in the room is the two deities that remain up on the dias, their stone-like vigils staring blankly into the void of the trees outside. That must be a miserable existence—living for so long that you have no desire to do anything but stare off into space while you swim through the abyss of your own mind. I'd find a way to fucking kill myself.

I sit up, rubbing my eyes before making my way to the outer ring of the temple. If I can't sleep, there is no point in my lying here under Teo'Kan's brief but frequent scrutiny.

When I reach the steps outside, I see Coli'hanu sitting against one of the pillars, as motionless as her counterparts inside. The flicker of consistent green flame that dances along her skin illuminates the night, encasing her in a small bubble of luminescence that bounces off the stone.

I sigh, rolling my eyes as I scratch under my chin in annoyance. I came out here to be alone for the love of her infuriating existence.

She's going to think I've gone rogue...

"Don't ever presume to know what I am going to think," she says, not even giving me the courtesy of turning around to address me.

She points to the spot beside her, the movement as smooth as silk. "Sit."

I let out a quick, sharp grumble, but do as I'm told. I lower myself down on the step beside her, feeling the cold that radiates off her skin. It's like sitting next to an ice sculpture.

We sit in a surprisingly comfortable silence for what feels like forever before I look down at my hands, wringing my fingers until the skin is angry and red.

"So, you really won't help?" I hate how desperate my voice sounds, the way it cracks against the emotions I've been hiding behind anger and irritation for the last two months.

Coli'hanu's pale lips part, then close once more as if she—a literal goddess—is trying to figure out how to put her thoughts into words. Her face tilts toward me, and I swear I can see regret flash through her features.

"No," she says simply, sighing as she turns her face back towards the outside world, "Sitara is exactly where fate needs her to be. And you are on the path to exactly where you need to go. There is no need for us this time."

I can't help but feel the harsh sting of anger well up in my chest, my hands clenching into fists in my lap. "But you already know what needs to be done." I don't try to hide the accusatory tone in my voice.

The goddess doesn't even react, doesn't give me so much as a glance or a flinch. And that pisses me off. Sitara is supposed to be some *prized* child to this woman, and she won't lift a finger to help her.

"When a child is born into one of the three tribes," her voice comes out in a soft murmur, "the parents bring that child to the temple, to be presented to their respective god. To show us the magnificence of growth within the tribe we preside over."

I have no idea what she's getting at, but I don't dare say a word. She continues after a short pause, finally removing herself from the pillar to a more natural-looking position–with her elbows propped on her knees.

"I have been presented with hundreds of children over my thousands of years of existence. And I can't seem to remember a single one, despite how hard I try." A small, self-deprecating smile tugs at the corner of her icy lips. "But I remember being presented with Sitara like it was yesterday. She was so small, hardly more than the size of her father's hand, yet the fire in her veins spoke to me even then."

She turns to face me, her jaw locking into one of pure defiance. "You may judge me now, but I have seen the path that girl shall walk since the day of her birth. I *do* know what needs to be done. And it is *being* done."

I feel my jaw working under my skin, the words I want to spout burning in my throat. I swallow them down and shake my head. Who am I to think I have any room to argue with a goddess? Regardless of how fucking insane I think this entire situation is.

This silence is less comfortable, the tension radiating between us palpable as I continue to swallow my own tongue. *For Sitara's benefit,*

I tell myself. When Coli'hanu finally breaks that silence, her voice is calm once more.

"People are wrong about him, you know," she mutters, a hint of old grief forming the words on her tongue, "My brother. People see him as a monster, uncaring and unfeeling. But it's quite the opposite. Hu'yimona is a product of caring *too* much. He was the most kind. The most gentle of us all. When he raised his hand, it was in the protection of those he loved the most. And he did it with a fierceness that could make the Earth itself quake."

I let her words sink in, unable to make the connection between who *she* says he is versus the man I have come to know through his actions towards Sitara.

"If that's so, then what changed him?" I look over at her, my eyes boring into the side of her face as she stares out into the night, "What happened that could make *him* a woman-napping, world-crumbling piece of work, but didn't make the *rest* of you that way?"

She surprises me by letting out a grating, stiff chuckle. "The rest of us care the *proper* amount," she says simply, then the subtle humor drops from her face like a stone tossed in a stream, "Many things happened in our time together. I suppose I could start with the fact that I had placed far too much on my little brother's shoulders when they brought us here to the temple. It wasn't fair to him. I should have been the one comforting him, but all I did was force him to make promises he couldn't possibly manage to keep."

"Not to mention, the death of Calandra," another voice resonates behind us, and I turn to see Gula'ci standing between two pillars, her face as hardened as ever, "She was our caretaker during our time growing up here."

"Calandra's death was the last straw for him, I think. They were very close, you see," Coli'hanu explains.

"Isn't he supposed to be '*the god of death*'?" I give them both a look of confusion, as though I can't even fathom what they are saying.

Why would death bother its god?

I watch as Gula'ci rolls her eyes at me, looking like she might actually slap me in the back of the head. The woman is irritatingly easy to annoy. I can't say anything right to please that woman. Ever.

"And you're a pirate. You plunder for a living, and yet, when your things are removed from your possession, you don't take kindly to it. Shouldn't a thief be used to theft?"

I swear she gets *pleasure* from watching me make an ass of myself.

"One of the things that makes us *living* gods is that we were all once human," Coli'hanu chimes in, "We still have human emotion, though sometimes buried under millennia of life. We can still feel the depths of what it meant to be mortal. Hu'yimona is no exception to that rule."

"You think so, do you, Coli'hanu?" A deep timbre cuts through the air, making me roll my eyes.

Teo'Kan.

"As I remember it, your brother has never really been normal. Even in mortality." His voice is tinged with a hint of bitter amusement.

"You are one to talk, Teo'Kan," Gula'ci snaps, venom dripping from her tongue like acid. "You were not exactly on the right path once yourself."

"And you think differently?" I cock a brow at Teo'Kan, inviting him to tell me more. I swear I can almost *feel* Gula'ci smacking me in the back of the head with her eyes. Unfortunately for her, it does nothing to deter me.

Teo'Kan rolls his eyes, huffing loudly as his tongue works in his mouth. I bet he's trying to decide how to word our mutual disdain for the god of death without incurring the wrath of his older sister.

"The man is completely unhinged. No one could possibly be granted the gift over *death* and war, let alone fall as far from grace as he has, and *not* already have a predisposition for the darkness," he flashes a glare down at Coli'hanu, who has stood from her place next to me with rigid movements.

"You know very well that Death is not an inherently evil concept, Teo'Kan. Your personal emotions cloud your judgment," she barks.

"Says who? Calandra?"

"Say the *universe*," Gula'ci snaps.

I feel like I'm watching a bear fight. I've never seen the three of them so... human.

Although this is one of the more interesting things I have seen in quite some time, I quickly stand up as the sky turns from onyx to deep navy. "Is there a reason you're telling me all of this? Or am I free to go back to moping through the remainder of my '*rest*' in peace?"

The three of them turn to face me, momentarily pulled from their own tense disagreement. Coli'hanu steps back away from Teo'Kan, flicking fire into his face as I have seen Sitara do many times.

So... that's where she gets that from.

"We are telling you this because you will be met with an unsettling amount of understanding for him where Sitara is concerned. Don't let it cloud your emotions," she says simply, then looks at the other two.

They both wander back into the temple, leaving us alone once more.

"And, a small part of me hopes that our story has given you some insight as well. I have no right to ask this. And he certainly doesn't deserve it, but... I'm hoping that when you step foot in front of my brother, you will fight him in the same way that he will fight you. Due to caring *too* much and not out of hatred for what he has become."

49

Sitara

I stare at myself in the mirror, continuously swallowing the lump that wants to keep lodging itself in my throat. Aren't weddings supposed to be happy occasions?

The sheer crimson of my gown cascades down my body in an intricate crossing of fabric, the skirt portion flaring out just before the small bulge that has formed at the base of my torso. My hand idly sweeps in slow circles over the space where my child is now growing and thriving as Eirian takes my hair and coils it away from my face.

"I wish you saw this as an honor," she murmurs softly behind me, "It would make me feel less guilty for being happy for you."

My eyes meet hers through our reflection, a gentle, wary smile forming on my lips. "I suppose it isn't all bad," *lies,* "I could be on my way toward another sacrifice."

That's all I have. The sliver of silver lining that keeps me grounded right now.

No, Hu'yimona isn't as bad as I believed him to be, but he's not *great.* And no, perhaps he wouldn't really make all that bad of a husband, but he's not the one I *want.*

Eirian continues pinning the mass of red curls, clearly not knowing what to say in response to that remark. I even feel a small amount of guilt for even bringing it up. I know it makes her uncomfortable knowing what some of the elder members had done in the past.

I stare as each strand is pulled away from my face one by one. Kiernan would have wanted it down, free and wild. He always told me it would be his undoing one day...

Damnit.

I blink frantically to keep the tears from spilling over my cheeks, convincing myself—in vain—that everyone cries at weddings.

I hadn't realized just how much I had been hoping that he would still come to save me. Or at least try. It is a silly notion, I know—to think that a Mundane man could harbor enough love for someone to walk into the den of his own death. Honestly, it probably makes me selfish for wishing he would.

But *no one* has come to look for me.

Not a single person.

Not Larkin.

Not Djar.

No one.

Just as she slides the last pin in and gives my shoulders a gentle squeeze, the door to my chambers is thrown open. There stands a slightly less disheveled Morana, staring in at us like a viper trying to decide which of us she should bite first.

Eirian and I never could figure out the significance of those letters that were found in her room. Frankly, I was too afraid to ask Hu'yimona if they were something of importance. *I* might have some level of immunity to Morana's murderous rage, but Eirian does *not*.

"Do you want me to go?" Eirian whispers, her silver-blue eyes snapping to the side to look at me. I immediately take hold of her hand, silently begging her to stay.

There is nowhere else I would rather she be right now. Alone with *her* is not how I want to start this day.

Morana comes further into the room, her movements predatory, like the snake she is. She eyes me, taking in my appearance with a critical eye. I've had about all I can take from this fucking woman. My composure is so close to snapping like a twig that all it will take is just a little bit of pressure.

"Well, don't you look..." the dumb bitch can't even compliment me without looking like she's in pain, "...different."

Better than you.

"Thanks, I guess?" I narrow my eyes at her, following her movements as she moves Eirian from my side to turn me toward the mirror. She rests her chin on my shoulder, her eyes flashing with threat.

"I do hope you remember the warning I gave you, hmm?"

There it is! The fucking pressure.

Something inside me snaps, and I whirl around so fast that, if I weren't being fueled by an absolute inferno of rage, I would probably be dizzy. My fingers wrap around her throat, where I squeeze hard enough to know I won't lose hold of her.

"You would do well to remember, *Shaman* Morana, that I am less than an hour away from being the wife of your *precious* Lord," I lean in, my hot breath fanning across her face, "And I swear to you that when I am... If you so much as *breathe* wrong in my general direction, I'll make sure that death finds you slowly."

Her eyes flash with crazed, barely contained violence, her words vibrating against my palm. "Is that a *treat*, Sitara?"

"No," I murmur, bringing our faces close enough that our noses touch, emerald flame licking along my fingers and onto her skin, "It's a fucking promise. So you should learn to *play nice*, otherwise, in less than a year, the first thing I do when I am a god is smite you where you stand."

I release her with a harsh flick of my wrist and turn back to Eirian before Morana has even a fraction of a second to respond.

"I'm finished in here. Thank you."

The communal chamber looks different than it normally does. At the far end of the room, where the head table normally sits, is a ceremonial arch that has been draped in crimson and onyx silks. It's lined with fern leaves and exotic flowers dipped in matching dyes, setting off a stark contrast against the gray stone that permeates every inch of this place. In the center sit our bowls of ink and feathered needles.

He must have gone out and gotten them last night. That's why he hadn't been sleeping in the bed with me.

Hu'yimona sits in the pooling fabric that is strewn along the base of the archway, like a victor sitting in his enemy's blood. He's in more colorful clothing today, the fabric around his legs still the same inky black, but the additional sash that wraps around his waist and chest is made of the same material as my dress. Banded silver ringlets sit on his upper arms and ankles. The same as what wraps around my own flesh.

The worst part is knowing that if I were just as unhinged or this were another life, he'd probably take my breath away...

My movements are jerky and uncomfortable, and I pull on the fabric slightly to hide it behind a malfunction in the cloth. I'm sure the woman who made it *really* loves seeing that.

I can see his eyes light up when he sees me, and it is almost endearing–the way he looks at me. Though he isn't the only one who has, and unfortunately for him, it doesn't have the same effect.

My eyes skim the room again, as if it's my last effort to find *him* among the crowd. But he isn't there.

I knew he wouldn't be.

Eirian stays back with the rest of those in attendance–the entirety of the Miqui'oh people assembled to watch me give my life away. I take my place across from him, looking up into his face as if he might actually see the uncertainty on my own.

He doesn't.

However, the longer I sit and stare at him, the longer I give myself time to accept the decisions *I* have made that lead me to this point. I begin to think maybe it won't be so bad. He has proven he can be kind. He has proven he doesn't lie. And he's never once gone back on his word to pull his people back into I'cuma and keep them from harming anyone outside these tunnels.

And with the idea of impending immortality only a few months away, I would be able to make him keep his word for the rest of eternity.

Perhaps my life is a small price to pay for all the good it could do.

Maybe, over time, he and I can become friends.

Maybe after a millennium or two of companionship, I could learn to even love him.

He extends his arm to me, nodding toward the feather needles and ink, anticipation shining through those dark orbs. "Shall we begin, my flower?"

I swallow that persistent lump in my throat and nod, taking the supplies into my hand. I pull his skin taut, beginning my work on the marital markings on his tattoo, starting at the base of his palm and working my way up his wrist.

I haven't been this shaky doing a tattoo since I was eight years old, when I gave my brother his Pe'aboros in the stead of my mother. I have to force myself to breathe, to keep my fingers steady as I etch the ruby ink into his skin.

When I am finished, the crimson color stands out vibrantly against the dark swirls of his other tattoos and the pale expanse of his skin. He admires it with a soft smile—one that makes my traitorous heart skip a beat just because of how happy his sad, sad man seems to be right now.

Then, it's my turn.

I watch him dip the needle into the ink and hold out his free hand for my arm. I steel myself against the vow I am about to make and place my wrist in his palm.

Just as Hu'yimona is about to slide the needle into my skin, every head in the room snaps toward the large double doors that lead out into one of the main corridors. My brows furrow deeply, my first thought being that Morana has begun to throw an absolute temper tantrum.

But that can't be right... She's standing right there, in the front row.

As the first resounding bang jostles the entrance, I rise to my feet slowly. Hu'yimona is immediately at my side, his arm protectively banded around my waist.

One... Two... Two bangs before everything goes eerily silent.

A draft, perhaps?

No sooner than I let out a breath, the doors splinter open, barely still on their hinges. My breathing quickens as a large majority of the room stumbles back onto one another with loud gasps and shouts.

I attempt to peer over their heads, trying to gain a decent look at the *massive* figure that now takes up the majority of the doorway. Seriously, this guy is gigantic.

As he takes a step into the chamber, I notice many things about his appearance that I don't recognize, yet seem so familiar to me. His auburn hair is a mess, unkept and overgrown into a jawline of disheveled facial hair. The butterscotch of his skin is smooth, save for the scars that faintly mar his skin under the shirt that has split at the seams and the dark smudges of purple under his eyes.

Underneath it all, I know that face–so familiar but so different. This is a Han'alli man, his dark black eyes rimmed with gold. It's the distinctive mark of one who possesses the power of Behemoth Physiology, a power marked by the use of earth energy to increase one's size and strength and decrease their vulnerability to physical attacks.

Behind him, I catch a glimpse of familiar figures I know very, *very* well. A mass of red hair peeks out from behind the colossal form, offering me a smile.

"Hangin' in there alright, Starlight?"

A choked, strangled sob rolls up my throat.

He came for me.

They all did.

50

Kiernan

My chest heaves with exertion and a surge of energy I've never felt before in my life. I scan the crowd, my eyes immediately landing on a soft visage draped in red.

Sitara.

I scan her for injury, for distress, but all I see is her, standing there with an expression of complete consolation. The air leaves my lungs, relief washing over me like a balm to a burn that I have so desperately needed these last two months. She's alive. She's alive and whole and perfect.

And tucked into the arm of that son of a bitch.

The room feels like it's closing in on me, shrinking as I make my way toward what is *mine.* The crowd parts like the Red Sea, only one man is brave enough to step into my path as if he will keep me away from them. Away from her.

He is sorely mistaken.

I don't take the time to really look at him, only registering the faintest hint of regret flashing through his eyes just before I hear the satisfying crack, feel the enjoyable snap of his neck breaking like a toothpick between my fingers.

That single act of violence erupts the room into chaos.

I can hear my men handling the mayhem that has erupted in my wake. The sounds of shouting and the blasts of magic are almost deafening in the once silent space.

"Sitara…" I damn near choke on her name as I make my way toward her. The tears that have welled up in her eyes are visible to me even from here. She's trembling, but I know her well enough to understand it isn't from fear. She's relieved. And I'm joyous to be able to say I lifted that burden off her shoulders.

The man who stands next to her moves as if to protect her, sliding his body in front of hers and passing her off to a dark skinned young woman with golden locks.

"She doesn't need protection from me," I growl and lengthen my stride.

Before I can reach them, he turns his face to my beloved, his expression as cold as the ice I'm going to shove up his ass. "I'm sorry, Flower, but our deal is null and void."

What the fuck *did he just call her?*

I watch as her eyes grow wide, panic etched into the fine lines of her features. "No, you can't do that!"

Her scream makes my blood boil, and his pet name sends me over some strange edge. I see red, my body hauling toward him with an impressive amount of speed thanks to the behemoth power behind my leg muscles.

Hu'yimona simply stares up at me coldly, a frigid fury ignited in his eyes. "I kept my word, Flower. I told you I wouldn't harm a hair on his head, so long as he stayed away."

Then his fist is in my gut, knocking the wind from my lungs. Well shit, for a little guy, the motherfucker is strong. I grunt, my heels skidding a few inches into the stone at my feet.

I regain my footing, but he is fast. Damn strong and fast. I'm going to need to figure my shit out right now if I want any hope of getting Sitara out of here.

I attempt to sweep his legs out from under him, but he sees it coming and dodges with such ease that a smarter man would have been discouraged. Good thing I'm stupid.

Before I have the chance to reposition myself, his elbow makes contact with my cheek. The bastard barely missed my nose, the flesh over my cheekbone splitting under his blow like fabric. My head snaps to the side, and I stumble, shaking off the pain like it's your average Friday night.

I trudge up all the fighting lessons of my early years with Ben, all the experience I have gained over the years. I'm too worked up, frantic to get passed him, and it isn't doing me any favors.

Calm down, Ben's voice blasts through my head with the memory of the countless times he had pissed me off just to show me how to focus. *Those meaty mittens won't land a single blow with you flailing them around like a raging bear.*

I force myself into that unnerving calm that Benedict had pushed until I perfected it. Lifting myself to my feet, I spit the blood that has trickled from my cheek into my mouth onto the floor. I manage to place myself in a better stance, lifting my fists to protect my upper body.

"I'm leaving here one of two ways. *With* Sitara or when she watches you drag my corpse away," I say through heaving breaths, "And I have no plans to die today."

He regards me with the same ice-cold analysis that has been on his face since I walked in, though a small smirk rises into the corners of his mouth. "Unfortunately for you, Kiernan Slater, Death has chosen you anyway."

He comes at me, his fist ready to strike. I managed to block the first blow, though the second lands with a thud against my shoulder.

With a speed that surprises even me, I manage to swing the other arm. I use the momentum of his punch to push my own, landing a blow to the side of his head. Good, I can say I hit him. At least once.

"I've cheated death a number of times. Today shall be no different," I grunt, aching to press my advantage. I know for a fact that it is a bad idea, though.

Off to the side, I hear Sitara screaming something over the roar of chaos around us. Her frantic voice breaks with a shrill screech. "Kiernan! Behind you!!"

I turn, finding myself sandwiched between Hu'yimona and... are those fucking shadows?

Well, I couldn't expect the guy not to use his power. This is a real fucking fight after all.

I reel, trying to decipher the best course of action here. I can't simply assume that the shadows can do anything, and I am barely holding my own against the god himself. I position myself so that my line of vision can easily swivel between him and his created henchmen.

Well, this isn't good. If I go for him, I'll have the shadows' nasty claws in my back before I can even blink.

Then, a flash of green barrels into the black masses, dispelling their forms with a sizzling gargle.

That's my girl.

I shoot her a glance of gratitude, which earns my jaw a good slam by Hu'yimona's...fist? Foot? Fuck, the stars in my vision aren't leaving much room for me to gain my bearings again. The next blow is to my ears, his palms bashing into my ears so hard that my eardrums might be bleeding. I reel, attempting to shake it off, but not before he pins me to the floor.

His breath ghosts over my face as I try to blink away the sudden headache from behind my eyes. His fingers dig into my temples, and I barely register his words before they become crystal clear.

"After I'm finished killing you, I'll be sure to erase any trace of your existence from this world," he snarls, giving me a good look at the rage behind that cool facade. "There will be nothing left of you for your child to learn of. No other sire of consequence but *me.*"

My eyes flare wide, my ears ringing in my skull painfully loud. I swear, as I'm trying to process what this sick fucker has just revealed, I can hear Benedict in the background mutter, "Ah shit..."

"My child?" I croak, my muscles growing taut. My breathing grows heavier, more ragged as it finally sinks in, "*My* child?!"

My vision narrows into one singular point. Nothing else matters until I feel this motherfucker's life in the palm of my hand. Irrational? Yes. He's a god after all. But I don't care. This rage is the only thing that will end this.

Without a second thought, I slam my forehead into his, my muscles hoisting his body from mine to throw him far enough that I can get to my feet. Everything is muted—the fighting, the shouting, the coppery tang of my own blood in my nose, and the acrid scent of it in my nose. One thing, however, is amplified. The sound of Hu'yimona's breath. An issue I plan to rectify momentarily.

I throw myself into him, my rage a driving force. I no longer feel his fists as they rain down on my ribs and face, my own knuckles driving forward to crack against his body with equal intensity.

Now we're fucking talking!

Blow after blow lands between us in a flurry of hands and feet and wild growls. Each dull thud and high-pitched snap resonates between us. There is no longer him and me. There are only the blows that are being exchanged.

We are both bloody and panting now, and I can't help feeling an overwhelming pride for managing to take the fucker down a peg, even if he's beaten my ass in the process.

He pushes back a few paces, planting his feet. It isn't until I hear it that I realize what is happening. My eyes flutter slightly, narrowing in on his wide swirling vortexes of shit water.

Ot t'zopua, Kiernan Slater, a voice, his voice, rings in my ears though his lips never move, *Ot mete no'ol laza ci'ia heuah me'eel ko'.*

Oh, hell no!

Is this motherfucker in my goddamn head right now?

I can feel my muscles and joints attempting to move on their own, to lock into place where I'll become a sitting duck, ripe for him to pluck my ass right out of existence. Just like he promised.

I'm not about to let that happen.

I have no idea what he's said to me, not fluent enough in the language. But it doesn't matter. I don't care what he has to say.

I attempt to push through it, my mind swimming, sharp streaks gliding across my vision. I have no idea what is happening, what I need to do to survive this. To break out of it. My panic mounts, breaths gushing out in strained, tight exhales. I can handle his punches, his kicks, his sheer power of strength. But this... I don't know if I can handle this.

Then, suddenly, my vision clears, and I blink the last of my agony from my eyes. What happened? Did I... No, no, it wasn't me at all.

I peer up to where I know Hu'yimona stands, my view of him obscured by tangles of fiery red hair.

Sitara...

Her hands cup his cheeks, shaking him out of his bloodlust. And... he complies. His eyes flick from me to her, and I have to strain to hear what is being said. I can't see her face, but I can hear the jagged, cutting edge to her breathing, as though she has sprinted with all her might from her place across the room.

"Please," she pants, her voice cracking as she pleads, "Please, don't."

I watch helplessly as Hu'yimona's hands come to rest between her shoulder blades, his head dipping to rest his forehead against hers. I grit my teeth, my palms itching to close the distance and rip his fucking hands off.

No one gets to touch her like that. No one but *me.*

My vision swims as I rise slowly to my feet. If I can just get my hands around his tiny fucking throat...

Sitara's voice breaks through the haze once more, her gentle tone confusing me. But then I remember what Coli'hanu had told me, and I quickly put two and two together.

"If you do this, you will be a monster to *me* too," she says firmly, the gentle glide of her thumb across his cheekbone almost too painful to watch.

To my surprise, the God of Death melts, his shoulders slumping in defeat. Seriously? That's all we had to do? Just let her handle it from the beginning?

It's almost laughable.

That's my girl, wrapping people around her tiny little finger.

51

Sitara

My heart pounds wildly in my chest as I stare up at the God of Death with every last ounce of pleading and begging that I can possibly convey through my eyes alone. That was close. Too close. And I know I wouldn't survive it, losing Kiernan after only just having him back at my side.

Kiernan is strong. But for all his newfound strength to top it off, even he can't withstand Hu'yimona's Spiritual Degradation. He would have turned Kiernan into a killing machine, would have had him kill his men, then leave him to pick up the pieces of his own shattered soul. It's not something I am willing to allow. Knowing that he is out there somewhere, knowing that he still loves me even if I can't have him... It's better than no Kiernan at all.

"I will send them away. I will still marry you and send them all away, but only if you stop this right now," I furrow my brow, part plea, part threat. I'm serious, and I know Hu'yimona can see that.

Kiernan's hoarse voice guts me like a knife as I hear him take a step toward us. "Sitara, no... Please, baby, don't... You can't stay here with him!"

The blade in my stomach twists tighter. It feels like someone has ripped my chest clean open and stolen my still-beating heart. He's only ever called me that one other time... with that same broken plea–the night he begged me to wake up from my nightmare.

My chin quivers involuntarily, and I turn my face so I can see him over my shoulder. I can't look at him directly. I know if I do, I won't be able to go through with it. I'll make the selfish decision and people–*my* people–will die.

"Yes. I can," my voice feels too tight, my clothes feel too tight, my very *skin* feels too tight, "If it means that you and everyone else can walk out of here alive... Yes, I can."

He takes another shaky step toward where Hu'yimona and I are standing, and I can practically feel his hand reaching toward me. I hold my breath, willing him not to touch me. I won't be able to hold my ground. I won't be able to save the people I love most if he touches me right now. I need time. I need time to steel my resolve.

"I said I wasn't leaving here alive unless you were with me." His voice drops into a low timbre that makes my body tense. If he takes one more step, I'm going to break, and then everything I've worked so hard to protect won't matter anymore. "I don't want a life without you in it. I can't go back to that version of myself... I can't."

"Then don't," my voice trembles as my hand lands on the small swell of my abdomen, "Be a version they can be proud of."

I can hear his breath hitch, the low, swallowed sob in his throat. I can't do this. I have to finish it before I can't go through with it.

"Sitara–"

"She's made her choice, Slater," Hu'yimona cuts in, his arm wrapping around my shoulders to pull me into his body as though I need shielding. Honestly, I've never been so grateful. One more second and I would have snapped. One more word from Kiernan's lips and I would have been finished, my determination to do the *right* thing, the safe thing, would have dissolved into dust at my feet.

"Come, Sitara, this drama isn't good for our baby. Let's get you back to your room," Hu'yimona murmurs against the top of my head.

But I need to say goodbye.

I can't leave knowing that I've left Kiernan believing I did this because I wanted to. Even if it's irrational. Even if my actions have spoken the opposite up until now, I need him to hear me *say* it.

"I just want to say goodbye. To my friends. Please." It isn't really a request, and the god knows it. He hesitates, as though I'm not going to fight him if he says no, then nods. His arm slides from my shoulders, and I step away, turning to rush toward the group of my family that has crowded at Kiernan's back.

I spread my arms wide, barreling straight for Kiernan when a high-pitched scream echoes through the chamber. I turn my head, my mother's face twisting into a crazed snarl. The flash of metal glints under the overhead candles, and everything seems to slow into a snail's crawl. Each turn of the dagger slices the air, making a distinct sound as it cuts through. Straight at me.

Well, I'm not really surprised. They *had* tried to kill me once before, after all. I can somewhat see the motion of Kiernan reaching to pull me out of the way. I can slightly register Hu'yimona barreling toward my mother.

Neither of them will make it in time. The dagger is already airborne and hurling its way right at me.

I close my eyes, bracing myself for the pain I know I'm going to inevitably endure. The only thought that crosses my mind is how beautiful I know our child would have looked, had we made it passed this point.

The sound of metal hitting flesh rings in my ears, but the pain never comes.

I open my eyes, my entire body beginning to shake as I catch sight of a tall, pale figure standing a few feet away from me, his arms outstretched, copper locks of long red hair cascading around his shoulders.

Arthur.

"No, no no no no no no!" It's the only thing that will come out of my mouth, the only word I can muster.

I watch him sway on his feet, his goofy grin laced with pain as he turns his face to look back at me.

"You're not the only one... who will be savin' someone today, Starlight."

No, no, this can't be happening! Not him!

I scramble to my hands and knees, my vision blurry as I rush to catch his head before it can crack against the stone below.

My hands fist into his shirt, using all my might to pull him into my lap. "What were you thinking?!"

I sob. I can't stop sobbing. My tears flow unabashed, dripping down onto his face and sliding across his skin. The knife is still lodged in his ribs, no doubt having punctured his lung. I want nothing more than to rip it out and fling it back at her, but I know she's already dead. Hu'yimona would have ended her the moment his hands met her flesh.

All I can do is hold him, cradle his head in my arms.

My fingertips and toes have gone numb, and I can't hear anything else but the garbled, wet breaths that rattle in Arthur's chest.

"I think..." his voice strains under the pressure, and I frantically try to get him to stop. To stop talking. To save his breath. To hold on just a little longer.

There's so much he wanted to do. So much he wanted to provide for Millie. He was so close. So *fucking* close, and he had to go be a hero.

"I think," he tries again, his hand coming up to cup the back of my head as I lay my forehead against his, "That I just saved two of my three favorite people in this world."

A sound escapes my lips, something between a forced laugh and a strangled choke. "Stupid."

I tap my forehead against his, my hands fisting into his hair. I can't make intelligent words, can't do anything but cry and hold him as he begins to gasp. The wet squelch of each of his breaths fills my ears. It's a sound that will haunt me for the rest of my life. And if Hu'yimona has his way... It will be a very, very long life.

"Sitara..." he gasps, and I can hear the panic begin to creep into his voice, "Promise me."

His hand wraps around my arm as each breath begins to come out in rapid succession. "Promise me you'll go get her."

I know exactly what he's asking of me.

I want to tell him not to be so silly. That he'll be there to pick Millicent up himself before he knows it. That she'll be safe in his arms and aboard the *Nureus* in no time.

But if the last two months have taught me anything... it's that I shouldn't lie. I shouldn't lie to myself. I shouldn't lie to him, especially when I can already see the truth accepted in his eyes.

I swallow, trying to make the words come out of my mouth, but they won't. He shakes me, his eyes growing wide until I can see every single fleck of color in his blue irises. "Sitara... Promise me!"

"I promise... I promise," I choke on the words as they tumble up my throat, broken up by sobs that I can't stop.

Arthur settles, his breathing beginning to slow, and my panic only mounts.

"Good... Good."

And then I can't hear anything. No gargling. No wheezing. No pulse as I lay my ear against his chest.

The only sound that permeates the air around us is my strangled scream and the pulsing fire that rips from my body as I stand.

52
Kiernan

The pure anguish in Sitara's scream curdles my stomach, my head still reeling due to what had just happened. I hardly have time to register the sacrifice Arthur has made on my behalf before the chamber is washed in emerald flames. Those of us who have not incurred her fury huddle together in the center of the room, praying like hell she has her wits about her enough not to accidentally engulf us in those waves of pure retribution.

That's what this is. Pure, unadulterated retribution.

Sitara's entire body is engulfed, her skin reflecting the green light as she lashes out. One by one, the enemy is consumed by ice-cold fire, their bodies turning red, then purple, then blue, then black, until they simply shatter like glass. Or rather... Ice.

I've never seen her like this before. And I never want to see it again.

Screams echo off the walls, some from her victims, some from her. The immeasurable pain that is laced in every sound, every expression... I knew Arthur meant a lot to her, and it is crystal clear now that he had become someone so irreplaceable in her life that even *I* can't bring myself to feel even the slightest bit of possessiveness at the display. She's hurting. And Arthur... He saved her life. And the life of my unborn child.

That is a debt I will never be able to repay. But I will start by making sure to uphold the promise Sitara made to him and take his woman to Rhazden.

More and more screams wail into the chamber, the echoes making it sound as though there are thousands rather than just a few left. Sitara's justice is swift and clean. She's not going to risk making things slow for them. She doesn't want torture; she just wants them dead.

Me on the other hand... Well, I might just have to torture whoever is left after this just for putting that look on her face.

As Sitara continues her annihilation, I pick up Arthur's cooling body and take him away from the initial destruction zone. Motioning for Benedict to follow, I quickly carry Arthur over toward the far end of the room.

"I need you to stay with him."

He nods silently. Knowing what the man meant to Sitara is more than enough for Ben.

I lay Pip down in the red cascading fabrics that Sitara had been sitting under with Hu'yimona, what feels like an eternity ago. I know it hasn't been nearly that long, though.

"Kiernan!" Larkin's voice shouts over the blasts of cold flame that are being thrown out in rapid fire. My head snaps over toward the sounds, and I see Larkin attempting to reach his sister without getting frostbite. He's not getting very far, though, as he keeps stumbling back every time he proceeds an inch too close to her.

Larkin points toward her, and I'm not sure what he's trying to tell me. I furrow my brows, looking her over carefully. I don't see anything wron–

"Her hands!"

My eyes immediately snap to Sitara's fingers, and I see it. Her fingertips are turning different shades of purple and black. She's lowering the temperature so much that even her own body can't handle it.

I need to get to her before she ends up going further than her bleeding heart will allow her to recover from.

"Sitara!" I call out to her, trying to get closer. My panic builds as I watch her continue her onslaught. She's so stricken with grief, I'm not sure she even comprehends the carnage she is inflicting. Not that the people she's killing don't completely deserve it. I know that if I don't break through to her before I try to touch her, it won't end well. I will be the next body turned to stone and shattered into a million fucking pieces. I know she doesn't want that.

I need to calm her down enough that her body doesn't give out. For so many more reasons than just not wanting frostbite.

"Sitara..."

Hu'yimona's voice must have pierced through her rage. Her chest is heaving, her hands trembling with the force of her emotions and the sting that has no doubt bloomed in her fingertips. Those big brown eyes that usually have such a warm glow are blazing now. Tears stream down her face, the liquid turning to tiny frozen diamonds before they hit the ground with a small clinking sound as they pass through the viridescent flames.

He extends his arms out to her to beckon her to him. I can see the flames flicker as recognition slides over her features and her shoulders begin to droop. The quiver of her chin breaks my heart. Sitara makes a small choked sound as he pulls her into his embrace.

"I'm right here..." he mutters, raking his fingers through her hair, which has all but fallen from the pins that had been placed in it.

She is so small in his arms. The room is beginning to feel less and less cramped as the rage and endorphins begin to disperse from my body, but Sitara still feels that way to me. She has always seemed so small and delicate compared to me.

Her size has never been indicative of her ability, though, and I know that. Honestly, right now *I'm* the one who feels helpless. And I know that my woman is anything *but.*

I watch her knees give out and Hu'yimona scoops her up into his arms, laying his cheek against the top of her head as she presses it to his chest. He lets her tears soak into the tattered remains of what used to be his shirt and just holds her.

That's all *I've* wanted to do for two long, excruciatingly long months.

"Why would he do that?" Her voice breaks through the silence that has fallen over the room. She's looking for answers. Some of those answers no one will ever be able to give her.

Like, why her mother did that in the first place when Sitara had already agreed to go with Hu'yimona and leave me behind.

Or, better yet, why she would even try to kill her daughter a second time to begin with.

But this question... I do have an answer to.

Because he loved you, Sitara.

The answer only brings heavier sobs, her body vibrating against his. The room is warming up now, and it isn't painful to breathe anymore. Thank the gods for that. Except for Hu'yimona. He can go straight to hell.

"Sitara..." Hu'yimona's voice cuts through their little bubble of connection, and it makes me grit my teeth. To my surprise, Sitara simply shifts her face against his chest and looks up. I follow her gaze, which is not hate-filled enough for my liking, only to find a deep, regretful resignation on his face.

"I know this isn't the best time, but I found something... concerning about your mother when I–"

When he killed her. It's the first noble fucking thing he's done in his forsaken life.

Well, obviously, I know that isn't true. I had listened to the Sacred Three intently last night, and I understand that there is probably more to that son of a bitch than I'd like to acknowledge.

"What?" Sitara sniffles, wiping tears off her cheeks with the back of her hand.

The god shifts uncomfortably on his feet and for a split second... I see it. The man who cares *too* much.

"She didn't have any blood in her system." He points a finger toward the corpse in question. The woman has a huge ass gaping hole in her chest, but she is only a few drops of coagulated blood around the wound and on the floor.

Well, that's just fucked up... but that means...

"She was already dead." Sitara's voice bites out, looking over at the crumbled woman on the floor.

My brows furrow so deeply I can feel the crease between them. He places his hand on her lower back as she turns to face him, making sure that some part of him remains touching her.

My eyes never leave *him*.

My mind is reeling. How in the hell did he *not* know she was dead already? Seriously, I thought this guy was supposed to be *the god of death*.

Hu'yimona nods solemnly, his face so perfectly human with that expression that I want to punch him in the nose. "Yes. The only way that could have been without my knowledge is if someone was keeping the cells and nerves in her body communicating and alive. She even had a heartbeat. The only one who could have done that is..."

He trails off, a realization sparking behind his eyes, though he doesn't continue.

"It was Morana," Sitara says with confidence, "I don't know how, but I know it was her."

"You're probably right," he says, nodding slowly.

The manner in which they both talk as though he *didn't* kidnap her and try to force her to marry him is eating away at my last nerve. Then again... I guess Sitara has a pattern. Hadn't I done the first of those things as well?

He looks at me. I grit my teeth, finally speaking. "Every fiber of the man I used to be–every morsel of him–is screaming at me to kill you. And I want to listen. I feel like I have every right after what you tried to steal from me, what you're currently *still* thinking you'll be taking from me. *My* woman. *My* child. I never claimed to be her knight in shining armor, her hero. She's never been a damsel in distress who needed me to save her from her monsters."

I look over at her, at my Sitara, and I can see the strength there. The strength that has always been there, even when she was at her most vulnerable. "I love you and I'm on your side... No matter what you choose to do."

"He's not a monster," she says softly, looking up at him, "Are you, Hu'yimona? You're just a man who has been hurt one too many times."

There's a gentle expression on her face. I realize now what has happened during her time here. Something about this man had caused her to develop feelings beyond hatred and fear. I know she doesn't feel for him the way she feels for me. She's never given me a single reason to doubt her. Not once. But that doesn't mitigate the fact that there is some level of care and understanding there. Something I probably will never fully understand myself.

"Please, just stop trying to go through with these plans of yours," Sitara begs, her hand reaching out to take his between her fingers, "You can do better. You *are* better than this. You could go home. I know they would listen if you just changed your mind about the way things are."

I can see the war playing out behind the man's eyes, and his words strike a chord with me–echo everything I feel toward her as well.

"There is next to none I wouldn't do for you, Sitara. Almost nothing I wouldn't give to make you happy," his voice breaks, and I have to clench my hands at my side, "But that... That is not one of them. However, my offer still stands. I won't touch anyone if only you'll stay with me."

I can hear the deep, rattling sigh that escapes her lips. "Alright... Then I'll stay with you, but this has to stop."

The God of Death nods, his eyes flicking toward me with resignation as he tells us to leave.

I'm frozen in place, watching her be led away. I can see the slight shudder in her shoulders, indicating the silent sobs that are most likely vibrating in her chest.

When they reach the exit, Hu'yimona finally looks down at her once more, pausing for a heartbeat before his head turns to look back at us once more. He's hesitating, contemplating. I can see that even from where I'm positioned, trying my damndest not to crumple into a heap in front of everyone.

He intakes a breath through his nose, turning back to her with an expression of pure grief. "No, Sitara," he murmurs, "You belong above ground. In the sun."

As his words carry through the space between us, I feel my knees give out, relief washing over me like a tidal wave. My entire body shudders, releasing the tension that's been pulling at my muscles for weeks now.

He's letting her go.

"Then I have to lock you away, and I would really like it if you wouldn't fight me. Can you give me that? Or is that yet another thing you cannot give me?" she asks.

Hu'yimona hesitates, torn between the truth behind Sitara's words and what he wants. He doesn't want to be locked up again. Honestly, I wouldn't want to be either, so I can't blame the guy. But we all know that if he doesn't stray from the path he has led himself down, then he leaves Sitara with no choice but to do it.

He looks around at the carnage surrounding us, as the clear manipulation that has been at play with the presence of Sitara's long-since dead mother on the floor, at the fact that his cult is all but completely obliterated. He has to make a choice. To accept his isolation once more or stand face to face with those he once called family.

It's clear he isn't willing to face them, to face his sister. He isn't willing to place himself on his knees and beg for forgiveness. I suppose, if I can grant Coli'hanu's request in some way, I can admit that he and I are a lot alike in that regard.

Hu'yimona is not the type to bow to anyone.

"I've come to know you as more than the beast history has made you to be," Sitara continues, "Will you really keep giving people a reason to fear you... Or will you allow me to change your story?"

The anguish written on his face is enough to make my eyes flick to Sitara for a reaction. I can tell that his responding reaction has torn some small piece of her heart out, the part she is willing to give him, the part that understands him.

I'm starting to understand what Coli'hanu meant by *she is right where she needs to be*.

"You will forget about me," Hu'yimona states simply, though the way his voice cracks isn't nearly as simple in its emotion.

Her expression softens, and I'm not sure I believe he deserves that sort of reverence from someone like her, but who am I to question? She pulls his face down to her, and I hold my breath, releasing it as she simply presses his forehead to hers. It's still an intimate gesture, but not one I would feel the need to rip his tongue out for.

"About the man who tried to kill me all those years ago? Absolutely," she murmurs, "But the man who showed he has a vast depth for care and love? No, that's not a person I can forget easily."

I know where I stand with her. Every facet of her belongs to me and me alone. I know that. But watching her with him now, it makes me realize just how vast Sitara's own capacity for understanding truly is.

The woman is practically a saint.

"Come on," she takes his hand, "Walk with me."

I look over my shoulder to make sure Benedict and the others are still with Arthur and nod toward the exit. I know my first mate knows what I'm asking of him, and he returns the gesture before I turn to follow Hu'yimona and Sitara. As much as I don't want to, I leave some space between myself and the two of them as I follow them, trying to remain respectful despite wanting to do the exact opposite.

I know they're talking. I know that the hushed tones are not because of any secret between them. She's comforting him. Reassuring him. And I'm left to wonder exactly what all happened in the last two months to change that dynamic so drastically.

When we reach what I am assuming is their destination, I lean myself against a shadowed wall to watch the scene unfold. Sitara opens the door, a bedroom coming into view between the jagged edges of stone on either side of the doorway. On the far wall is a natural hole carved into the wall that lets in the sounds and smells of the salty ocean breezes.

They turn to face one another, and Sitara's lips curve up into an understanding smile. "I want you to be able to see the sun, unlike the last time."

"Why?" Hu'yimona asks, just as confused as I am by her choice in location. Then again, my girl has always been gracious like that.

"Because, in a world full of wolves in sheep's clothing... You have only ever been the wolf. And for that raw honesty, you have earned my respect."

I can see the mixture of acceptance and gratitude that slides onto Hu'yimona's face as he takes one last chance to hug her. And she lets him.

Once they've parted, Sitara begins the process of sealing him away with her Cold Fire.

53

Sitara

I know I should feel relieved to be walking out of these tunnels.

I should be elated that Kiernan had come for me, that Larkin hadn't left me to my own devices forever.

I should feel grateful that every single one of them had risked everything to make sure I had the support I needed to end this.

But all I feel is numb as I watch Benedict and Henry carry Arthur's prone form out into the sunlight.

His face is serene, like he's sleeping. If not for the pale parlor of his skin and the crimson patch in his shirt, I might be able to convince myself that's what he's doing...

Just napping.

It doesn't feel right that I'm standing here unscathed while he is lifeless and broken. I know that's what he wanted, but I still can't shake the wrongness of it.

As our little group begins to trek through the jungle, completely silent and sullen, I can feel Kiernan's hand searing through the back of the thin fabric of my gown. It's grounding, a reminder that not all was lost. My hands slide down to the swell of my stomach, and I finally allow myself to truly feel it.

I hadn't realized until now how detached I truly was.

Of course, I had acknowledged it. And, yes, I had already felt a deep maternal protectiveness. However, with everything happening, I hadn't given myself time to really soak in the life I was bringing into this world.

But Arthur had.

He had moved into the path of that dagger without a second thought.

I think I just saved two of my three favorite people, he had said, acknowledging my child's existence so quickly and so completely.

He would have made a wonderful uncle.

Through the haze of my own thought process, I can feel Kiernan's hand shift from the small of my back to my waist. He pulls me closer, tucking me under his arm. This is where I belong, right here, surrounded by him and all the others I had spent the last two months trying to protect.

I can feel his gaze as he watches the movement of my hand. He's trying to be subtle, but Kiernan has never been a subtle man.

I look up at him, our eyes locking together. I can see the relief in his eyes, which are still slowly speckling back to that vibrant blue.

It's an elephant in the room, so to speak—knowing that Kiernan has Kana'te blood is a heady realization, one none of us has had time to process yet.

He offers me a soft, reassuring smile, his thumb brushing slow circles on my skin. "Where do you want us to take him?"

The question is simple, and I feel the immense responsibility that comes with it.

Not to mention the fact that I greatly appreciate it.

There is no way in hell I'm letting them give Pip a *pirate funeral*. He deserves better than being laid to rest in the murky depths of the ocean.

"Djar's hut," I say simply. At least there we can clean him up and figure out what our next move will be.

When we finally reach the village, I lead the men toward Djar's home, where the shaman allows them to lay Arthur's body down on the thick rugs lining the floor.

As they all shuffle out, Kiernan turns me to face him. He rests his forehead against mine, his hands sliding up to cup my cheeks. "Do you need me to help you with what needs to be done?"

"No," I murmur, shaking my head gently. I would rather do this on my own, or at least without my ever-endearing Kiernan hovering over me the entire time.

As much as I appreciate it, I don't know if I can handle it right now.

"If you're sure... I'm going to go assess the damage to the crew. See what wounds I can help mend and get a head count."

He straightens up just as another comes in through the flaps in the hut door. Larkin. I'm not sure how, but their body language claims that whatever canyon had been between them before has finally been mended.

I move to Arthur's body as Kiernan brushes passed my brother, exiting the hut without another word.

We don't say anything as we move to cut away at the clothes on Pip's form, bringing him down to nothing but the cloth Larkin helps me wrap around his hips.

The wet sponge in my hand glides over Arthur's cold skin, each detail accounted for as I am handed the needle and thread to sew the gaping wound in his ribs closed. Once I've begun doing so, Larkin finally speaks, his voice low and soothing.

"Sitara..." he hesitates for a fraction of a second, his words shaky and uneven. "Sitara, I'm so sorry..."

Every visible muscle in his body is taut, almost trembling. His movements are stiff and jerky as he attempts to help me cleanse Arthur of the horrors that we carried back with us. I don't remove my focus from the stitching, though that blasted lump in my throat decides to make its appearance again.

"It's not your fault."

That much I can say with certainty.

Yes, Larkin was the one who took me down into that cave to begin with, but even I had been fooled by the carefully constructed plan Hu'yimona had created.

"I should have known better," he says quietly, ringing out a dirty rag. "If I had just... If I had looked passed what I *wanted* to be true, we wouldn't be doing this."

His shoulders drop in defeat, the pain etched into the lines of his face giving me pause. "You would have been off living your life in Rhazden or sailing. Arthur would be with–"

"But he's not," I cut him off, though there is no real malice in my voice. I don't blame Larkin for any of it. Truly, I don't. I hardly blame Hu'yimona for it at this point.

Now, Morana on the other hand... I'll smite her dead where she stands if I ever find her.

I take a deep, steadying breath and set the stitching supplies down next to the bucket of water and rags. "You wanted us to be whole again. There's nothing wrong with that. Besides, Hu'yimona would have found a way to get out of the Cavern of Light one way or another."

That is another thing I can say with utmost certainty. Hu'yimona is far too clever and far too resourceful to have stayed in that prison forever, allowing himself to rot away into that tree.

Still, the offer of an apology hangs in the air between us, a fragile olive branch extended by my brother after years of silence. I know he's apologizing for more than just the last two months. He's apologizing for everything since we were children—the anger, the distance, the self-destruction, the misplaced blame... All of it.

It's not that I reject the gesture entirely. A part of me, still weary from the weight of our strained relationship, even craves it. In all honesty, the mere fact that Larkin acknowledges his wrongdoing, that he feels compelled to voice those words to me, tells me there is a certain maturity that has taken place in my absence.

But the apology, no matter how much I appreciate it, feels hollow and powerless against the gaping wound Arthur's death has left. Words can't resurrect a life, can't fill the void left by laughter or wisdom or his unwavering presence. The sting of losing him, of knowing that I will never get to sit on the deck in the middle of the night and talk about our futures, leaves a dull ache that throbs deep in my chest.

Larkin seems to understand this unspoken connection I had with Pip.

As we work together, meticulously wrapping Athur's body in a pristine white linen shroud–my final act of respect–he breaks the silence that has settled around us like a blanket all its own.

"He was someone very special to you, wasn't he?" His question, softly spoken, hangs in the air, heavy with unspoken understanding.

"Yes," I say simply. I don't elaborate, don't delve into the irreplaceable role Arthur played in my life. The emotions are too raw, too overwhelming.

After a few more moments of silence, something that has become so normal for me and Larkin over the course of our lives, he helps me braid Arthur's hair into a tightly woven braid. I had cut it a few times after he had asked me, but it had gotten long again.

"I'm glad he was for you what I *should* have been." It is all my brother has left to say to me before he tucks out of the hut flap and leaves me to finish the process of caring for my friend in peace.

The metallic tang of blood clings to the air, a grim reminder of the recent events. My hands, still slightly trembling, are slick with the residual oils and water I've used on Arthur's body.

Finally, I can do no more.

Leaning heavily against the rough wall of the hut, I close my eyes, allowing the wood to dig into my back.

Gods, I'm so tired.

It's not just physical fatigue, but a soul-deep weariness that has settled into my bones. Emotionally, I am a raw, frayed wire. Mentally, my thoughts are a tangled mess, spinning and looping back on themselves with maddening repetition. These last two months have offered no respite, no solace. Sleep is a battlefield instead of a refuge, haunted by choking anxieties.

I linger in the shadowed corners of the hut, enjoying the quiet—however fleeting that quiet might be. Outside, the sounds of the living world intrude. The rustle of leaves in the wind, the chirping of unseen insects, and then... the unmistakable shuffle of approaching feet, accompanied by hushed whispers.

Kiernan's voice, carrying a fragile hope that threatens to shatter against the truth, rings out into the air. "Is Sitara ready for me?" he asks, the question a hesitant plea.

My stomach clenches.

No. No, I'm not ready.

Not ready to face his grief alongside my own.

Not ready to feel the relief wash over me like a balm without feeling guilty for the enjoyment of being in his arms when I know Millicent will never feel that again.

I'm not ready to navigate the minefield of emotions that lies ahead. I'm not ready to have the conversations we both know we need to have, the conversations that will undoubtedly come.

"She's nearly finished in there, but let's not rush her," Djar's voice resonates through the thin wooden walls, a soothing sound against Kiernan's raw anticipation. Djar has always had a way of smoothing ruffled feathers, his voice a low, steady rumble that can quell the fiercest storm.

But even in his comforting tone, I can feel the note of solemnity, a quiet gravity that speaks volumes. He knows what I have been doing and how much the man in the center of his hut meant to me. He understands the weight I carry.

The air expelled from Kiernan's lungs is a ragged expulsion, a mixture of contrasting emotions. It is a gush of relief, a silent acknowledgement that I am okay, even if it is intertwined with his signature, stinging impatience.

"Then... you need something?" Kiernan's voice, once it reemerges, is raspy and worn.

He *sounds* as tired as I feel. I'm sure he's been pushing himself and the men as hard as they could physically handle.

I'm sure he doesn't look half as bad as I do, though. Kiernan has always carried himself with that strength and power–that put-togeth-erness.

"Oh, I just thought I would give you the courtesy of my fantastic company," Djar announces, injecting a playful tone into the somber air. He's trying to make a joke, a feeble attempt at lightening the atmosphere, knowing that some levity is so greatly needed right now. But the words feel hollow, like a cheap imitation of genuine cheer.

When Kiernan says nothing, the silence stretches once more, thick and uncomfortable. Fucking gods, I can practically feel the tension radiating off of him in waves. Kiernan has always been intense, but damn...

I can hear Djar shift, the rustle of his clothing, the only sound breaking the quiet. He settles down beside Kiernan, who had moved to sitting once more a while ago, in the dirt.

"I am sorry about your friend," the elder says, his voice soft and reverent, laced with genuine sympathy. I can hear the faint patting of his hand gently landing on Kiernan's shoulder, a small, imperceptible gesture of comfort and support.

Kiernan lets out a long sigh, the sound raspy and laden with fatigue. "He was a good man... All three of the men we lost were. But Arthur," his voice cracks slightly as he says the name, "he was something special to her."

He pauses, as though he's trying to gain some sort of bearing. "I'll have to figure out what to tell the families of the other two when we get back to Rhazden."

The weight of his words settles heavily, a tangible blanket of sorrow and responsibility pressing down around us. All three? We lost three of them?

The realization hits me like a physical blow. Not just Arthur, but two others. My breath hitches in my throat, a silent gasp of horror catching in my lungs. My heart clenched tightly, a painful knot forming in my chest. Tears prick at the corners of my eyes, blurring my vision as the images of who it could be flood through me. I hadn't exactly paid attention to who had left with us.

Who else do I have to say goodbye to? The first name that comes to mind is Benedict, and my entire head spins. He's about to have a baby. His wife would be left alone to raise a child all by herself. All because I decided to drag a Mundane–well, not so mundane now–man into my world. I sit here, practically hyperventilating, but I can't make myself move. I don't want to pay the piper just yet.

"On that matter," Djar says, his voice piercing through my panic, "I'd like to convince the two of you to stay. Obviously, the decision is solely Sitara's, but I *had* trained her with the intention of naming her the next shaman of our village."

"Staying…" Kiernan's voice comes out softly, barely audible above the rustle of leaves and the distant call of some unseen bird. I can sense the war waging inside of him, a silent battle between the life he knows and the unknown of creating a life here with me. After all, my seaworthy sailor isn't quite as majestic here in the jungle as he is out on the waves. But he knows I would love to raise our child in my world, to ensure they could use whatever magic ends up a part of them unabashed and unashamed. To be connected to the place and the magic I grew up around.

"I'd be allowed to stay with her? Not just in Puka'qui, but beyond the treeline? Here in the village?" The plea in his voice is unmistakable, a subtle hint of desperation that only I would be able to pick up on.

"My dear boy," Djar says almost affectionately, "You gained your blessing–not that you needed it. But more importantly, you took the rite. You are as much a member of this tribe as Sitara now."

The weight in my chest is almost unbearable. I know what he must be thinking, the worry that is probably gnawing at him.

Rhazden. His home. The people he cares about who live and thrive within its borders. More specifically, his sister and niece–the family he clearly adores. To ask him to leave all of that, everything he's built with his own two hands, all for me? It feels monstrously selfish.

I bite into my lip, trying to swallow the guilt that threatens to choke me. No, I can't ask any more of him. It just wouldn't be fair.

Then, breaking the heavy silence that seems to pierce through this place every chance it fucking gets, comes his voice, laced with bewilderment. "What do you mean, I didn't *need* it? I thought all Mundanes needed the blessing to cross?"

The words are so perfectly, endearingly clueless that I can't help but groan internally. I lift my hand to my forehead with a soft 'thud', the sound echoing in the quiet hut.

Oh, my sweet, beautifully stupid man... He hasn't figured it out yet. He hasn't grasped the significance of what he had done in I'cuma.

From inside the hut, I hear Djar start to chuckle. "*Mundane* people do need the blessing, Kiernan." The amusement in his voice only serves to amplify Kiernan's confusion, if I know my love at all.

I can practically picture his face: the furrowed brow, the slightly parted lips, the realization that is so, so, *so* close yet so far away.

With a deep breath, I rise to my feet, willing my weary muscles to move. I step out of the hut, out into the cool of the night, the moonlight a heavy, shimmering blanket cast across the landscape now. The moment I emerge, Kiernan's eyes lock onto me. He jumps immediately to his feet, concern and relief etched onto his features.

"Sitara."

I give him a soft, tremulous smile. My feet move almost of their own volition, covering the remaining distance between us until I have managed to wrap my arms tightly around his waist. The instantaneous relief is almost overwhelming. It's crazy, completely irrational, to think that a single person can bring you so much peace, can anchor you so completely.

"I heard," I say simply, my voice untrustworthy as it shakes slightly. I bury my face into the tattered remains of his shirt and sigh. We have plenty of time to talk about all of this. Right?

I'm so. Fucking. Tired. At this moment, I just want to be cradled in the warmth of Kiernan's presence. All I want is to lay it all down.

He wraps me gently in his arms and presses his lips to the top of my head. We both inhale at the same time, and I savor every sensation.

Gods, I've missed him.

Missed feeling his arms around me.

Missed the smell of him.

"You don't have to decide now," he murmurs, his voice slightly muffled by my hair, "You don't need to rush."

I know with bone-deep certainty that he would give me whatever I wanted. Go wherever I wanted to go, be that on the ship, on this island, in Rhazden. It doesn't matter to him. But it matters to me that we make the decision together.

"*We* don't have to decide now," I correct him, and tighten my arms around him imperceptibly.

"Well, I, for one, think there is no one better to take the roll," a familiarly airy voice catches the air and drifts toward us.

The three of us lift our heads to see Coli'hanu making her way toward us. Kiernan loosens his grip, but he doesn't let go, his words—when uttered—laced with confusion. "She... left the temple."

A small smile crooks the corner of my mouth, the genuine use of those muscles more foreign to me at this point than I would like to admit. "They do that from time to time. Though... Never when you expect it."

I lift my brow as I gaze toward the Goddess of Cold Fire and her billowing trusses of white hair that seem to flow behind her like silk.

"To what do we owe the pleasure, my lady?" Djar smiles, lowering his head in respect.

Coli'hanu smiles at him, then turns her smile to the two of us. "I've simply come to see how my favorite girl is doing."

The look on Kiernan's face says something between '*don't push her*' and '*are you fucking kidding me*' as he holds me a little closer.

It's endearing, really, how his muscles tense and he draws my body to his as if he would wrestle a bear for me. In a way, he has. The look of protectiveness warms my chest. It isn't like it was in the beginning, that possessive streak as if I were an item to be owned. It's different now.

I am *his*, yes. But now...now he is truly *mine* in return.

"I'm doing alright, thank you," I respond, giving my goddess a soft smile.

She nods slowly, as though she has something she wants to say. Her glowing eyes soften, the corner of her mouth pressing inward. "I hope my brother treated you well?"

"He did," I say with confidence, "Actually...he was very...kind."

"I'm sure that was very confusing for you." She looks at me as though she feels pity for me. It's the first time in my life I've ever wanted to tell her to get fucked.

"No, not really. It's not confusing at all once you get to know him." I answer simply, wrapping my arm back around Kiernan's waist and tucking myself back under his arm.

As a look of relief and gratitude slides onto her face, I can hear a familiar voice calling–no, scratch that, *screaming*–my name.

All our heads snap toward the sounds as a familiar visage takes form on the edge of the village. Her ringlet mass of blonde curls whips around as she searches for me.

Eirian.

She drags along the five children that belong to the next generation of the Miqui'oh people. A small hint of guilt takes hold of my chest as the knowledge that I ended their parents' lives in a fit of rage sinks in, but deep down... I can't bring myself to regret it.

Does that make me a bad person? Maybe.

I pull away from Kiernan's grasp, racing toward the frantic, disheveled woman I've come to call a friend.

"Eirian! What are you doing here? What happened?"

She's out of breath after picking up the smallest of the children to make it to my side just a bit faster, her chest heaving heavily. "Morana..." she shakes her head and tries to catch her breath as the last of the children takes a seat at her feet, "She...She took Ardere..."

The sound of my father's name makes my shoulders bunch instinctively. I haven't allowed myself to even think about the implication that he very well may already be dead in the same fashion as my mother was. Eirian sits the smallest down and puts her hand on her own chest, taking in another deep breath.

"I heard her telling him...that they were leaving...going to your island... Sitara, they're going to burn it to the ground."

My blood runs cold, my breath hitching in my throat as I hear the unmistakable growl rumble up Kiernan's chest from behind me. After everything...

I swear to the gods I'm going to kill her!

I spin around toward Kiernan, my grim expression met with one of pure fury, his body beginning to grow in size almost instantaneously.

He looks down at me, his jaw working under his skin. "I have to go. I have to get Rielle and Neoma." I freeze at his words, everything in me screaming not to be separated again. He kisses the top of my head roughly, his movements jerky. "You deal with Arthur."

"You're mental if you think I'm staying here," I take a step toward him, glancing toward Coli'hanu.

The goddess nods, a small smile spreading across her face. "I think you two have done more than enough. I will preserve your friend until you can return safely home."

54

Benedict

I'm too old for this shit.

Granted, I'm not *that* old, but I'm old enough.

If there is one thing I hate more than anything else in this gods-for-saken world, it's being rushed.

And waiting.

It feels like that is all I've done lately—rushed around trying to save someone's ass or waiting on this fucking ship to get to where I need to be to save someone's ass.

Not that I wouldn't have jumped at the opportunity to save Sitara; of course, I would. But damn, the waiting and the rushing have me gnawing on the inside of my cheek until I can taste the tangy copper of my own blood on my tongue.

The worst part is that this time... It's my Enna and my own unborn child's lives I'm being forced to wait to save.

That's made me very, very cranky.

I think I have made three men piss themselves since we set sail from Puka'qui. Then, I made them mop the piss up off the deck.

Do I feel bad? Absolutely not.

Did Kiernan get on my ass about it? Yeah, a little.

The tension on the ship has been so thick the last couple of days that I can probably scrape it out of the air and use it like butter on my toast. Honestly, I'm wound tighter than a spring, and I can't seem to get my muscles to relax. I'm not above being a big man and saying that I'm terrified.

I am terrified.

I'm terrified of what I'm going to find when we finally dock in Rhazden.

I'm terrified that I'm going to find my house crumbled to the ground with my wife still inside, charred to a fucking crisp.

Even the thought makes a low growl rumble up my throat, which makes Becket skitter away from me like a scolded puppy. As I stand here, leaning up against the railing of the ship, peering into the deep blue like an old man trying to watch birds, I can hear the heavy footsteps of my favorite oaf walking toward me.

Kiernan approaches with a glass decanter from his cabin. We keep this specific whiskey locked away from the rest of the crew, bought only for us. It's aged and bloody fucking expensive. This crew would have it destroyed, container and all, wasting a precious slice of chest hair-growing gold like the savages they are. So instead, he and I save it for moments like this, when it's needed the most, either as a celebratory shot or a slow, solemn drink amongst the two of us.

"You look like you could use this," he mutters, handing me a glass and pouring a small amount of the amber liquid into it.

I nod, shifting my eyes back toward the water, and Kiernan does the same. We both let out a sigh and take a nice, healthy dose of our preferred medicine.

We sit like this for some time before I finally turn to him, a subtle grin pulling at the corner of my mouth. I have to keep things light, even though I feel far from it. If I don't, I'll end up sending someone to join Gerald, and I'm not particularly inclined to lose a man right now. Not when we don't know what the hell we are sailing into right now.

That seems to be the common theme of the last few months.

"So, feel better now that we have Starlight back where she belongs?" I ask.

At least we can check one thing off our to-do list.

Too bad we added another. One that makes me want to hurl my own best friend off the fucking ship and tell his gigantic ass to start pushing.

I watch as his shoulders sag, the relief evident as he nods. "One weight lifted. Though there is a lot we need to talk about. I was just trying to give her a second to breathe."

K swirls the whiskey in his glass, and we both watch as it dances around the edges. I've watched the guy exhaust himself these last few weeks, and if I know Kiernan Slater—which I do—he's eventually going to drop dead on his feet and end up sleeping for a week straight.

Which will leave more work for me in the long run.

Work is good right now, honestly.

It'll keep my mind busy.

"Between everything that she's been through on her own over the last two months, and then losing Arthur..."

We both look back over the water at that.

A better man than Kiernan.

And worlds better than me.

We both know it, and, deep down, so does everyone else.

He takes a deep breath, in through his nose, and continues. "And now the offer of taking over Djar's role... She's got a lot on her plate."

"Yeah." I nod, closing my eyes to savor the burn that comes with drinking from my cup. "She's a tough cookie, though. I don't think I know anyone who would have been able to handle what she has in her lifetime and remain so... kind? Except for maybe my Enna."

He gives me a sympathetic look.

Less than a week ago, he had been in the same position as I am now. My worry is evident in every tightened twitch of my muscles, every tick of my jaw, every... well, fucking everything.

I'm a fucking mess, wrapped up in a nice blanket of false composure.

"Enna is a good woman. I've given you a lot of shit about her over the years, but now I get it. I probably owe you an apology," he murmurs.

My brows lift slightly as he takes another swig of his drink. That concept is almost more unsettling than facing the God of Death and his horde of followers. My discomfort is quickly placated by the crooked grin he gives me as he continues. "But that's not how we work, so just know that the sentiment is there."

"Thank fuck for that," I sigh teasingly, swishing my next drink in my mouth for a moment before swallowing. "You had me going there for a second. I thought I was going to have to go find that voodoo doctor again and have him stab you with a needle."

We both laugh at that, bringing our glasses to our lips in unison before sombering out once more.

As the two of us finish off our drinks, Sitara walks barefoot across the deck, her hand running up Kiernan's back. He turns to pull her to him, and I can't help but smile a little.

This man was a fucking hazard to society before she came along. Though I suppose I don't have much room to talk.

Seeing him this happy though... I guess that's the kind of thing only a mentor can be this happy to see.

"Welcome to the party," Kiernan smiles, planting a kiss on the top of her head. "I'm sorry, but I won't be sharing tonight."

I roll my eyes, a chuckle coating my throat. Sitara didn't drink *before* knowing about the child. The big guy is just being dramatic for the sake of it at this point.

"That's alright, you can keep it." She teases back.

I can't help but notice the maturity in Sitara. Whatever happened down in those caves, it changed her. Seemingly for the better.

"Doin' alright over there, Starlight?" I smile down at her warmly. "How's the tot doing?"

She leans into K, smiling over at me with a warmth I've missed. Sitara has certainly brought a level of camaraderie to this ship that wasn't there before. Sure, we all lived and worked together, but that was as far as it went. Until a fiery-haired young woman decided to challenge the status quo, that is.

"As well as can be expected, I suppose," she answers almost whimsically, laying her head against Kiernan's chest.

I can tell she appreciated me asking. K has probably kept the topic pretty much out of his line of communication over the last several days.

He's gotten to the point that we all get to when we fall for a woman who can handle us. He doesn't want to push, doesn't want to keep the topic in the forefront of her mind.

I, on the other hand, have absolutely no qualms about pushing.

"That's good to hear." I grin. "Got baby names picked out? Gonna name it after a special tree in that jungle of yours or something?"

Yeah, it's a lame joke, but it got her laughing.

"We haven't talked about names yet," she says, peering up at K.

"It's kind of hard to choose a name before you know what it is, isn't it?" Kiernan offers in response.

I roll my eyes, shaking my head. I could have sworn I taught him to be smarter than this. Enna and I already picked a name for each.

Kiernan hasn't spent any real time around babies.

Children, yes.

Tiny, immobile infants who can't so much as lift their head without assistance? Absolutely no experience.

He was sailing with me and the crew most of Neoma's early infancy, so he didn't get to really enjoy that.

He turns to me with that stupid, cocky grin. "I'm sure Enna has had your child's name chosen since before it was conceived."

Well, it's official.

My wife and I have spent far too much time with this man since she became an article in my life all those years ago.

"You know my wife well." I chuckle, leaning back against the railing and folding my arms over my chest. "But, yes, we do have a name picked out for either gender."

"I'd ask what they are, but knowing her, she's sworn you to secrecy," he laughs, pulling Sitara just a little closer to his side. She runs her hands along his arm until her hand finds his, and I practically watch the big lug melt.

Ah... Karma is a bitch, isn't she?

"I'm sure names will come to us." Sitara keeps the flow of the conversation going as she leans back into him.

"Oh, without a doubt, Enna had her brilliant idea for a girl's name while peeling an orange," I grin, looking up at the sky as my impatience to get to Rhazden in time only grows.

The sun has fallen below the horizon now, and, honestly, I am thanking Sitara's infernal gods for the amount of whiskey I've just ingested. It seems to be the only thing that helps ebb the fear that's continuously building in my gut. Most of the crew has long since gone to bed, but a few of us continue to sprawl out on the deck, filling our bellies with liquid fire.

Kiernan and Sitara are leaning against the mast, her petite frame between his legs with a blanket wrapped around her shoulders. I can't help but feel a small ball of guilt drop into my gut as it wars with my paternal pride as he runs his hands in small circles over her stomach, whispering something in her ear that makes her smile.

I have yet to have a moment like that with my own pregnant wife...

I take another drink from my cup to chase that line of thinking away. Alcohol doesn't mix well with irritation, yet here I am... drinking to my heart's content.

Viktor and Henry burst from the kitchen with arms full of jerky for the lot of us, grinning from ear to ear as Henry offers Sitara some with an exaggerated bow. Those two are thick as thieves and just as fucking ornery.

"So Cap', a few of us were wonderin'," Viktor starts, his scrawny ass swaying slightly as he lands ass first too hard onto the deck.

"Seeing as you don't seem to be going to say anything about it yourself," Henry grandly butts in, sitting down in the same fashion next to his brother.

"What was all that back at the caves anyway?" Viktor finishes.

Becket, Todd, and Joffrey all look over at K as though they had the same thought, each one giving Kiernan their full attention.

I find it fucking comical that Sitara has been on this ship all this time–not to mention we just fought a hundred of them–and they haven't been able to put two and two together yet.

Kiernan's face is almost enough to send me into a fit of laughter... or coughing due to the dumb I know is going to come out of his mouth. I can see the wheels turning, see the strain of his poor, wee little brain. I realize now I have failed him in one thing, and that was giving him some common fucking sense to work with.

"I'm not really sure. It just kind of happened," he answers, looking down at Sitara, "Maybe something to do with the rites... or the blessing from the gods?"

I almost spit out my drink at the laughter that cackles up Sitara's throat. Nope... scratch that, I've now spittled on myself as she starts rolling in his lap.

I can't help following her contagiousness right over the fucking cliff.

My head falls back as I roar, Sitara pointing her finger at me when she realizes I'm thinking the same thing.

The others are completely oblivious to why she and I are dying, and I think that might actually make it funnier.

"Seems to make sense to me," Becket shrugs, scratching his mop of brown hair in confusion.

"Don't you think we would all have gotten powers if it were the blessing?" I ask then, praying that one of these lousy halfwits has some brains.

"And the rites have nothing to do with our magic besides the fact that some might use it to catch the Coa'Hesa," Sitara adds, grinning widely once she's done gasping for air.

Kiernan furrows his brows and throws a piece of jerky at me, to which I proceed to munch on it.

"Maybe the gods just like me more than the rest of you heathens!" he grumbles, practically pouting as he lays his chin back down on Sitara's shoulder.

"Oh, for fuck's sake, K," I roll my eyes, chewing the tough morsel of meat. "The only way you could have been able to use Kana'te magic is if you *are* Kana'te."

Sitara's confirmation nod makes me smirk with smug satisfaction. I just can't help proving time and time again that I'm the smartest man on this fucking ship, and K knows it.

I can see the realization hit him like a brick to the side of the face. If he were any more obvious, his lips would be making that dumb ass '*O*'. "That's what Djar meant when he said I never really needed the blessing..." *There we go, he's finally getting it.* "How the hell did I not know?"

In his defense, the boy never really knew his parents. He's given me small, fuzzy retellings of memories in the past, but that has always been as far as it has gone.

It's clear that one of them had to have been Kana'te at least.

I had always had my suspicions, with the way he'd seem to grow larger during times of stress or anger. Though he had never become fully realized in that power until we were down in those fucking tunnels.

"It makes sense," Todd drones, leaning against the railing where he's decided to occupy. "You always were a big ass fucker."

True enough.

When I had brought Kiernan onto this ship at a meager age of seventeen, he was every bit as big as I am already. Still, I'll never forget the look on his face when he realized size isn't everything.

"So whatcha sayin' is Cap' is a..." Joffrey sputters, pointing a meaty finger in K's direction. I can see the fucker's face pale, replaying every nasty thing he's ever said about the tribes people.

Kiernan starts laughing. All of the lightheartedness is so desperately needed on my end, though it doesn't soothe the frayed wire that is my brain completely.

Sitara turns in his lap as if to assess what exactly is happening with him, her brows lifting to her hairline.

"So, I'm guessing you know the answer to their question then, Darling?" He looks down at her with an infinite gentleness I never thought I would see from him of all people.

"Yes," Sitara begins, sitting up a little straighter as though she's about to give a lecture to children. Honestly, she might as well be. "It's called Behemoth Physiology. It's an earth-based ability from the Han'alli tribe."

He closes his eyes briefly, shaking his head as though she has just said something amusing. "So, it came from the goddess who basically made me lick the temple floor... Of course it did, 'cause why not?"

So, the stone-skinned gal had done the same thing to him the first time he had gone to the temple. Honestly, I'm not surprised in the slightest. She seemed a bit of a prickly dame.

"It sure did," Sitara chuckles, wrapping her hands around his arms as he pulls her back into him and grabs another piece of jerky.

"Well, who would have thought," Henry starts.

"That the Cap' would have fit right in on that island to start with," Viktor finishes, the two of them grinning at one another.

Honestly, anyone could have guessed it if we had known what we were looking at. Until recently, none of us had ever seen some of the more combatant abilities on the island, having only been given small glimpses in Puka'qui.

Still, looking at him now... I find it hard to believe he's the same wet-eared boy I took off that ship all those years ago.

He's changed and has become better.

Better than I ever thought he would.

And it's all thanks to the wildly vibrant woman in his arms.

You know, the one I tried so hard to get him to walk away from.

Well, a man is allowed to be wrong from time to time.

And I've also realized I've had far too much to drink. I suppose sappy is better than throwing Joffrey off the side of the ship just because his face pisses me off.

We should arrive today.

I *need* to arrive today.

I can't take the fucking waiting any longer.

Fuck's sake... I'm about to jump the fuck overboard and swim my way there. Not that the idea is rational or smart.

I stand at the bow of the ship, my muscles vibrating as they coil tightly. Rhazden should come into view any time now. I'm dreading what we will see from afar, let alone once we are actually there. My breathing comes out in shallow, forced breaths as I try to remember that my lungs need air.

I've already thrown one man overboard just for trying to ask me a question.

Not my finest moment, but it made me feel better.

For a second.

Luckily, he was a new guy Kiernan picked up not long ago from a port hardly big enough to mention. He wouldn't have even been on the ship at this point if K hadn't cared about his rule at the moment.

Looks like I've saved him the trouble.

My eyes scan the seas, looking for the reinforcements we sent missives for at the start of this journey. Even if there are survivors, and every person present better hope there are, there's no way we will be able to get them all off the island with just a single ship. It's never been an issue before. Rhazden is supposed to be the safest place, only next to the jungle of Capulli'ana.

I can hear Sitara walking up from behind. The sound of her bare feet padding across the wooden deck gives her away every time. She's not changed back into her Mundane clothes, and I don't blame her for it. In all honesty, her native fabrics suit her better anyway.

"Benedict..." Her voice is soft and soothing, which isn't new. She's always been that way. Always been gentle when she needs to be.

My fingers dig into the railing, and one of two things needs to happen. Either this wood needs to give, or my bones do. "Hey there,

Starlight. What can I do for you?" I'm trying to keep the conversation light, to put on airs, but I know my attempt falls short. I'm too tense, my words coming out half growled.

She runs her hand up my back, rubbing the tension between my shoulder blades in a soothing circle. "We will be there soon..."

I know this already.

It doesn't help, though.

She continues with: "Kiernan says he saw the burgee from the *Spindler's Web* on the horizon this morning..."

Well, I can breathe a little easier, knowing that we won't be going in entirely without help.

Captain Odessa '*Ginger*' Marsh has been a long-standing ally to the Nereus, dating back to my time as its captain.

"Good... Good," I mutter, looking out over the waves as I try to slow the speed of my heartbeats.

I'm going to give myself a fucking stroke at this rate.

"Rhazden ho!" Kiernan's voice booms over the sound of the ocean crashing under us. I strain my eyes, realizing my vision probably isn't as great as it once was. Rhazden is still just a smudge on the horizon, but sure enough, it's there.

"He'll get us there in no time," Sitara offers in comfort.

As much as I appreciate the gesture, the only thing that is going to comfort me is having Enna in my arms.

I need to see her safe and unharmed with my own eyes.

55

Kiernan

When Rhazden comes into view, the entire ship goes silent. The smoke billowing up from over the cliff walls makes my stomach drop into my toes and my blood boil with a rage I'm not sure even Sitara could temper. I can see Benedict physically vibrating at the bow, his shoulders jerking with as much barely contained violence as what is swirling in my own gut. If that bitch and her fucked up meat puppets are still on that island, there is no way in hell *anyone* is going to manage to contain us.

Ben looks over his shoulder at me, his eyes swimming with a blood-lust I haven't seen in years. Actually, this might be worse, seeing as he has a wife and an unborn child to worry about.

He's in no place to be helping command the crew right now, so I begin barking orders, and the men immediately get to work. Everyone is worried about what we will find when we finally tie in. Who have we lost? Who was spared? The questions alone are enough to dry out my throat and rip a growl from it.

Sitara is at the helm with me now. She joined just as we saw the smoke. Her face is twisted with disbelief and horror, her eyes moving frantically to take in the entire scene. Or what we can see of it from here, that is.

"Ginger should be waiting for us at the entrance," I tell her, mostly to keep myself calm. "Her ship will be anchored just outside the walls. She and a few of the women from her crew will be following behind in some of their tenders."

I continue to tell her that those boats will be used to transport some of the women and children to her ship, the *Spindler's Web*, to help us get them to safety. I watch her lips move in silent words as she shuffles through her thoughts, focusing on the mottle of freckles that dust over the bridge of her nose.

I've seen them a million times, from a million different angles, but it's what is keeping me calm right now—taking in the details of her face.

"There still won't be enough room between the two ships..." She points this out, having done the calculations in that pretty little head of hers. That must have been what she was silently muttering.

Perceptive as always.

"Yes, I know," I mutter, steering the ship toward the passage in the side of the cliffs just as Ginger's lot comes into view. "Which is why Maximilian Hujo and his ship will be here soon as well."

She looks at me, her lips parting as if impressed that I have actually managed to obtain as many friends as I have. If I weren't so focused on not crashing us into the side of the rock, I might have found it comical.

I give Ginger a nod as we pass by her and her crew, who are loading into the ship boats to follow.

"Don't look so shocked." I side-eye Sitara. "Being in the same line of work does wonders for friendships."

I barely miss one large cluster of rock, doing my best to get us through as quickly as possible while maintaining enough safety to keep us from crashing. The men are already waiting at their posts, prepared to anchor us down the moment we reach our destination.

The ones who aren't stationed are waiting to help Ginger's crew to shore, and a few already have the gangplank in their hands.

Everyone is giving Benedict a wide berth, as not to die themselves before we ever even get there. I can't blame them; he's already thrown one of my men off the side of the ship. Some of them also have families in Rhazden, their faces etched in dread. The men we lost in the fight in Capulli'ana also had families here.

It's all just one big cluster fuck of bad, no matter how you look at it.

I don't even have to yell out any orders as we reach the docks, all of the men accomplishing their assigned tasks without me having to say a word. I look to Sitara, giving her a once-over to assess her condition.

"You remember the plan?"

"Yes," she states simply, then glances at me as I give her an expectant expression. I want her, need her to relay the plan back to me, to ease my own mind. "You are going to find your sister and niece. I am to stay close to Ginger and help her assess the damage to the wounded."

"Good girl," I nod, turning to see Benedict burst into a full sprint off the ship without even waiting for the gangplank to be lowered. The motherfucker just jumped off the side like a fucking gazelle, his feet moving the moment they hit the dock.

It's nothing more than I expected, and I can't blame him for his impatience. After all, I went up against a full-fledged god for my own woman.

Once the gangplank is lowered, everyone starts doing their respective jobs. Sitara and I work our way off the ship, heading toward the mouth of the cavern that will lead us into town.

The sight before us makes an audible gasp escape her, my own jaw clenching in disbelief. Everything is gone. The entire village has been turned to ashes and rubble. Homes are still burning, angry black smoke billowing up from their depths. The trees have been charred to charcoal, and the cobblestone roads have been scorched with black soot.

I glance over at Sitara, the look of pure horror and guilt washing over her face. She has nothing to feel guilty about, but knowing her, that's exactly what she's doing—blaming herself. I wish I could take the time to comfort her the way I'd like to, but with her and my child safe and sound, I have other priorities screaming for my attention. So, I simply grab her face in my hands, kissing the top of her head.

"Don't do that," I say, kissing her head a second time. "I need to go find Rielle and Neoma. Promise me you'll stay near the ship. I need to know I can focus on finding my sister without worrying that you'll be missing when I get back."

She nods, and I plan a quick kiss to her lips before sprinting toward my sister's little cabin in the sliver of woods that sits along the edge of the northeast cliff wall.

The entire trip goes by in a blur. I ignore everything—the burn of my muscles, the ache in my lungs, the slight tilt of my run due to sea legs. I don't have time to worry about it, or acknowledge it, or give it energy.

Bursting into the clearing, a bubble of panic pops in my throat. Seeing the still burning embers of the place my sister has called home for years fills me with a deep, burning rage I can barely control.

"Fuck!" I snarl, kicking through the rubble and debris in a desperate attempt to make sure there is no one underneath. Coals and splinters burn and dig into my hands, but I don't care. I have to know. I have to.

My breathing comes easier once I've discovered the worst-case scenario has not come to pass. There are no bones, no pieces of bodies, no burnt flesh.

Next, I hurry toward Benedict and Enna's house, which isn't far from here—only a tier down the side of the cliff. Maybe their house has been spared. Maybe my sister and her daughter are there with Enna right now.

Before I even make it to my destination, I collide with Benedict. I can tell by the heaviness of his breathing and the panic in his eyes that they had left nothing of the home he had put his own blood, sweat, and (possibly) tears into building for his wife.

"It's gone," he growls. "There's nothing left."

"Rielle's is basically a pile of charred rubble," I inform him, shaking my head.

This is not good, not at all.

"Luckily for every soul on this planet, Enna was nowhere to be found inside," he snarls, the molten steel in his eyes a blatant indication that he would hold to that unspoken threat if she had been, or if he finds her somewhere else no longer breathing.

"I haven't seen many bodies," I tell him, starting to pace the few feet in front of him. "There were none in Rielle's house, and you had said Enna wasn't in yours, which means they have to be *somewhere*."

The sudden look of realization on Benedict's face gives me pause, a growing sense of hope blooming that there may be a way to find them. He scratches the stubble on his jaw, a glimmer of amusement flashing across his eyes.

"The little guy did it," he mutters, "I told Emery to find a place to hide in case something like this were ever to happen. I told him not to say a word of it, not even to me or you. The last thing we needed was someone cutting the location out of us."

Relief washes over me, threatening to weaken my knees. I clap him on the shoulder and laugh. "You brilliant bastard!"

"Well, your arrogant ass wasn't going to have him do it," he grins.

"I guess we either wait him out, or we start calling out for him," I muse, running my hand through my hair. I look around at the crumbled remains of the city once more, trying to determine where to even begin. "Around the perimeter, maybe?"

"I'd say that's the best course of action. *I'm* not sitting around waiting for them to come out on their own," he agrees.

I didn't figure he would be willing to wait.

I know Benedict won't stop until he has Enna physically before him, unharmed.

"You circle left, and I'll go toward the right. We will meet back up near the ship." I point in each direction, then pause with a furrowed brow. "What kind of signal should we send when we find them?"

There is no *if* we find them.

There is only *when.*

I refuse to accept any other answer, any other outcome.

"Mate, I don't care if we squawk like fucking chickens, just as long as we find them," Ben grunts, his muscles twitching to begin the search. "The island isn't that big. Just use that loud mouth of yours and holler."

I spend the next hour calling out Emery's name. I have been listening to Ben shout from across the village, his voice growing increasingly strained as his panic sets in. I know that Emergy will be the only one to answer whichever one of us finds them, seeing as he is the way he is. The sun is getting low in the sky, painting it in a mix of orange and pink, when I finally hear something move.

"Emery?" I spin around, my eyes scanning the small grove of trees along the outer cavernous wall. I nearly drop when the man comes into view, his silken ebony baby curls and contrasting porcelain skin covered in soot and dirt.

I pull his small frame into a tight hug, feeling his muscles relax slightly. I pull back just enough to hold him at arm's length, assessing him for any potential injuries.

"Are you okay? Where are the others?"

"They are in a cave on the eastern side," he responds, his higher-pitched voice weary from exhaustion and raspy from what smoke her might have inhaled. "I tried to get as many of the villagers as I could."

"You did well. Ben and I only found a few people, and most of them were near the dock," I console him. "I'm assuming they were on or near them when the attack started."

I look down at the man, his honey-gold eyes sunken in and haunted by whatever it is he's seen. Emery has never had a problem witnessing conflict, but being in the middle of it...

Gods, I wish you were here right about now, Zyran...

"Take me to everyone. I need to get Enna to Benedict before he sinks what's left of Rhazden," I command, receiving a frantic nod in return.

Emery had spent far too much time working under Benedict before me not to know how serious that statement is.

"It's this way." He motions for me to follow, scurrying toward the eastern portion of town.

My longer strides eat up the distance, keeping pace with his willowy frame easily. My eyes never leave his back as he takes me to what seems like an average, everyday rock wall. Curious, I lean over his shoulder, watching as he pushes aside some overgrown vines. There's a hold in the cliff, just big enough for a person to squeeze through. Well, a me-sized person would have to squeeze. Someone the size of Emergy has no problem slipping through.

"Emery, you resourceful little fucker," I praise, lowering myself down enough to follow him through the entrance.

By the time I've led all the survivors to the docks, Sitara has already started a fire. I can smell the food cooking from a mile away, long before I can even see her.

As we all approach, I catch sight of her standing next to Ginger, chatting away about something I can't quite make out. The two redheaded women snap their heads toward the sound of our shuffled footsteps in unison, both seeming to visibly relax their shoulders.

A warmth spreads through me as I watch Sitara rush to Enna's side, the two embracing in a familial hug as she begins to bombard her with questions like '*Are you okay?*' and '*Are you hungry?*'. It's just like Sitara to meet the woman once and already hold a place for her in her heart.

The woman's capacity for genuine care is boundless.

She does the same with Saolo'ki, who looks like he's seen better days. According to Emery, he was a key factor in the mass survival of the village, using his power to hold off the cult for as long as he could before finally being forced to retreat.

I sent out a signal to Ben over an hour ago, so he should be here any time now. I can already imagine his tall, lanky ass bursting through rubble just so he can make a straight beeline here.

In the meantime, I suppose it's time I finally introduced my fiancé to Rielle and Neoma.

I motion for Sitara, beckoning her with a crook of my finger. As she makes her way toward where I stand with the rest of my family, I catch sight of Ginger turning to pull Emery into her crushing embrace, her chin quivering slightly as she holds onto him for dear life. It's not often they get to see one another, and I'm sure this isn't the circumstances either one of them wanted to reunite under.

My sister stiffens imperceptibly beside me, her head on a swivel as she looks from me to my woman, then back to me again. She's already putting two and two together. I can see it in her eyes, which are incredibly clear today.

Well, I guess it's been a hot second since I got my ass chewed.

No time like the present.

Neoma, however, is still clinging to my arm as she has been since I arrived at the cave. Her tiny fingers are trembling as she holds on with a death-grip I'm not sure any child should have the strength for. I can't imagine what all this poor girl has witnessed recently.

I turn to my sister, opening my mouth to explain. "Rielle—"

"You better not say two words to me, Kiernan Slater." She puts her finger in the center of my chest. "You have some introductions to make and, then, you have some *serious* explaining to do."

Once Sitara has made it to my side, a bright, friendly smile on her face, I pull her into my side and brace myself for a good old-fashioned tongue lashing.

"Sitara, this is Rielle." I nod toward my sister since both of my arms are currently occupied. Then I jerk my head down at my niece. "And this is her daughter, Neoma."

If Rielle stares at the slight swell of Sitara's lower abdomen any harder, I might have to worry about my child's safety.

However, Sitara doesn't seem to notice, giving Rielle a wider smile before crouching down to level herself with Neoma. Her face softens as the normally extroverted child only barely peeks out from around my arm.

Sitara holds out her hand, and an emerald flame, barely larger than that on a lit candle, flickers to life. At first, I have no idea what she's doing, but then the flame molds itself into a likeness of Neoma and waves.

Neoma loosens her grip on my arm, moving closer to Sitara with an awe-inspired smile.

"It's me!" she exclaims, pointing at it as Sitara makes the flame follow her movements and point back. I can see my niece's shoulders begin to relax as she continues to make gestures, Sitara keeping up with each one until Neoma and the flame are dancing in tiny circles.

After a few moments of drinking in the scene, I tear my eyes away to look back at Rielle. She's still irritated with me, even despite the adorable moment happening right under her nose.

"Is this *the* woman, Kiernan?" She interrogates, folding her arms over her chest. She already knows the answer, or she wouldn't be asking, and we both know it. "As in, *Benedict telling you to get a hooker and move on*, woman?! *That* woman?"

"Uh..." I rub my palm into my neck sheepishly. "The very same woman, yes."

"Are you kidding me, Kiernan Matthew Slater?!" she bellows furiously. Rielle rarely raises her voice, but when she does... well... Let's just say that before Sitara, she was the only woman whose anger made me flinch a little.

Sitara pulls herself away from the moment she's having with Neoma after seemingly working the temperature enough for the girl to hold the flame herself. She turns to Rielle, then lifts a brow at me before flicking her eyes back to my sister again.

There seems to be a lot of that right now, doesn't there?

"It's nice to finally meet you," she says calmly, though I know I'm going to get a good talking to from her, too, depending on how the rest of this interaction goes.

Over the next few minutes, the girls interact with one another, warming up into a steady stream of conversation.

"So, he didn't mention the fact that I was on the ship the first time we came here?" Sitara asks, almost insulted by the fact.

"No, he did *not*," Rielle responds, which elicits a side-eyed glare from both of them.

I'm fucking confused... Did I actually do anything wrong?

I'm incredibly relieved when I hear Enna's name being flung across the wind in desperation.

Thank the gods for Benedict and his impeccable timing.

"Enna!" he yells frantically. "Somebody better hand me my wife before heads begin to roll!"

"Ben!" Enna calls out, and Ben's head snaps toward the sound like a hound scenting a target. "Benedict!"

We all watch as the entire remaining populace of Rhazden parts like they are avoiding the plague, which Ben might as well be in his fragile state. Enna hurries as fast as her waddling body will allow, and he quickly makes up for it by pummeling poor Becket into the soup Sitara has made for everyone.

He should know by now that getting in the way of Benedict Leighton will usually land you in shit. Or, in this case, scalding hot stew.

If it wasn't for Benedict's almost bruising grip on her, Enna probably would have fallen backwards with the force the man had hauled his ass to her. His relief is damn near breathable in the air as his lips find probably every inch of exposed skin on the woman's body. He'd probably kiss her damn toes if she'd take off her shoes. Ben's hands hover over her body with a hesitant uncertainty as he checks her over for injuries.

"You're alright? The baby's alright?"

I don't think I've ever heard Benedict's voice quiver like that before.

Enna grabs his face, making him meet her eyes as she shakes him just enough to slow his breathing. "I'm fine, Benedict. We're both okay."

She wraps her arms around his shoulder and pulls him tightly against her. I don't think a single one of us is willing to move or speak or even breathe. We all just stare as her hand runs down his arm to guide his hand to her belly.

Ben's head falls to her chest, and he damn near drops to his knees in relief. After a few heartbeats and a couple of deep breaths on his part, Benedict looks around with a grin even as the exhaustion he's been fighting off begins to win out.

"Don't you guys have something better to do than stand there staring like a pond full of dyin' fish?"

And with that, the usual Benedict is right back at it.

56
Sitara

With everything that has happened lately, it feels good to simply lie here, in bed, wrapped up in Kiernan's warmth. The beating of waves under the *Nureus* comes filtering through the slightly ajar window, which was opened late last night due to a sudden bout of motion sickness. Or perhaps it is morning sickness—I can't be sure.

Probably the latter.

It doesn't really matter. Either way, I felt horrible and couldn't hold in the contents of my stomach any longer. The only thing that *matters* right now is allowing myself some sort of comfort in being back where I belong. It isn't about the ship or the bed, not really. It's about the man lying next to me, his lips parted slightly as he sleeps, his eyelashes fanned over his cheekbones.

I can hear the rest of the crew outside, bustling about the deck, going about their daily routine. However, the roar of voices is louder on this journey, seeing as we have doubled the number of bodies on this ship. There are so many of them, in fact, that some have opted to sleep on the upper deck to keep from being elbow to elbow with each other on the cannon decks. It wouldn't be quite as cramped, however, if Benedict hadn't threatened the lives of anyone who crossed the five-foot radius he's demanded to be around Enna at all times.

I like seeing him with her.

She makes him seem... less feral, in a way, yet even more so in his protection of her.

I let my eyes drift out the window, a small smile tugging at my lips as I think about that. I had never seen Ben crumple to his knees like that before, and judging by the looks on everyone's faces that day, neither had anyone else. It's good, though, that there is someone to bring that vulnerability out in him.

If I've learned nothing else in the last few months, it's that we all need someone to keep us humble, grounded.

Not to mention, I love watching her put that big man in his place any chance she gets.

I feel a stirring at my side, pulling me from my thoughts. I turn to see a pair of electric blue eyes staring back at me. His hair is adorably mussed from sleep—I never thought a man the size of a brick wall could be adorable, but he's proven me wrong—and a slight sheen of nighttime sweat glistens on his sun-kissed skin.

I love these early mornings, before the lines of stress slide back over his brow. I can't blame him for it, not with everything that's been going on. We have a lot that we have to do once we get back to Capulli'ana.

Like building enough shelter for the entirety of Rhazden.

"You're supposed to be resting, Darling," he rasps out in that sleepy timbre that makes my toes curl. "We will be docking in Saint Dubois before noon."

He pulls me closer, his hands immediately moving to rest on the little swell of my abdomen. I use the term '*little*' loosely. It's begun to have that roundness to it, but it's not nearly as big as poor Enna, who is desperately waddling at this point.

"I can rest *and* sit up, Kiernan. That is a thing, you know." I chuckle, though I allow him to pull me back into his arms, which lays me back down into the mattress. "If you make me stay in this bed too long, I'll become more restless than you can handle."

I say that, but I know it is about as hollow a threat as Enna threatening to withhold sex from Benedict. Being with child has done nothing to put a damper on this man's drive. Actually, I think it might have made it worse.

Now, he truly *is* insatiable.

"I don't think you could ever be too much for me to handle," he murmurs, nuzzling into my hair. "I'm not *making* you do anything. The sun isn't even awake yet, my love."

I look out the window, quirking my mouth to the side. He's right. There is only the faintest of purple in the inky sky. The sun is still a few hours from breaking over the horizon, and the crew I keep hearing outside the door must be those of them who decided to drink themselves stupid until dawn.

I'm already restless, itching to do *something* productive. Enna says it's the start of the '*nesting*' phase. I'm not sure what I'm supposed to be nesting. The dark corner of the captain's quarters?

Maybe I'll scrub the upper deck later and bicker with Kiernan about the necessity of it later today.

"Besides..." He rubs soothing circles over my belly. "You can't leave yet. I'm bonding."

An indignant snort falls out of my face, followed by the flutter of a foot against his hand. Well, now I'm *really* not getting out of this bed. He's going to be gushing about this for the next three hours and antagonizing the wee one to move more.

If I pee myself, I'm making him clean it up.

I watch with amusement as his eyes widen and his mouth falls open. This is the first time he's managed to feel anything, even though I have been feeling little flutters for a week or so now.

"See?! He doesn't want you to get up either!"

"He?" I cock a brow at him. I've had the feeling the baby is a boy myself, but I can't very well admit that if my love is going to be so blatantly confident about it himself.

Where's the fun in that?

"With a right hook like that, there's no way that is a girl." He pokes a single finger into the spot where we have just felt movement, and I roll my eyes, feigning offense. "Do it again, buddy."

"Oh, really?" I hold up a fist with a playful smirk. "Give me your jaw, *darling*, and let us find out."

He put his cheek against my stomach, whispering conspiratorially. "You and hormones make Mommy think she's capable of being mean. It's almost scary."

"You're gonna think '*scary*' in a minute." I puff out my cheeks, folding my arms to rest them on the swell.

Perks, I suppose.

Another kick catches Kiernan right in the face, and I grin, patting what eventually will be a little bottom. "Good job! Show him not to be a bully."

"It's not bullying when it's true," he grumbles, moving his lips to talk directly into my skin. I roll my eyes, shaking my head with a smile. I love seeing him this way, so carefree and lovable.

As Kiernan continues to poke and play, my mind drifts to the letter I had found in Arthur's possessions when I had gathered his belongings from the cannon deck. It's the only real clue we have to finding Millicent, whom I have refused to go back to Puka'qui without. I had made a promise, and I intend to keep that promise. I will not go back on that. Not now, not ever.

The letter is addressed to someone named Jonas Halling, whoever that may be. When I opened it to figure out if it was important enough to keep and deliver, I became more confused than ever. Despite the mailing name on the outside, the contents are addressed to Millie.

As confusing as that is, I suspect whoever this Jonas Halling is will lead us right to Millicent. Then, I can finally offer her what Arthur had been striving for, what he was so close to achieving.

I've been pacing the deck for the last hour while we anchor down at the port. Finally, I go motionless long enough to help Enna mend one of Benedict's shirts, which I'm pretty sure *she* tore to give me something to do.

At least it had done its intended job...

"Not long now, Starlight," Enna reassures, snipping the end of the thread off as I hold it out for her.

Starlight... It's an alias I hold close to my heart now. Pip had been the first of many to call me that, and it has spread on this ship like wildfire.

I nod, chewing on the inside of my cheek as I bob my knee frantically. I'm ready to go. I'm ready to feel like I have done the one thing he had asked of me. I'm ready to feel... I don't know, like I have fulfilled a purpose?

Kiernan has tried to convince me not to go alone, but I have stayed steadfast in my decision. He can come with me to help find this *'Jonas'* character, but when it comes to actually approaching Millie... I want—no, I need—to do it alone.

I've made subtle jabs about how I don't want him to scare the poor girl, but that's not really the reason. My reasoning is so much more unfair than that. I'm hoping that by finding her and bringing her home to a safe place, I can relieve some of my own guilt. I think somewhere deep inside, I'm hoping she'll tell me it wasn't my fault, even though it was.

Once *Nureus* is tied off, Kiernan turns to me as I disappear like an apparition from his side. I'm already halfway down the gangplank to the dock, careful to accommodate the change in my balance as I race off like a bat right out of I'cuma.

"Sitara!" I hear him shout as he hurries to catch up.

"You were too slow," I say simply, determined to find the address written on the front of the letter, which is clutched painfully tight in my right hand. Mundanes do have one thing I simply don't understand. That's addresses. Which, to my secret source of self-loathing, is the only reason why I agreed to let him come with me in the first place.

"I was helping dock the sh–"

I don't allow him to finish before I shove the envelope into his hand, tapping the scribbled pen marks with a finger. He looks down at it, then up at the street signs, resigning to the fact that I am not in the mood to stand around. Chewing into my inner cheek once more, a habit that has developed recently, I wait not all too patiently for him to give us a heading. I'm practically vibrating by the time Kiernan points up the road in front of us.

"Temptest Lane is that way." He reaches down to take my free hand in his, lacing our fingers together. "We are getting to her. That won't change even if you slow down just a little."

I know he's right.

I know that all I'm doing is putting unnecessary stress on myself, but I can't help it.

I need this.

I need to know I've done my part.

We turn down the lane, our eyes roving over the buildings for the right set of numbers.

453...453...453...

I've memorized the address, even though I don't know anything about the system they use for said addresses. All I have to do is find the '*big ol' numbers above the door*', according to Viktor.

When we finally find it, I can't do anything but stand there and stare. It's not a home... or at least, it certainly doesn't look like one. The large picture window at the front gives a full view of the small room inside, which is littered with books, parchment, and desks. Above the worn grey wood of the outside reads a sign that says *Halling & Son* in bold golden letters

"What is this place?" I ask, my neck craning to get a better view of the inside.

Kiernan furrows his brow, shaking his head lightly. "I'm not sure. Do you want me to knock on the door?"

He loosens his grip on my hand and rubs my back. I take that opportunity to walk up to the door myself and tap my knuckles on the wood. I can hear the deep sigh behind me, and I know I'll have to apologize later for being a butthole.

But that is later, and this is now.

I feel Kiernan's body heat at my back as the door swings open with a jingle of the bell above the door.

Standing on the other side is a middle-aged gentleman, approximately in his late forties. A lump forms in my throat as I take in the uncanny red hair, the dusting of prominent freckles, and the gentleness of his blue eyes. It doesn't take a genius to see that Arthur is... was... the spitting image of the man before us.

"Jonas Halling?" Kiernan asks, probably sensing my sudden inability to speak.

"Yes, I would be he," Jonas smiles kindly. He even has the same dimples... "What can I help you with?" He looks between the two of us, stepping aside to offer us entry.

"We need some help finding someone," Kiernan tells the man, most likely to give me a moment to regain my tongue. He looks down at me, his hand making grounding circles between my shoulder blades. He urges me forward, my feet feeling heavy with every step through the door.

After a moment of taking in the clean wooden floors and the array of books scattered around everywhere—mostly ledgers from the looks of it—I finally turn to look at Jonas. I know I'm not doing a very good job of keeping my guilt off my face, though I try really hard to. When neither Kiernan nor I immediately goes into an explanation, Jonas takes it upon himself to continue.

"Who is it that you are looking for?" I can see the way he shifts slightly from foot to foot. I'm not sure what is causing his nervous fidgeting, but something about it tells me we are on the right track to finding Millicent.

Jonas offers me a seat, his eyes briefly glancing down at my condition before he looks to Kiernan, who is still holding my hand despite my seated position.

"We are looking for Millicent Rolan," Kiernan explains, motioning to me, "My fiancé has something of hers."

The man's face immediately shifts, his shoulders stiffening like a maturing oak. "And, if I may ask, what exactly is this *something*?"

I hold up the letter I have been clutching in my free hand this entire time and watch as Jonas's face changes from stern warning to surprise to sudden understanding.

His jaw works vigorously beneath his skin, his eyes dewy with unshed tears. "Is that from my Arthur?"

When his voice cracks, I feel my own eyes grow damp. I look up to the ceiling, blinking them away furiously. I have no right to sit here in front of his father and cry. Jonas, being the intelligent man he's proving himself to be, is putting the puzzle pieces together at a rapid pace.

"It is," Kiernan answers when my own voice continues to fail me. I need to get it together, to muscle through the sudden muteness that has wrapped itself around my vocal chords. I swallow down the lumpy blockage in my throat and clench my jaw enough to keep my chin from quivering.

"We found it... when we were gathering his things." I can't bring myself to say it any other way.

We were gathering his things.

Nothing more.

Nothing less.

Jonas nods solemnly, his eyes falling to the floor in resignation. "I see..."

"He spoke of Millie so often that... we wanted to make sure she received everything he promised her." My tone is somewhere between explanatory and pleading. Kiernan helps me from the chair as I move to offer a hug to the teary, grieving father.

I know he doesn't know me, but I can't help but try to bring some sort of... I don't know. I know comfort can't be given. I know that sympathy does no one any good. Relatability? Even that is a far stretch. I haven't lost a child, so I can't even begin to understand Jonas's pain.

"Will you take me to her?" I ask, my voice barely above a murmur.

Jonas nods, looking between the two of us. "How did it happen?"

My chest clenches, my voice lost to me again. How do I even begin to explain what had happened? How can I possibly look his father in the eye and tell him his son jumped in front of a blade for me?

Kiernan clears his throat, saving me from the anguished scrutiny. It doesn't make me feel any better, but at least Jonas can get his answer without watching me try to regain myself for ten minutes.

"Arthur went with me and the rest of the crew to rescue Sitara." He shakes his head. "Your son stood in the way of steel to save Sitara and my child."

Jonas processes the revelation, his eyes drifting to me once more. Something akin to pride begins to mix with the grief—or perhaps that's just my own wishful thinking.

"I suppose, there is no more honorable way to go."

Jonas had closed his place of business and led us to where we needed to go. The walk there had been mostly quiet, nothing more than the sound of his and Kiernan's boots on the ground and the slight rustle of our clothing. I don't think any of us really knew what to say. There really is nothing we can say.

When we finally draw closer, Jonas abruptly stops, gently grabbing my arm. "This will not be a pleasant thing to witness. Millie's situation has deteriorated significantly since my son's departure."

I give him a stiff nod. If only he knew that this would not be my first unpleasant experience. It's not even my first unpleasant experience involving another human being. It never makes it easier to see, but at least this time, I know I have the power to change it rather than *hoping* I can figure it out.

At the end of the path he has taken us down sits a farm. It's not very large, but it harbors enough to ensure they can supply meat and such to the townspeople, I assume. Several servants mill about, tending to the small herds of cattle and hogs that dot the pens lining the property.

"Look for the mousy hair. She normally wears it in a scarf," Jonas says, "She will probably be in one of the barns."

With those parting words, I know this is as far as he will be going. I nod slowly, storing his description in my memory. "Thank you, Jonas."

I want to say I'm sorry, but I know it's not something that will lessen the pain. He doesn't need to hear words that will do him no good in the long run. He nods, then mimics the action with Kiernan before heading back the way we had come. I watch his back, counting his footsteps as he rounds the corner until his copper locks are no longer visible. Then I turn back toward the farm, trying to determine which of the three barns I'm going to look in first.

"You're sure you don't want me to go with you?" Kiernan asks, kissing the top of my head.

"No," I respond, my throat suddenly very dry, "I can do it on my own."

Either I've grown to know him very well, or his thoughts are written all over his face. *You try to do everything on your own.*

Yes, yes, I do.

I'll fix that unflattering personality trait after this.

Probably.

My feet feel like lead as I surge forward, forcing myself to take that first step. I have no idea where to begin, so I just pick a barn and go. It's the largest of the three, most likely where they shelter the cattle and keep their straw and hay—by the smell of it.

I receive a few stares, which I had already anticipated. I'm not exactly a local. That fact is evident due to my clothing, as I had refused to wear anything but my own clothes from my tent after making my way out of I'cuma. Not that I would fit in the dresses Kiernan had bought for me now anyway. I might as well be a three-headed sow with the way some of them are gawking. It's clear that women don't exactly walk around with their bellies bare around here.

Or anywhere outside of Capulli'ana, as I'm beginning to understand.

I pay it no more mind than that, my hand scraping against the rough wood of the barn door as I pull it open enough to slip inside.

Looking around the barn's interior, I can't see a single soul. There are a few cows that have come inside the open stalls to graze, and an old herding dog lies in the corner. Realizing I'm not getting anywhere in here, I turn and move to look in the next barn, which is small and looks as though it may contain chickens.

Inside this one, the scent of chicken hits my nose and makes me nauseous. I muscle through it, looking around for the mousy blonde hair that Jonas described.

A small woman bustles about in the far left corner of the barn, and my heart slams up into my throat. She's filthy... Her hair looks like it hasn't been washed in an unholy amount of time, and her clothes have probably required burning in a fire for even longer. She's moving through each designated area in search of eggs, her hand delving into each nest.

Oh, Pip, if you could only see her right now...

I clear my throat, mostly to keep my tears from overwhelming me. Millicent turns, looking up at where I'm standing with a weary exhaustion that almost breaks my heart.

"The stable is the next barn down. The front door is a better entrance to the main house, miss," she says, setting a handful of eggs into a basket before reaching into another nesting box without even flinching when the brooding hen pecks at her hand.

"Actually," I finally muster up the courage to speak, the sheer drive to get her out of this situation overriding any other emotion, "I'm a friend of Arthur's... I-I... You're Millicent Rolan, yes?"

She immediately stops what she's doing, turning to face me fully. "Arthur?"

Her brows furrow, and she steps out of the hen's nesting area. Quickly moving to where I stand, she sets the full basket down to wring her hands before wiping them on her apron. "Arthur sent you?"

"W-Well... Sort of..." I struggle, unsure of how to tell her.

How would I want someone to tell me Kiernan was gone?

The answer is simple.

I wouldn't.

Nothing I say is going to make it better. Nothing I do will take it away or make it as if it never happened. I'm the villain in her story, here to rip away her happily ever after with my own two hands.

"He, um," I take a deep breath, trying to steady myself. "Something happened and..."

Millicent's chin quivers, tears blooming and spilling over. She immediately holds up her hand to silence me. "Stop... Please just stop..."

I snap my mouth closed, my own chin quivering before I stomp it down deep, deep into my chest. The way she wipes her tears with the backs of her grim-covered hands leaves mud along her cheeks. I want to run and hide and never show my face again, but I can't. I have to take what she dishes, even if it means my guilt is never alleviated. Even if I have to live with it for the rest of my life.

"I'd rather be stuck here, in hell, with the hope of him returning... so please... stop," she croaks, the break of her voice threatening to mute me once more.

"I made him a promise," I say, my voice barely audible over the sounds of the animals shifting around us, "I promised him I would get you out of here..."

"You..." Another tear slides down her cheek. "What did you do with–" She chokes on another sob, closing her eyes. The action causes the salty streams to flow. "Where is he now?"

"I... He's being preserved in my village. I didn't– I wanted to wait for you..." I explain, looking anywhere but at her face. I know I don't have a right to look away, but I can't watch it anymore, or my resolve to do this without tears of my own will dissolve like sand through my fingers.

"He isn't going to let me leave... It's the reason Arthur left in the first place." She lifts her apron to blow her nose, her words forcing my gaze back to her. "When Arthur asked for my hand, the first time, my father rejected him. He said he had daughters because we were worth a hefty sum. He said Arthur couldn't afford his price..."

My gut twists as though that dagger had reached its mark. So far, that has been the largest difference between our people. A mixture of anger and disbelief churns inside me. Millicent fidgets with the fabric of her dirty apron, her eyes locked on her fingers as they tangle in the cloth.

"I should have run away with him when we had the chance," she sobs, her shoulders heaving with despair. "He said he wanted to do it the right way."

That's all the cracked damn of emotions inside me needed to burst and crumble. Watching her, seeing her here like this, realizing the truth behind how some Mundane families treat their women... It's all too much. Tears stream down my face violently, a strangled sob rattling in my chest.

"I'm so sorry..." I can't seem to stop the flow of my words, every ounce of guilt spewing out of me like a flood, "He wanted so much for you. I-I never wanted it to be this way... Pip, he... He loved you so much..."

She wraps her arms around herself as she listens to my verbal vomit, my chest tightening until it's difficult to breathe. I hadn't even realized I had called him by his nickname until her eyes snap up to look at me, wide with recognition.

"Pip? You... You're her then?" she sniffs, using the apron again as a makeshift wipe. "The girl he calls Starlight?"

I nod, her visage blurry through the immense emotions clouding my vision. When she takes that first step toward me, I brace myself. I half expect there to be some sort of blow to my face, her screaming that I was supposed to have been his friend, that I shouldn't have let him die the way he had...

But when her arms wrap around my shoulders, the damp streaks of continued tears wetting the side of my face, I freeze, my brain trying to catch up.

"Thank you..." she whispers, her voice muffled in my hair, "Thank you for being his friend. He felt so alone on that ship... Thank you for being there..."

My body trembles, my shaking arms coming up to wrap around her slender body tightly. My own cries vibrate through us in tandem with hers, and I hold tighter. This is what I needed. It doesn't take the pain away, doesn't fill that hole or ease the loss... But this is what I needed.

After helping Millie gather her meager belongings, mostly a dress or two and the letters from Pip, I may or may not have lit a fire under her father's ass when he tried to protest. Again, I may have. Either way, I walk out of that farm with Millicent Rolan's hand interlaced with my own and the promise that she will never have to set foot in that place again.

Arthur can rest easy, his struggles finally over, his burdens lifted. And now, knowing he's at peace and that his fight is done, so can I.

The weight I carried for him, the worry and the sorrow, can finally be set down.

Epilogue
Sitara

Three Years Later

Walking down the familiar, dimly lit tunnels of I'cuma, I can feel the anticipation building. I know he's aware of my presence within the depths of the tunnels as the sconces flicker on every few feet to light my way down the path. In my current state, being pregnant with my and Kiernan's fourth child—fifth if you count the child we adopted from I'cuma not long after the birth of our first—I'm finding it harder to make this journey than usual.

Everything is quiet; the oppressive atmosphere that had lingered here all those years ago is now gone. The air is stale, stagnant, with the emptiness that now inhabits this place.

Rounding the corner, I can see the light filtering out into the hallway from his prison, my cold fire still firmly placed around Hu'yimona's gilded cage. It takes me longer than I would like to admit to make it, but when I finally do, I can see him standing right along the edge of the barrier, waiting for me.

"Hello, Flower," he greets me, a small, relieved smile forming on his face. His voice is rough with disuse, as I'm the only one who comes to visit him, to my knowledge. I had once asked Coli'hanu why she remained so distant from her brother, but she never gave me a straight answer.

"Hello." I return the smile and take a seat on the chair that my husband had so lovingly brought down here during one of my visits when I was pregnant with Arthur, our firstborn, who is now a toddling little three-year-old.

He loves his siblings, my Arthur, who are two twin girls we had conceived not long after his birth. I swear, Kiernan can't be stopped when he is determined. I do believe it has given a whole new meaning to '*barefoot and pregnant*'.

"They have taken down the barrier?" He murmurs, getting straight to the point this morning. He tilts his head, watching me curiously as I settle into the chair. Luckily, there is no malice on his face or in his tone, only a need to be informed. I knew he would feel it the moment the Kana'te people and the Mundanes were no longer separated by the magic that had once kept our worlds separated.

I nod, letting out a long, worn-out sigh. "Yes. Well... Mostly." A chuckle bubbles up as I shift my position slightly in my seat, taking some of the strain away from my back and hips. "The part of the barrier that keeps the Mundanes out is no more. However, the bit that keeps the wildlife of the jungle safe is still intact."

Hu'yimona leans against the doorframe, his pale, shadow-inked skin rippling in the dim light as he folds his arms over his chest in a relaxed, conversational manner. "Ah, yes. We wouldn't want them crying over a few Coa'Hesa getting into their produce, now would we?"

We share a laugh, the companionship between us effortless at this point. Without all the tension and the war, Hu'yimona is just about the kindest soul I've ever come into contact with. Apart from Arthur, whose death continues to leave its mark on those who knew him best.

I stare at him as he stares right back, taking in my general state. "You look lovely, Sitara. As always. Though it might be nice to see you with a child in your arms more often, rather than in your womb."

It's a tease. I know it is. But, like always, he isn't wrong. I think I've managed to come all of one time without being with child.

"Perhaps, I will bring the children to visit soon," I offer.

I have brought Arthur with me a time or two in the past, and, to Kiernan's surprise—or rather, dismay—the child seemed fairly comfortable with the God of Death. A few months ago, Arthur even attempted to break through the barrier to the room, determined to tug on Hu'yimona's clothes. I think, in some strange way, perhaps the boy recognizes him from the earlier months after his conception, as silly as that may seem.

"I would enjoy it greatly," Hu'yimona nods, "It's been some time since I have seen any of them."

I try to come visit as often as I can manage. It was difficult in the beginning, with the expansion of Puka'qui to harbor all of the Rhazden refugees and the shifts in the workings of the world, however subtle.

Now that everything has settled down, I try my best to make an appearance at least once a week. I can't imagine how lonely it must be down here for him, to be all alone with no one to talk to or confide in.

With that thought in mind, I look up at him, my eyes almost pleading with him to rethink his ideology. "Still set on your master plan?"

"You already know the answer to that."

Yes, I do.

It's the same answer he has given me every time I've come for the last three years.

He has no intention of playing nice with the Mundanes any time soon.

"I was afraid you would say that. *Again*," I mutter, running my hand along my stomach in a soothing motion. This child is restless, constantly moving as if they can't sit still already.

I have a feeling Kiernan and I will have our hands full.

"Old ideals die hard, Flower. Normally, only doing so alongside those who have them. Unfortunately for the world, I will not be dying anytime soon."

We fall into silence once more, the voided conversation ending between us. Sometimes, we simply stay like this, taking in the comfort of one another's presence. Although I have never been *in love* with Hu'yimona, there is still a special place for him.

There always will be.

"What of the children who were taken from I'cuma?" he finally asks, breaking the silence.

This is just another example of how twisted the misconceptions of the God of Death have become. We were always taught he was not capable of care or worry, but here he is, concerned with the children of his own tribe, as messed up as that tribe was.

"They are well," I reassure him, giving him a placating smile. "Eirian has taken great care of them. Many have been adopted into the tribes and even Mundane families."

His face scrunches as I knew it would. "Well, I suppose as long as they are cared for, I can live with the knowledge that some have had the misfortune of being raised by—"

"Hu." I scold him, not allowing his sentence to be finished with an insult.

"You know, you wound my pride when you talk to me as though I'm one of your children."

"Then don't behave like a child."

A low, rumbling laugh passes through the barrier, his face filled with a heartwarming mirth that I have grown to love seeing. I'm glad I'm able to bring some sort of comfort to him, if even just a little.

After everything, he deserves at least that much.

We both do.

"Some of them have even decided to learn the Mundane language." I grin, unable to keep from teasing him further. "Millie is a very good teacher."

He places his hand on his chest, feigning insult. "You wound me, Flower. Have you come as friend or foe?"

Walking out into the boiling sun after spending every bit of an hour or two inside the dim tunnels, I squint as I break through the shadowed depths of the entryway. The sun burns in my eyes, forcing me to blink rapidly. Kiernan, ever the possessive—I'm sorry, I was told to call him *'protective'* —husband that he is, is waiting for me all of a few feet away.

He opens his arms for me, a ritual that has been in place for so long it almost seems like a habit at this point, and I allow him to wrap his arms around me. He presses a kiss to the top of my head, his hand automatically coming to rest on the flutters in my midsection.

This might very well be the *exact* same greeting it has been for the last three years, baby included.

"How was your visit?" he asks. It is the same question every time, and every time, there is always a slight hint of that grudge he simply will *not* let go of.

"Pleasant. He wishes to see the children soon."

I watch his electric blue eyes roll, a sigh escaping his lips to add to the effect of his annoyance. This causes me to roll my own eyes and pinch his side.

"I still, for the life of me, cannot figure out why you would want to go visit him after everything that has happened," he grumbles, tightening his hold on me slightly.

This is a constant topic of discussion.

At least once a week.

After every visit to I'cuma.

"How would you feel if your life were confined to a meager space of four walls?" I furrow my brow, finding it more exhausting each time I have to explain my reasons. I don't blame him for not understanding. He hadn't spent that time with Hu'yimona like I had. However, he could at least let it go and stop behaving like I'm making the biggest mistake of my life by going to visit the god.

Some people once thought he was the biggest mistake of my life as well, and look at us now.

"*My* life is pretty damn good, so I don't care to think about *his*."

I roll my eyes again, taking in a deep, heavy sigh.

Trying to make him understand the unexplainable fondness I have for Hu'yimona is about as pointless as convincing said god that not all Mundanes are the scum of the Earth.

It's not something I can explain with mere words alone. There is something about Hu'yimona that no one has dared to take the time to see. It's as if he's a wounded puppy, having been kicked enough times that now he simply lashes out. But underneath all of that fear and pain, there is someone worth taking the time for.

I move to walk back toward home, a cozy little cottage Kiernan and Benedict had built that sits between the Ma'tawi tribe and Puka'qui. I no longer wish to have this conversation, one that only leads us in circles. I'm far too pregnant and far too tired to try to make him understand any of it.

His hand suddenly wraps around my wrist, gently to halt me. I turn to look up at him, finding his eyes soft and warm as they meet mine.

"I'm sorry, Darling." He brushes a strand of my hair, which is still his favorite thing for some reason, and tucks it behind my ear, his fingertips grazing my skin tenderly. "I simply can't help myself."

He's gotten better with apologies, though they are still few and far between.

The stubborn brute.

"Because your life is *so* fantastic, you can't imagine anyone else's?" I grin, a mockery of sarcasm lacing my tone.

"I've tricked the world's most perfect woman into falling in love with me." He flashes me that roguish grin that, still to this day, makes my knees weak, and leans down to brush his nose against mine. "I think my life is going pretty well."

Bonus

Millicent

It has been a long journey. I have never been anywhere but home, so needless to say, I'm a bit overwhelmed with it all. The ship—term I was corrected on by Kiernan when I had originally called it a *'boat'* —is larger than most homes in the surrounding area around the farm. Throughout the entire trip, my stomach had done nothing but turn and flip with the swaying *Nureus*.

Sitara had tended to me the majority of the journey, and everyone had been kind to me. Though I can't honestly say I left the pallet on the floor of Kiernan and Sitara's cabin, other than to relieve myself or bathe when Sitara had insisted on it.

She had said I am worth being clean.

It's very clear to see why Arthur had bonded so easily with her.

She's easy to like.

I wrap my shoulders in a shawl that is among the items Sitara had forced Kiernan to buy me before leaving my home port. Even though I could have probably lived on that pallet, I can't say I'm not curious enough to move myself to the deck as the men shout and rush around trying to secure us to the dock. After all, Capulli'ana has been nothing but a child's bedtime story where I am from. We knew it existed, but to see it in person...

Sitara had explained during our journey that the place my Arthur had wanted to take me to, Rhazden, had been reduced to ash very recently. However, she assured me that I will be safe here, although it is not where Arthur had planned for us to build a home.

"It's fairly hot here on the island," Sitara says, walking up beside me to rest herself on the railing. "Are you sure you won't get too hot in that? We have a bit of walking to do."

"I don't mind carrying it if it gets too hot. Thank you for telling me about the walk, though. It may change my choice of shoes." I look down at my feet, forcing a small smile for her kind gesture.

As the gangplank is lowered to allow us to shore, I rub my arm and watch as the others exit the ship. "You're going to take me to him? First thing?"

She looks back toward the treeline and nods. I can tell she's hurting just the same as I am, though in a different way. He was everything to me, but he was something to her, too. I suppose that's one reason why the camaraderie is easy with her.

After a long pause, she looks back over at me, nodding again as if to confirm the truth behind the first. "Yeah. First thing."

Sitara hooks her arm through mine and leads me to solid land, my stomach thanking whatever force is out there for the reprieve. My body slowly relaxes as it adjusts to the lack of swaying. The bustling little village is very familiar in layout, which I had not expected, even if it is a mundane establishment. The building materials are the same as those from my hometown: brick, wood, and glass.

However, I know we are not staying here.

It's the looming jungle beyond that seems foreign and unwelcoming.

As our journey begins, I'm grateful for the comfortable silence that lingers between the two of us. I, myself, am not a woman of many words. I never have been. Arthur always spoke enough for both of us, and he never let the silence become awkward.

Sitara seems to be the same in that aspect.

Sometimes, it's difficult to even look at her. If one didn't know the situation behind these strange circumstances, they would think the two of them were siblings in almost every way. The only definitive difference between the two is their eyes. Arthur's were a soft, opalescent blue, while Sitara's are like earthen rubies.

There are several people following us, the group consisting of Sitara's captain, three male crewmembers, and the first mate and his wife, as far as I can tell. I don't know their names. Honestly, I haven't had the energy to try. Well... that isn't completely true. I know Kiernan's name because he is the captain and is directly linked to the generous woman at my side. The others, though? Their faces may as well be composed of wet, smudged paint.

Kiernan's name sticks because he is also the one who had made my Arthur so many promises, and filled his sweet mind with so many pretty dreams for our future. He's the one who led him into a fight that cost him his life. Rationally, logically, I know that Arthur had made his own choices. I know that the captain hadn't twisted Arthur's arm or forced him into any of those decisions. But I need someone to blame, and after meeting Sitara for more than five seconds, I can't bring myself to blame her.

After what feels like an eternity of silent walking, we break through the treeline and into a completely different world. Sitara's village is filled with strangely dressed individuals, much like herself, weaving and working between structures of hide and wood.

I am led to a small hut, though it seems bigger than the others around it. Suddenly, my feet refuse to carry me any further. The halt in my movement is abrupt enough that Sitara's grip on my arm fails, and she stumbles ahead a step or two. If I weren't so petrified in place,

I would have tried to reach out and hold her steady, but I simply can't bring myself to.

"Millie?" she offers, her voice so soft, so kind... so concerned.

My vision blurs as I shake my head. "I need–" I choke on my words as tears begin to roll freely down my cheek for the hundredth time since I found myself face to face with her in that barn. I pull my shawl tighter around my shoulders, as if it could shield me from whatever lay inside that hut. "I can't–"

If I go in there, if I see him, it makes everything real. I won't have any room for denial anymore. Can't I just stay here, in this moment, where I can tell myself that this is all just a cruel joke? I want to keep believing that this is all just a horrible nightmare, that I will wake up and find myself back in that awful barn, hanging on to tentative hope.

An old, withered figure of a man, with gray braids and a face full of white facial hair, steps out of the hut. After looking at me and Sitara for a moment, he tells the rest of the group to give us some space. I need a moment to collect myself. A moment to breathe before my lungs no longer work for the foreseeable future.

Once they all have been taken to wherever it is the old gentleman had indicated, Sitara rests herself on the ground by the doorway, her head lowered and her eyes closed. It's her way of giving me privacy without removing her calming presence from my side.

All I can do is stare at the entryway. I can hear the muffled voices of village people talking around me, using a language I can't understand, nor do I wish to. Even as a new figure joins the two of us, I am too stuck in my fog to listen to their murmured words to the red-haired woman on the ground.

I don't know how long I have been standing here, staring as if he's going to walk out at any moment and wrap me up in his arms. It must have been long enough to cause some kind of concern because I can hear Sitara say my name through the haze. I turn to face her, blinking a few times to clear my vision.

"Okay, take me in..." The words '*I'm ready*' will never apply here. I'm not ready.

But I can't just stand here forever.

Sitara moves the flap that hangs in the doorway, standing aside to allow me to walk in first. When I don't move after a few heartbeats, the individual who had approached earlier—a dark-haired man with the same ruby irises as Sitara—moves to take the fabric in his own hands and hold it open for us. I feel her warm hand wrap around mine and gently coax me forward.

The tears rolling down my cheeks continue their relentless path along my skin, and I don't know how there are any left to cry. I squeeze her hand and allow her to lead me toward him. My body feels like it's made of lead, heavy and slow.

At first, I don't see him, not until the encasement of green fire is fizzled away by Sitara's waving hand. There, lying on a mat of woven reeds, lies the human-shaped form wrapped in clean white linens.

"Arthur..." I choke out a sob, his name dropping from my throat in a hoarse, garbled mess of syllables.

"My brother and I cleaned him," Sitara explains, dropping to her knees at the edge of the mat, "I can- I can remove the linen... If you want to see his face..." I can tell, even through my own grief, that she had taken such immense care with him.

I kneel next to her, reaching out toward where his face lies hidden. My hand strokes his face through the linen, but I can't bring my fingers to close around the fabric to pull it away.

She knows. I can tell by the look on her face as she reaches out to him, my eyes watching her fingers find purchase. My jaw works as I force my eyes to his face, taking in all the new and old details of him. His cheeks are more gaunt than they had been when he left. Hard manual labor and rationed food will do that to a man. His skin has been touched by the sun, his freckles more prominent now than they had been throughout our childhood. Even his hair is a lighter hue, having been bleached by the harsh ocean sun.

But he's still my Arthur.

And now reality sets in at full.

I haven't been able to take a solid breath since yesterday, and now the time has come to place everything I have put my hopes, my dreams, and my love into the ground. The village people have been welcoming, though it hasn't helped the bitter taste that comes with food and drink. Sitara had asked me if it was okay that they placed him in their burial grounds and perform the traditions of their people. As much as I appreciate her considerate question, I don't know if I can make that decision.

So I told her I didn't mind.

The morning sun has barely risen high enough to wash dappled shards of light through the trees when Sitara comes out of her tent, Kiernan at her heels. She's in what I assume is the traditional clothing.

All of her jewelry is gone, the braids in her hair removed until all that is left is a long, brown tunic of roughly woven material. The only other thing adorning her body, and the bodies of all the others I've seen pass by, is the inky face paint placed over her skin from the bridge of her nose down her neck, from ear to ear. Her fingers have been painted the same, the dried pigment a stark contrast to her ivory skin.

She takes my hand, leading me toward where some of the men will carry Arthur on their shoulders down the path that leads to his final rest.

I cling to the one person Arthur had told me would be my friend, and she has faithfully delivered. When we reach where they are going to place him, my only thought is to beg them to bury me with him. No part of me thought my last view of him would be so soon, so abrupt. And I'm not ready.

I will *never* be ready.

Each person who knew him takes a turn digging into the dirt, creating the gaping hole in the earth that will serve as his bed. When they lower him, I follow, my knees giving out on me until they hit the grass-covered dirt. It's as far as I can go with him, and I know that.

As I keep my eyes toward the ground, watching pile after pile of dirt being filled in over the top of him, the tribe's people all face toward the northwest, prostrating themselves to the ground in prayer. When the ground is level once more, I watch the entirety of the Ma'tawi tribe turn and face his grave, all their heads pressed against the earth as they pay their respects to the man who had saved one of their own.

9 798218 828066